An Introduction to Fiction

FOURTH EDITION

X. J. KENNEDY

LITTLE, BROWN AND COMPANY

Boston · Toronto

Library of Congress Cataloging-in-Publication Data

An introduction to fiction.

Includes index.
1. Fiction—Collections.   I. Kennedy, X. J.
PN6120.2.I5   1987   808.3   86–18592
ISBN 0–316–48883–6

Library of Congress Catalog Card No. 86-18592

ISBN 0-316-48883-6

9 8 7 6 5 4 3 2

DON

Published simultaneously in Canada
by Little, Brown & Company (Canada) Limited

Printed in the United States of America

Acknowledgments

Cover art: Detail from "Enchanted Wood, 1983" by Thomas McKnight. From the collection of Mr. and Mrs. Morton
J. Stark, Baltimore. Photograph © 1985 Thomas McKnight.

Toni Cade Bambara. "My Man Bovanne." Copyright © 1971 by Toni Cade Bambara. Reprinted from Gorilla, My
Love, by Toni Cade Bambara, by permission of Random House, Inc.
T. Coraghessan Boyle. "Greasy Lake" from Greasy Lake & Other Stories by T. Coraghessan Boyle. Copyright © 1982
by T. Coraghessan Boyle. Reprinted by permission of Viking Penguin Inc.
Willa Cather. "Paul's Case" from Youth and the Bright Medusa by Willa Cather (Alfred A. Knopf, 1920).
Walter Van Tilburg Clark. "The Portable Phonograph." Reprinted by permission of International Creative Manage-
ment, Inc. Copyright 1941, 1969 by Walter Van Tilburg Clark.
Isak Dinesen. "A Sailor Boy's Tale" from Winter's Tales by Isak Dinesen. Copyright 1942 by Random House, Inc.,
and renewed 1970 by Johan Philip Thomas Ingerslev c/o The Rungstedlund Foundation. Reprinted by permission of the
publisher, Random House, Inc., and The Rungstedlund Foundation of Denmark.
William Faulkner. "A Rose for Emily." Copyright 1930 and renewed 1958 by William Faulkner. "Barn Burning,"
copyright 1939 and renewed 1967 by Estelle Faulkner and Jill Faulkner Summers. Reprinted from Collected Stories of William
Faulkner, by permission of Random House, Inc.
Stanley Fish. Excerpt from Is There a Text in This Class? Reprinted by permission of the publishers from Is There a
Text in This Class? by Stanley Fish, Cambridge, Mass.: Harvard University Press, Copyright © 1980 by the President and
Fellows of Harvard College.
Gustave Flaubert. Excerpt from Madame Bovary by Gustave Flaubert, translated by Francis Steegmuller, Copyright
© 1957 by Francis Steegmuller. Reprinted by permission of Random House, Inc.
E. M. Forster. Excerpt from Aspects of the Novel by E. M. Forster Copyright 1927 Harcourt Brace Jovanovich, Inc.;
renewed 1955 by E. M. Forster. Reprinted by permission of Harcourt Brace Jovanovich, Inc., and Edward Arnold, London.
Jakob and Wilhelm Grimm. "Godfather Death" from The Juniper Tree and Other Tales from the Brothers Grimm, translated by
Lore Segal and Randall Jarrell. Copyright © 1973 by Lore Segal. Reprinted by permission of Farrar, Straus & Giroux, Inc.
Dashiell Hammett. Excerpt from The Maltese Falcon by Dashiell Hammett. Copyright 1929, 1930 by Alfred A. Knopf,
Inc., and renewed 1957, 1958 by Dashiell Hammett. Reprinted by permission of the publisher.
Ernest Hemingway. "A Clean, Well-Lighted Place" from The Short Stories of Ernest Hemingway. Copyright 1933 Charles
Scribner's Sons; copyright © 1961 Mary Hemingway. Reprinted with the permission of Charles Scribner's Sons.
Shirley Jackson. "The Lottery" from The Lottery by Shirley Jackson. Copyright 1948, 1949 by Shirley Jackson.
Copyright renewed © 1976 1977 by Laurence Hyman, Barry Hyman, Mrs. Sarah Webster, and Mrs. Joanne Schnurer.
Reprinted by permission of Farrar, Straus & Giroux, Inc. "The Lottery" originally appeared in The New Yorker.
James Joyce. "Araby" from Dubliners by James Joyce. Originally published by B. W. Huebsch, Inc. in 1916.
Definitive text Copyright © 1967 by the Estate of James Joyce. Reprinted by permission of Viking Penguin Inc. Excerpt
from Stephen Hero reprinted by permission of The Society of Authors as the literary representative of the Estate of James
Joyce, Jonathan Cape Ltd, and the Executors of the James Joyce Estate.
Franz Kafka. "A Hunger Artist." Reprinted by permission of Schocken Books Inc. from The Penal Colony by Franz
Kafka, translated by Willa and Edwin Muir. Copyright © 1948, 1975 by Schocken Books Inc.
D. H. Lawrence. "The Rocking-Horse Winner" from The Complete Short Stories of D. H. Lawrence, Volume Three.
Copyright 1933 by the Estate of D. H. Lawrence. Copyright renewed 1961 by Angelo Ravagli and C. M. Weekley, as
Executors of the Estate of Frieda Lawrence Ravagli. Copyright © 1974 The Estate of Frieda Lawrence Ravagli. Reprinted
by permission of Viking Penguin Inc., Laurence Pollinger Ltd., and the Estate of Frieda Lawrence Ravagli.

(continued on page 448)

PREFACE

Here is a story, one of the shortest ever written and one of the most difficult to forget:

A woman is sitting in her old, shuttered house. She knows that she is alone in the whole world; every other thing is dead.
The doorbell rings.

In a brief space this small tale of terror, credited to Thomas Bailey Aldrich, makes itself memorable. It sets a promising scene—is this a haunted house? —introduces a character, and places her in a strange and intriguing situation. Although in reading a story that is over so soon we don't come to know the character well, for a moment we enter her thoughts and begin to share her feelings. Then something surprising happens. The story leaves us to wonder: who or what rang? Like many richer, longer, more complicated stories, this one—in its few words—engages the imagination.

Evidently, how much a story contains and suggests doesn't depend on its size. In the opening chapter of this book, we will look first at other brief stories—examples of two ancient kinds of fiction, a fable and a tale —then at a modern short story. One at a time, we will consider the elements of fiction. By seeing a few short stories broken into their parts, you will come to a keener appreciation of how a story is put together. Not all stories are short, of course; later you will find a chapter on reading novels.

All in all, here are forty-one stories. Among them, may you meet at least a few you'll enjoy and care to remember.

A Word about Careers

Most students agree that to read celebrated writers such as Faulkner and Tolstoi is probably good for the spirit, and most even take some pleasure in the experience. But many, not planning to teach English and impatient to begin some other career, wonder if studying literature, however enjoyable, isn't a waste of time—or at least, an annoying obstacle.

This objection, reasonable though it may seem, rests on a shaky assumption. On the contrary, it can be argued, success in a career is not merely a matter of learning the information and skills required to join a profession. In most careers, according to one senior business executive, people often fail not because they don't understand their jobs, but because they don't understand the people they work with, or their clients or customers. They don't ever see the world from another person's point of view. Their problem is a failure of imagination.

To leap over the wall of self, to look through another's eyes—this is valuable experience, which fiction offers. If you are lucky, you may never meet (or have to do business with) anyone *exactly* like Mrs. Turpin in the story "Revelation," and yet you will learn much about the kind of person she is from Flannery O'Connor's fictional portrait of her. In reading Tolstoi's "The Death of Ivan Ilych," you will enter the mind and heart of another human being. He is someone unlike you: a Russian petty bureaucrat of the last century. Still, you may find him amazingly similar to many people now living in America.

What is it like to be black, a white may wonder? Alice Walker and Toni Cade Bambara have knowledge to impart. What is it like to be a woman? If a man would learn, let him read (for a start) those writers, and Doris Lessing, Katherine Anne Porter, Flannery O'Connor, Edith Wharton, Kate Chopin, Tillie Olsen, Alice Munro—perhaps, too, John Steinbeck's story "The Chrysanthemums."

Plodding single-mindedly toward careers, some people walk like horses wearing blinders. To many, the goals look fixed and predictable, for competent nurses, accountants, and dental technicians seem always in demand. Others may find that in our society some careers, like waves in the sea, will rise or fall unexpectedly. Think how many professions we now take for granted, which only a few years ago didn't even exist: computer programming, energy conservation, tofu manufacture, videotape rental. Others that once looked like lifetime meal tickets have been cut back and nearly ruined: shoe repairing, commercial fishing, railroading.

In a society perpetually in change, it may be risky to lock yourself onto one track to a career, refusing to consider any other. "We are moving," writes John Naisbitt in *Megatrends,* a study of our changing society, "from the specialist, soon obsolete, to the generalist who can adapt." Perhaps your greatest opportunity in your whole life may lie in a career that has yet to be invented. If you do change your career plans as you go along, you will be like most people. According to U.S. Department of Labor statistics, the average person in a working life changes occupations three times. When for some unforeseen reason you have to make such a change, basic skills may be your most valuable credentials—and a knowledge of humanity.

Literature has much practical knowledge to offer you. An art of words, it can help you become more sensitive to language, both your own and other people's. It can make you aware of the difference between the word that is exactly right and the word that is merely good enough—Mark Twain calls it "the difference between the lightning and the lightning-bug." Read a fine work of literature alertly, and some of its writer's sensitivity to words may grow on you. A Supreme Court justice, John Paul Stevens, gave his opinion (informally) that the best preparation for law school is to study poetry. Why? George D. Gopen, an English professor with a law degree, said it may be because "no other discipline so closely replicates the central question asked in the study of legal thinking: Here is a text; in how many ways can it have meaning?"

Many careers today, besides law, call for close reading and for clear thinking expressed on paper. Lately, college placement directors have reported increased demand for graduates who are good readers and writers. The reason is evident: employers need people who can handle words. In a recent survey conducted by Cornell University, business executives were asked to rank in importance the traits they look for when hiring. Leadership ranked first, but skill in writing and speaking came in fourth, ahead of managerial skill, ahead of skill in analysis. Times change, but to think cogently and to express yourself well are abilities the world still has need for.

That is why most colleges, however thorough the career training they may provide, still insist on general training as well, including basic courses in the humanities. No one can promise that your study of literature will result in cash profit, but at least the kind of wealth that literature provides is immune to fluctuations of the Dow Jones average. A highly paid tool and die maker, asked by his community college English instructor why he had enrolled in an evening literature course, said, "Oh, I just decided there has to be more to life than work, a few beers, and the bowling alley." If you should discover in yourself a fondness for great reading, then in no season of your life are you likely to become incurably bored or feel totally alone —even after you make good in your career, even when there is nothing on television.

Changes in This Edition

Of the forty-one stories included, eighteen are new to this edition. Nine women writers not in the book last time are now represented: Toni Cade Bambara, Willa Cather, Kate Chopin, Isak Dinesen, Ursula K. Le-Guin, Katherine Mansfield, Alice Munro, Alice Walker, and Virginia Woolf. In all, the number of stories by women writers both classic and contemporary has been increased from nine to seventeen.

Two new chapters have been added: "Setting," now offered in response to the wishes of many instructors, and "Irony," promoted from a mere note in "Tone and Style." Like the old chapters, each new chapter begins with a story most students will find engaging and absorbing, one that raises no discouraging difficulties.

Instructors who feel that their students need more background information will be pleased to find that every story is now accompanied by a
biographical note. To gain space, "Reading a Novel" has been rendered
more concise. Now we have seventeen (not fifteen) "Stories for Further
Reading."

Using This Book to Teach Writing

Deep changes have occurred, too, in the "Supplement: Writing,"
especially in "Writing about Literature." In the past, this book's advice on
writing has been conventional, quite uninformed by recent advances in
composition theory. In preparing earlier editions, I used to see the writing
of a paper as a lockstep trip through stages, with an always-foreseeable
product at the end. This advice has now been recast, to describe real life
more accurately. Strategies for discovering material are given priority.
Students are still told they may find it helpful to state a thesis, but this
advice is offered as only one possible way to write. Editing and mechanics,
though given careful attention, take a back seat to more vital matters, such
as the tendency of fresh ideas to arrive when it's time to revise. The
directions for documenting sources now follow the latest *MLA Handbook for
Writers of Research Papers.*

Recently, many instructors have been using this book in a combined
literature-and-writing course. To serve their needs, I have tried to improve
the guidance offered to student writers—improve, but not lengthen it. This
book keeps the essential focus on literature; apparatus is not permitted to
intrude or dominate. The editor's prose, I believe, matters less to the study
of fiction than William Faulkner's or Tillie Olsen's.

The suggestions for writing, at the end of each main chapter, have
been freshened and rethought. Some instructors prefer to let students
discover their own topics, and these suggestions may be helpful to start
them thinking on their own. The well-received section "Criticism: On
Fiction" remains, and although an instructor need not do anything about
it, it can provide not only ideas for class discussion but also further writing
possibilities. (For these, please see the *Instructor's Manual to Accompany An
Introduction to Fiction, Fourth Edition.*)

Besides lending support to the student creative writer, the section
"Writing a Story" may interest others: it has remarks by celebrated fiction
writers, telling how they write.

Texts and Dates

Every effort has been made to supply these stories in their most
accurate texts and in lively, faithful translations. For the reader who wishes
to know when the stories were written, at the right of each title appears
the date of the story's first publication in book form. Parentheses around

a date indicate that the story was written much earlier than it was first printed, but that its exact date of composition is not known.

Thanks

Besides the debts this editor has contracted over the past eleven years, he owes profound thanks to nearly a hundred instructors who taught from this book's previous edition. (Some used its contents in its companion, *Literature: An Introduction to Fiction, Poetry, and Drama.*) Among those who made comments and suggestions for book or manual are Jaquita Albin, Carol Bachman, M. LeRoy Badger, Sheila C. Bailey, William H. Blanchard, Wilson C. Boynton, Margaret Broderick, Lurene Brooks, Duane Bruce, John J. Brugaletta, Ed Buban, Jerrold E. Buchholz, Terre Burton, George F. Butler, Michael Calvello, Helen Caudill, Lynda Corbin, Peter Cousins, Charles E. Cowdrick, Virginia P. Critchlow, Robert Con Davis, Brian J. Delaney, Linda Donahue, Natalie Dunn, William D. Eisenberg, Ed Eleazer, Julie Fay, Marilyn Fisher, J. L. Funston, Silas H. Garrison, John M. Gissendanner, Sue Grady, Helen E. Harris, Louise E. Harris, Terry Heller, Donald J. Herzog, Steven Hind, James Hoogenakker, Frederick W. Hopkins, Dorothy G. Horwitz, R. A. Hughes, Darrell W. Hurst, Anne Johnson, Sandra Katz, Terrance B. Kearns, David Kerner, Enno Klammer, Arlene E. Kuhner, Juliann Lange, Richard Leveroni, Carolyn S. Lightsey, Nancy G. Little, Marcus López, Clarinda Lott, Celeste Loughman, Nancy Adams Malone, Lawrence W. Manglintz, Charles E. May, Gunhild T. Miller, Michael Miller, Sylvia T. Miner, Laura Moffet, Edward F. Murphy, M. G. O'Hara, Ghita Orth, Janice J. Osterholm, Joe Parks, Margie Presley, Jules Ryckebusch, Julie Launhardt Ryden, B. Sandlin, Epifanio San Juan, Jr., Gerald J. Schiffhorst, Nicola Seed, Cynthia L. Selfe, Theresa Showalter, Robert Slaughter, Barbara Sloan, Helen M. Sloan, Donald M. Smith, Frank P. Steele, Carol D. Stevens, R. E. Stratton, Stan Sulkes, Patrick Sullivan, Shirley D. Sykes, Debra Tenney, T. J. Trout, B. Verwiel, Theodore A. Wiebe, Gary Williams, Trudy Williams, Tom Windt, and Neal Woodruff. I remain grateful to the host of instructors named in the prefaces to earlier editions, much of whose advice is still evident. Scores of students, some of them using the questionnaire at the back of the book, wrote reactions and suggestions. I wish there were space to name them all, and to thank properly all the students at Tufts, Michigan, North Carolina (Greensboro), and Leeds who let me read stories with them.

On the publisher's staff, Carolyn Potts has for a long time given her firm but kindly guidance. David W. Lynch, Janice Friedman, Amy Johnson, Adrienne Weiss, and Sarah Clark made extraordinary contributions as well. To Dorothy M. Kennedy (coauthor of the *Instructor's Manual*), I am indebted for some of the new questions, and for immeasurably more besides.

TOPICAL CONTENTS

CONTENTS

LEO TOLSTOI, *The Death of Ivan Ilych* (Translated by Louise and Aylmer Maude) 235

A supreme Russian writer tells how a petty, ambitious judge, near the end of his wasted life, discovers a harrowing truth.

NATHANIEL HAWTHORNE, *The Birthmark* 274

Superscientist Aylmer's young, beautiful wife has just one flaw. What if he were to remove it by his powerful alchemy?

VIRGINIA WOOLF, *A Haunted House* 286

Whatever hour you woke a door was shutting. From room to room went the ghostly couple, hand in hand.

KATHERINE MANSFIELD, *The Garden-Party* 287

Just beyond the pleasant world of her wealthy family, a young girl has an experience that opens her eyes.

FRANZ KAFKA, *A Hunger Artist* (Translated by Willa and Edwin Muir) 298

Right this way, ladies and gentlemen! Hurry, hurry, get your tickets for the most amazing spectacle in the world!

D. H. LAWRENCE, *The Rocking-Horse Winner* 305

When the boy, "wild-eyed and strange, as if something were going to explode in him," predicts a winning racehorse, shrewd gamblers rush to bet a thousand pounds.

EDITH WHARTON, *Roman Fever* 316

In Europe, two American women examine each other, "each through the wrong end of her little telescope," until one lets fall a secret she had kept for years.

EUDORA WELTY, *A Worn Path* 325

Cagey, strong-willed old Aunt Phoenix has made the journey many times before. A Mississippi writer draws a character impossible to forget.

WALTER VAN TILBURG CLARK, *The Portable Phonograph* 331

In a world left devastated by a final war, an old wind-up record-player becomes a treasure beyond price.

ISAK DINESEN, *A Sailor Boy's Tale* 336

In one night, young Simon experiences all that life can offer. A celebrated Danish writer tells a tale of first love, sudden death, and magical transformation.

CRITICISM: ON FICTION   395

1 Reading a Story

After the shipwreck that marooned him on his desert island, Robinson Crusoe, in the story by Daniel Defoe, stood gazing over the water where pieces of cargo from his ship were floating by. Along came "two shoes, not mates." It is the qualification *not mates* that makes the detail memorable. We could well believe that a thing so striking and odd must have been seen, and not invented. But in truth Defoe, like other masters of the art of fiction, had the power to make us believe his imaginings. Borne along by the art of the storyteller, we trust what we are told, even though the story may be sheer fantasy.

Fiction (from the Latin *fictio,* "a shaping, a counterfeiting") is a name for stories not entirely factual, but at least partially shaped, made up, imagined. It is true that in some fiction, such as a historical novel, a writer draws upon factual information in presenting scenes, events, and characters. But the factual information in a historical novel, unlike that in a history book, is of secondary importance. Many firsthand accounts of the American Civil War were written by men who had fought in it, but few eyewitnesses give us so keen a sense of actual life on the battlefront as the author of *The Red Badge of Courage,* Stephen Crane, born after the war was over. In fiction, the "facts" may or may not be true, and a story is none the worse for their being entirely imaginary. We expect from fiction a sense of how people act, not an authentic chronicle of how, at some past time, a few people acted.

As children, we used to read (if we were lucky and formed the habit) to steep ourselves in romance, mystery, and adventure. As adults, we still do: at an airport, perhaps, while waiting for a flight, we pass the time with some newsstand paperback full of fast action and brisk dialogue. Certain fiction, of course, calls for closer attention. To read a novel by the Russian master Dostoevsky instead of a thriller about secret agent James Bond is somewhat like playing chess instead of a game of tic-tac-toe. Not that a great novel does not provide entertainment. In fact, it may offer more deeply satisfying entertainment than a novel of violence and soft-core pornography, in which stick figures connive, go to bed, and kill one another in accord with some market-tested formula. Reading **literary fiction** (as distinguished from fiction as a commercial product — the formula kind of spy, detective, Western, love, jungle, or other adventure story), we are not necessarily led on by the promise of thrills; we do not keep reading mainly to find out what happens next. Indeed, a literary story might even disclose in its opening lines everything that happened, then spend the rest of its length revealing what that happening meant. Reading literary fiction is no merely passive activity, but one that demands both attention and insight-lending participation. In return, it offers rewards. In some works of literary fiction, in Stephen Crane's "The Open Boat" and Leo Tolstoi's "The Death of Ivan Ilych," we see more deeply into the minds and hearts of the characters than we ever see into those of our family, our close friends, our lovers — or even ourselves.

FABLE AND TALE

Modern literary fiction in English has been dominated by two forms: the novel and the short story. The two have many elements in common (and in this book a further discussion of the novel as a special form will be given in Chapter Ten). Perhaps we will be able to define the short story more meaningfully — for it has traits more essential than just a particular length — if first, for comparison, we consider some related varieties of fiction: the fable and the tale. Ancient forms whose origins date back to the time of word-of-mouth storytelling, the fable and the tale are relatively simple in structure; in them we can plainly see elements also found in the short story (and in the novel). To begin, here is a **fable:** a brief story that sets forth some pointed statement of truth. The writer, W. Somerset Maugham, an English novelist and playwright (1874 – 1965), is retelling an Arabian folk story. (Samarra, by the way, is a city sixty miles from Bagdad.)

W. Somerset Maugham
THE APPOINTMENT IN SAMARRA   1933

Death speaks: There was a merchant in Bagdad who sent his servant to market to buy provisions and in a little while the servant came back, white and trembling, and said, Master, just now when I was in the market-place I was jostled by a woman in the crowd and when I turned I saw it was Death that jostled me. She looked at me and made a threatening gesture; now, lend me your horse, and I will ride away from this city and avoid my fate. I will go to Samarra and there Death will not find me. The merchant lent him his horse, and the servant mounted it, and he dug his spurs in its flanks and as fast as the horse could gallop he went. Then the merchant went down to the market-place and he saw me standing in the crowd and he came to me and said, Why did you make a threatening gesture to my servant when you saw him this morning? That was not a threatening gesture, I said, it was only a start of surprise. I was astonished to see him in Bagdad, for I had an appointment with him tonight in Samarra.

This brief story seems practically all skin and bones; that is, it contains little decoration. For in a fable everything leads directly to the **moral,** or message, sometimes stated at the end ("Moral: Haste makes waste"). In "The Appointment in Samarra" the moral isn't stated outright, it is merely implied. How would you state it in your own words?

You are probably acquainted with some of the fables credited to the Greek slave Aesop (about 620 – 560 B.C.), whose stories seem designed to teach lessons about human life. Such is the fable of "The Fox and the Grapes," in which a fox, unable to reach a bunch of grapes that hangs too high, decides that they were sour anyway. (Implied moral: It is easy to spurn what we cannot attain.) Another is the fable of "The Tortoise and the Hare" (implied moral: "Slow, steady plodding wins the race"). The characters in a fable may be talking animals (as in many of Aesop's fables), inanimate objects, or people and supernatural beings (as in "The Appointment in Samarra"). Whoever they may be, these characters are merely sketched, not greatly developed. Evidently, it would not have helped Maugham's fable to put across its point if he had portrayed the merchant, the servant, and Death in fuller detail. A more elaborate description of the market-place would not have improved the story. Probably, such a description would strike us as unnecessary and distracting. By its very bareness and simplicity, a fable fixes itself — and its message — in memory.

The name *tale* (from the Old English *talu,* "speech") is sometimes applied to any story, whether short or long, true or fictitious. *Tale* being a more evocative name than *story,* writers sometimes call their stories "tales" as if to imply something handed down from the past (as Nathaniel Hawthorne did in naming his *Twice-Told Tales*). But defined in a more limited sense, a **tale** is a story, usually short, that sets forth strange and wonderful events in more or less bare summary, without detailed character-drawing. "Tale" is pretty much synonymous with "yarn," for it implies a story in which the goal is revelation of the marvelous rather than revelation of character. In the English folk tale "Jack and the Beanstalk," we take away a more vivid impression of the miraculous beanstalk and the giant who dwells at its top than of Jack's mind or personality. Because such venerable stories were told aloud before someone set them down in writing, the storytellers had to limit themselves to brief descriptions. Probably spoken around a fire or hearth, such a tale tends to be less complicated and less closely detailed than a story written for the printed page, whose reader can linger over it. Still, such tales *can* be complicated. It is not merely greater length that makes a short story different from a tale or a fable: a mark of a short story is a fully delineated character.

Even modern tales favor supernatural or fantastic events: for instance, the **tall tale,** that variety of folk story which recounts the deeds of a superhero (Paul Bunyan, John Henry, Mike Fink) or of the storyteller. If the storyteller is telling about his own imaginary experience, his bragging yarn is usually told with a straight face to listeners who take pleasure in scoffing at it. Although the **fairy tale,** set in a world of magic and enchantment, is sometimes the work of a modern author (notably Hans Christian Andersen), well-known examples are those German folktales probably originated in the Middle Ages, collected by the brothers Grimm. The label *fairy tale* is something of an English misnomer, for in the Grimm stories, though witches and goblins abound, fairies are a minority.

Jakob and Wilhelm Grimm

GODFATHER DEATH   1812 (from oral tradition)

Translated by Lore Segal

Jakob Grimm (1785 – 1863) and Wilhelm Grimm (1786 – 1859), brothers and scholars, were born near Frankfurt-am-Main, Germany. For most of their lives they worked together — lived together, too, even when in 1825 Wilhelm married. In 1838, as librarians, they began toiling on their Deutsch Wörterbuch, *or German dictionary, a vast project that was to outlive them by a century. (It was completed only in 1960.) In 1840 King Friedrich Wilhelm IV appointed both brothers to the Royal Academy of Sciences, and both taught at the University of Berlin for the rest of their days. Although Jakob had a side-career as a diplomat, wrote a great* Deutsche Grammatik, *or German grammar (1819 – 37), and propounded Grimm's Law (an explanation of shifts in consonant sounds, of interest to students of linguistics), the name Grimm is best known to us for that splendid collection of ancient German folk stories we call* Grimm's Fairy Tales — *in German,* Kinder- und Hausmärchen *("Childhood and Household Tales," 1812 – 15). This classic work spread German children's stories around the world. Many tales we hear early in life were collected by the Grimms: "Hansel and Gretel," "Snow White and the Seven Dwarfs," "Rapunzel," "Puss-in-Boots," "Little Red Riding Hood," "Rumpelstiltskin." Versions of some of these tales had been written down as early as the sixteenth century, but mainly the brothers relied on the memories of Hessian peasants who recited the stories aloud for them.*

A poor man had twelve children and worked night and day just to get enough bread for them to eat. Now when the thirteenth came into the world, he did not know what to do and in his misery ran out onto the great highway to ask the first person he met to be godfather. The first to come along was God, and he already knew what it was that weighed on the man's mind and said, "Poor man, I pity you. I will hold your child at the font and I will look after it and make it happy upon earth." "Who are you?" asked the man. "I am God." "Then I don't want you for a godfather," the man said. "You give to the rich and let the poor go hungry." That was how the man talked because he did not understand how wisely God shares out wealth and poverty, and thus he turned from the Lord and walked on. Next came the Devil and said, "What is it you want? If you let me be godfather to your child, I will give him gold as much as he can use, and all the pleasures of the world besides." "Who are you?" asked the man. "I am the Devil." "Then I don't want you for a godfather," said the man. "You deceive and mislead mankind." He walked on and along came spindle-legged Death striding toward him and said, "Take me as godfather." The man asked, "Who are you?" "I am Death who makes all men equal." Said the man, "Then you're the one for me; you take rich and poor without distinction. You shall be godfather." Answered Death, "I will make your child rich and famous, because the one who has me for a friend shall want for nothing." The man said, "Next Sunday is the baptism. Be there in good time." Death appeared as he had promised and made a perfectly fine godfather.

When the boy was of age, the godfather walked in one day, told him to come along, and led him out into the woods. He showed him an herb which grew there and said, "This is your christening gift. I shall make you into a famous doctor. When you are called to a patient's bedside I will appear and if I stand at the sick man's head you can boldly say that you will cure him and if you give him some of this herb he will recover. But if I stand at the sick man's feet, then he is mine, and you must say there is no help for him and no doctor on this earth could save him. But take care not to use the herb against my will or it could be the worse for you."

It wasn't long before the young man had become the most famous doctor in the whole world. "He looks at a patient and right away he knows how things stand, whether he will get better or if he's going to die." That is what they said about him, and from near and far the people came, took him to see the sick, and gave him so much money he became a rich man. Now it happened that the king fell ill. The doctor was summoned to say if he was going to get well. When he came to the bed, there stood Death at the feet of the sick man, so that no herb on earth could have done him any good. If I could only just this once outwit Death! thought the doctor. He'll be annoyed, I know, but I am his godchild and he's sure to turn a blind eye. I'll take my chance. And so he lifted the sick man and laid him the other way around so that Death was standing at his head. Then he gave him some of the herb and the king began to feel better and was soon in perfect health. But Death came toward the doctor, his face dark and angry, threatened him with raised forefinger, and said, "You have tricked me. This time I will let it pass because you are my godchild, but if you ever dare do such a thing again, you put your own head in the noose and it is you I shall carry away with me."

Soon after that, the king's daughter lapsed into a deep illness. She was his only child, he wept day and night until his eyes failed him and he let it be known that whoever saved the princess from death should become her husband and inherit the crown. When the doctor came to the sick girl's bed, he saw Death at her feet. He ought to have remembered his godfather's warning, but the great beauty of the princess and the happiness of becoming her husband so bedazzled him that he threw caution to the winds, nor did he see Death's angry glances and how he lifted his hand in the air and threatened him with his bony fist. He picked the sick girl up and laid her head where her feet had lain, then he gave her some of the herb and at once her cheeks reddened and life stirred anew.

When Death saw himself cheated of his property the second time, he 5 strode toward the doctor on his long legs and said, "It is all up with you, and now it is your turn," grasped him harshly with his ice-cold hand so that the doctor could not resist, and led him to an underground cave, and here he saw thousands upon thousands of lights burning in rows without end, some big, some middle-sized, others small. Every moment some went out and others lit up so that the little flames seemed to be jumping here and there in perpetual exchange. "Look," said Death, "these are the life lights of mankind. The big ones belong to children, the middle-sized ones to married couples in their best years, the little ones belong to very old people. Yet children and the young often have only little lights." "Show me my life light," said the doctor, imagining that it must be one of the big ones. Death pointed to a little stub threatening to go out and said, "Here it is." "Ah, dear godfather," said the terrified doctor, "light me a new one, do it, for my sake, so that I may enjoy my life and become king and marry the beautiful princess." "I cannot," answered Death. "A light must go out before a new one lights up." "Then set the old on top of a new one so it can go on burning when the first is finished," begged the doctor. Death made as if to grant his wish, reached for a tall new taper, but because he wanted revenge he purposely fumbled and the little stub fell over and went out. Thereupon the doctor sank to the ground and had himself fallen into the hands of death.

PLOT

Like a fable, the Grimm brothers' tale seems stark in its lack of detail and in the swiftness of its telling. Compared with the fully portrayed characters of many modern stories, the characters of father, son, king, princess, and even Death himself seem hardly more than stick figures. It may have been that to draw ample characters would not have contributed to the storytellers' design; that, indeed, to have done so would have been inartistic. Yet "Godfather Death" is a compelling story. By what methods does it arouse and sustain our interest?

From the opening sentence of the tale, we watch the unfolding of a **dramatic situation:** a person is involved in some conflict. First, this character is a poor man with children to feed, in conflict with the world; very soon, we find him in conflict with God and with the Devil besides. Drama in fiction occurs in any clash of wills, desires, or powers — whether it be a conflict of character against character, character against society, character against some natural force, or, as in "Godfather Death," character against some supernatural entity.

Like any shapely tale, "Godfather Death" has a beginning, a middle, and an end. In fact, it is unusual to find a story so clearly displaying the elements of structure that critics have found in many classic works of fiction and drama. The tale begins with an **exposition:** the opening portion that sets the scene (if any), introduces the main characters, tells us what happened before the story opened, and provides any other background information that we need in order to understand and care about the events to follow. In "Godfather Death," the exposition is brief — all in the opening paragraph. The middle section of the story begins with Death's giving the herb to the boy, and his warning not to defy him. This moment introduces a new conflict (a **complication**), and by this time it is clear that the son and not the father is to be the central human character of the story. Death's godson is the principal person who strives: the **protagonist** (a better term than **hero,** for it may apply equally well to a central character who is not especially brave or virtuous).

The **suspense,** the pleasurable anxiety we feel that heightens our attention to the story, inheres in our wondering how it will all turn out. Will the doctor triumph over Death? Even though we suspect, early in the story, that the doctor stands no chance against such a superhuman **antagonist,** we want to see for ourselves the outcome of his defiance. A storyteller can try to incite our anticipation by giving us some **foreshadowing** or indication of events to come. In "Godfather Death" the foreshadowings are apparent in Death's warnings ("but if you ever dare do such a thing again, you put your own head in the noose"). When the doctor defies his godfather for the first time — when he saves the king — we have a **crisis,** a moment of high tension. The tension is momentarily resolved when Death lets him off. Then an even greater crisis — the turning point in the action — occurs with the doctor's second defiance in restoring the princess to life. In the last section of the story, with the doctor in the underworld, events come to a **climax,** the moment of greatest tension at which the outcome is to be decided, when the terrified doctor begs for a new candle. Will Death grant him one? Will he live, become king, and marry the princess? The outcome or **conclusion** — also called the **resolution** or **denouement** ("the untying of the knot") — quickly follows as Death allows the little candle to go out.

Such a structure of events arising out of a conflict may be called the plot of the story. Like many terms used in literary discussion, *plot* is blessed with several meanings. Sometimes it refers simply to the events in a story. In this book, **plot** will mean the artistic arrangement of those events. Different arrangements of the same material are possible. A writer might decide to tell of the events in chronological order, beginning with the earliest; or he might open his story with the last event, then tell what led up to it. Sometimes a writer chooses to skip rapidly over the exposition and begin **in medias res** (Latin, "in the midst of things"), first presenting some exciting or significant moment, then filling in what happened earlier. This method is by no means a modern invention: Homer begins the *Odyssey* with his hero mysteriously late in returning from war and his son searching for him; John Milton's *Paradise Lost* opens with Satan already defeated in his revolt against the Lord. A device useful to writers for filling in what happened earlier is the **flashback** (or **retrospect**), a scene relived in a character's memory.

To have a plot, a story does not need an intense, sustained conflict such as we find in "Godfather Death," a tale especially economical in its structure of crisis, climax, and conclusion. Although a highly dramatic story may tend to assume such a clearly recognizable structure, many contemporary writers avoid it, considering it too contrived and arbitrary. In commercial fiction, in which exciting conflict is everything and in which the writer has to manufacture all possible suspense, such a structure is often obvious. In popular detective, Western, and adventure novels; in juvenile fiction (the perennial Hardy Boys and Nancy Drew books); and in popular series on television (soap operas, police and hospital thrillers, mysteries, and cowboy stories), it is often easy to recognize crisis, climax, and conclusion. The presence of these elements does not necessarily indicate inferior literature (as "Godfather Death" shows); yet when reduced to parts of a formula, the result may seem stale and contrived.[1] Such plots may be (as contemporary French novelist Alain Robbe-Grillet describes them) mere anecdotes, providing trumped-up surprises for "the panting reader."

THE SHORT STORY

The teller of a tale relies heavily upon the method of **summary:** terse, general narration as in "Godfather Death" ("It wasn't long before the young man had become the most famous doctor in the whole world"). But in a **short story,** a form more realistic than the tale and of modern origin, the writer usually presents the main events in greater fullness. Fine writers of short stories, although they may use summary at times (often to give some portion of a story less emphasis), are skilled in rendering a **scene:** a vivid or dramatic moment described in enough detail to create the illusion that the reader is practically there. Avoiding long summary, they try to *show* rather than simply to *tell;* as if following Mark Twain's advice to authors: "Don't say, 'The old lady screamed.' Bring her on and let her scream."

A short story is more than just a sequence of happenings. A finely wrought short story has the richness and conciseness of an excellent lyric poem. Spontaneous and natural as the finished story may seem, the writer

---

[1] In the heyday of the **pulp magazines** (so called for their cheap paper), some professional writers even relied on a mechanical device called Plotto: a tin arrow-spinner pointed to numbers and the writer looked them up in a book that listed necessary ingredients — type of hero, type of villain, sort of conflict, crisis, climax, conclusion.

has written it so artfully that there is meaning in even seemingly casual speeches and apparently trivial details. If we skim it hastily, skipping the descriptive passages, we miss significant parts. Some literary short stories, unlike commercial fiction in which the main interest is in physical action or conflict, tell of an **epiphany:** some moment of insight, discovery, or revelation by which a character's life, or view of life, is greatly altered.[2] (For such moments in fiction, see the stories in this book by James Joyce, Leo Tolstoi, John Steinbeck, Edith Wharton, and Joyce Carol Oates.) Other short stories tell of a character initiated into experience or maturity: one such **story of initiation** is William Faulkner's "Barn Burning" (Chapter Five), in which a boy finds it necessary to defy his father and suddenly to grow into manhood. Less obviously dramatic, perhaps, than "Godfather Death," such a story may be no less powerful.

The fable and the tale are ancient forms; the short story is of more recent origin. In the nineteenth century, writers of fiction were encouraged by a large, literate audience of middle-class readers who wanted to see their lives reflected in faithful mirrors. Skillfully representing ordinary life, many writers perfected the art of the short story: in Russia, Anton Chekhov; in France, Honoré de Balzac, Gustave Flaubert, and Guy de Maupassant; and in America, Nathaniel Hawthorne and Edgar Allan Poe (although the Americans seem less fond of everyday life than of dream and fantasy). It would be false to claim that, in passing from the fable and the tale to the short story, fiction has made a triumphant progress; or to claim that, because short stories are modern, they are superior to fables and tales. Fable, tale, and short story are distinct forms, each achieving its own effects. (Incidentally, fable and tale are far from being extinct today: you can find many recent examples.) Lately, in the hands of Donald Barthelme, Joyce Carol Oates, John Barth, and other innovative writers, the conventions of the short story have been changing; and at the moment, stories of epiphany and initiation have become scarcer.

But let us begin with a contemporary short story whose protagonist *does* undergo an initiation into maturity. To notice the difference between a short story and a tale, you may find it helpful to compare John Updike's "A & P" with "Godfather Death." Although Updike's short story is centuries distant from the Grimm tale in its method of telling and in its setting, you may be reminded of "Godfather Death" in the main character's dramatic situation. To defend a young woman, a young man has to defy his mentor — here, the boss of a supermarket! So doing, he places himself in jeopardy. Updike has the protagonist tell his own story, amply and with humor. How does it differ from a tale?

[2]From the Greek *epiphainein,* "to show forth." In Christian tradition, the Feast of the Epiphany commemorates the revelation to the Magi of the birth of Christ. For James Joyce's description of epiphanies in everyday life, see page 400.

John Updike
A & P

John Updike, born in Shillingford, Pennsylvania in 1932, received his B.A. from Harvard, then studied drawing and fine art at Oxford. But writing soon became his main interest. From 1955 to 1957 he worked on the staff of The New Yorker, *sometimes doing errands for the aged James Thurber. Though he quit to be a full-time writer, he has continued to supply the magazine with bright stories and searching book reviews. Author of more than two dozen books, including both clever light verse and serious poetry, Updike is best known as a hardworking, versatile, highly productive novelist. (Hardly a fall goes by without a new Updike novel.) For* The Centaur *(1963) he received a National Book Award, and for* Rabbit Is Rich *(1982), a Pulitzer prize and an American Book Award.*

In walks these three girls in nothing but bathing suits. I'm in the third check-out slot, with my back to the door, so I don't see them until they're over by the bread. The one that caught my eye first was the one in the plaid green two-piece. She was a chunky kid, with a good tan and a sweet broad soft-looking can with those two crescents of white just under it, where the sun never seems to hit, at the top of the backs of her legs. I stood there with my hand on a box of HiHo crackers trying to remember if I rang it up or not. I ring it up again and the customer starts giving me hell. She's one of these cash-register-watchers, a witch about fifty with rouge on her cheekbones and no eyebrows, and I know it made her day to trip me up. She'd been watching cash registers for fifty years and probably never seen a mistake before.

By the time I got her feathers smoothed and her goodies into a bag — she gives me a little snort in passing, if she'd been born at the right time they would have burned her over in Salem — by the time I get her on her way the girls had circled around the bread and were coming back, without a push-cart, back my way along the counters, in the aisle between the check-outs and the Special bins. They didn't even have shoes on. There was this chunky one, with the two-piece — it was bright green and the seams on the bra were still sharp and her belly was still pretty pale so I guessed she just got it (the suit) — there was this one, with one of those chubby berry-faces, the lips all bunched together under her nose, this one, and a tall one, with black hair that hadn't quite frizzed right, and one of these sunburns right across under the eyes, and a chin that was too long — you know, the kind of girl other girls think is very "striking" and "attractive" but never quite makes it, as they very well know, which is why they like her so much — and then the third one, that wasn't quite so tall. She was the queen. She kind of led them, the other two peeking around and making their shoulders round. She didn't look around, not this queen, she just walked straight on slowly, on these long white prima-donna legs. She came down a little hard on her heels, as if she didn't walk in her bare feet that much, putting down her heels and then letting the weight move along to her toes as if she was testing the floor with every step, putting a little deliberate extra action into it. You never know for sure how girls' minds

12   Reading a Story

work (do you really think it's a mind in there or just a little buzz like a bee in a glass jar?) but you got the idea she had talked the other two into coming in here with her, and now she was showing them how to do it, walk slow and hold yourself straight.

She had on a kind of dirty-pink — beige maybe, I don't know — bathing suit with a little nubble all over it and, what got me, the straps were down. They were off her shoulders looped loose around the cool tops of her arms, and I guess as a result the suit had slipped a little on her, so all around the top of the cloth there was this shining rim. If it hadn't been there you wouldn't have known there could have been anything whiter than those shoulders. With the straps pushed off, there was nothing between the top of the suit and the top of her head except just *her*, this clean bare plane of the top of her chest down from the shoulder bones like a dented sheet of metal tilted in the light. I mean, it was more than pretty.

She had sort of oaky hair that the sun and salt had bleached, done up in a bun that was unravelling, and a kind of prim face. Walking into the A & P with your straps down, I suppose it's the only kind of face you *can* have. She held her head so high her neck, coming up out of those white shoulders, looked kind of stretched, but I didn't mind. The longer her neck was, the more of her there was.

She must have felt in the corner of her eye me and over my shoulder Stokesie in the second slot watching, but she didn't tip. Not this queen. She kept her eyes moving across the racks, and stopped, and turned so slow it made my stomach rub the inside of my apron, and buzzed to the other two, who kind of huddled against her for relief, and they all three of them went up the cat-and-dog-food-breakfast-cereal-macaroni-rice-raisins-seasonings-spreads-spaghetti-soft-drinks-crackers-and-cookies aisle. From the third slot I look straight up this aisle to the meat counter, and I watched them all the way. The fat one with the tan sort of fumbled with the cookies, but on second thought she put the packages back. The sheep pushing their carts down the aisle — the girls were walking against the usual traffic (not that we have one-way signs or anything) — were pretty hilarious. You could see them, when Queenie's white shoulders dawned on them, kind of jerk, or hop, or hiccup, but their eyes snapped back to their own baskets and on they pushed. I bet you could set off dynamite in an A & P and the people would by and large keep reaching and checking oatmeal off their lists and muttering "Let me see, there was a third thing, began with A, asparagus, no, ah, yes, applesauce!" or whatever it is they do mutter. But there was no doubt, this jiggled them. A few houseslaves in pin curlers even looked around after pushing their carts past to make sure what they had seen was correct.

You know, it's one thing to have a girl in a bathing suit down on the beach, where what with the glare nobody can look at each other much anyway, and another thing in the cool of the A & P, under the fluorescent lights, against all those stacked packages, with her feet paddling along naked over our checkerboard green-and-cream rubber-tile floor.

"Oh Daddy," Stokesie said beside me. "I feel so faint."

"Darling," I said. "Hold me tight." Stokesie's married, with two babies chalked up on his fuselage already, but as far as I can tell that's the only difference. He's twenty-two, and I was nineteen this April.

"Is it done?" he asks, the responsible married man finding his voice. I forgot to say he thinks he's going to be manager some sunny day, maybe in 1990 when it's called the Great Alexandrov and Petrooshki Tea Company or something.

What he meant was, our town is five miles from a beach, with a big summer colony out on the Point, but we're right in the middle of town, and the women generally put on a shirt or shorts or something before they get out of the car into the street. And anyway these are usually women with six children and varicose veins mapping their legs and nobody, including them, could care less. As I say, we're right in the middle of town, and if you stand at our front doors you can see two banks and the Congregational church and the newspaper store and three real-estate offices and about twenty-seven old freeloaders tearing up Central Street because the sewer broke again. It's not as if we're on the Cape; we're north of Boston and there's people in this town haven't seen the ocean for twenty years.

The girls had reached the meat counter and were asking McMahon something. He pointed, they pointed, and they shuffled out of sight behind a pyramid of Diet Delight peaches. All that was left for us to see was old McMahon patting his mouth and looking after them sizing up their joints. Poor kids, I began to feel sorry for them, they couldn't help it.

Now here comes the sad part of the story, at least my family says it's sad but I don't think it's sad myself. The store's pretty empty, it being Thursday afternoon, so there was nothing much to do except lean on the register and wait for the girls to show up again. The whole store was like a pinball machine and I didn't know which tunnel they'd come out of. After a while they come around out of the far aisle, around the light bulbs, records at discount of the Caribbean Six or Tony Martin Sings or some such gunk you wonder they waste the wax on, sixpacks of candy bars, and plastic toys done up in cellophane that fall apart when a kid looks at them anyway. Around they come, Queenie still leading the way, and holding a little gray jar in her hand. Slots Three through Seven are unmanned and I could see her wondering between Stokes and me, but Stokesie with his usual luck draws an old party in baggy gray pants who stumbles up with four giant cans of pineapple juice (what do these bums *do* with all that pineapple juice? I've often asked myself) so the girls come to me. Queenie puts down the jar and I take it into my fingers icy cold. Kingfish Fancy Herring Snacks in Pure Sour Cream: 49¢. Now her hands are empty, not a ring or a bracelet, bare as God made them, and I wonder where the money's coming from. Still with that prim look she lifts a folded dollar bill out of the hollow at the center of her nubbled pink top. The jar went heavy in my hand. Really, I thought that was so cute.

Then everybody's luck begins to run out. Lengel comes in from haggling with a truck full of cabbages on the lot and is about to scuttle into that door marked MANAGER behind which he hides all day when the girls touch his eye. Lengel's pretty dreary, teaches Sunday school and the rest, but he doesn't miss that much. He comes over and says, "Girls, this isn't the beach."

Queenie blushes, though maybe it's just a brush of sunburn I was noticing for the first time, now that she was so close. "My mother asked me to pick up a jar of herring snacks." Her voice kind of startled me, the way voices do when you see the people first, coming out so flat and dumb yet kind of tony, too, the way it ticked over "pick up" and "snacks." All of a sudden I slid right down her voice into her living room. Her father and the other men were standing around in ice-cream coats and bow ties and the women were in sandals picking up herring snacks on toothpicks off a big plate and they were all holding drinks the color of water with olives and sprigs of mint in them. When my parents have somebody over they get lemonade and if it's a real racy affair Schlitz in tall glasses with "They'll Do It Every Time" cartoons stencilled on.

"That's all right," Lengel said. "But this isn't the beach." His repeating   15
this struck me as funny, as if it had just occurred to him, and he had been thinking all these years the A & P was a great big dune and he was the head lifeguard. He didn't like my smiling — as I say he doesn't miss much — but he concentrates on giving the girls that sad Sunday-school-superintendent stare.

Queenie's blush is no sunburn now, and the plump one in plaid, that I liked better from the back — a really sweet can — pipes up, "We weren't doing any shopping. We just came in for the one thing."

"That makes no difference," Lengel tells her, and I could see from the way his eyes went that he hadn't noticed she was wearing a two-piece before. "We want you decently dressed when you come in here."

"We *are* decent," Queenie says suddenly, her lower lip pushing, getting sore now that she remembers her place, a place from which the crowd that runs the A & P must look pretty crummy. Fancy Herring Snacks flashed in her very blue eyes.

"Girls, I don't want to argue with you. After this come in here with your shoulders covered. It's our policy." He turns his back. That's policy for you. Policy is what the kingpins want. What the others want is juvenile delinquency.

All this while, the customers had been showing up with their carts but,   20
you know, sheep, seeing a scene, they had all bunched up on Stokesie, who shook open a paper bag as gently as peeling a peach, not wanting to miss a word. I could feel in the silence everybody getting nervous, most of all Lengel, who asks me, "Sammy, have you rung up this purchase?"

I thought and said "No" but it wasn't about that I was thinking. I go through the punches, 4, 9, GROC, TOT — it's more complicated than you think, and after you do it often enough, it begins to make a little song, that you hear words to, in my case "Hello *(bing)* there, you *(gung)* hap-py *pee*-pul *(splat)!*" — the *splat* being the drawer flying out. I uncrease the bill, tenderly as you may imagine, it just having come from between the two smoothest scoops of vanilla I had ever known were there, and pass a half and a penny into her narrow pink palm, and nestle the herrings in a bag and twist its neck and hand it over, all the time thinking.

The girls, and who'd blame them, are in a hurry to get out, so I say "I quit" to Lengel quick enough for them to hear, hoping they'll stop and watch me, their unsuspected hero. They keep right on going, into the electric eye; the door flies open and they flicker across the lot to their car, Queenie and Plaid and Big Tall Goony-Goony (not that as raw material she was so bad), leaving me with Lengel and a kink in his eyebrow.

"Did you say something, Sammy?"

"I said I quit."

"I thought you did."

"You didn't have to embarrass them."

"It was they who were embarrassing us."

I started to say something that came out "Fiddle-de-doo." It's a saying of my grandmother's, and I know she would have been pleased.

"I don't think you know what you're saying," Lengel said.

"I know you don't," I said. "But I do." I pull the bow at the back of my apron and start shrugging it off my shoulders. A couple customers that had been heading for my slot begin to knock against each other, like scared pigs in a chute.

Lengel sighs and begins to look very patient and old and gray. He's been a friend of my parents for years. "Sammy, you don't want to do this to your Mom and Dad," he tells me. It's true, I don't. But it seems to me that once you begin a gesture it's fatal not to go through with it. I fold the apron, "Sammy" stitched in red on the pocket, and put it on the counter, and drop the bow tie on top of it. The bow tie is theirs, if you've ever wondered. "You'll feel this for the rest of your life," Lengel says, and I know that's true, too, but remembering how he made that pretty girl blush makes me so scrunchy inside I punch the No Sale tab and the machine whirs "pee-pul" and the drawer splats out. One advantage to this scene taking place in summer, I can follow this up with a clean exit, there's no fumbling around getting your coat and galoshes, I just saunter into the electric eye in my white shirt that my mother ironed the night before, and the door heaves itself open, and outside the sunshine is skating around on the asphalt.

I look around for my girls, but they're gone, of course. There wasn't anybody but some young married screaming with her children about some candy they didn't get by the door of a powder-blue Falcon station wagon. Looking back in the big windows, over the bags of peat moss and aluminum lawn furniture stacked on the pavement, I could see Lengel in my place in the slot, checking the sheep through. His face was dark gray and his back stiff, as if he'd just had an injection of iron, and my stomach kind of fell as I felt how hard the world was going to be to me hereafter.

Questions

1. Notice how artfully Updike arranges details to set the story in a perfectly ordinary supermarket. What details stand out for you as particularly true to life? What does this close attention to detail contribute to the story?
2. How fully does Updike draw the character of Sammy? What traits (admirable or otherwise) does Sammy show? Is he any less a hero for wanting the girls to notice his heroism? To what extent is he more thoroughly and fully portrayed than the doctor in "Godfather Death"?
3. What part of the story seems exposition? (See the definition of *exposition* on page 9.) Of what value to the story is the carefully detailed portrait of Queenie, the leader of the three girls?
4. As the story develops, do you detect any change in Sammy's feelings toward the girls?
5. Where in "A & P" does the dramatic conflict become apparent? What moment in the story brings the crisis? What is the climax of the story?

6. Why, exactly, does Sammy quit his job?
7. Does anything lead you to *expect* Sammy to make some gesture of sympathy for the three girls? What incident earlier in the story (before Sammy quits) seems a foreshadowing?
8. What do you understand from the conclusion of the story? What does Sammy mean when he acknowledges "how hard the world was going to be . . . hereafter"?
9. What comment does Updike — through Sammy — make on supermarket society?

Suggestions for Writing

1. In a paragraph or two, referring to John Updike's "A & P," consider this remark: "Sammy is a sexist pig who suddenly sees the light." What evidence supporting (or refuting) this comment do you find in the story?
2. Imagining you are Sammy, write a brief letter to a friend explaining why you quit your job.
3. Look up Anne Sexton's retelling of the Grimm tale "Godfather Death" in her book of poems *Transformations* (1971); also included in *The Complete Poems of Anne Sexton* (1981). In a short essay of three to five paragraphs, discuss the differences you find between the Grimm and Sexton versions. What is the effect of Sexton's retelling? What does she retain from the original? Which version of the story do you prefer? Why?
4. If you have had any experience in telling stories aloud (to children or to others), write a brief but detailed account of your experience, giving tips to adults who wish to become storytellers.
5. Write a brief fable of your own invention, perhaps illustrating some familiar proverb ("Too many cooks spoil the broth," "A rolling stone gathers no moss"). Your fable might be inspired by "The Appointment in Samarra" or by a fable of Aesop. You can state a moral at the end, or, if you prefer, let the moral be unstated but obvious.
6. After you have written such a fable, write a short account of your writing process. Tell of the problems you encountered in thinking up your fable and in writing it, and how you surmounted them.

2 Point of View

In the opening lines of *The Adventures of Huckleberry Finn,* Mark Twain takes care to separate himself from the leading character, who is to tell his own story:

> You don't know about me, without you have read a book by the name of *The Adventures of Tom Sawyer,* but that ain't no matter. That book was made by Mr. Mark Twain, and he told the truth, mainly.

Twain wrote the novel, but the **narrator** or speaker is Huck Finn, the one from whose perspective the story is told. Obviously, in *Huckleberry Finn,* the narrator of a story is not the same person as the "real-life" author, the one given the by-line. In employing Huck as his narrator, Twain selects a special angle of vision: not his own, exactly, but that of a resourceful boy moving through the thick of events, with a mind at times shrewd, at other times innocent. Through Huck's eyes, Twain takes in certain scenes, actions, and characters and — as only Huck's angle of vision could have enabled Twain to do so well — records them memorably.

Not every narrator in fiction is, like Huck Finn, a main character, one in the thick of events. Some narrators play only minor parts in the stories they tell; others take no active part at all. In the tale of "Godfather Death," we have a narrator who does not participate in the events he recounts. He is not a character in the story but is someone not even named, who stands at some distance from the action recording what the main characters say and do; recording also, at times, what they think, feel, or desire. He seems to have unlimited knowledge: he even knows the mind of Death, who "because he wanted revenge" let the doctor's candle go out. More humanly restricted in their knowledge, other narrators can see into the mind of only one character. They may be less willing to express opinions than the narrator of "Godfather Death" ("He ought to have remembered his godfather's warning"). A story may even be told by a narrator who seems so impartial and aloof that he limits himself to reporting only overheard conversation and to describing, without comment or opinion, the appearances of things. Evidently, narrators greatly differ in kind; however, because stories usually are told by someone, almost every story has some kind of narrator.[1] It is rare in modern fiction for the "real-life" author to try to step out from behind the typewriter and tell the story. Real persons can tell stories, but when such a story is *written*, the result is usually *non*fiction: a memoir, an account of travels, an autobiography.[2]

To identify the narrator of a story, describing any part he or she plays in the events and any limits placed upon his knowledge, is to identify the story's **point of view.** In a short story, it is usual for the writer to maintain one point of view from beginning to end, but there is nothing to stop him from introducing other points of view as well. In his long, panoramic novel *War and Peace,* Leo Tolstoi, encompassing the vast drama of Napoleon's invasion of Russia, freely shifts the point of view in and out of the minds of many characters, among them Napoleon himself.

Theoretically, a great many points of view are possible. A narrator who says "I" might conceivably be involved in events to a much greater or a much lesser degree: as the protagonist, as some other major character, as some minor character, as a mere passive spectator, or even as a character who arrives late upon the scene and then tries to piece together what happened. Evidently, too, a narrator's knowledge might vary in gradations from total omniscience to almost total ignorance. But in reading fiction, again and again we encounter familiar and recognizable points of view. Here is a list of them — admittedly just a rough abstraction — that may provide a few terms with which to discuss the stories that you read and to describe their points of view:

Narrator a participant (writing in the first person):
   1. a major character
   2. a minor character

Narrator a nonparticipant (writing in the third person):
   3. all-knowing (seeing into any of the characters)
   4. seeing into one major character
   5. seeing into one minor character
   6. objective (not seeing into any characters)

When the narrator is cast as a **participant** in the events of the story, he or she is a dramatized character who says "I." Such a narrator may be

---

[1]Some theorists reserve the term *narrator* for a character who tells a story in the first person. We use it in a wider sense: to mean a recording consciousness that an author creates, who may or may not be a participant in the events of the story. In the view of Wayne C. Booth, the term *narrator* can be dispensed with in dealing with a rigorously impersonal "fly-on-the-wall" story, containing no editorializing and confined to the presentation of surfaces: "In Hemingway's 'The Killers,' for example, there is no narrator other than the implicit second self that Hemingway creates as he writes" *(The Rhetoric of Fiction* [Chicago: U of Chicago P, 1961] 151).

[2]Another relationship between the author and the story will be discussed in Chapter Five, "Tone and Style."

the protagonist (Huck Finn) or may be an **observer,** a minor character standing a little to one side, watching a story unfold that mainly involves someone else.

A narrator who remains a **nonparticipant** does not appear in the story as a character. Viewing the characters, perhaps seeing into the minds of one or more of them, such a narrator refers to them as "he," "she," or "they." When **all-knowing** (or **omniscient**), the narrator sees into the minds of all (or some) characters, moving when necessary from one to another. This is the point of view in "Godfather Death," whose narrator knows the feelings and motives of the father, of the doctor, and even of Death himself. In that he adds an occasional comment or opinion, this narrator may be said also to show **editorial omniscience** (as we can tell from his disapproving remark that the doctor "ought to have remembered" and his observation that the father did not understand "how wisely God shares out wealth and poverty"). A narrator who shows **impartial omniscience** presents the thoughts and actions of the characters, but does not judge them or comment on them.

When a nonparticipating narrator sees events through the eyes of a single character, whether a major character or a minor one, the resulting point of view is sometimes called **limited omniscience** or **selective omniscience.** The author, of course, selects which character to see through; the omniscience is his and not the narrator's. In William Faulkner's "Barn Burning" (Chapter Five), the narrator is almost entirely confined to knowing the thoughts and perceptions of a boy, the central character. Here is another example. Early in his novel *Madame Bovary*, Gustave Flaubert tells of the first time a young country doctor, Charles Bovary, meets Emma, the woman later to become his wife. The doctor has been summoned late at night to set the broken leg of a farmer, Emma's father.

> A young woman wearing a blue merino dress with three flounces came to the door of the house to greet Monsieur Bovary, and she ushered him into the kitchen, where a big open fire was blazing. Around its edges the farm hands' breakfast was bubbling in small pots of assorted sizes. Damp clothes were drying inside the vast chimney-opening. The fire shovel, the tongs, and the nose of the bellows, all of colossal proportions, shone like polished steel; and along the walls hung a lavish array of kitchen utensils, glimmering in the bright light of the fire and in the first rays of the sun that were now beginning to come in through the window-panes.
>
> Charles went upstairs to see the patient. He found him in bed, sweating under blankets, his nightcap lying where he had flung it. He was a stocky little man of fifty, fair-skinned, blue-eyed, bald in front and wearing earrings. On a chair beside him was a big decanter of brandy: he had been pouring himself drinks to keep up his courage. But as soon as he saw the doctor he dropped his bluster, and instead of cursing as he had been doing for the past twelve hours he began to groan weakly.
>
> The fracture was a simple one, without complications of any kind.

Charles couldn't have wished for anything easier. Then he recalled his teachers' bedside manner in accident cases, and proceeded to cheer up his patient with all kinds of facetious remarks — a truly surgical attention, like the oiling of a scalpel. For splints, they sent someone to bring a bundle of laths from the carriage shed. Charles selected one, cut it into lengths and smoothed it down with a piece of broken window glass, while the maidservant tore sheets for bandages and Mademoiselle Emma tried to sew some pads. She was a long time finding her workbox, and her father showed his impatience. She made no reply; but as she sewed she kept pricking her fingers and raising them to her mouth to suck.

Charles was surprised by the whiteness of her fingernails. They were almond-shaped, tapering, as polished and shining as Dieppe ivories. Her hands, however, were not pretty — not pale enough, perhaps, a little rough at the knuckles; and they were too long, without softness of line. The finest thing about her was her eyes. They were brown, but seemed black under the long eyelashes; and she had an open gaze that met yours with fearless candor.[3]

In this famous scene, Charles Bovary is beholding people and objects in a natural sequence. On first meeting Emma, he notices only her dress, as though less interested in the woman who opens the door than in passing through to the warm fire. Needing pads for his patient's splint, the doctor observes just the hands of the woman sewing them. Obliged to wait for the splints, he then has the leisure to notice her face, her remarkable eyes. (By the way, notice the effect of the word *yours* in the last sentence of the passage. It is as if the reader, seeing through the doctor's eyes, suddenly became one with him.) Who is the narrator? Not Charles Bovary, nor Gustave Flaubert, but someone able to enter the minds of others — here limited to knowing the thoughts and perceptions of one character.

In the **objective** point of view, the narrator does not enter the mind of any character but describes events from the outside. Telling us what people say and how their faces look, he leaves us to infer their thoughts and feelings. So inconspicuous is the narrator that this point of view has been called "the fly on the wall." This metaphor assumes the existence of a fly with a highly discriminating gaze, who knows which details to look for to communicate the deepest meaning. Some critics would say that in the objective point of view, the narrator disappears altogether. Consider this passage by a writer famous for remaining objective, Dashiell Hammett, in his mystery novel *The Maltese Falcon,* describing his private detective Sam Spade:

Spade's thick fingers made a cigarette with deliberate care, sifting a measured quantity of tan flakes down into curved paper, spreading the flakes so that they lay equal at the ends with a slight depression in the middle, thumbs rolling the paper's inner edge down and up under the outer edge as forefingers pressed it over, thumb and fingers sliding

[3]*Madame Bovary,* translated by Francis Steegmuller (New York: Random, 1957) 16 – 17.

to the paper cylinder's ends to hold it even while tongue licked the flap, left forefinger and thumb pinching their ends while right forefinger and thumb smoothed the damp seam, right forefinger and thumb twisting their end and lifting the other to Spade's mouth.[4]

In Hammett's novel, this sentence comes at a moment of crisis: just after Spade has been roused from bed in the middle of the night by a phone call telling him that his partner has been murdered. Even in time of stress (we infer) Spade is deliberate, cool, efficient, and painstaking. Hammett refrains from applying all those adjectives to Spade; to do so would be to exercise editorial omniscience and to destroy the objective point of view.

Besides the common points of view just listed, uncommon points of view are possible. In *Flush,* a fictional biography of Elizabeth Barrett Browning, Virginia Woolf employs an unusual observer as narrator: the poet's pet cocker spaniel. In "The Circular Valley," a short story by Paul Bowles, a man and a woman are watched by a sinister spirit trying to take possession of them, and we see the human characters through the spirit's vague consciousness. The narrator, however, is human and a nonparticipant. Possible also, but unusual, is a story written in the second person, *you.* This point of view results in an attention-getting directness, as in Jay McInerney's novel *Bright Lights, Big City* (1985), which begins:

> You are not the kind of guy who would be at a place like this at this time of the morning. But here you are, and you cannot say that the terrain is entirely unfamiliar, although the details are fuzzy. You are at a nightclub talking to a girl with a shaved head.

This arresting way to tell a story is effective, too, in a novel by Carlos Fuentes, *Aura* (1962), in some startling stories by Lorrie Moore in *Self-Help* (1985), and (apparently with great popular success) in a recent line of juvenile paperbound books, "The Adventures of You Series."[5]

The attitudes and opinions of a narrator aren't necessarily those of the author; in fact, we may notice a lively conflict between what we are told and what, apparently, we are meant to believe. A story may be told by an **innocent narrator** or a **naive narrator,** a character who fails to understand all the implications of the story. One such innocent narrator (despite his sometimes shrewd perceptions) is Huckleberry Finn. Because Huck accepts without question the morality and lawfulness of slavery, he feels guilty about helping Jim, a runaway slave. But, far from condemning Huck for his defiance of the law — "All right, then, I'll *go* to hell," Huck

[4]Chapter Two, "Death in the Fog," *The Maltese Falcon* (New York: Knopf, 1929).
[5]Each book starts out with you, the main character, facing some challenge or danger. Then you are offered a choice: "Will you leap forward and struggle with the vampire? Turn to page 20. Will you flee? Turn to page 22." If you choose badly, you may be told, "Suddenly you feel the searing pain of a spear in your back. You sink to the ground — finished for good" (from Edward Packard, *Sugarcane Island* [New York: Pocket, 1978] 60).

tells himself, deciding against returning Jim to captivity — the author, and the reader along with him, silently applaud. Naive in the extreme is the narrator of one part of William Faulkner's novel *The Sound and the Fury,* the idiot Benjy, a grown man with the intellect of a child. In a story told by an **unreliable narrator,** the point of view is that of a person who, we perceive, is deceptive, self-deceptive, deluded, or deranged. As though seeking ways to be faithful to uncertainty, contemporary writers have been particularly fond of unreliable narrators.

Virginia Woolf compared life to "a luminous halo, a semi-transparent envelope surrounding us from the beginning of consciousness to the end."[6] To capture such a reality, modern writers of fiction have employed many strategies. One is the method of writing called **stream of consciousness,** from a phrase coined by psychologist William James to describe the procession of thoughts passing through the mind. In fiction, stream of consciousness is a kind of selective omniscience: the presentation of thoughts and sense impressions in a lifelike fashion — not in a sequence arranged by logic, but mingled randomly. When in his novel *Ulysses* James Joyce takes us into the mind of Leopold Bloom, an ordinary Dublin mind well-stocked with trivia and fragments of odd learning, the reader may have an impression not of a smoothly flowing stream but of an ocean of miscellaneous things, all crowded and jostling.

> As he set foot on O'Connell bridge a puffball of smoke plumed up from the parapet. Brewery barge with export stout. England. Sea air sours it, I heard. Be interesting some day to get a pass through Hancock to see the brewery. Regular world in itself. Vats of porter, wonderful. Rats get in too. Drink themselves bloated as big as a collie floating.[7]

Perceptions — such as the smoke from the brewery barge — trigger Bloom's reflections. A moment later, as he casts a crumpled paper ball off the bridge, he recalls a bit of science he learned in school, the rate of speed of a falling body: "thirty-two feet per sec."

Stream-of-consciousness writing usually occurs in relatively short passages, but in *Ulysses* Joyce employs it extensively. Similar in method, an **interior monologue** is an extended presentation of a character's thoughts, not in the seemingly helter-skelter order of a stream of consciousness, but in an arrangement as if the character were speaking out loud to himself, for us to overhear. A famous interior monologue comes at the end of *Ulysses* when Joyce gives us the rambling memories and reflections of earth-mother Molly Bloom.

Every point of view has limitations. Even **total omniscience,** a knowledge of the minds of all the characters, has its disadvantages. Such

[6]"Modern Fiction," in *Collected Essays* (New York: Harcourt, 1967). For the entire statement, see page 401.
[7]*Ulysses* (New York: Random, 1934) 150.

a point of view requires high skill to manage, without the storyteller's losing his way in a multitude of perspectives. In fact, there are evident advantages in having a narrator not know everything. We are accustomed to seeing the world through one pair of eyes, to having truths gradually occur to us. Henry James, whose theory and practice of fiction have been influential, held that an excellent way to tell a story was through the fine but bewildered mind of an observer. "It seems probable," James wrote, "that if we were never bewildered there would never be a story to tell about us; we should partake of the superior nature of the all-knowing immortals whose annals are dreadfully dull so long as flurried humans are not, for the positive relief of bored Olympians, mixed up with them."[8]

By using a particular point of view, an author may artfully withhold information, if need be, rather than immediately present it to us. If, for instance, the suspense in a story depends upon our not knowing until the end that the protagonist is a secret agent, the author would be ill advised to tell the story from the protagonist's point of view. If a character acts as the narrator, the author must make sure that the character possesses (or can obtain) enough information to tell the story adequately. Clearly, the author makes a fundamental decision in selecting, from many possibilities, a story's point of view. What we readers admire, if the story is effective, is not only skill in execution, but also powers of choice.

Here is a short story memorable for many reasons, among them for its point of view.

William Faulkner

A ROSE FOR EMILY
1931

William Faulkner (1897 – 1962) spent most of his days in Oxford, Mississippi, where he attended the University of Mississippi and where he served as postmaster until angry townspeople ejected him after they had long failed to receive mail. During World War I he served with the Royal Canadian Air Force, and afterward worked as a feature writer for the New Orleans Times-Picayune. *Faulkner's private life was a long struggle to stay solvent: even after fame came to him, he had to write Hollywood scripts and teach at the University of Virginia. The violent comic novel* Sanctuary *(1931) caused a stir and turned a profit, but critics tend most to admire* The Sound and the Fury *(1929), a tale partially told through the eyes of an idiot;* As I Lay Dying *(1930);* Light in August *(1932);* Absalom, Absalom *(1936); and* The Hamlet *(1940). Beginning with* Sartoris *(1929), Faulkner in his fiction imagines a Mississippi county named Yoknapatawpha*

---

[8]Preface to *The Princess Casamassima*, reprinted in *The Art of the Novel*, ed. R. P. Blackmur (New York: Scribner's, 1934).

and traces the fortunes of several of its families, including the aristocratic Compsons and Sartorises and the white-trash, dollar-grubbing Snopeses, from the Civil War to modern times. His influence on his fellow southern writers (and others) has been profound. In 1950 he received the Nobel prize for literature with a stirring speech (quoted on page 403). Although we think of Faulkner primarily as a novelist, he wrote nearly a hundred short stories. Forty-two of the best are available in his Collected Stories *(1950).*

I

When Miss Emily Grierson died, our whole town went to her funeral: the men through a sort of respectful affection for a fallen monument, the women mostly out of curiosity to see the inside of her house, which no one save an old manservant — a combined gardener and cook — had seen in at least ten years.

It was a big, squarish frame house that had once been white, decorated with cupolas and spires and scrolled balconies in the heavily lightsome style of the seventies, set on what had once been our most select street. But garages and cotton gins had encroached and obliterated even the august names of that neighborhood; only Miss Emily's house was left, lifting its stubborn and coquettish decay above the cotton wagons and the gasoline pumps — an eyesore among eyesores. And now Miss Emily had gone to join the representatives of those august names where they lay in the cedar-bemused cemetery among the ranked and anonymous graves of Union and Confederate soldiers who fell at the battle of Jefferson.

Alive, Miss Emily had been a tradition, a duty, and a care; a sort of hereditary obligation upon the town, dating from that day in 1894 when Colonel Sartoris, the mayor — he who fathered the edict that no Negro woman should appear on the streets without an apron — remitted her taxes, the dispensation dating from the death of her father on into perpetuity. Not that Miss Emily would have accepted charity. Colonel Sartoris invented an involved tale to the effect that Miss Emily's father had loaned money to the town, which the town, as a matter of business, preferred this way of repaying. Only a man of Colonel Sartoris' generation and thought could have invented it, and only a woman could have believed it.

When the next generation, with its more modern ideas, became mayors and aldermen, this arrangement created some little dissatisfaction. On the first of the year they mailed her a tax notice. February came, and there was no reply. They wrote her a formal letter, asking her to call at the sheriff's office at her convenience. A week later the mayor wrote her himself, offering to call or to send his car for her, and received in reply a note on paper of an archaic shape, in a thin, flowing calligraphy in faded ink, to the effect that she no longer went out at all. The tax notice was also enclosed, without comment.

They called a special meeting of the Board of Aldermen. A deputation ⁵ waited upon her, knocked at the door through which no visitor had passed since she ceased giving china-painting lessons eight or ten years earlier. They were admitted by the old Negro into a dim hall from which a stairway mounted into still more shadow. It smelled of dust and disuse — a close, dank smell. The Negro led them into the parlor. It was furnished in heavy, leather-covered furniture. When the Negro opened the blinds of one window, they could see that the leather was cracked; and when they sat down, a faint dust rose sluggishly about their thighs, spinning with slow motes in the single sun-ray. On a tarnished gilt easel before the fireplace stood a crayon portrait of Miss Emily's father.

They rose when she entered — a small, fat woman in black, with a thin gold chain descending to her waist and vanishing into her belt, leaning on an ebony cane with a tarnished gold head. Her skeleton was small and spare; perhaps that was why what would have been merely plumpness in another was obesity in her. She looked bloated, like a body long submerged in motion-less water, and of that pallid hue. Her eyes, lost in the fatty ridges of her face, looked like two small pieces of coal pressed into a lump of dough as they moved from one face to another while the visitors stated their errand.

She did not ask them to sit. She just stood in the door and listened quietly until the spokesman came to a stumbling halt. Then they could hear the invisible watch ticking at the end of the gold chain.

Her voice was dry and cold. "I have no taxes in Jefferson. Colonel Sartoris explained it to me. Perhaps one of you can gain access to the city records and satisfy yourselves."

"But we have. We are the city authorities, Miss Emily. Didn't you get a notice from the sheriff, signed by him?"

"I received a paper, yes," Miss Emily said. "Perhaps he considers himself   10
the sheriff . . . I have no taxes in Jefferson."

"But there is nothing on the books to show that, you see. We must go by the — "

"See Colonel Sartoris. I have no taxes in Jefferson."

"But, Miss Emily — "

"See Colonel Sartoris." (Colonel Sartoris had been dead almost ten years.) "I have no taxes in Jefferson. Tobe!" The Negro appeared. "Show these gentlemen out."

II

So she vanquished them, horse and foot, just as she had vanquished their   15
fathers thirty years before about the smell. That was two years after her father's death and a short time after her sweetheart — the one we believed would marry her — had deserted her. After her father's death she went out very little; after her sweetheart went away, people hardly saw her at all. A few of the ladies had the temerity to call, but were not received, and the only sign of life about the place was the Negro man — a young man then — going in and out with a market basket.

"Just as if a man — any man — could keep a kitchen properly," the ladies said; so they were not surprised when the smell developed. It was another link between the gross, teeming world and the high and mighty Griersons.

A neighbor, a woman, complained to the mayor, Judge Stevens, eighty years old.

"But what will you have me do about it, madam?" he said.

"Why, send her word to stop it," the woman said. "Isn't there a law?"

"I'm sure that won't be necessary," Judge Stevens said. "It's probably   20
just a snake or a rat that nigger of hers killed in the yard. I'll speak to him about
it."

The next day he received two more complaints, one from a man who
came in diffident deprecation. "We really must do something about it, Judge.
I'd be the last one in the world to bother Miss Emily, but we've got to do
something." That night the Board of Aldermen met — three graybeards and
one younger man, a member of the rising generation.

"It's simple enough," he said. "Send her word to have her place cleaned
up. Give her a certain time to do it in, and if she don't . . ."

"Dammit, sir," Judge Stevens said, "will you accuse a lady to her face
of smelling bad?"

So the next night, after midnight, four men crossed Miss Emily's lawn
and slunk about the house like burglars, sniffing along the base of the brick-
work and at the cellar openings while one of them performed a regular sowing
motion with his hand out of a sack slung from his shoulder. They broke open
the cellar door and sprinkled lime there, and in all the outbuildings. As they
recrossed the lawn, a window that had been dark was lighted and Miss Emily
sat in it, the light behind her, and her upright torso motionless as that of an
idol. They crept quietly across the lawn and into the shadow of the locusts that
lined the street. After a week or two the smell went away.

That was when people had begun to feel really sorry for her. People in   25
our town, remembering how old lady Wyatt, her great-aunt, had gone completely crazy at last, believed that the Griersons held themselves a little too
high for what they really were. None of the young men were quite good
enough for Miss Emily and such. We had long thought of them as a tableau,
Miss Emily a slender figure in white in the background, her father a spraddled
silhouette in the foreground, his back to her and clutching a horsewhip, the
two of them framed by the back-flung front door. So when she got to be thirty
and was still single, we were not pleased exactly, but vindicated; even with
insanity in the family she wouldn't have turned down all of her chances if they
had really materialized.

When her father died, it got about that the house was all that was left
to her; and in a way, people were glad. At last they could pity Miss Emily.
Being left alone, and a pauper, she had become humanized. Now she too would
know the old thrill and the old despair of a penny more or less.

The day after his death all the ladies prepared to call at the house and
offer condolence and aid, as is our custom. Miss Emily met them at the door,
dressed as usual and with no trace of grief on her face. She told them that her
father was not dead. She did that for three days, with the ministers calling on
her, and the doctors, trying to persuade her to let them dispose of the body.
Just as they were about to resort to law and force, she broke down, and they
buried her father quickly.

We did not say she was crazy then. We believed she had to do that. We
remembered all the young men her father had driven away, and we knew that
with nothing left, she would have to cling to that which had robbed her, as
people will.

III

She was sick for a long time. When we saw her again, her hair was cut short, making her look like a girl, with a vague resemblance to those angels in colored church windows — sort of tragic and serene.

The town had just let the contracts for paving the sidewalks, and in the summer after her father's death they began the work. The construction company came with niggers and mules and machinery, and a foreman named Homer Barron, a Yankee — a big, dark, ready man, with a big voice and eyes lighter than his face. The little boys would follow in groups to hear him cuss the niggers, and the niggers singing in time to the rise and fall of picks. Pretty soon he knew everybody in town. Whenever you heard a lot of laughing anywhere about the square, Homer Barron would be in the center of the group. Presently we began to see him and Miss Emily on Sunday afternoons driving in the yellow-wheeled buggy and the matched team of bays from the livery stable.

At first we were glad that Miss Emily would have an interest, because the ladies all said, "Of course a Grierson would not think seriously of a Northerner, a day laborer." But there were still others, older people, who said that even grief could not cause a real lady to forget *noblesse oblige*° — without calling it *noblesse oblige*. They just said, "Poor Emily. Her kinsfolk should come to her." She had some kin in Alabama; but years ago her father had fallen out with them over the estate of old lady Wyatt, the crazy woman, and there was no communication between the two families. They had not even been represented at the funeral.

And as soon as the old people said, "Poor Emily," the whispering began. "Do you suppose it's really so?" they said to one another. "Of course it is. What else could . . ." This behind their hands; rustling of craned silk and satin behind jalousies closed upon the sun of Sunday afternoon as the thin, swift clop-clop-clop of the matched team passed: "Poor Emily."

She carried her head high enough — even when we believed that she was fallen. It was as if she demanded more than ever the recognition of her dignity as the last Grierson; as if it had wanted that touch of earthiness to reaffirm her imperviousness. Like when she bought the rat poison, the arsenic. That was over a year after they had begun to say "Poor Emily," and while the two female cousins were visiting her.

"I want some poison," she said to the druggist. She was over thirty then, still a slight woman, though thinner than usual, with cold, haughty black eyes in a face the flesh of which was strained across the temples and about the eye-sockets as you imagine a lighthouse-keeper's face ought to look. "I want some poison," she said.

"Yes, Miss Emily. What kind? For rats and such? I'd recom — "

"I want the best you have. I don't care what kind."

The druggist named several. "They'll kill anything up to an elephant. But what you want is — "

"Arsenic," Miss Emily said. "Is that a good one?"

"Is . . . arsenic? Yes, ma'am. But what you want — "

noblesse oblige: the obligation of a member of the nobility to behave with honor and dignity.

"I want arsenic."

The druggist looked down at her. She looked back at him, erect, her face like a strained flag. "Why, of course," the druggist said. "If that's what you want. But the law requires you to tell what you are going to use it for."

Miss Emily just stared at him, her head tilted back in order to look him eye for eye, until he looked away and went and got the arsenic and wrapped it up. The Negro delivery boy brought her the package; the druggist didn't come back. When she opened the package at home there was written on the box, under the skull and bones: "For rats."

IV

So the next day we all said, "She will kill herself"; and we said it would be the best thing. When she had first begun to be seen with Homer Barron, we had said, "She will marry him." Then we said, "She will persuade him yet," because Homer himself had remarked — he liked men, and it was known that he drank with the younger men in the Elks' Club — that he was not a marrying man. Later we said, "Poor Emily" behind the jalousies as they passed on Sunday afternoon in the glittering buggy, Miss Emily with her head high and Homer Barron with his hat cocked and a cigar in his teeth, reins and whip in a yellow glove.

Then some of the ladies began to say that it was a disgrace to the town and a bad example to the young people. The men did not want to interfere, but at last the ladies forced the Baptist minister — Miss Emily's people were Episcopal — to call upon her. He would never divulge what happened during that interview, but he refused to go back again. The next Sunday they again drove about the streets, and the following day the minister's wife wrote to Miss Emily's relations in Alabama.

So she had blood-kin under her roof again and we sat back to watch developments. At first nothing happened. Then we were sure that they were to be married. We learned that Miss Emily had been to the jeweler's and ordered a man's toilet set in silver, with the letters H. B. on each piece. Two days later we learned that she had bought a complete outfit of men's clothing, including a nightshirt, and we said, "They are married." We were really glad. We were glad because the two female cousins were even more Grierson than Miss Emily had ever been.

So we were not surprised when Homer Barron — the streets had been finished some time since — was gone. We were a little disappointed that there was not a public blowing-off, but we believed that he had gone on to prepare for Miss Emily's coming, or to give her a chance to get rid of the cousins. (By that time it was a cabal, and we were all Miss Emily's allies to help circumvent the cousins.) Sure enough, after another week they departed. And, as we had expected all along, within three days Homer Barron was back in town. A neighbor saw the Negro man admit him at the kitchen door at dusk one evening.

And that was the last we saw of Homer Barron. And of Miss Emily for some time. The Negro man went in and out with the market basket, but the front door remained closed. Now and then we would see her at a window for a moment, as the men did that night when they sprinkled the lime, but for almost six months she did not appear on the streets. Then we knew that this was to be expected too; as if that quality of her father which had thwarted her woman's life so many times had been too virulent and too furious to die.

When we next saw Miss Emily, she had grown fat and her hair was turning gray. During the next few years it grew grayer and grayer until it attained an even pepper-and-salt iron-gray, when it ceased turning. Up to the day of her death at seventy-four it was still that vigorous iron-gray, like the hair of an active man.

From that time on her front door remained closed, save for a period of six or seven years, when she was about forty, during which she gave lessons in china-painting. She fitted up a studio in one of the downstairs rooms, where the daughters and granddaughters of Colonel Sartoris' contemporaries were sent to her with the same regularity and in the same spirit that they were sent to church on Sundays with a twenty-five-cent piece for the collection plate. Meanwhile her taxes had been remitted.

Then the newer generation became the backbone and the spirit of the town, and the painting pupils grew up and fell away and did not send their children to her with boxes of color and tedious brushes and pictures cut from the ladies' magazines. The front door closed upon the last one and remained closed for good. When the town got free postal delivery, Miss Emily alone refused to let them fasten the metal numbers above her door and attach a mailbox to it. She would not listen to them.

Daily, monthly, yearly we watched the Negro grow grayer and more stooped, going in and out with the market basket. Each December we sent her a tax notice, which would be returned by the post office a week later, un-claimed. Now and then we would see her in one of the downstairs windows — she had evidently shut up the top floor of the house — like the carven torso of an idol in a niche, looking or not looking at us, we could never tell which. Thus she passed from generation to generation — dear, inescapable, impervious, tranquil, and perverse.

And so she died. Fell ill in the house filled with dust and shadows, with only a doddering Negro man to wait on her. We did not even know she was sick; we had long since given up trying to get any information from the Negro. He talked to no one, probably not even to her, for his voice had grown harsh and rusty, as if from disuse.

She died in one of the downstairs rooms, in a heavy walnut bed with a curtain, her gray head propped on a pillow yellow and moldy with age and lack of sunlight.

V

The Negro met the first of the ladies at the front door and let them in, with their hushed, sibilant voices and their quick, curious glances, and then he disappeared. He walked right through the house and out the back and was not seen again.

The two female cousins came at once. They held the funeral on the second day, with the town coming to look at Miss Emily beneath a mass of bought flowers, with the crayon face of her father musing profoundly above the bier and the ladies sibilant and macabre; and the very old men — some in their brushed Confederate uniforms — on the porch and the lawn, talking of

Miss Emily as if she had been a contemporary of theirs, believing that they had danced with her and courted her perhaps, confusing time with its mathematical progression, as the old do, to whom all the past is not a diminishing road but, instead, a huge meadow which no winter ever quite touches, divided from them now by the narrow bottle-neck of the most recent decade of years.

Already we knew that there was one room in that region above stairs which no one had seen in forty years, and which would have to be forced. They waited until Miss Emily was decently in the ground before they opened it.

The violence of breaking down the door seemed to fill this room with pervading dust. A thin, acrid pall as of the tomb seemed to lie everywhere upon this room decked and furnished as for a bridal: upon the valance curtains of faded rose color, upon the rose-shaded lights, upon the dressing table, upon the delicate array of crystal and the man's toilet things backed with tarnished silver, silver so tarnished that the monogram was obscured. Among them lay collar and tie, as if they had just been removed, which, lifted, left upon the surface a pale crescent in the dust. Upon a chair hung the suit, carefully folded; beneath it the two mute shoes and the discarded socks.

The man himself lay in the bed.

For a long while we just stood there, looking down at the profound and fleshless grin. The body had apparently once lain in the attitude of an embrace, but now the long sleep that outlasts love, that conquers even the grimace of love, had cuckolded him. What was left of him, rotted beneath what was left of the nightshirt, had become inextricable from the bed in which he lay; and upon him and upon the pillow beside him lay that even coating of the patient and biding dust.

Then we noticed that in the second pillow was the indentation of a head. 60 One of us lifted something from it, and leaning forward, that faint and invisible dust dry and acrid in the nostrils, we saw a long strand of iron-gray hair.

QUESTIONS

1. What is meaningful in the final detail that the strand of hair on the second pillow is *iron-gray?*
2. Who is the unnamed narrator? For whom does he profess to be speaking?
3. Why does "A Rose for Emily" seem better told from his point of view than if it were told (like John Updike's "A & P") from the point of view of the main character?
4. What foreshadowings of the discovery of the body of Homer Barron are we given earlier in the story? Share your experience in reading "A Rose for Emily": did the foreshadowings give away the ending for you? Did they heighten your interest?
5. What contrasts does the narrator draw between changing reality and Emily's refusal or inability to recognize change?
6. How do the character and background of Emily Grierson differ from those of Homer Barron? What general observations about the society that Faulkner depicts can be made from his portraits of these two characters and from his account of life in this one Mississippi town?
7. Does the story seem to you totally grim, or do you find any humor in it?
8. What do you infer to be the author's attitude toward Emily Grierson? Is she simply a murderous madwoman? Why do you suppose Faulkner calls his story "A Rose . . ."?

Frank O'Connor

FIRST CONFESSION 1952

*Frank O'Connor was the pen name that Michael O'Donovan (1903 –
1966) adopted when he feared that to be known as a writer would hurt his
career in civil service. He was born in Cork, Ireland's second city. Desperate
poverty forced his parents to take him out of school after he had completed
only fourth grade. During the troubles of 1918 – 21 that led to the new Irish
Free State, he served in the Republican Army. After peace came, he worked
as a librarian and for several years served as a director of Dublin's influential
Abbey Theatre. America offered O'Connor-O'Donovan early hospitality: in
1931 The Atlantic printed his first story. In the 1950s he lived in America, teaching at Northwestern and Harvard. For a time he regularly appeared
on CBS television on Sunday mornings, just sitting and telling stories. A
fine literary critic, besides, he wrote* The Mirror in the Roadway *(1956),
a study of the novel, and* The Lonely Voice *(1963), a study of the short
story. In* Kings, Lords & Commons *(1959), he proved himself a master
translator of Gaelic poetry. O'Connor toiled hard over his stories, trying to
polish each to the perfection of a good lyric. "First Confession" appeared in
print in three versions because he kept rewriting it. The story is based upon
his boyhood memories.*

All the trouble began when my grandfather died and my grandmother
— my father's mother — came to live with us. Relations in the one house are
a strain at the best of times, but, to make matters worse, my grandmother was
a real old countrywoman and quite unsuited to the life in town. She had a fat,
wrinkled old face, and, to Mother's great indignation, went round the house
in bare feet — the boots had her crippled, she said. For dinner she had a jug
of porter and a pot of potatoes with — sometimes — a bit of salt fish, and she
poured out the potatoes on the table and ate them slowly, with great relish,
using her fingers by way of a fork.

Now, girls are supposed to be fastidious, but I was the one who suffered
most from this. Nora, my sister, just sucked up to the old woman for the penny
she got every Friday out of the old-age pension, a thing I could not do. I was
too honest, that was my trouble; and when I was playing with Bill Connell,
the sergeant-major's son, and saw my grandmother steering up the path with
the jug of porter sticking out from beneath her shawl I was mortified. I made
excuses not to let him come into the house, because I could never be sure what
she would be up to when we went in.

When Mother was at work and my grandmother made the dinner I
wouldn't touch it. Nora once tried to make me, but I hid under the table from
her and took the bread-knife with me for protection. Nora let on to be very
indignant (she wasn't, of course, but she knew Mother saw through her, so she
sided with Gran) and came after me. I lashed out at her with the bread-knife,
and after that she left me alone. I stayed there till Mother came in from work
and made my dinner, but when Father came in later Nora said in a shocked

voice: "Oh, Dadda, do you know what Jackie did at dinnertime?" Then, of course, it all came out; Father gave me a flaking; Mother interfered, and for days after that he didn't speak to me and Mother barely spoke to Nora. And all because of that old woman! God knows, I was heart-scalded.

Then, to crown my misfortunes, I had to make my first confession and communion. It was an old woman called Ryan who prepared us for these. She was about the one age with Gran; she was well-to-do, lived in a big house on Montenotte, wore a black cloak and bonnet, and came every day to school at three o'clock when we should have been going home, and talked to us of hell. She may have mentioned the other place as well, but that could only have been by accident, for hell had the first place in her heart.

She lit a candle, took out a new half-crown, and offered it to the first boy who would hold one finger — only one finger! — in the flame for five minutes by the school clock. Being always very ambitious I was tempted to volunteer, but I thought it might look greedy. Then she asked were we afraid of holding one finger — only one finger! — in a little candle flame for five minutes and not afraid of burning all over in roasting hot furnaces for all eternity. "All eternity! Just think of that! A whole lifetime goes by and it's nothing, not even a drop in the ocean of your sufferings." The woman was really interesting about hell, but my attention was all fixed on the half-crown. At the end of the lesson she put it back in her purse. It was a great disappointment; a religious woman like that, you wouldn't think she'd bother about a thing like a half-crown.

Another day she said she knew a priest who woke one night to find a fellow he didn't recognize leaning over the end of his bed. The priest was a bit frightened — naturally enough — but he asked the fellow what he wanted, and the fellow said in a deep, husky voice that he wanted to go to confession. The priest said it was an awkward time and wouldn't it do in the morning, but the fellow said that last time he went to confession, there was one sin he kept back, being ashamed to mention it, and now it was always on his mind. Then the priest knew it was a bad case, because the fellow was after making a bad confession and committing a mortal sin. He got up to dress, and just then the cock crew in the yard outside, and — lo and behold! — when the priest looked round there was no sign of the fellow, only a smell of burning timber, and when the priest looked at his bed didn't he see the print of two hands burned in it? That was because the fellow had made a bad confession. This story made a shocking impression on me.

But the worst of all was when she showed us how to examine our conscience. Did we take the name of the Lord, our God, in vain? Did we honor our father and our mother? (I asked her did this include grandmothers and she said it did.) Did we love our neighbors as ourselves? Did we covet our neighbor's goods? (I thought of the way I felt about the penny that Nora got every Friday.) I decided that, between one thing and another, I must have broken the whole ten commandments, all on account of that old woman, and so far as I could see, so long as she remained in the house I had no hope of ever doing anything else.

I was scared to death of confession. The day the whole class went I let on to have a toothache, hoping my absence wouldn't be noticed; but at three o'clock, just as I was feeling safe, along comes a chap with a message from Mrs. Ryan that I was to go to confession myself on Saturday and be at the chapel for communion with the rest. To make it worse, Mother couldn't come with me and sent Nora instead.

Now, that girl had ways of tormenting me that Mother never knew of. She held my hand as we went down the hill, smiling sadly and saying how sorry she was for me, as if she were bringing me to the hospital for an operation.

"Oh, God help us!" she moaned. "Isn't it a terrible pity you weren't a 10 good boy? Oh, Jackie, my heart bleeds for you! How will you ever think of all your sins? Don't forget you have to tell him about the time you kicked Gran on the shin."

"Lemme go!" I said, trying to drag myself free of her. "I don't want to go to confession at all."

"But sure, you'll have to go to confession, Jackie," she replied in the same regretful tone. "Sure, if you didn't, the parish priest would be up to the house, looking for you. 'Tisn't, God knows, that I'm not sorry for you. Do you remember the time you tried to kill me with the bread-knife under the table? And the language you used to me? I don't know what he'll do with you at all, Jackie. He might have to send you up to the bishop."

I remember thinking bitterly that she didn't know the half of what I had to tell — if I told it. I knew I couldn't tell it, and understood perfectly why the fellow in Mrs. Ryan's story made a bad confession; it seemed to me a great shame that people wouldn't stop criticizing him. I remember that steep hill down to the church, and the sunlit hillsides beyond the valley of the river, which I saw in the gaps between the houses like Adam's last glimpse of Paradise.

Then, when she had maneuvered me down the long flight of steps to the chapel yard, Nora suddenly changed her tone. She became the raging malicious devil she really was.

"There you are!" she said with a yelp of triumph, hurling me through 15 the church door. "And I hope he'll give you the penitential psalms, you dirty little caffler."

I knew then I was lost, given up to eternal justice. The door with the colored-glass panels swung shut behind me, the sunlight went out and gave place to deep shadow, and the wind whistled outside so that the silence within seemed to crackle like ice under my feet. Nora sat in front of me by the confession box. There were a couple of old women ahead of her, and then a miserable-looking poor devil came and wedged me in at the other side, so that I couldn't escape even if I had the courage. He joined his hands and rolled his eyes in the direction of the roof, muttering aspirations in an anguished tone, and I wondered had he a grandmother too. Only a grandmother could account for a fellow behaving in that heartbroken way, but he was better off than I, for he at least could go and confess his sins; while I would make a bad confession and then die in the night and be continually coming back and burning people's furniture.

Nora's turn came, and I heard the sound of something slamming, and then her voice as if butter wouldn't melt in her mouth, and then another slam, and out she came. God, the hypocrisy of women! Her eyes were lowered, her head was bowed, and her hands were joined very low down on her stomach, and she walked up the aisle to the side altar looking like a saint. You never saw such an exhibition of devotion; and I remembered the devilish malice with which she had tormented me all the way from our door, and wondered were all religious people like that, really. It was my turn now. With the fear of damnation in my soul I went in, and the confessional door closed of itself behind me.

It was pitch-dark and I couldn't see priest or anything else. Then I really began to be frightened. In the darkness it was a matter between God and me, and He had all the odds. He knew what my intentions were before I even started; I had no chance. All I had ever been told about confession got mixed up in my mind, and I knelt to one wall and said: "Bless me, father, for I have sinned; this is my first confession." I waited for a few minutes, but nothing happened, so I tried it on the other wall. Nothing happened there either. He had me spotted all right.

It must have been then that I noticed the shelf at about one height with my head. It was really a place for grown-up people to rest their elbows, but in my distracted state I thought it was probably the place you were supposed to kneel. Of course, it was on the high side and not very deep, but I was always good at climbing and managed to get up all right. Staying up was the trouble. There was room only for my knees, and nothing you could get a grip on but a sort of wooden moulding a bit above it. I held on to the moulding and repeated the words a little louder, and this time something happened all right. A slide was slammed back; a little light entered the box, and a man's voice said: "Who's there?"

" 'Tis me, father," I said for fear he mightn't see me and go away again. 20 I couldn't see him at all. The place the voice came from was under the moulding, about level with my knees, so I took a good grip of the moulding and swung myself down till I saw the astonished face of a young priest looking up at me. He had to put his head on one side to see me, and I had to put mine on one side to see him, so we were more or less talking to one another upside-down. It struck me as a queer way of hearing confessions, but I didn't feel it my place to criticize.

"Bless me, father, for I have sinned; this is my first confession," I rattled off all in one breath, and swung myself down the least shade more to make it easier for him.

"What are you doing up there?" he shouted in an angry voice, and the strain the politeness was putting on my hold of the moulding, and the shock of being addressed in such an uncivil tone, were too much for me. I lost my grip, tumbled, and hit the door an unmerciful wallop before I found myself flat on my back in the middle of the aisle. The people who had been waiting stood up with their mouths open. The priest opened the door of the middle box and came out, pushing his biretta back from his forehead; he looked something terrible. Then Nora came scampering down the aisle.

"Oh, you dirty little caffler!" she said. "I might have known you'd do it. I might have known you'd disgrace me. I can't leave you out of my sight for one minute."

Before I could even get to my feet to defend myself she bent down and gave me a clip across the ear. This reminded me that I was so stunned I had even forgotten to cry, so that people might think I wasn't hurt at all, when in fact I was probably maimed for life. I gave a roar out of me.

"What's all this about?" the priest hissed, getting angrier than ever and pushing Nora off me. "How dare you hit the child like that, you little vixen?" ²⁵

"But I can't do my penance with him, father," Nora cried, cocking an outraged eye up at him.

"Well, go and do it, or I'll give you some more to do," he said, giving me a hand up. "Was it coming to confession you were, my poor man?" he asked me.

" 'Twas, father," said I with a sob.

"Oh," he said respectfully, "a big hefty fellow like you must have terrible sins. Is this your first?"

" 'Tis, father," said I. ³⁰

"Worse and worse," he said gloomily. "The crimes of a life-time. I don't know will I get rid of you at all today. You'd better wait now till I'm finished with these old ones. You can see by the looks of them they haven't much to tell."

"I will, father," I said with something approaching joy.

The relief of it was really enormous. Nora stuck out her tongue at me from behind his back, but I couldn't even be bothered retorting. I knew from the very moment that man opened his mouth that he was intelligent above the ordinary. When I had time to think, I saw how right I was. It only stood to reason that a fellow confessing after seven years would have more to tell than people that went every week. The crimes of a lifetime, exactly as he said. It was only what he expected, and the rest was the cackle of old women and girls with their talk of hell, the bishop, and the penitential psalms. That was all they knew. I started to make my examination of conscience, and barring the one bad business of my grandmother it didn't seem so bad.

The next time, the priest steered me into the confession box himself and left the shutter back the way I could see him get in and sit down at the further side of the grille from me.

"Well, now," he said, "what do they call you?" ³⁵

"Jackie, father," said I.

"And what's a-trouble to you, Jackie?"

"Father," I said, feeling I might as well get it over while I had him in good humor, "I had it all arranged to kill my grandmother."

He seemed a bit shaken by that, all right, because he said nothing for quite a while.

"My goodness," he said at last, "that'd be a shocking thing to do. What ⁴⁰ put that into your head?"

"Father," I said, feeling very sorry for myself, "she's an awful woman."

"Is she?" he asked. "What way is she awful?"

"She takes porter, father," I said, knowing well from the way Mother talked of it that this was a mortal sin, and hoping it would make the priest take a more favorable view of my case.

"Oh, my!" he said, and I could see he was impressed.

"And snuff, father," said I. ⁴⁵

"That's a bad case, sure enough, Jackie," he said.

"And she goes round in her bare feet, father," I went on in a rush of self-pity, "and she knows I don't like her, and she gives pennies to Nora and none to me, and my da sides with her and flakes me, and one night I was so heart-scalded I made up my mind I'd have to kill her."

"And what would you do with the body?" he asked with great interest.

"I was thinking I could chop that up and carry it away in a barrow I have," I said.

"Begor, Jackie," he said, "do you know you're a terrible child?" 50

"I know, father," I said, for I was just thinking the same thing myself. "I tried to kill Nora too with a bread-knife under the table, only I missed her."

"Is that the little girl that was beating you just now?" he asked.

" 'Tis, father."

"Someone will go for her with a bread-knife one day, and he won't miss her," he said rather cryptically. "You must have great courage. Between ourselves, there's a lot of people I'd like to do the same to but I'd never have the nerve. Hanging is an awful death."

"Is it, father?" I asked with the deepest interest — I was always very 55 keen on hanging. "Did you ever see a fellow hanged?"

"Dozens of them," he said solemnly. "And they all died roaring."

"Jay!" I said.

"Oh, a horrible death!" he said with great satisfaction. "Lots of the fellows I saw killed their grandmothers too, but they all said 'twas never worth it."

He had me there for a full ten minutes talking, and then walked out the chapel yard with me. I was genuinely sorry to part with him, because he was the most entertaining character I'd ever met in the religious line. Outside, after the shadow of the church, the sunlight was like the roaring of waves on a beach; it dazzled me; and when the frozen silence melted and I heard the screech of trams on the road my heart soared. I knew now I wouldn't die in the night and come back, leaving marks on my mother's furniture. It would be a great worry to her, and the poor soul had enough.

Nora was sitting on the railing, waiting for me, and she put on a very 60 sour puss when she saw the priest with me. She was mad jealous because a priest had never come out of the church with her.

"Well," she asked coldly, after he left me, "what did he give you?"

"Three Hail Marys," I said.

"Three Hail Marys," she repeated incredulously. "You mustn't have told him anything."

"I told him everything," I said confidently.

"About Gran and all?" 65

"About Gran and all."

(All she wanted was to be able to go home and say I'd made a bad confession.)

"Did you tell him you went for me with the bread-knife?" she asked with a frown.

"I did to be sure."

"And he only gave you three Hail Marys?" 70

"That's all."

She slowly got down from the railing with a baffled air. Clearly, this was beyond her. As we mounted the steps back to the main road she looked at me suspiciously.

"What are you sucking?" she asked.

"Bullseyes."

"Was it the priest gave them to you?" 75

" 'Twas."

"Lord God," she wailed bitterly, "some people have all the luck! 'Tis no advantage to anybody trying to be good. I might just as well be a sinner like you."

QUESTIONS

1. Does the narrator of "First Confession" seem a boy — an innocent or naive narrator — or a grown-up looking back through seven-year-old eyes?
2. At what moments in the story did you sense a discrepancy between the boy's view of things and Frank O'Connor's? What is *funny* in the following moments (or in any others you care to point out)?

   Jackie's attitude toward his grandmother and her terrible vices.

   His reaction to Mrs. Ryan's yarn about the spirit with burning hands.

   His explanation for the long silence that follows his confessing his plot to kill his grandmother.

   (Why do *you* suppose the priest was silent for such a long time?)

   His plan for disposing of the body ("I could chop that up and carry it away in a barrow I have").

3. Imagine "First Confession" retold from a *different* point of view: that of the priest, say, or that of an objective narrator (the "fly on the wall"). What would be lost?
4. In what ways is Jackie not entirely naive, but sometimes shrewd and perceptive? (Suggestion: Take a close look at what he says about Mrs. Ryan and about his sister Nora.)
5. What traits of character do you find in the priest? How does he differ from Mrs. Ryan as a teacher of the young?
6. Do you believe Frank O'Connor to be saying — as Nora says at the end — that there is no use in trying to live a virtuous life?

Edgar Allan Poe

THE TELL-TALE HEART   1850

Edgar Allan Poe (1809 – 1849), orphaned child of traveling actors, was raised by well-off foster parents, John and Frances Allan, in Richmond, Virginia. At eighteen he published his first book of poems. When Poe ran up heavy gambling debts as a student at the University of Virginia, Allan called him home and eventually disowned him. After two years in the army and a brief stay at West Point, Poe became a successful editor in Richmond, Philadelphia, and New York and an industrious contributor to newspapers and magazines. Marriage in 1836 to his thirteen-year-old cousin Virginia Clemm increased his happiness but also his burdens; mercilessly, he drove his pen to support wife, self, and mother-in-law. Virginia, five years an invalid, died of tuberculosis in 1847. Poe, whose tolerance for alcohol was low, increased his drinking. He was found dead in a street in Baltimore. As a writer, Poe was a true innovator. His bizarre, macabre tales have held generations spellbound, as have some of his highly musical poems ("The

Raven," "Annabel Lee"). His tales of private sleuth C. Auguste Dupin ("The Murders in the Rue Morgue," "The Purloined Letter") have earned him the title of father of the modern detective story. Other tales and his one novel, The Narrative of Arthur Gordon Pym, figure in the history of science fiction. A trail-blazing critic, Poe laid down laws for the short story (see page 397). His work has profoundly influenced not only American literature but European literature through French translations by Charles Baudelaire.

True! — nervous — very, very dreadfully nervous I had been and am; but why will you say that I am mad? The disease had sharpened my senses — not destroyed — not dulled them. Above all was the sense of hearing acute. I heard all things in the heaven and in the earth. I heard many things in hell. How, then, am I mad? Hearken! and observe how healthily — how calmly I can tell you the whole story.

It is impossible to say how first the idea entered my brain; but once conceived, it haunted me day and night. Object there was none. Passion there was none. I loved the old man. He had never wronged me. He had never given me insult. For his gold I had no desire. I think it was his eye! yes, it was this! One of his eyes resembled that of a vulture — a pale blue eye, with a film over it. Whenever it fell upon me, my blood ran cold; and so by degrees — very gradually — I made up my mind to take the life of the old man, and thus rid myself of the eye for ever.

Now this is the point. You fancy me mad. Madmen know nothing. But you should have seen me. You should have seen how wisely I proceeded — with what caution — with what foresight — with what dissimulation I went to work! I was never kinder to the old man than during the whole week before I killed him. And every night, about midnight, I turned the latch of his door and opened it — oh, so gently! And then, when I had made an opening sufficient for my head, I put in a dark lantern, all closed, closed, so that no light shone out, and then I thrust in my head. Oh, you would have laughed to see how cunningly I thrust it in! I moved it slowly — very, very slowly, so that I might not disturb the old man's sleep. It took me an hour to place my whole head within the opening so far that I could see him as he lay upon his bed. Ha! — would a madman have been so wise as this? And then, when my head was well in the room, I undid the lantern cautiously — oh, so cautiously — cautiously (for the hinges creaked) — I undid it just so much that a single thin ray fell upon the vulture eye. And this I did for seven long nights — every night just at midnight — but I found the eye always closed; and so it was impossible to do the work; for it was not the old man who vexed me, but his Evil Eye. And every morning, when the day broke, I went boldly into the chamber, and spoke courageously to him, calling him by name in a hearty tone, and inquiring how he had passed the night. So you see he would have been a very profound old man, indeed, to suspect that every night, just at twelve, I looked in upon him while he slept.

Upon the eighth night I was more than usually cautious in opening the door. A watch's minute hand moves more quickly than did mine. Never before that night had I felt the extent of my own powers — of my sagacity. I could scarcely contain my feelings of triumph. To think that there I was, opening the door, little by little, and he not even to dream of my secret deeds or thoughts. I fairly chuckled at the idea; and perhaps he heard me; for he moved on the bed suddenly, as if startled. Now you may think that I drew back — but no. His room was as black as pitch with the thick darkness (for the shutters were close fastened, through fear of robbers), and so I knew that he could not see the opening of the door, and I kept pushing it on steadily, steadily.

I had my head in, and was about to open the lantern, when my thumb 5 slipped upon the tin fastening, and the old man sprang up in the bed, crying out — "Who's there?"

I kept quite still and said nothing. For a whole hour I did not move a muscle, and in the meantime I did not hear him lie down. He was still sitting up in the bed listening; — just as I have done, night after night, hearkening to the death watches° in the wall.

Presently I heard a slight groan, and I knew it was the groan of mortal terror. It was not a groan of pain or of grief — oh, no! — it was the low stifled sound that arises from the bottom of the soul when overcharged with awe. I knew the sound well. Many a night, just at midnight, when all the world slept, it has welled up from my own bosom, deepening, with its dreadful echo, the terrors that distracted me. I say I knew it well. I knew what the old man felt, and pitied him, although I chuckled at heart. I knew that he had been lying awake ever since the first slight noise, when he had turned in the bed. His fears had been ever since growing upon him. He had been trying to fancy them causeless, but could not. He had been saying to himself — "It is nothing but the wind in the chimney — it is only a mouse crossing the floor," or "it is merely a cricket which has made a single chirp." Yes, he had been trying to comfort himself with these suppositions; but he had found all in vain. *All in vain;* because Death, in approaching him, had stalked with his black shadow before him, and enveloped the victim. And it was the mournful influence of the unperceived shadow that caused him to feel — although he neither saw nor heard — to *feel* the presence of my head within the room.

When I had waited a long time, very patiently, without hearing him lie down, I resolved to open a little — a very, very little crevice in the lantern. So I opened it — you cannot imagine how stealthily, stealthily — until, at length, a single dim ray, like the thread of the spider, shot from out the crevice and full upon the vulture eye.

It was open — wide, wide open — and I grew furious as I gazed upon it. I saw it with perfect distinctness — all a dull blue, with a hideous veil over it that chilled the very marrow in my bones; but I could see nothing else of the old man's face or person: for I had directed the ray as if by instinct, precisely upon the damned spot.

And now have I not told you that what you mistake for madness is but 10 over-acuteness of the senses? — now, I say, there came to my ears a low, dull, quick sound, such as a watch makes when enveloped in cotton. I knew *that* sound well too. It was the beating of the old man's heart. It increased my fury, as the beating of a drum stimulates the soldier into courage.

death watches: beetles that infest timbers. Their clicking sound was thought to be an omen of death.

But even yet I refrained and kept still. I scarcely breathed. I held the lantern motionless. I tried how steadily I could maintain the ray upon the eye. Meantime the hellish tattoo of the heart increased. It grew quicker and quicker, and louder and louder every instant. The old man's terror *must* have been extreme! It grew louder, I say, louder every moment! — do you mark me well? I have told you that I am nervous: so I am. And now at the dead hour of the night, amid the dreadful silence of that old house, so strange a noise as this excited me to uncontrollable terror. Yet, for some minutes longer I refrained and stood still. But the beating grew louder, louder! I thought the heart must burst. And now a new anxiety seized me — the sound would be heard by a neighbor! The old man's hour had come! With a loud yell, I threw open the lantern and leaped into the room. He shrieked once — once only. In an instant I dragged him to the floor, and pulled the heavy bed over him. I then smiled gaily, to find the deed so far done. But, for many minutes, the heart beat on with a muffled sound. This, however, did not vex me; it would not be heard through the wall. At length it ceased. The old man was dead. I removed the bed and examined the corpse. Yes, he was stone, stone dead. I placed my hand upon the heart and held it there many minutes. There was no pulsation. He was stone dead. His eye would trouble me no more.

If still you think me mad, you will think so no longer when I describe the wise precautions I took for the concealment of the body. The night waned, and I worked hastily, but in silence. First of all I dismembered the corpse. I cut off the head and the arms and the legs.

I then took up three planks from the flooring of the chamber, and deposited all between the scantlings. I then replaced the boards so cleverly, so cunningly, that no human eye — not even *his* — could have detected anything wrong. There was nothing to wash out — no stain of any kind — no blood-spot whatever. I had been too wary for that. A tub had caught all — ha! ha!

When I had made an end of these labors, it was four o'clock — still dark as midnight. As the bell sounded the hour, there came a knocking at the street door. I went down to open it with a light heart, — for what had I *now* to fear? There entered three men, who introduced themselves, with perfect suavity, as officers of the police. A shriek had been heard by a neighbor during the night; suspicion of foul play had been aroused; information had been lodged at the police office, and they (the officers) had been deputed to search the premises.

I smiled, — for *what* had I to fear? I bade the gentlemen welcome. The shriek, I said, was my own in a dream. The old man, I mentioned, was absent in the country. I took my visitors all over the house. I bade them search — search *well*. I led them, at length, to *his* chamber. I showed them his treasures, secure, undisturbed. In the enthusiasm of my confidence, I brought chairs into the room, and desired them *here* to rest from their fatigues, while I myself, in the wild audacity of my perfect triumph, placed my own seat upon the very spot beneath which reposed the corpse of the victim.

The officers were satisfied. My *manner* had convinced them. I was singularly at ease. They sat, and while I answered cheerily, they chatted familiar things. But, ere long, I felt myself getting pale and wished them gone. My head ached, and I fancied a ringing in my ears: but still they sat and still chatted. The ringing became more distinct: — it continued and became more distinct: I talked more freely to get rid of the feeling: but it continued and gained

15

definitiveness — until, at length, I found that the noise was *not* within my ears.

No doubt I now grew *very* pale: — but I talked more fluently, and with a heightened voice. Yet the sound increased — and what could I do? It was *a low, dull, quick sound — much such a sound as a watch makes when enveloped in cotton.* I gasped for breath — and yet the officers heard it not. I talked more quickly — more vehemently; but the noise steadily increased. I arose and argued about trifles, in a high key and with violent gesticulations, but the noise steadily increased. Why *would* they not be gone? I paced the floor to and fro with heavy strides, as if excited to fury by the observation of the men — but the noise steadily increased. Oh God! what *could* I do? I foamed — I raved — I swore! I swung the chair upon which I had been sitting, and grated it upon the boards, but the noise arose over all and continually increased. It grew louder — louder — *louder!* And still the men chatted pleasantly, and smiled. Was it possible they heard not? Almighty God! — no, no! They heard! — they suspected! — they *knew!* — they were making a mockery of my horror! — this I thought, and this I think. But any thing was better than this agony! Any thing was more tolerable than this derision! I could bear those hypocritical smiles no longer! I felt that I must scream or die! — and now — again! — hark! louder! louder! louder! *louder!* —

"Villains!" I shrieked, "dissemble no more! I admit the deed! — tear up the planks! — here, here! — it is the beating of his hideous heart!"

QUESTIONS

1. From what point of view is Poe's story told? Why is this point of view particularly effective for "The Tell-Tale Heart"?
2. Point to details in the story that identify its speaker as an unreliable narrator.
3. What do we know about the old man in the story? What motivates the narrator to kill him?
4. In spite of all his precautions, the narrator does not commit the perfect crime. What trips him up?
5. How do you account for the police officers' chatting calmly with the murderer instead of reacting to the sound that stirs the murderer into a frenzy?
6. See the students' comments on this story on pages 426 and 430. What do they point out that enlarges your own appreciation of Poe's art?

Doris Lessing

A WOMAN ON A ROOF   1963

Doris Lessing was born Doris Taylor in Iran in 1919. At five she moved with her family to a remote farm in the white-controlled British colony of Rhodesia (today Zimbabwe). She attended a convent school in Salisbury, the capital city. Like Isak Dinesen, Lessing found that her African experience nurtured her early writing: her experience led to her first novel, The Grass Is Singing (1950), and two collections of short stories. In her teens she quit school, an act of defiance against her mother's plans to give her a proper, ladylike British education. In 1949, with her third child, she settled in

London to earn her living as a writer. For a short time she belonged to the British Communist party, working as an organizer. Soon Lessing attracted a following in Britain and America for her five-novel series, Children of Violence *(1950 – 69), based on her own varied experiences, and* The Golden Notebook *(1962), exploring the lives of intelligent women who struggle for independence. Though Lessing became a heroine to feminists, she has declared herself mainly interested in larger social and cultural issues. Lately these questions have led her to write a five-volume series of science-fiction novels,* Canopus in Argus: Archives *(1979 – 83). With* The Good Terrorist *(1985), Lessing returned to the realistic vein of fiction that made her famous.*

It was during the week of hot sun, that June.

Three men were at work on the roof, where the leads got so hot they had the idea of throwing water on to cool them. But the water steamed, then sizzled; and they made jokes about getting an egg from some woman in the flats under them, to poach it for their dinner. By two it was not possible to touch the guttering they were replacing, and they speculated about what workmen did in regularly hot countries. Perhaps they should borrow kitchen gloves with the egg? They were all a bit dizzy, not used to the heat; and they shed their coats and stood side by side squeezing themselves into a foot-wide patch of shade against a chimney, careful to keep their feet in the thick socks and boots out of the sun. There was a fine view across several acres of roofs. Not far off a man sat in a deck chair reading the newspapers. Then they saw her, between chimneys, about fifty yards away. She lay face down on a brown blanket. They could see the top part of her: black hair, a flushed solid back, arms spread out.

"She's stark naked," said Stanley, sounding annoyed.

Harry, the oldest, a man of about forty-five, said: "Looks like it."

Young Tom, seventeen, said nothing, but he was excited and grinning.   5

Stanley said: "Someone'll report her if she doesn't watch out."

"She thinks no one can see," said Tom, craning his head all ways to see more.

At this point the woman, still lying prone, brought her two hands up behind her shoulders with the ends of a scarf in them, tied it behind her back, and sat up. She wore a red scarf tied around her breasts and brief red bikini pants. This being the first day of the sun she was white, flushing red. She sat smoking, and did not look up when Stanley let out a wolf whistle. Harry said: "Small things amuse small minds," leading the way back to their part of the roof, but it was scorching. Harry said: "Wait, I'm going to rig up some shade," and disappeared down the skylight into the building. Now that he'd gone, Stanley and Tom went to the farthest point they could to peer at the woman. She had moved, and all they could see were two pink legs stretched on the blanket. They whistled and shouted but the legs did not move. Harry came back with a blanket and shouted: "Come on, then." He sounded irritated with them. They clambered back to him and he said to Stanley: "What about your missus?" Stanley was newly married, about three months. Stanley said, jeering: "What about my missus?" — preserving his independence. Tom said nothing, but his mind was full of the nearly naked woman. Harry slung the blanket, which he had borrowed from a friendly woman downstairs, from the stem of a television aerial to a row of chimney-pots. This shade fell across the piece of gutter they had to replace. But the shade kept moving, they had to adjust the blanket, and not much progress was made. At last some of the heat left the roof, and they worked fast, making up for lost time. First Stanley, then Tom, made a trip to the end of the roof to see the woman. "She's on her back," Stanley said, adding a jest which made Tom snicker, and the older man smile tolerantly. Tom's report was that she hadn't moved, but it was a lie. He wanted to keep what he had seen to himself: he had caught her in the act of rolling down the little red pants over her hips, till they were no more than a small triangle. She was on her back, fully visible, glistening with oil.

Next morning, as soon as they came up, they went to look. She was already there, face down, arms spread out, naked except for the little red pants. She had turned brown in the night. Yesterday she was a scarlet-and-white woman, today she was a brown woman. Stanley let out a whistle. She lifted her head, startled, as if she'd been asleep, and looked straight over at them. The sun was in her eyes, she blinked and stared, then she dropped her head again. At this gesture of indifference, they all three, Stanley, Tom and old Harry, let out whistles and yells. Harry was doing it in parody of the younger men, making fun of them, but he was also angry. They were all angry because of her utter indifference to the three men watching her.

"Bitch," said Stanley.   10

"She should ask us over," said Tom, snickering.

Harry recovered himself and reminded Stanley: "If she's married, her old man wouldn't like that."

"Christ," said Stanley virtuously, "if my wife lay about like that, for everyone to see, I'd soon stop her."

Harry said, smiling: "How do you know, perhaps she's sunning herself at this very moment?"

"Not a chance, not on our roof." The safety of his wife put Stanley into   15
a good humor, and they went to work. But today it was hotter than yesterday; and several times one or the other suggested they should tell Matthew, the foreman, and ask to leave the roof until the heat wave was over. But they didn't. There was work to be done in the basement of the big block of flats, but up here they felt free, on a different level from ordinary humanity shut in the streets or the buildings. A lot more people came out on to the roofs that day, for an hour at midday. Some married couples sat side by side in deck chairs, the women's legs stockingless and scarlet, the men in vests with reddening shoulders.

The woman stayed on her blanket, turning herself over and over. She ignored them, no matter what they did. When Harry went off to fetch more screws, Stanley said: "Come on." Her roof belonged to a different system of roofs, separated from theirs at one point by about twenty feet. It meant a scrambling climb from one level to another, edging along parapets, clinging to chimneys, while their big boots slipped and slithered, but at last they stood on a small square projecting roof looking straight down at her, close. She sat smoking, reading a book. Tom thought she looked like a poster, or a magazine cover, with the blue sky behind her and her legs stretched out. Behind her a great crane at work on a new building in Oxford Street° swung its black arm across roofs in a great arc. Tom imagined himself at work on the crane, adjusting the arm to swing over and pick her up and swing her back across the sky to drop her near him.

They whistled. She looked up at them, cool and remote, then went on reading. Again, they were furious. Or, rather, Stanley was. His sun-heated face was screwed into a rage as he whistled again and again, trying to make her look up. Young Tom stopped whistling. He stood beside Stanley, excited, grinning; but he felt as if he were saying to the woman: Don't associate me with *him,* for his grin was apologetic. Last night he had thought of the unknown woman before he slept, and she had been tender with him. This tenderness he was remembering as he shifted his feet by the jeering, whistling Stanley, and watched the indifferent, healthy brown woman a few feet off, with the gap that plunged to the street between them. Tom thought it was romantic, it was like being high on two hilltops. But there was a shout from Harry, and they clambered back. Stanley's face was hard, really angry. The boy kept looking at him and wondered why he hated the woman so much, for by now he loved her.

They played their little games with the blanket, trying to trap shade to work under; but again it was not until nearly four that they could work seriously, and they were exhausted, all three of them. They were grumbling about the weather by now. Stanley was in a thoroughly bad humor. When they made their routine trip to see the woman before they packed up for the day, she was apparently asleep, face down, her back all naked save for the scarlet triangle on her buttocks. "I've got a good mind to report her to the police," said Stanley, and Harry said: "What's eating you? What harm's she doing?"

"I tell you, if she was my wife!"

"But she isn't, is she?" Tom knew that Harry, like himself, was uneasy   20
at Stanley's reaction. He was normally a sharp young man, quick at his work, making a lot of jokes, good company.

"Perhaps it will be cooler tomorrow," said Harry.

But it wasn't; it was hotter, if anything, and the weather forecast said the good weather would last. As soon as they were on the roof, Harry went over to see if the woman was there, and Tom knew it was to prevent Stanley going, to put off his bad humor. Harry had grownup children, a boy the same age as Tom, and the youth trusted and looked up to him.

Harry came back and said: "She's not there."

"I bet her old man has put his foot down," said Stanley, and Harry and Tom caught each other's eyes and smiled behind the young married man's back.

Harry suggested they should get permission to work in the basement,   25
and they did, that day. But before packing up Stanley said: "Let's have a breath of fresh air." Again Harry and Tom smiled at each other as they followed Stanley up to the roof. Tom in the devout conviction that he was there to protect the woman from Stanley. It was about five-thirty, and a calm, full

Oxford Street: busy shopping street in central London.

sunlight lay over the roofs. The great crane still swung its black arm from Oxford Street to above their heads. She was not there. Then there was a flutter of white from behind a parapet, and she stood up, in a belted, white dressing-gown. She had been there all day, probably, but on a different patch of roof, to hide from them. Stanley did not whistle; he said nothing, but watched the woman bend to collect papers, books, cigarettes, then fold the blanket over her arm. Tom was thinking: If they weren't here, I'd go over and say . . . what? But he knew from his nightly dreams of her that she was kind and friendly. Perhaps she would ask him down to her flat? Perhaps . . . He stood watching her disappear down the skylight. As she went, Stanley let out a shrill derisive yell; she started, and it seemed as if she nearly fell. She clutched to save herself, they could hear things falling. She looked straight at them, angry. Harry said, facetiously: "Better be careful on those slippery ladders, love." Tom knew he said it to save her from Stanley, but she could not know it. She vanished, frowning. Tom was full of a secret delight, because he knew her anger was for the others, not for him.

"Roll on some rain," said Stanley, bitter, looking at the blue evening sky.

Next day was cloudless, and they decided to finish the work in the basement. They felt excluded, shut in the grey cement basement fitting pipes, from the holiday atmosphere of London in a heat wave. At lunchtime they came up for some air, but while the married couples, and the men in shirt-sleeves or vests, were there, she was not there, either on her usual patch of roof or where she had been yesterday. They all, even Harry, clambered about, between chimney-pots, over parapets, the hot leads stinging their fingers. There was not a sign of her. They took off their shirts and vests and exposed their chests, feeling their feet sweaty and hot. They did not mention the woman. But Tom felt alone again. Last night she had him into her flat: it was big and had fitted white carpets and a bed with a padded white leather head-board. She wore a black filmy negligée and her kindness to Tom thickened his throat as he remembered it. He felt she had betrayed him by not being there.

And again after work they climbed up, but still there was nothing to be seen of her. Stanley kept repeating that if it was as hot as this tomorrow he wasn't going to work and that's all there was to it. But they were all there next day. By ten the temperature was in the middle seventies, and it was eighty long before noon. Harry went to the foreman to say it was impossible to work on the leads in that heat; but the foreman said there was nothing else he could put them on, and they'd have to. At midday they stood, silent, watching the skylight on her roof open, and then she slowly emerged in her white gown, holding a bundle of blanket. She looked at them, gravely, then went to the part of the roof where she was hidden from them. Tom was pleased. He felt she was more his when the other men couldn't see her. They had taken off their shirts and vests, but now they put them back again, for they felt the sun bruising their flesh. "She must have the hide of a rhino," said Stanley, tugging at guttering and swearing. They stopped work, and sat in the shade, moving around behind chimney stacks. A woman came to water a yellow window box opposite them. She was middleaged, wearing a flowered summer dress. Stanley said to her: "We need a drink more than them." She smiled and said: "Better drop down to the pub quick, it'll be closing in a minute." They exchanged pleasantries, and she left them with a smile and a wave.

"Not like Lady Godiva°," said Stanley. "She can give us a bit of a chat and a smile."

"You didn't whistle at _her,_" said Tom, reproving.

"Listen to him," said Stanley, "you didn't whistle, then?"

But the boy felt as if he hadn't whistled, as if only Harry and Stanley had. He was making plans, when it was time to knock off work, to get left behind and somehow make his way over to the woman. The weather report said the hot spell was due to break, so he had to move quickly. But there was no chance of being left. The other two decided to knock off work at four, because they were exhausted. As they went down, Tom quickly climbed a parapet and hoisted himself higher by pulling his weight up a chimney. He caught a glimpse of her lying on her back, her knees up, eyes closed, a brown woman lolling in the sun. He slipped and clattered down, as Stanley looked for information: "She's gone down," he said. He felt as if he had protected her from Stanley, and that she must be grateful to him. He could feel the bond between the woman and himself.

Next day, they stood around on the landing below the roof, reluctant to climb up into the heat. The woman who had lent Harry the blanket came out and offered them a cup of tea. They accepted gratefully, and sat around Mrs. Pritchett's kitchen an hour or so, chatting. She was married to an airline pilot. A smart blonde, of about thirty, she had an eye for the handsome sharp-faced Stanley; and the two teased each other while Harry sat in a corner, watching, indulgent, though his expression reminded Stanley that he was married. And young Tom felt envious of Stanley's ease in badinage°; felt, too, that Stanley's getting off with Mrs. Pritchett left his romance with the woman on the roof safe and intact.

"I thought they said the heat wave'd break," said Stanley, sullen, as the time approached when they really would have to climb up into the sunlight.

"You don't like it, then?" asked Mrs. Pritchett.

"All right for some," said Stanley. "Nothing to do but lie about as if it was a beach up there. Do you ever go up?"

"Went up once," said Mrs. Pritchett. "But it's a dirty place up there, and it's too hot."

"Quite right too," said Stanley.

Then they went up, leaving the cool neat little flat and the friendly Mrs. Pritchett.

As soon as they were up they saw her. The three men looked at her, resentful at her ease in this punishing sun. Then Harry said, because of the expression on Stanley's face: "Come on, we've got to pretend to work, at least."

They had to wrench another length of guttering that ran beside a parapet out of its bed, so that they could replace it. Stanley took it in his two hands, tugged, swore, stood up. "Fuck it," he said, and sat down under a chimney.

Lady Godiva: Stanley compares the woman on the roof to the heroine of a medieval English legend. On a bet with her husband, to make him abolish a heavy tax on the people of Coventry, Godiva rode naked through the streets. No one was supposed to look at her. (Peeping Tom looked, and was struck blind.)

badinage: (French), teasing, playful conversation.

He lit a cigarette. "Fuck them," he said. "What do they think we are, lizards? I've got blisters all over my hands." Then he jumped up and climbed over the roofs and stood with his back to them. He put his fingers either side of his mouth and let out a shrill whistle. Tom and Harry squatted, not looking at each other, watching him. They could just see the woman's head, the beginnings of her brown shoulders. Stanley whistled again. Then he began stamping with his feet, and whistled and yelled and screamed at the woman, his face getting scarlet. He seemed quite mad, as he stamped and whistled, while the woman did not move, she did not move a muscle.

"Barmy," said Tom.

"Yes," said Harry, disapproving.

Suddenly the older man came to a decision. It was, Tom knew, to save some sort of scandal or real trouble over the woman. Harry stood up and began packing tools into a length of oily cloth. "Stanley," he said, commanding. At first Stanley took no notice, but Harry said: "Stanley, we're packing it in, I'll tell Matthew."

Stanley came back, cheeks mottled, eyes glaring.   45

"Can't go on like this," said Harry. "It'll break in a day or so. I'm going to tell Matthew we've got sunstroke, and if he doesn't like it, it's too bad." Even Harry sounded aggrieved, Tom noted. The small, competent man, the family man with his grey hair, who was never at a loss, sounded really off balance. "Come on," he said, angry. He fitted himself into the open square in the roof, and went down, watching his feet on the ladder. Then Stanley went, with not a glance at the woman. Then Tom, who, his throat beating with excitement, silently promised her on a backward glance: Wait for me, wait, I'm coming.

On the pavement Stanley said: "I'm going home." He looked white now, so perhaps he really did have sunstroke. Harry went off to find the foreman, who was at work on the plumbing of some flats down the street. Tom slipped back, not into the building they had been working on, but the building on whose roof the woman lay. He went straight up, no one stopping him. The skylight stood open, with an iron ladder leading up. He emerged on to the roof a couple of yards from her. She sat up, pushing back her black hair with both hands. The scarf across her breasts bound them tight, and brown flesh bulged around it. Her legs were brown and smooth. She stared at him in silence. The boy stood grinning, foolish, claiming the tenderness he expected from her.

"What do you want?" she asked.

"I . . . I came to . . . make your acquaintance," he stammered, grinning, pleading with her.

They looked at each other, the slight, scarlet-faced excited boy, and the   50
serious, nearly naked woman. Then, without a word, she lay down on her brown blanket, ignoring him.

"You like the sun, do you?" he enquired of her glistening back.

Not a word. He felt panic, thinking of how she had held him in her arms, stroked his hair, brought him where he sat, lordly, in her bed, a glass of some exhilarating liquor he had never tasted in life. He felt that if he knelt down, stroked her shoulders, her hair, she would turn and clasp him in her arms.

He said: "The sun's all right for you, isn't it?"

She raised her head, set her chin on two small fists. "Go away," she said.

He did not move. "Listen," she said, in a slow reasonable voice, where anger was kept in check, though with difficulty; looking at him, her face weary with anger, "if you get a kick out of seeing women in bikinis, why don't you take a sixpenny bus ride to the Lido°? You'd see dozens of them, without all this mountaineering."

She hadn't understood him. He felt her unfairness pale him. He stammered: "But I like you, I've been watching you and . . ." 55

"Thanks," she said, and dropped her face again, turned away from him.

She lay there. He stood there. She said nothing. She had simply shut him out. He stood, saying nothing at all, for some minutes. He thought: She'll have to say something if I stay. But the minutes went past, with no sign of them in her, except in the tension of her back, her thighs, her arms — the tension of waiting for him to go.

He looked up at the sky, where the sun seemed to spin in heat; and over the roofs where he and his mates had been earlier. He could see the heat quivering where they had worked. And they expect us to work in these conditions! he thought, filled with righteous indignation. The woman hadn't moved. A bit of hot wind blew her black hair softly; it shone, and was iridescent. He remembered how he had stroked it last night.

Resentment of her at last moved him off and away down the ladder, through the building, into the street. He got drunk then, in hatred of her.

Next day when he woke the sky was grey. He looked at the wet grey 60 and thought, vicious: Well, that's fixed you, hasn't it now? That's fixed you good and proper.

The three men were at work early on the cool leads, surrounded by damp drizzling roofs where no one came to sun themselves, black roofs, slimy with rain. Because it was cool now, they would finish the job that day, if they hurried.

Questions

1. What do you understand from the story's last line?
2. What is a *protagonist*? (See the definition on page 9, if necessary.) Who is the protagonist in this story?
3. Who tells the story? Does this narrator take us into the mind of each character? Of specific characters? Of one?
4. Suppose "A Woman on a Roof" were told in the first person, from the point of view of the sunbather herself. What do you think the story would lose, or gain?
5. Pay special notice to the setting in this story. How does weather help account for the behavior of the characters? Comment on the effectiveness of the descriptions of the heat wave; of the final rain.
6. Recall Stanley's calling the sunbather Lady Godiva. What is meaningful in Tom's name? How accurate is a critic's remark that this is "a recent rooftop version of the Godiva story"?
7. What do you think Doris Lessing is saying? Do you find her story a comment on any familiar attitudes of men toward women? Does she show any sympathy for the three men?

Lido: a section of London's Hyde Park.

Suggestions for Writing

1. Here is a writing exercise to help you sense what a difference a point of view makes. Write a short statement from the point of view of one of these characters:

   William Faulkner's Homer Barron (on "My Affair with Miss Emily").

   Frank O'Connor's Nora (on "Why My Brother Jackie Deserves Damnation").

   Doris Lessing's woman on the roof (on "The Difficulties of Sunbathing").

2. Write a brief narrative account of a decisive moment in your life — one that changed your outlook or your future — from two quite different, contrasting points of view. One instance: a memory of buying a first car, told in two ways: from the first-person point of view of the buyer and from the third-person point of view of a worried parent or a gloating car dealer. Another example: An account of meeting a person who profoundly affected your life, from (1) your point of view and then (2) from the point of view of that other person.

3. Topic for an essay of two or three paragraphs: How William Faulkner Sees North and South in "A Rose for Emily."

4. Taking examples from short stories you have read, point out some differences between male and female ways of looking at things. Some stories especially to consider: "A & P" and "First Confession"; also "The Jilting of Granny Weatherall" (in Chapter Four) and "I Stand Here Ironing" (in "Stories for Further Reading"). (Note: Because a character holds a certain attitude in a specific situation doesn't oblige you to argue that such an attitude is universally held by women and men.)

5. Adopt the point of view of a naive, innocent commentator — either a younger, less-knowing version of yourself, or some imagined character. From this point of view, discuss the proposed ban of nuclear weapons, the case for legislation against the sale of pornography, or another issue in the news. Sound off like a true ignoramus. An effective paper will make clear to your reader that your speaker is full of malarkey. (This task means that you, the knowing writer, and not the uninformed speaker who is your mask, will need to know something about your subject.)

6. Choosing one of the "Stories for Further Reading" (pages 233 – 393), briefly describe whatever point of view you find in it. Then, in a paragraph or two, explain why this angle of vision seems right and fitting to the telling of this story. If you like, you may argue that the story might be told more effectively from some other point of view.

7. Write a one-paragraph story in the first person. Some recent small event in your life is a possible subject. Then rewrite your story from the *objective,* or "fly-on-the-wall," point of view. (See the passage by Dashiell Hammett on page 21 for an illustration.) Following your two terse stories, make a comment summing up what this exercise told you about point of view.

3 Setting

By the **setting** of a story, we mean its time and place. The word might remind you of the metal that holds a diamond in a ring, or of a *set* used in a play — perhaps a bare chair in front of a slab of painted canvas. But often, in an effective short story, setting may figure as more than mere background or underpinning. It can make things happen. It can prompt characters to act, bring them to realizations, or cause them to reveal their inmost natures.

To be sure, the idea of setting includes the physical environment of a story: a house, a street, a city, a landscape, a region. (*Where* a story takes place is sometimes called its **locale**.) Physical places mattered so greatly to French novelist Honoré de Balzac that sometimes, before writing a story set in a town, he would visit that town, select a few houses, and describe them in detail, down to their very smells. "The place in which an event occurred," Henry James admiringly said of him, "was in his view of equal moment with the event itself . . . it had a part to play; it needed to be made as definite as anything else."

But besides place, setting may crucially involve the *time* of the story — hour, year, or century. It might matter greatly that a story takes place at dawn, or on the day of the first moon landing. When we begin to read a historical novel, we are soon made aware that we aren't reading about life in the 1980s. In *The Scarlet Letter,* nineteenth-century author Nathaniel Hawthorne, by a long introduction and a vivid opening scene at a prison door, prepares us to witness events in the Puritan community of Boston in the earlier seventeenth century. This setting, together with scenes of Puritan times we recall from high school history, helps us understand what happens in the novel. We can appreciate the shocked agitation in town when a woman is accused of adultery: she has given illegitimate birth. Such an event might seem more nearly common today, but in the stern, God-fearing New England Puritan community, it was a flagrant defiance of church and state, which are all-powerful (and are all one). That reader will make no sense of *The Scarlet Letter* who ignores its setting — if to ignore the setting is possible, so much attention does Hawthorne pay to it.

That Hawthorne's novel takes place in a time remote from our own leads us to expect different customs, different attitudes. Some critics and teachers regard the setting of a story as its whole society, including the beliefs and assumptions of its characters, which might well be a helpful way of looking at *The Scarlet Letter.* From this view, the setting of Frank O'Connor's "First Confession" might be said to include not just a church and a confessional, but turn-of-the-century Irish Catholicism and the ritual of going to confession. Still, we suggest that for now you keep your working definition of *setting* simple. Call it time and place. If later you should feel that your definition needs widening and deepening, you can always widen and deepen it.

Besides time and place, setting may also include the weather — which indeed, in some stories, may be crucial. Climate seems as substantial as any character in William Faulkner's "Dry September." After sixty-two rainless days, a long-unbroken spell of late-summer heat has frayed every nerve in a small town and caused the main character, a hotheaded white supremacist, to feel more and more irritation. The weather, someone remarks, is "enough to make a man do anything." When a false report circulates that a woman has been raped by a black man, the rumor, like a match flung into a dry field, ignites rage and provokes a lynching. Evidently, to understand the story we have to recognize its locale, a small town in Mississippi. The action (the 1930s) and that infernal heat wave matter, too. Fully to take in the meaning of Faulkner's story, we have to take in the setting in its entirety.

Physical place, by the way, is especially vital to a **regional writer,** who usually sets stories (or other work) in one geographic area. Such a writer, often a native of the place, tries to bring it alive to readers who live no matter where. William Faulkner, a distinguished regional writer, almost always sets his novels and stories in his native Mississippi. Though born in St. Louis, Kate Chopin became known as a regional writer for writing about Louisiana in many of her short stories and in her novel *The Awakening.* Willa Cather, for her novels of frontier Nebraska, often is regarded as another outstanding regionalist (though she also set fiction in Quebec, the Southwest, and in "Paul's Case," in Pittsburgh and New York). The expression is generally heard only in discussions of American and Canadian writing. (In a sense, we might think of James Joyce as a regional writer, in that all his fiction takes place in the city of Dublin, but instead we usually call him an Irish one.)

As such writers show, a place can profoundly affect the character who grew up in it. Willa Cather is fond of portraying strong-minded, independent women, such as the heroine of her novel *My Ántonia,* strengthened in part by years of coping with the hardships of life on the wind-lashed prairie. Not that every writer of stories in which a place matters greatly will draw the characters as helpless puppets of their environment. Few writers do so, although that may be what you find in novels of **naturalism** — fiction of grim realism, in which the writer observes human characters like a scientist observing ants, seeing them as the products and victims of environment and heredity.[1] Theodore Dreiser carries on the tradition of naturalism in novels such as *The Financier* (1912). It begins in a city setting. A young lad (who will grow up to be a ruthless industrialist) is watching a battle to death between a lobster and a squid in a fish-market tank. Dented for the rest of his life by this grim scene, he decides that's exactly the way to live in human society.

Setting may operate more subtly than that fish tank. Often, setting and character will reveal each other. Recall how Faulkner, at the start of "A Rose for Emily," depicts Emily Grierson's house, once handsome but now "an eyesore among eyesores" surrounded by gas stations. Still standing, refusing to yield its old-time horse-and-buggy splendor to the age of the automobile, the house in "its stubborn and coquettish decay" embodies the character of its owner. In some fiction, setting is closely bound with theme (what the story is saying) — as you will find in John Steinbeck's "The Chrysanthemums" (Chapter 8), a story beginning with a fog that has sealed off a valley from the rest of the world — a fog like the lid on a pot. In *The Scarlet Letter*, even small details contain powerful hints. At the beginning of his story, Hawthorne remarks of a colonial jailhouse:

> Before this ugly edifice, and between it and the wheel-track of the street, was a grass-plot, much overgrown with burdock, pigweed, apple-peru, and such unsightly vegetation, which evidently found something congenial in the soil that had so early borne the black flower of civilized society, a prison. But, on one side of the portal, and rooted almost at the threshold, was a wild rose-bush, covered, in this month of June, with its delicate gems, which might be imagined to offer their fragrance and fragile beauty to the prisoner as he went in, and to the condemned criminal as he came forth to his doom, in token that the deep heart of Nature could pity and be kind to him.

Apparently, Hawthorne wishes to show us that Puritan Boston, a town of rutted streets and an ugly jail with a tangled grass-plot, may be rough but has beauty in it. As the story unfolds, he will further suggest (among other things) that secret sin and a beautiful child may go together like pigweed and wild roses. In his artfully crafted novel, setting is one with — not separate from — characters, theme, and symbols.

In some stories, a writer will seem to draw a setting mainly to evoke atmosphere. In such a story, setting starts us feeling whatever the storyteller would have us feel. In "The Tell-Tale Heart," Poe's setting the action in an old, dark, lantern-lit house greatly contributes to our sense of unease — and so helps the story's effectiveness. (Old, dark mansions are favorite

[1]The founder of naturalism in fiction was French novelist Émile Zola (1840 – 1902), who in a vast series of twenty novels about the family Rougon-Macquart traced a case of syphilis through several generations. In America, Stephen Crane wrote an early naturalist novel, *Maggie: A Girl of the Streets* (1893), and showed the way for later novelists such as Dreiser, Frank Norris, Upton Sinclair, and James T. Farrell.

settings for the Gothic story, a long-popular kind of fiction mentioned again on page 223.)

But be warned: you'll meet stories in which setting appears hardly to matter. In W. Somerset Maugham's fable, "The Appointment in Samarra," all we need be told about the setting is that it is a marketplace in Bagdad. In that brief fable, the inevitability of death is the point, not an exotic setting. In this chapter, though, you will meet three fine stories in which setting, for one reason or another, counts greatly. Without it, none of these stories could happen.

James Joyce

ARABY 1905

James Joyce (1884 – 1941) quit Ireland at twenty to spend his mature life in voluntary exile on the continent, writing of nothing but Dublin, where he was born. In Trieste, Zurich, and Paris, he supported his family with difficulty, sometimes teaching in Berlitz language schools, until his writing won him fame and wealthy patrons. At first Joyce met difficulty in getting his work printed and circulated. Publication of Dubliners *(1914), the collection of stories that includes "Araby," was delayed seven years because its prospective Irish publisher feared libel suits. (The book depicts local citizens, some of them recognizable, and views Dubliners mostly as a thwarted, self-deceived lot.)* Portrait of the Artist as a Young Man *(1916), a novel of thinly veiled autobiography, recounts a young intellectual's breaking away from country, church, and home. Joyce's immense comic novel,* Ulysses *(1922), a parody of the Odyssey, spans eighteen hours in the life of a wandering Jew, a Dublin seller of advertising. Frank about sex but untitillating, the book was banned at one time by the U.S. Post Office. Joyce's later work stepped up its demands on readers. The challenging* Finnegans Wake *(1939), if read aloud, sounds as though a learned comic poet were sleep-talking, jumbling several languages. Joyce was an innovator whose bold experiments showed many other writers possibilities in fiction that had not earlier been imagined.*

North Richmond Street, being blind°, was a quiet street except at the hour when the Christian Brothers' School set the boys free. An uninhabited house of two stories stood at the blind end, detached from its neighbors in a square ground. The other houses of the street, conscious of decent lives within them, gazed at one another with brown imperturbable faces.

The former tenant of our house, a priest, had died in the back drawing-room. Air, musty from having long been enclosed, hung in all the rooms, and the waste room behind the kitchen was littered with old useless papers.

being blind: being a dead-end street.

Among these I found a few paper-covered books, the pages of which were curled and damp: *The Abbot,* by Walter Scott, *The Devout Communicant* and *The Memoirs of Vidocq°.* I liked the last best because its leaves were yellow. The wild garden behind the house contained a central apple-tree and a few straggling bushes under one of which I found the late tenant's rusty bicycle-pump. He had been a very charitable priest; in his will he had left all his money to institutions and the furniture of his house to his sister.

When the short days of winter came dusk fell before we had well eaten our dinners. When we met in the street the houses had grown somber. The space of sky above us was the color of ever-changing violet and towards it the lamps of the street lifted their feeble lanterns. The cold air stung us and we played till our bodies glowed. Our shouts echoed in the silent street. The career of our play brought us through the dark muddy lanes behind the houses where we ran the gantlet of the rough tribes from the cottages, to the back doors of the dark dripping gardens where odors arose from the ashpits, to the dark odorous stables where a coachman smoothed and combed the horse or shook music from the buckled harness. When we returned to the street light from the kitchen windows had filled the areas. If my uncle was seen turning the corner we hid in the shadow until we had seen him safely housed. Or if Mangan's sister° came out on the doorstep to call her brother in to his tea we watched her from our shadow peer up and down the street. We waited to see whether she would remain or go in and, if she remained, we left our shadow and walked up to Mangan's steps resignedly. She was waiting for us, her figure defined by the light from the half-opened door. Her brother always teased her before he obeyed and I stood by the railings looking at her. Her dress swung as she moved her body and the soft rope of her hair tossed from side to side.

Every morning I lay on the floor in the front parlor watching her door. The blind was pulled down within an inch of the sash so that I could not be seen. When she came out on the doorstep my heart leaped. I ran to the hall, seized my books and followed her. I kept her brown figure always in my eye and, when we came near the point at which our ways diverged, I quickened my pace and passed her. This happened morning after morning. I had never spoken to her, except for a few casual words, and yet her name was like a summons to all my foolish blood.

Her image accompanied me even in places the most hostile to romance. 5 On Saturday evenings when my aunt went marketing I had to go to carry some of the parcels. We walked through the flaring streets, jostled by drunken men and bargaining women, amid the curses of laborers, the shrill litanies of shop-boys who stood on guard by the barrels of pigs' cheeks, the nasal chanting of street singers, who sang a *come-all-you* about O'Donovan Rossa°, or a ballad

---

The Abbot . . . Vidocq: a popular historical romance (1820); a book of pious meditations by an eighteenth-century English Franciscan, Pacificus Baker; and the autobiography of François-Jules Vidocq (1775 – 1857), a criminal who later turned detective.

Mangan's sister: an actual young woman in this story, but the phrase recalls Irish poet James Clarence Mangan (1803 – 1849) and his best-known poem, "Dark Rosaleen," which personifies Ireland as a beautiful woman for whom the poet yearns.

come-all-you about O'Donovan Rossa: the street singers earned their living by singing timely songs that usually began, "Come all you gallant Irishmen / And listen to my song." Their subject, about the troubles in our native land. These noises converged in a single sensation of life for me: I imagined that I bore my chalice safely through the throng of foes. Her name sprang to my lips at moments in strange prayers and praises which I myself did not understand. My eyes were often full of tears (I could not tell why) and at times a flood from my heart seemed to pour itself out into my bosom. I thought little of the future. I did not know whether I would ever speak to her or not or, if I spoke to her, how I could tell her of my confused adoration. But my body was like a harp and her words and gestures were like fingers running upon the wires.

One evening I went into the back drawing-room in which the priest had died. It was a dark rainy evening and there was no sound in the house. Through one of the broken panes I heard the rain impinge upon the earth, the fine incessant needles of water playing in the sodden beds. Some distant lamp or lighted window gleamed below me. I was thankful that I could see so little. All my senses seemed to desire to veil themselves and, feeling that I was about to slip from them, I pressed the palms of my hands together until they trembled, murmuring: *O love! O love!* many times.

At last she spoke to me. When she addressed the first words to me I was so confused that I did not know what to answer. She asked me was I going to *Araby.* I forget whether I answered yes or no. It would be a splendid bazaar, she said; she would love to go.

— And why can't you? I asked.

While she spoke she turned a silver bracelet round and round her wrist. She could not go, she said, because there would be a retreat that week in her convent°. Her brother and two other boys were fighting for their caps and I was alone at the railings. She held one of the spikes, bowing her head towards me. The light from the lamp opposite our door caught the white curve of her neck, lit up her hair that rested there and, falling, lit up the hand upon the railing. It fell over one side of her dress and caught the white border of a petticoat, just visible as she stood at ease.

— It's well for you, she said.

— If I go, I said, I will bring you something.

What innumerable follies laid waste my waking and sleeping thoughts after that evening! I wished to annihilate the tedious intervening days. I chafed against the work of school. At night in my bedroom and by day in the classroom her image came between me and the page I strove to read. The syllables of the word *Araby* were called to me through the silence in which my soul luxuriated and cast an Eastern enchantment over me. I asked for leave to go to the bazaar on Saturday night. My aunt was surprised and hoped it was not some Freemason° affair. I answered few questions in class. I watched my master's face pass from amiability to sternness; he hoped I was

10

---

also called Dynamite Rossa, was a popular hero jailed by the British for advocating violent rebellion.

a retreat . . . in her convent: a week devoted to religious observances more intense than usual, at the convent school Miss Mangan attends; probably she will have to listen to a number of Hellfire sermons.

Freemason: Catholics in Ireland viewed the masonic order as a Protestant conspiracy against them.

not beginning to idle. I could not call my wandering thoughts together. I had hardly any patience with the serious work of life which, now that it stood between me and my desire, seemed to me child's play, ugly monotonous child's play.

On Saturday morning I reminded my uncle that I wished to go to the bazaar in the evening. He was fussing at the hall-stand, looking for the hat-brush, and answered me curtly:

— Yes, boy, I know.

As he was in the hall I could not go into the front parlor and lie at the window. I left the house in bad humor and walked slowly towards the school. The air was pitilessly raw and already my heart misgave me.

When I came home to dinner my uncle had not yet been home. Still it was early. I sat staring at the clock for some time and, when its ticking began to irritate me, I left the room. I mounted the staircase and gained the upper part of the house. The high cold empty gloomy rooms liberated me and I went from room to room singing. From the front window I saw my companions playing below in the street. Their cries reached me weakened and indistinct and, leaning my forehead against the cool glass, I looked over at the dark house where she lived. I may have stood there for an hour, seeing nothing but the brown-clad figure cast by my imagination, touched discreetly by the lamplight at the curved neck, at the hand upon the railings and at the border below the dress.

When I came downstairs again I found Mrs. Mercer sitting at the fire. She was an old garrulous woman, a pawnbroker's widow, who collected used stamps for some pious purpose. I had to endure the gossip of the tea-table. The meal was prolonged beyond an hour and still my uncle did not come. Mrs. Mercer stood up to go: she was sorry she couldn't wait any longer, but it was after eight o'clock and she did not like to be out late, as the night air was bad for her. When she had gone I began to walk up and down the room, clenching my fists. My aunt said:

— I'm afraid you may put off your bazaar for this night of Our Lord.

At nine o'clock I heard my uncle's latchkey in the halldoor. I heard him talking to himself and heard the hall-stand rocking when it had received the weight of his overcoat. I could interpret these signs. When he was midway through his dinner I asked him to give me the money to go to the bazaar. He had forgotten.

— The people are in bed and after their first sleep now, he said.

I did not smile. My aunt said to him energetically:

— Can't you give him the money and let him go? You've kept him late enough as it is.

My uncle said he was very sorry he had forgotten. He said he believed in the old saying: *All work and no play makes Jack a dull boy.* He asked me where I was going and, when I had told him a second time he asked me did I know *The Arab's Farewell to His Steed*°. When I left the kitchen he was about to recite the opening lines of the piece to my aunt.

The Arab's Farewell to His Steed: This sentimental ballad by a popular poet, Caroline Norton (1808 – 1877), tells the story of a nomad of the desert who, in a fit of greed, sells his beloved horse, then regrets the loss and flings away the gold he has received. Notice the echo of "Araby" in the song title.

I held a florin tightly in my hand as I strode down Buckingham Street towards the station. The sight of the streets thronged with buyers and glaring with gas recalled to me the purpose of my journey. I took my seat in a third-class carriage of a deserted train. After an intolerable delay the train moved out of the station slowly. It crept onward among ruinous houses and over the twinkling river. At Westland Row Station a crowd of people pressed to the carriage doors; but the porters moved them back, saying that it was a special train for the bazaar. I remained alone in the bare carriage. In a few minutes the train drew up beside an improvised wooden platform. I passed out on to the road and saw by the lighted dial of a clock that it was ten minutes to ten. In front of me was a large building which displayed the magical name.

I could not find any sixpenny entrance and, fearing that the bazaar would   25
be closed, I passed in quickly through a turnstile, handing a shilling to a weary-looking man. I found myself in a big hall girdled at half its height by a gallery. Nearly all the stalls were closed and the greater part of the hall was in darkness. I recognized a silence like that which pervades a church after a service. I walked into the center of the bazaar timidly. A few people were gathered about the stalls which were still open. Before a curtain, over which the words *Café Chantant*° were written in colored lamps, two men were counting money on a salver°. I listened to the fall of the coins.

Remembering with difficulty why I had come I went over to one of the stalls and examined porcelain vases and flowered tea-sets. At the door of the stall a young lady was talking and laughing with two young gentlemen. I remarked their English accents and listened vaguely to their conversation.

— O, I never said such a thing!

— O, but you did!

— O, but I didn't!

— Didn't she say that?   30

— Yes. I heard her.

— O, there's a . . . fib!

Observing me the young lady came over and asked me did I wish to buy anything. The tone of her voice was not encouraging; she seemed to have spoken to me out of a sense of duty. I looked humbly at the great jars that stood like eastern guards at either side of the dark entrance to the stall and murmured:

— No, thank you.

The young lady changed the position of one of the vases and went back   35
to the two young men. They began to talk of the same subject. Once or twice the young lady glanced at me over her shoulder.

I lingered before her stall, though I knew my stay was useless, to make my interest in her wares seem the more real. Then I turned away slowly and walked down the middle of the bazaar. I allowed the two pennies to fall against the sixpence in my pocket. I heard a voice call from one end of the gallery that the light was out. The upper part of the hall was now completely dark.

Gazing up into the darkness I saw myself as a creature driven and derided by vanity; and my eyes burned with anguish and anger.

Café Chantant: name for a Paris nightspot featuring topical songs.
salver: a tray like that used in serving Holy Communion.

1. In general, how would you describe the physical setting of "Araby" as Joyce details it in the opening five paragraphs? Does he make Dublin strike you as a beautiful place, a merry place, an ugly place, or what? What do you make of the detail, in the opening sentence, that the boy's street has a dead-end?
2. What images are conjured up by the name of the bazaar?
3. At what other moments in the story does the boy romanticize, or project an air of enchantment upon the commonplace?
4. Exactly what, in his visit to the bazaar, does the boy find so bitterly disillusioning? Does his confrontation with reality take place only at the end? At what moments in the story — and in what details — does he confront the actual?
5. From what point of view does James Joyce tell this story? Does the narrator of "Araby" seem a boy — a naive or innocent narrator — or a mature man looking back through a boy's eyes?
6. Imagine "Araby" told from some other point of view. Why would the story probably be less moving and less effective?
7. Who besides the boy is a major character in the story? How do we know that the boy's view of this character is not the author's view? (It may help to look closely at some of the narrator's descriptions of the other major character, and of his own feelings.)
8. How does the time of day matter to this story? What is meaningful or suggestive, in the end, about the fall of night?

Kate Chopin

THE STORM   1898

Kate Chopin (1851 – 1904) was born Katherine O'Flaherty in St. Louis, daughter of an Irish immigrant grown wealthy in retailing. On his death, young Kate was raised by her mother's family: aristocratic Creoles, descendants of the French and Spaniards who had colonized Louisiana. Young Kate received a convent schooling, and at nineteen married Oscar Chopin, a Creole cotton broker from New Orleans. Later, the Chopins lived on a plantation near Cloutierville, Louisiana, a region whose varied people — Creoles, Cajuns, blacks — Kate Chopin was later to write about with loving care in Bayou Folk *(1894) and* A Night in Arcadie *(1897). The shock of her husband's sudden death in 1883, which left her with the raising of six children, seems to have plunged Kate Chopin into writing. She read and admired fine woman writers of her day, such as the Maine realist Sarah Orne Jewett. She also read Maupassant, Zola, and other new (and scandalous) French naturalist writers. She began to bring into American fiction some of their hard-eyed observation and their passion for telling unpleasant truths. Determined, in defiance of her times, frankly to show the sexual feelings of her characters, Chopin suffered from neglect and censorship. When her major novel,* The Awakening, *appeared in 1899, critics were outraged by her candid portrait of a woman who seeks sexual and professional independence. After causing such a literary scandal, Chopin was unable to get her later work published, and wrote little more before she died.* The Awakening *and many of her stories had to wait seven decades for a sympathetic audience.*

I

The leaves were so still that even Bibi thought it was going to rain. Bobinôt, who was accustomed to converse on terms of perfect equality with his little son, called the child's attention to certain somber clouds that were rolling with sinister intention from the west, accompanied by a sullen, threatening roar. They were at Friedheimer's store and decided to remain there till the storm had passed. They sat within the door on two empty kegs. Bibi was four years old and looked very wise.

"Mama'll be 'fraid, yes," he suggested with blinking eyes.

"She'll shut the house. Maybe she got Sylvie helpin' her this evenin'," Bobinôt responded reassuringly.

"No; she ent got Sylvie. Sylvie was helpin' her yistiday," piped Bibi.

Bobinôt arose and going across to the counter purchased a can of   5 shrimps, of which Calixta was very fond. Then he returned to his perch on the keg and sat stolidly holding the can of shrimps while the storm burst. It shook the wooden store and seemed to be ripping great furrows in the distant field. Bibi laid his little hand on his father's knee and was not afraid.

II

Calixta, at home, felt no uneasiness for their safety. She sat at a side window sewing furiously on a sewing machine. She was greatly occupied and did not notice the approaching storm. But she felt very warm and often stopped to mop her face on which the perspiration gathered in beads. She unfastened her white sacque at the throat. It began to grow dark, and suddenly realizing the situation she got up hurriedly and went about closing windows and doors.

Out on the small front gallery she had hung Bobinôt's Sunday clothes to air and she hastened out to gather them before the rain fell. As she stepped outside, Alcée Laballière rode in at the gate. She had not seen him very often since her marriage, and never alone. She stood there with Bobinôt's coat in her hands, and the big rain drops began to fall. Alcée rode his horse under the shelter of a side projection where the chickens had huddled and there were plows and a harrow piled up in the corner.

"May I come and wait on your gallery till the storm is over, Calixta?" he asked.

"Come 'long in, M'sieur Alcée."

His voice and her own startled her as if from a trance, and she seized   10 Bobinôt's vest. Alcée, mounting to the porch, grabbed the trousers and snatched Bibi's braided jacket that was about to be carried away by a sudden gust of wind. He expressed an intention to remain outside, but it was soon apparent that he might as well have been out in the open: the water beat in upon the boards in driving sheets, and he went inside, closing the door after him. It was even necessary to put something beneath the door to keep the water out.

"My! what a rain! It's good two years sence it rain' like that," exclaimed Calixta as she rolled up a piece of bagging and Alcée helped her to thrust it beneath the crack.

She was a little fuller of figure than five years before when she married; but she had lost nothing of her vivacity. Her blue eyes still retained their melting quality; and her yellow hair, dishevelled by the wind and rain, kinked more stubbornly than ever about her ears and temples.

The rain beat upon the low, shingled roof with a force and clatter that threatened to break an entrance and deluge them there. They were in the dining room — the sitting room — the general utility room. Adjoining was her bed room, with Bibi's couch along side her own. The door stood open, and the room with its white, monumental bed, its closed shutters, looked dim and mysterious.

Alcée flung himself into a rocker and Calixta nervously began to gather up from the floor the lengths of a cotton sheet which she had been sewing.

"If this keeps up, *Dieu sait*° if the levees goin' to stan' it!" she exclaimed. 15

"What have you got to do with the levees?"

"I got enough to do! An' there's Bobinôt with Bibi out in that storm — if he only didn' left Friedheimer's!"

"Let us hope, Calixta, that Bobinôt's got sense enough to come in out of a cyclone."

She went and stood at the window with a greatly disturbed look on her face. She wiped the frame that was clouded with moisture. It was stiflingly hot. Alcée got up and joined her at the window, looking over her shoulder. The rain was coming down in sheets obscuring the view of far-off cabins and enveloping the distant wood in a gray mist. The playing of the lightning was incessant. A bolt struck a tall chinaberry tree at the edge of the field. It filled all visible space with a blinding glare and the crash seemed to invade the very boards they stood upon.

Calixta put her hands to her eyes, and with a cry, staggered backward. 20 Alcée's arm encircled her, and for an instant he drew her close and spasmodically to him.

"Bonte!°" she cried, releasing herself from his encircling arm and retreating from the window, "the house'll go next! If I only knew w'ere Bibi was!" She would not compose herself; she would not be seated. Alcée clasped her shoulders and looked into her face. The contact of her warm, palpitating body when he had unthinkingly drawn her into his arms, had aroused all the old-time infatuation and desire for her flesh.

"Calixta," he said, "don't be frightened. Nothing can happen. The house is too low to be struck, with so many tall trees standing about. There! aren't you going to be quiet? say, aren't you?" He pushed her hair back from her face that was warm and steaming. Her lips were as red and moist as pomegranate seed. Her white neck and a glimpse of her full, firm bosom disturbed him

Dieu sait: God only knows.
Bonte!: Heavens!

powerfully. As she glanced up at him the fear in her liquid blue eyes had given place to a drowsy gleam that unconsciously betrayed a sensuous desire. He looked down into her eyes and there was nothing for him to do but to gather her lips in a kiss. It reminded him of Assumption°.

"Do you remember — in Assumption, Calixta?" he asked in a low voice broken by passion. Oh! she remembered; for in Assumption he had kissed her and kissed and kissed her; until his senses would well nigh fail, and to save her he would resort to a desperate flight. If she was not an immaculate dove in those days, she was still inviolate; a passionate creature whose very defenselessness had made her defense, against which his honor forbade him to prevail. Now — well, now — her lips seemed in a manner free to be tasted, as well as her round, white throat and her whiter breasts.

They did not heed the crashing torrents, and the roar of the elements made her laugh as she lay in his arms. She was a revelation in that dim, mysterious chamber; as white as the couch she lay upon. Her firm, elastic flesh that was knowing for the first time its birthright, was like a creamy lily that the sun invites to contribute its breath and perfume to the undying life of the world.

The generous abundance of her passion, without guile or trickery, was   25
like a white flame which penetrated and found response in depths of his own sensuous nature that had never yet been reached.

When he touched her breasts they gave themselves up in quivering ecstasy, inviting his lips. Her mouth was a fountain of delight. And when he possessed her, they seemed to swoon together at the very borderland of life's mystery.

He stayed cushioned upon her, breathless, dazed, enervated, with his heart beating like a hammer upon her. With one hand she clasped his head, her lips lightly touching his forehead. The other hand stroked with a soothing rhythm his muscular shoulders.

The growl of the thunder was distant and passing away. The rain beat softly upon the shingles, inviting them to drowsiness and sleep. But they dared not yield.

The rain was over; and the sun was turning the glistening green world into a palace of gems. Calixta, on the gallery, watched Alcée ride away. He turned and smiled at her with a beaming face; and she lifted her pretty chin in the air and laughed aloud.

III

Bobinôt and Bibi, trudging home, stopped without at the cistern to make   30
themselves presentable.

"My! Bibi, w'at will yo' mama say! You ought to be ashame'. You oughtn' put on those good pants. Look at 'em! An' that mud on yo' collar! How you got that mud on yo' collar, Bibi? I never saw such a boy!" Bibi was the picture of pathetic resignation. Bobinôt was the embodiment of serious solicitude as he strove to remove from his own person and his son's the signs of their tramp over heavy roads and through wet fields. He scraped the mud off Bibi's

Assumption: Feast day, August 15, to celebrate Mary's bodily rising to Heaven.

bare legs and feet with a stick and carefully removed all traces from his heavy brogans. Then, prepared for the worst — the meeting with an over-scrupulous housewife, they entered cautiously at the back door.

Calixta was preparing supper. She had set the table and was dripping coffee at the hearth. She sprang up as they came in.

"Oh, Bobinôt! You back! My! but I was uneasy. W'ere you been during the rain? An' Bibi? he ain't wet? he ain't hurt?" She had clasped Bibi and was kissing him effusively. Bobinôt's explanations and apologies which he had been composing all along the way, died on his lips as Calixta felt him to see if he were dry, and seemed to express nothing but satisfaction at their safe return.

"I brought you some shrimps, Calixta," offered Bobinôt, hauling the can from his ample side pocket and laying it on the table.

"Shrimps! Oh, Bobinôt! you too good fo' anything!" and she gave him a smacking kiss on the cheek that resounded. *"J'vous reponds*°, we'll have a feas' to night! umph-umph!" 35

Bobinôt and Bibi began to relax and enjoy themselves, and when the three seated themselves at table they laughed much and so loud that anyone might have heard them as far away as Laballière's.

IV

Alcée Laballière wrote to his wife, Clarisse, that night. It was a loving letter, full of tender solicitude. He told her not to hurry back, but if she and the babies liked it at Biloxi, to stay a month longer. He was getting on nicely; and though he missed them, he was willing to bear the separation a while longer — realizing that their health and pleasure were the first things to be considered.

V

As for Clarisse, she was charmed upon receiving her husband's letter. She and the babies were doing well. The society was agreeable; many of her old friends and acquaintances were at the bay. And the first free breath since her marriage seemed to restore the pleasant liberty of her maiden days. Devoted as she was to her husband, their intimate conjugal life was something which she was more than willing to forego for a while.

So the storm passed and everyone was happy.

Questions

1. Exactly where does Chopin's story take place? How can you tell?
2. What circumstances introduced in Part I turn out to have a profound effect on events in the story?
3. What details in "The Storm" emphasize the fact that Bobinôt loves his wife? What details reveal how imperfectly he comprehends her nature?
4. What general attitudes toward sex, love, and marriage does Chopin imply? Cite evidence to support your answer.

J'vous reponds: Let me tell you.

5. What meanings do you find in the title "The Storm"?

6. In the story as a whole, how do setting and plot reinforce each other?

T. Coraghessan Boyle

GREASY LAKE   1985

T. Coraghessan Boyle (the "T" stands for Tom) was born in 1948 in Peekskill, New York, in the Hudson River Valley, a region about which he has been writing a novel that involves the lives of three families and spans three hundred years. A graduate of the University of Iowa Writers' Workshop, he now lives in Woodland Hills, California, and teaches creative writing at the University of Southern California. Winner of the St. Lawrence Award for Short Fiction and an Aga Khan Award from The Paris Review, *he contributes stories to* Antaeus, Esquire, The Atlantic, Iowa Review, Paris Review, TriQuarterly, *and other leading magazines. Boyle has published two novels: a ribald historical saga,* Water Music *(1982), which makes fiction out of an actual expedition to Africa led by Scottish explorer Mungo Park, and* Budding Prospects *(1984), a picaresque (or scoundrel-adventure) novel of life among marijuana growers. Boyle has also written two remarkable volumes of short stories:* The Descent of Man *(1979) and* Greasy Lake and Other Stories *(1985). His work has quickly won attention for its macabre humor, verve, and inventiveness — or, as critics have said, "tumbling exuberance" and "a raw ability to make one laugh." Another recent story imagines a love affair between Mrs. Nina Khrushchev and Dwight D. Eisenhower.*

It's about a mile down on the dark side of Route 88.
                                                              — Bruce Springsteen

There was a time when courtesy and winning ways went out of style, when it was good to be bad, when you cultivated decadence like a taste. We were all dangerous characters then. We wore torn-up leather jackets, slouched around with toothpicks in our mouths, sniffed glue and ether and what somebody claimed was cocaine. When we wheeled our parents' whining station wagons out into the street we left a patch of rubber half a block long. We drank gin and grape juice, Tango, Thunderbird, and Bali Hai. We were nineteen. We were bad. We read André Gide° and struck elaborate poses to show that we didn't give a shit about anything. At night, we went up to Greasy Lake.

Through the center of town, up the strip, past the housing developments and shopping malls, street lights giving way to the thin streaming illumination of the headlights, trees crowding the asphalt in a black unbroken wall: that was the way out to Greasy Lake. The Indians had called it Wakan, a reference to

André Gide: controversial French writer (1869 – 1951) whose novels, including *The Counterfeiters* and *Lafcadio's Adventures,* often show individuals in conflict with accepted morality.

the clarity of its waters. Now it was fetid and murky, the mud banks glittering with broken glass and strewn with beer cans and the charred remains of bonfires. There was a single ravaged island a hundred yards from shore, so stripped of vegetation it looked as if the air force had strafed it. We went up to the lake because everyone went there, because we wanted to snuff the rich scent of possibility on the breeze, watch a girl take off her clothes and plunge into the festering murk, drink beer, smoke pot, howl at the stars, savor the incongruous full-throated roar of rock and roll against the primeval susurrus of frogs and crickets. This was nature.

I was there one night, late, in the company of two dangerous characters. Digby wore a gold star in his right ear and allowed his father to pay his tuition at Cornell; Jeff was thinking of quitting school to become a painter/musician/head-shop proprietor. They were both expert in the social graces, quick with a sneer, able to manage a Ford with lousy shocks over a rutted and gutted blacktop road at eighty-five while rolling a joint as compact as a Tootsie Roll Pop stick. They could lounge against a bank of booming speakers and trade "man"s with the best of them or roll out across the dance floor as if their joints worked on bearings. They were slick and quick and they wore their mirror shades at breakfast and dinner, in the shower, in closets and caves. In short, they were bad.

I drove. Digby pounded the dashboard and shouted along with Toots & the Maytals while Jeff hung his head out the window and streaked the side of my mother's Bel Air with vomit. It was early June, the air soft as a hand on your cheek, the third night of summer vacation. The first two nights we'd been out till dawn, looking for something we never found. On this, the third night, we'd cruised the strip sixty-seven times, been in and out of every bar and club we could think of in a twenty-mile radius, stopped twice for bucket chicken and forty-cent hamburgers, debated going to a party at the house of a girl Jeff's sister knew, and chucked two dozen raw eggs at mailboxes and hitchhikers. It was 2:00 A.M.; the bars were closing. There was nothing to do but take a bottle of lemon-flavored gin up to Greasy Lake.

The taillights of a single car winked at us as we swung into the dirt lot with its tufts of weed and washboard corrugations; '57 Chevy, mint, metallic blue. On the far side of the lot, like the exoskeleton of some gaunt chrome insect, a chopper leaned against its kickstand. And that was it for excitement: some junkie half-wit biker and a car freak pumping his girlfriend. Whatever it was we were looking for, we weren't about to find it at Greasy Lake. Not that night.

But then all of a sudden Digby was fighting for the wheel. "Hey, that's Tony Lovett's car! Hey!" he shouted, while I stabbed at the brake pedal and the Bel Air nosed up to the gleaming bumper of the parked Chevy. Digby leaned on the horn, laughing, and instructed me to put my brights on. I flicked on the brights. This was hilarious. A joke. Tony would experience premature withdrawal and expect to be confronted by grim-looking state troopers with flashlights. We hit the horn, strobed the lights, and then jumped out of the car to press our witty faces to Tony's windows; for all we knew we might even catch a glimpse of some little fox's tit, and then we could slap backs with red-faced Tony, roughhouse a little, and go on to new heights of adventure and daring.

The first mistake, the one that opened the whole floodgate, was losing my grip on the keys. In the excitement, leaping from the car with the gin in one hand and a roach clip in the other, I spilled them in the grass — in the dark, rank, mysterious nighttime grass of Greasy Lake. This was a tactical error, as damaging and irreversible in its way as Westmoreland's decision to dig in at Khe Sanh°. I felt it like a jab of intuition, and I stopped there by the open door, peering vaguely into the night that puddled up round my feet.

The second mistake — and this was inextricably bound up with the first — was identifying the car as Tony Lovett's. Even before the very bad character in greasy jeans and engineer boots ripped out of the driver's door, I began to realize that this chrome blue was much lighter than the robin's-egg of Tony's car, and that Tony's car didn't have rear-mounted speakers. Judging from their expressions, Digby and Jeff were privately groping toward the same inevitable and unsettling conclusion as I was.

In any case, there was no reasoning with this bad greasy character — clearly he was a man of action. The first lusty Rockette° kick of his steel-toed boot caught me under the chin, chipped my favorite tooth, and left me sprawled in the dirt. Like a fool, I'd gone down on one knee to comb the stiff hacked grass for the keys, my mind making connections in the most dragged-out, testudineous way, knowing that things had gone wrong, that I was in a lot of trouble, and that the lost ignition key was my grail and my salvation. The three or four succeeding blows were mainly absorbed by my right buttock and the tough piece of bone at the base of my spine.

Meanwhile, Digby vaulted the kissing bumpers and delivered a savage kung-fu blow to the greasy character's collarbone. Digby had just finished a course in martial arts for phys-ed credit and had spent the better part of the past two nights telling us apocryphal tales of Bruce Lee types and of the raw power invested in lightning blows shot from coiled wrists, ankles, and elbows. The greasy character was unimpressed. He merely backed off a step, his face like a Toltec mask, and laid Digby out with a single whistling roundhouse blow . . . but by now Jeff had got into the act, and I was beginning to extricate myself from the dirt, a tinny compound of shock, rage, and impotence wadded in my throat.

Jeff was on the guy's back, biting at his ear. Digby was on the ground, cursing. I went for the tire iron I kept under the driver's seat. I kept it there because bad characters always keep tire irons under the driver's seat, for just such an occasion as this. Never mind that I hadn't been involved in a fight since sixth grade, when a kid with a sleepy eye and two streams of mucus depending from his nostrils hit me in the knee with a Louisville slugger°, never mind that I'd touched the tire iron exactly twice before, to change tires: it was there. And I went for it.

10

I was terrified. Blood was beating in my ears, my hands were shaking, my heart turning over like a dirtbike in the wrong gear. My antagonist was shirtless, and a single cord of muscle flashed across his chest as he bent forward to peel Jeff from his back like a wet overcoat. "Motherfucker," he spat, over and over, and I was aware in that instant that all four of us — Digby, Jeff, and myself included — were chanting "motherfucker, motherfucker," as if it were a battle cry. (What happened next? the detective asks the murderer from beneath the turned-down brim of his porkpie hat. I don't know, the murderer says, something came over me. Exactly.)

Digby poked the flat of his hand in the bad character's face and I came at him like a kamikaze, mindless, raging, stung with humiliation — the whole thing, from the initial boot in the chin to this murderous primal instant involving no more than sixty hyperventilating, gland-flooding seconds — I came at him and brought the tire iron down across his ear. The effect was instantaneous, astonishing. He was a stunt man and this was Hollywood, he was a big grimacing toothy balloon and I was a man with a straight pin. He collapsed. Wet his pants. Went loose in his boots.

A single second, big as a zeppelin, floated by. We were standing over him in a circle, gritting our teeth, jerking our necks, our limbs and hands and feet twitching with glandular discharges. No one said anything. We just stared down at the guy, the car freak, the lover, the bad greasy character laid low. Digby looked at me; so did Jeff. I was still holding the tire iron, a tuft of hair clinging to the crook like dandelion fluff, like down. Rattled, I dropped it in the dirt, already envisioning the headlines, the pitted faces of the police inquisitors, the gleam of handcuffs, clank of bars, the big black shadows rising from the back of the cell . . . when suddenly a raw torn shriek cut through me like all the juice in all the electric chairs in the country.

It was the fox. She was short, barefoot, dressed in panties and a man's shirt. "Animals!" she screamed, running at us with her fists clenched and wisps of blow-dried hair in her face. There was a silver chain round her ankle, and her toenails flashed in the glare of the headlights. I think it was the toenails that did it. Sure, the gin and the cannabis and even the Kentucky Fried may have had a hand in it, but it was the sight of those flaming toes that set us off — the toad emerging from the loaf in *Virgin Spring*°, lipstick smeared on a child: she was already tainted. We were on her like Bergman's deranged brothers — see no evil, hear none, speak none — panting, wheezing, tearing at her clothes, grabbing for flesh. We were bad characters, and we were scared and hot and three steps over the line — anything could have happened.

It didn't.

Before we could pin her to the hood of the car, our eyes masked with lust and greed and the purest primal badness, a pair of headlights swung into the lot. There we were, dirty, bloody, guilty, dissociated from humanity and civilization, the first of the Ur-crimes behind us, the second in progress, shreds of nylon panty and spandex brassiere dangling from our fingers, our flies open, lips licked — there we were, caught in the spotlight. Nailed.

We bolted. First for the car, and then, realizing we had no way of starting

Virgin Spring: film by Swedish director Ingmar Bergman.

it, for the woods. I thought nothing. I thought escape. The headlights came at me like accusing fingers. I was gone.

Ram-bam-bam, across the parking lot, past the chopper and into the feculent undergrowth at the lake's edge, insects flying up in my face, weeds whipping, frogs and snakes and red-eyed turtles splashing off into the night: I was already ankle-deep in muck and tepid water and still going strong. Behind me, the girl's screams rose in intensity, disconsolate, incriminating, the screams of the Sabine women°, the Christian martyrs, Anne Frank° dragged from the garret. I kept going, pursued by those cries, imagining cops and bloodhounds. The water was up to my knees when I realized what I was doing: I was going to swim for it. Swim the breadth of Greasy Lake and hide myself in the thick clot of woods on the far side. They'd never find me there.

I was breathing in sobs, in gasps. The water lapped at my waist as I looked out over the moon-burnished ripples, the mats of algae that clung to the surface like scabs. Digby and Jeff had vanished. I paused. Listened. The girl was quieter now, screams tapering to sobs, but there were male voices, angry, excited, and the high-pitched ticking of the second car's engine. I waded deeper, stealthy, hunted, the ooze sucking at my sneakers. As I was about to take the plunge — at the very instant I dropped my shoulder for the first slashing stroke — I blundered into something. Something unspeakable, obscene, something soft, wet, moss-grown. A patch of weed? A log? When I reached out to touch it, it gave like a rubber duck, it gave like flesh.

In one of those nasty little epiphanies for which we are prepared by films and TV and childhood visits to the funeral home to ponder the shrunken painted forms of dead grandparents, I understood what it was that bobbed there so inadmissibly in the dark. Understood, and stumbled back in horror and revulsion, my mind yanked in six different directions (I was nineteen, a mere child, an infant, and here in the space of five minutes I'd struck down one greasy character and blundered into the waterlogged carcass of a second), thinking, The keys, the keys, why did I have to go and lose the keys? I stumbled back, but the muck took hold of my feet — a sneaker snagged, balance lost — and suddenly I was pitching face forward into the buoyant black mass, throwing out my hands in desperation while simultaneously conjuring the image of reeking frogs and muskrats revolving in slicks of their own deliquescing juices. AAAAArrrgh! I shot from the water like a torpedo, the dead man rotating to expose a mossy beard and eyes cold as the moon. I must have shouted out, thrashing around in the weeds, because the voices behind me suddenly became animated.

"What was that?"

"It's them, it's them: they tried to, tried to . . . *rape* me!" Sobs.

A man's voice, flat Midwestern accent. "You sons a bitches, we'll kill you!"

Sabine women: members of an ancient tribe in Italy, according to legend, forcibly carried off by the early Romans under Romulus to be their wives. The incident is depicted in a famous painting, "The Rape of the Sabine Women," by seventeenth-century French artist Nicolas Poussin.

Anne Frank: German Jewish girl (1929 – 1945) whose diary written during the Nazi occupation of the Netherlands later became world famous. She hid with her family in a secret attic in Amsterdam, but was caught by storm troopers and sent to the concentration camp at Belsen, where she died.

Frogs, crickets.

Then another voice, harsh, r-less, Lower East Side: "Motherfucker!" I recognized the verbal virtuosity of the bad greasy character in the engineer boots. Tooth chipped, sneakers gone, coated in mud and slime and worse, crouching breathless in the weeds waiting to have my ass thoroughly and definitively kicked and fresh from the hideous stinking embrace of a three-days-dead-corpse, I suddenly felt a rush of joy and vindication: the son of a bitch was alive! Just as quickly, my bowels turned to ice. "Come on out of there, you pansy mothers!" the bad greasy character was screaming. He shouted curses till he was out of breath.

The crickets started up again, then the frogs. I held my breath. All at once there was a sound in the reeds, a swishing, a splash: thunk-a-thunk. They were throwing rocks. The frogs fell silent. I cradled my head. Swish, swish, thunk-a-thunk. A wedge of feldspar the size of a cue ball glanced off my knee. I bit my finger.

It was then that they turned to the car. I heard a door slam, a curse, and then the sound of the headlights shattering — almost a good-natured sound, celebratory, like corks popping from the necks of bottles. This was succeeded by the dull booming of the fenders, metal on metal, and then the icy crash of the windshield. I inched forward, elbows and knees, my belly pressed to the muck, thinking of guerrillas and commandos and *The Naked and the Dead*°. I parted the weeds and squinted the length of the parking lot.

The second car — it was a Trans-Am — was still running, its high beams washing the scene in a lurid stagy light. Tire iron flailing, the greasy bad character was laying into the side of my mother's Bel Air like an avenging demon, his shadow riding up the trunks of the trees. Whomp. Whomp. Whomp-whomp. The other two guys — blond types, in fraternity jackets — were helping out with tree branches and skull-sized boulders. One of them was gathering up bottles, rocks, muck, candy wrappers, used condoms, pop-tops, and other refuse and pitching it through the window on the driver's side. I could see the fox, a white bulb behind the windshield of the '57 Chevy. "Bobbie," she whined over the thumping, "come *on*." The greasy character paused a moment, took one good swipe at the left taillight, and then heaved the tire iron halfway across the lake. Then he fired up the '57 and was gone.

Blond head nodded at blond head. One said something to the other, too low for me to catch. They were no doubt thinking that in helping to annihilate my mother's car they'd committed a fairly rash act, and thinking too that there were three bad characters connected with that very car watching them from the woods. Perhaps other possibilities occurred to them as well — police, jail cells, justices of the peace, reparations, lawyers, irate parents, fraternal censure. Whatever they were thinking, they suddenly dropped branches, bottles, and rocks and sprang for their car in unison, as if they'd choreographed it. Five seconds. That's all it took. The engine shrieked, the tires squealed, a cloud of dust rose from the rutted lot and then settled back on darkness.

I don't know how long I lay there, the bad breath of decay all around me, my jacket heavy as a bear, the primordial ooze subtly reconstituting itself to accommodate my upper thighs and testicles. My jaws ached, my knee throbbed, my coccyx was on fire. I contemplated suicide, wondered if I'd need

The Naked and the Dead: novel (1948) by Norman Mailer, of U.S. Army life in World War II.

bridgework, scraped the recesses of my brain for some sort of excuse to give my parents — a tree had fallen on the car, I was blindsided by a bread truck, hit and run, vandals had got to it while we were playing chess at Digby's. Then I thought of the dead man. He was probably the only person on the planet worse off than I was. I thought about him, fog on the lake, insects chirring eerily, and felt the tug of fear, felt the darkness opening up inside me like a set of jaws. Who was he, I wondered, this victim of time and circumstance bobbing sorrowfully in the lake at my back. The owner of the chopper, no doubt, a bad older character come to this. Shot during a murky drug deal, drowned while drunkenly frolicking in the lake. Another headline. My car was wrecked; he was dead.

When the eastern half of the sky went from black to cobalt and the trees began to separate themselves from the shadows, I pushed myself up from the mud and stepped out into the open. By now the birds had begun to take over for the crickets, and dew lay slick on the leaves. There was a smell in the air, raw and sweet at the same time, the smell of the sun firing buds and opening blossoms. I contemplated the car. It lay there like a wreck along the highway, like a steel sculpture left over from a vanished civilization. Everything was still. This was nature.

I was circling the car, as dazed and bedraggled as the sole survivor of an air blitz, when Digby and Jeff emerged from the trees behind me. Digby's face was crosshatched with smears of dirt; Jeff's jacket was gone and his shirt was torn across the shoulder. They slouched across the lot, looking sheepish, and silently came up beside me to gape at the ravaged automobile. No one said a word. After a while Jeff swung open the driver's door and began to scoop the broken glass and garbage off the seat. I looked at Digby. He shrugged. "At least they didn't slash the tires," he said.

It was true: the tires were intact. There was no windshield, the headlights were staved in, and the body looked as if it had been sledge-hammered for a quarter a shot at the county fair, but the tires were inflated to regulation pressure. The car was drivable. In silence, all three of us bent to scrape the mud and shattered glass from the interior. I said nothing about the biker. When we were finished, I reached in my pocket for the keys, experienced a nasty stab of recollection, cursed myself, and turned to search the grass. I spotted them almost immediately, no more than five feet from the open door, glinting like jewels in the first tapering shaft of sunlight. There was no reason to get philosophical about it: I eased into the seat and turned the engine over.

It was at that precise moment that the silver Mustang with the flame decals rumbled into the lot. All three of us froze; then Digby and Jeff slid into the car and slammed the door. We watched as the Mustang rocked and bobbed across the ruts and finally jerked to a halt beside the forlorn chopper at the far end of the lot. "Let's go," Digby said. I hesitated, the Bel Air wheezing beneath me.

Two girls emerged from the Mustang. Tight jeans, stiletto heels, hair like frozen fur. They bent over the motorcycle, paced back and forth aimlessly, glanced once or twice at us, and then ambled over to where the reeds sprang up in a green fence round the perimeter of the lake. One of them cupped her hands to her mouth. "Al," she called. "Hey, Al!"

"Come on," Digby hissed. "Let's get out of here."

But it was too late. The second girl was picking her way across the lot, unsteady on her heels, looking up at us and then away. She was older — twenty-five or -six — and as she came closer we could see there was something wrong with her: she was stoned or drunk, lurching now and waving her arms for balance. I gripped the steering wheel as if it were the ejection lever of a flaming jet, and Digby spat out my name, twice, terse and impatient.

"Hi," the girl said.

We looked at her like zombies, like war veterans, like deaf-and-dumb pencil peddlers. [40]

She smiled, her lips cracked and dry. "Listen," she said, bending from the waist to look in the window, "you guys seen Al?" Her pupils were pin-points, her eyes glass. She jerked her neck. "That's his bike over there — Al's. You seen him?"

Al. I didn't know what to say. I wanted to get out of the car and retch, I wanted to go home to my parents' house and crawl into bed. Digby poked me in the ribs. "We haven't seen anybody," I said.

The girl seemed to consider this, reaching out a slim veiny arm to brace herself against the car. "No matter," she said, slurring the *t*'s, "he'll turn up." And then, as if she'd just taken stock of the whole scene — the ravaged car and our battered faces, the desolation of the place — she said: "Hey, you guys look like some pretty bad characters — been fightin', huh?" We stared straight ahead, rigid as catatonics. She was fumbling in her pocket and muttering something. Finally she held out a handful of tablets in glassine wrappers: "Hey, you want to party, you want to do some of these with me and Sarah?"

I just looked at her. I thought I was going to cry. Digby broke the silence. "No, thanks," he said, leaning over me. "Some other time."

I put the car in gear and it inched forward with a groan, shaking off [45] pellets of glass like an old dog shedding water after a bath, heaving over the ruts on its worn springs, creeping toward the highway. There was a sheen of sun on the lake. I looked back. The girl was still standing there, watching us, her shoulders slumped, hand outstretched.

QUESTIONS

1. Around what year, would you say, was it that "courtesy and winning ways went out of style, when it was good to be bad, when you cultivated decadence like a taste"?
2. What is it about Digby and Jeff that inspires the narrator to call them "bad"?
3. Twice in "Greasy Lake" — in paragraphs 2 and 32 — appear the words, "This was nature." What contrasts do you find between the "nature" of the narrator's earlier and later views?
4. What makes the narrator and his friends run off into the woods?
5. How does the heroes' encounter with the two girls at the end of the story differ from their earlier encounter with the girl from the blue Chevy? How do you account for the difference? When at the end of the story the girl offers to party with the three friends, what makes the narrator say, "I thought I was going to cry"?
6. How important to what happens in this story is Greasy Lake itself? What details about the lake and its shores strike you as particularly memorable (whether funny, disgusting, or both)?

7. The setting of Boyle's story is very different from that of James Joyce's "Araby." But in what ways do the two stories resemble each other?

SUGGESTIONS FOR WRITING

1. In a few paragraphs, not necessarily a complete essay or story, recreate a time and place you know intimately. Write about it like a fiction writer, giving reality to a setting in which a story is about to unfold. Imagine this setting in detail — or, if you can, go take a fresh look at it. Ensure that your reader can virtually see, hear, smell, and taste your chosen time and place.

   You might find it revealing to choose for your subject some nearby, present-day place that your audience will recognize, then read your paper aloud in class. If, without your dropping place names or giving them other obvious clues, your listeners can identify your subject, then you have written well.

2. From a different chapter of this book, or from the Stories for Further Reading, choose a story that particularly interests you. Start out by defining for your reader its exact time and place. Then, in two or three more paragraphs, go on to show how this setting functions in the story. Does the setting supply atmosphere? Make things happen? Reveal the natures of certain people? Prompt a character to a realization? Suggested stories to work on (but your instructor may be saving some stories for other purposes and may wish to narrow or add to this list): "Gimpel the Fool" (Chapter 4); "A Clean, Well-Lighted Place," "Barn Burning" (Chapter 5); "Revelation," "The Open Boat" (Chapter 7); "The Chrysanthemums," "Wild Swans" (Chapter 8); "The Death of Ivan Ilych," "The Birthmark," "A Haunted House," "The Garden-Party," "Roman Fever," "A Worn Path," "The Portable Phonograph" (Stories for Further Reading).

3. Rewrite the first page or two of a story you have read, picking up the characters and putting them down in an entirely different setting. This new time and place might be the setting of another story, or it might be some actual place your readers will recognize. As you write, you might find yourself deciding to seek laughs, or you might decide to make the rewrite serious. You might try, for instance, a satire in the vein of *Monty Python*, shifting Hawthorne's "The Birthmark" to the setting of Updike's "A & P." Or, without trying to be funny, you might rewrite the opening of Joyce's "Araby," setting the story in the neighborhood where you grew up.

   End with a short comment in answer to the question, "What did this exercise prove to you?" If your attempt should seem to you a failure, try to explain why the original story proved so reluctant to give up its time and place. (The purpose of this exercise is not to produce a new masterpiece, but to experience at first hand how the setting of a story works.)

4 Character

From popular fiction and drama, both classic and contemporary, we are acquainted with many stereotyped characters. Called **stock characters,** they are often known by some outstanding trait or traits: the *bragging* soldier of Greek and Roman comedy, the prince *charming* of fairy tales, the *mad* scientist of horror movies, the *loyal* sidekick of Westerns, the *greedy* explorer of Tarzan films, the *brilliant but alcoholic* brain surgeon of medical thrillers on television. Stock characters are especially convenient for writers of commercial fiction: they require little detailed portraiture, for we already know them well. Most writers of the literary story, however, attempt to create characters who strike us not as stereotypes but as unique individuals. Although stock characters tend to have single dominant virtues and vices, characters in the finest contemporary short stories tend to have many facets, like people we meet.

A **character,** then, is presumably an imagined person who inhabits a story — although that simple definition may admit to a few exceptions. In George Stewart's novel *Storm,* the protagonist is the wind; in Richard Adams's *Watership Down,* the main characters are rabbits. But usually we recognize, in the main characters of a story, human personalities that become familiar to us. If the story seems "true to life," we generally find that its characters act in a reasonably consistent manner, and that the author has provided them with **motivation:** sufficient reason to behave as they do. Should a character behave in a sudden and unexpected way, seeming to deny what we have been told about his nature or personality, we trust that he had a reason, and that sooner or later we will discover it. This is not to claim that *all* authors insist that their characters behave with absolute consistency, for (as we shall see later in this chapter) some contemporary stories feature characters who sometimes act without apparent reason. Nor can we say that, in good fiction, characters never change or develop. In "A Christmas Carol," Charles Dickens tells how Ebeneezer Scrooge, a tightfisted miser, reforms overnight, suddenly gives to the poor, and endeavors to assist his clerk's struggling family. But Dickens amply demonstrates why Scrooge had such a change of heart: four ghostly visitors, stirring kind memories the old miser had forgotten and also warning him of the probable consequences of his habits, provide the character (and hence the story) with adequate motivation.

To borrow the useful terms of the English novelist E. M. Forster, characters may seem **flat** or **round,** depending on whether a writer sketches or sculptures them. A flat character usually has only one outstanding trait or feature, or at most a few distinguishing marks: for example, the familiar stock character of the mad scientist, with his lust for absolute power and his crazily gleaming eyes. Flat characters, however, need not be stock characters: in all of literature there is probably only one Tiny Tim, though his functions in "A Christmas Carol" are mainly to invoke blessings and to remind others of their Christian duties. Some writers, notably Balzac, who peopled his many novels with hosts of characters, try to distinguish the flat ones by giving each a single odd physical feature or mannerism — a nervous twitch, a piercing gaze, an obsessive fondness for oysters. Round characters, however, present us with more facets — that is, their authors portray them in greater depth and in more generous detail. Such a round character may appear to us only as he appears to the other characters in the story. If their views of him differ, we will see him from more than one side. In other stories, we enter a character's mind and come to know him through his own thoughts, feelings, and perceptions. By the time we finish reading James Joyce's "Araby" (page 54), we are well acquainted with the boy who tells his story and probably find him amply three-dimensional.

Flat characters tend to stay the same throughout a story, but round characters often change — learn or become enlightened, grow or deteriorate. In William Faulkner's "Barn Burning" (Chapter Five), the boy Sarty Snopes, driven to defy his proud and violent father, becomes at the story's end more knowing and more mature. (Some critics call a fixed character **static;** a changing one, **dynamic.**) This is not to damn a flat character as an inferior work of art. In most fiction — even the greatest — minor characters tend to be flat instead of round. Why? Rounding them would cost time and space; and so enlarged, they might only distract us from the main characters.

"A character, first of all, is the noise of his name," according to novelist William Gass.[1] Names, chosen artfully, can indicate natures. A simple illustration is the completely virtuous Squire Allworthy, the foster father in *Tom Jones* by Henry Fielding. Subtler, perhaps, is the custom of giving a character a name that makes an **allusion:** a reference to some famous person, place, or thing in history, in other fiction, or in actuality. For his central characters in *Moby-Dick,* Herman Melville chose names from the Old Testament, calling his tragic and domineering Ahab after a biblical tyrant who came to a bad end, and his wandering narrator Ishmael after a biblical outcast. Whether or not it includes an allusion, a good name often

[1]"The Concept of Character in Fiction," in *Fiction and the Figures of Life* (New York: Knopf, 1970).

reveals the character of the character. Charles Dickens, a vigorous and richly suggestive christener, named a charming confidence man Mr. Jingle (suggesting something jingly, light, and superficially pleasant), named a couple of shyster lawyers Dodgson and Fogg (suggesting dodging evasiveness and foglike obfuscation), and named two heartless educators, who grimly drill their schoolchildren in "hard facts," Gradgrind and M'Choakumchild. Henry James, who so loved names that he kept lists of them for characters he might someday conceive, chose for a sensitive, cultured gentleman the name of Lambert Strether; for a down-to-earth, benevolent individual, the name of Mrs. Bread. (But James may have wished to indicate that names cannot be identified with people absolutely, in giving the fragile, considerate heroine of *The Spoils of Poynton* the harsh-sounding name of Fleda Vetch.)

Instead of a hero, many a recent novel has featured an **antihero**: an ordinary, unglorious twentieth-century citizen, usually drawn (according to Sean O'Faolain) as someone "groping, puzzled, cross, mocking, frustrated, and isolated.[2] (Evidently, there are antiheroines too.) If epic poets once drew their heroes as decisive leaders of their people, embodying their people's highest ideals, antiheroes tend to be loners, without perfections, just barely able to survive. Antiheroes lack "character," as defined by psychologist Anthony Quinton to mean a person's conduct or "persistence and consistency in seeking to realize his long-term aims."[3] A gulf separates Leopold Bloom, antihero of James Joyce's novel *Ulysses*, from the hero of the Greek *Odyssey*. In Homer's epic, Ulysses wanders the Mediterranean, battling monsters and overcoming enchantments. In Joyce's novel, Bloom wanders the littered streets of Dublin, peddling advertising space. In recent fiction, by the way, female antiheroes abound.

Evidently, not only fashions in heroes but also attitudes toward human nature have undergone change. In the eighteenth century, Scottish philosopher David Hume argued that the nature of an individual is relatively fixed and unalterable. Hume mentioned, however, a few exceptions: "A person of an obliging disposition gives a peevish answer; but he has the toothache or has not dined. A stupid fellow discovers an obvious alacrity in his carriage; but he has met with a sudden piece of good fortune." For a long time after Hume, novelists and short-story writers seem to have assumed that characters behave nearly always in a predictable fashion and that their actions ought to be consistent with their personalities. Now and again, a writer differed: Jane Austen in *Pride and Prejudice* has her protagonist Elizabeth Bennet remark to the citified Mr. Darcy, who fears that life in the country cannot be amusing, "But people themselves alter so much, that there is something to be observed in them forever."

---

[2]*The Vanishing Hero* (Boston: Little, 1957).
[3]"The Continuity of Persons," *Times Literary Supplement* issue on "The Nature of Character," 27 July 1973.

Many contemporary writers of fiction would deny even that people have definite selves to alter. Following Sigmund Freud and other modern psychologists, they assume that a large part of human behavior is shaped in the unconscious — that, for instance, a person might fear horses not because of a basically timid nature, but because of unconscious memories of having been nearly trampled by a horse when a child. To some writers it now appears that what Hume called a "disposition" (now called a "personality") is more vulnerable to change from such causes as age, disease, neurosis, psychic shock, or brainwashing than was once believed. Hence, some characters in twentieth-century fiction appear to be shifting bundles of impulses. "You mustn't look in my novel for the old stable ego of character," wrote D. H. Lawrence to a friend about *The Rainbow;* and in that novel and other novels Lawrence demonstrated his view of individuals as bits of one vast Life Force, spurred to act by incomprehensible passions and urges — the "dark gods" in them. The idea of the **gratuitous act,** a deed without cause or motive, is explored in André Gide's novel *Lafcadio's Adventures,* in which an ordinary young man without homicidal tendencies abruptly and for no reason pushes a stranger from a speeding train. The usual limits of character are playfully violated by Virginia Woolf in *Orlando,* a novel whose protagonist, defying time, lives right on from Elizabethan days into the present, changing in midstory from a man into a woman. Characterization, as practiced by nineteenth-century novelists, almost entirely disappears in Franz Kafka's *The Castle,* whose protagonist has no home, no family, no definite appearance — not even a name, just the initial *K.* Characters are things of the past, insists the contemporary French novelist Alain Robbe-Grillet. Still, many writers of fiction go on portraying them.

James Thurber
THE CATBIRD SEAT   1945

James Thurber (1894 – 1961), a humorist sometimes mentioned in the same breath with Mark Twain, was born in Columbus, Ohio and took a degree from Ohio State University. As a young man he gravitated to New York, where he became a prolific contributor to The New Yorker *along with E. B. White, his collaborator on a book-length spoof of popular psychology,* Is Sex Necessary? *(1929). Despite weak eyesight, Thurber gained fame as a cartoonist known for his childlike drawings of timid little men and hound dogs with floppy ears. As blindness descended in his last years, Thurber drew less and less, wrote more and more. Besides essays and stories, his works include a fable for children,* The Thirteen Clocks *(1950); a memoir of working on the* New Yorker *staff,* The Years with Ross *(1959); and with Elliott Nugent, a comedy,* The Male Animal, *produced on Broadway in 1940.*

Mr. Martin bought the pack of Camels on Monday night in the most crowded cigar store on Broadway. It was theater time and seven or eight men were buying cigarettes. The clerk didn't even glance at Mr. Martin, who put the pack in his overcoat pocket and went out. If any of the staff at F & S had seen him buy the cigarettes, they would have been astonished, for it was generally known that Mr. Martin did not smoke, and never had. No one saw him.

It was just a week to the day since Mr. Martin had decided to rub out Mrs. Ulgine Barrows. The term "rub out" pleased him because it suggested nothing more than the correction of an error — in this case an error of Mr. Fitweiler. Mr. Martin had spent each night of the past week working out his plan and examining it. As he walked home now he went over it again. For the hundredth time he resented the element of imprecision, the margin of guess-work that entered into the business. The project as he had worked it out was casual and bold, the risks were considerable. Something might go wrong any-where along the line. And therein lay the cunning of his scheme. No one would ever see in it the cautious, painstaking hand of Erwin Martin, head of the filing department at F & S, of whom Mr. Fitweiler had once said, "Man is fallible but Martin isn't." No one would see his hand, that is, unless it were caught in the act.

Sitting in his apartment, drinking a glass of milk, Mr. Martin reviewed his case against Mrs. Ulgine Barrows, as he had every night for seven nights. He began at the beginning. Her quacking voice and braying laugh had first profaned the halls of F & S on March 7, 1941 (Mr. Martin had a head for dates). Old Roberts, the personnel chief, had introduced her as the newly appointed special adviser to the president of the firm, Mr. Fitweiler. The woman had appalled Mr. Martin instantly, but he hadn't shown it. He had given her his dry hand, a look of studious concentration, and a faint smile. "Well," she had said, looking at the papers on his desk, "are you lifting the oxcart out of the ditch?" As Mr. Martin recalled that moment, over his milk, he squirmed slightly. He must keep his mind on her crimes as a special adviser, not on her peccadillos as a personality. This he found difficult to do, in spite of entering an objection and sustaining it. The faults of the woman as a woman kept chattering on in his mind like an unruly witness. She had, for almost two years now, baited him. In the halls, in the elevator, even in his own office, into which she romped now and then like a circus horse, she was constantly shouting out these silly questions at him. "Are you lifting the oxcart out of the ditch? Are you tearing up the pea patch? Are you hollering down the rain barrel? Are you scraping around the bottom of the pickle barrel? Are you sitting in the catbird seat?"

It was Joey Hart, one of Mr. Martin's two assistants, who had explained what the gibberish meant. "She must be a Dodger fan°," he had said. "Red

Dodger fan: At the time of this story, the Dodgers were the Brooklyn Dodgers.

Barber announces the Dodger games over the radio and he uses those expressions — picked 'em up down South." Joey had gone on to explain one or two. "Tearing up the pea patch" meant going on a rampage; "sitting in the catbird seat" meant sitting pretty, like a batter with three balls and no strikes on him. Mr. Martin dismissed all this with an effort. It had been annoying, it had driven him near to distraction, but he was too solid a man to be moved to murder by anything so childish. It was fortunate, he reflected as he passed on to the important charges against Mrs. Barrows, that he had stood up under it so well. He had maintained always an outward appearance of polite tolerance. "Why, I even believe you like the woman," Miss Paird, his other assistant, had once said to him. He had simply smiled.

A gavel rapped in Mr. Martin's mind and the case proper was resumed. 5 Mrs. Ulgine Barrows stood charged with willful, blatant, and persistent attempts to destroy the efficiency and system of F & S. It was competent, material, and relevant to review her advent and rise to power. Mr. Martin had got the story from Miss Paird, who seemed always able to find things out. According to her, Mrs. Barrows had met Mr. Fitweiler at a party, where she had rescued him from the embraces of a powerfully built drunken man who had mistaken the president of F & S for a famous retired Middle Western football coach. She had led him to a sofa and somehow worked upon him a monstrous magic. The aging gentleman had jumped to the conclusion there and then that this was a woman of singular attainments, equipped to bring out the best in him and in the firm. A week later he had introduced her into F & S as his special adviser. On that day confusion got its foot in the door. After Miss Tyson, Mr. Brundage, and Mr. Bartlett had been fired and Mr. Munson had taken his hat and stalked out, mailing in his resignation later, old Roberts had been emboldened to speak to Mr. Fitweiler. He mentioned that Mr. Munson's department had been "a little disrupted" and hadn't they perhaps better resume the old system there? Mr. Fitweiler had said certainly not. He had the greatest faith in Mrs. Barrows' ideas. "They require a little seasoning, a little seasoning, is all," he had added. Mr. Roberts had given it up. Mr. Martin reviewed in detail all the changes wrought by Mrs. Barrows. She had begun chipping at the cornices of the firm's edifice and now she was swinging at the foundation stones with a pickaxe.

Mr. Martin came now, in his summing up, to the afternoon of Monday, November 2, 1942 — just one week ago. On that day, at 3 P.M., Mrs. Barrows had bounced into his office. "Boo!" she had yelled. "Are you scraping around the bottom of the pickle barrel?" Mr. Martin had looked at her from under his green eyeshade, saying nothing. She had begun to wander about the office, taking it in with her great, popping eyes. "Do you really need *all* these filing cabinets?" she had demanded suddenly. Mr. Martin's heart had jumped. "Each of these files," he had said, keeping his voice even, "plays an indispensable part in the system of F & S." She had brayed at him, "Well, don't tear up the pea patch!" and gone to the door. From there she had bawled, "But you sure have got a lot of fine scrap in here!" Mr. Martin could no longer doubt that the finger was on his beloved department. Her pickaxe was on the upswing, poised for the first blow. It had not come yet; he had received no blue memo from the enchanted Mr. Fitweiler bearing nonsensical instructions deriving from the obscene woman. But there was no doubt in Mr. Martin's mind that one would be forthcoming. He must act quickly. Already a precious week had gone by. Mr. Martin stood up in his living room, still holding his milk glass. "Gentlemen of the jury," he said to himself, "I demand the death penalty for this horrible person."

The next day Mr. Martin followed his routine, as usual. He polished his glasses more often and once sharpened an already sharp pencil, but not even Miss Paird noticed. Only once did he catch sight of his victim; she swept past him in the hall with a patronizing "Hi!" At five-thirty he walked home, as usual, and had a glass of milk, as usual. He had never drunk anything stronger in his life — unless you could count ginger ale. The late Sam Schlosser, the S of F & S, had praised Mr. Martin at a staff meeting several years before for his temperate habits. "Our most efficient worker neither drinks nor smokes," he had said. "The results speak for themselves." Mr. Fitweiler had sat by, nodding approval.

Mr. Martin was still thinking about that red-letter day as he walked over to the Schrafft's on Fifth Avenue near Forty-sixth Street. He got there, as he always did, at eight o'clock. He finished his dinner and the financial page of the *Sun* at a quarter to nine, as he always did. It was his custom after dinner to take a walk. This time he walked down Fifth Avenue at a casual pace. His gloved hands felt moist and warm, his forehead cold. He transferred the Camels from his overcoat to a jacket pocket. He wondered, as he did so, if they did not represent an unnecessary note of strain. Mrs. Barrows smoked only Luckies. It was his idea to puff a few puffs on a Camel (after the rubbing-out), stub it out in the ashtray holding her lipstick-stained Luckies, and thus drag a small red herring across the trail. Perhaps it was not a good idea. It would take time. He might even choke, too loudly.

Mr. Martin had never seen the house on West Twelfth Street where Mrs. Barrows lived, but he had a clear enough picture of it. Fortunately, she had bragged to everybody about her ducky first-floor apartment in the perfectly darling three-story redbrick. There would be no doorman or other attendants; just the tenants of the second and third floors. As he walked along, Mr. Martin realized that he would get there before nine-thirty. He had considered walking north on Fifth Avenue from Schrafft's to a point from which it would take him until ten o'clock to reach the house. At that hour people were less likely to be coming in or going out. But the procedure would have made an awkward loop in the straight thread of his casualness, and he had abandoned it. It was impossible to figure when people would be entering or leaving the house, anyway. There was a great risk at any hour. If he ran into anybody, he would simply have to place the rubbing-out of Ulgine Barrows in the inactive file forever. The same thing would hold true if there were someone in her apartment. In that case he would just say that he had been passing by, recognized her charming house and thought to drop in.

It was eighteen minutes after nine when Mr. Martin turned into Twelfth 10 Street. A man passed him, and a man and a woman talking. There was no one within fifty paces when he came to the house, halfway down the block. He was up the steps and in the small vestibule in no time, pressing the bell under the card that said "Mrs. Ulgine Barrows." When the clicking in the lock started, he jumped forward against the door. He got inside fast, closing the door behind him. A bulb in a lantern hung from the hall ceiling on a chain seemed to give a monstrously bright light. There was nobody on the stair, which went up ahead of him along the left wall. A door opened down the hall in the wall on the right. He went toward it swiftly, on tiptoe.

"Well, for God's sake, look who's here!" bawled Mrs. Barrows, and her braying laugh rang out like the report of a shotgun. He rushed past her like a football tackle, bumping her. "Hey, quit shoving!" she said, closing the door behind them. They were in her living room, which seemed to Mr. Martin to be lighted by a hundred lamps. "What's after you?" she said. "You're as jumpy as a goat." He found he was unable to speak. His heart was wheezing in his throat. "I — yes," he finally brought out. She was jabbering and laughing as she started to help him off with his coat. "No, no," he said. "I'll put it there." He took it off and put it on a chair near the door. "Your hat and gloves, too," she said. "You're in a lady's house." He put his hat on top of the coat. Mrs. Barrows seemed larger than he had thought. He kept his gloves on. "I was passing by," he said. "I recognized — is there anyone here?" She laughed louder than ever. "No," she said, "we're all alone. You're as white as a sheet, you funny man. Whatever *has* come over you? I'll mix you a toddy." She started toward a door across the room. "Scotch-and-soda be all right? But say, you don't drink, do you?" She turned and gave him her amused look. Mr. Martin pulled himself together. "Scotch-and-soda will be all right," he heard himself say. He could hear her laughing in the kitchen.

Mr. Martin looked quickly around the living room for the weapon. He had counted on finding one there. There were andirons and a poker and something in a corner that looked like an Indian club. None of them would do. It couldn't be that way. He began to pace around. He came to a desk. On it lay a metal paper knife with an ornate handle. Would it be sharp enough? He reached for it and knocked over a small brass jar. Stamps spilled out of it and it fell to the floor with a clatter. "Hey," Mrs. Barrows yelled from the kitchen, "are you tearing up the pea patch?" Mr. Martin gave a strange laugh. Picking up the knife, he tried its point against his left wrist. It was blunt. It wouldn't do.

When Mrs. Barrows reappeared, carrying two highballs, Mr. Martin, standing there with his gloves on, became acutely conscious of the fantasy he had wrought. Cigarettes in his pocket, a drink prepared for him — it was all too grossly improbable. It was more than that; it was impossible. Somewhere in the back of his mind a vague idea stirred, sprouted. "For heaven's sake, take off those gloves," said Mrs. Barrows. "I always wear them in the house," said Mr. Martin. The idea began to bloom, strange and wonderful. She put the glasses on a coffee table in front of a sofa and sat on the sofa. "Come over here, you odd little man," she said. Mr. Martin went over and sat beside her. It was difficult getting a cigarette out of the pack of Camels, but he managed it. She held a match for him, laughing. "Well," she said, handing him his drink, "this is perfectly marvelous. You with a drink and a cigarette."

Mr. Martin puffed, not too awkwardly, and took a gulp of the highball. "I drink and smoke all the time," he said. He clinked his glass against hers. "Here's nuts to that old windbag, Fitweiler," he said, and gulped again. The stuff tasted awful, but he made no grimace. "Really, Mr. Martin," she said, her voice and posture changing, "you are insulting our employer." Mrs. Barrows was now all special adviser to the president. "I am preparing a bomb," said Mr. Martin, "which will blow the old goat higher than hell." He had only had a little of the drink, which was not strong. It couldn't be that. "Do you take dope or something?" Mrs. Barrows asked coldly. "Heroin," said Mr. Martin. "I'll be coked to the gills when I bump that old buzzard off." "Mr. Martin!" she shouted, getting to her feet. "That will be all of that. You must go at once." Mr. Martin took another swallow of his drink. He tapped his cigarette out in the ashtray and put the pack of Camels on the coffee table. Then he got up. She stood glaring at him. He walked over and put on his hat and coat. "Not a word about this," he said, and laid an index finger against his lips. All Mrs. Barrows could bring out was "Really!" Mr. Martin put his hand on the doorknob. "I'm sitting in the catbird seat," he said. He stuck his tongue out at her and left. Nobody saw him go.

Mr. Martin got to his apartment, walking, well before eleven. No one saw him go in. He had two glasses of milk after brushing his teeth, and he felt elated. It wasn't tipsiness, because he hadn't been tipsy. Anyway, the walk had worn off all effects of the whisky. He got in bed and read a magazine for a while. He was asleep before midnight.

Mr. Martin got to the office at eight-thirty the next morning, as usual. At a quarter to nine, Ulgine Barrows, who had never before arrived at work before ten, swept into his office. "I'm reporting to Mr. Fitweiler now!" she shouted. "If he turns you over to the police, it's no more than you deserve!" Mr. Martin gave her a look of shocked surprise. "I beg your pardon?" he said. Mrs. Barrows snorted and bounced out of the room, leaving Miss Paird and Joey Hart staring after her. "What's the matter with that old devil now?" asked Miss Paird. "I have no idea," said Mr. Martin, resuming his work. The other two looked at him and then at each other. Miss Paird got up and went out. She walked slowly past the closed door of Mr. Fitweiler's office. Mrs. Barrows was yelling inside, but she was not braying. Miss Paird could not hear what the woman was saying. She went back to her desk.

Forty-five minutes later, Mrs. Barrows left the president's office and went into her own, shutting the door. It wasn't until half an hour later that Mr. Fitweiler sent for Mr. Martin. The head of the filing department, neat, quiet, attentive, stood in front of the old man's desk. Mr. Fitweiler was pale and nervous. He took his glasses off and twiddled them. He made a small, bruffing sound in his throat. "Martin," he said, "you have been with us more than twenty years." "Twenty-two, sir," said Mr. Martin. "In that time," pursued the president, "your work and your — uh — manner have been exemplary." "I trust so, sir," said Mr. Martin. "I have understood, Martin," said Mr. Fitweiler, "that you have never taken a drink or smoked." "That is correct, sir," said Mr. Martin. "Ah, yes." Mr. Fitweiler polished his glasses. "You may describe what you did after leaving the office yesterday, Martin," he said. Mr. Martin allowed less than a second for his bewildered pause. "Certainly, sir," he said. "I walked home. Then I went to Schrafft's for dinner. Afterward I walked home again. I went to bed early, sir, and read a magazine for a while. I was asleep before eleven." "Ah, yes," said Mr. Fitweiler again. He was silent for a moment, searching for the proper words to say to the head of the filing department. "Mrs. Barrows," he said finally, "Mrs. Barrows has worked hard,

Martin, very hard. It grieves me to report that she has suffered a severe breakdown. It has taken the form of a persecution complex accompanied by distressing hallucinations." "I am very sorry, sir," said Mr. Martin. "Mrs. Barrows is under the delusion," continued Mr. Fitweiler, "that you visited her last evening and behaved yourself in an — uh — unseemly manner." He raised his hand to silence Mr. Martin's little pained outcry. "It is the nature of these psychological diseases," Mr. Fitweiler said, "to fix upon the least likely and most innocent party as the — uh — source of persecution. These matters are not for the lay mind to grasp, Martin. I've just had my psychiatrist, Dr. Fitch, on the phone. He would not, of course, commit himself, but he made enough generalizations to substantiate my suspicions. I suggested to Mrs. Barrows when she had completed her — uh — story to me this morning, that she visit Dr. Fitch, for I suspected a condition at once. She flew, I regret to say, into a rage, and demanded — uh — requested that I call you on the carpet. You may not know, Martin, but Mrs. Barrows had planned a reorganization of your department — subject to my approval, of course, subject to my approval. This brought you, rather than anyone else, to her mind — but again that is a phenomenon for Dr. Fitch and not for us. So, Martin, I am afraid Mrs. Barrows' usefulness here is at an end." "I am dreadfully sorry, sir," said Mr. Martin.

It was at this point that the door to the office blew open with the suddenness of a gas-main explosion and Mrs. Barrows catapulted through it. "Is the little rat denying it?" she screamed. "He can't get away with that!" Mr. Martin got up and moved discreetly to a point beside Mr. Fitweiler's chair. "You drank and smoked at my apartment," she bawled at Mr. Martin, "and you know it! You called Mr. Fitweiler an old windbag and said you were going to blow him up when you got coked to the gills on your heroin!" She stopped yelling to catch her breath and a new glint came into her popping eyes. "If you weren't such a drab, ordinary little man," she said, "I'd think you'd planned it all. Sticking your tongue out, saying you were sitting in the catbird seat, because you thought no one would believe me when I told it! My God, it's really too perfect!" She brayed loudly and hysterically, and the fury was on her again. She glared at Mr. Fitweiler. "Can't you see how he has tricked us, you old fool? Can't you see his little game?" But Mr. Fitweiler had been surreptitiously pressing all the buttons under the top of his desk and employees of F & S began pouring into the room. "Stockton," said Mr. Fitweiler, "you and Fishbein will take Mrs. Barrows to her home. Mrs. Powell, you will go with them." Stockton, who had played a little football in high school, blocked Mrs. Barrows as she made for Mr. Martin. It took him and Fishbein together to force her out of the door into the hall, crowded with stenographers and office boys. She was still screaming imprecations at Mr. Martin, tangled and contradictory imprecations. The hubbub finally died out down the corridor.

"I regret that this has happened," said Mr. Fitweiler. "I shall ask you to dismiss it from your mind, Martin." "Yes, sir," said Mr. Martin, anticipating his chief's "That will be all" by moving to the door. "I will dismiss it." He went out and shut the door, and his step was light and quick in the hall. When he entered his department he had slowed down to his customary gait, and he walked quietly across the room to the W20 file, wearing a look of studious concentration.

1. What are the outstanding traits of Mr. Martin's character, as others in the story see him? What false impressions of himself does he leave with Mrs. Barrows after he visits her apartment?
2. What do we know about Mr. Martin's inner self that is unknown to the other characters in the story? Why *isn't* he a stock character — merely the fussy, colorless, mild-mannered little man familiar from comic strips and television comedy?
3. Sum up your impressions of Mrs. Ulgine Barrows. What peculiarities does Thurber give her? What elements of her character lead her into conflict with Mr. Martin?
4. How convincing is the motivation that the author gives Mr. Martin? For what reasons does Martin go to Mrs. Barrows's apartment with the notion of killing her? Why does he then pretend to vices he doesn't have, insult his employer, and stick out his tongue at Mrs. Barrows?
5. What is the point of view, and how is it appropriate to this story? Why could not the story be told equally well from the point of view of Mrs. Barrows, or from that of a totally objective narrator, who could not see into the mind of any character?
6. Recall the definition of an *antihero* (page 75). Would you call Mr. Martin an antihero? What do you take to be James Thurber's attitude toward him? How can you tell?

Katherine Anne Porter

THE JILTING OF GRANNY WEATHERALL   1930

Katherine Anne Porter (1890 – 1980) was born in Indian Creek, Texas. Her mother died when she was two, and Porter was raised by a grandmother who surrounded the growing girl with books. At sixteen, apparently bored with her studies at an Ursuline convent, Porter ran away from home. Three years later, she began supporting herself as a news reporter in Chicago, Denver, and Forth Worth, and sometimes as an actress and ballad singer traveling through the South. Sojourns in Europe and in Mexico supplied her with matter for some of her finest stories. Her brilliant, sensitive short fiction, first collected in Flowering Judas *(1930), won her a high reputation. Her one novel,* Ship of Fools *(1962), with which she had struggled for twenty years, received harsh critical notices, but proved a commercial success. Made into a movie, it ended Porter's lifelong struggle to earn a living. In 1965 her* Collected Stories *received a Pulitzer prize and a National Book Award.*

She flicked her wrist neatly out of Doctor Harry's pudgy careful fingers and pulled the sheet up to her chin. The brat ought to be in knee breeches. Doctoring around the country with spectacles on his nose! "Get along now, take your schoolbooks and go. There's nothing wrong with me."

Doctor Harry spread a warm paw like a cushion on her forehead where the forked green vein danced and made her eyelids twitch. "Now, now, be a good girl, and we'll have you up in no time."

"That's no way to speak to a woman nearly eighty years old just because she's down. I'd have you respect your elders, young man."

"Well, Missy, excuse me." Doctor Harry patted her cheek. "But I've got to warn you, haven't I? You're a marvel, but you must be careful or you're going to be good and sorry."

"Don't tell me what I'm going to be. I'm on my feet now, morally speaking. It's Cornelia. I had to go to bed to get rid of her." 5

Her bones felt loose, and floated around in her skin, and Doctor Harry floated like a balloon around the foot of the bed. He floated and pulled down his waistcoat and swung his glasses on a cord. "Well, stay where you are, it certainly can't hurt you."

"Get along and doctor your sick," said Granny Weatherall. "Leave a well woman alone. I'll call for you when I want you. . . . Where were you forty years ago when I pulled through milk-leg and double pneumonia? You weren't even born. Don't let Cornelia lead you on," she shouted, because Doctor Harry appeared to float up to the ceiling and out. "I pay my own bills, and I don't throw my money away on nonsense!"

She meant to wave good-by, but it was too much trouble. Her eyes closed of themselves, it was like a dark curtain drawn around the bed. The pillow rose and floated under her, pleasant as a hammock in a light wind. She listened to the leaves rustling outside the window. No, somebody was swishing newspapers: no, Cornelia and Doctor Harry were whispering together. She leaped broad awake, thinking they whispered in her ear.

"She was never like this, *never* like this!" "Well, what can we expect?" "Yes, eighty years old. . . ."

Well, and what if she was? She still had ears. It was like Cornelia to 10 whisper around doors. She always kept things secret in such a public way. She was always being tactful and kind. Cornelia was dutiful; that was the trouble with her. Dutiful and good: "So good and dutiful," said Granny, "that I'd like to spank her." She saw herself spanking Cornelia and making a fine job of it.

"What'd you say, Mother?"

Granny felt her face tying up in hard knots.

"Can't a body think, I'd like to know?"

"I thought you might want something."

"I do. I want a lot of things. First off, go away and don't whisper." 15

She lay and drowsed, hoping in her sleep that the children would keep out and let her rest a minute. It had been a long day. Not that she was tired. It was always pleasant to snatch a minute now and then. There was always so much to be done, let me see: tomorrow.

Tomorrow was far away and there was nothing to trouble about. Things were finished somehow when the time came; thank God there was always a little margin over for peace: then a person could spread out the plan of life and tuck in the edges orderly. It was good to have everything clean and folded away, with the hair brushes and tonic bottles sitting straight on the white embroidered linen: the day started without fuss and the pantry shelves laid out with rows of jelly glasses and brown jugs and white stone-china jars with blue whirligigs and words painted on them: coffee, tea, sugar, ginger, cinnamon, allspice: and the bronze clock with the lion on top nicely dusted off. The dust that lion could collect in twenty-four hours! The box in the attic with all those letters tied up, well, she'd have to go through that tomorrow. All those letters — George's letters and John's letters and her letters to them both — lying around for the children to find afterwards made her uneasy. Yes, that would be tomorrow's business. No use to let them know how silly she had been once.

While she was rummaging around she found death in her mind and it felt clammy and unfamiliar. She had spent so much time preparing for death there was no need for bringing it up again. Let it take care of itself now. When she was sixty she had felt very old, finished, and went around making farewell trips to see her children and grandchildren, with a secret in her mind: This is the very last of your mother, children! Then she made her will and came down with a long fever. That was all just a notion like a lot of other things, but it was lucky too, for she had once for all got over the idea of dying for a long time. Now she couldn't be worried. She hoped she had better sense now. Her father had lived to be one hundred and two years old and had drunk a noggin of strong hot toddy on his last birthday. He told the reporters it was his daily habit, and he owed his long life to that. He had made quite a scandal and was very pleased about it. She believed she'd just plague Cornelia a little.

"Cornelia! Cornelia!" No footsteps, but a sudden hand on her cheek. "Bless you, where have you been?"

"Here, Mother." 20

"Well, Cornelia, I want a noggin of hot toddy."

"Are you cold, darling?"

"I'm chilly, Cornelia. Lying in bed stops the circulation. I must have told you that a thousand times."

Well, she could just hear Cornelia telling her husband that Mother was getting a little childish and they'd have to humor her. The thing that most annoyed her was that Cornelia thought she was deaf, dumb, and blind. Little hasty glances and tiny gestures tossed around her and over her head saying, "Don't cross her, let her have her way, she's eighty years old," and she sitting there as if she lived in a thin glass cage. Sometimes Granny almost made up her mind to pack up and move back to her own house where nobody could remind her every minute that she was old. Wait, wait, Cornelia, till your own children whisper behind your back!

In her day she had kept a better house and had got more work done. She 25 wasn't too old yet for Lydia to be driving eighty miles for advice when one of the children jumped the track, and Jimmy still dropped in and talked things over: "Now, Mammy, you've a good business head, I want to know what you think of this? . . ." Old. Cornelia couldn't change the furniture around without asking. Little things, little things! They had been so sweet when they were little. Granny wished the old days were back again with the children young and everything to be done over. It had been a hard pull, but not too much for her. When she thought of all the food she had cooked, and all the clothes she had cut and sewed, and all the gardens she had made — well, the children showed it. There they were, made out of her, and they couldn't get away from that. Sometimes she wanted to see John again and point to them and say, Well, I didn't do so badly, did I? But that would have to wait. That was for tomorrow. She used to think of him as a man, but now all the children were older than their father, and he would be a child beside her if she saw him now. It seemed strange and there was something wrong in the idea. Why, he couldn't possibly recognize her. She had fenced in a hundred acres once, digging the post holes herself and clamping the wires with just a negro boy to help. That changed a woman. John would be looking for a young woman with the peaked Spanish comb in her hair and the painted fan. Digging post holes changed a woman. Riding country roads in the winter when women had their babies was another thing: sitting up nights with sick horses and sick negroes and sick children and hardly ever losing one. John, I hardly ever lost one of them! John would see that in a minute, that would be something he could understand, she wouldn't have to explain anything!

It made her feel like rolling up her sleeves and putting the whole place to rights again. No matter if Cornelia was determined to be everywhere at once, there were a great many things left undone on this place. She would start tomorrow and do them. It was good to be strong enough for everything, even if all you made melted and changed and slipped under your hands, so that by the time you finished you almost forgot what you were working for. What was it I set out to do? she asked herself intently, but she could not remember. A fog rose over the valley, she saw it marching across the creek swallowing the trees and moving up the hill like an army of ghosts. Soon it would be at the near edge of the orchard, and then it was time to go in and light the lamps. Come in, children, don't stay out in the night air.

Lighting the lamps had been beautiful. The children huddled up to her and breathed like little calves waiting at the bars in the twilight. Their eyes followed the match and watched the flame rise and settle in a blue curve, then they moved away from her. The lamp was lit, they didn't have to be scared and hang on to mother any more. Never, never, never more. God, for all my life I thank Thee. Without Thee, my God, I could never have done it. Hail, Mary, full of grace.

I want you to pick all the fruit this year and see that nothing is wasted. There's always someone who can use it. Don't let good things rot for want of using. You waste life when you waste good food. Don't let things get lost. It's bitter to lose things. Now, don't let me get to thinking, not when I am tired and taking a little nap before supper. . . .

The pillow rose about her shoulders and pressed against her heart and the memory was being squeezed out of it: oh, push down the pillow, somebody: it would smother her if she tried to hold it. Such a fresh breeze blowing and such a green day with no threats in it. But he had not come, just the same. What does a woman do when she has put on the white veil and set out the white cake for a man and he doesn't come? She tried to remember. No, I swear he never harmed me but in that. He never harmed me but in that . . . and what if he did? There was the day, the day, but a whirl of dark smoke rose and covered it, crept up and over into the bright field where everything was planted so carefully in orderly rows. That was hell, she knew hell when she saw it. For sixty years she had prayed against remembering him and against losing her soul in the deep pit of hell, and now the two things were mingled in one and the thought of him was a smoky cloud from hell that moved and crept in her head when she had just got rid of Doctor Harry and was trying to rest a minute. Wounded vanity, Ellen, said a sharp voice in the top of her mind. Don't let your wounded vanity get the upper hand of you. Plenty of girls get jilted. You were jilted, weren't you? Then stand up to it. Her eyelids wavered and let in streamers of blue-gray light like tissue paper over her eyes. She must get up and pull the shades down or she'd never sleep. She was in bed again and the shades were not down. How could that happen? Better turn over, hide from the light, sleeping in the light gave you nightmares. "Mother, how do you feel now?" and a stinging wetness on her forehead. But I don't like having my face washed in cold water!

Hapsy? George? Lydia? Jimmy? No, Cornelia, and her features were 30 swollen and full of little puddles. "They're coming, darling, they'll all be here soon." Go wash your face, child, you look funny.

Instead of obeying, Cornelia knelt down and put her head on the pillow. She seemed to be talking but there was no sound. "Well, are you tongue-tied? Whose birthday is it? Are you going to give a party?"

Cornelia's mouth moved urgently in strange shapes. "Don't do that, you bother me, daughter."

"O, no, Mother. Oh, no. . . ."

Nonsense. It was strange about children. They disputed your every word. "No what, Cornelia?"

"Here's Doctor Harry." 35

"I won't see that boy again. He just left five minutes ago."

"That was this morning, Mother. It's night now. Here's the nurse."

"This is Doctor Harry, Mrs. Weatherall. I never saw you look so young and happy!"

"Ah, I'll never be young again — but I'd be happy if they'd let me lie in peace and get rested."

She thought she spoke up loudly, but no one answered. A warm weight 40 on her forehead, a warm bracelet on her wrist, and a breeze went on whispering, trying to tell her something. A shuffle of leaves in the everlasting hand of God. He blew on them and they danced and rattled. "Mother, don't mind, we're going to give you a little hypodermic." "Look here, daughter, how do ants get in this bed? I saw sugar ants yesterday." Did you send for Hapsy too?

It was Hapsy she really wanted. She had to go a long way back through a great many rooms to find Hapsy standing with a baby on her arm. She seemed to herself to be Hapsy also, and the baby on Hapsy's arm was Hapsy and himself and herself, all at once, and there was no surprise in the meeting. Then Hapsy melted from within and turned flimsy as gray gauze and the baby was a gauzy shadow, and Hapsy came up close and said, "I thought you'd never come," and looked at her very searchingly and said, "You haven't changed a bit!" They leaned forward to kiss, when Cornelia began whispering from a long way off, "Oh, is there anything you want to tell me? Is there anything I can do for you?"

Yes, she had changed her mind after sixty years and she would like to see George. I want you to find George. Find him and be sure to tell him I forgot him. I want him to know I had my husband just the same and my children and my house like any other woman. A good house too and a good husband that I loved and fine children out of him. Better than I hoped for even. Tell him I was given back everything he took away and more. Oh, no, oh, God, no, there was something else besides the house and the man and the children. Oh, surely they were not all? What was it? Something not given back. . . . Her breath crowded down under her ribs and grew into a monstrous frightening shape with cutting edges; it bored up into her head, and the agony was unbelievable: Yes, John, get the Doctor now, no more talk, my time has come.

When this one was born it should be the last. The last. It should have been born first, for it was the one she had truly wanted. Everything came in good time. Nothing left out, left over. She was strong, in three days she would be as well as ever. Better. A woman needed milk in her to have her full health.

"Mother, do you hear me?"

"I've been telling you — "

"Mother, Father Connolly's here."

"I went to Holy Communion only last week. Tell him I'm not so sinful as all that."

"Father just wants to speak to you."

He could speak as much as he pleased. It was like him to drop in and inquire about her soul as if it were a teething baby, and then stay on for a cup of tea and a round of cards and gossip. He always had a funny story of some sort, usually about an Irishman who made his little mistakes and confessed them, and the point lay in some absurd thing he would blurt out in the confessional showing his struggles between native piety and original sin. Granny felt easy about her soul. Cornelia, where are your manners? Give Father Connolly a chair. She had her secret comfortable understanding with a few favorite saints who cleared a straight road to God for her. All as surely signed and sealed as the papers for the new Forty Acres. Forever . . . heirs and assigns forever. Since the day the wedding cake was not cut, but thrown out and wasted. The whole bottom dropped out of the world, and there she was blind and sweating with nothing under her feet and the walls falling away. His hand had caught her under the breast, she had not fallen, there was the freshly polished floor with the green rug on it, just as before. He had cursed like a sailor's parrot and said, "I'll kill him for you." Don't lay a hand on him, for my sake leave something to God. "Now, Ellen, you must believe what I tell you. . . ."

So there was nothing, nothing to worry about any more, except some- times in the night one of the children screamed in a nightmare, and they both hustled out shaking and hunting for the matches and calling, "There, wait a minute, here we are!" John, get the doctor now, Hapsy's time has come. But there was Hapsy standing by the bed in a white cap. "Cornelia, tell Hapsy to take off her cap. I can't see her plain."

Her eyes opened very wide and the room stood out like a picture she had seen somewhere. Dark colors with the shadows rising towards the ceiling in long angles. The tall black dresser gleamed with nothing on it but John's picture, enlarged from a little one, with John's eyes very black when they should have been blue. You never saw him, so how do you know how he looked? But the man insisted the copy was perfect, it was very rich and handsome. For a picture, yes, but it's not my husband. The table by the bed had a linen cover and a candle and a crucifix. The light was blue from Cor- nelia's silk lampshades. No sort of light at all, just frippery. You had to live forty years with kerosene lamps to appreciate honest electricity. She felt very strong and she saw Doctor Harry with a rosy nimbus around him.

"You look like a saint, Doctor Harry, and I vow that's as near as you'll ever come to it."

Character

"She's saying something."

"I heard you, Cornelia. What's all this carrying-on?"

"Father Connolly's saying — "

Cornelia's voice staggered and bumped like a cart in a bad road. It rounded corners and turned back again and arrived nowhere. Granny stepped up in the cart very lightly and reached for the reins, but a man sat beside her and she knew him by his hands, driving the cart. She did not look in his face, for she knew without seeing, but looked instead down the road where the trees leaned over and bowed to each other and a thousand birds were singing a Mass. She felt like singing too, but she put her hand in the bosom of her dress and pulled out a rosary, and Father Connolly murmured Latin in a very solemn voice and tickled her feet. My God, will you stop that nonsense? I'm a married woman. What if he did run away and leave me to face the priest by myself? I found another a whole world better. I wouldn't have exchanged my husband for anybody except St. Michael himself, and you may tell him that for me with a thank you in the bargain.

Light flashed on her closed eyelids, and a deep roaring shook her. Cornelia, is that lightning? I hear thunder. There's going to be a storm. Close all the windows. Call the children in. . . . "Mother, here we are, all of us." "Is that you, Hapsy?" "Oh, no, I'm Lydia. We drove as fast as we could." Their faces drifted above her, drifted away. The rosary fell out of her hands and Lydia put it back. Jimmy tried to help, their hands fumbled together, and Granny closed two fingers around Jimmy's thumb. Beads wouldn't do, it must be something alive. She was so amazed her thoughts ran round and round. So, my dear Lord, this is my death and I wasn't even thinking about it. My children have come to see me die. But I can't, it's not time. Oh, I always hated surprises. I wanted to give Cornelia the amethyst set — Cornelia, you're to have the amethyst set, but Hapsy's to wear it when she wants, and, Doctor Harry, do shut up. Nobody sent for you. Oh, my dear Lord, do wait a minute. I meant to do something about the Forty Acres, Jimmy doesn't need it and Lydia will later on, with that worthless husband of hers. I meant to finish the altar cloth and send six bottles of wine to Sister Borgia for her dyspepsia. I want to send six bottles of wine to Sister Borgia, Father Connolly, now don't let me forget.

Cornelia's voice made short turns and tilted over and crashed. "Oh, Mother, oh, Mother, oh, Mother. . . ."

"I'm not going, Cornelia. I'm taken by surprise. I can't go."

You'll see Hapsy again. What about her? "I thought you'd never come." Granny made a long journey outward, looking for Hapsy. What if I don't find her? What then? Her heart sank down and down, there was no bottom to death, she couldn't come to the end of it. The blue light from Cornelia's lampshade drew into a tiny point in the center of her brain, it flickered and winked like an eye, quietly it fluttered and dwindled. Granny lay curled down within herself, amazed and watchful, staring at the point of light that was herself; her body was now only a deeper mass of shadow in an endless darkness and this darkness would curl around the light and swallow it up. God, give a sign!

For the second time there was no sign. Again no bridegroom and the priest in the house. She could not remember any other sorrow because this grief wiped them all away. Oh, no, there's nothing more cruel than this —

I'll never forgive it. She stretched herself with a deep breath and blew out the light.

QUESTIONS

1. In the very first paragraph, what does the writer tell us about Ellen (Granny) Weatherall?
2. What does the name of Weatherall have to do with Granny's nature (or her life story)? What other traits or qualities do you find in her?
3. "Her bones felt loose, and floated around in her skin, and Doctor Harry floated like a balloon" (paragraph 6). What do you understand from this statement? By what other remarks does the writer indicate Granny's condition? In paragraph 56, why does Father Connolly tickle Granny's feet? At what other moments in the story does she fail to understand what is happening, or confuse the present with the past?
4. Exactly what happened to Ellen Weatherall sixty years earlier? What effects did this event have on her?
5. In paragraph 49, who do you guess to be the man who "cursed like a sailor's parrot"? In paragraph 56, who do you assume to be the man driving the cart? Is the fact that these persons are not clearly labeled and identified a failure on the author's part?
6. What is stream of consciousness? (The term is discussed on page 23.) Would you call "The Jilting of Granny Weatherall" a stream of consciousness story? Refer to the story in your reply.
7. Sum up the character of the daughter Cornelia.
8. Why doesn't Granny's last child Hapsy come to her mother's deathbed?
9. Would you call the character of Doctor Harry "flat" or "round"? Why is his flatness (or roundness) appropriate to the story?
10. How is this the story of another "jilting"? What is similar between that fateful day of sixty years ago (described in paragraphs 29, 49, and 61) and the moment when Granny is dying? This time, who is the "bridegroom" not in the house?
11. "This is the story of an eighty-year-old woman lying in bed, getting groggy, and dying; I can't see why it should interest anybody." How would you answer this critic?

Willa Cather
PAUL'S CASE   1905

Willa Cather (1876 – 1947) was born in Gore, Virginia, but at nine moved to Webster County, Nebraska, where pioneer sod houses still clung to the windswept plains. There, mainly in the town of Red Cloud, she grew up among Scandinavians, Czechs, Bohemians, and other immigrant settlers, for whom she felt a quick kinship: they too had been displaced from their childhood homes. After graduation from the University of Nebraska, Cather went east to spend ten years in Pittsburgh, where the story "Paul's Case" opens. (When she wrote the story, she was a high school teacher of Latin and English and music critic for a newspaper.) Then, because her early stories had attracted notice, New York beckoned. A job on the staff of McClure's led to her becoming managing editor of the popular magazine. Her early

novels of Nebraska won immense popularity: O Pioneers! *(1913),* My
Ántonia *(1918), and* A Lost Lady *(1923). In her later novels Cather
explores other regions of the North American past: in* Death Comes to the
Archbishop *(1927), frontier New Mexico; in* Shadows on the Rock
*(1931), seventeenth-century Quebec. She does not romanticize the rugged
lives of farm people on the plains, or glamorize village life. Often, as in*
The Song of the Lark *(1915), the story of a Colorado girl who becomes
an opera singer, she depicts a small town as stifling. With remarkable skill,
she may tell a story from a man's point of view, but her favorite characters
are likely to be women of strong will who triumph over obstacles.*

It was Paul's afternoon to appear before the faculty of the Pittsburgh
High School to account for his various misdemeanors. He had been suspended
a week ago, and his father had called at the Principal's office and confessed his
perplexity about his son. Paul entered the faculty room suave and smiling. His
clothes were a trifle outgrown and the tan velvet on the collar of his open
overcoat was frayed and worn; but for all that there was something of the
dandy about him, and he wore an opal pin in his neatly knotted black four-in-
hand, and a red carnation in his buttonhole. This latter adornment the faculty
somehow felt was not properly significant of the contrite spirit befitting a boy
under the ban of suspension.

Paul was tall for his age and very thin, with high, cramped shoulders and
a narrow chest. His eyes were remarkable for a certain hysterical brilliancy and
he continually used them in a conscious, theatrical sort of way, peculiarly
offensive in a boy. The pupils were abnormally large, as though he were
addicted to belladonna, but there was a glassy glitter about them which that
drug does not produce.

When questioned by the Principal as to why he was there, Paul stated,
politely enough, that he wanted to come back to school. This was a lie, but
Paul was quite accustomed to lying; found it, indeed, indispensable for overcoming friction. His teachers were asked to state their respective charges
against him, which they did with such a rancor and aggrievedness as evinced
that this was not a usual case. Disorder and impertinence were among the
offenses named, yet each of his instructors felt that it was scarcely possible to
put into words the real cause of the trouble, which lay in a sort of hysterically
defiant manner of the boy's; in the contempt which they all knew he felt for
them, and which he seemingly made not the least effort to conceal. Once, when
he had been making a synopsis of a paragraph at the blackboard, his English
teacher had stepped to his side and attempted to guide his hand. Paul had
started back with a shudder and thrust his hands violently behind him. The
astonished woman could scarcely have been more hurt and embarrassed had
he struck at her. The insult was so involuntary and definitely personal as to
be unforgettable. In one way and another, he had made all his teachers, men
and women alike, conscious of the same feeling of physical aversion. In one
class he habitually sat with his hand shading his eyes; in another he always
looked out of the window during the recitation; in another he made a running
commentary on the lecture, with humorous intention.

His teachers felt this afternoon that his whole attitude was symbolized by his shrug and his flippantly red carnation flower, and they fell upon him without mercy, his English teacher leading the pack. He stood through it smiling, his pale lips parted over his white teeth. (His lips were continually twitching, and he had a habit of raising his eyebrows that was contemptuous and irritating to the last degree.) Older boys than Paul had broken down and shed tears under that baptism of fire, but his set smile did not once desert him, and his only sign of discomfort was the nervous trembling of the fingers that toyed with the buttons of his overcoat, and an occasional jerking of the other hand that held his hat. Paul was always smiling, always glancing about him, seeming to feel that people might be watching him and trying to detect something. This conscious expression, since it was as far as possible from boyish mirthfulness, was usually attributed to insolence or "smartness."

As the inquisition proceeded, one of his instructors repeated an impertinent remark of the boy's, and the Principal asked him whether he thought that a courteous speech to have made a woman. Paul shrugged his shoulders slightly and his eyebrows twitched. 5

"I don't know," he replied. "I didn't mean to be polite or impolite, either. I guess it's a sort of way I have of saying things regardless."

The Principal, who was a sympathetic man, asked him whether he didn't think that a way it would be well to get rid of. Paul grinned and said he guessed so. When he was told that he could go, he bowed gracefully and went out. His bow was but a repetition of the scandalous red carnation.

His teachers were in despair, and his drawing master voiced the feeling of them all when he declared there was something about the boy which none of them understood. He added: "I don't really believe that smile of his comes altogether from insolence; there's something sort of haunted about it. The boy is not strong, for one thing. I happen to know that he was born in Colorado, only a few months before his mother died out there of a long illness. There is something wrong about the fellow."

The drawing master had come to realize that, in looking at Paul, one saw only his white teeth and the forced animation of his eyes. One warm afternoon the boy had gone to sleep at his drawing-board, and his master had noted with amazement what a white, blue-veined face it was; drawn and wrinkled like an old man's about the eyes, the lips twitching even in his sleep, and stiff with a nervous tension that drew them back from his teeth.

His teachers left the building dissatisfied and unhappy; humiliated to have felt so vindictive toward a mere boy, to have uttered this feeling in cutting terms, and to have set each other on, as it were, in the gruesome game of intemperate reproach. Some of them remembered having seen a miserable street cat set at bay by a ring of tormentors. 10

As for Paul, he ran down the hill whistling the Soldiers' Chorus from *Faust*° looking wildly behind him now and then to see whether some of his teachers were not there to writhe under this light-heartedness. As it was now late in the afternoon and Paul was on duty that evening as usher at Carnegie Hall°, he decided that he would not go home to supper. When he reached the

---

Faust: tragic grand opera (1859) by French composer Charles Gounod.

Carnegie Hall: concert hall endowed by Pittsburgh steel manufacturer Andrew Carnegie, not to be confused with the better-known Carnegie Hall in New York City.

concert hall the doors were not yet open and, as it was chilly outside, he decided to go up into the picture gallery — always deserted at this hour — where there were some of Raffaelli's° gay studies of Paris streets and an airy blue Venetian scene or two that always exhilarated him. He was delighted to find no one in the gallery but the old guard, who sat in one corner, a newspaper on his knee, a black patch over one eye and the other closed. Paul possessed himself of the place and walked confidently up and down, whistling under his breath. After a while he sat down before a blue Rico° and lost himself. When he bethought him to look at his watch, it was after seven o'clock, and he rose with a start and ran downstairs, making a face at Augustus, peering out from the cast-room°, and an evil gesture at the Venus of Milo as he passed her on the stairway.

When Paul reached the ushers' dressing-room half-a-dozen boys were there already, and he began excitedly to tumble into his uniform. It was one of the few that at all approached fitting, and Paul thought it very becoming — though he knew that the tight, straight coat accentuated his narrow chest, about which he was exceedingly sensitive. He was always considerably excited while he dressed, twanging all over to the tuning of the strings and the preliminary flourishes of the horns in the music-room; but to-night he seemed quite beside himself, and he teased and plagued the boys until, telling him that he was crazy, they put him down on the floor and sat on him.

Somewhat calmed by his suppression, Paul dashed out to the front of the house to seat the early comers. He was a model usher; gracious and smiling he ran up and down the aisles; nothing was too much trouble for him; he carried messages and brought programmes as though it were his greatest pleasure in life, and all the people in his section thought him a charming boy, feeling that he remembered and admired them. As the house filled, he grew more and more vivacious and animated, and the color came to his cheeks and lips. It was very much as though this were a great reception and Paul were the host. Just as the musicians came out to take their places, his English teacher arrived with checks for the seats which a prominent manufacturer had taken for the season. She betrayed some embarrassment when she handed Paul the tickets, and a *hauteur*° which subsequently made her feel very foolish. Paul was startled for a moment, and had the feeling of wanting to put her out; what business had she here among all these fine people and gay colors? He looked her over and decided that she was not appropriately dressed and must be a fool to sit downstairs in such togs. The tickets had probably been sent her out of kindness, he reflected as he put down a seat for her, and she had about as much right to sit there as he had.

When the symphony began Paul sank into one of the rear seats with a long sigh of relief, and lost himself as he had done before the Rico. It was not that symphonies, as such, meant anything in particular to Paul, but the

---

Raffaelli: Jean-François Raffaelli (1850 – 1921), painter and graphic artist, native and lifelong resident of Paris, attained great popularity for his paintings and drawings of that city.

Rico: Andreas Rico (flourished 1500 – 1550), painter of the Byzantine school, a native of Crete.

Augustus . . . cast-room: Paul mocks a plaster cast of the Vatican Museum's famous statue of the first Roman emperor (63 B.C. – A.D. 14), whom an unknown sculptor posed sternly pointing an index finger at his beholders.

hauteur: haughtiness.

first sigh of the instruments seemed to free some hilarious and potent spirit within him; something that struggled there like the Genius in the bottle found by the Arab fisherman°. He felt a sudden zest of life; the lights danced before his eyes and the concert hall blazed into unimaginable splendor. When the soprano soloist came on, Paul forgot even the nastiness of his teacher's being there and gave himself up to the peculiar stimulus such personages always had for him. The soloist chanced to be a German woman, by no means in her first youth, and the mother of many children; but she wore an elaborate gown and a tiara, and above all she had that indefinable air of achievement, that world-shine upon her, which, in Paul's eyes, made her a veritable queen of Romance.

After a concert was over Paul was always irritable and wretched until he 15 got to sleep, and tonight he was even more than usually restless. He had the feeling of not being able to let down, of its being impossible to give up this delicious excitement which was the only thing that could be called living at all. During the last number he withdrew and, after hastily changing his clothes in the dressing-room, slipped out to the side door where the soprano's carriage stood. Here he began pacing rapidly up and down the walk, waiting to see her come out.

Over yonder the Schenley, in its vacant stretch, loomed big and square through the fine rain, the windows of its twelve stories glowing like those of a lighted cardboard house under a Christmas tree. All the actors and singers of the better class stayed there when they were in the city, and a number of the big manufacturers of the place lived there in the winter. Paul had often hung about the hotel, watching the people go in and out, longing to enter and leave school-masters and dull care behind him forever.

At last the singer came out, accompanied by the conductor, who helped her into her carriage and closed the door with a cordial *auf wiedersehen*° which set Paul to wondering whether she were not an old sweetheart of his. Paul followed the carriage over to the hotel, walking so rapidly as not to be far from the entrance when the singer alighted and disappeared behind the swinging glass doors that were opened by a negro in a tall hat and a long coat. In the moment that the door was ajar it seemed to Paul that he, too, entered. He seemed to feel himself go after her up the steps, into the warm, lighted building, into an exotic, a tropical world of shiny, glistening surfaces and basking ease. He reflected upon the mysterious dishes that were brought into the dining-room, the green bottles in buckets of ice, as he had seen them in the supper party pictures of the *Sunday World* supplement. A quick gust of wind brought the rain down with sudden vehemence, and Paul was startled to find that he was still outside in the slush of the gravel driveway; that his boots were letting in the water and his scanty overcoat was clinging wet about him; that the lights in front of the concert hall were out, and that the rain was driving in sheets between him and the orange glow of the windows above him. There it was, what he wanted — tangibly before him, like the fairy world of a Christmas pantomime, but mocking spirits stood guard at the doors, and, as

Genius: genie in a tale from *The Arabian Nights.*
auf wiedersehen: German equivalent of *au revoir,* or, "here's to seeing you again."

the rain beat in his face, Paul wondered whether he were destined always to shiver in the black night outside, looking up at it.

He turned and walked reluctantly toward the car tracks. The end had to come sometime; his father in his night-clothes at the top of the stairs, explanations that did not explain, hastily improvised fictions that were forever tripping him up, his upstairs room and its horrible yellow wall-paper, the creaking bureau with the greasy plush collar-box, and over his painted wooden bed the pictures of George Washington and John Calvin°, and the framed motto, "Feed my Lambs," which had been worked in red worsted by his mother.

Half an hour later, Paul alighted from his car and went slowly down one of the side streets off the main thoroughfare. It was a highly respectable street, where all the houses were exactly alike, and where businessmen of moderate means begot and reared large families of children, all of whom went to Sabbath-school and learned the shorter catechism, and were interested in arithmetic; all of whom were as exactly alike as their homes, and of a piece with the monotony in which they lived. Paul never went up Cordelia Street without a shudder of loathing. His home was next to the house of the Cumberland° minister. He approached it tonight with the nerveless sense of defeat, the hopeless feeling of sinking back forever into ugliness and commonness that he had always had when he came home. The moment he turned into Cordelia Street he felt the waters close above his head. After each of these orgies of living, he experienced all the physical depression which follows a debauch; the loathing of respectable beds, of common food, of a house penetrated by kitchen odors; a shuddering repulsion for the flavorless, colorless mass of every-day existence; a morbid desire for cool things and soft lights and fresh flowers.

The nearer he approached the house, the more absolutely unequal Paul   20
felt to the sight of it all; his ugly sleeping chamber; the cold bathroom with the grimy zinc tub, the cracked mirror, the dripping spiggots; his father, at the top of the stairs, his hairy legs sticking out from his night-shirt, his feet thrust into carpet slippers. He was so much later than usual that there would certainly be inquiries and reproaches. Paul stopped short before the door. He felt that he could not be accosted by his father tonight; that he could not toss again on that miserable bed. He would not go in. He would tell his father that he had no car fare, and it was raining so hard he had gone home with one of the boys and stayed all night.

Meanwhile, he was wet and cold. He went around to the back of the house and tried one of the basement windows, found it open, raised it cautiously, and scrambled down the cellar wall to the floor. There he stood, holding his breath, terrified by the noise he had made, but the floor above him was silent, and there was no creak on the stairs. He found a soap-box, and carried it over to the soft ring of light that streamed from the furnace door, and sat down. He was horribly afraid of rats, so he did not try to sleep, but sat looking distrustfully at the dark, still terrified lest he might have awakened his father. In such reactions, after one of the experiences which made days and

John Calvin: French Protestant theologian of the Reformation (1509 – 1564) whose teachings are the basis of Presbyterianism.

Cumberland: industrial city in western Maryland.

nights out of the dreary blanks of the calendar, when his senses were dead-ened, Paul's head was always singularly clear. Suppose his father had heard him getting in at the window and had come down and shot him for a burglar? Then, again, suppose his father had come down, pistol in hand, and he had cried out in time to save himself, and his father had been horrified to think how nearly he had killed him? Then, again, suppose a day should come when his father would remember that night, and wish there had been no warning cry to stay his hand? With this last supposition Paul entertained himself until daybreak.

The following Sunday was fine; the sodden November chill was broken by the last flash of autumnal summer. In the morning Paul had to go to church and Sabbath-school, as always. On seasonable Sunday afternoons the burgh-ers of Cordelia Street always sat out on their front "stoops," and talked to their neighbors on the next stoop, or called to those across the street in neighborly fashion. The men usually sat on gay cushions placed upon the steps that led down to the sidewalk, while the women, in their Sunday "waists," sat in rockers on the cramped porches, pretending to be greatly at their ease. The children played in the streets; there were so many of them that the place resembled the recreation grounds of a kindergarten. The men on the steps — all in their shirt sleeves, their vests unbuttoned — sat with their legs well apart, their stomachs comfortably protruding, and talked of the prices of things, or told anecdotes of the sagacity of their various chiefs and overlords. They occasionally looked over the multitude of squabbling children, listened affectionately to their high-pitched, nasal voices, smiling to see their own proclivities reproduced in their offspring, and interspersed their legends of the iron kings with remarks about their sons' progress at school, their grades in arithmetic, and the amounts they had saved in their toy banks.

On this last Sunday of November, Paul sat all the afternoon on the lowest step of his "stoop," staring into the street, while his sisters, in their rockers, were talking to the minister's daughters next door about how many shirt-waists they had made in the last week, and how many waffles some one had eaten at the last church supper. When the weather was warm, and his father was in a particularly jovial frame of mind, the girls made lemonade, which was always brought out in a red-glass pitcher, ornamented with forget-me-nots in blue enamel. This the girls thought very fine, and the neighbors always joked about the suspicious color of the pitcher.

Today Paul's father sat on the top step, talking to a young man who shifted a restless baby from knee to knee. He happened to be the young man who was daily held up to Paul as a model, and after whom it was his father's dearest hope that he would pattern. This young man was of a ruddy complex-ion, with a compressed, red mouth, and faded, near-sighted eyes, over which he wore thick spectacles, with gold bows that curved about his ears. He was clerk to one of the magnates of a great steel corporation, and was looked upon in Cordelia Street as a young man with a future. There was a story that, some five years ago — he was now barely twenty-six — he had been a trifle dis-sipated but in order to curb his appetites and save the loss of time and strength that a sowing of wild oats might have entailed, he had taken his chief's advice, oft reiterated to his employees, and at twenty-one had married the first woman whom he could persuade to share his fortunes. She happened to be an angular school-mistress, much older than he, who also wore thick glasses, and who had now borne him four children, all near-sighted, like herself.

The young man was relating how his chief, now cruising in the Mediterranean, kept in touch with all the details of the business, arranging his office hours on his yacht just as though he were at home, and "knocking off work enough to keep two stenographers busy." His father told, in turn, the plan his corporation was considering, of putting in an electric railway plant at Cairo. Paul snapped his teeth; he had an awful apprehension that they might spoil it all before he got there. Yet he rather liked to hear these legends of the iron kings, that were told and retold on Sundays and holidays; these stories of palaces in Venice, yachts on the Mediterranean, and high play at Monte Carlo appealed to his fancy, and he was interested in the triumphs of these cash boys who had become famous, though he had no mind for the cash-boy stage.

After supper was over, and he had helped to dry the dishes, Paul nervously asked his father whether he could go to George's to get some help in his geometry, and still more nervously asked for car fare. This latter request he had to repeat, as his father, on principle, did not like to hear requests for money, whether much or little. He asked Paul whether he could not go to some boy who lived nearer, and told him that he ought not to leave his school work until Sunday; but he gave him the dime. He was not a poor man, but he had a worthy ambition to come up in the world. His only reason for allowing Paul to usher was, that he thought a boy ought to be earning a little.

Paul bounded upstairs, scrubbed the greasy odor of the dish-water from his hands with the ill-smelling soap he hated, and then shook over his fingers a few drops of violet water from the bottle he kept hidden in his drawer. He left the house with his geometry conspicuously under his arm, and the moment he got out of Cordelia Street and boarded a downtown car, he shook off the lethargy of two deadening days, and began to live again.

The leading juvenile of the permanent stock company which played at one of the downtown theatres was an acquaintance of Paul's, and the boy had been invited to drop in at the Sunday-night rehearsals whenever he could. For more than a year Paul had spent every available moment loitering about Charley Edwards's dressing-room. He had won a place among Edwards's following not only because the young actor, who could not afford to employ a dresser, often found him useful, but because he recognized in Paul something akin to what churchmen term "vocation."

It was at the theatre and at Carnegie Hall that Paul really lived; the rest was but a sleep and a forgetting. This was Paul's fairy tale, and it had for him all the allurement of a secret love. The moment he inhaled the gassy, painty, dusty odor behind the scenes, he breathed like a prisoner set free, and felt within him the possibility of doing or saying splendid, brilliant, poetic things. The moment the cracked orchestra beat out the overture from *Martha*°, or jerked at the serenade from *Rigoletto*°, all stupid and ugly things slid from him, and his senses were deliciously, yet delicately fired.

Perhaps it was because, in Paul's world, the natural nearly always wore

Martha: grand opera about romance among English aristocrats (1847) by German composer Friedrich von Flotow.
Rigoletto: tragic grand opera (1851) by Italian composer Giuseppe Verdi.

the guise of ugliness, that a certain element of artificiality seemed to him necessary in beauty. Perhaps it was because his experience of life elsewhere was so full of Sabbath-school picnics, petty economies, wholesome advice as to how to succeed in life, and the unescapable odors of cooking, that he found this existence so alluring, these smartly-clad men and women so attractive, that he was so moved by these starry apple orchards that bloomed perennially under the lime-light.

It would be difficult to put it strongly enough how convincingly the stage entrance of that theatre was for Paul the actual portal of Romance. Certainly none of the company ever suspected it, least of all Charley Edwards. It was very like the old stories that used to float about London of fabulously rich Jews, who had subterranean halls there, with palms, and fountains, and soft lamps and richly apparelled women who never saw the disenchanting light of London day. So, in the midst of that smoke-palled city, enamored of figures and grimy toil, Paul had his secret temple, his wishing carpet, his bit of blue-and-white Mediterranean shore bathed in perpetual sunshine.

Several of Paul's teachers had a theory that his imagination had been perverted by garish fiction, but the truth was that he scarcely ever read at all. The books at home were not such as would either tempt or corrupt a youthful mind, and as for reading the novels that some of his friends urged upon him — well, he got what he wanted much more quickly from music; any sort of music, from an orchestra to a barrel organ. He needed only the spark, the indescribable thrill that made his imagination master of his senses, and he could make plots and pictures enough of his own. It was equally true that he was not stage struck — not, at any rate, in the usual acceptation of that expression. He had no desire to become an actor, any more than he had to become a musician. He felt no necessity to do any of these things; what he wanted was to see, to be in the atmosphere, float on the wave of it, to be carried out, blue league after blue league, away from everything.

After a night behind the scenes, Paul found the school-room more than ever repulsive; the bare floors and naked walls; the prosy men who never wore frock coats, or violets in their buttonholes; the women with their dull gowns, shrill voices, and pitiful seriousness about prepositions that govern the dative. He could not bear to have the other pupils think, for a moment, that he took these people seriously; he must convey to them that he considered it all trivial, and was there only by way of a jest, anyway. He had autographed pictures of all the members of the stock company which he showed his classmates, telling them the most incredible stories of his familiarity with these people, of his acquaintance with the soloists who came to Carnegie Hall, his suppers with them and the flowers he sent them. When these stories lost their effect, and his audience grew listless, he became desperate and would bid all the boys good-bye, announcing that he was going to travel for a while; going to Naples, to Venice, to Egypt. Then, next Monday, he would slip back, conscious and nervously smiling; his sister was ill, and he should have to defer his voyage until spring.

Matters went steadily worse with Paul at school. In the itch to let his instructors know how heartily he despised them and their homilies, and how thoroughly he was appreciated elsewhere, he mentioned once or twice that he had no time to fool with theorems; adding — with a twitch of the eyebrows and a touch of that nervous bravado which so perplexed them — that he was helping the people down at the stock company; they were old friends of his.

The upshot of the matter was that the Principal went to Paul's father, and Paul was taken out of school and put to work. The manager at Carnegie Hall was told to get another usher in his stead; the door-keeper at the theatre was warned not to admit him to the house; and Charley Edwards remorsefully promised the boy's father not to see him again.

The members of the stock company were vastly amused when some of Paul's stories reached them — especially the women. They were hardworking women, most of them supporting indigent husbands or brothers, and they laughed rather bitterly at having stirred the boy to such fervid and florid inventions. They agreed with the faculty and with his father that Paul's was a bad case.

The east-bound train was ploughing through a January snow-storm; the dull dawn was beginning to show grey when the engine whistled a mile out of Newark. Paul started up from the seat where he had lain curled in uneasy slumber, rubbed the breath-misted window glass with his hand, and peered out. The snow was whirling in curling eddies above the white bottom lands, and the drifts lay already deep in the fields and along the fences, while here and there the long dead grass and dried weed stalks protruded black above it. Lights shone from the scattered houses, and a gang of laborers who stood beside the track waved their lanterns.

Paul had slept very little, and he felt grimy and uncomfortable. He had made the all-night journey in a day coach, partly because he was ashamed, dressed as he was, to go into a Pullman, and partly because he was afraid of being seen there by some Pittsburgh businessmen, who might have noticed him in Denny & Carson's office. When the whistle awoke him, he clutched quickly at his breast pocket, glancing about him with an uncertain smile. But the little, clay-bespattered Italians were still sleeping, the slatternly women across the aisle were in open-mouthed oblivion, and even the crumby, crying babies were for the nonce stilled. Paul settled back to struggle with his impatience as best he could.

When he arrived at the Jersey City station, he hurried through his breakfast, manifestly ill at ease and keeping a sharp eye about him. After he reached the Twenty-third Street station°, he consulted a cabman, and had himself driven to a men's furnishing establishment that was just opening for the day. He spent upward of two hours there, buying with endless reconsidering and great care. His new street suit he put on in the fitting-room; the frock coat and dress clothes he had bundled into the cab with his linen. Then he drove to a hatter's and a shoe house. His next errand was at Tiffany's, where he selected his silver and a new scarf-pin. He would not wait to have his silver marked, he said. Lastly, he stopped at a trunk shop on Broadway, and had his purchases packed into various travelling bags.

It was a little after one o'clock when he drove up to the Waldorf, and after settling with the cabman, went into the office. He registered from Washington; said his mother and father had been abroad, and that he had come

Twenty-third Street station: The scene is now New York City.

down to await the arrival of their steamer. He told his story plausibly and had no trouble, since he volunteered to pay for them in advance, in engaging his rooms; a sleeping-room, sitting-room and bath.

Not once, but a hundred times Paul had planned this entry into New York. He had gone over every detail of it with Charley Edwards, and in his scrap book at home there were pages of description about New York hotels, cut from the Sunday papers. When he was shown to his sitting-room on the eighth floor, he saw at a glance that everything was as it should be; there was but one detail in his mental picture that the place did not realize, so he rang for the bell boy and sent him down for flowers. He moved about nervously until the boy returned, putting away his new linen and fingering it delightedly as he did so. When the flowers came, he put them hastily into water, and then tumbled into a hot bath. Presently he came out of his white bath-room, resplendent in his new silk underwear, and playing with the tassels of his red robe. The snow was whirling so fiercely outside his windows that he could scarcely see across the street, but within the air was deliciously soft and fragrant. He put the violets and jonquils on the taboret beside the couch, and threw himself down, with a long sigh, covering himself with a Roman blanket. He was thoroughly tired; he had been in such haste, he had stood up to such a strain, covered so much ground in the last twenty-four hours, that he wanted to think how it had all come about. Lulled by the sound of the wind, the warm air, and the cool fragrance of the flowers, he sank into deep, drowsy retrospection.

It had been wonderfully simple; when they had shut him out of the theatre and concert hall, when they had taken away his bone, the whole thing was virtually determined. The rest was a mere matter of opportunity. The only thing that at all surprised him was his own courage — for he realized well enough that he had always been tormented by fear, a sort of apprehensive dread that, of late years, as the meshes of the lies he had told closed about him, had been pulling the muscles of his body tighter and tighter. Until now, he could not remember the time when he had not been dreading something. Even when he was a little boy, it was always there — behind him, or before, or on either side. There had always been the shadowed corner, the dark place into which he dared not look, but from which something seemed always to be watching him — and Paul had done things that were not pretty to watch, he knew.

But now he had a curious sense of relief, as though he had at last thrown down the gauntlet to the thing in the corner.

Yet it was but a day since he had been sulking in the traces; but yesterday afternoon that he had been sent to the bank with Denny & Carson's deposit, as usual — but this time he was instructed to leave the book to be balanced. There was above two thousand dollars in checks, and nearly a thousand in the bank notes which he had taken from the book and quietly transferred to his pocket. At the bank he had made out a new deposit slip. His nerves had been steady enough to permit of his returning to the office, where he had finished his work and asked for a full day's holiday tomorrow, Saturday, giving a perfectly reasonable pretext. The bank book, he knew, would not be returned before Monday or Tuesday, and his father would be out of town for the next week. From the time he slipped the bank notes into his pocket until he boarded the night train for New York, he had not known a moment's hesitation. It was not the first time Paul had steered through treacherous waters.

How astonishingly easy it had all been; here he was, the thing done; and this time there would be no awakening, no figure at the top of the stairs. He watched the snow flakes whirling by his window until he fell asleep. 45

When he awoke, it was three o'clock in the afternoon. He bounded up with a start; half of one of his precious days gone already! He spent more than an hour in dressing, watching every stage of his toilet carefully in the mirror. Everything was quite perfect; he was exactly the kind of boy he had always wanted to be.

When he went downstairs, Paul took a carriage and drove up Fifth Avenue toward the Park. The snow had somewhat abated; carriages and tradesmen's wagons were hurrying soundlessly to and fro in the winter twilight; boys in woollen mufflers were shovelling off the doorsteps; the avenue stages made fine spots of color against the white street. Here and there on the corners were stands, with whole flower gardens blooming under glass cases, against the sides of which the snow flakes stuck and melted; violets, roses, carnations, lilies of the valley — somewhat vastly more lovely and alluring that they blossomed thus unnaturally in the snow. The Park itself was a wonderful stage winterpiece.

When he returned, the pause of the twilight had ceased, and the tune of the streets had changed. The snow was falling faster, lights streamed from the hotels that reared their dozen stories fearlessly up into the storm, defying the raging Atlantic winds. A long, black stream of carriages poured down the avenue, intersected here and there by other streams, tending horizontally. There were a score of cabs about the entrance of his hotel, and his driver had to wait. Boys in livery were running in and out of the awning stretched across the sidewalk, up and down the red velvet carpet laid from the door to the street. Above, about, within it all was the rumble and roar, the hurry and toss of thousands of human beings as hot for pleasure as himself, and on every side of him towered the glaring affirmation of the omnipotence of wealth.

The boy set his teeth and drew his shoulders together in a spasm of realization: the plot of all dramas, the text of all romances, the nerve-stuff of all sensations was whirling about him like the snow flakes. He burnt like a faggot in a tempest.

When Paul went down to dinner, the music of the orchestra came floating up the elevator shaft to greet him. His head whirled as he stepped into the thronged corridor, and he sank back into one of the chairs against the wall to get his breath. The lights, the chatter, the perfumes, the bewildering medley of color — he had, for a moment, the feeling of not being able to stand it. But only for a moment; these were his own people, he told himself. He went slowly about the corridors, through the writing-rooms, smoking-rooms, reception-rooms, as though he were exploring the chambers of an enchanted palace, built and peopled for him alone. 50

When he reached the dining-room he sat down at a table near a window. The flowers, the white linen, the many-colored wine glasses, the gay toilettes of the women, the low popping of corks, the undulating repetitions of the *Blue Danube* from the orchestra, all flooded Paul's dream with bewildering radiance. When the roseate tinge of his champagne was added — that cold, precious, bubbling stuff that creamed and foamed in his glass — Paul wondered that there were honest men in the world at all. This was what all the world was fighting for, he reflected; this was what all the struggle was about. He doubted the reality of his past. Had he ever known a place called Cordelia Street, a place where fagged-looking businessmen got on the early car; mere rivets in a machine they seemed to Paul — sickening men, with combings of children's hair always hanging to their coats, and the smell of cooking in their clothes. Cordelia Street — Ah! that belonged to another time and country; had he not always been thus, had he not sat here night after night, from as far back as he could remember, looking pensively over just such shimmering textures, and slowly twirling the stem of a glass like this one between his thumb and middle finger? He rather thought he had.

He was not in the least abashed or lonely. He had no especial desire to meet or to know any of these people; all he demanded was the right to look on and conjecture, to watch the pageant. The mere stage properties were all he contended for. Nor was he lonely later in the evening, in his loge at the Metropolitan. He was now entirely rid of his nervous misgivings, of his forced aggressiveness, of the imperative desire to show himself different from his surroundings. He felt now that his surroundings explained him. Nobody questioned the purple; he had only to wear it passively. He had only to glance down at his attire to reassure himself that here it would be impossible for anyone to humiliate him.

He found it hard to leave his beautiful sitting-room to go to bed that night, and sat long watching the raging storm from his turret window. When he went to sleep it was with the lights turned on in his bedroom; partly because of his old timidity, and partly so that, if he should wake in the night, there would be no wretched moment of doubt, no horrible suspicion of yellow wall-paper, or of Washington and Calvin above his bed.

Sunday morning the city was practically snow-bound. Paul breakfasted late, and in the afternoon he fell in with a wild San Francisco boy, a freshman at Yale, who said he had run down for a "little flyer" over Sunday. The young man offered to show Paul the night side of the town, and the two boys went out together after dinner, not returning to the hotel until seven o'clock the next morning. They had started out in the confiding warmth of a champagne friendship, but their parting in the elevator was singularly cool. The freshman pulled himself together to make his train, and Paul went to bed. He awoke at two o'clock in the afternoon, very thirsty and dizzy, and rang for ice-water, coffee, and the Pittsburgh papers.

On the part of the hotel management, Paul excited no suspicion. There was this to be said for him, that he wore his spoils with dignity and in no way made himself conspicuous. Even under the glow of his wine he was never boisterous, though he found the stuff like a magician's wand for wonder-building. His chief greediness lay in his ears and eyes, and his excesses were not offensive ones. His dearest pleasures were the grey winter twilights in his sitting-room; his quiet enjoyment of his flowers, his clothes, his wide divan, his cigarette, and his sense of power. He could not remember a time when he had felt so at peace with himself. The mere release from the necessity of petty lying, lying every day and every day, restored his self-respect. He had never lied for pleasure, even at school; but to be noticed and admired, to assert his difference from other Cordelia Street boys; and he felt a good deal more manly, more honest, even, now that he had no need for boastful pretensions, now that he could, as his actor friends used to say, "dress the part." It was characteristic that remorse did not occur to him. His golden days went by without a shadow, and he made each as perfect as he could.

On the eighth day after his arrival in New York, he found the whole affair exploited in the Pittsburgh papers, exploited with a wealth of detail which indicated that local news of a sensational nature was at a low ebb. The firm of Denny & Carson announced that the boy's father had refunded the full amount of the theft, and that they had no intention of prosecuting. The Cumberland minister had been interviewed, and expressed his hope of yet reclaiming the motherless lad, and his Sabbath-school teacher declared that she would spare no effort to that end. The rumor had reached Pittsburgh that the boy had been seen in a New York hotel, and his father had gone East to find him and bring him home.

Paul had just come in to dress for dinner; he sank into a chair, weak to the knees, and clasped his head in his hands. It was to be worse than jail, even; the tepid waters of Cordelia Street were to close over him finally and forever. The grey monotony stretched before him in hopeless, unrelieved years; Sabbath-school, Young People's Meeting, the yellow-papered room, the damp dish-towels; it all rushed back upon him with a sickening vividness. He had the old feeling that the orchestra had suddenly stopped, the sinking sensation that the play was over. The sweat broke out on his face, and he sprang to his feet, looked about him with his white, conscious smile, and winked at himself in the mirror. With something of the old childish belief in miracles with which he had so often gone to class, all his lessons unlearned, Paul dressed and dashed whistling down the corridor to the elevator.

He had no sooner entered the dining-room and caught the measure of the music than his remembrance was lightened by his old elastic power of claiming the moment, mounting with it, and finding it all sufficient. The glare and glitter about him, the mere scenic accessories had again, and for the last time, their old potency. He would show himself that he was game, he would finish the thing splendidly. He doubted, more than ever, the existence of Cordelia Street, and for the first time he drank his wine recklessly. Was he not, after all, one of those fortunate beings born to the purple, was he not still himself and in his own place? He drummed a nervous accompaniment to the Pagliacci music and looked about him, telling himself over and over that it had paid.

He reflected drowsily, to the swell of the music and the chill sweetness of his wine, that he might have done it more wisely. He might have caught an outboard steamer and been well out of their clutches before now. But the other side of the world had seemed too far away and too uncertain then; he could not have waited for it; his need had been too sharp. If he had to choose over again, he would do the same thing tomorrow. He looked affectionately about the dining-room, now gilded with a soft mist. Ah, it had paid indeed!

Paul was awakened next morning by a painful throbbing in his head and feet. He had thrown himself across the bed without undressing, and had slept with his shoes on. His limbs and hands were lead heavy, and his tongue and throat were parched and burnt. There came upon him one of those fateful attacks of clear-headedness that never occurred except when he was physically exhausted and his nerves hung loose. He lay still and closed his eyes and let the tide of things wash over him.

His father was in New York; "stopping at some joint or other," he told himself. The memory of successive summers on the front stoop fell upon him like a weight of black water. He had not a hundred dollars left; and he knew now, more than ever, that money was everything, the wall that stood between all he loathed and all he wanted. The thing was winding itself up; he had thought of that on his first glorious day in New York, and had even provided a way to snap the thread. It lay on his dressing-table now; he had got it out last night when he came blindly up from dinner, but the shiny metal hurt his eyes, and he disliked the looks of it.

He rose and moved about with a painful effort, succumbing now and again to attacks of nausea. It was the old depression exaggerated; all the world had become Cordelia Street. Yet somehow he was not afraid of anything, was absolutely calm; perhaps because he had looked into the dark corner at last and knew. It was bad enough, what he saw there, but somehow not so bad as his long fear of it had been. He saw everything clearly now. He had a feeling that he had made the best of it, that he had lived the sort of life he was meant to live, and for half an hour he sat staring at the revolver. But he told himself that was not the way, so he went downstairs and took a cab to the ferry.

When Paul arrived at Newark, he got off the train and took another cab, directing the driver to follow the Pennsylvania tracks out of the town. The snow lay heavy on the roadways and had drifted deep in the open fields. Only here and there the dead grass or dried weed stalks projected, singularly black, above it. Once well into the country, Paul dismissed the carriage and walked, floundering along the tracks, his mind a medley of irrelevant things. He seemed to hold in his brain an actual picture of everything he had seen that morning. He remembered every feature of both his drivers, of the toothless old woman from whom he had bought the red flowers in his coat, the agent from whom he had got his ticket, and all of his fellow-passengers on the ferry. His mind, unable to cope with vital matters near at hand, worked feverishly and deftly at sorting and grouping these images. They made for him a part of the ugliness of the world, of the ache in his head, and the bitter burning on his tongue. He stooped and put a handful of snow into his mouth as he walked, but that, too, seemed hot. When he reached a little hillside, where the tracks ran through a cut some twenty feet below him, he stopped and sat down.

The carnations in his coat were drooping with the cold, he noticed; their red glory all over. It occurred to him that all the flowers he had seen in the glass cases that first night must have gone the same way, long before this. It was only one splendid breath they had, in spite of their brave mockery at the winter outside the glass; and it was a losing game in the end, it seemed, this revolt against the homilies by which the world is run. Paul took one of the blossoms carefully from his coat and scooped a little hole in the snow, where he covered it up. Then he dozed a while, from his weak condition, seemingly insensible to the cold.

The sound of an approaching train awoke him, and he started to his feet, remembering only his resolution, and afraid lest he should be too late. He stood watching the approaching locomotive, his teeth chattering, his lips drawn away from them in a frightened smile; once or twice he glanced nervously sidewise, as though he were being watched. When the right moment came, he jumped. As he fell, the folly of his haste occurred to him with merciless clearness, the vastness of what he had left undone. There flashed through his brain, clearer than ever before, the blue of Adriatic water, the yellow of Algerian sands.

He felt something strike his chest, and that his body was being thrown swiftly through the air, on and on, immeasurably far and fast, while his limbs were gently relaxed. Then, because the picture making mechanism was crushed, the disturbing visions flashed into black, and Paul dropped back into the immense design of things.

QUESTIONS

1. What is it about Paul that so disturbs his teachers? Recall any of his traits that they find irritating, any actions that trouble them. Do they irritate or trouble *you?*
2. How does Paul relate to his father, his neighbors, and his fellow students?
3. What do the arts — music, painting, theater — mean to Paul? How does he react when exposed to them? Is he himself an artist?
4. In what different places do we follow Paul throughout the story? How do these settings (and the boy's reactions to them) help us understand him, his attitudes, his personality?
5. What, exactly, does Paul want out of life? Cite evidence for your answer, paying attention to what most pleases him in New York.
6. What is the point of view in "Paul's Case"? Does it ever change, or does it remain the same throughout the story? Imagine the story told in the first person. Why wouldn't that point of view have been so effective?
7. Does Cather's brief introduction into the story of the wild Yale freshman from San Francisco (in paragraph 54) serve any purpose? If you had been writing this story, would you have given this minor character more importance? Why do you suppose he and Paul have such a "singularly cool" parting? What is Cather's point?
8. Is Paul a static character or a dynamic one? (If you find him changing and developing in the story, can you indicate what changes him?)
9. Comment on some of the concrete details Cather dwells on. What, for instance, do you make of the portraits of Washington and Calvin and the motto placed over Paul's bed (paragraph 18)? Of the carnation Paul buries in the snow (paragraph 64)?
10. What implications, if any, does the title "Paul's Case" have for this story? Is Paul mentally ill, or does Cather place the roots of his malaise elsewhere?
11. What motivates Paul to commit suicide? To what extent does his decision to kill himself seem to grow from his character? (Suggestion: Consider what Paul reveals about himself by his earlier behavior: his lies to his father and teachers, the exaggerated tales he tells his schoolmates about his acquaintance with theater people, his frequent attendance at the stock theater productions, his runaway trip to New York.)
12. Does this story contain any message, stated or implied? Do you get any sense of how the author feels toward Paul? How far does she appear to sympathize with him? Point to any passages in the story that seem to reveal her attitude.
13. When Cather first published "Paul's Case" in 1905, she subtitled it "A Study in Temperament." Three of the possible meanings of temperament (according

to *Webster's New Collegiate Dictionary*) are "peculiar or distinguishing mental or physical character," "characteristic or habitual inclination or mode of emotional response ['he is of a nervous temperament'])," and "extremely high sensibility, especially excessive sensitiveness." Which of these definitions seems to you best to fit the story? How do you describe Paul's temperament?

14. What circumstances of Paul's boyhood environment make his temperament a particularly dangerous and unfortunate one for him?

Isaac Bashevis Singer

GIMPEL THE FOOL   1953

Translated by Saul Bellow

Isaac Bashevis Singer, born in Poland in 1904, the son of a rabbi, grew up in the Jewish ghetto in Warsaw in a family where money was scarce, but intellectual stimuli plentiful. "My father's house," he recalls, "was a study house, a court of justice, a house of prayer, of storytelling." For a time he pursued rabbinical studies. In 1935, when the Nazi invasion of Poland was imminent, he came to New York and became a journalist for the Jewish Daily Forward, *a Yiddish-language newspaper for which, ever since, he has continued to write. For years he contributed a daily serial story to the* Forward *and for a time wrote scripts for a Yiddish soap opera on radio station WEVD. He became a naturalized United States citizen in 1943. Only in 1950 when* The Family Moskat, *a novel of three generations of Warsaw Jews, appeared in English translation, did a larger audience become aware of him. (Singer, whose command of English is excellent, has always worked closely with his translators.) In 1978 he was awarded the Nobel prize for literature. Singer's work often (as in "Gimpel the Fool") recreates the vanished world of the* shtetl, *or Jewish village of Eastern Europe. Traditional Jewish legends inform many of his novels, including* Satan in Goray *(1955),* The Magician of Lublin *(1960), and* The Golem *(1982). Singer has also written many volumes of short fiction (see* Collected Stories, *1982), children's books, the play* Yentl *(1975), and three volumes of autobiography.*

I

I am Gimpel the fool. I don't think myself a fool. On the contrary. But that's what folks call me. They gave me the name while I was still in school. I had seven names in all: imbecile, donkey, flax-head, dope, glump, ninny, and fool. The last name stuck. What did my foolishness consist of? I was easy to take in. They said, "Gimpel, you know the rabbi's wife has been brought to childbed?" So I skipped school. Well, it turned out to be a lie. How was I supposed to know? She hadn't had a big belly. But I never looked at her belly. Was that really so foolish? The gang laughed and hee-hawed, stomped and danced and chanted a good-night prayer. And instead of the raisins they give when a woman's lying in, they stuffed my hand full of goat turds. I was no weakling. If I slapped someone he'd see all the way to Cracow. But I'm really not a slugger by nature. I think to myself, Let it pass. So they take advantage of me.

I was coming home from school and heard a dog barking. I'm not afraid of dogs, but of course I never want to start up with them. One of them may be mad, and if he bites there's not a Tartar in the world who can help you. So I made tracks. Then I looked around and saw the whole market place wild with laughter. It was no dog at all but Wolf-Leib the thief. How was I supposed to know it was he? It sounded like a howling bitch.

When the pranksters and leg-pullers found that I was easy to fool, every one of them tried his luck with me. "Gimpel, the Czar is coming to Frampol; Gimpel, the moon fell down in Turbeen; Gimpel, little Hodel Furpiece found a treasure behind the bathhouse." And I like a *golem*° believed everyone. In the first place, everything is possible, as it is written in the Wisdom of the Fathers, I've forgotten just how. Second, I had to believe when the whole town came down on me! If I ever dared to say, "Ah, you're kidding!" there was trouble. People got angry. "What do you mean! You want to call everyone a liar?" What was I to do? I believed them, and I hope at least that did them some good.

I was an orphan. My grandfather who brought me up was already bent toward the grave. So they turned me over to a baker, and what a time they gave me there! Every woman or girl who came to bake a pan of cookies or dry a batch of noodles had to fool me at least once. "Gimpel, there's a fair in heaven; Gimpel, the rabbi gave birth to a calf in the seventh month; Gimpel, a cow flew over the roof and laid brass eggs." A student from the *yeshiva*° came once to buy a roll, and he said, "You, Gimpel, while you stand here scraping with your baker's shovel the Messiah has come. The dead have arisen." "What do you mean?" I said. "I heard no one blowing the ram's horn!" He said, "Are you deaf?" And all began to cry, "We heard it, we heard!" Then in came Reitze the candle-dipper and called out in her hoarse voice, "Gimpel, your father and mother have stood up from the grave. They're looking for you."

To tell the truth, I knew very well that nothing of the sort had happened, but all the same, as folks were talking, I threw on my wool vest and went out. Maybe something had happened. What did I stand to lose by looking? Well, what a cat music went up! And then I took a vow to believe nothing more. But that was no go either. They confused me so that I didn't know the big end from the small.

I went to the rabbi to get some advice. He said, "It is written, better to be a fool all your days than for one hour to be evil. You are not a fool. They are the fools. For he who causes his neighbor to feel shame loses Paradise himself." Nevertheless the rabbi's daughter took me in. As I left the rabbinical court she said, "Have you kissed the wall yet?" I said, "No; what for?" She answered, "It's a law; you've got to do it after every visit." Well, there didn't

5

---

golem: simpleton. From the Hebrew: "a yet-unformed thing" (*Psalms* 139:16); a mere robot, a shapeless mass.
yeshiva: school of theology.

seem to be any harm in it. And she burst out laughing. It was a fine trick. She put one over on me, all right.

I wanted to go off to another town, but then everyone got busy match-making, and they were after me so they nearly tore my coat tails off. They talked at me and talked until I got water on the ear. She was no chaste maiden, but they told me she was virgin pure. She had a limp, and they said it was deliberate, from coyness. She had a bastard, and they told me the child was her little brother. I cried, "You're wasting your time. I'll never marry that whore." But they said indignantly, "What a way to talk! Aren't you ashamed of yourself? We can take you to the rabbi and have you fined for giving her a bad name." I saw then that I wouldn't escape them so easily and I thought, They're set on making me their butt. But when you're married the husband's the master, and if that's all right with her it's agreeable to me too. Besides, you can't pass through life unscathed, nor expect to.

I went to her clay house, which was built on the sand, and the whole gang, hollering and chorusing, came after me. They acted like bearbaiters. When we came to the well they stopped all the same. They were afraid to start anything with Elka. Her mouth would open as if it were on a hinge, and she had a fierce tongue. I entered the house. Lines were strung from wall to wall and clothes were drying. Barefoot she stood by the tub, doing the wash. She was dressed in a worn hand-me-down gown of plush. She had her hair put up in braids and pinned across her head. It took my breath away, almost, the reek of it all.

Evidently she knew who I was. She took a look at me and said, "Look who's here! He's come, the drip. Grab a seat."

I told her all; I denied nothing. "Tell me the truth," I said, "are you really a virgin, and is that mischievous Yechiel actually your little brother? Don't be deceitful with me, for I'm an orphan."

"I'm an orphan myself," she answered, "and whoever tries to twist you up, may the end of his nose take a twist. But don't let them think they can take advantage of me. I want a dowry of fifty guilders, and let them take up a collection besides. Otherwise they can kiss my you-know-what." She was very plain-spoken. I said, "It's the bride and not the groom who gives a dowry." Then she said, "Don't bargain with me. Either a flat 'yes' or a flat 'no' — go back where you came from."

I thought, No bread will ever be baked from *this* dough. But ours is not a poor town. They consented to everything and proceeded with the wedding. It so happened that there was a dysentery epidemic at the time. The ceremony was held at the cemetery gates, near the little corpse-washing hut. The fellows got drunk. While the marriage contract was being drawn up I heard the most pious high rabbi ask, "Is the bride a widow or a divorced woman?" And the sexton's wife answered for her, "Both a widow and divorced." It was a black moment for me. But what was I to do, run away from under the marriage canopy?

There was singing and dancing. An old granny danced opposite me, hugging a braided white *chalah*°. The master of revels made a "God 'a mercy" in memory of the bride's parents. The schoolboys threw burrs, as on *Tishe b'*

chalah: loaf of bread glazed with egg white, a Sabbath and holiday delicacy.

Av fast day°. There were a lot of gifts after the sermon: a noodle board, a kneading trough, a bucket, brooms, ladles, household articles galore. Then I took a look and saw two strapping young men carrying a crib. "What do we need this for?" I asked. So they said, "Don't rack your brains about it. It's all right, it'll come in handy." I realized I was going to be rooked. Take it another way though, what did I stand to lose? I reflected, I'll see what comes of it. A whole town can't go altogether crazy.

II

At night I came where my wife lay, but she wouldn't let me in. "Say, look here, is this what they married us for?" I said. And she said, "My monthly has come." "But yesterday they took you to the ritual bath, and that's afterward, isn't it supposed to be?" "Today isn't yesterday," said she, "and yesterday's not today. You can beat it if you don't like it." In short, I waited.

Not four months later she was in childbed. The townsfolk hid their laughter with their knuckles. But what could I do? She suffered intolerable pains and clawed at the walls. "Gimpel," she cried, "I'm going. Forgive me!" The house filled with women. They were boiling pans of water. The screams rose to the welkin.

The thing to do was to go to the House of Prayer to repeat Psalms, and that was what I did.

The townsfolk liked that, all right. I stood in a corner saying Psalms and prayers, and they shook their heads at me. "Pray, pray!" they told me. "Prayer never made any woman pregnant." One of the congregation put a straw to my mouth and said, "Hay for the cows." There was something to that too, by God!

She gave birth to a boy. Friday at the synagogue the sexton stood up before the Ark, pounded on the reading table, and announced, "The wealthy Reb Gimpel invites the congregation to a feast in honor of the birth of a son." The whole House of Prayer rang with laughter. My face was flaming. But there was nothing I could do. After all, I *was* the one responsible for the circumcision honors and rituals.

Half the town came running. You couldn't wedge another soul in. Women brought peppered chick-peas, and there was a keg of beer from the tavern. I ate and drank as much as anyone, and they all congratulated me. Then there was a circumcision, and I named the boy after my father, may he rest in peace. When all were gone and I was left with my wife alone, she thrust her head through the bed-curtain and called me to her.

"Gimpel," said she, "why are you silent? Has your ship gone and sunk?"

"What shall I say?" I answered. "A fine thing you've done to me! If my mother had known of it she'd have died a second time."

She said, "Are you crazy, or what?"

"How can you make such a fool," I said, "of one who should be the lord and master?"

"What's the matter with you?" she said. "What have you taken it into your head to imagine?"

Tishe b' Av: day of mourning that commemorates disasters and persecutions.

I saw that I must speak bluntly and openly. "Do you think this is the 25
way to use an orphan?" I said. "You have borne a bastard."

She answered, "Drive this foolishness out of your head. The child is
yours."

"How can he be mine?" I argued. "He was born seventeen weeks after
the wedding."

She told me then that he was premature. I said, "Isn't he a little too
premature?" She said she had had a grandmother who carried just as short a
time and she resembled this grandmother of hers as one drop of water does
another. She swore to it with such oaths that you would have believed a
peasant at the fair if he had used them. To tell the plain truth, I didn't believe
her; but when I talked it over next day with the schoolmaster he told me that
the very same thing had happened to Adam and Eve. Two they went up to
bed, and four they descended.

"There isn't a woman in the world who is not the granddaughter of Eve,"
he said.

That was how it was — they argued me dumb. But then, who really 30
knows how such things are?

I began to forget my sorrow. I loved the child madly, and he loved me
too. As soon as he saw me he'd wave his little hands and want me to pick him
up, and when he was colicky I was the only one who could pacify him. I
bought him a little bone teething ring and a little gilded cap. He was forever
catching the evil eye from someone, and then I had to run to get one of those
abracadabras for him that would get him out of it. I worked like an ox. You
know how expenses go up when there's an infant in the house. I don't want
to lie about it; I didn't dislike Elka either, for that matter. She swore at me and
cursed, and I couldn't get enough of her. What strength she had! One of her
looks could rob you of the power of speech. And her orations! Pitch and
sulphur, that's what they were full of, and yet somehow also full of charm.
I adored her every word. She gave me bloody wounds though.

In the evening I brought her a white loaf as well as a dark one, and also
poppyseed rolls I baked myself. I thieved because of her and swiped everything I could lay hands on, macaroons, raisins, almonds, cakes. I hope I may
be forgiven for stealing from the Saturday pots the women left to warm in the
baker's oven. I would take out scraps of meat, a chunk of pudding, a chicken
leg or head, a piece of tripe, whatever I could nip quickly. She ate and became
fat and handsome.

I had to sleep away from home all during the week, at the bakery. On
Friday nights when I got home she always made an excuse of some sort. Either
she had heartburn, or a stitch in the side, or hiccups, or headaches. You know
what women's excuses are. I had a bitter time of it. It was rough. To add to
it, this little brother of hers, the bastard, was growing bigger. He'd put lumps
on me, and when I wanted to hit back she'd open her mouth and curse so
powerfully I saw a green haze floating before my eyes. Ten times a day she
threatened to divorce me. Another man in my place would have taken French
leave and disappeared. But I'm the type that bears it and says nothing. What's
one to do? Shoulders are from God, and burdens too.

One night there was a calamity in the bakery; the oven burst, and we
almost had a fire. There was nothing to do but go home, so I went home. Let

me, I thought, also taste the joy of sleeping in bed in midweek. I didn't want to wake the sleeping mite and tiptoed into the house. Coming in, it seemed to me that I heard not the snoring of one but, as it were, a double snore, one a thin enough snore and the other like the snoring of a slaughtered ox. Oh, I didn't like that! I didn't like it at all. I went up to the bed, and things suddenly turned black. Next to Elka lay a man's form. Another in my place would have made an uproar, and enough noise to rouse the whole town, but the thought occurred to me that I might wake the child. A little thing like that — why frighten a little swallow like that, I thought. All right then, I went back to the bakery and stretched out on a sack of flour, and till morning I never shut an eye. I shivered as if I had had malaria. "Enough of being a donkey," I said to myself. "Gimpel isn't going to be a sucker all his life. There's a limit even to the foolishness of a fool like Gimpel."

In the morning I went to the rabbi to get advice, and it made a great commotion in the town. They sent the beadle for Elka right away. She came, carrying the child. And what do you think she did? She denied it, denied everything, bone and stone! "He's out of his head," she said. "I know nothing of dreams or divinations." They yelled at her, warned her, hammered on the table, but she stuck to her guns: it was a false accusation, she said.

The butchers and the horse-traders took her part. One of the lads from the slaughterhouse came by and said to me, "We've got our eye on you, you're a marked man." Meanwhile the child started to bear down and soiled itself. In the rabbinical court there was an Ark of the Covenant, and they couldn't allow that, so they sent Elka away.

I said to the rabbi, "What shall I do?"

"You must divorce her at once," said he.

"And what if she refuses?" I asked.

He said, "You must serve the divorce, that's all you'll have to do."

I said, "Well, all right, Rabbi. Let me think about it."

"There's nothing to think about," said he. "You mustn't remain under the same roof with her."

"And if I want to see the child?" I asked.

"Let her go, the harlot," said he, "and her brood of bastards with her."

The verdict he gave was that I mustn't even cross her threshold — never again, as long as I should live.

During the day it didn't bother me so much. I thought, It was bound to happen, the abscess had to burst. But at night when I stretched out upon the sacks I felt it all very bitterly. A longing took me, for her and for the child. I wanted to be angry, but that's my misfortune exactly, I don't have it in me to be really angry. In the first place — this was how my thoughts went — there's bound to be a slip sometimes. You can't live without errors. Probably that lad who was with her led her on and gave her presents and what not, and women are often long on hair and short on sense, and so he got around her. And then since she denies it so, maybe I was only seeing things? Hallucinations do happen. You see a figure or a mannikin or something, but when you come up closer it's nothing, there's not a thing there. And if that's so, I'm doing her an injustice. And when I got so far in my thoughts I started to weep. I sobbed so that I wet the flour where I lay. In the morning I went to the rabbi and told him that I had made a mistake. The rabbi wrote on with his quill, and he said that if that were so he would have to reconsider the whole case. Until he had finished I wasn't to go near my wife, but I might send her bread and money by messenger.

III

Nine months passed before all the rabbis could come to an agreement. Letters went back and forth. I hadn't realized that there could be so much erudition about a matter like this.

Meantime Elka gave birth to still another child, a girl this time. On the Sabbath I went to the synagogue and invoked a blessing on her. They called me up to the Torah, and I named the child for my mother-in-law, may she rest in peace. The louts and loudmouths of the town who came into the bakery gave me a going over. All Frampol refreshed its spirits because of my trouble and grief. However, I resolved that I would always believe what I was told. What's the good of *not* believing? Today it's your wife you don't believe; tomorrow it's God Himself you won't take stock in.

By an apprentice who was her neighbor I sent her daily a corn or a wheat loaf, or a piece of pastry, rolls or bagels, or, when I got the chance, a slab of pudding, a slice of honeycake, or wedding strudel — whatever came my way. The apprentice was a goodhearted lad, and more than once he added something on his own. He had formerly annoyed me a lot, plucking my nose and digging me in the ribs, but when he started to be a visitor to my house he became kind and friendly. "Hey, you, Gimpel," he said to me, "you have a very decent little wife and two fine kids. You don't deserve them."

"But the things people say about her," I said.   50

"Well, they have long tongues," he said, "and nothing to do with them but babble. Ignore it as you ignore the cold of last winter."

One day the rabbi sent for me and said, "Are you certain, Gimpel, that you were wrong about your wife?"

I said, "I'm certain."

"Why, but look here! You yourself saw it."

"It must have been a shadow," I said.   55

"The shadow of what?"

"Just of one of the beams, I think."

"You can go home then. You owe thanks to the Yanover rabbi. He found an obscure reference in Maimonides that favored you."

I seized the rabbi's hand and kissed it.

I wanted to run home immediately. It's no small thing to be separated   60
for so long a time from wife and child. Then I reflected, I'd better go back to work now, and go home in the evening. I said nothing to anyone, although as far as my heart was concerned it was like one of the Holy Days. The women teased and twitted me as they did every day, but my thought was, Go on, with your loose talk. The truth is out, like the oil upon the water. Maimonides says it's right, and therefore it is right!

At night, when I had covered the dough to let it rise, I took my share of bread and a little sack of flour and started homeward. The moon was full and the stars were glistening, something to terrify the soul. I hurried onward, and before me darted a long shadow. It was winter, and a fresh snow had fallen. I had a mind to sing, but it was growing late and I didn't want to wake the householders. Then I felt like whistling, but remembered that you don't whistle at night because it brings the demons out. So I was silent and walked as fast as I could.

Dogs in the Christian yards barked at me when I passed, but I thought, Bark your teeth out! What are you but mere dogs? Whereas I am a man, the husband of a fine wife, the father of promising children.

As I approached the house my heart started to pound as though it were the heart of a criminal. I felt no fear, but my heart went thump! thump! Well, no drawing back. I quietly lifted the latch and went in. Elka was asleep. I looked at the infant's cradle. The shutter was closed, but the moon forced its way through the cracks. I saw the newborn child's face and loved it as soon as I saw it — immediately — each tiny bone.

Then I came nearer to the bed. And what did I see but the apprentice lying there beside Elka. The moon went out all at once. It was utterly black, and I trembled. My teeth chattered. The bread fell from my hands and my wife waked and said, "Who is that, ah?"

I muttered, "It's me."   65

"Gimpel?" she asked. "How come you're here? I thought it was forbidden."

"The rabbi said," I answered and shook as with a fever.

"Listen to me, Gimpel," she said, "go out to the shed and see if the goat's all right. It seems she's been sick." I have forgotten to say that we had a goat. When I heard she was unwell I went into the yard. The nannygoat was a good little creature. I had a nearly human feeling for her.

With hesitant steps I went up to the shed and opened the door. The goat stood there on her four feet. I felt her everywhere, drew her by the horns, examined her udders, and found nothing wrong. She had probably eaten too much bark. "Good night, little goat," I said. "Keep well." And the little beast answered with a "Maa" as though to thank me for the good will.

I went back. The apprentice had vanished.   70

"Where," I asked, "is the lad?"

"What lad?" my wife answered.

"What do you mean?" I said. "The apprentice. You were sleeping with him."

"The things I have dreamed this night and the night before," she said, "may they come true and lay you low, body and soul! An evil spirit has taken root in you and dazzles your sight." She screamed out, "You hateful creature! You moon calf! You spook! You uncouth man! Get out, or I'll scream all Frampol out of bed!"

Before I could move, her brother sprang out from behind the oven and   75
struck me a blow on the back of the head. I thought he had broken my neck. I felt that something about me was deeply wrong, and I said, "Don't make a scandal. All that's needed now is that people should accuse me of raising spooks and *dybbuks*°." For that was what she had meant. "No one will touch bread of my baking."

In short, I somehow calmed her.

---

dybbuks: demons, or souls of the dead, who take possession of people.

"Well," she said, "that's enough. Lie down, and be shattered by wheels."

Next morning I called the apprentice aside. "Listen here, brother!" I said. And so on and so forth. "What do you say?" He stared at me as though I had dropped from the roof or something.

"I swear," he said, "you'd better go to an herb doctor or some healer. I'm afraid you have a screw loose, but I'll hush it up for you." And that's how the thing stood.

To make a long story short, I lived twenty years with my wife. She bore me six children, four daughters and two sons. All kinds of things happened, but I neither saw nor heard. I believed, and that's all. The rabbi recently said to me, "Belief in itself is beneficial. It is written that a good man lives by his faith." 80

Suddenly my wife took sick. It began with a trifle, a little growth upon the breast. But she evidently was not destined to live long; she had no years. I spent a fortune on her. I have forgotten to say that by this time I had a bakery of my own and in Frampol was considered to be something of a rich man. Daily the healer came, and every witch doctor in the neighborhood was brought. They decided to use leeches, and after that to try cupping. They even called a doctor from Lublin, but it was too late. Before she died she called me to her bed and said, "Forgive me, Gimpel."

I said, "What is there to forgive? You have been a good and faithful wife."

"Woe, Gimpel!" she said. "It was ugly how I deceived you all these years. I want to go clean to my Maker, and so I have to tell you that the children are not yours."

If I had been clouted on the head with a piece of wood it couldn't have bewildered me more.

"Whose are they?" I asked. 85

"I don't know," she said, "there were a lot. . . . But they're not yours." And as she spoke she tossed her head to the side, her eyes turned glassy, and it was all up with Elka. On her whitened lips there remained a smile.

I imagined that, dead as she was, she was saying, "I deceived Gimpel. That was the meaning of my brief life."

IV

One night, when the period of mourning was done, as I lay dreaming on the flour sacks, there came the Spirit of Evil himself and said to me, "Gimpel, why do you sleep?"

I said, "What should I be doing? Eating *kreplach*°?"

"The whole world deceives you," he said, "and you ought to deceive the world in your turn." 90

"How can I deceive all the world?" I asked him.

He answered, "You might accumulate a bucket of urine every day and at night pour it into the dough. Let the sages of Frampol eat filth."

"What about judgment in the world to come?" I said.

kreplach: a kind of dumpling containing meat, cheese, or other filling.

"There is no world to come," he said. "They've sold you a bill of goods and talked you into believing you carried a cat in your belly. What nonsense!"

"Well then," I said, "and is there a God?"

He answered, "There is no God either."

"What," I said, *"is* there, then?"

"A thick mire."

He stood before my eyes with a goatish beard and horns, longtoothed, and with a tail. Hearing such words, I wanted to snatch him by the tail, but I tumbled from the flour sacks and nearly broke a rib. Then it happened that I had to answer the call of nature, and, passing, I saw the risen dough, which seemed to say to me, "Do it!" In brief, I let myself be persuaded.

At dawn the apprentice came. We kneaded the bread, scattered caraway seeds on it, and set it to bake. Then the apprentice went away, and I was left sitting in the little trench by the oven, on a pile of rags. Well, Gimpel, I thought, you've revenged yourself on them for all the shame they've put on you. Outside the frost glittered, but it was warm beside the oven. The flames heated my face. I bent my head and fell into a doze.

I saw in a dream, at once, Elka in her shroud. She called to me, "What have you done, Gimpel?"

I said to her, "It's all your fault," and started to cry.

"You fool!" she said. "You fool! Because I was false is everything false too? I never deceived anyone but myself. I'm paying for it all, Gimpel. They spare you nothing here."

I looked at her face. It was black. I was startled and waked, and remained sitting dumb. I sensed that everything hung in the balance. A false step now and I'd lose Eternal Life. But God gave me His help. I seized the long shovel and took out the loaves, carried them into the yard, and started to dig a hole in the frozen earth.

My apprentice came back as I was doing it. "What are you doing, boss?" he said, and grew pale as a corpse.

"I know what I'm doing," I said, and I buried it all before his very eyes.

Then I went home, took my hoard from its hiding place, and divided it among the children. "I saw your mother tonight," I said. "She's turning black, poor thing."

They were so astounded they couldn't speak a word.

"Be well," I said, "and forget that such a one as Gimpel ever existed." I put on my short coat, a pair of boots, took the bag that held my prayer shawl in one hand, my stick in the other, and kissed the *mezzuzah*°. When people saw me in the street they were greatly surprised.

"Where are you going?" they said.

I answered, "Into the world." And so I departed from Frampol.

I wandered over the land, and good people did not neglect me. After many years I became old and white; I heard a great deal, many lies and falsehoods, but the longer I lived the more I understood that there were really

---

mezzuzah: a small oblong container, affixed near the front door of the house, which holds copies of Biblical verses (including a reminder to obey God's laws when traveling away from home).

no lies. Whatever doesn't really happen is dreamed at night. It happens to one if it doesn't happen to another, tomorrow if not today, or a century hence if not next year. What difference can it make? Often I heard tales of which I said, "Now this is a thing that cannot happen." But before a year had elapsed I heard that it actually had come to pass somewhere.

Going from place to place, eating at strange tables, it often happens that I spin yarns — improbable things that could never have happened — about devils, magicians, windmills, and the like. The children run after me, calling, "Grandfather, tell us a story." Sometimes they ask for particular stories, and I try to please them. A fat young boy once said to me, "Grandfather, it's the same story you told us before." The little rogue, he was right.

So it is with dreams too. It is many years since I left Frampol, but as soon as I shut my eyes I am there again. And whom do you think I see? Elka. She is standing by the washtub, as at our first encounter, but her face is shining and her eyes are radiant as the eyes of a saint, and she speaks outlandish words to me, strange things. When I wake I have forgotten it all. But while the dream lasts I am comforted. She answers all my queries, and what comes out is that all is right. I weep and implore, "Let me be with you." And she consoles me and tells me to be patient. The time is nearer than it is far. Sometimes she strokes and kisses me and weeps upon my face. When I awaken I feel her lips and taste the salt of her tears.

No doubt the world is entirely an imaginary world, but it is only once removed from the true world. At the door of the hovel where I lie, there stands the plank on which the dead are taken away. The gravedigger Jew has his spade ready. The grave waits and the worms are hungry; the shrouds are prepared — I carry them in my beggar's sack. Another *shnorrer*° is waiting to inherit my bed of straw. When the time comes I will go joyfully. Whatever may be there, it will be real, without complication, without ridicule, without deception. God be praised: there even Gimpel cannot be deceived.

QUESTIONS

1. In what ways does Gimpel appear to deserve his nickname *the fool?* In what other ways is Gimpel not foolish at all?
2. What does Gimpel find to love in the character of Elka? Consider in particular the scene of her deathbed confession and her later appearance in Gimpel's dreams.
3. Why does Gimpel momentarily listen to the Devil? How is he delivered from temptation? For what reasons does he finally divide his wealth and become a poor wanderer? Would you call him a dynamic character, or a static character — one who grows and develops in the course of the story, or one who remains unchanged?
4. "No doubt the world is entirely an imaginary world, but it is only once removed from the true world." Comment on this statement in the closing paragraph. What do you think it means?
5. What elements of the supernatural do you find in "Gimpel the Fool"? What details of down-to-earth realism?
6. In what respects does the story resemble a fable? Is it possible to draw any moral from it?

shnorrer: a beggar, a traveling panhandler.

Suggestions for Writing

1. Here is a topic for a lively essay if you are familiar with some variety of popular fiction — detective stories, science fiction, Gothic novels, romances, "adolescent agony" novels written for teenagers, or other kinds of paperback storytelling. Portray some of the stock characters you find prevalent in it. Suggestion: It might be simplistic to condemn stock characters as bad. They have long been valuable ingredients in much excellent literature. (For a discussion of stock characters, see page 73).

2. Alternate topic: Portray a few stock characters we meet in current television programs. It might focus your essay to confine it to just one variety of stock character (for instance, the little man who peddles information to the police, the glamorous Russian spy), or to just one kind of program (situation comedies, say, or soap operas, or police thrillers).

3. In a brief essay, study a dynamic character in a story, showing exactly how that character changed, or grew and developed. Possible subjects: Granny Weatherall, Gimpel, Sammy in John Updike's "A & P," Paul in "Paul's Case," the boy Sarty Snopes in William Faulkner's "Barn Burning" (in Chapter 5). (For a discussion of dynamic characters, see page 74.)

4. Alternate topic: Have you ever in your life known anyone whose character, over months or years, has altered deeply? If so, try to explain what may have caused that person to be a "dynamic character."

5. Topics for brief papers:

   The motivation of Gimpel in leaving Frampol to wander the world.

   The motivation of Sammy in quitting his job (in "A & P").

   The motivation of someone (whether in your reading or in your experience) who made a similar gesture of throwing over everything and taking off.

6. Here are topics for an essay you can write by the method of comparison and contrast (explained in "Writing about a Story," page 425).

   Compare the characters of two forceful women: Granny Weatherall and Mrs. Ulgine Barrows (in "The Catbird Seat").

   Compare two sly deceivers: Mr. Martin (in "The Catbird Seat") and Elka (in "Gimpel the Fool").

   Compare two black mothers in their attitudes toward young people: Mama (in "Everyday Use") and Miss Hazel (in "My Man Bovanne").

   Look up Emily Dickinson's poem "I heard a Fly buzz – when I died" and compare it with "The Jilting of Granny Weatherall" in its account of a woman's deathbed experience.

5 Tone and Style

In many Victorian novels it was customary for some commentator, presumably the author, to interrupt the story from time to time, remarking upon the action, offering philosophic asides, or explaining the procedures to be followed in telling the story.

> Two hours later, Dorothea was seated in an inner room or boudoir of a handsome apartment in the Via Sistina. I am sorry to add that she was sobbing bitterly. . . .
> — George Eliot in *Middlemarch* (1873)

> But let the gentle-hearted reader be under no apprehension whatsoever. It is not destined that Eleanor shall marry Mr. Slope or Bertie Stanhope.
> — Anthony Trollope in *Barchester Towers* (1857)

> And, as we bring our characters forward, I will ask leave, as a man and a brother, not only to introduce, but occasionally to step down from the platform, and talk about them: if they are good and kindly, to love them and shake them by the hand; if they are silly, to laugh at them confidentially in the reader's sleeve; if they are wicked and heartless, to abuse them in the strongest terms which politeness admits of.
> — William Makepeace Thackeray in *Vanity Fair* (1847 – 1848)

Of course, the voice of this commentator was not identical with that of the "real life" author — the one toiling over an inkpot, worrying about publication deadlines and whether the rent would be paid. At times the living author might have been far different in personality from that usually wise and cheerful intruder who kept addressing the reader of the book. Much of the time, to be sure, the author probably agreed with whatever attitudes his alter ego expressed. But, in effect, the author created the character of a commentator to speak for him and throughout the novel artfully sustained that character's voice.

Such intrusions, although sometimes useful to the "real" author and enjoyable to the reader, are today rare. Modern storytellers, carefully keeping out of sight, seldom comment on their plots and characters. Apparently they agree with Anton Chekhov that a writer should not judge the characters but should serve as their "impartial witness." And yet, no less definitely than Victorian novelists who introduced commentators, writers of effective stories no doubt have feelings toward their characters and events. The authors presumably care about these imaginary people and, in order for the story to grasp and sustain our interest, have to make us see these people in such a way that we, too, will care about them. When at the beginning of the short story "In Exile" Chekhov introduces us to a character, he does so with a description that arouses sympathy:

> The Tartar was worn out and ill, and, wrapping himself in his rags, he talked about how good it was in the province of Simbirsk, and what a beautiful and clever wife he had left at home. He was not more than twenty-five, and in the firelight his pale, sickly face and woebegone expression made him seem like a boy.

Other than the comparison of the Tartar to a child, the details in this passage seem mostly factual: the young man's illness, ragged clothes, facial expression, and topics of conversation. But these details form a portrait that stirs pity. By his selection of these imaginary details out of countless others that he might have included, Chekhov firmly directs our feelings about the Tartar, so miserable and pathetic in his sickness and his homesickness. We cannot know, of course, exactly what the living Chekhov felt; but at least we can be sure that we are supposed to share the compassion and tenderness of the narrator — Chekhov's impartial (but human) witness.

Not only the author's choice of details may lead us to infer his attitude, but also his choice of characters, events, and situations, and his choice of words. When the narrator of Joseph Conrad's *Heart of Darkness* comes upon an African outpost littered with abandoned machines and notices "a boiler wallowing in the grass," the exact word *wallowing* conveys an attitude: that there is something swinish about this scene of careless waste. Whatever leads us to infer the author's attitude is commonly called **tone.** Like a tone of voice, the tone of a story may communicate amusement, anger, affection, sorrow, contempt. It implies the feelings of the author, so far as we can sense them. Those feelings may be similar to feelings expressed by the narrator of the story (or by any character), but sometimes they may be dissimilar, even sharply opposed. The characters in a story may regard an event as sad, but we sense that the author regards it as funny. To understand the tone of a story, then, is to understand some attitude more fundamental to the story than whatever attitude the characters explicitly declare.

The tone of a story, like a tone of voice, may convey not simply one attitude, but a medley. Reading "Gimpel the Fool" (Chapter Four), we have mingled feelings toward Gimpel and his "foolishness": amusement that Gimpel is so easily deceived; sympathy, perhaps, for his excessive innocence; admiration for his unwavering faith in God and fellow man. Often the tone of a literary story will be too rich and complicated to sum up in one or two words. But to try to describe the tone of such a story may be a useful way to penetrate to its center and to grasp the whole of it.

One of the clearest indications of the tone of a story is the **style** in which it is written. In general, style refers to the individual traits or characteristics of a piece of writing; to a writer's particular ways of managing words that we come to recognize as habitual or customary. A distinctive style marks the work of a fine writer: we can tell his or her work from that of anyone else. From one story to another, however, the writer may fittingly change style; and in some stories, style may be altered meaningfully as the story goes along. In his novel *As I Lay Dying,* William Faulkner changes narrators with every chapter, and he distinguishes the narrators one from another by giving each an individual style or manner of speaking. Though each narrator has his own style, the book as a whole demonstrates Faulkner's style as well. For instance, one chapter is written from the point of view of a small boy, Vardaman Bundren, member of a family of poor Mississippi tenant farmers, whose view of a horse in a barn reads like this:

> It is as though the dark were resolving him out of his integrity, into an unrelated scattering of components — snuffings and stampings; smells of cooling flesh and ammoniac hair; an illusion of a coordinated whole of splotched hide and strong bones within which, detached and secret and familiar, an *is* different from my is.[1]

How can a small boy unaccustomed to libraries use words like *integrity, components, illusion,* and *coordinated?* Elsewhere in the story, Vardaman says aloud, with no trace of literacy, "Hit was a-laying right there on the ground." Apparently, in the passage it is not the voice of the boy that we are hearing, but something resembling the voice of William Faulkner, elevated and passionate, expressing the boy's thoughts in a style that admits Faulknerian words.

Usually, *style* indicates a mode of expression: the language a writer uses. In this sense, the notion of style includes such traits as the length and complexity of sentences, and **diction,** or choice of words: abstract or concrete, bookish ("unrelated scattering of components") or close to speech ("Hit was a-laying right there on the ground"). Involved in the idea of style, too, is any habitual use of imagery, patterns of sound, figures of speech, or other devices.

To see what style means, compare the stories in this chapter by William Faulkner ("Barn Burning") and by Ernest Hemingway ("A Clean, Well-Lighted Place"). Faulkner frequently falls into a style in which a statement, as soon as uttered, is followed by another statement expressing

[1]Modern Library edition (New York: Random, 1930) 379.

the idea in a more emphatic way. Sentences are interrupted with parenthetical elements (asides, like this) thrust into them unexpectedly. At times, Faulkner writes of seemingly ordinary matters as if giving a speech in a towering passion. Here, from "Barn Burning," is a description of how a boy's father delivers a rug:

> "Don't you want me to help?" he whispered. His father did not answer and now he heard again that stiff foot striking the hollow portico with that wooden and clocklike deliberation, that outrageous overstatement of the weight it carried. The rug, hunched, not flung (the boy could tell that even in the darkness) from his father's shoulder struck the angle of wall and floor with a sound unbelievably loud, thunderous, then the foot again, unhurried and enormous; a light came on in the house and the boy sat, tense, breathing steadily and quietly and just a little fast, though the foot itself did not increase its beat at all, descending the steps now; now the boy could see him.

Faulkner is not merely indulging in language for its own sake. As you will find when you read the whole story, this rug delivery is vital to the story, and so too is the father's profound defiance — indicated by his walk. By devices of style — by *metaphor* and *simile* ("wooden and clocklike"), by exact qualification ("not flung"), by emphatic adjectives ("loud, thunderous") — Faulkner is carefully placing his emphases. By the words he selects to describe the father's stride, Faulkner directs how we feel toward the man and perhaps also indicates his own wondering but skeptical attitude toward a character whose very footfall is "outrageous" and "enormous." (Fond of long sentences like the last one in the quoted passage, Faulkner remarked that there are sentences that need to be written in the way a circus acrobat pedals a bicycle on a high wire: rapidly, so as not to fall off.)

Hemingway's famous style includes both short sentences and long, but when the sentences are long they tend to be relatively simple in construction. Hemingway likes long compound sentences (clause plus clause plus clause), sometimes joined with "and's." He interrupts such a sentence with a dependent clause or a parenthetical element much less frequently than Faulkner does. The effect is like listening to speech:

> In the day time the street was dusty, but at night the dew settled the dust and the old man liked to sit late because he was deaf and now at night it was quiet and he felt the difference.

Hemingway is a master of swift, terse dialogue, and often casts whole scenes in the form of conversation. As if he were a closemouthed speaker unwilling to let his feelings loose, the narrator of a Hemingway story often addresses us in understatement, implying greater depths of feeling than he puts into words. Read the following story and you will see that its style and tone cannot be separated.

Ernest Hemingway

A Clean, Well-Lighted Place   1933

Ernest Hemingway (1898 – 1961), born in Oak Park, Illinois, bypassed college to be a cub reporter. In World War I, as an eighteen-year-old volunteer ambulance driver in Italy, he was wounded in action. In 1922 he settled in Paris, then aswarm with writers: days he later recalled in A Moveable Feast *(1964). Hemingway won swift acclaim for his early stories,* In Our Time *(1925), and for his first, perhaps finest novel,* The Sun Also Rises *(1926), portraying a "lost generation" of postwar American drifters in France and Spain.* For Whom the Bell Tolls *(1940) depicts life during the Spanish Civil War. Hemingway became a celebrity, often photographed as a marlin fisherman or a lion hunter. A fan of bullfighting, he wrote two nonfiction books on the subject:* Death in the Afternoon *(1932) and* The Dangerous Summer *(1985). After World War II, with his fourth wife, journalist Mary Welsh, he made his home in Cuba, where he wrote* The Old Man and the Sea *(1952). The Nobel prize for literature came to him in 1954. In 1961, mentally distressed and physically ailing, he shot himself. Hemingway brought a hard-bitten realism into American fiction. His heroes live dangerously, by personal codes of honor, courage, and endurance. Hemingway's distinctively crisp, unadorned style left American literature permanently changed.*

It was late and every one had left the café except an old man who sat in the shadow the leaves of the tree made against the electric light. In the day time the street was dusty, but at night the dew settled the dust and the old man liked to sit late because he was deaf and now at night it was quiet and he felt the difference. The two waiters inside the café knew that the old man was a little drunk, and while he was a good client they knew that if he became too drunk he would leave without paying, so they kept watch on him.

"Last week he tried to commit suicide," one waiter said.

"Why?"

"He was in despair."

"What about?"

"Nothing."   5

"How do you know it was nothing?"

"He has plenty of money."

They sat together at a table that was close against the wall near the door of the café and looked at the terrace where the tables were all empty except where the old man sat in the shadow of the leaves of the tree that moved slightly in the wind. A girl and a soldier went by in the street. The street light shone on the brass number on his collar. The girl wore no head covering and hurried beside him.

"The guard will pick him up," one waiter said.   10

"What does it matter if he gets what he's after?"

"He had better get off the street now. The guard will get him. They went by five minutes ago."

The old man sitting in the shadow rapped on his saucer with his glass. The younger waiter went over to him.

"What do you want?"

The old man looked at him. "Another brandy," he said. 15

"You'll be drunk," the waiter said. The old man looked at him. The waiter went away.

"He'll stay all night," he said to his colleague. "I'm sleepy now. I never get into bed before three o'clock. He should have killed himself last week."

The waiter took the brandy bottle and another saucer from the counter inside the café and marched out to the old man's table. He put down the saucer and poured the glass full of brandy.

"You should have killed yourself last week," he said to the deaf man. The old man motioned with his finger. "A little more," he said. The waiter poured on into the glass so that the brandy slopped over and ran down the stem into the top saucer of the pile. "Thank you," the old man said. The waiter took the bottle back inside the café. He sat down at the table with his colleague again.

"He's drunk now," he said. 20

"He's drunk every night."°

"What did he want to kill himself for?"

"How should I know."

"How did he do it?"

"He hung himself with a rope." 25

"Who cut him down?"

"His niece."

"Why did they do it?"

"Fear for his soul."

"How much money has he got?" 30

"He's got plenty."

"He must be eighty years old."

"Anyway I should say he was eighty."°

"I wish he would go home. I never get to bed before three o'clock. What kind of hour is that to go to bed?"

"He stays up because he likes it." 35

"He's lonely. I'm not lonely. I have a wife waiting in bed for me."

"He had a wife once too."

"A wife would be no good to him now."

"You can't tell. He might be better with a wife."

"His niece looks after him." 40

"I know. You said she cut him down."

"I wouldn't want to be that old. An old man is a nasty thing."

"Not always. This old man is clean. He drinks without spilling. Even now, drunk. Look at him."

"I don't want to look at him. I wish he would go home. He has no regard for those who must work."

"He's drunk now," he said. "He's drunk every night": The younger waiter says both these lines. A device of Hemingway's style is sometimes to have a character pause, then speak again — as often happens in actual speech.

"He must be eighty years old." "Anyway I should say he was eighty": Is this another instance of the same character's speaking twice? Clearly, it is the younger waiter who says the next line, "I wish he would go home."

The old man looked from his glass across the square, then over at the 45 waiters.

"Another brandy," he said, pointing to his glass. The waiter who was in a hurry came over.

"Finished," he said, speaking with that omission of syntax stupid people employ when talking to drunken people or foreigners. "No more tonight. Close now."

"Another," said the old man.

"No. Finished." The waiter wiped the edge of the table with a towel and shook his head.

The old man stood up, slowly counted the saucers, took a leather coin 50 purse from his pocket and paid for the drinks, leaving half a peseta tip.

The waiter watched him go down the street, a very old man walking unsteadily but with dignity.

"Why didn't you let him stay and drink?" the unhurried waiter asked. They were putting up the shutters. "It is not half-past two."

"I want to go home to bed."

"What is an hour?"

"More to me than to him." 55

"An hour is the same."

"You talk like an old man yourself. He can buy a bottle and drink at home."

"It's not the same."

"No, it is not," agreed the waiter with a wife. He did not wish to be unjust. He was only in a hurry.

"And you? You have no fear of going home before your usual hour?" 60

"Are you trying to insult me?"

"No, hombre, only to make a joke."

"No," the waiter who was in a hurry said, rising from pulling down the metal shutters. "I have confidence. I am all confidence."

"You have youth, confidence, and a job," the older waiter said. "You have everything."

"And what do you lack?" 65

"Everything but work."

"You have everything I have."

"No. I have never had confidence and I am not young."

"Come on. Stop talking nonsense and lock up."

"I am of those who like to stay late at the café," the older waiter said. 70 "With all those who do not want to go to bed. With all those who need a light for the night."

"I want to go home and into bed."

"We are of two different kinds," the older waiter said. He was now dressed to go home. "It is not only a question of youth and confidence although those things are very beautiful. Each night I am reluctant to close up because there may be some one who needs the café."

"Hombre, there are bodegas° open all night long."

"You do not understand. This is a clean and pleasant café. It is well

bodegas: wineshops.

lighted. The light is very good and also, now, there are shadows of the leaves."

"Good night," said the younger waiter. ₇₅

"Good night," the other said. Turning off the electric light he continued the conversation with himself. It is the light of course but it is necessary that the place be clean and pleasant. You do not want music. Certainly you do not want music. Nor can you stand before a bar with dignity although that is all that is provided for these hours. What did he fear? It was not fear or dread. It was a nothing that he knew too well. It was all a nothing and a man was nothing too. It was only that and light was all it needed and a certain cleanness and order. Some lived in it and never felt it but he knew it all was nada y pues nada y nada y pues nada°. Our nada who art in nada, nada be thy name thy kingdom nada thy will be nada in nada as it is in nada. Give us this nada our daily nada and nada us our nada as we nada our nadas and nada us not into nada but deliver us from nada; pues nada. Hail nothing full of nothing, nothing is with thee. He smiled and stood before a bar with a shining steam pressure coffee machine.

"What's yours?" asked the barman.

"Nada."

"Otro loco más°," said the barman and turned away.

"A little cup," said the waiter. ₈₀

The barman poured it for him.

"The light is very bright and pleasant but the bar is unpolished," the waiter said.

The barman looked at him but did not answer. It was too late at night for conversation.

"You want another copita°?" the barman asked.

"No, thank you," said the waiter and went out. He disliked bars and ₈₅ bodegas. A clean, well-lighted café was a very different thing. Now, without thinking further, he would go home to his room. He would lie in the bed and finally, with daylight, he would go to sleep. After all, he said to himself, it is probably only insomnia. Many must have it.

Questions

1. What besides insomnia makes the older waiter reluctant to go to bed? Comment especially on his meditation with its *nada* refrain. Why does he so well understand the old man's need for a café? What does the café represent for the two of them?
2. Compare the younger waiter and the older waiter in their attitudes toward the old man. Whose attitude do you take to be closer to that of the author? Even though Hemingway does not editorially state his own feelings, how does he make them clear to us?
3. Point to sentences that establish the style of the story. What is distinctive in them? What repetitions of words or phrases seem particularly effective? Does Hemingway seem to favor a simple or an erudite vocabulary?
4. What is the story's point of view? Discuss its appropriateness.

nada y pues . . . nada: nothing and then nothing and nothing and then nothing.
Otro loco más: another lunatic.
copita: little cup.

William Faulkner

Barn Burning 1939

William Faulkner (1897 – 1962) receives a capsule biography on page 24, along with his story "A Rose for Emily." His "Barn Burning" is among his many contributions to the history of Yoknapatawpha, an imaginary Mississippi county in which the Sartorises and the de Spains are landed aristocrats living by a code of honor and the Snopeses — most of them — shiftless ne'er-do-wells.

The store in which the Justice of the Peace's court was sitting smelled of cheese. The boy, crouched on his nail keg at the back of the crowded room, knew he smelled cheese, and more: from where he sat he could see the ranked shelves close-packed with the solid, squat, dynamic shapes of tin cans whose labels his stomach read, not from the lettering which meant nothing to his mind but from the scarlet devils and the silver curve of fish — this, the cheese which he knew he smelled and the hermetic meat which his intestines believed he smelled coming in intermittent gusts momentary and brief between the other constant one, the smell and sense just a little of fear because mostly of despair and grief, the old fierce pull of blood. He could not see the table where the Justice sat and before which his father and his father's enemy *(our enemy* he thought in that despair; *ourn! mine and hisn both! He's my father!)* stood, but he could hear them, the two of them that is, because his father had said no word yet:

"But what proof have you, Mr. Harris?"

"I told you. The hog got into my corn. I caught it up and sent it back to him. He had no fence that would hold it. I told him so, warned him. The next time I put the hog in my pen. When he came to get it I gave him enough wire to patch up his pen. The next time I put the hog up and kept it. I rode down to his house and saw the wire I gave him still rolled on to the spool in his yard. I told him he could have the hog when he paid me a dollar pound fee. That evening a nigger came with the dollar and got the hog. He was a strange nigger. He said, 'He say to tell you wood and hay kin burn.' I said, 'What?' 'That whut he say to tell you,' the nigger said. 'Wood and hay kin burn.' That night my barn burned. I got the stock out but I lost the barn."

"Where is the nigger? Have you got him?"

"He was a strange nigger, I tell you. I don't know what became of him." 5

"But that's not proof. Don't you see that's not proof?"

"Get that boy up here. He knows." For a moment the boy thought too that the man meant his older brother until Harris said, "Not him. The little one. The boy," and, crouching, small for his age, small and wiry like his father, in patched and faded jeans even too small for him, with straight, uncombed, brown hair and eyes gray and wild as storm scud, he saw the men between himself and the table part and become a lane of grim faces, at the end of which he saw the Justice, a shabby, collarless, graying man in spectacles, beckoning him. He felt no floor under his bare feet; he seemed to walk beneath the palpable weight of the grim turning faces. His father, still in his black Sunday coat donned not for the trial but for the moving, did not even look at him. *He aims for me to lie,* he thought, again with that frantic grief and despair. *And I will have to do hit.*

"What's your name, boy?" the Justice said.

"Colonel Sartoris Snopes," the boy whispered.

"Hey?" the Justice said. "Talk louder. Colonel Sartoris? I reckon any- 10 body named for Colonel Sartoris in this country can't help but tell the truth, can they?" The boy said nothing. *Enemy! Enemy!* he thought; for a moment he could not even see, could not see that the Justice's face was kindly nor discern that his voice was troubled when he spoke to the man named Harris: "Do you want me to question this boy?" But he could hear, and during those subsequent long seconds while there was absolutely no sound in the crowded little room save that of quiet and intent breathing it was as if he had swung outward at the end of a grape vine, over a ravine, and at the top of the swing had been caught in a prolonged instant of mesmerized gravity, weightless in time.

"No!" Harris said violently, explosively. "Damnation! Send him out of here!" Now time, the fluid world, rushed beneath him again, the voices coming to him again through the smell of cheese and sealed meat, the fear and despair and the old grief of blood:

"This case is closed. I can't find against you, Snopes, but I can give you advice. Leave this country and don't come back to it."

His father spoke for the first time, his voice cold and harsh, level, without emphasis: "I aim to. I don't figure to stay in a country among people who . . ." he said something unprintable and vile, addressed to no one.

"That'll do," the Justice said. "Take your wagon and get out of this country before dark. Case dismissed."

His father turned, and he followed the stiff black coat, the wiry figure 15 walking a little stiffly from where a Confederate provost's man's musket ball had taken him in the heel on a stolen horse thirty years ago, followed the two backs now, since his older brother had appeared from somewhere in the crowd, no taller than the father but thicker, chewing tobacco steadily, between the two lines of grim-faced men and out of the store and across the worn gallery and down the sagging steps and among the dogs and half-grown boys in the mild May dust, where as he passed a voice hissed:

"Barn burner!"

Again he could not see, whirling; there was a face in a red haze, moonlike, bigger than the full moon, the owner of it half again his size, he leaping in the red haze toward the face, feeling no blow, feeling no shock when his head struck the earth, scrabbling up and leaping again, feeling no blow this time either and tasting no blood, scrabbling up to see the other boy in full flight and himself already leaping into pursuit as his father's hand jerked him back, the harsh, cold voice speaking above him: "Go get in the wagon."

It stood in a grove of locusts and mulberries across the road. His two hulking sisters in their Sunday dresses and his mother and her sister in calico and sunbonnets were already in it, sitting on and among the sorry residue of the dozen and more movings which even the boy could remember — the battered stove, the broken beds and chairs, the clock inlaid with mother-of-pearl, which would not run, stopped at some fourteen minutes past two o'clock of a dead and forgotten day and time, which had been his mother's dowry. She was crying, though when she saw him she drew her sleeve across her face and began to descend from the wagon. "Get back," the father said.

"He's hurt. I got to get some water and wash his . . ."

"Get back in the wagon," his father said. He got in too, over the tail-gate. His father mounted to the seat where the older brother already sat and struck the gaunt mules two savage blows with the peeled willow, but without heat. It was not even sadistic; it was exactly that same quality which in later years would cause his descendants to over-run the engine before putting a motor car into motion, striking and reining back in the same movement. The wagon went on, the store with its quiet crowd of grimly watching men dropped behind; a curve in the road hid it. *Forever* he thought. *Maybe he's done satisfied now, now that he has . . .* stopping himself, not to say it aloud even to himself. His mother's hand touched his shoulder.

"Does hit hurt?" she said.

"Naw," he said. "Hit don't hurt. Lemme be."

"Can't you wipe some of the blood off before hit dries?"

"I'll wash to-night," he said. "Lemme be, I tell you."

The wagon went on. He did not know where they were going. None of them ever did or ever asked, because it was always somewhere, always a house of sorts waiting for them a day or two days or even three days away. Likely his father had already arranged to make a crop on another farm before he . . . Again he had to stop himself. He (the father) always did. There was something about his wolflike independence and even courage when the advantage was at least neutral which impressed strangers, as if they got from his latent ravening ferocity not so much a sense of dependability as a feeling that his ferocious conviction in the rightness of his own actions would be of advantage to all whose interest lay with his.

That night they camped, in a grove of oaks and beeches where a spring ran. The nights were still cool and they had a fire against it, of a rail lifted from a nearby fence and cut into lengths — a small fire, neat, niggard almost, a shrewd fire; such fires were his father's habit and custom always, even in freezing weather. Older, the boy might have remarked this and wondered why not a big one; why should not a man who had not only seen the waste and extravagance of war, but who had in his blood an inherent voracious prodigality with material not his own, have burned everything in sight? Then he might have gone a step farther and thought that that was the reason: that niggard blaze was the living fruit of nights passed during those four years in the woods hiding from all men, blue or gray, with his strings of horses (captured horses, he called them). And older still, he might have divined the true reason: that the element of fire spoke to some deep mainspring of his father's being, as the element of steel or of powder spoke to other men, as the one weapon for the preservation of integrity, else breath were not worth the breathing, and hence to be regarded with respect and used with discretion.

But he did not think this now and he had seen those same niggard blazes all his life. He merely ate his supper beside it and was already half asleep over his iron plate when his father called him, and once more he followed the stiff back, the stiff and ruthless limp, up the slope and on to the starlit road where, turning, he could see his father against the stars but without face or depth — a shape black, flat, and bloodless as though cut from tin in the iron folds of the frockcoat which had not been made for him, the voice harsh like tin and without heat like tin:

"You were fixing to tell them. You would have told him."

He didn't answer. His father struck him with the flat of his hand on the side of the head, hard but without heat, exactly as he had struck the two mules at the store, exactly as he would strike either of them with any stick in order to kill a horse fly, his voice still without heat or anger: "You're getting to be a man. You got to learn. You got to learn to stick to your own blood or you ain't going to have any blood to stick to you. Do you think either of them, any man there this morning, would? Don't you know all they wanted was a chance to get at me because they knew I had them beat? Eh?" Later, twenty years later, he was to tell himself, "If I had said they wanted only truth, justice, he would have hit me again." But now he said nothing. He was not crying. He just stood there. "Answer me," his father said.

"Yes," he whispered. His father turned. 30

"Get on to bed. We'll be there tomorrow."

Tomorrow they were there. In the early afternoon the wagon stopped before a paintless two-room house identical almost with the dozen others it had stopped before even in the boy's ten years, and again, as on the other dozen occasions, his mother and aunt got down and began to unload the wagon, although his two sisters and his father and brother had not moved.

"Likely hit ain't fitten for hawgs," one of the sisters said.

"Nevertheless, fit it will and you'll hog it and like it," his father said. "Get out of them chairs and help your Ma unload."

The two sisters got down, big, bovine, in a flutter of cheap ribbons; one 35 of them drew from the jumbled wagon bed a battered lantern, the other a worn broom. His father handed the reins to the older son and began to climb stiffly over the wheel. "When they get unloaded, take the team to the barn and feed them." Then he said, and at first the boy thought he was still speaking to his brother: "Come with me."

"Me?" he said.

"Yes," his father said. "You."

"Abner," his mother said. His father paused and looked back — the harsh level stare beneath the shaggy, graying, irascible brows.

"I reckon I'll have a word with the man that aims to begin tomorrow owning me body and soul for the next eight months."

They went back up the road. A week ago — or before last night, that is 40 — he would have asked where they were going, but not now. His father had struck him before last night but never before had he paused afterward to explain why; it was as if the blow and the following calm, outrageous voice still rang, repercussed, divulging nothing to him save the terrible handicap of being young, the light weight of his few years, just heavy enough to prevent his soaring free of the world as it seemed to be ordered but not heavy enough to keep him footed solid in it, to resist it and try to change the course of its events.

Presently he could see the grove of oaks and cedars and the other flowering trees and shrubs where the house would be, though not the house yet. They walked beside a fence massed with honeysuckle and Cherokee roses and came to a gate swinging open between two brick pillars, and now, beyond a sweep of drive, he saw the house for the first time and at that instant he forgot his father and the terror and despair both, and even when he remembered his father again (who had not stopped) the terror and despair did not return. Because, for all the twelve movings, they had sojourned until now in a poor country, a land of small farms and fields and houses, and he had never seen a house like this before. *Hit's big as a courthouse* he thought quietly, with a surge of peace and joy whose reason he could not have thought into words, being too young for that: *They are safe from him. People whose lives are a part of this peace and dignity are beyond his touch, he no more to them than a buzzing wasp: capable of stinging for a little moment but that's all; the spell of this peace and dignity rendering even the barns and stable and cribs which belong to it impervious to the puny flames he might contrive . . .* this, the peace and joy, ebbing for an instant as he looked again at the stiff black back, the stiff and implacable limp of the figure which was not dwarfed by the house, for the reason that it had never looked big anywhere and which now, against the serene columned backdrop, had more than ever that impervious quality of something cut ruthlessly from tin, depthless, as though, sidewise to the sun, it would cast no shadow. Watching him, the boy remarked the absolutely undeviating course which his father held and saw the stiff foot come squarely down in a pile of fresh droppings where a horse had stood in the drive and which his father could have avoided by a simple change of stride. But it ebbed only for a moment, though he could not have thought this into words either, walking on in the spell of the house, which he could even want but without envy, without sorrow, certainly never with that ravening and jealous rage which unknown to him walked in the ironlike black coat before him: *Maybe he will feel it too. Maybe it will even change him now from what maybe he couldn't help but be.*

They crossed the portico. Now he could hear his father's stiff foot as it came down on the boards with clocklike finality, a sound out of all proportion to the displacement of the body it bore and which was not dwarfed either by the white door before it, as though it had attained to a sort of vicious and ravening minimum not to be dwarfed by anything — the flat, wide, black hat, the formal coat of broadcloth which had once been black but which had now that friction-glazed greenish cast of the bodies of old house flies, the lifted sleeve which was too large, the lifted hand like a curled claw. The door opened so promptly that the boy knew the Negro must have been watching them all the time, an old man with neat grizzled hair, in a linen jacket, who stood barring the door with his body, saying, "Wipe yo foots, white man, fo you come in here. Major ain't home nohow."

"Get out of my way, nigger," his father said, without heat too, flinging the door back and the Negro also and entering, his hat still on his head. And now the boy saw the prints of the stiff foot on the doorjamb and saw them appear on the pale rug behind the machinelike deliberation of the foot which seemed to bear (or transmit) twice the weight which the body compassed. The Negro was shouting "Miss Lula! Miss Lula!" somewhere behind them, then the boy, deluged as though by a warm wave by a suave turn of the carpeted stair and a pendant glitter of chandeliers and a mute gleam of gold frames, heard the swift feet and saw her too, a lady — perhaps he had never seen her like before either — in a gray, smooth gown with lace at the throat and an apron tied at the waist and the sleeves turned back, wiping cake or biscuit dough from her hands with a towel as she came up the hall, looking not at his father at all but at the tracks on the blond rug with an expression of incredulous amazement.

"I tried," the Negro cried. "I tole him to . . ."

"Will you please go away?" she said in a shaking voice. "Major de Spain is not at home. Will you please go away?"

His father had not spoken again. He did not speak again. He did not even look at her. He just stood stiff in the center of the rug, in his hat, the shaggy iron-gray brows twitching slightly above the pebble-colored eyes as he appeared to examine the house with brief deliberation. Then with the same deliberation he turned; the boy watched him pivot on the good leg and saw the stiff foot drag around the arc of the turning, leaving a final long and fading smear. His father never looked at it, he never once looked down at the rug. The Negro held the door. It closed behind them, upon the hysteric and indistinguishable woman-wail. His father stopped at the top of the steps and scraped his boot clean on the edge of it. At the gate he stopped again. He stood for a moment, planted stiffly on the stiff foot, looking back at the house. "Pretty and white, ain't it?" he said. "That's sweat. Nigger sweat. Maybe it ain't white enough yet to suit him. Maybe he wants to mix some white sweat with it."

Two hours later the boy was chopping wood behind the house within which his mother and aunt and the two sisters (the mother and aunt, not the two girls, he knew that; even at this distance and muffled by walls the flat loud voices of the two girls emanated an incorrigible idle inertia) were setting up the stove to prepare a meal, when he heard the hooves and saw the linen-clad man on a fine sorrel mare, whom he recognized even before he saw the rolled rug in front of the Negro youth following on a fat bay carriage horse — a suffused, angry face vanishing, still at full gallop, beyond the corner of the house where his father and brother were sitting in the two tilted chairs; and a moment later, almost before he could have put the axe down, he heard the hooves again and watched the sorrel mare go back out of the yard, already galloping again. Then his father began to shout one of the sisters' names, who presently emerged backward from the kitchen door dragging the rolled rug along the ground by one end while the other sister walked behind it.

"If you ain't going to tote, go on and set up the wash pot," the first said.

"You, Sarty!" the second shouted. "Set up the wash pot!" His father appeared at the door, framed against that shabbiness, as he had been against that other bland perfection, impervious to either, the mother's anxious face at his shoulder.

"Go on," the father said. "Pick it up." The two sisters stooped, broad, lethargic; stooping, they presented an incredible expanse of pale cloth and a flutter of tawdry ribbons.

"If I thought enough of a rug to have to git hit all the way from France I wouldn't keep hit where folks coming in would have to tromp on hit," the first said. They raised the rug.

"Abner," the mother said. "Let me do it."

"You go back and git dinner," his father said. "I'll tend to this."

From the woodpile through the rest of the afternoon the boy watched them, the rug spread flat in the dust beside the bubbling wash pot, the two sisters stooping over it with that profound and lethargic reluctance, while the father stood over them in turn, implacable and grim, driving them though never raising his voice again. He could smell the harsh homemade lye they were using; he saw his mother come to the door once and look toward them with an expression not anxious now but very like despair; he saw his father turn, and he fell to with the axe and saw from the corner of his eye his father raise from the ground a flattish fragment of field stone and examine it and return to the pot, and this time his mother actually spoke: "Abner. Abner. Please don't. Please, Abner."

Then he was done too. It was dusk; the whippoorwills had already 55 begun. He could smell coffee from the room where they would presently eat the cold food remaining from the mid-afternoon meal, though when he entered the house he realized they were having coffee again probably because there was a fire on the hearth, before which the rug now lay spread over the backs of the two chairs. The tracks of his father's foot were gone. Where they had been were now long, water-cloudy scoriations resembling the sporadic course of a lilliputian mowing machine.

It still hung there while they ate the cold food and then went to bed, scattered without order or claim up and down the two rooms, his mother in one bed, where his father would later lie, the older brother in the other, himself, the aunt, and the two sisters on pallets on the floor. But his father was not in bed yet. The last thing the boy remembered was the depthless, harsh silhouette of the hat and coat bending over the rug and it seemed to him that he had not even closed his eyes when the silhouette was standing over him, the fire almost dead behind it, the stiff foot prodding him awake. "Catch up the mule," his father said.

When he returned with the mule his father was standing in the black door, the rolled rug over his shoulder. "Ain't you going to ride?" he said.

"No. Give me your foot."

He bent his knee into his father's hand, the wiry, surprising power flowed smoothly, rising, he rising with it, on to the mule's bare back (they had owned a saddle once; the boy could remember it though not when or where) and with the same effortlessness his father swung the rug up in front of him. Now in the starlight they retraced the afternoon's path, up the dusty road rife with honeysuckle, through the gate and up the black tunnel of the drive to the lightless house, where he sat on the mule and felt the rough warp of the rug drag across his thighs and vanish.

"Don't you want me to help?" he whispered. His father did not answer 60 and now he heard again that stiff foot striking the hollow portico with that wooden and clocklike deliberation, that outrageous overstatement of the weight it carried. The rug, hunched, not flung (the boy could tell that even in the darkness) from his father's shoulder struck the angle of wall and floor with a sound unbelievably loud, thunderous, then the foot again, unhurried and enormous; a light came on in the house and the boy sat, tense, breathing steadily and quietly and just a little fast, though the foot itself did not increase its beat at all, descending the steps now; now the boy could see him.

"Don't you want to ride now?" he whispered. "We kin both ride now," the light within the house altering now, flaring up and sinking. *He's coming down the stairs now,* he thought. He had already ridden the mule up beside the horse block; presently his father was up behind him and he doubled the reins over and slashed the mule across the neck, but before the animal could begin to trot the hard, thin arm came around him, the hard, knotted hand jerking the mule back to a walk.

In the first red rays of the sun they were in the lot, putting plow gear on the mules. This time the sorrel mare was in the lot before he heard it at all, the rider collarless and even bareheaded, trembling, speaking in a shaking voice as the woman in the house had done, his father merely looking up once before stooping again to the hame he was buckling, so that the man on the mare spoke to his stooping back:

"You must realize you have ruined that rug. Wasn't there anybody here, any of your women . . ." he ceased, shaking, the boy watching him, the older brother leaning now in the stable door, chewing, blinking slowly and steadily at nothing apparently. "It cost a hundred dollars. But you never had a hundred dollars. You never will. So I'm going to charge you twenty bushels of corn against your crop. I'll add it in your contract and when you come to the commissary you can sign it. That won't keep Mrs. de Spain quiet but maybe it will teach you to wipe your feet off before you enter her house again."

Then he was gone. The boy looked at his father, who still had not spoken or even looked up again, who was now adjusting the logger-head in the hame.

"Pap," he said. His father looked at him — the inscrutable face, the   65
shaggy brows beneath which the gray eyes glinted coldly. Suddenly the boy went toward him, fast, stopping as suddenly. "You done the best you could!" he cried. "If he wanted hit done different why didn't he wait and tell you how? He won't git no twenty bushels! He won't git none! We'll gether hit and hide hit! I kin watch . . ."

"Did you put the cutter back in that straight stock like I told you?"

"No, sir," he said.

"Then go do it."

That was Wednesday. During the rest of that week he worked steadily, at what was within his scope and some which was beyond it, with an industry that did not need to be driven nor even commanded twice; he had this from his mother, with the difference that some at least of what he did he liked to do, such as splitting wood with the half-size axe which his mother and aunt had earned, or saved money somehow, to present him with at Christmas. In company with the two older women (and on one afternoon, even one of the sisters), he built pens for the shoat and the cow which were a part of his father's contract with the landlord, and one afternoon, his father being absent, gone somewhere on one of the mules, he went to the field.

They were running a middle buster now, his brother holding the plow   70
straight while he handled the reins, and walking beside the straining mule, the rich black soil shearing cool and damp against his bare ankles, he thought *Maybe this is the end of it. Maybe even that twenty bushels that seems hard to have to pay for just a rug will be a cheap price for him to stop forever and always from being what he used to be;* thinking, dreaming now, so that his brother had to speak sharply to him to mind the mule: *Maybe he even won't collect the twenty bushels. Maybe it will all add up and balance and vanish — corn, rug, fire; the terror and grief; the being pulled two ways like between two teams of horses — gone, done with for ever and ever.*

Then it was Saturday; he looked up from beneath the mule he was harnessing and saw his father in the black coat and hat. "Not that," his father said. "The wagon gear." And then, two hours later, sitting in the wagon bed behind his father and brother on the seat, the wagon accomplished a final curve, and he saw the weathered paintless store with its tattered tobacco- and patent-medicine posters and the tethered wagons and saddle animals below the gallery. He mounted the gnawed steps behind his father and brother, and there again was the lane of quiet, watching faces for the three of them to walk through. He saw the man in spectacles sitting at the plank table and he did not need to be told this was a Justice of the Peace; he sent one glare of fierce, exultant, partisan defiance at the man in collar and cravat now, whom he had seen but twice before in his life, and that on a galloping horse, who now wore on his face an expression not of rage but of amazed unbelief which the boy could not have known was at the incredible circumstance of being sued by one of his own tenants, and came and stood against his father and cried at the Justice: "He ain't done it! He ain't burnt . . ."

"Go back to the wagon," his father said.

"Burnt?" the Justice said. "Do I understand this rug was burned too?"

"Does anybody here claim it was?" his father said. "Go back to the wagon." But he did not, he merely retreated to the rear of the room, crowded as that other had been, but not to sit down this time, instead, to stand pressing among the motionless bodies, listening to the voices:

"And you claim twenty bushels of corn is too high for the damage you   75
did to the rug?"

"He brought the rug to me and said he wanted the tracks washed out of it. I washed the tracks out and took the rug back to him."

"But you didn't carry the rug back to him in the same condition it was in before you made the tracks on it."

His father did not answer, and now for perhaps half a minute there was no sound at all save that of breathing, the faint, steady suspiration of complete and intent listening.

"You decline to answer that, Mr. Snopes?" Again his father did not answer. "I'm going to find against you, Mr. Snopes. I'm going to find that you were responsible for the injury to Major de Spain's rug and hold you liable for it. But twenty bushels of corn seems a little high for a man in your circumstances to have to pay. Major de Spain claims it cost a hundred dollars. October corn will be worth about fifty cents. I figure that if Major de Spain can stand a ninety-five dollar loss on something he paid cash for, you can stand a five-dollar loss you haven't earned yet. I hold you in damages to Major de Spain to the amount of ten bushels of corn over and above your contract with him, to be paid to him out of your crop at gathering time. Court adjourned."

It had taken no time hardly, the morning was but half begun. He thought   80
they would return home and perhaps back to the field, since they were late, far behind all other farmers. But instead his father passed on behind the wagon, merely indicating with his hand for the older brother to follow with it, and crossed the road toward the blacksmith shop opposite, pressing on after his father, overtaking him, speaking, whispering up at the harsh, calm face beneath the weathered hat: "He won't git no ten bushels neither. He won't git one. We'll . . ." until his father glanced for an instant down at him, the face

absolutely calm, the grizzled eyebrows tangled above the cold eyes, the voice almost pleasant, almost gentle:

"You think so? Well, we'll wait till October anyway."

The matter of the wagon — the setting of a spoke or two and the tightening of the tires — did not take long either, the business of the tires accomplished by driving the wagon into the spring branch behind the shop and letting it stand there, the mules nuzzling into the water from time to time, and the boy on the seat with the idle reins, looking up the slope and through the sooty tunnel of the shed where the slow hammer rang and where his father sat on an upended cypress bolt, easily, either talking or listening, still sitting there when the boy brought the dripping wagon up out of the branch and halted it before the door.

"Take them on to the shade and hitch," his father said. He did so and returned. His father and the smith and a third man squatting on his heels inside the door were talking, about crops and animals; the boy, squatting too in the ammoniac dust and hoof-parings and scales of rust, heard his father tell a long and unhurried story out of the time before the birth of the older brother even when he had been a professional horsetrader. And then his father came up beside him where he stood before a tattered last year's circus poster on the other side of the store, gazing rapt and quiet at the scarlet horses, the incredible poisings and convolutions of tulle and tights and the painted leers of comedians, and said, "It's time to eat."

But not at home. Squatting beside his brother against the front wall, he watched his father emerge from the store and produce from a paper sack a segment of cheese and divide it carefully and deliberately into three with his pocket knife and produce crackers from the same sack. They all three squatted on the gallery and ate, slowly, without talking; then in the store again, they drank from a tin dipper tepid water smelling of the cedar bucket and of living beech trees. And still they did not go home. It was a horse lot this time, a tall rail fence upon and along which men stood and sat and out of which one by one horses were led, to be walked and trotted and then cantered back and forth along the road while the slow swapping and buying went on and the sun began to slant westward, they — the three of them — watching and listening, the older brother with his muddy eyes and his steady, inevitable tobacco, the father commenting now and then on certain of the animals, to no one in particular.

It was after sundown when they reached home. They ate supper by lamplight, then, sitting on the doorstep, the boy watched the night fully accomplish, listening to the whippoorwills and the frogs, when he heard his mother's voice: "Abner! No! No! Oh, God. Oh, God. Abner!" and he rose, whirled, and saw the altered light through the door where a candle stub now burned in a bottle neck on the table and his father, still in the hat and coat, at once formal and burlesque as though dressed carefully for some shabby and ceremonial violence, emptying the reservoir of the lamp back into the five-gallon kerosene can from which it had been filled, while the mother tugged at his arm until he shifted the lamp to the other hand and flung her back, not savagely or viciously, just hard, into the wall, her hands flung out against the wall for balance, her mouth open and in her face the same quality of hopeless despair as had been in her voice. Then his father saw him standing in the door.

"Go to the barn and get that can of oil we were oiling the wagon with," he said. The boy did not move. Then he could speak.

"What . . ." he cried. "What are you . . ."

"Go get that oil," his father said. "Go."

Then he was moving, running, outside the house, toward the stable: this the old habit, the old blood which he had not been permitted to choose for himself, which had been bequeathed him willy nilly and which had run for so long (and who knew where, battening on what of outrage and savagery and lust) before it came to him. *I could keep on,* he thought. *I could run on and on and never look back, never need to see his face again. Only I can't. I can't,* the rusted can in his hand now, the liquid sploshing in it as he ran back to the house and into it, into the sound of his mother's weeping in the next room, and handed the can to his father.

"Ain't you going to even send a nigger?" he cried. "At least you sent a nigger before!" 90

This time his father didn't strike him. The hand came even faster than the blow had, the same hand which had set the can on the table with almost excruciating care flashing from the can toward him too quick for him to follow it, gripping him by the back of his shirt and on to tiptoe before he had seen it quit the can, the face stooping at him in breathless and frozen ferocity, the cold, dead voice speaking over him to the older brother who leaned against the table, chewing with that steady, curious, sidewise motion of cows:

"Empty the can into the big one and go on. I'll catch up with you."

"Better tie him up to the bedpost," the brother said.

"Do like I told you," the father said. Then the boy was moving, his bunched shirt and the hard, bony hand between his shoulder-blades, his toes just touching the floor, across the room and into the other one, past the sisters sitting with spread heavy thighs in the two chairs over the cold hearth, and to where his mother and aunt sat side by side on the bed, the aunt's arms about his mother's shoulders.

"Hold him," the father said. The aunt made a startled movement. "Not 95 you," the father said. "Lennie. Take hold of him. I want to see you do it." His mother took him by the wrist. "You'll hold him better than that. If he gets loose don't you know what he is going to do? He will go up yonder." He jerked his head toward the road. "Maybe I'd better tie him."

"I'll hold him," his mother whispered.

"See you do then." Then his father was gone, the stiff foot heavy and measured upon the boards, ceasing at last.

Then he began to struggle. His mother caught him in both arms, he jerking and wrenching at them. He would be stronger in the end, he knew that. But he had no time to wait for it. "Lemme go!" he cried. "I don't want to have to hit you!"

"Let him go!" the aunt said. "If he don't go, before God, I am going up there myself!"

"Don't you see I can't?" his mother cried. "Sarty! Sarty! No! No! Help 100 me, Lizzie!"

Then he was free. His aunt grasped at him but it was too late. He whirled, running, his mother stumbled forward on to her knees behind him, crying to the nearer sister: "Catch him, Net! Catch him!" But that was too late too, the sister (the sisters were twins, born at the same time, yet either of them now gave the impression of being, encompassing as much living meat and volume and weight as any other two of the family) not yet having begun to rise from the chair, her head, face, alone merely turned, presenting to him in the flying instant an astonishing expanse of young female features untroubled by any surprise even, wearing only an expression of bovine interest. Then he was out of the room, out of the house, in the mild dust of the starlit road and the heavy rifeness of honeysuckle, the pale ribbon unspooling with terrific slowness under his running feet, reaching the gate at last and turning in, running, his heart and lungs drumming, on up the drive toward the lighted house, the lighted door. He did not knock, he burst in, sobbing for breath, incapable for the moment of speech; he saw the astonished face of the Negro in the linen jacket without knowing when the Negro had appeared.

"De Spain!" he cried, panted. "Where's . . ." then he saw the white man too emerging from a white door down the hall. "Barn!" he cried. "Barn!"

"What?" the white man said. "Barn?"

"Yes!" the boy cried. "Barn!"

"Catch him!" the white man shouted.   105

But it was too late this time too. The Negro grasped his shirt, but the entire sleeve, rotten with washing, carried away, and he was out that door too and in the drive again, and had actually never ceased to run even while he was screaming into the white man's face.

Behind him the white man was shouting, "My horse! Fetch my horse!" and he thought for an instant of cutting across the park and climbing the fence into the road, but he did not know the park nor how high the vine-massed fence might be and he dared not risk it. So he ran on down the drive, blood and breath roaring; presently he was in the road again though he could not see it. He could not hear either: the galloping mare was almost upon him before he heard her, and even then he held his course, as if the very urgency of his wild grief and need must in a moment more find him wings, waiting until the ultimate instant to hurl himself aside and into the weed-choked roadside ditch as the horse thundered past and on, for an instant in furious silhouette against the stars, the tranquil early summer night sky which, even before the shape of the horse and rider vanished, stained abruptly and violently upward: a long, swirling roar incredible and soundless, blotting the stars, and he springing up and into the road again, running again, knowing it was too late yet still running even after he heard the shot and an instant later, two shots, pausing now without knowing he had ceased to run, crying "Pap! Pap!", running again before he knew he had begun to run, stumbling, tripping over something and scrabbling up again without ceasing to run, looking backward over his shoulder at the glare as he got up, running on among the invisible trees, panting, sobbing, "Father! Father!"

At midnight he was sitting on the crest of a hill. He did not know it was midnight and he did not know how far he had come. But there was no glare behind him now and he sat now, his back toward what he had called home for four days anyhow, his face toward the dark woods which he would enter when breath was strong again, small, shaking steadily in the chill darkness, hugging himself into the remainder of his thin, rotten shirt, the grief and despair now no longer terror and fear but just grief and despair. *Father. My father,* he thought.

"He was brave!" he cried suddenly, aloud but not loud, no more than a whisper. "He was! He was in the war! He was in Colonel Sartoris' cav'ry!" not knowing that his father had gone to that war a private in the fine old European sense, wearing no uniform, admitting the authority of and giving fidelity to no man or army or flag, going to war as Malbrouck himself did: for booty — it meant nothing and less than nothing to him if it were enemy booty or his own.

The slow constellations wheeled on. It would be dawn and then sun-up after a while and he would be hungry. But that would be tomorrow and now he was only cold, and walking would cure that. His breathing was easier now and he decided to get up and go on, and then he found that he had been asleep because he knew it was almost dawn, the night almost over. He could tell that from the whippoorwills. They were everywhere now among the dark trees below him, constant and inflectioned and ceaseless, so that, as the instant for giving over to the day birds drew nearer and nearer, there was no interval at all between them. He got up. He was a little stiff, but walking would cure that too as it would the cold, and soon there would be the sun. He went on down the hill, toward the dark woods within which the liquid silver voices of the birds called unceasing — the rapid and urgent beating of the urgent and quiring heart of the late spring night. He did not look back.

QUESTIONS

1. After delivering his warning to Major de Spain, the boy Snopes does not actually witness what happens to his father and brother, nor what happens to the Major's barn. But what do you assume does happen? What evidence is given in the story?
2. What do you understand to be Faulkner's opinion of Abner Snopes? Make a guess, indicating details in the story that convey attitudes.
3. Which adjectives best describe the general tone of the story: calm, amused, disinterested, scornful, marveling, excited, impassioned? Point out passages that may be so described. What do you notice about the style in which these passages are written?
4. In tone and style, how does "Barn Burning" compare with Faulkner's story "A Rose for Emily" (Chapter Two)? To what do you attribute any differences?
5. Suppose that, instead of "Barn Burning," Faulkner had written another story told by Abner Snopes in the first person. Why would such a story need a style different from that of "Barn Burning"? (Suggestion: Notice Faulkner's descriptions of Abner Snopes's voice.)
6. Although "Barn Burning" takes place some thirty years after the Civil War, how does the war figure in it?

Alice Walker

EVERYDAY USE   1973

Alice Walker, a leading black writer and social activist, was born in 1944 in Eatonton, Georgia, the youngest of eight children. Her father, a sharecropper and dairy farmer, usually earned about $300 a year; her mother helped by working as a maid. Both entertained their children by telling stories.

When Alice Walker was eight, accidentally struck by a pellet from a brother's BB gun, she lost the sight of one eye because the Walkers had no car to rush her to the hospital. Later she attended Spelman College in Atlanta and finished college at Sarah Lawrence on a scholarship. While working for the civil rights movement in Mississippi, she met a young lawyer, Melvyn Leventhal; and in 1967 they settled in Jackson, Mississippi, the first legally married interracial couple in town. They returned to New York in 1974, and were later divorced. First known as a poet, Walker has published four books of her verse. She also has edited a collection of the work of neglected black woman author Zora Neale Hurston, and has written a study of Langston Hughes. She has collected her essays as In Search of Our Mothers' Gardens: Womanist Prose *(1983), in which she recalls her mother and addresses her own daughter. (By* womanist *she means "black feminist.") But the largest part of Walker's reading audience knows her fiction: two story collections,* In Love and Trouble *(1973), from which "Everyday Use" is taken, and* You Can't Keep a Good Woman Down *(1981); and her novels,* The Third Life of Grange Copeland *(1970);* Meridian *(1976); and, best known,* The Color Purple *(1982), which won a Pulitzer prize. In 1985 Steven Spielberg made it into a film.*

for your grandmama

I will wait for her in the yard that Maggie and I made so clean and wavy yesterday afternoon. A yard like this is more comfortable than most people know. It is not just a yard. It is like an extended living room. When the hard clay is swept clean as a floor and the fine sand around the edges lined with tiny, irregular grooves, anyone can come and sit and look up into the elm tree and wait for the breezes that never come inside the house.

Maggie will be nervous until after her sister goes: she will stand hopelessly in corners, homely and ashamed of the burn scars down her arms and legs, eying her sister with a mixture of envy and awe. She thinks her sister has held life always in the palm of one hand, that "no" is a word the world never learned to say to her.

You've no doubt seen those TV shows where the child who has "made it" is confronted, as a surprise, by her own mother and father, tottering in weakly from backstage. (A pleasant surprise, of course: What would they do if parent and child came on the show only to curse out and insult each other?) On TV mother and child embrace and smile into each other's faces. Sometimes the mother and father weep, the child wraps them in her arms and leans across the table to tell how she would not have made it without their help. I have seen these programs°.

Sometimes I dream a dream in which Dee and I are suddenly brought

these programs: The NBC television show "This Is Your Life," with Ralph Edwards as producer and master of ceremonies, publicly and often tearfully reunited people with friends, relatives, and teachers they had not seen in years. It was aired 1952 – 61 and 1970 – 73.

together on a TV program of this sort. Out of a dark and soft-seated limousine I am ushered into a bright room filled with many people. There I meet a smiling, gray, sporty man like Johnny Carson who shakes my hand and tells me what a fine girl I have. Then we are on the stage and Dee is embracing me with tears in her eyes. She pins on my dress a large orchid, even though she has told me once that she thinks orchids are tacky flowers.

In real life I am a large, big-boned woman with rough, man-working hands. In the winter I wear flannel nightgowns to bed and overalls during the day. I can kill and clean a hog as mercilessly as a man. My fat keeps me hot in zero weather. I can work outside all day, breaking ice to get water for washing; I can eat pork liver cooked over the open fire minutes after it comes steaming from the hog. One winter I knocked a bull calf straight in the brain between the eyes with a sledge hammer and had the meat hung up to chill before nightfall. But of course all this does not show on television. I am the way my daughter would want me to be: a hundred pounds lighter, my skin like an uncooked barley pancake. My hair glistens in the hot bright lights. Johnny Carson has much to do to keep up with my quick and witty tongue.

But that is a mistake. I know even before I wake up. Who ever knew a Johnson with a quick tongue? Who can even imagine me looking a strange white man in the eye? It seems to me I have talked to them always with one foot raised in flight, with my head turned in whichever way is farthest from them. Dee, though. She would always look anyone in the eye. Hesitation was no part of her nature.

"How do I look, Mama?" Maggie says, showing just enough of her thin body enveloped in pink skirt and red blouse for me to know she's there, almost hidden by the door.

"Come out into the yard," I say.

Have you ever seen a lame animal, perhaps a dog run over by some careless person rich enough to own a car, sidle up to someone who is ignorant enough to be kind to him? That is the way my Maggie walks. She has been like this, chin on chest, eyes on ground, feet in shuffle, ever since the fire that burned the other house to the ground.

Dee is lighter than Maggie, with nicer hair and a fuller figure. She's a woman now, though sometimes I forget. How long ago was it that the other house burned? Ten, twelve years? Sometimes I can still hear the flames and feel Maggie's arms sticking to me, her hair smoking and her dress falling off her in little black papery flakes. Her eyes seemed stretched open, blazed open by the flames reflected in them. And Dee. I see her standing off under the sweet gum tree she used to dig gum out of; a look of concentration on her face as she watched the last dingy gray board of the house fall in toward the red-hot brick chimney. Why don't you do a dance around the ashes? I'd wanted to ask her. She had hated the house that much.

I used to think she hated Maggie, too. But that was before we raised the money, the church and me, to send her to Augusta to school. She used to read to us without pity; forcing words, lies, other folks' habits, whole lives upon us two, sitting trapped and ignorant underneath her voice. She washed us in a river of make-believe, burned us with a lot of knowledge we didn't necessarily need to know. Pressed us to her with the serious way she read, to shove us away at just the moment, like dimwits, we seemed about to understand.

Dee wanted nice things. A yellow organdy dress to wear to her graduation from high school; black pumps to match a green suit she'd made from an old suit somebody gave me. She was determined to stare down any disaster in her efforts. Her eyelids would not flicker for minutes at a time. Often I fought off the temptation to shake her. At sixteen she had a style of her own, and knew what style was.

I never had an education myself. After second grade the school was closed down. Don't ask me why: in 1927 colored asked fewer questions than they do now. Sometimes Maggie reads to me. She stumbles along good-naturedly but can't see well. She knows she is not bright. Like good looks and money, quickness passed her by. She will marry John Thomas (who has mossy teeth in an earnest face) and then I'll be free to sit here and I guess just sing church songs to myself. Although I never was a good singer. Never could carry a tune. I was always better at a man's job. I used to love to milk till I was hooked in the side in '49. Cows are soothing and slow and don't bother you, unless you try to milk them the wrong way.

I have deliberately turned my back on the house. It is three rooms, just like the one that burned, except the roof is tin; they don't make shingle roofs any more. There are no real windows, just some holes cut in the sides, like the portholes in a ship, but not round and not square, with rawhide holding the shutters up on the outside. This house is in a pasture, too, like the other one. No doubt when Dee sees it she will want to tear it down. She wrote me once that no matter where we "choose" to live, she will manage to come see us. But she will never bring her friends. Maggie and I thought about this and Maggie asked me, "Mama, when did Dee ever *have* any friends?"

She had a few. Furtive boys in pink shirts hanging about on washday 15 after school. Nervous girls who never laughed. Impressed with her they worshiped the well-turned phrase, the cute shape, the scalding humor that erupted like bubbles in lye. She read to them.

When she was courting Jimmy T she didn't have much time to pay to us, but turned all her faultfinding power on him. He *flew* to marry a cheap city girl from a family of ignorant flashy people. She hardly had time to recompose herself.

When she comes I will meet — but there they are!

Maggie attempts to make a dash for the house, in her shuffling way, but I stay her with my hand. "Come back here," I say. And she stops and tries to dig a well in the sand with her toe.

It is hard to see them clearly through the strong sun. But even the first glimpse of leg out of the car tells me it is Dee. Her feet were always neat-looking, as if God himself had shaped them with a certain style. From the other side of the car comes a short, stocky man. Hair is all over his head a foot long and hanging from his chin like a kinky mule tail. I hear Maggie suck in her breath. "Uhnnnh," is what it sounds like. Like when you see the wriggling end of a snake just in front of your foot on the road. "Uhnnnh."

Dee next. A dress down to the ground, in this hot weather. A dress so loud 20 it hurts my eyes. There are yellows and oranges enough to throw back the light of the sun. I feel my whole face warming from the heat waves it throws out. Earrings gold, too, and hanging down to her shoulders. Bracelets dangling and making noises when she moves her arm up to shake the folds of the dress out of her armpits. The dress is loose and flows, and as she walks closer, I like it. I hear Maggie go "Uhnnnh" again. It is her sister's hair. It stands straight up like the wool on a sheep. It is black as night and around the edges are two long pigtails that rope about like small lizards disappearing behind her ears.

"Wa-su-zo-Tean-o!"° she says, coming on in that gliding way the dress makes her move. The short stocky fellow with the hair to his navel is all grinning and he follows up with "Asalamalakim°, my mother and sister!" He moves to hug Maggie but she falls back, right up against the back of my chair. I feel her trembling there and when I look up I see the perspiration falling off her chin.

"Don't get up," says Dee. Since I am stout it takes something of a push. You can see me trying to move a second or two before I make it. She turns, showing white heels through her sandals, and goes back to the car. Out she peeks next with a Polaroid. She stoops down quickly and lines up picture after picture of me sitting there in front of the house with Maggie cowering behind me. She never takes a shot without making sure the house is included. When a cow comes nibbling around the edge of the yard she snaps it and me and Maggie *and* the house. Then she puts the Polaroid in the back seat of the car, and comes up and kisses me on the forehead.

Meanwhile Asalamalakim is going through motions with Maggie's hand. Maggie's hand is as limp as a fish, and probably as cold, despite the sweat, and she keeps trying to pull it back. It looks like Asalamalakim wants to shake hands but wants to do it fancy. Or maybe he don't know how people shake hands. Anyhow, he soon gives up on Maggie.

"Well," I say. "Dee."

"No, Mama," she says. "Not 'Dee,' Wangero Leewanika Kemanjo!"   25

"What happened to 'Dee'?" I wanted to know.

"She's dead," Wangero said. "I couldn't bear it any longer, being named after the people who oppress me."

"You know as well as me you was named after your aunt Dicie," I said. Dicie is my sister. She named Dee. We called her "Big Dee" after Dee was born.

"But who was *she* named after?" asked Wangero.

"I guess after Grandma Dee," I said.   30

"And who was she named after?" asked Wangero.

"Her mother," I said, and saw Wangero was getting tired. "That's about as far back as I can trace it," I said. Though, in fact, I probably could have carried it back beyond the Civil War through the branches.

"Well," said Asalamalakim, "there you are."

"Uhnnnh," I heard Maggie say.

"There I was not," I said, "before 'Dicie' cropped up in our family, so   35 why should I try to trace it that far back?"

Wa-su-zo-Tean-o!: Salutation in Swahili, an African language. Notice that Dee has to sound it out, syllable by syllable.

Asalamalakim: Salutation in Arabic: "Peace be upon you."

He just stood there grinning, looking down on me like somebody inspecting a Model A car°. Every once in a while he and Wangero sent eye signals over my head.

"How do you pronounce this name?" I asked.

"You don't have to call me by it if you don't want to," said Wangero.

"Why shouldn't I?" I asked. "If that's what you want us to call you, we'll call you."

"I know it might sound awkward at first," said Wangero. 40

"I'll get used to it," I said. "Ream it out again."

Well, soon we got the name out of the way. Asalamalakim had a name twice as long and three times as hard. After I tripped over it two or three times he told me to just call him Hakim-a-barber. I wanted to ask him was he a barber, but I didn't really think he was, so I didn't ask.

"You must belong to those beef-cattle peoples down the road," I said. They said "Asalamalakim" when they met you, too, but they didn't shake hands. Always too busy: feeding the cattle, fixing the fences, putting up salt-lick shelters, throwing down hay. When the white folks poisoned some of the herd the men stayed up all night with rifles in their hands. I walked a mile and a half just to see the sight.

Hakim-a-barber said, "I accept some of their doctrines, but farming and raising cattle is not my style." (They didn't tell me, and I didn't ask, whether Wangero (Dee) had really gone and married him.)

We sat down to eat and right away he said he didn't eat collards and pork 45 was unclean. Wangero, though, went on through the chitlins and corn bread, the greens and everything else. She talked a blue streak over the sweet potatoes. Everything delighted her. Even the fact that we still used the benches her daddy made for the table when we couldn't afford to buy chairs.

"Oh, Mama!" she cried. Then turned to Hakim-a-barber. "I never knew how lovely these benches are. You can feel the rump prints," she said, running her hands underneath her and along the bench. Then she gave a sigh and her hand closed over Grandma Dee's butter dish. "That's it!" she said. "I knew there was something I wanted to ask you if I could have." She jumped up from the table and went over in the corner where the churn stood, the milk in it clabber° by now. She looked at the churn and looked at it.

"This churn top is what I need," she said. "Didn't Uncle Buddy whittle it out of a tree you all used to have?"

"Yes," I said.

"Uh huh," she said happily. "And I want the dasher, too."

"Uncle Buddy whittle that, too?" asked the barber. 50

Dee (Wangero) looked up at me.

"Aunt Dee's first husband whittled the dash," said Maggie so low you almost couldn't hear her. "His name was Henry, but they called him Stash."

"Maggie's brain is like an elephant's," Wangero said, laughing. "I can use the churn top as a centerpiece for the alcove table," she said, sliding a plate over the churn, "and I'll think of something artistic to do with the dasher."

When she finished wrapping the dasher the handle stuck out. I took it

Model A car: popular low-priced automobile introduced by the Ford Motor Company in 1927.
clabber: sour milk or buttermilk.

for a moment in my hands. You didn't even have to look close to see where hands pushing the dasher up and down to make butter had left a kind of sink in the wood. In fact, there were a lot of small sinks; you could see where thumbs and fingers had sunk into the wood. It was beautiful light yellow wood, from a tree that grew in the yard where Big Dee and Stash had lived.

After dinner Dee (Wangero) went to the trunk at the foot of my bed and started rifling through it. Maggie hung back in the kitchen over the dishpan. Out came Wangero with two quilts. They had been pieced by Grandma Dee and then Big Dee and me had hung them on the quilt frames on the front porch and quilted them. One was in the Lone Star pattern. The other was Walk Around the Mountain. In both of them were scraps of dresses Grandma Dee had worn fifty and more years ago. Bits and pieces of Grandpa Jarrell's Paisley shirts. And one teeny faded blue piece, about the size of a penny matchbox, that was from Great Grandpa Ezra's uniform that he wore in the Civil War.

"Mama," Wangero said sweet as a bird. "Can I have these old quilts?"

I heard something fall in the kitchen, and a minute later the kitchen door slammed.

"Why don't you take one or two of the others?" I asked. "These old things was just done by me and Big Dee from some tops your grandma pieced before she died."

"No," said Wangero. "I don't want those. They are stitched around the borders by machine."

"That'll make them last better," I said.

"That's not the point," said Wangero. "These are all pieces of dresses Grandma used to wear. She did all this stitching by hand. Imagine!" She held the quilts securely in her arms, stroking them.

"Some of the pieces, like those lavender ones, come from old clothes her mother handed down to her," I said, moving up to touch the quilts. Dee (Wangero) moved back just enough so that I couldn't reach the quilts. They already belonged to her.

"Imagine!" she breathed again, clutching them closely to her bosom.

"The truth is," I said, "I promised to give them quilts to Maggie, for when she marries John Thomas."

She gasped like a bee had stung her.

"Maggie can't appreciate these quilts!" she said. "She'd probably be backward enough to put them to everyday use."

"I reckon she would," I said. "God knows I been saving 'em for long enough with nobody using 'em. I hope she will!" I didn't want to bring up how I had offered Dee (Wangero) a quilt when she went away to college. Then she had told me they were old-fashioned, out of style.

"But they're *priceless!*" she was saying now, furiously; for she has a temper. "Maggie would put them on the bed and in five years they'd be in rags. Less than that!"

"She can always make some more," I said. "Maggie knows how to quilt."

Dee (Wangero) looked at me with hatred. "You just will not understand. The point is these quilts, *these* quilts!"

"Well," I said, stumped. "What would *you* do with them?"

"Hang them," she said. As if that was the only thing you *could* do with quilts.

Maggie by now was standing in the door. I could almost hear the sound her feet made as they scraped over each other.

"She can have them, Mama," she said, like somebody used to never winning anything, or having anything reserved for her. "I can 'member Grandma Dee without the quilts."

I looked at her hard. She had filled her bottom lip with checkerberry snuff and it gave her face a kind of dopey, hangdog look. It was Grandma Dee and Big Dee who taught her how to quilt herself. She stood there with her scarred hands hidden in the folds of her skirt. She looked at her sister with something like fear but she wasn't mad at her. This was Maggie's portion. This was the way she knew God to work.

When I looked at her like that something hit me in the top of my head and ran down to the soles of my feet. Just like when I'm in church and the spirit of God touches me and I get happy and shout. I did something I never had done before: hugged Maggie to me, then dragged her on into the room, snatched the quilts out of Miss Wangero's hands and dumped them into Maggie's lap. Maggie just sat there on my bed with her mouth open.

"Take one or two of the others," I said to Dee.

But she turned without a word and went out to Hakim-a-barber.

"You just don't understand," she said, as Maggie and I came out to the car.

"What don't I understand?" I wanted to know.

"Your heritage," she said. And then she turned to Maggie, kissed her, and said, "You ought to try to make something of yourself, too, Maggie. It's really a new day for us. But from the way you and Mama still live you'd never know it."

She put on some sunglasses that hid everything above the tip of her nose and her chin.

Maggie smiled; maybe at the sunglasses. But a real smile, not scared. After we watched the car dust settle I asked Maggie to bring me a dip of snuff. And then the two of us sat there just enjoying, until it was time to go in the house and go to bed.

QUESTIONS

1. What is the basic conflict in "Everyday Use"?
2. What is the tone of Walker's story? By what means does the author communicate it?
3. From whose point of view is "Everyday Use" told? What does the story gain from this point of view — instead of, say, from the point of view of Dee (Wangero)?
4. How does the narrator of the story feel toward Dee? What seems to be Dee's present attitude toward her mother and sister?
5. What do you take to be the author's attitude toward each of her characters? How does she convey it?
6. What levels of meaning do you find in the story's title?
7. Contrast Dee's attitude toward her heritage with the attitudes of her mother and sister. How much truth is there in Dee's accusation that her mother and sister don't understand their heritage?
8. Does the knowledge that "Everyday Use" was written by a black writer in any way influence your reactions to it? Explain.

Suggestions for Writing

1. This is an exercise in communicating your feelings. Choose a subject you greatly admire — some person, place, film, sports team, or work of fiction — and in a paragraph, describe it so that you forcefully indicate your admiration. Then rewrite the paragraph from the point of view of someone who *detests* your subject. Try not to declare "I love this" or "I hate this," but choose details and characteristics of your subject that make the tone of each paragraph clear.

2. Consider a short story in which the narrator is the central character (perhaps "A & P," "First Confession," "Araby," "I Stand Here Ironing," "My Man Bovanne," or "The Wife's Story." In a brief essay, show how the character of the narrator determines the language of the story. What words or phrases, slang expressions, figures of speech, local or regional speech do you find the narrator using? In general, how would you describe the style of the story?

3. Take a short story or novel not included in this book: one by a writer of high reputation and distinctive style, such as William Faulkner, Ernest Hemingway, Flannery O'Connor, Joyce Carol Oates, or another writer suggested by your instructor. Write a passage of your own, and insert it somewhere in the story. Imitate the writer's style as closely as possible, paying attention to vocabulary, length and variety of sentences, amount of description, and tone. Then type out two or three pages of the story, including your forgery, and make copies for the other members of the class. See if anyone can tell where the writer's prose stops and yours begins.

6 Irony

If a friend declares, "Oh, sure, I just *love* to have four papers fall due on the same day," you detect that the statement contains **irony.** This is **verbal irony,** the most familiar kind, in which we understand the speaker's meaning to be far from the usual meaning of the words — in this case, quite the opposite. (When the irony is, as here, a somewhat sour statement tinged with mockery, it is usually called **sarcasm.**)

Irony, of course, occurs in writing as well as in conversation. When in a comic moment in Isaac Bashevis Singer's "Gimpel the Fool" (Chapter Four) the sexton announces, "The wealthy Reb Gimpel invites the congregation to a feast in honor of the birth of a son," the people at the synagogue burst into laughter. They know that Gimpel, in contrast to the sexton's words, is not a wealthy man but a humble baker; that the son is not his own but his wife's lover's; and that the birth brings no honor to anybody. Verbal irony, then, implies a contrast or discrepancy between what is *said* and what is *meant*. But stories often contain other kinds of irony besides such verbal irony. A situation, for example, can be ironic if it contains some wry contrast or incongruity. In James Thurber's "The Catbird Seat" (Chapter Four), it is an **ironic situation** that the mildest, most apparently harmless man in an office should plot murder, claim to be a heroin addict, and cause the firing of the office tyrant.

An entire story may be told from an **ironic point of view.** Whenever we sense a sharp distinction between the narrator of a story and the author, irony is likely to occur — especially when the narrator is telling us something that we are clearly expected to doubt or to interpret very differently. In "Gimpel the Fool," Gimpel (who tells his own story) keeps insisting on trusting people; but the author, a shrewder observer, makes it clear to us that the people Gimpel trusts are only tricking him. (This irony, by the way, does not prevent Gimpel from expressing a few things that Isaac Bashevis Singer believes, and perhaps expects us to believe.) And when we read Hemingway's "A Clean, Well-Lighted Place," surely we feel that most of the time the older waiter speaks for the author. Though the waiter gives us a respectful, compassionate view of a lonely old man, and we don't doubt that the view is Hemingway's, still, in the closing lines of the story we are reminded that author and waiter are not identical. Musing on the sleepless night ahead of him, the waiter tries to shrug off his problem — "After all, it is probably only insomnia" — but the reader, who recalls the waiter's bleak view of *nada,* nothingness, knows that it certainly isn't mere insomnia that keeps him awake, but a dread of solitude and death. At that crucial moment, Hemingway and the older waiter part company, and we perceive an ironic point of view, and also a verbal irony, "After all, it is probably only insomnia."

Storytellers are sometimes fond of ironic twists of fate — developments that reveal a terrible distance between what people deserve and what they get, between what is and what ought to be. In the novels of Thomas Hardy, some hostile fate keeps playing tricks to thwart the main characters. In *Tess of the D'Urbervilles,* an all-important letter, thrust under a door, by chance slides beneath a carpet and is not received. An obvious prank of fate occurs in O. Henry's short story "The Gift of the Magi," in which a young wife sells her beautiful hair to buy her poor young husband a watch chain for Christmas, not knowing that, to buy combs for her hair, he has sold his watch. Such an irony is sometimes called an **irony of fate** or a **cosmic irony,** for it suggests that some malicious fate (or other spirit in the universe) is deliberately frustrating human efforts. (In O. Henry's story, however, the twist of fate leads to a happy ending; for the author suggests that, by their futile sacrifices, the lovers are drawn closer together.) Evidently, there is an irony of fate in the servant's futile attempt to escape Death in the fable "The Appointment in Samarra."

To notice an irony gives pleasure. It may move us to laughter, make us feel wonder, or arouse our sympathy. By so involving us, irony — whether in a statement, a situation, an unexpected event, or a point of view — can render a story more likely to strike us, to affect us, and to be remembered.

Shirley Jackson
THE LOTTERY   1948

Shirley Jackson (1919 – 1965), a native of San Francisco, moved in her teens to Rochester, New York. She started college at the University of Rochester, but had to drop out, stricken by severe depression, a problem that was to recur at intervals throughout her life. Later she was graduated from Syracuse University. With her husband Stanley Edgar Hyman, a literary critic, she settled in Bennington, Vermont, in a sprawling house built in the nineteenth century. There Jackson conscientiously set herself to produce a fixed number of words each day. She wrote novels: The Road Through the Wall *(1948), and three psychological thrillers —* Hangsaman *(1951),* The Haunting of Hill House *(1959), and* We Have Always Lived in the

Castle (1962). She wrote light, witty articles for Good Housekeeping *and other popular magazines about the horrors of housekeeping and rearing four children, collected in* Life among the Savages *(1953) and* Raising Demons *(1957); but she claimed to have written these only for money. When in 1948 "The Lottery" appeared in* The New Yorker, *that issue of the magazine quickly sold out. Her purpose in writing the story, Jackson declared, had been "to shock the story's readers with a graphic demonstration of the pointless violence and general inhumanity in their own lives."*

The morning of June 27th was clear and sunny, with the fresh warmth of a full-summer day; the flowers were blossoming profusely and the grass was richly green. The people of the village began to gather in the square, between the post office and the bank, around ten o'clock; in some towns there were so many people that the lottery took two days and had to be started on June 26th, but in this village, where there were only about three hundred people, the whole lottery took less than two hours, so it could begin at ten o'clock in the morning and still be through in time to allow the villagers to get home for noon dinner.

The children assembled first, of course. School was recently over for the summer, and the feeling of liberty sat uneasily on most of them; they tended to gather together quietly for a while before they broke into boisterous play, and their talk was still of the classroom and the teacher, of books and reprimands. Bobby Martin had already stuffed his pockets full of stones, and the other boys soon followed his example, selecting the smoothest and roundest stones; Bobby and Harry Jones and Dickie Delacroix — the villagers pronounced this name "Dellacroy" — eventually made a great pile of stones in one corner of the square and guarded it against the raids of the other boys. The girls stood aside, talking among themselves, looking over their shoulders at the boys, and the very small children rolled in the dust or clung to the hands of their older brothers or sisters.

Soon the men began to gather, surveying their own children, speaking of planting and rain, tractors and taxes. They stood together, away from the pile of stones in the corner, and their jokes were quiet and they smiled rather than laughed. The women, wearing faded house dresses and sweaters, came shortly after their menfolk. They greeted one another and exchanged bits of gossip as they went to join their husbands. Soon the women, standing by their husbands, began to call to their children, and the children came reluctantly, having to be called four or five times. Bobby Martin ducked under his mother's grasping hand and ran, laughing, back to the pile of stones. His father spoke up sharply, and Bobby came quickly and took his place between his father and his oldest brother.

The lottery was conducted — as were the square dances, the teenage club, the Halloween program — by Mr. Summers, who had time and energy to devote to civic activities. He was a roundfaced, jovial man and he ran the coal business, and people were sorry for him, because he had no children and his wife was a scold. When he arrived in the square, carrying the black wooden box, there was a murmur of conversation among the villagers and he waved and called, "Little late today, folks." The postmaster, Mr. Graves, followed him, carrying a three-legged stool, and the stool was put in the center of the square and Mr. Summers set the black box down on it. The villagers kept their distance, leaving a space between themselves and the stool, and when Mr. Summers said, "Some of you fellows want to give me a hand?" there was a hesitation before two men, Mr. Martin and his oldest son, Baxter, came forward to hold the box steady on the stool while Mr. Summers stirred up the papers inside it.

The original paraphernalia for the lottery had been lost long ago, and the black box now resting on the stool had been put into use even before Old Man Warner, the oldest man in town, was born. Mr. Summers spoke frequently to the villagers about making a new box, but no one liked to upset even as much tradition as was represented by the black box. There was a story that the present box had been made with some pieces of the box that had preceded it, the one that had been constructed when the first people settled down to make a village here. Every year, after the lottery, Mr. Summers began talking again about a new box, but every year the subject was allowed to fade off without anything's being done. The black box grew shabbier each year; by now it was no longer completely black but splintered badly along one side to show the original wood color, and in some places faded or stained.

Mr. Martin and his oldest son, Baxter, held the black box securely on the stool until Mr. Summers had stirred the papers thoroughly with his hand. Because so much of the ritual had been forgotten or discarded, Mr. Summers had been successful in having slips of paper substituted for the chips of wood that had been used for generations. Chips of wood, Mr. Summers had argued, had been all very well when the village was tiny, but now that the population was more than three hundred and likely to keep on growing, it was necessary to use something that would fit more easily into the black box. The night before the lottery, Mr. Summers and Mr. Graves made up the slips of paper and put them in the box, and it was then taken to the safe of Mr. Summers's coal company and locked up until Mr. Summers was ready to take it to the square next morning. The rest of the year, the box was put away, sometimes one place, sometimes another; it had spent one year in Mr. Graves's barn and another year underfoot in the post office, and sometimes it was set on a shelf in the Martin grocery and left there.

There was a great deal of fussing to be done before Mr. Summers declared the lottery open. There were lists to make up — of heads of families, heads of households in each family, members of each household in each family. There was the proper swearing-in of Mr. Summers by the postmaster, as the official of the lottery; at one time, some people remembered, there had been a recital of some sort, performed by the official of the lottery, a perfunctory, tuneless chant that had been rattled off duly each year; some people believed that the official of the lottery used to stand just so when he said or sang it, others believed that he was supposed to walk among the people, but years and years ago this part of the ritual had been allowed to lapse. There had been, also, a ritual salute, which the official of the lottery had had to use in addressing each person who came up to draw from the box, but this also had changed with time, until now it was felt necessary only for the official to speak to each person approaching. Mr. Summers was very good at all this; in his clean white shirt and blue jeans, with one hand resting carelessly on the black box, he seemed very proper and important as he talked interminably to Mr. Graves and the Martins.

Just as Mr. Summers finally left off talking and turned to the assembled villagers, Mrs. Hutchinson came hurriedly along the path to the square, her sweater thrown over her shoulders, and slid into place in the back of the crowd. "Clean forgot what day it was," she said to Mrs. Delacroix, who stood next to her, and they both laughed softly. "Thought my old man was out back stacking wood," Mrs. Hutchinson went on, "and then I looked out the window and the kids were gone, and then I remembered it was the twenty-seventh and came a-running." She dried her hands on her apron, and Mrs. Delacroix said, "You're in time, though. They're still talking away up there."

Mrs. Hutchinson craned her neck to see through the crowd and found her husband and children standing near the front. She tapped Mrs. Delacroix on the arm as a farewell and began to make her way through the crowd. The people separated good-humoredly to let her through; two or three people said, in voices just loud enough to be heard across the crowd, "Here comes your Missus, Hutchinson," and "Bill, she made it after all." Mrs. Hutchinson reached her husband, and Mr. Summers, who had been waiting, said cheerfully, "Thought we were going to have to get on without you, Tessie." Mrs. Hutchinson said, grinning, "Wouldn't have me leave m'dishes in the sink, now would you, Joe?" and soft laughter ran through the crowd as the people stirred back into position after Mrs. Hutchinson's arrival.

"Well, now," Mr. Summers said soberly, "guess we better get started, get this over with, so's we can go back to work. Anybody ain't here?" 10

"Dunbar," several people said. "Dunbar, Dunbar."

Mr. Summers consulted his list. "Clyde Dunbar," he said. "That's right. He's broke his leg, hasn't he? Who's drawing for him?"

"Me, I guess," a woman said, and Mr. Summers turned to look at her. "Wife draws for her husband," Mr. Summers said. "Don't you have a grown boy to do it for you, Janey?" Although Mr. Summers and everyone else in the village knew the answer perfectly well, it was the business of the official of the lottery to ask such questions formally. Mr. Summers waited with an expression of polite interest while Mrs. Dunbar answered.

"Horace's not but sixteen yet," Mrs. Dunbar said regretfully. "Guess I gotta fill in for the old man this year."

"Right," Mr. Summers said. He made a note on the list he was holding. 15 Then he asked, "Watson boy drawing this year?"

A tall boy in the crowd raised his hand. "Here," he said. "I'm drawing for m'mother and me." He blinked his eyes nervously and ducked his head as several voices in the crowd said things like "Good fellow, Jack," and "Glad to see your mother's got a man to do it."

"Well," Mr. Summers said, "guess that's everyone. Old Man Warner make it?"

"Here," a voice said, and Mr. Summers nodded.

A sudden hush fell on the crowd as Mr. Summers cleared his throat and looked at the list. "All ready?" he called. "Now, I'll read the names — heads of families first — and the men come up and take a paper out of the box. Keep the paper folded in your hand without looking at it until everyone has had a turn. Everything clear?"

The people had done it so many times that they only half listened to the directions; most of them were quiet, wetting their lips, not looking around. Then Mr. Summers raised one hand high and said, "Adams." A man disengaged himself from the crowd and came forward. "Hi, Steve," Mr. Summers said, and Mr. Adams said, "Hi, Joe." They grinned at one another humorlessly and nervously. Then Mr. Adams reached into the black box and took out a folded paper. He held it firmly by one corner as he turned and went hastily back to his place in the crowd, where he stood a little apart from his family, not looking down at his hand.

"Allen," Mr. Summers said. "Anderson. . . . Bentham."

"Seems like there's no time at all between lotteries any more," Mrs. Delacroix said to Mrs. Graves in the back row. "Seems like we got through with the last one only last week."

"Time sure goes fast," Mrs. Graves said.

"Clark. . . . Delacroix."

"There goes my old man," Mrs. Delacroix said. She held her breath while her husband went forward.

"Dunbar," Mr. Summers said, and Mrs. Dunbar went steadily to the box while one of the women said, "Go on, Janey," and another said, "There she goes."

"We're next," Mrs. Graves said. She watched while Mr. Graves came around from the side of the box, greeted Mr. Summers gravely, and selected a slip of paper from the box. By now, all through the crowd there were men holding the small folded papers in their large hands, turning them over and over nervously. Mrs. Dunbar and her two sons stood together, Mrs. Dunbar holding the slip of paper.

"Harburt. . . . Hutchinson."

"Get up there, Bill," Mrs. Hutchinson said, and the people near her laughed.

"Jones."

"They do say," Mr. Adams said to Old Man Warner, who stood next to him, "that over in the north village they're talking of giving up the lottery."

Old Man Warner snorted, "Pack of crazy fools," he said. "Listening to the young folks, nothing's good enough for *them*. Next thing you know, they'll be wanting to go back to living in caves, nobody work any more, live *that* way for a while. Used to be a saying about 'Lottery in June, corn be heavy soon.' First thing you know, we'd all be eating stewed chickweed and acorns. There's *always* been a lottery," he added petulantly. "Bad enough to see young Joe Summers up there joking with everybody."

"Some places have already quit lotteries," Mrs. Adams said.

"Nothing but trouble in *that,*" Old Man Warner said stoutly. "Pack of young fools."

"Martin." And Bobby Martin watched his father go forward. "Overdyke. . . . Percy."

"I wish they'd hurry," Mrs. Dunbar said to her older son. "I wish they'd hurry."

"They're almost through," her son said.

"You get ready to run tell Dad," Mrs. Dunbar said.

Mr. Summers called his own name and then stepped forward precisely and selected a slip from the box. Then he called, "Warner."

"Seventy-seventh year I been in the lottery," Old Man Warner said as he went through the crowd. "Seventy-seventh time."

"Watson." The tall boy came awkwardly through the crowd. Someone said, "Don't be nervous, Jack," and Mr. Summers said, "Take your time, son."

"Zanini."

After that, there was a long pause, a breathless pause, until Mr. Summers, holding his slip of paper in the air, said, "All right, fellows." For a minute, no one moved, and then all the slips of paper were opened. Suddenly, all women began to speak at once, saying, "Who is it?" "Who's got it?" "Is it the Dunbars?" "Is it the Watsons?" Then the voices began to say, "It's Hutchinson. It's Bill." "Bill Hutchinson's got it."

"Go tell your father," Mrs. Dunbar said to her older son.

People began to look around to see the Hutchinsons. Bill Hutchinson was standing quiet, staring down at the paper in his hand. Suddenly, Tessie Hutchinson shouted to Mr. Summers, "You didn't give him time enough to take any paper he wanted. I saw you. It wasn't fair!"

"Be a good sport, Tessie," Mrs. Delacroix called, and Mrs. Graves said, "All of us took the same chance."

"Shut up, Tessie," Bill Hutchinson said.

"Well, everyone," Mr. Summers said, "that was done pretty fast, and now we've got to be hurrying a little more to get done in time." He consulted his next list. "Bill," he said, "you draw for the Hutchinson family. You got any other households in the Hutchinsons?"

"There's Don and Eva," Mrs. Hutchinson yelled. "Make *them* take their chance!"

"Daughters draw with their husbands' families, Tessie," Mr. Summers said gently. "You know that as well as anyone else."

"It wasn't fair," Tessie said.

"I guess not, Joe," Bill Hutchinson said regretfully. "My daughter draws with her husband's family, that's only fair. And I've got no other family except the kids."

"Then, as far as drawing for families is concerned, it's you," Mr. Summers said in explanation, "and as far as drawing for households is concerned, that's you, too. Right?"

"Right," Bill Hutchinson said.

"How many kids, Bill?" Mr. Summers asked formally.

"Three," Bill Hutchinson said. "There's Bill, Jr., and Nancy, and little Dave. And Tessie and me."

"All right, then," Mr. Summers said. "Harry, you got their tickets back?"

Mr. Graves nodded and held up the slips of paper. "Put them in the box, then," Mr. Summers directed. "Take Bill's and put it in."

"I think we ought to start over," Mrs. Hutchinson said, as quietly as she could. "I tell you it wasn't *fair.* You didn't give him time enough to choose. *Every*body saw that."

Mr. Graves had selected the five slips and put them in the box, and he dropped all the papers but those onto the ground, where the breeze caught them and lifted them off.

"Listen, everybody," Mrs. Hutchinson was saying to the people around her.

"Ready, Bill?" Mr. Summers asked, and Bill Hutchinson, with one quick glance around at his wife and children, nodded.

"Remember," Mr. Summers said, "take the slips and keep them folded until each person has taken one. Harry, you help little Dave." Mr. Graves took the hand of the little boy, who came willingly with him up to the box. "Take a paper out of the box, Davy," Mr. Summers said. Davy put his hand into the box and laughed. "Take just *one* paper," Mr. Summers said. "Harry, you hold it for him." Mr. Graves took the child's hand and removed the folded paper from the tight fist and held it while little Dave stood next to him and looked up at him wonderingly.

"Nancy next," Mr. Summers said. Nancy was twelve, and her school friends breathed heavily as she went forward, switching her skirt, and took a slip daintily from the box. "Bill, Jr.," Mr. Summers said, and Billy, his face red and his feet over-large, nearly knocked the box over as he got a paper out. "Tessie," Mr. Summers said. She hesitated for a minute, looking around defiantly, and then set her lips and went up to the box. She snatched a paper out and held it behind her.

"Bill," Mr. Summers said, and Bill Hutchinson reached into the box and felt around, bringing his hand out at last with the slip of paper in it.   65

The crowd was quiet. A girl whispered, "I hope it's not Nancy," and the sound of the whisper reached the edges of the crowd.

"It's not the way it used to be," Old Man Warner said clearly. "People ain't the way they used to be."

"All right," Mr. Summers said. "Open the papers. Harry, you open little Dave's."

Mr. Graves opened the slip of paper and there was a general sigh through the crowd as he held it up and everyone could see that it was blank. Nancy and Bill, Jr., opened theirs at the same time, and both beamed and laughed, turning around to the crowd and holding their slips of paper above their heads.

"Tessie," Mr. Summers said. There was a pause, and then Mr. Summers   70 looked at Bill Hutchinson, and Bill unfolded his paper and showed it. It was blank.

"It's Tessie," Mr. Summers said, and his voice was hushed. "Show us her paper, Bill."

Bill Hutchinson went over to his wife and forced the slip of paper out of her hand. It had a black spot on it, the black spot Mr. Summers had made the night before with the heavy pencil in the coal-company office. Bill Hutchinson held it up, and there was a stir in the crowd.

"All right, folks," Mr. Summers said, "let's finish quickly."

Although the villagers had forgotten the ritual and lost the original black box, they still remembered to use stones. The pile of stones the boys had made earlier was ready; there were stones on the ground with the blowing scraps of paper that had come out of the box. Mrs. Delacroix selected a stone so large she had to pick it up with both hands and turned to Mrs. Dunbar. "Come on," she said. "Hurry up."

Mrs. Dunbar had small stones in both hands, and she said, gasping for   75 breath, "I can't run at all. You'll have to go ahead and I'll catch up with you."

The children had stones already, and someone gave little Davy Hutchinson a few pebbles.

Tessie Hutchinson was in the center of a cleared space by now, and she held her hands out desperately as the villagers moved in on her. "It isn't fair," she said. A stone hit her on the side of the head.

Old Man Warner was saying, "Come on, come on, everyone." Steve Adams was in the front of the crowd of villagers, with Mrs. Graves beside him.

"It isn't fair, it isn't right," Mrs. Hutchinson screamed, and then they were upon her.

QUESTIONS

1. Where do you think "The Lottery" takes place? What purpose do you suppose the writer has in making this setting appear so familiar and ordinary?
2. In paragraphs 2 and 3, what details foreshadow the ending of the story?
3. What is ironic in this statement (in paragraph 76): "The children had stones already, and someone gave little Davy Hutchinson a few pebbles"?
4. What else did you notice in the story that strikes you as an irony?
5. What particular details lend vividness to the story? Take a close look at Jackson's description of the black wooden box (paragraph 5) and of the black spot on the fatal slip of paper (paragraph 72).
6. From what point of view is the story told? Why does Jackson's choice of this point of view seem effective?
7. What do you understand to be the writer's own attitude toward the lottery and the stoning? Exactly what in the story makes her attitude clear to us?
8. What do you make of Old Man Warner's saying, "Lottery in June, corn be heavy soon"?
9. What do you think Shirley Jackson is driving at? Consider each of the following interpretations and, looking at the story, see if you can find any evidence for it.

> Jackson takes a primitive fertility rite and playfully transfers it to a small town in North America.
>
> Jackson, writing her story soon after World War II, indirectly expresses her horror at the Holocaust. She assumes that the massacre of the Jews was carried out by unwitting, obedient people, like these villagers. (This suggestion has been advanced by critic Richard Moore.)
>
> Jackson is satirizing our own society, in which men are selected for the army by lottery.
>
> Jackson is just writing a memorable, entertaining story that signifies nothing at all.

Flann O'Brien
TWO IN ONE   1978

Flann O'Brien (1911 – 1966), whose real name was Brian O'Nolan, was born in County Tyrone, Ireland. After his graduation from University College, Dublin (where he edited a magazine called Blather*), he spent eighteen years as a civil servant. As a writer, so prolific was O'Nolan that he needed more than one pen name. Under the byline of Miles na Gopaleen,* *for twenty-five years he contributed a much-beloved column to* The Irish Times, *which James Thurber considered the funniest newspaper feature he knew. O'Nolan's masterpiece (as Flann O'Brien) was the wildly inventive comic novel,* At Swim-Two-Birds *(1939) — "just the book to give to your sister," said poet Dylan Thomas, "if she is a wild, dirty, boozy girl." The novel at first escaped notice, having appeared on the day Hitler invaded Poland, precipitating World War II. O'Brien also produced stories, essays, plays, and four other novels:* The Hard Life *(1962);* The Dalkey Archive *(1964);* The Third Policeman *(1967); and one novel written in Irish,* An Beál Bocht *(1941), translated as* The Poor Mouth *(1973). Characteristically, the author died on April Fool's Day. Flann O'Brien has long been cherished by his countrymen, and by an international audience that keeps growing.* A Flann O'Brien Reader, *edited by Stephen Jonas (1978), affords an overall glimpse of him.*

The story I have to tell is a strange one, perhaps unbelievable. I will try to set it down as simply as I can. I do not expect to be disturbed in my literary labors, for I am writing this in the condemned cell.

Let us say my name is Murphy. The unusual occurrence which led me here concerns my relations with another man whom we shall call Kelly. Both of us were taxidermists.

I will not attempt a treatise on what a taxidermist is. The word is ugly and inadequate. Certainly it does not convey to the layman that such an operator must combine the qualities of zoologist, naturalist, chemist, sculptor, artist and carpenter. Who would blame such a person for showing some temperament now and again, as I did?

It is necessary, however, to say a brief word about this science. First, there is no such thing in modern practice as "stuffing" an animal. There is a record of stuffed gorillas having been in Carthage in the 5th century, and it is a fact that an Austrian prince, Siegmund Herberstein, had stuffed bison in the great hall of his castle in the 16th century — it was then the practice to draw the entrails of animals and to substitute spices and various preservative substances. There is a variety of methods in use today but, except in particular cases — snakes, for example, where preserving the translucency of the skin is a problem calling for special measures — the basis of all modern methods is simply this: you skin the animal very carefully according to a certain pattern, and you encase the skinless body in plaster of Paris. You bisect the plaster when cast providing yourself with two complementary moulds from which you can make a casting of the animal's body — there are several substances, all very light, from which such castings can be made. The next step, calling for infinite skill and patience, is to mount the skin on the casting of the body. That is all I need explain here, I think.

Kelly carried on a taxidermy business and I was his assistant. He was the boss — a swinish, overbearing mean boss, a bully, a sadist. He hated me, but enjoyed his hatred too much to sack me. He knew I had a real interest in the work, and a desire to broaden my experience. For that reason, he threw me all the commonplace jobs that came in. If some old lady sent her favorite terrier to be done, that was me; foxes and cats and Shetland ponies and white rabbits — they were all strictly *my* department. I could do a perfect job on such animals in my sleep, and got to hate them. But if a crocodile came in, or a Great Borneo spider, or (as once happened) a giraffe — Kelly kept them all for himself. In the meantime he would treat my own painstaking work with sourness and sneers and complaints.

One day the atmosphere in the workshop had been even fouler than usual, with Kelly in a filthier temper than usual. I had spent the forenoon finishing a cat, and at about lunch-time put it on the shelf where he left completed orders.

I could nearly *hear* him glaring at it. Where was the tail? I told him there was no tail, that it was a Manx cat. How did I know it was a Manx cat, how did I know it was not an ordinary cat which had lost its tail in a motor accident or something? I got so mad that I permitted myself a disquisition on cats in general, mentioning the distinctions as between *felis manul, felis silvestris* and *felis lybica,* and on the unique structure of the Manx cat. His reply to that? He called me a slob. That was the sort of life *I* was having.

On this occasion something within me snapped. I was sure I could hear the snap. I had moved up to where he was to answer his last insult. The loathsome creature had his back to me, bending down to put on his bicycle clips. Just to my hand on the bench was one of the long, flat steel instruments we use for certain operations with plaster. I picked it up and hit him a blow with it on the back of the head. He gave a cry and slumped forward. I hit him again. I rained blow after blow on him. Then I threw the tool away. I was upset. I went out into the yard and looked around. I remembered he had a weak heart. Was he dead? I remember adjusting the position of a barrel we had in the yard to catch rainwater, the only sort of water suitable for some of the mixtures we used. I found I was in a cold sweat but strangely calm. I went back into the workshop.

Kelly was just as I had left him. I could find no pulse. I rolled him over on his back and examined his eyes, for I have seen more lifeless eyes in my day than most people. Yes, there was no doubt: Kelly was dead. I had killed him. I was a murderer. I put on my coat and hat and left the place. I walked the streets for a while, trying to avoid panic, trying to think rationally. Inevitably, I was soon in a public house. I drank a lot of whiskey and finally went home to my digs. The next morning I was very sick indeed from this terrible mixture of drink and worry. Was the Kelly affair merely a fancy, a drunken fancy? No, there was no consolation in that sort of hope. He was dead all right.

It was as I lay in bed there, shaking, thinking and smoking, that the mad   10 idea came into my head. No doubt this sounds incredible, grotesque, even disgusting, but I decided I would treat Kelly the same as any other dead creature that found its way to the workshop.

Once one enters a climate of horror, distinction of degree as between one infamy and another seems slight, sometimes undetectable. That evening I went to the workshop and made my preparations. I worked steadily all next day. I will not appall the reader with gruesome detail. I need only say that I applied the general technique and flaying pattern appropriate to apes. The job took me four days at the end of which I had a perfect skin, face and all. I made the usual castings before committing the remains of, so to speak, the remains, to the furnace. My plan was to have Kelly on view asleep on a chair, for the benefit of anybody who might call. Reflection convinced me that this would be far too dangerous. I had to think again.

A further idea began to form. It was so macabre that it shocked even myself. For days I had been treating the inside of the skin with the usual preservatives — cellulose acetate and the like — thinking all the time. The new illumination came upon me like a thunderbolt. *I would don his skin and, when the need arose, BECOME Kelly!* His clothes fitted me. So would his skin. Why not?

Another day's agonized work went on various alterations and adjustments but that night I was able to look into a glass and see Kelly looking back at me, perfect in every detail except for the teeth and eyes, which had to be my own but which I knew other people would never notice.

Naturally I wore Kelly's clothes, and had no trouble in imitating his unpleasant voice and mannerisms. On the second day, having "dressed," so to speak, I went for a walk, receiving salutes from newsboys and other people who had known Kelly. And on the day after, I was foolhardy enough to visit Kelly's lodgings. Where on earth had I been, his landlady wanted to know. (She had noticed nothing.) What, I asked — had that fool Murphy not told her that I had to go to the country for a few days? No? I had told the good-for-nothing to convey the message.

I slept that night in Kelly's bed. I was a little worried about what the other landlady would think of my own absence. I decided not to remove Kelly's skin the first night I spent in his bed but to try to get the rest of my plan of campaign perfected and into sharper focus. I eventually decided that Kelly should announce to various people that he was going to a very good job in Canada, and that he had sold his business to his assistant Murphy. I would then burn the skin, I would own a business and — what is more stupid than vanity! — I could secretly flatter myself that I had committed the perfect crime.

Need I say that I had overlooked something?

The mummifying preparation with which I had dressed the inside of the skin was, of course, quite stable for the ordinary purposes of taxidermy. It had not occurred to me that a night in a warm bed would make it behave differently. The horrible truth dawned on me the next day when I reached the workshop and tried to take the skin off. *It wouldn't come off!* It had literally fused with my own! And in the days that followed, this process kept rapidly advancing. Kelly's skin got to live again, to breathe, to perspire.

Then followed more days of terrible tension. My own landlady called one day, inquiring about me of "Kelly." I told her I had been on the point of calling on *her* to find out where I was. She was disturbed about my disappearance — it was so unlike me — and said she thought she should inform the police. I thought it wise not to try to dissuade her. My disappearance would eventually come to be accepted, I thought. My Kelliness, so to speak, was permanent. It was horrible, but it was a choice of that or the scaffold.

I kept drinking a lot. One night, after many drinks, I went to the club for a game of snooker°. This club was in fact one of the causes of Kelly's bitterness towards me. I had joined it without having been aware that Kelly was a member. His resentment was boundless. He thought I was watching him, and taking note of the attentions he paid the lady members.

15

snooker: billiard game played with fifteen red balls and six balls of other colors.

On this occasion I nearly made a catastrophic mistake. It is a simple fact that I am a very good snooker player, easily the best in that club. As I was standing watching another game in progress awaiting my turn for the table, *I suddenly realised that Kelly did not play snooker at all!* For some moments, a cold sweat stood out on Kelly's brow at the narrowness of this escape. I went to the bar. There, a garrulous lady (who thinks her unsolicited conversation is a fair exchange for a drink) began talking to me. She remarked the long absence of my nice Mr. Murphy. She said he was missed a lot in the snooker room. I was hot and embarrassed and soon went home. To Kelly's place, of course.

Not embarrassment, but a real sense of danger, was to be my next portion in this adventure. One afternoon, two very casual strangers strolled into the workshop, saying they would like a little chat with me. Cigarettes were produced. Yes indeed, they were plain-clothesmen making a few routine inquiries. This man Murphy had been reported missing by several people. Any idea where he was? None at all. When had I last seen him? Did he seem upset or disturbed? No, but he was an impetuous type. I had recently reprimanded him for bad work. On similar other occasions he had threatened to leave and seek work in England. Had I been away for a few days myself? Yes, down in Cork for a few days. On business. Yes . . . yes . . . some people thinking of starting a natural museum down there, technical school people — that sort of thing.

The casual manner of these men worried me, but I was sure they did not suspect the truth and that they were genuinely interested in tracing Murphy. Still, I knew I was in danger, without knowing the exact nature of the threat I had to counter. Whiskey cheered me somewhat.

Then it happened. The two detectives came back accompanied by two other men in uniform. They showed me a search warrant. It was purely a formality; it had to be done in the case of all missing persons. They had already searched Murphy's digs and had found nothing of interest. They were very sorry for upsetting the place during my working hours.

A few days later the casual gentlemen called and put me under arrest for the willful murder of Murphy, of myself. They proved the charge in due course with all sorts of painfully amassed evidence, including the remains of human bones in the furnace. I was sentenced to be hanged. Even if I could now prove that Murphy still lived by shedding the accursed skin, what help would that be? Where, they would ask, is Kelly?

That is my strange and tragic story. And I end it with the thought that if Kelly and I must each be either murderer or murdered, it is perhaps better to accept my present fate as philosophically as I can and be cherished in the public mind as the victim of this murderous monster, Kelly. He *was* a murderer, anyway.

QUESTIONS

1. With what details does O'Brien establish the verisimilitude of his narrator — show us that, indeed, Murphy would be entirely capable of pulling off this perfect-seeming crime?
2. What is the narrator's motivation for killing his employer? For deciding to "treat Kelly the same as any other dead creature that found its way to the workshop"? For donning the dead man's skin?
3. At what moment — and for what reason — does Murphy's neat plan go askew?

4. In the end, the narrator says of Kelly, "He *was* a murderer, anyway." In what sense is this remark to be taken?

5. When does it begin to dawn on you that the whole story just might be a preposterous lot of cock and bull and that O'Brien may be pulling your leg? Do you resent the absurdity of the story — that it couldn't possibly happen? (There is, of course, no one right answer to this last question.)

6. What sorts of irony do you find in "Two in One"? What is ironic about the "macabre idea" that Murphy determines to try out (paragraphs 12 – 15)? What is ironic in the narrator's situation at the end? Is the story told from an ironic point of view? Explain.

7. What similarities do you find between "Two in One" and Edgar Allan Poe's "The Telltale Heart" (page 38)? Did you find any irony in Poe's story? In what important ways do the two stories differ?

8. Would you care to read any more of Flann O'Brien's work, or have you had enough? (If you care to pursue him further, see any of the books listed in the biographical note at the start of the story.)

Suggestions for Writing

1. Freewrite for fifteen or twenty minutes, rapidly jotting down any thoughts you may have in answer to this question: From your daily contacts with people, what ironies do you at times become aware of? Consider ironies of language (in deliberately misleading or sarcastic remarks), ironies of situation (here you are, a trained computer programmer unable to convince a counterperson in a fast-food joint that you can correctly add up a check). Then, using any good perceptions you have generated, write and polish a short answer to the question, illustrating your remarks by reference to your own recalled experience and recent observations. You might find it useful too, of course, to cite some ironies in any stories about everyday life you know.

2. Inspired by Flann O'Brien's "Two in One," write a brief tall tale, keeping an absolutely straight poker face. Make your tale as convincing as possible, by including plenty of convincing detail and perhaps openly recognizing that your readers are likely to be skeptical. Then, following your tale, write a comment recalling the problems you had in telling the story and how you coped with them.

3. Write an answer to the last question on "The Lottery." Try to show, by referring to particulars in the story, what if anything you think Shirley Jackson is driving at.

4. Here are some other topics: "Irony in 'A Rose for Emily.'" "Irony in 'Greasy Lake.'" "Irony in 'The Jilting of Granny Weatherall.'" (Or what other story have you read that more keenly interests you?) What sorts of irony make the story more effective? In dealing with any of them, you may find the method of analysis a help to you. Before you write, read about this useful method in "Writing about a Story" (page 425).

7 Theme

The **theme** of a story is whatever general idea or insight the entire story reveals. In some stories the theme is unmistakable. At the end of Aesop's fable about the council of the mice that can't decide who will bell the cat, the theme is stated in the moral: *It is easier to propose a thing than to carry it out.* In a work of commercial fiction, too, the theme (if any) is usually obvious. Consider a typical detective thriller in which, say, a rookie police-man trained in scientific methods of crime detection sets out to solve a mystery sooner than his rival, a veteran sleuth whose only laboratory is carried under his hat. Perhaps the veteran solves the case, leading to the conclusion (and the theme), "The old ways are the best ways after all." Another story by the same writer might dramatize the same rivalry but reverse the outcome, having the rookie win, thereby reversing the theme: "The times are changing! Let's shake loose from old-fashioned ways." In such commercial entertainments, a theme is like a length of rope with which the writer, patently and mechanically, trusses the story neatly (usu-ally too neatly) into meaningful shape.

In literary fiction, a theme is seldom so obvious. That is, a theme need not be a moral or a message; it may be what the happenings add up to, what the story is about. When we come to the end of a finely wrought short story such as Ernest Hemingway's "A Clean, Well-Lighted Place" (Chap-ter Five), it may be easy to sum up the plot — to say what happens — but it is more difficult to sum up the story's main idea. Evidently, Heming-way relates events — how a younger waiter gets rid of an old man and how an older waiter then goes to a coffee bar — but in themselves these events seem relatively slight, though the story as a whole seems large (for its size) and full of meaning. For the meaning, we must look to other elements in the story besides what happens in it. And it is clear that Hemingway is most deeply interested in the thoughts and feelings of the older waiter, the character who has more and more to say as the story progresses, until at the end the story is entirely confined to his thoughts and perceptions. What is meaningful in these thoughts and perceptions? The older waiter understands the old man and sympathizes with his need for a clean, well-lighted place. If we say that, we are still talking about what happens in the story, though we have gone beyond merely recording its external events. But a theme is usually stated in *general* words. Another try: "Solitary people who cannot sleep need a cheerful, orderly place where they can drink with dignity." That's a little better. We have indicated, at least, that Hemingway's story is about more than just an old man and a couple of waiters. But what about the older waiter's meditation on *nada,* nothingness? Coming near the end of the story, it takes great emphasis; and probably no good statement of Hemingway's theme can leave it out. Still another try at a statement: "Solitary people need a place of refuge from their terrible awareness that their lives (or perhaps, human lives) are essentially meaningless." Neither this nor any other statement of the story's theme is unarguably right, but at least the sentence helps the reader to bring into focus one primary idea that Hemingway seems to be driving at. When we finish reading "A Clean, Well-Lighted Place," we feel that there *is* such a theme, a unifying vision, even though we cannot reduce it absolutely to a tag. Like some freshwater lake alive with creatures, Hemingway's story is a broad expanse, reflecting in many directions. No wonder that many readers will view it differently.

Moral inferences may be drawn from the story, no doubt — for Hemingway is indirectly giving us advice for properly regarding and sympathizing with the lonely, the uncertain, and the old. But the story doesn't set forth a lesson that we are supposed to put into practice. One could argue that "A Clean, Well-Lighted Place" contains *several* themes — and other statements could be made to take in Hemingway's views of love, of communication between people, of dignity. Great short stories, like great symphonies, frequently have more than one theme.

In many a fine short story, theme is the center, the moving force, the principle of unity. Clearly, such a theme is something other than the characters and events of its story. To say of James Joyce's "Araby" (page 54) that it is about a boy who goes to a bazaar to buy a gift for a young woman, only to arrive too late, is to summarize plot, not theme. (The theme *might* be put, "The illusions of a romantic child are vulnerable," or it might be put in any of a few hundred other ways.) Although the title of Isaac Bashevis Singer's "Gimpel the Fool" (Chapter Four) indicates the main character and suggests the subject (his "foolishness"), the theme — the larger realization that the story leaves us with — has to do not with foolishness, but with how to be wise.

Sometimes you will hear it said that the theme of a story (say, Faulkner's "Barn Burning") is "loss of innocence" or "initiation into maturity"; or that the theme of some other story (Thurber's "The Catbird Seat," for instance) is "the revolt of the downtrodden." This is to use *theme* in a larger and more abstract sense than we use it here. Although such general descriptions of theme can be useful — as in sorting a large number of stories into rough categories — we suggest that, in the beginning, you look for whatever truth or insight you think the writer of a story reveals. Try to sum it up *in a sentence.* By doing so, you will find yourself looking closely at the story, trying to define its principal meaning. You may find it helpful, in making your sentence-statement of theme, to consider these points:

1. Look back once more at the title of the story. From what you have read, what does it indicate?

2. Does the main character in any way change in the story? Does this character arrive at any eventual realization or understanding? Are you left with any realization or understanding you did not have before?

3. Does the author make any general observations about life or human nature? Do the characters make any? (Caution: Characters now and again will utter opinions with which the reader is not necessarily supposed to agree.)

4. Does the story contain any especially curious objects, mysterious flat characters, significant animals, repeated names, song titles, or whatever, that hint toward meanings larger than such things ordinarily have? In literary stories, such symbols may point to central themes. (For a short discussion of symbolism and a few illustrations, see Chapter Eight.)

5. When you have worded your statement of theme, have you cast your statement into general language, not just given a plot summary?

6. Does your statement hold true for the story as a whole, not for just part of it?

In distilling a statement of theme from a rich and complicated story, we have, of course, no more encompassed the whole story than a paleontologist taking a plaster mold of a petrified footprint has captured a living brontosaurus. A writer (other than a fabulist) does not usually set out with theme in hand, determined to make every detail in the story work to demonstrate it. Well then, the skeptical reader may ask, if only *some* stories have themes, if those themes may be hard to sum up, and if readers will probably disagree in their summations, why bother to state themes? Isn't it too much trouble? Surely it is, unless the effort to state a theme ends in pleasure and profit. Trying to sum up the point of a story in our own words is merely one way to make ourselves better aware of whatever we may have understood vaguely and tentatively. Attempted with loving care, such statements may bring into focus our scattered impressions of a rewarding story, may help to clarify and hold fast whatever wisdom the storyteller has offered us.

Flannery O'Connor

REVELATION   1965

Mary Flannery O'Connor (she dropped the first name from her byline) spent most of her life (1925 – 1964) in Milledgeville, Georgia. While she was a student at Georgia State College for Women, in her home town, her fledgling stories won her local fame. She went on to study at the Writers

Workshop of the University of Iowa, from which in 1946 she obtained her M.F.A. degree. On discovering that she was afflicted with lupus erythematosus, the progressive and incurable blood disease that had killed her father, O'Connor returned to Milledgeville to live with her mother, undergo treatment, raise peacocks, and write. The bulk of her work consists of two novels, Wise Blood *(1952) and* The Violent Bear It Away *(1960);* Complete Stories of Flannery O'Connor *(1971); a book of essays and talks,* Mystery and Manners *(1961); her brilliant, modest, cheerful letters, collected in* The Habit of Being *(1979); and terse book reviews written for Catholic newspapers in Georgia, collected in* The Presence of Grace *(1983). Since O'Connor's early death, her fiction, once blamed as gratuitously violent and jarringly grotesque, has enjoyed a steady and triumphant rise in critical favor. Its themes derive from her devoutly Christian faith, but its dark and often hilarious humor derives from her own view — perhaps also from a native Georgian tradition of tall-taletelling.*

The doctor's waiting room, which was very small, was almost full when the Turpins entered and Mrs. Turpin, who was very large, made it look even smaller by her presence. She stood looming at the head of the magazine table set in the center of it, a living demonstration that the room was inadequate and ridiculous. Her little bright black eyes took in all the patients as she sized up the seating situation. There was one vacant chair and a place on the sofa occupied by a blond child in a dirty blue romper who should have been told to move over and make room for the lady. He was five or six, but Mrs. Turpin saw at once that no one was going to tell him to move over. He was slumped down in the seat, his arms idle at his sides and his eyes idle in his head; his nose ran unchecked.

Mrs. Turpin put a firm hand on Claud's shoulder and said in a voice that included anyone who wanted to listen, "Claud, you sit in that chair there," and gave him a push down into the vacant one. Claud was florid and bald and sturdy, somewhat shorter than Mrs. Turpin, but he sat down as if he were accustomed to doing what she told him to.

Mrs. Turpin remained standing. The only man in the room besides Claud was a lean stringy old fellow with a rusty hand spread out on each knee, whose eyes were closed as if he were asleep or dead or pretending to be so as not to get up and offer her his seat. Her gaze settled agreeably on a well-dressed grey-haired lady whose eyes met hers and whose expression said: if that child belonged to me, he would have some manners and move over — there's plenty of room there for you and him too.

Claud looked up with a sigh and made as if to rise.

"Sit down," Mrs. Turpin said. "You know you're not supposed to stand on that leg. He has an ulcer on his leg," she explained.   5

Claud lifted his foot onto the magazine table and rolled his trouser leg up to reveal a purple swelling on a plump marble-white calf.

"My!" the pleasant lady said. "How did you do that?"

"A cow kicked him," Mrs. Turpin said.

"Goodness!" said the lady.

Claud rolled his trouser leg down.

"Maybe the little boy would move over," the lady suggested, but the child did not stir.

"Somebody will be leaving in a minute," Mrs. Turpin said. She could not understand why a doctor — with as much money as they made charging five dollars a day to just stick their head in the hospital door and look at you — couldn't afford a decent-sized waiting room. This one was hardly bigger than a garage. The table was cluttered with limp-looking magazines and at one end of it there was a big green glass ash tray full of cigaret butts and cotton wads with little blood spots on them. If she had had anything to do with the running of the place, that would have been emptied every so often. There were no chairs against the wall at the head of the room. It had a rectangular-shaped panel in it that permitted a view of the office where the nurse came and went and the secretary listened to the radio. A plastic fern in a gold pot sat in the opening and trailed its fronds down almost to the floor. The radio was softly playing gospel music.

Just then the inner door opened and a nurse with the highest stack of yellow hair Mrs. Turpin had ever seen put her face in the crack and called for the next patient. The woman sitting beside Claud grasped the two arms of her chair and hoisted herself up; she pulled her dress free from her legs and lumbered through the door where the nurse had disappeared.

Mrs. Turpin eased into the vacant chair, which held her tight as a corset. "I wish I could reduce," she said, and rolled her eyes and gave a comic sigh.

"Oh, *you* aren't fat," the stylish lady said.

"Ooooo I am too," Mrs. Turpin said. "Claud he eats all he wants to and never weighs over one hundred and seventy-five pounds, but me I just look at something good to eat and I gain some weight," and her stomach and shoulders shook with laughter. "You can eat all you want to, can't you, Claud?" she asked, turning to him.

Claud only grinned.

"Well, as long as you have such a good disposition," the stylish lady said, "I don't think it makes a bit of difference what size you are. You just can't beat a good disposition."

Next to her was a fat girl of eighteen or nineteen, scowling into a thick blue book which Mrs. Turpin saw was entitled *Human Development.* The girl raised her head and directed her scowl at Mrs. Turpin as if she did not like her looks. She appeared annoyed that anyone should speak while she tried to read. The poor girl's face was blue with acne and Mrs. Turpin thought how pitiful it was to have a face like that at that age. She gave the girl a friendly smile but the girl only scowled the harder. Mrs. Turpin herself was fat but she had always had good skin, and, though she was forty-seven years old, there was not a wrinkle in her face except around her eyes from laughing too much.

Next to the ugly girl was the child, still in exactly the same position, and next to him was a thin leathery old woman in a cotton print dress. She and Claud had three sacks of chicken feed in their pump house that was in the same print. She had seen from the first that the child belonged with the old woman. She could tell by the way they sat — kind of vacant and white-trashy, as if they would sit there until Doomsday if nobody called and told them to get up. And at right angles but next to the well-dressed pleasant lady was a lank-faced woman who was certainly the child's mother. She had on a yellow sweat shirt and wine-colored slacks, both gritty-looking, and the rims of her lips were stained with snuff. Her dirty yellow hair was tied behind with a little piece of red paper ribbon. Worse than niggers any day, Mrs. Turpin thought.

The gospel hymn playing was, "When I looked up and He looked down," and Mrs. Turpin, who knew it, supplied the last line mentally, "And wona these days I know I'll we-eara crown."

Without appearing to, Mrs. Turpin always noticed people's feet. The well-dressed lady had on red and grey suede shoes to match her dress. Mrs. Turpin had on her good black patent leather pumps. The ugly girl had on Girl Scout shoes and heavy socks. The old woman had on tennis shoes and the white-trashy mother had on what appeared to be bedroom slippers, black straw with gold braid threaded through them — exactly what you would have expected her to have on.

Sometimes at night when she couldn't go to sleep, Mrs. Turpin would occupy herself with the question of who she would have chosen to be if she couldn't have been herself. If Jesus had said to her before he made her, "There's only two places available for you. You can either be a nigger or white-trash," what would she have said? "Please, Jesus, please," she would have said, "just let me wait until there's another place available," and he would have said, "No, you have to go right now and I have only those two places so make up your mind." She would have wiggled and squirmed and begged and pleaded but it would have been no use and finally she would have said, "All right, make me a nigger then — but that don't mean a trashy one." And he would have made her a neat clean respectable Negro-woman, herself but black.

Next to the child's mother was a red-headed youngish woman, reading one of the magazines and working a piece of chewing gum, hell for leather, as Claud would say. Mrs. Turpin could not see the woman's feet. She was not white-trash, just common. Sometimes Mrs. Turpin occupied herself at night naming the classes of people. On the bottom of the heap were most colored people, not the kind she would have been if she had been one, but most of them; then next to them — not above, just away from — were the white-trash; then above them were the home-owners, and above them the home-and-land owners, to which she and Claud belonged. Above she and Claud° were people with a lot of money and much bigger houses and much more land. But here the complexity of it would begin to bear in on her, for some of the people with a lot of money were common and ought to be below she and Claud and some of the people who had good blood had lost their money and had to rent and then there were colored people who owned their homes and land as well. There was a colored dentist in town who had two red Lincolns and a swimming pool and a farm with registered white-face cattle on it. Usually by the time she had fallen asleep all the classes of people were moiling and roiling around in her head, and she would dream they were all crammed in together in a box car, being ridden off to be put in a gas oven.

"That's a beautiful clock," she said and nodded to her right. It was a big wall clock, the face encased in a brass sunburst. 25

Above she and Claud: ungrammatical construction. Putting herself first, Mrs. Turpin presumably would say (if she were speaking aloud), "Above I and Claud . . ."

"Yes, it's very pretty," the stylish lady said agreeably. "And right on the dot too," she added, glancing at her watch.

The ugly girl beside her cast an eye upward at the clock, smirked, then looked directly at Mrs. Turpin and smirked again. Then she returned her eyes to her book. She was obviously the lady's daughter because, although they didn't look anything alike as to disposition, they both had the same shape of face and the same blue eyes. On the lady they sparkled pleasantly but in the girl's seared face they appeared alternately to smolder and to blaze.

What if Jesus had said, "All right, you can be white-trash or a nigger or ugly"!

Mrs. Turpin felt an awful pity for the girl, though she thought it was one thing to be ugly and another to act ugly.

The woman with the snuff-stained lips turned around in her chair and looked up at the clock. Then she turned back and appeared to look a little to the side of Mrs. Turpin. There was a cast in one of her eyes. "You want to know wher you can get you one of themther clocks?" she asked in a loud voice.

"No, I already have a nice clock," Mrs. Turpin said. Once somebody like her got a leg in the conversation, she would be all over it.

"You can get you one with green stamps," the woman said. "That's most likely wher he got hisn. Save you up enough, you can get you most anythang. I got me some joo'ry."

Ought to have got you a wash rag and some soap, Mrs. Turpin thought.

"I get contour sheets with mine," the pleasant lady said.

The daughter slammed her book shut. She looked straight in front of her, directly through Mrs. Turpin and on through the yellow curtain and the plate glass window which made the wall behind her. The girl's eyes seemed lit all of a sudden with a peculiar light, an unnatural light like night road signs give. Mrs. Turpin turned her head to see if there was anything going on outside that she should see, but she could not see anything. Figures passing cast only a pale shadow through the curtain. There was no reason the girl should single her out for her ugly looks.

"Miss Finley," the nurse said, cracking the door. The gum-chewing woman got up and passed in front of her and Claud and went into the office. She had on red high-heeled shoes.

Directly across the table, the ugly girl's eyes were fixed on Mrs. Turpin as if she had some very special reason for disliking her.

"This is wonderful weather, isn't it?" the girl's mother said.

"It's good weather for cotton if you can get the niggers to pick it," Mrs. Turpin said, "but niggers don't want to pick cotton any more. You can't get the white folks to pick it and now you can't get the niggers — because they got to be right up there with the white folks."

"They gonna *try* anyways," the white-trash woman said, leaning forward.

"Do you have one of those cotton-picking machines?" the pleasant lady asked.

"No," Mrs. Turpin said, "they leave half the cotton in the field. We don't have much cotton anyway. If you want to make it farming now, you have to have a little of everything. We got a couple of acres of cotton and a few hogs and chickens and just enough white-face that Claud can look after them himself."

"One thang I don't want," the white-trash woman said, wiping her mouth with the back of her hands. "Hogs. Nasty stinking things, a-gruntin and a-rootin all over the place."

Mrs. Turpin gave her the merest edge of her attention. "Our hogs are not dirty and they don't stink," she said. "They're cleaner than some children I've seen. Their feet never touch the ground. We have a pig-parlor — that's where you raise them on concrete," she explained to the pleasant lady, "and Claud scoots them down with the hose every afternoon and washes off the floor." Cleaner by far than that child right there, she thought. Poor nasty little thing. He had not moved except to put the thumb of his dirty hand into his mouth.

The woman turned her face away from Mrs. Turpin. "I know I wouldn't scoot down no hog with no hose," she said to the wall. 45

You wouldn't have no hog to scoot down, Mrs. Turpin said to herself.

"A-gruntin and a-rootin and a-groanin," the woman muttered.

"We got a little of everything," Mrs. Turpin said to the pleasant lady. "It's no use in having more than you can handle yourself with help like it is. We found enough niggers to pick our cotton this year but Claud he has to go after them and take them home again in the evening. They can't walk that half a mile. No they can't. I tell you," she said and laughed merrily, "I sure am tired of buttering up niggers, but you got to love em if you want em to work for you. When they come in the morning, I run out and I say, 'Hi yawl this morning?' and when Claud drives them off to the field I just wave to beat the band and they just wave back." And she waved her hand rapidly to illustrate.

"Like you read out of the same book," the lady said, showing she understood perfectly.

"Child, yes," Mrs. Turpin said. "And when they come in from the field, 50 I run out with a bucket of icewater. That's the way it's going to be from now on," she said. "You may as well face it."

"One thang I know," the white-trash woman said. "Two thangs I ain't going to do: love no niggers or scoot down no hog with no hose." And she let out a bark of contempt.

The look that Mrs. Turpin and the pleasant lady exchanged indicated they both understood that you had to *have* certain things before you could *know* certain things. But every time Mrs. Turpin exchanged a look with the lady, she was aware that the ugly girl's peculiar eyes were still on her, and she had trouble bringing her attention back to the conversation.

"When you got something," she said, "you got to look after it." And when you ain't got a thing but breath and britches, she added to herself, you can afford to come to town every morning and just sit on the Court House coping and spit.

A grotesque revolving shadow passed across the curtain behind her and was thrown palely on the opposite wall. Then a bicycle clattered down against the outside of the building. The door opened and a colored boy glided in with a tray from the drug store. It had two large red and white paper cups on it with tops on them. He was a tall, very black boy in discolored white pants and a green nylon shirt. He was chewing gum slowly, as if to music. He set the tray down in the office opening next to the fern and stuck his head through to look for the secretary. She was not in there. He rested his arms on the ledge and waited, his narrow bottom stuck out, swaying slowly to the left and right. He raised a hand over his head and scratched the base of his skull.

"You see that button there, boy?" Mrs. Turpin said. "You can punch that and she'll come. She's probably in the back somewhere." 55

"Is thas right?" the boy said agreeably, as if he had never seen the button before. He leaned to the right and put his finger on it. "She sometime out," he said and twisted around to face his audience, his elbows behind him on the counter. The nurse appeared and he twisted back again. She handed him a dollar and he rooted in his pocket and made the change and counted it out to her. She gave him fifteen cents for a tip and he went out with the empty tray. The heavy door swung to slowly and closed at length with the sound of suction. For a moment no one spoke.

"They ought to send all them niggers back to Africa," the white-trash woman said. "That's wher they come from in the first place."

"Oh, I couldn't do without my good colored friends," the pleasant lady said.

"There's a heap of things worse than a nigger," Mrs. Turpin agreed. "It's all kinds of them just like it's all kinds of us."

"Yes, and it takes all kinds to make the world go round," the lady said 60 in her musical voice.

As she said it, the raw-complexioned girl snapped her teeth together. Her lower lip turned downwards and inside out, revealing the pale pink inside of her mouth. After a second it rolled back up. It was the ugliest face Mrs. Turpin had ever seen anyone make and for a moment she was certain that the girl had made it at her. She was looking at her as if she had known and disliked her all her life — all of Mrs. Turpin's life, it seemed too, not just all the girl's life. Why, girl, I don't even know you, Mrs. Turpin said silently.

She forced her attention back to the discussion. "It wouldn't be practical to send them back to Africa," she said. "They wouldn't want to go. They got it too good here."

"Wouldn't be what they wanted — if I had anythang to do with it," the woman said.

"It wouldn't be a way in the world you could get all the niggers back over there," Mrs. Turpin said. "They'd be hiding out and lying down and turning sick on you and wailing and hollering and raring and pitching. It wouldn't be a way in the world to get them over there."

"They got over here," the trashy woman said. "Get back like they got 65 over."

"It wasn't so many of them then," Mrs. Turpin explained.

The woman looked at Mrs. Turpin as if here was an idiot indeed but Mrs. Turpin was not bothered by the look, considering where it came from.

"Nooo," she said, "they're going to stay here where they can go to New York and marry white folks and improve their color. That's what they all want to do, every one of them, improve their color."

"You know what comes of that, don't you?" Claud asked.

"No, Claud, what?" Mrs. Turpin said. 70

Claud's eyes twinkled. "White-faced niggers," he said with never a smile.

Everybody in the office laughed except the white-trash and the ugly girl. The girl gripped the book in her lap with white fingers. The trashy woman looked around her from face to face as if she thought they were all idiots. The old woman in the feed sack dress continued to gaze expressionless across the floor at the high-top shoes of the man opposite her, the one who had been pretending to be asleep when the Turpins came in. He was laughing heartily, his hands still spread out on his knees. The child had fallen to the side and was lying now almost face down in the old woman's lap.

While they recovered from their laughter, the nasal chorus on the radio kept the room from silence.

> *"You go to blank blank*
> *And I'll go to mine*
> *But we'll all blank along*
> *To-geth-ther,*
> *And all along the blank*
> *We'll hep each other out*
> *Smile-ling in any kind of*
> *Weath-ther!"*

Mrs. Turpin didn't catch every word but she caught enough to agree with the spirit of the song and it turned her thoughts sober. To help anybody out that needed it was her philosophy of life. She never spared herself when she found somebody in need, whether they were white or black, trash or decent. And of all she had to be thankful for, she was most thankful that this was so. If Jesus had said, "You can be high society and have all the money you want and be thin and svelte-like, but you can't be a good woman with it," she would have had to say, "Well don't make me that then. Make me a good woman and it don't matter what else, how fat or how ugly or how poor!" Her heart rose. He had not made her a nigger or white-trash or ugly! He had made her herself and given her a little of everything. Jesus, thank you! she said. Thank you thank you thank you! Whenever she counted her blessings she felt as buoyant as if she weighed one hundred and twenty-five pounds instead of one hundred and eighty.

"What's wrong with your little boy?" the pleasant lady asked the white-trashy woman.

"He has a ulcer," the woman said proudly. "He ain't give me a minute's peace since he was born. Him and her are just alike," she said, nodding at the old woman, who was running her leathery fingers through the child's pale hair. "Look like I can't get nothing down them two but Co' Cola and candy."

That's all you try to get down em, Mrs. Turpin said to herself. Too lazy to light the fire. There was nothing you could tell her about people like them that she didn't know already. And it was not just that they didn't have anything. Because if you gave them everything, in two weeks it would all be broken or filthy or they would have chopped it up for lightwood. She knew all this from her own experience. Help them you must, but help them you couldn't.

All at once the ugly girl turned her lips inside out again. Her eyes were fixed like two drills on Mrs. Turpin. This time there was no mistaking that there was something urgent behind them.

Girl, Mrs. Turpin exclaimed silently, I haven't done a thing to you! The girl might be confusing her with somebody else. There was no need to sit by and let herself be intimidated. "You must be in college," she said boldly, looking directly at the girl. "I see you reading a book there."

The girl continued to stare and pointedly did not answer.

Her mother blushed at this rudeness. "The lady asked you a question, Mary Grace," she said under her breath.

"I have ears," Mary Grace said.

The poor mother blushed again. "Mary Grace goes to Wellesley College," she explained. She twisted one of the buttons on her dress. "In Massachusetts," she added with a grimace. "And in the summer she just keeps right on studying. Just reads all the time, a real book worm. She's done real well at Wellesley; she's taking English and Math and History and Psychology and Social Studies," she rattled on, "and I think it's too much. I think she ought to get out and have fun."

The girl looked as if she would like to hurl them all through the plate glass window.

"Way up north," Mrs. Turpin murmured and thought, well, it hasn't done much for her manners.

"I'd almost rather to have him sick," the white-trash woman said, wrenching the attention back to herself. "He's so mean when he ain't. Look like some children just take natural to meanness. It's some gets bad when they get sick but he was the opposite. Took sick and turned good. He don't give me no trouble now. It's me waitin to see the doctor," she said.

If I was going to send anybody back to Africa, Mrs. Turpin thought, it would be your kind, woman. "Yes, indeed," she said aloud, but looking up at the ceiling, "it's a heap of things worse than a nigger." And dirtier than a hog, she added to herself.

"I think people with bad dispositions are more to be pitied than anyone on earth," the pleasant lady said in a voice that was decidedly thin.

"I thank the Lord he has blessed me with a good one," Mrs. Turpin said. "The day has never dawned that I couldn't find something to laugh at."

"Not since she married me anyways," Claud said with a comical straight face.

Everybody laughed except the girl and the white-trash.

Mrs. Turpin's stomach shook. "He's such a caution," she said, "that I can't help but laugh at him."

The girl made a loud ugly noise through her teeth.

Her mother's mouth grew thin and tight. "I think the worst thing in the world," she said, "is an ungrateful person. To have everything and not appreciate it. I know a girl," she said, "who has parents who would give her anything, a little brother who loves her dearly, who is getting a good education, who wears the best clothes, but who can never say a kind word to anyone, who never smiles, who just criticizes and complains all day long."

"Is she too old to paddle?" Claud asked.

The girl's face was almost purple.

"Yes," the lady said, "I'm afraid there's nothing to do but leave her to her folly. Some day she'll wake up and it'll be too late."

"It never hurt anyone to smile," Mrs. Turpin said. "It just makes you feel better all over."

"Of course," the lady said sadly, "but there are just some people you   100
can't tell anything to. They can't take criticism."

"If it's one thing I am," Mrs. Turpin said with feeling, "it's grateful.
When I think who all I could have been besides myself and what all I got, a
little of everything, and a good disposition besides, I just feel like shouting,
'Thank you, Jesus, for making everything the way it is!' It could have been
different!" For one thing, somebody else could have got Claud. At the thought
of this, she was flooded with gratitude and a terrible pang of joy ran through
her. "Oh thank you, Jesus, Jesus, thank you!" she cried aloud.

The book struck her directly over her left eye. It struck almost at the
same instant that she realized the girl was about to hurl it. Before she could
utter a sound, the raw face came crashing across the table toward her, howling.
The girl's fingers sank like clamps into the soft flesh of her neck. She heard
the mother cry out and Claud shout, "Whoa!" There was an instant when she
was certain that she was about to be in an earthquake.

All at once her vision narrowed and she saw everything as if it were
happening in a small room far away, or as if she were looking at it through
the wrong end of a telescope. Claud's face crumpled and fell out of sight. The
nurse ran in, then out, then in again. Then the gangling figure of the doctor
rushed out of the inner door. Magazines flew this way and that as the table
turned over. The girl fell with a thud and Mrs. Turpin's vision suddenly
reversed itself and she saw everything large instead of small. The eyes of the
white-trashy woman were staring hugely at the floor. There the girl, held
down on one side by the nurse and on the other by her mother, was wrenching
and turning in their grasp. The doctor was kneeling astride her, trying to hold
her arm down. He managed after a second to sink a long needle into it.

Mrs. Turpin felt entirely hollow except for her heart which swung from
side to side as if it were agitated in a great empty drum of flesh.

"Somebody that's not busy call for the ambulance," the doctor said in   105
the off-hand voice young doctors adopt for terrible occasions.

Mrs. Turpin could not have moved a finger. The old man who had been
sitting next to her skipped nimbly into the office and made the call, for the
secretary still seemed to be gone.

"Claud!" Mrs. Turpin called.

He was not in his chair. She knew she must jump up and find him but
she felt like some one trying to catch a train in a dream, when everything
moves in slow motion and the faster you try to run the slower you go.

"Here I am," a suffocated voice, very unlike Claud's, said.

He was doubled up in the corner on the floor, pale as paper, holding his   110
leg. She wanted to get up and go to him but she could not move. Instead, her
gaze was drawn slowly downward to the churning face on the floor, which she
could see over the doctor's shoulder.

The girl's eyes stopped rolling and focused on her. They seemed a much
lighter blue than before, as if a door that had been tightly closed behind them
was now open to admit light and air.

Mrs. Turpin's head cleared and her power of motion returned. She leaned
forward until she was looking directly into the fierce brilliant eyes. There was
no doubt in her mind that the girl did know her, knew her in some intense
and personal way, beyond time and place and condition. "What you got to say

to me?" she asked hoarsely and held her breath, waiting, as for a revelation.

The girl raised her head. Her gaze locked with Mrs. Turpin's. "Go back to hell where you came from, you old wart hog," she whispered. Her voice was low but clear. Her eyes burned for a moment as if she saw with pleasure that her message had struck its target.

Mrs. Turpin sank back in her chair.

After a moment the girl's eyes closed and she turned her head wearily to the side.

The doctor rose and handed the nurse the empty syringe. He leaned over and put both hands for a moment on the mother's shoulders, which were shaking. She was sitting on the floor, her lips pressed together, holding Mary Grace's hand in her lap. The girl's fingers were gripped like a baby's around her thumb. "Go on to the hospital," he said. "I'll call and make the arrangements."

"Now let's see that neck," he said in a jovial voice to Mrs. Turpin. He began to inspect her neck with his first two fingers. Two little moon-shaped lines like pink fish bones were indented over her windpipe. There was the beginning of an angry red swelling above her eye. His fingers passed over this also.

"Lea' me be," she said thickly and shook him off. "See about Claud. She kicked him."

"I'll see about him in a minute," he said and felt her pulse. He was a thin grey-haired man, given to pleasantries. "Go home and have yourself a vacation the rest of the day," he said and patted her on the shoulder.

Quit your pattin me, Mrs. Turpin growled to herself.

"And put an ice pack over that eye," he said. Then he went and squatted down beside Claud and looked at his leg. After a moment he pulled him up and Claud limped after him into the office.

Until the ambulance came, the only sounds in the room were the tremulous moans of the girl's mother, who continued to sit on the floor. The white-trash woman did not take her eyes off the girl. Mrs. Turpin looked straight ahead at nothing. Presently the ambulance drew up, a long dark shadow, behind the curtain. The attendants came in and set the stretcher down beside the girl and lifted her expertly onto it and carried her out. The nurse helped the mother gather up her things. The shadow of the ambulance moved silently away and the nurse came back in the office.

"That ther girl is going to be a lunatic, ain't she?" the white-trash woman asked the nurse, but the nurse kept on to the back and never answered her.

"Yes, she's going to be a lunatic," the white-trash woman said to the rest of them.

"Po' critter," the old woman murmured. The child's face was still in her lap. His eyes looked idly out over her knees. He had not moved during the disturbance except to draw one leg up under him.

"I thank Gawd," the white-trash woman said fervently, "I ain't a lunatic."

Claud came limping out and the Turpins went home.

As their pick-up truck turned into their own dirt road and made the crest of the hill, Mrs. Turpin gripped the window ledge and looked out suspiciously. The land sloped gracefully down through a field dotted with lavender weeds and at the start of the rise their small yellow frame house, with its little flower beds spread out around it like a fancy apron, sat primly in its accustomed place between two giant hickory trees. She would not have been startled to see a burnt wound between two blackened chimneys.

Neither of them felt like eating so they put on their house clothes and lowered the shade in the bedroom and lay down, Claud with his leg on a pillow and herself with a damp washcloth over her eye. The instant she was flat on her back, the image of a razor-backed hog with warts on its face and horns coming out behind its ears snorted into her head. She moaned, a low quiet moan.

"I am not," she said tearfully, "a wart hog. From hell." But the denial had no force. The girl's eyes and her words, even the tone of her voice, low but clear, directed only to her, brooked no repudiation. She had been singled out for the message, though there was trash in the room to whom it might justly have been applied. The full force of this fact struck her only now. There was a woman there who was neglecting her own child but she had been overlooked. The message had been given to Ruby Turpin, a respectable, hard-working, church-going woman. The tears dried. Her eyes began to burn instead with wrath.

She rose on her elbow and the washcloth fell into her hand. Claud was lying on his back, snoring. She wanted to tell him what the girl had said. At the same time, she did not wish to put the image of herself as a wart hog from hell into his mind.

"Hey, Claud," she muttered and pushed his shoulder.

Claud opened one pale baby blue eye.

She looked into it warily. He did not think about anything. He just went his way.

"Wha, whasit?" he said and closed the eye again.

"Nothing," she said. "Does your leg pain you?"

"Hurts like hell," Claud said.

"It'll quit terreckly," she said and lay back down. In a moment Claud was snoring again. For the rest of the afternoon they lay there. Claud slept. She scowled at the ceiling. Occasionally she raised her fist and made a small stabbing motion over her chest as if she was defending her innocence to invisible guests who were like the comforters of Job, reasonable-seeming but wrong.

About five-thirty Claud stirred. "Got to go after those niggers," he sighed, not moving.

She was looking straight up as if there were unintelligible handwriting on the ceiling. The protuberance over her eye had turned a greenish-blue. "Listen here," she said.

"What?"

"Kiss me."

Claud leaned over and kissed her loudly on the mouth. He pinched her side and their hands interlocked. Her expression of ferocious concentration did not change. Claud got up, groaning and growling, and limped off. She continued to study the ceiling.

She did not get up until she heard the pick-up truck coming back with the Negroes. Then she rose and thrust her feet in her brown oxfords, which she did not bother to lace, and stumped out onto the back porch and got her red plastic bucket. She emptied a tray of ice cubes into it and filled it half full of water and went out into the back yard. Every afternoon after Claud brought the hands in, one of the boys helped him put out hay and the rest waited in the back of the truck until he was ready to take them home. The truck was parked in the shade under one of the hickory trees.

"Hi yawl this evening?" Mrs. Turpin asked grimly, appearing with the 145 bucket and the dipper. There were three women and a boy in the truck.

"Us doin nicely," the oldest woman said. "Hi you doin?" and her gaze stuck immediately on the dark lump on Mrs. Turpin's forehead. "You done fell down, ain't you?" she asked in a solicitous voice. The old woman was dark and almost toothless. She had on an old felt hat of Claud's set back on her head. The other two women were younger and lighter and they both had new bright green sun hats. One of them had hers on her head; the other had taken hers off and the boy was grinning beneath it.

Mrs. Turpin set the bucket down on the floor of the truck. "Yawl hep yourselves," she said. She looked around to make sure Claud had gone. "No. I didn't fall down," she said, folding her arms. "It was something worse than that."

"Ain't nothing bad happen to you!" the old woman said. She said it as if they all knew that Mrs. Turpin was protected in some special way by Divine Providence. "You just had you a little fall."

"We were in town at the doctor's office for where the cow kicked Mr. Turpin," Mrs. Turpin said in a flat tone that indicated they could leave off their foolishness. "And there was this girl there. A big fat girl with her face all broke out. I could look at that girl and tell she was peculiar but I couldn't tell how. And me and her mama were just talking and going along and all of a sudden WHAM! She throws this big book she was reading at me and . . ."

"Naw!" the old woman cried out. 150

"And then she jumps over the table and commences to choke me."

"Naw!" they all exclaimed, "naw!"

"Hi come she do that?" the old woman asked. "What ail her?"

Mrs. Turpin only glared in front of her.

"Something ail her," the old woman said. 155

"They carried her off in an ambulance," Mrs. Turpin continued, "but before she went she was rolling on the floor and they were trying to hold her down to give her a shot and she said something to me." She paused. "You know what she said to me?"

"What she say?" they asked.

"She said," Mrs. Turpin began, and stopped, her face very dark and heavy. The sun was getting whiter and whiter, blanching the sky overhead so that the leaves of the hickory tree were black in the face of it. She could not bring forth the words. "Something real ugly," she muttered.

"She sho shouldn't said nothin ugly to you," the old woman said. "You so sweet. You the sweetest lady I know."

"She pretty too," the one with the hat on said. 160

"And stout," the other one said. "I never knowed no sweeter white lady."

"That's the truth befo' Jesus," the old woman said. "Amen! You des as sweet and pretty as you can be."

Mrs. Turpin knew just exactly how much Negro flattery was worth and it added to her rage. "She said," she began again and finished this time with a fierce rush of breath, "that I was an old wart hog from hell."

There was an astounded silence.

"Where she at?" the youngest woman cried in a piercing voice. 165

"Lemme see her. I'll kill her!"

"I'll kill her with you!" the other one cried.

"She b'long in the sylum," the old woman said emphatically. "You the sweetest white lady I know."

"She pretty too," the other two said. "Stout as she can be and sweet. Jesus satisfied with her!"

"Deed he is," the old woman declared. 170

Idiots! Mrs. Turpin growled to herself. You could never say anything intelligent to a nigger. You could talk at them but not with them. "Yawl ain't drunk your water," she said shortly. "Leave the bucket in the truck when you're finished with it. I got more to do than just stand around and pass the time of day," and she moved off and into the house.

She stood for a moment in the middle of the kitchen. The dark protuberance over her eye looked like a miniature tornado cloud which might any moment sweep across the horizon of her brow. Her lower lip protruded dangerously. She squared her massive shoulders. Then she marched into the front of the house and out the side door and started down the road to the pig parlor. She had the look of a woman going single-handed, weaponless, into battle.

The sun was a deep yellow now like a harvest moon and was riding westward very fast over the far tree line as if it meant to reach the hogs before she did. The road was rutted and she kicked several good-sized stones out of her path as she strode along. The pig parlor was on a little knoll at the end of a lane that ran off from the side of the barn. It was a square of concrete as large as a small room, with a board fence about four feet high around it. The concrete floor sloped slightly so that the hog wash could drain off into a trench where it was carried to the field for fertilizer. Claud was standing on the outside, on the edge of the concrete, hanging onto the top board, hosing down the floor inside. The hose was connected to the faucet of a water trough nearby.

Mrs. Turpin climbed up beside him and glowered down at the hogs inside. There were seven long-snouted bristly shoats in it — tan with liver-colored spots — and an old sow a few weeks off from farrowing. She was lying on her side grunting. The shoats were running about shaking themselves like idiot children, their little slit pig eyes searching the floor for anything left. She had read that pigs were the most intelligent animal. She doubted it. They were supposed to be smarter than dogs. There had even been a pig astronaut. He had performed his assignment perfectly but died of a heart attack afterwards because they left him in his electric suit, sitting upright throughout his examination when naturally a hog should be on all fours.

A-gruntin and a-rootin and a-groanin. 175

"Gimme that hose," she said, yanking it away from Claud. "Go on and carry them niggers home and then get off that leg."

"You look like you might have swallowed a mad dog," Claud observed, but he got down and limped off. He paid no attention to her humors.

Until he was out of earshot, Mrs. Turpin stood on the side of the pen, holding the hose and pointing the stream of water at the hind quarters of any shoat that looked as if it might try to lie down. When he had had time to get over the hill, she turned her head slightly and her wrathful eyes scanned the path. He was nowhere in sight. She turned back again and seemed to gather herself up. Her shoulders rose and she drew in her breath.

"What do you send me a message like that for?" she said in a low fierce voice, barely above a whisper but with the force of a shout in its concentrated fury. "How am I a hog and me both? How am I saved and from hell too?" Her free fist was knotted and with the other she gripped the hose, blindly pointing the stream of water in and out of the eye of the old sow whose outraged squeal she did not hear.

The pig parlor commanded a view of the back pasture where their twenty beef cows were gathered around the hay-bales Claud and the boy had put out. The freshly cut pasture sloped down to the highway. Across it was their cotton field and beyond that a dark green dusty wood which they owned as well. The sun was behind the wood, very red, looking over the paling of trees like a farmer inspecting his own hogs.

"Why me?" she rumbled. "It's no trash around here, black or white, that I haven't given to. And break my back to the bone every day working. And do for the church."

She appeared to be the right size woman to command the arena before her. "How am I a hog?" she demanded. "Exactly how am I like them?" and she jabbed the stream of water at the shoats. "There was plenty of trash there. It didn't have to be me.

"If you like trash better, go get yourself some trash then," she railed. "You could have made me trash. Or a nigger. If trash is what you wanted why didn't you make me trash?" She shook her fist with the hose in it and a watery snake appeared momentarily in the air. "I could quit working and take it easy and be filthy," she growled. "Lounge about the sidewalks all day drinking root beer. Dip snuff and spit in every puddle and have it all over my face. I could be nasty.

"Or you could have made me a nigger. It's too late for me to be a nigger," she said with deep sarcasm, "but I could act like one. Lay down in the middle of the road and stop traffic. Roll on the ground."

In the deepening light everything was taking on a mysterious hue. The pasture was growing a peculiar glassy green and the streak of highway had turned lavender. She braced herself for a final assault and this time her voice rolled out over the pasture. "Go on," she yelled, "call me a hog! Call me a hog again. From hell. Call me a wart hog from hell. Put that bottom rail on top. There'll still be a top and bottom!"

A garbled echo returned to her.

A final surge of fury shook her and she roared, "Who do you think you are?"

The color of everything, field and crimson sky, burned for a moment with a transparent intensity. The question carried over the pasture and across the highway and the cotton field and returned to her clearly like an answer from beyond the wood.

She opened her mouth but no sound came out of it.

A tiny truck, Claud's, appeared on the highway, heading rapidly out of sight. Its gears scraped thinly. It looked like a child's toy. At any moment a bigger truck might smash into it and scatter Claud's and the niggers' brains all over the road.

Mrs. Turpin stood there, her gaze fixed on the highway, all her muscles rigid, until in five or six minutes the truck reappeared, returning. She waited until it had had time to turn into their own road. Then like a monumental statue coming to life, she bent her head slowly and gazed, as if through the very heart of mystery, down into the pig parlor at the hogs. They had settled all in one corner around the old sow who was grunting softly. A red glow suffused them. They appeared to pant with a secret life.

Until the sun slipped finally behind the tree line, Mrs. Turpin remained there with her gaze bent to them as if she were absorbing some abysmal life-giving knowledge. At last she lifted her head. There was only a purple streak in the sky, cutting through a field of crimson and leading, like an extension of the highway, into the descending dusk. She raised her hands from the side of the pen in a gesture hieratic and profound. A visionary light settled in her eyes. She saw the streak as a vast swinging bridge extending upward from the earth through a field of living fire. Upon it a vast horde of souls were rumbling toward heaven. There were whole companies of white-trash, clean for the first time in their lives, and bands of black niggers in white robes, and battalions of freaks and lunatics shouting and clapping and leaping like frogs. And bringing up the end of the procession was a tribe of people whom she recognized at once as those who, like herself and Claud, had always had a little of everything and the God-given wit to use it right. She leaned forward to observe them closer. They were marching behind the others with great dignity, accountable as they had always been for good order and common sense and respectable behavior. They alone were on key. Yet she could see by their shocked and altered faces that even their virtues were being burned away. She lowered her hands and gripped the rail of the hog pen, her eyes small but fixed unblinkingly on what lay ahead. In a moment the vision faded but she remained where she was, immobile.

At length she got down and turned off the faucet and made her slow way on the darkening path to the house. In the woods around her the invisible cricket choruses had struck up, but what she heard were the voices of the souls climbing upward into the starry field and shouting hallelujah.

QUESTIONS

1. How does Mrs. Turpin see herself before Mary Grace calls her a wart hog?
2. What is the narrator's attitude toward Mrs. Turpin in the beginning of the story? How can you tell? Does this attitude change, or stay the same, at the end?
3. Describe the relationship between Mary Grace and her mother. What annoying platitudes does the mother mouth? Which of Mrs. Turpin's opinions seem especially to anger Mary Grace?
4. Sketch the plot of the story. What moment or event do you take to be the crisis, or turning point? What is the climax? What is the conclusion?
5. What do you infer from Mrs. Turpin's conversation with the black farm workers? Is she their friend? Why does she now find their flattery unacceptable ("Jesus satisfied with her")?

6. When, near the end of the story, Mrs. Turpin roars, "Who do you think you are?" an echo "returned to her clearly like an answer from beyond the wood" (paragraph 188). Explain.
7. What is the final revelation given to Mrs. Turpin? (To state it is to state the theme of the story.) What new attitude does the revelation impart? (How is Mrs. Turpin left with a new vision of humanity?)
8. Other stories in this book contain revelations: "Gimpel the Fool," "The Death of Ivan Ilych." If you have read them, try to sum up the supernatural revelation made to the central character in each story. In each, is the revelation the same as a statement of the story's main theme?

E. B. White
THE DOOR   1939

Elwyn Brooks White (1899 – 1985) was one of America's most widely admired craftsmen of the English language, and indeed, so he remains. For a half-century beginning in 1926, White steadily contributed to The New Yorker, *turning out essays, stories, editorials, verse, and unsigned fillers, and reporting for a weekly feature, "The Talk of the Town." His work helped the magazine erect a reputation for trenchant wit and lively writing. Besides, White wrote the lastingly popular children's stories* Stuart Little *(1945),* Charlotte's Web *(1952), and* The Trumpet of the Swan *(1970), and he successfully revised a textbook of grammar and usage he had used as a college student at Cornell:* The Elements of Style *by William Strunk, Jr. (republished as by Strunk and White in 1959). In 1976 White's* Letters *were collected, in 1977 his* Essays, *and in 1981 his* Poems and Sketches. *In later life, White quit Manhattan for a farm in North Brooklin, Maine.*

Everything (he kept saying) is something it isn't. And everybody is always somewhere else. Maybe it was the city, being in the city, that made him feel how queer everything was and that it was something else. Maybe (he kept thinking) it was the names of the things. The names were tex and frequently koid. Or they were flex and oid or they were duroid (sani) or flexsan (duro), but everything was glass (but not quite glass) and the thing that you touched (the surface, washable, crease-resistant) was rubber, only it wasn't quite rubber and you didn't quite touch it but almost. The wall, which was glass but thrutex, turned out on being approached not to be a wall, it was something else, it was an opening or doorway — and the doorway (through which he saw himself approaching) turned out to be something else, it was a wall. And what he had eaten not having agreed with him.

He was in a washable house, but he wasn't sure. Now about those rats, he kept saying to himself. He meant the rats that the Professor had driven crazy by forcing them to deal with problems which were beyond the scope of rats, the insoluble problems. He meant the rats that had been trained to jump at the square card with the circle in the middle, and the card (because it was something it wasn't) would give way and let the rat into a place where the food was, but then one day it would be a trick played on the rat, and the card would be changed, and the rat would jump but the card wouldn't give way, and it was an impossible situation (for a rat) and the rat would go insane and into its eyes would come the unspeakably bright imploring look of the frustrated, and after the convulsions were over and the frantic racing around, then the passive stage would set in and the willingness to let anything be done to it, even if it was something else.

He didn't know which door (or wall) or opening in the house to jump at, to get through, because one was an opening that wasn't a door (it was a void, or koid) and the other was a wall that wasn't an opening, it was a sanitary cupboard of the same color. He caught a glimpse of his eyes staring into his eyes, in the thrutex, and in them was the expression he had seen in the picture of the rats — weary after convulsions and the frantic racing around, when they were willing and did not mind having anything done to them. More and more (he kept saying) I am confronted by a problem which is incapable of solution (for this time even if he chose the right door, there would be no food behind it) and that is what madness is, and things seeming different from what they are. He heard, in the house where he was, in the city to which he had gone (as toward a door which might, or might not, give way), a noise — not a loud noise but more of a low prefabricated humming. It came from a place in the base of the wall (or stat) where the flue carrying the filterable air was, and not far from the Minipiano, which was made of the same material nailbrushes are made of, and which was under the stairs. "This, too, has been tested," she said, pointing, but not at it, "and found viable." It wasn't a loud noise, he kept thinking, sorry that he had seen his eyes, even though it was through his own eyes that he had seen them.

First will come the convulsions (he said), then the exhaustion, then the willingness to let anything be done. "And you better believe it *will* be."

All his life he had been confronted by situations which were incapable   5
of being solved, and there was a deliberateness behind all this, behind this changing of the card (or door), because they would always wait till you had learned to jump at the certain card (or door) — the one with the circle — and then they would change it on you. There have been so many doors changed on me, he said, in the last twenty years, but it is now becoming clear that it is an impossible situation, and the question is whether to jump again, even though they ruffle you in the rump with a blast of air — to make you jump. He wished he wasn't standing by the Minipiano. First they would teach you the prayers and the Psalms, and that would be the right door (the one with the circle), and the long sweet words with the holy sound, and that would be the one to jump at to get where the food was. Then one day you jumped and it didn't give way, so that all you got was the bump on the nose, and the first bewilderment, the first young bewilderment.

I don't know whether to tell her about the door they substituted or not, he said, the one with the equation on it and the picture of the amoeba reproducing itself by division. Or the one with the photostatic copy of the check for thirty-two dollars and fifty cents. But the jumping was so long ago, although the bump is . . . how those old wounds hurt! Being crazy this way wouldn't be so bad if only, if only. If only when you put your foot forward to take a step, the ground wouldn't come up to meet your foot the way it does. And the same way in the street (only I may never get back to the street unless I jump at the right door), the curb coming up to meet your foot, anticipating ever so delicately the weight of the body, which is somewhere else. "We could take your name," she said, "and send it to you." And it wouldn't be so bad if only you could read a sentence all the way through without jumping (your eye) to something else on the same page; and then (he kept thinking) there was that man out in Jersey, the one who started to chop his trees down, one by one, the man who began talking about how he would take his house to pieces, brick by brick, because he faced a problem incapable of solution, probably, so he began to hack at the trees in the yard, began to pluck with trembling fingers at the bricks in the house. Even if a house is not washable, it is worth taking down. It is not till later that the exhaustion sets in.

But it is inevitable that they will keep changing the doors on you, he said, because that is what they are for; and the thing is to get used to it and not let it unsettle the mind. But that would mean not jumping, and you can't. Nobody can not jump. There will be no not-jumping. Among rats, perhaps, but among people never. Everybody has to keep jumping at a door (the one with the circle on it) because that is the way everybody is, specially some people. You wouldn't want me, standing here, to tell you, would you, about my friend the poet (deceased) who said, "My heart has followed all my days something I cannot name"? (It had the circle on it.) And like many poets, although few so beloved, he is gone. It killed him, the jumping. First, of course, there were the preliminary bouts, the convulsions, and the calm and the willingness.

I remember the door with the picture of the girl on it (only it was spring), her arms outstretched in loveliness, her dress (it was the one with the circle on it) uncaught, beginning the slow, clear, blinding cascade — and I guess we would all like to try that door again, for it seemed like the way and for a while it was the way, the door would open and you would go through winged and exalted (like any rat) and the food would be there, the way the Professor had it arranged, everything O.K., and you had chosen the right door for the world was young. The time they changed that door on me, my nose bled for a hundred hours — how do you like that, Madam? Or would you prefer to show me further through this so strange house, or you could take my name and send it to me, for although my heart has followed all my days something I cannot name, I am tired of the jumping and I do not know which way to go, Madam, and I am not even sure that I am not tried beyond the endurance of man (rat, if you will) and have taken leave of sanity. What are you following these days, old friend, after your recovery from the last bump? What is the name, or is it something you cannot name? The rats have a name for it by this time, perhaps, but I don't know what they call it. I call it plexikoid and it comes in sheets, something like insulating board, unattainable and ugli-proof.

And there was the man out in Jersey, because I keep thinking about his terrible necessity and the passion and trouble he had gone to all those years in the indescribable abundance of a householder's detail, building the estate and the planting of the trees and in spring the lawn dressing and in fall the bulbs for the spring burgeoning, and the watering of the grass on the long light evenings in summer and the gravel for the driveway (all had to be thought out, planned) and the decorative borders, probably, the perennials and the bug spray, and the building of the house from plans of the architect, first the sills, then the studs, then the full corn in the ear, the floors laid on the floor timbers, smoothed, and then the carpets upon the smooth floors and the curtains and the rods therefor. And then, almost without warning, he would be jumping at the same old door and it wouldn't give: they had changed it on him, making life no longer supportable under the elms in the elm shade, under the maples in the maple shade.

"Here you have the maximum of openness in a small room."   10

It was impossible to say (maybe it was the city) what made him feel the way he did, and I am not the only one either, he kept thinking — ask any doctor if I am. The doctors, they know how many there are, they even know where the trouble is only they don't like to tell you about the prefrontal lobe because that means making a hole in your skull and removing the work of centuries. It took so long coming, this lobe, so many, many years. (Is it something you read in the paper, perhaps?) And now, the strain being so great, the door having been changed by the Professor once too often . . . but it only means a whiff of ether, a few deft strokes, and the higher animal becomes a little easier in his mind and more like the lower one. From now on, you see, that's the way it will be, the ones with the small prefrontal lobes will win because the other ones are hurt too much by this incessant bumping. They can stand just so much, eh, Doctor? (And what is that, pray, that you have in your hand?) Still, you never can tell, eh, Madam?

He crossed (carefully) the room, the thick carpet under him softly, and went toward the door carefully, which was glass and he could see himself in it, and which, at his approach, opened to allow him to pass through; and beyond he half expected to find one of the old doors that he had known, perhaps the one with the circle, the one with the girl her arms outstretched in loveliness and beauty before him. But he saw instead a moving stairway, and descended in light (he kept thinking) to the street below and to the other people. As he stepped off, the ground came up slightly, to meet his foot.

Questions

1. Who is the "I" in "The Door"?
2. Where does this story take place?
3. In the opening paragraphs, what is suggested by the odd un-English-sounding language — *tex, koid, duroid (sani), flexsan (duro), thrutex, stat,* and *Minipiano?* Where have you heard words (or parts of words) like those before? Would you expect a lover of the English language, like White, to be fond of such words? Why or why not?
4. In paragraph 2, White refers to "the rats that the Professor had driven crazy." Where else in his story does he refer to these rats? What do rats and the Professor have to do with you and me?
5. What does the main character mean when he suggests that at first the door with the prayers, Psalms, and "long sweet words with the holy sound" was "the one to jump at" (paragraph 5)? What do you understand him to mean by "the first young bewilderment"?
6. What does the author suggest by the doors bearing the equation and picture of the amoeba, the photostatic copy of the check (paragraph 6), and the picture of the girl (paragraph 8)? Who are "they," the ones who keep changing these doors on you?

7. What does the man in New Jersey who set out to destroy his trees and house have to do with the rest of the story?
8. What does the main character mean by "There will be no not-jumping" (paragraph 7)?
9. ". . . But it only means a whiff of ether, a few deft strokes, and the higher animal becomes a little easier in his mind and more like the lower one" (paragraph 11). Explain what you understand by this remark.
10. How would you sum up the story's theme or themes?

Stephen Crane
THE OPEN BOAT   1897

Stephen Crane (1871 – 1900) was born in Newark, New Jersey, a Methodist minister's last and fourteenth child. After flunking out of both Lafayette College and Syracuse University, he became a journalist in New York, specializing in grim life among the down-and-out who people his early self-published novel Maggie: A Girl of the Streets *(1893). Restlessly generating material for stories, Crane trekked to the Southwest, New Orleans, and Mexico. "The Open Boat" is based on experience. En route to Havana to report the Cuban revolution for the New York* Press, *Crane was shipwrecked when the S.S.* Commodore *sank in heavy seas east of New Smyrna, Florida, on January 2, 1897. He escaped in a ten-foot lifeboat with the captain and two members of the crew. Later that year, Crane moved into a stately home in England with Cora Taylor, former Madam of a Florida brothel, hobnobbed with literary greats, and lived beyond his means. Hounded by creditors, afflicted by tuberculosis, he died in Germany at twenty-eight. Crane has been called the first writer of American realism. His famed novel* The Red Badge of Courage *(1895) gives an imagined but convincing account of a young Union soldier's initiation into battle. A handful of his short stories appear immortal. He was an original poet, too, writing terse, sardonic poems in open forms, at the time considered radical. In his short life, Crane greatly helped American literature to come of age.*

A Tale Intended to be after the Fact:
Being the Experience of Four Men from the Sunk Steamer Commodore

I

None of them knew the color of the sky. Their eyes glanced level, and were fastened upon the waves that swept toward them. These waves were of the hue of slate, save for the tops, which were of foaming white, and all of the men knew the colors of the sea. The horizon narrowed and widened, and dipped and rose, and at all times its edge was jagged with waves that seemed thrust up in points like rocks.

Many a man ought to have a bathtub larger than the boat which here rode upon the sea. These waves were most wrongfully and barbarously abrupt and tall, and each frothtop was a problem in small-boat navigation.

The cook squatted in the bottom, and looked with both eyes at the six inches of gunwale which separated him from the ocean. His sleeves were rolled over his fat forearms, and the two flaps of his unbuttoned vest dangled as he bent to bail out the boat. Often he said, "Gawd! that was a narrow clip." As he remarked it he invariably gazed eastward over the broken sea.

The oiler, steering with one of the two oars in the boat, sometimes raised himself suddenly to keep clear of water that swirled in over the stern. It was a thin little oar, and it seemed often ready to snap.

The correspondent°, pulling at the other oar, watched the waves and   5
wondered why he was there.

The injured captain, lying in the bow, was at this time buried in that profound dejection and indifference which comes, temporarily at least, to even the bravest and most enduring when, willy-nilly, the firm fails, the army loses, the ship goes down. The mind of the master of a vessel is rooted deep in the timbers of her, though he command for a day or a decade; and this captain had on him the stern impression of a scene in the grays of dawn of seven turned faces, and later a stump of a topmast with a white ball on it, that slashed to and fro at the waves, went low and lower, and down. Thereafter there was something strange in his voice. Although steady, it was deep with mourning, and of a quality beyond oration or tears.

"Keep 'er a little more south, Billie," said he.

"A little more south, sir," said the oiler in the stern.

A seat in this boat was not unlike a seat upon a bucking broncho, and by the same token a broncho is not much smaller. The craft pranced and reared and plunged like an animal. As each wave came, and she rose for it, she seemed like a horse making at a fence outrageously high. The manner of her scramble over these walls of water is a mystic thing, and, moreover, at the top of them were ordinarily these problems in white water, the foam racing down from the summit of each wave requiring a new leap, and a leap from the air. Then, after scornfully bumping a crest, she would slide and race and splash down a long incline, and arrive bobbing and nodding in front of the next menace.

A singular disadvantage of the sea lies in the fact that after successfully   10
surmounting one wave you discover that there is another behind it just as important and just as nervously anxious to do something effective in the way of swamping boats. In a ten-foot dinghy one can get an idea of the resources of the sea in the line of waves that is not probable to the average experience which is never at sea in a dinghy. As each slaty wall of water approached, it shut all else from the view of the men in the boat, and it was not difficult to imagine that this particular wave was the final outburst of the ocean, the last effort of the grim water. There was a terrible grace in the move of the waves, and they came in silence, save for the snarling of the crests.

In the wan light the faces of the men must have been gray. Their eyes must have glinted in strange ways as they gazed steadily astern. Viewed from a balcony, the whole thing would doubtless have been weirdly picturesque.

correspondent: foreign correspondent, newspaper reporter.

But the men in the boat had no time to see it, and if they had had leisure, there were other things to occupy their minds. The sun swung steadily up the sky, and they knew it was broad day because the color of the sea changed from slate to emerald green streaked with amber lights, and the foam was like tumbling snow. The process of the breaking day was unknown to them. They were aware only of this effect upon the color of the waves that rolled toward them.

In disjointed sentences the cook and the correspondent argued as to the difference between a life-saving station and a house of refuge. The cook had said: "There's a house of refuge just north of the Mosquito Inlet Light, and as soon as they see us they'll come off in their boat and pick us up."

"As soon as who see us?" said the correspondent.

"The crew," said the cook.

"Houses of refuge don't have crews," said the correspondent. "As I understand them, they are only places where clothes and grub are stored for the benefit of shipwrecked people. They don't carry crews." 15

"Oh, yes, they do," said the cook.

"No, they don't," said the correspondent.

"Well, we're not there yet, anyhow," said the oiler, in the stern.

"Well," said the cook, "perhaps it's not a house of refuge that I'm thinking of as being near Mosquito Inlet Light; perhaps it's a life-saving station."

"We're not there yet," said the oiler in the stern. 20

II

As the boat bounced from the top of each wave the wind tore through the hair of the hatless men, and as the craft plopped her stern down again the spray slashed past them. The crest of each of these waves was a hill, from the top of which the men surveyed for a moment a broad tumultuous expanse, shining and wind-riven. It was probably splendid, it was probably glorious, this play of the free sea, wild with lights of emerald and white and amber.

"Bully good thing it's an on-shore wind," said the cook. "If not, where would we be? Wouldn't have a show."

"That's right," said the correspondent.

The busy oiler nodded his assent.

Then the captain, in the bow, chuckled in a way that expressed humor, contempt, tragedy, all in one. "Do you think we've got much of a show now, boys?" said he. 25

Whereupon the three were silent, save for a trifle of hemming and hawing. To express any particular optimism at this time they felt to be childish and stupid, but they all doubtless possessed this sense of the situation in their minds. A young man thinks doggedly at such times. On the other hand, the ethics of their condition was decidedly against any open suggestion of hopelessness. So they were silent.

"Oh, well," said the captain, soothing his children, "we'll get ashore all right."

But there was that in his tone which made them think; so the oiler quoth, "Yes! if this wind holds."

The cook was bailing. "Yes! if we don't catch hell in the surf."

Canton-flannel gulls flew near and far. Sometimes they sat down on the   30
sea, near patches of brown seaweed that rolled over the waves with a movement like carpets on a line in a gale. The birds sat comfortably in groups, and
they were envied by some in the dinghy, for the wrath of the sea was no more
to them than it was to a covey of prairie chickens a thousand miles inland.
Often they came very close and stared at the men with black bead-like eyes.
At these times they were uncanny and sinister in their unblinking scrutiny,
and the men hooted angrily at them, telling them to be gone. One came, and
evidently decided to alight on the top of the captain's head. The bird flew
parallel to the boat and did not circle, but made short sidelong jumps in the
air in chicken-fashion. His black eyes were wistfully fixed upon the captain's
head. "Ugly brute," said the oiler to the bird. "You look as if you were made
with a jackknife." The cook and the correspondent swore darkly at the creature. The captain naturally wished to knock it away with the end of the heavy
painter, but he did not dare do it, because anything resembling an emphatic
gesture would have capsized this freighted boat; and so, with his open hand,
the captain gently and carefully waved the gull away. After it had been
discouraged from the pursuit the captain breathed easier on account of his hair,
and others breathed easier because the bird struck their minds at this time as
being somehow gruesome and ominous.

In the meantime the oiler and the correspondent rowed. And also they
rowed. They sat together in the same seat, and each rowed an oar. Then the
oiler took both oars; then the correspondent took both oars; then the oiler; then
the correspondent. They rowed and they rowed. The very ticklish part of the
business was when the time came for the reclining one in the stern to take his
turn at the oars. By the very last star of truth, it is easier to steal eggs from
under a hen than it was to change seats in the dinghy. First the man in the stern
slid his hand along the thwart and moved with care, as if he were of
Sèvres°. Then the man in the rowing-seat slid his hand along the other thwart.
It was all done with the most extraordinary care. As the two sidled past each
other, the whole party kept watchful eyes on the coming wave, and the captain
cried: "Look out, now! Steady, there!"

The brown mats of seaweed that appeared from time to time were like
islands, bits of earth. They were travelling, apparently, neither one way nor
the other. They were, to all intents, stationary. They informed the men in the
boat that it was making progress slowly toward the land.

The captain, rearing cautiously in the bow after the dinghy soared on a
great swell, said that he had seen the lighthouse at Mosquito Inlet. Presently
the cook remarked that he had seen it. The correspondent was at the oars then,
and for some reason he too wished to look at the lighthouse; but his back was
toward the far shore, and the waves were important, and for some time he
could not seize an opportunity to turn his head. But at last there came a wave
more gentle than the others, and when at the crest of it he swiftly scoured the
western horizon.

"See it?" said the captain.

"No," said the correspondent, slowly; "I didn't see anything."   35

Sèvres: chinaware made in this French town.

"Look again," said the captain. He pointed. "It's exactly in that direction."

At the top of another wave the correspondent did as he was bid, and this time his eyes chanced on a small, still thing on the edge of the swaying horizon. It was precisely like the point of a pin. It took an anxious eye to find a lighthouse so tiny.

"Think we'll make it, Captain?"

"If this wind holds and the boat don't swamp, we can't do much else," said the captain.

The little boat, lifted by each towering sea and splashed viciously by the crests, made progress that in the absence of seaweed was not apparent to those in her. She seemed just a wee thing wallowing, miraculously top up, at the mercy of five oceans. Occasionally a great spread of water, like white flames, swarmed into her.

"Bail her, cook," said the captain, serenely.

"All right, Captain," said the cheerful cook.

III

It would be difficult to describe the subtle brotherhood of men that was here established on the seas. No one said that it was so. No one mentioned it. But it dwelt in the boat, and each man felt it warm him. They were a captain, an oiler, a cook, and a correspondent, and they were friends — friends in a more curiously iron-bound degree than may be common. The hurt captain, lying against the water-jar in the bow, spoke always in a low voice and calmly; but he could never command a more ready and swiftly obedient crew than the motley three of the dinghy. It was more than a mere recognition of what was best for the common safety. There was surely in it a quality that was personal and heart-felt. And after this devotion to the commander of the boat, there was this comradeship, that the correspondent, for instance, who had been taught to be cynical of men, knew even at the time was the best experience of his life. But no one said that it was so. No one mentioned it.

"I wish we had a sail," remarked the captain. "We might try my overcoat on the end of an oar, and give you two boys a chance to rest." So the cook and the correspondent held the mast and spread wide the overcoat; the oiler steered; and the little boat made good way with her new rig. Sometimes the oiler had to scull sharply to keep a sea from breaking into the boat, but otherwise sailing was a success.

Meanwhile the lighthouse had been growing slowly larger. It had now almost assumed color, and appeared like a little gray shadow on the sky. The man at the oars could not be prevented from turning his head rather often to try for a glimpse of this little gray shadow.

At last, from the top of each wave, the men in the tossing boat could see land. Even as the lighthouse was an upright shadow on the sky, this land seemed but a long black shadow on the sea. It certainly was thinner than paper. "We must be about opposite New Smyrna," said the cook, who had coasted this shore often in schooners. "Captain, by the way, I believe they abandoned that life-saving station there about a year ago."

"Did they?" said the captain.

The wind slowly died away. The cook and the correspondent were not now obliged to slave in order to hold high the oar. But the waves continued their old impetuous swooping at the dinghy, and the little craft, no longer under way, struggled woundily over them. The oiler or the correspondent took the oars again.

Shipwrecks are apropos of nothing. If men could only train for them and have them occur when the men had reached pink condition, there would be less drowning at sea. Of the four in the dinghy none had slept any time worth mentioning for two days and two nights previous to embarking in the dinghy, and in the excitement of clambering about the deck of a foundering ship they had also forgotten to eat heartily.

For these reasons, and for others, neither the oiler nor the correspondent 50 was fond of rowing at this time. The correspondent wondered ingenuously how in the name of all that was sane could there be people who thought it amusing to row a boat. It was not an amusement; it was a diabolical punishment, and even a genius of mental aberrations could never conclude that it was anything but a horror to the muscles and a crime against the back. He mentioned to the boat in general how the amusement of rowing struck him, and the weary-faced oiler smiled in full sympathy. Previously to the foundering, by the way, the oiler had worked double watch in the engine-room of the ship.

"Take her easy now, boys," said the captain. "Don't spend yourselves. If we have to run a surf you'll need all your strength, because we'll sure have to swim for it. Take your time."

Slowly the land arose from the sea. From a black line it became a line of black and a line of white — trees and sand. Finally the captain said that he could make out a house on the shore. "That's the house of refuge, sure," said the cook. "They'll see us before long, and come out after us."

The distant lighthouse reared high. "The keeper ought to be able to make us out now, if he's looking through a glass," said the captain. "He'll notify the life-saving people."

"None of those other boats could have got ashore to give word of the wreck," said the oiler, in a low voice, "else the life-boat would be out hunting us."

Slowly and beautifully the land loomed out of the sea. The wind came 55 again. It had veered from the north-east to the south-east. Finally a new sound struck the ears of the men in the boat. It was the low thunder of the surf on the shore. "We'll never be able to make the lighthouse now," said the captain. "Swing her head a little more north, Billie."

"A little more north, sir," said the oiler.

Whereupon the little boat turned her nose once more down the wind, and all but the oarsman watched the shore grow. Under the influence of this expansion doubt and direful apprehension were leaving the minds of the men. The management of the boat was still most absorbing, but it could not prevent a quiet cheerfulness. In an hour, perhaps, they would be ashore.

Their backbones had become thoroughly used to balancing in the boat, and they now rode this wild colt of a dinghy like circus men. The correspondent thought that he had been drenched to the skin, but happening to feel in the top pocket of his coat, he found therein eight cigars. Four of them were soaked with sea-water; four were perfectly scatheless. After a search, somebody produced three dry matches; and thereupon the four waifs rode impudently in their little boat and, with an assurance of an impending rescue shining in their eyes, puffed at the big cigars, and judged well and ill of all men. Everybody took a drink of water.

IV

"Cook," remarked the captain, "there don't seem to be any signs of life about your house of refuge."

"No," replied the cook. "Funny they don't see us!"

A broad stretch of lowly coast lay before the eyes of the men. It was of low dunes topped with dark vegetation. The roar of the surf was plain, and sometimes they could see the white lip of a wave as it spun up the beach. A tiny house was blocked out black upon the sky. Southward, the slim lighthouse lifted its little gray length.

Tide, wind, and waves were swinging the dinghy northward. "Funny they don't see us," said the men.

The surf's roar was here dulled, but its tone was nevertheless thunderous and mighty. As the boat swam over the great rollers the men sat listening to this roar. "We'll swamp sure," said everybody.

It is fair to say here that there was not a life-saving station within twenty miles in either direction; but the men did not know this fact, and in consequence they made dark and opprobrious remarks concerning the eyesight of the nation's life-savers. Four scowling men sat in the dinghy and surpassed records in the invention of epithets.

"Funny they don't see us."

The light-heartedness of a former time had completely faded. To their sharpened minds it was easy to conjure pictures of all kinds of incompetency and blindness and, indeed, cowardice. There was the shore of the populous land, and it was bitter and bitter to them that from it came no sign.

"Well," said the captain, ultimately, "I suppose we'll have to make a try for ourselves. If we stay out here too long, we'll none of us have strength left to swim after the boat swamps."

And so the oiler, who was at the oars, turned the boat straight for the shore. There was a sudden tightening of muscles. There was some thinking.

"If we don't all get ashore," said the captain — "if we don't all get ashore, I suppose you fellows know where to send news of my finish?"

They then briefly exchanged some addresses and admonitions. As for the reflections of the men, there was a great deal of rage in them. Perchance they might be formulated thus: "If I am going to be drowned — if I am going to be drowned — if I am going to be drowned, why, in the name of the seven mad gods who rule the sea, was I allowed to come thus far and contemplate sand and trees? Was I brought here merely to have my nose dragged away as I was about to nibble the sacred cheese of life? It is preposterous. If this old ninny-woman, Fate, cannot do better than this, she should be deprived of the management of men's fortunes. She is an old hen who knows not her intention. If she has decided to drown me, why did she not do it in the beginning and save me all this trouble? The whole affair is absurd. — But no; she cannot mean

60

65

70

to drown me. She dare not drown me. She cannot drown me. Not after all this work." Afterward the man might have had an impulse to shake his fist at the clouds. "Just you drown me, now, and then hear what I call you!"

The billows that came at this time were more formidable. They seemed always just about to break and roll over the little boat in a turmoil of foam. There was a preparatory and long growl in the speech of them. No mind unused to the sea would have concluded that the dinghy could ascend these sheer heights in time. The shore was still afar. The oiler was a wily surfman. "Boys," he said swiftly, "she won't live three minutes more, and we're too far out to swim. Shall I take her to sea again, Captain?"

"Yes; go ahead!" said the captain.

This oiler, by a series of quick miracles and fast and steady oarsmanship, turned the boat in the middle of the surf and took her safely to sea again.

There was a considerable silence as the boat bumped over the furrowed sea to deeper water. Then somebody in gloom spoke: "Well, anyhow, they must have seen us from the shore by now."

The gulls went in slanting flight up the wind toward the gray, desolate east. A squall, marked by dingy clouds and clouds brick-red like smoke from a burning building, appeared from the south-east. ⁊⁵

"What do you think of those life-saving people? Ain't they peaches?"

"Funny they haven't seen us."

"Maybe they think we're out here for sport! Maybe they think we're fishin'. Maybe they think we're damned fools."

It was a long afternoon. A changed tide tried to force them southward, but wind and wave said northward. Far ahead, where coast-line, sea, and sky formed their mighty angle, there were little dots which seemed to indicate a city on the shore.

"St. Augustine?" 80

The captain shook his head. "Too near Mosquito Inlet."

And the oiler rowed, and then the correspondent rowed; then the oiler rowed. It was a weary business. The human back can become the seat of more aches and pains than are registered in books for the composite anatomy of a regiment. It is a limited area, but it can become the theatre of innumerable muscular conflicts, tangles, wrenches, knots, and other comforts.

"Did you ever like to row, Billie?" asked the correspondent.

"No," said the oiler; "hang it!"

When one exchanged the rowing-seat for a place in the bottom of the 85 boat, he suffered a bodily depression that caused him to be careless of every- thing save an obligation to wiggle one finger. There was cold sea-water swash- ing to and fro in the boat, and he lay in it. His head, pillowed on a thwart, was within an inch of the swirl of a wave-crest, and sometimes a particularly obstreperous sea came inboard and drenched him once more. But these matters did not annoy him. It is almost certain that if the boat had capsized he would have tumbled comfortably upon the ocean as if he felt sure that it was a great soft mattress.

"Look! There's a man on the shore!"

"Where?"

"There! See 'im?"

"Yes, sure! He's walking along."

"Now he's stopped. Look! He's facing us!"

"He's waving at us!"

"So he is! By thunder!"

"Ah, now we're all right! Now we're all right! There'll be a boat out here for us in half an hour."

"He's going on. He's running. He's going up to that house there."

The remote beach seemed lower than the sea, and it required a searching glance to discern the little black figure. The captain saw a floating stick, and they rowed to it. A bath towel was by some weird chance in the boat, and, tying this on the stick, the captain waved it. The oarsman did not dare turn his head, so he was obliged to ask questions.

"What's he doing now?"

"He's standing still again. He's looking, I think. — There he goes again — toward the house. — Now he's stopped again."

"Is he waving at us?"

"No, not now; he was, though."

"Look! There comes another man!"

"He's running."

"Look at him go, would you!"

"Why, he's on a bicycle. Now he's met the other man. They're both waving at us. Look!"

"There comes something up the beach."

"What the devil is that thing?"

"Why, it looks like a boat."

"Why, certainly, it's a boat."

"No; it's on wheels."

"Yes, so it is. Well, that must be the life-boat. They drag them along shore on a wagon."

"That's the life-boat, sure."

"No, by God, it's — it's an omnibus."

"I tell you it's a life-boat."

"It is not! It's an omnibus. I can see it plain. See? One of these big hotel omnibuses."

"By thunder, you're right. It's an omnibus, sure as fate. What do you suppose they are doing with an omnibus? Maybe they are going around collecting the life-crew, hey?"

"That's it, likely. Look! There's a fellow waving a little black flag. He's standing on the steps of the omnibus. There come those other two fellows. Now they're all talking together. Look at the fellow with the flag. Maybe he ain't waving it!"

"That ain't a flag, is it? That's his coat. Why, certainly, that's his coat."

"So it is; it's his coat. He's taken it off and is waving it around his head. But would you look at him swing it!"

"Oh, say, there isn't any life-saving station there. That's just a winter-resort hotel omnibus that has brought over some of the boarders to see us drown."

"What's that idiot with the coat mean? What's he signalling, anyhow?"

"It looks as if he were trying to tell us to go north. There must be a life-saving station up there."

"No; he thinks we're fishing. Just giving us a merry hand. See? Ah, there, Willie!"

"Well, I wish I could make something out of those signals. What do you suppose he means?"

"He don't mean anything; he's just playing."

"Well, if he'd just signal us to try the surf again, or to go to sea and wait, or go north, or go south, or go to hell, there would be some reason in it. But look at him! He just stands there and keeps his coat revolving like a wheel. The ass!"

"There come more people." 125

"Now there's quite a mob. Look! Isn't that a boat?"

"Where? Oh, I see where you mean. No, that's no boat."

"That fellow is still waving his coat."

"He must think we like to see him do that. Why don't he quit it? It don't mean anything."

"I don't know. I think he is trying to make us go north. It must be that 130 there's a life-saving station there somewhere."

"Say, he ain't tired yet. Look at 'im wave!"

"Wonder how long he can keep that up. He's been revolving his coat ever since he caught sight of us. He's an idiot. Why aren't they getting men to bring a boat out? A fishingboat — one of those big yawls — could come out here all right. Why don't he do something?"

"Oh, it's all right now."

"They'll have a boat out here for us in less than no time, now that they've seen us."

A faint yellow tone came into the sky over the low land. The shadows 135 on the sea slowly deepened. The wind bore coldness with it, and the men began to shiver.

"Holy smoke!" said one, allowing his voice to express his impious mood, "If we keep on monkeying out here! If we've got to flounder out here all night!"

"Oh, we'll never have to stay here all night! Don't you worry. They've seen us now, and it won't be long before they'll come chasing out after us."

The shore grew dusky. The man waving a coat blended gradually into this gloom, and it swallowed in the same manner the omnibus and the group of people. The spray, when it dashed uproariously over the side, made the voyagers shrink and swear like men who were being branded.

"I'd like to catch the chump who waved the coat. I feel like socking him one, just for luck."

"Why? What did he do?" 140

"Oh, nothing, but then he seemed so damned cheerful."

In the meantime the oiler rowed, and then the correspondent rowed, and then the oiler rowed. Gray-faced and bowed forward, they mechanically, turn by turn, plied the leaden oars. The form of the lighthouse had vanished from the southern horizon, but finally a pale star appeared, just lifting from the sea. The streaked saffron in the west passed before the all-merging darkness, and the sea to the east was black. The land had vanished, and was expressed only by the low and drear thunder of the surf.

"If I am going to be drowned — if I am going to be drowned — if I am going to be drowned, why, in the name of the seven gods who rule the sea, was I allowed to come thus far and contemplate sand and trees? Was I brought here merely to have my nose dragged away as I was about to nibble the sacred cheese of life?"

The patient captain, drooped over the water-jar, was sometimes obliged to speak to the oarsman.

"Keep her head up! Keep her head up!"   145

"Keep her head up, sir." The voices were weary and low.

This was surely a quiet evening. All save the oarsman lay heavily and listlessly in the boat's bottom. As for him, his eyes were just capable of noting the tall black waves that swept forward in a most sinister silence, save for an occasional subdued growl of a crest.

The cook's head was on a thwart, and he looked without interest at the water under his nose. He was deep in other scenes. Finally he spoke. "Billie," he murmured, dreamfully, "what kind of pie do you like best?"

V

"Pie!" said the oiler and the correspondent, agitatedly. "Don't talk about those things, blast you!"

"Well," said the cook, "I was just thinking about ham sandwiches,   150
and — "

A night on the sea in an open boat is a long night. As darkness settled finally, the shine of the light, lifting from the sea in the south, changed to full gold. On the northern horizon a new light appeared, a small bluish gleam on the edge of the waters. These two lights were the furniture of the world. Otherwise there was nothing but waves.

Two men huddled in the stern, and distances were so magnificent in the dinghy that the rower was enabled to keep his feet partly warm by thrusting them under his companions. Their legs indeed extended far under the rowing-seat until they touched the feet of the captain forward. Sometimes, despite the efforts of the tired oarsman, a wave came piling into the boat, an icy wave of the night, and the chilling water soaked them anew. They would twist their bodies for a moment and groan, and sleep the dead sleep once more, while the water in the boat gurgled about them as the craft rocked.

The plan of the oiler and the correspondent was for one to row until he lost the ability, and then arouse the other from his sea-water couch in the bottom of the boat.

The oiler plied the oars until his head drooped forward and the overpowering sleep blinded him; and he rowed yet afterward. Then he touched a man in the bottom of the boat, and called his name. "Will you spell me for a little while?" he said meekly.

"Sure, Billie," said the correspondent, awaking and dragging himself to   155
a sitting position. They exchanged places carefully, and the oiler, cuddling down in the sea-water at the cook's side, seemed to go to sleep instantly.

The particular violence of the sea had ceased. The waves came without snarling. The obligation of the man at the oars was to keep the boat headed so that the tilt of the rollers would not capsize her, and to preserve her from filling when the crests rushed past. The black waves were silent and hard to be seen in the darkness. Often one was almost upon the boat before the oarsman was aware.

In a low voice the correspondent addressed the captain. He was not sure that the captain was awake, although this iron man seemed to be always awake. "Captain, shall I keep her making for that light north, sir?"

The same steady voice answered him. "Yes. Keep it about two points off the port bow."

The cook had tied a life-belt around himself in order to get even the warmth which this clumsy cork contrivance could donate, and he seemed almost stove-like when a rower, whose teeth invariably chattered wildly as soon as he ceased his labor, dropped down to sleep.

The correspondent, as he rowed, looked down at the two men sleeping underfoot. The cook's arm was around the oiler's shoulders, and, with their fragmentary clothing and haggard faces, they were the babes of the sea — a grotesque rendering of the old babes in the wood. 160

Later he must have grown stupid at his work, for suddenly there was a growling of water, and a crest came with a roar and a swash into the boat, and it was a wonder that it did not set the cook afloat in his life-belt. The cook continued to sleep, but the oiler sat up, blinking his eyes and shaking with the new cold.

"Oh, I'm awful sorry, Billie," said the correspondent, contritely.

"That's all right, old boy," said the oiler, and lay down again and was asleep.

Presently it seemed that even the captain dozed, and the correspondent thought that he was the one man afloat on all the oceans. The wind had a voice as it came over the waves, and it was sadder than the end.

There was a long, loud swishing astern of the boat, and a gleaming trail of phosphorescence, like blue flame, was furrowed on the black waters. It might have been made by a monstrous knife. 165

Then there came a stillness, while the correspondent breathed with open mouth and looked at the sea.

Suddenly there was another swish and another long flash of bluish light, and this time it was alongside the boat, and might almost have been reached with an oar. The correspondent saw an enormous fin speed like a shadow through the water, hurling the crystalline spray and leaving the long glowing trail.

The correspondent looked over his shoulder at the captain. His face was hidden, and he seemed to be asleep. He looked at the babes of the sea. They certainly were asleep. So, being bereft of sympathy, he leaned a little way to one side and swore softly into the sea.

But the thing did not then leave the vicinity of the boat. Ahead or astern, on one side or the other, at intervals long or short, fled the long sparkling streak, and there was to be heard the *whirroo* of the dark fin. The speed and power of the thing was greatly to be admired. It cut the water like a gigantic and keen projectile.

The presence of this biding thing did not affect the man with the same horror that it would if he had been a picnicker. He simply looked at the sea dully and swore in an undertone. 170

Nevertheless, it is true that he did not wish to be alone with the thing. He wished one of his companions to awake by chance and keep him company with it. But the captain hung motionless over the water-jar, and the oiler and the cook in the bottom of the boat were plunged in slumber.

VI

"If I am going to be drowned — if I am going to be drowned — if I am going to be drowned, why, in the name of the seven mad gods who rule the sea, was I allowed to come thus far and contemplate sand and trees?"

During this dismal night, it may be remarked that a man would conclude that it was really the intention of the seven mad gods to drown him, despite the abominable injustice of it. For it was certainly an abominable injustice to drown a man who had worked so hard, so hard. The man felt it would be a crime most unnatural. Other people had drowned at sea since galleys swarmed with painted sails, but still ——

When it occurs to a man that nature does not regard him as important, and that she feels she would not maim the universe by disposing of him, he at first wishes to throw bricks at the temple, and he hates deeply the fact that there are no bricks and no temples. Any visible expression of nature would surely be pelleted with his jeers.

Then, if there be no tangible thing to hoot, he feels, perhaps, the desire   175
to confront a personification and indulge in pleas, bowed to one knee, and with hands supplicant, saying, "Yes, but I love myself."

A high cold star on a winter's night is the word he feels that she says to him. Thereafter he knows the pathos of his situation.

The men in the dinghy had not discussed these matters, but each had, no doubt, reflected upon them in silence and according to his mind. There was seldom any expression upon their faces save the general one of complete weariness. Speech was devoted to the business of the boat.

To chime the notes of his emotion, a verse mysteriously entered the correspondent's head. He had even forgotten that he had forgotten this verse, but it suddenly was in his mind.

A soldier of the Legion lay dying in Algiers;
There was lack of woman's nursing, there was dearth of woman's
    tears;
But a comrade stood beside him, and he took that comrade's hand,
And he said, "I never more shall see my own, my native land°."

In his childhood the correspondent had been made acquainted with the   180
fact that a soldier of the Legion lay dying in Algiers, but he had never regarded the fact as important. Myriads of his school-fellows had informed him of the soldier's plight, but the dinning had naturally ended by making him perfectly indifferent. He had never considered it his affair that a soldier of the Legion lay dying in Algiers, nor had it appeared to him as a matter for sorrow. It was less to him than the breaking of a pencil's point.

A soldier of the Legion . . . native land: The correspondent remembers a Victorian ballad about a German dying in the French Foreign Legion, "Bingen on the Rhine" by Caroline Norton.

Now, however, it quaintly came to him as a human, living thing. It was no longer merely a picture of a few throes in the breast of a poet, meanwhile drinking tea and warming his feet at the grate; it was an actuality — stern, mournful, and fine.

The correspondent plainly saw the soldier. He lay on the sand with his feet out straight and still. While his pale left hand was upon his chest in an attempt to thwart the going of his life, the blood came between his fingers. In the far Algerian distance, a city of low square forms was set against a sky that was faint with the last sunset hues. The correspondent, plying the oars and dreaming of the slow and slower movements of the lips of the soldier, was moved by a profound and perfectly impersonal comprehension. He was sorry for the soldier of the Legion who lay dying in Algiers.

The thing which had followed the boat and waited had evidently grown bored at the delay. There was no longer to be heard the slash of the cutwater, and there was no longer the flame of the long trail. The light in the north still glimmered, but it was apparently no nearer to the boat. Sometimes the boom of the surf rang in the correspondent's ears, and he turned the craft seaward then and rowed harder. Southward, some one had evidently built a watch-fire on the beach. It was too low and too far to be seen, but it made a shimmering, roseate reflection upon the bluff in back of it, and this could be discerned from the boat. The wind came stronger, and sometimes a wave suddenly raged out like a mountain cat, and there was to be seen the sheen and sparkle of a broken crest.

The captain, in the bow, moved on his water-jar and sat erect. "Pretty long night," he observed to the correspondent. He looked at the shore. "Those life-saving people take their time."

"Did you see that shark playing around?"   185

"Yes, I saw him. He was a big fellow, all right."

"Wish I had known you were awake."

Later the correspondent spoke into the bottom of the boat.

"Billie!" There was a slow and gradual disentanglement.

"Billie, will you spell me?"   190

"Sure," said the oiler.

As soon as the correspondent touched the cold, comfortable sea-water in the bottom of the boat and had huddled close to the cook's life-belt he was deep in sleep, despite the fact that his teeth played all the popular airs. This sleep was so good to him that it was but a moment before he heard a voice call his name in a tone that demonstrated the last stages of exhaustion. "Will you spell me?"

"Sure, Billie."

The light in the north had mysteriously vanished, but the correspondent took his course from the wide-awake captain.

Later in the night they took the boat farther out to sea, and the captain   195
directed the cook to take one oar at the stern and keep the boat facing the seas. He was to call out if he should hear the thunder of the surf. This plan enabled the oiler and the correspondent to get respite together. "We'll give those boys a chance to get into shape again," said the captain. They curled down and, after a few preliminary chatterings and trembles, slept once more the dead sleep. Neither knew they had bequeathed to the cook the company of another shark, or perhaps the same shark.

As the boat caroused on the waves, spray occasionally bumped over the side and gave them a fresh soaking, but this had no power to break their repose. The ominous slash of the wind and the water affected them as it would have affected mummies.

"Boys," said the cook, with the notes of every reluctance in his voice, "she's drifted in pretty close. I guess one of you had better take her to sea again." The correspondent, aroused, heard the crash of the toppled crests.

As he was rowing, the captain gave him some whisky-and-water, and this steadied the chills out of him. "If I ever get ashore and anybody shows me even a photograph of an oar ——"

At last there was a short conversation.

"Billie! — Billie, will you spell me?" 200

"Sure," said the oiler.

VII

When the correspondent again opened his eyes, the sea and the sky were each of the gray hue of the dawning. Later, carmine and gold was painted upon the waters. The morning appeared finally, in its splendor, with a sky of pure blue, and the sunlight flamed on the tips of the waves.

On the distant dunes were set many little black cottages, and a tall white windmill reared above them. No man, nor dog, nor bicycle appeared on the beach. The cottages might have formed a deserted village.

The voyagers scanned the shore. A conference was held in the boat. "Well," said the captain, "if no help is coming, we might better try a run through the surf right away. If we stay out here much longer we will be too weak to do anything for ourselves at all." The others silently acquiesced in this reasoning. The boat was headed for the beach. The correspondent wondered if none ever ascended the tall wind-tower, and if then they never looked seaward. This tower was a giant, standing with its back to the plight of the ants. It represented in a degree, to the correspondent, the serenity of nature amid the struggles of the individual — nature in the wind, and nature in the vision of men. She did not seem cruel to him then, nor beneficent, nor treacherous, nor wise. But she was indifferent, flatly indifferent. It is, perhaps, plausible that a man in this situation, impressed with the unconcern of the universe, should see the innumerable flaws of his life, and have them taste wickedly in his mind, and wish for another chance. A distinction between right and wrong seems absurdly clear to him, then, in this new ignorance of the grave-edge, and he understands that if he were given another opportunity he would mend his conduct and his words, and be better and brighter during an introduction or at a tea.

"Now, boys," said the captain, "she is going to swamp sure. All we can 205 do is to work her in as far as possible, and then when she swamps, pile out and scramble for the beach. Keep cool now, and don't jump until she swamps sure."

The oiler took the oars. Over his shoulders he scanned the surf. "Captain," he said, "I think I'd better bring her about and keep her head-on to the seas and back her in."

"All right, Billie," said the captain. "Back her in." The oiler swung the boat then, and, seated in the stern, the cook and the correspondent were obliged to look over their shoulders to contemplate the lonely and indifferent shore.

The monstrous inshore rollers heaved the boat high until the men were again enabled to see the white sheets of water scudding up the slanted beach. "We won't get in very close," said the captain. Each time a man could wrest his attention from the rollers, he turned his glance toward the shore, and in the expression of the eyes during this contemplation there was a singular quality. The correspondent, observing the others, knew that they were not afraid, but the full meaning of their glances was shrouded.

As for himself, he was too tired to grapple fundamentally with the fact. He tried to coerce his mind into thinking of it, but the mind was dominated at this time by the muscles, and the muscles said they did not care. It merely occurred to him that if he should drown it would be a shame.

There were no hurried words, no pallor, no plain agitation. The men ₂₁₀ simply looked at the shore. "Now, remember to get well clear of the boat when you jump," said the captain.

Seaward the crest of a roller suddenly fell with a thunderous crash, and the long white comber came roaring down upon the boat.

"Steady now," said the captain. The men were silent. They turned their eyes from the shore to the comber and waited. The boat slid up the incline, leaped at the furious top, bounced over it, and swung down the long back of the wave. Some water had been shipped, and the cook bailed it out.

But the next crest crashed also. The tumbling, boiling flood of white water caught the boat and whirled it almost perpendicular. Water swarmed in from all sides. The correspondent had his hands on the gunwale at this time, and when the water entered at that place he swiftly withdrew his fingers, as if he objected to wetting them.

The little boat, drunken with this weight of water, reeled and snuggled deeper into the sea.

"Bail her out, cook! Bail her out!" said the captain. ₂₁₅

"All right, Captain," said the cook.

"Now, boys, the next one will do for us sure," said the oiler. "Mind to jump clear of the boat."

The third wave moved forward, huge, furious, implacable. It fairly swallowed the dinghy, and almost simultaneously the men tumbled into the sea. A piece of life-belt had lain in the bottom of the boat, and as the correspondent went overboard he held this to his chest with his left hand.

The January water was icy, and he reflected immediately that it was colder than he had expected to find it off the coast of Florida. This appeared to his dazed mind as a fact important enough to be noted at the time. The coldness of the water was sad; it was tragic. This fact was somehow mixed and confused with his opinion of his own situation, so that it seemed almost a proper reason for tears. The water was cold.

When he came to the surface he was conscious of little but the noisy ₂₂₀ water. Afterward he saw his companions in the sea. The oiler was ahead in the race. He was swimming strongly and rapidly. Off to the correspondent's left, the cook's great white and corked back bulged out of the water; and in the rear the captain was hanging with his one good hand to the keel of the overturned dinghy.

There is a certain immovable quality to a shore, and the correspondent wondered at it amid the confusion of the sea.

It seemed also very attractive; but the correspondent knew that it was a long journey, and he paddled leisurely. The piece of life-preserver lay under him, and sometimes he whirled down the incline of a wave as if he were on a hand-sled.

But finally he arrived at a place in the sea where travel was beset with difficulty. He did not pause swimming to inquire what manner of current had caught him, but there his progress ceased. The shore was set before him like a bit of scenery on a stage, and he looked at it and understood with his eyes each detail of it.

As the cook passed, much farther to the left, the captain was calling to him, "Turn over on your back, cook! Turn over on your back and use the oar."

"All right, sir." The cook turned on his back, and, paddling with an oar, went ahead as if he were a canoe.   225

Presently the boat also passed to the left of the correspondent, with the captain clinging with one hand to the keel. He would have appeared like a man raising himself to look over a board fence if it were not for the extraordinary gymnastics of the boat. The correspondent marvelled that the captain could still hold to it.

They passed on nearer to shore—the oiler, the cook, the captain — and following them went the water-jar, bouncing gaily over the seas.

The correspondent remained in the grip of this strange new enemy — a current. The shore, with its white slope of sand and its green bluff topped with little silent cottages, was spread like a picture before him. It was very near to him then, but he was impressed as one who, in a gallery, looks at a scene from Brittany or Algiers.

He thought: "I am going to drown? Can it be possible? Can it be possible? Can it be possible?" Perhaps an individual must consider his own death to be the final phenomenon of nature.

But later a wave perhaps whirled him out of this small deadly current,   230
for he found suddenly that he could again make progress toward the shore. Later still he was aware that the captain, clinging with one hand to the keel of the dinghy, had his face turned away from the shore and toward him, and was calling his name. "Come to the boat! Come to the boat!"

In his struggle to reach the captain and the boat, he reflected that when one gets properly wearied drowning must really be a comfortable arrangement — a cessation of hostilities accompanied by a large degree of relief; and he was glad of it, for the main thing in his mind for some moments had been horror of the temporary agony. He did not wish to be hurt.

Presently he saw a man running along the shore. He was undressing with most remarkable speed. Coat, trousers, shirt, everything flew magically off him.

"Come to the boat!" called the captain.

"All right, Captain." As the correspondent paddled, he saw the captain let himself down to bottom and leave the boat. Then the correspondent performed his one little marvel of the voyage. A large wave caught him and flung him with ease and supreme speed completely over the boat and far beyond it. It struck him even then as an event in gymnastics and a true miracle of the sea. An overturned boat in the surf is not a plaything to a swimming man.

The correspondent arrived in water that reached only to his waist, but 235 his condition did not enable him to stand for more than a moment. Each wave knocked him into a heap, and the undertow pulled at him.

Then he saw the man who had been running and undressing, and undressing and running, come bounding into the water. He dragged ashore the cook, and then waded toward the captain; but the captain waved him away and sent him to the correspondent. He was naked — naked as a tree in winter; but a halo was about his head, and he shone like a saint. He gave a strong pull, and a long drag, and a bully heave at the correspondent's hand. The correspondent, schooled in the minor formulae, said, "Thanks, old man." But suddenly the man cried, "What's that?" He pointed a swift finger. The correspondent said, "Go."

In the shallows, face downward, lay the oiler. His forehead touched sand that was periodically, between each wave, clear of the sea.

The correspondent did not know all that transpired afterward. When he achieved safe ground he fell, striking the sand with each particular part of his body. It was as if he had dropped from a roof, but the thud was grateful to him.

It seems that instantly the beach was populated with men with blankets, clothes, and flasks, and women with coffee-pots and all the remedies sacred to their minds. The welcome of the land to the men from the sea was warm and generous; but a still and dripping shape was carried slowly up the beach, and the land's welcome for it could only be the different and sinister hospitality of the grave.

When it came night, the white waves paced to and fro in the moonlight, 240 and the wind brought the sound of the great sea's voice to the men on the shore, and they felt that they could then be interpreters.

QUESTIONS

1. In actuality, Crane, the captain of the *Commodore,* and the two crew members spent nearly thirty hours in the open boat. William Higgins, the oiler, was drowned as Crane describes. Does a knowledge of these facts in any way affect your response to the story? Would you admire the story less if you believed it to be pure fiction?
2. Sum up the personalities of each of the four men in the boat: captain, cook, oiler, and correspondent.
3. What is the point of view of the story?
4. In paragraph 9, we are told that as each wave came, the boat "seemed like a horse making for a fence outrageously high." Point to other vivid similes or figures of speech. What do they contribute to the story's effectiveness?
5. Notice some of the ways in which Crane, as a storyteller conscious of plot, builds suspense. What enemies or obstacles do the men in the boat confront? What is the effect of the scene of the men who wave from the beach (paragraphs 86 – 141)? What is the climax of the story? (If you need to be refreshed on the meaning of *climax,* see page 9.)

6. In paragraph 70 (and again in paragraph 143), the men wonder, "Was I brought here merely to have my nose dragged away as I was about to nibble the sacred cheese of life?" What variety of irony do you find in this quotation?
7. Why does the scrap of verse about the soldier dying in Algiers (paragraph 179) suddenly come to mean so much to the correspondent?
8. What theme in "The Open Boat" seems most important to you? Where is it stated?
9. What secondary themes also enrich the story? See for instance paragraph 43 (the thoughts on comradeship).
10. How do you define *heroism?* Who is a hero in "The Open Boat"?

Suggestions for Writing

1. In "The Door" E. B. White expresses a theme or two worth thinking on. Once you feel sure you know what point or points White is making (and if you aren't yet sure, discuss the story further with your instructor or your peers), write a letter to White. Take him to task for failing to get with modern high-tech civilization, or thank him for making you aware of things you have noticed but which haven't quite landed home. Tell him your own recollections or observations of city life.
2. Have you, like the narrator of "The Open Boat," ever been in physical danger? Not that your life needs to be as thrilling as an episode of *Miami Vice;* but think and see what you can recall. What have you learned from your experience? Tell of it, comparing your memory with what Crane observes of people in danger, with what Crane's reporter notices within himself.

   Note: In a sense, you are often in real danger from forces sometimes beyond your control (storms, rapists and other criminals, crazed souls who tamper with capsules in drugstores, disease carriers). In a way, passively to face such ordinary perils may seem less heroic than rowing an open boat in a heaving sea. In another way — well, if you're looking for a danger to recall, you might think about this comparison. Reading Crane's story, do you feel that, in any sense, you and the news correspondent are in the same boat?
3. In "The Open Boat," recall the poem that comes to matter greatly to the correspondent (paragraphs 179 – 182). Have you ever been in a situation when a story, an Aesop fable, a saying, a line of poetry, or a song lyric took on fresh and immediate meaning for you? If so, relate your experience. (If no such experience has befallen you, don't make one up.)
4. Compare Mrs. Turpin's defiance of God in "Revelation" ("Who do you think you are?" — paragraph 187) with the urge of a shipwrecked man in "The Open Boat" to shake his fist at the clouds ("Just you drown me, now, and then hear what I call you!" — paragraph 70). Do Flannery O'Connor and Stephen Crane express similar or different concepts of Whoever runs the universe?
5. Pick a story not included in this chapter and, in your own words, sum up its main theme. Then indicate what you find in the story that makes this theme clear. Among stories whose themes stand out are "Gimpel the Fool," "Barn Burning," "Paul's Case," "Everyday Use," "The Chrysanthemums," "I Stand Here Ironing," "The Death of Ivan Ilych," and "The Birthmark." Is the author making any statement you can agree or disagree with? Why do you feel the way you do? Suggestion: Before you write, refresh your memory of the method of analysis (in "Writing about a Story," page 425). This useful method might come in handy.
6. Compare two stories similar in theme. Both Joyce in "Araby" and Singer in "Gimpel the Fool" set forth a conflict between illusion and reality. Poe in "The Tell-Tale Heart" and O'Brien in "Two in One" show us that murder, even

ingeniously clever murder, will out. Browse in other chapters and in "Stories for Further Reading" and see what other pairs of stories go together in theme. Then set them side by side and point out their similarities and differences. This topic will lead you to use the method of comparison and contrast, discussed in "Writing a Story" on page 439.

7. Here is a topic for science fiction fans: Trace a general theme in two or more science fiction novels or stories you know. Choose works that express similar views. Suggestion: If you know two science fiction writers who distrust the benefits of technology, or who take a keen interest in the future of women, look closely at their work and you will probably find an intriguing theme.

8 Symbol

In F. Scott Fitzgerald's novel *The Great Gatsby,* a huge pair of bespectacled eyes stares across a wilderness of ash heaps, from a billboard advertising the services of an oculist. Repeatedly entering into the story, the advertisement comes to mean more than simply the availability of eye examinations. Fitzgerald has a character liken it to the eyes of God; he hints that some sad, compassionate spirit is brooding as it watches the passing procession of mankind. Such an object is a **symbol:** in literature, a thing that suggests more than its literal meaning. Symbols generally do not "stand for" any one meaning, nor for anything absolutely definite; they point, they hint, or, as Henry James put it, they cast long shadows. To take a large example: in Herman Melville's *Moby-Dick,* the great white whale of the book's title apparently means more than the literal dictionary-definition meaning of an aquatic mammal. He also suggests more than the devil, to whom some of the characters liken him. The great whale, as the story unfolds, comes to imply an amplitude of meanings: among them the forces of nature and the whole created universe. This indefinite multiplicity of meanings is characteristic of a symbolic story and distinguishes it from an **allegory,** a story in which persons, places, and things form a system of clearly labeled equivalents.

In a simple allegory, characters and other ingredients often stand for other definite meanings, which are often abstractions. Supreme allegories are found in some biblical parables ("The kingdom of Heaven is like a man who sowed good seed in his field . . . ," Matthew 13:24 – 30).[1] A classic allegory is the medieval play *Everyman,* whose hero represents us all, and who, deserted by false friends called Kindred and Goods, faces the judgment of God accompanied only by a faithful friend called Good Deeds. In John Bunyan's seventeenth-century *Pilgrim's Progress,* the protagonist, Christian, struggles along the difficult road toward salvation, meeting along the way persons such as Mr. Worldly Wiseman, who directs him into a more comfortable path (a wrong turn), and the residents of a town called Fair Speech, among them a hypocrite named Mr. Facing-both-ways. Not

---

[1]A **parable** is a brief story that teaches a lesson. Some (but not all) parables are allegories.

all allegories are simple: Dante's *Divine Comedy,* written in the Middle Ages, continues to reveal new meanings to careful readers. Allegory was much beloved in the Middle Ages, but in contemporary fiction it is rare. One modern instance is George Orwell's long fable *Animal Farm,* in which (among its double meanings) barnyard animals stand for human victims and totalitarian oppressors.

Symbols in fiction are not generally abstract terms like *love* or *truth,* but are likely to be perceptible objects (or worded descriptions that cause us to imagine them). In William Faulkner's "A Rose for Emily" (Chapter Two), Miss Emily's invisible watch ticking at the end of a golden chain not only indicates the passage of time, but suggests that time passes without even being noticed by the watch's owner, and the golden chain carries suggestions of wealth and authority. Often the symbols we meet in fiction are inanimate objects, but other things also may function symbolically. In James Joyce's "Araby" (page 54), the very name of the bazaar, Araby — the poetic name for Arabia — suggests magic, romance, and *The Arabian Nights;* its syllables (the narrator tells us) "cast an Eastern enchantment over me." Even a locale, or a feature of physical topography, can provide rich suggestions. Recall Ernest Hemingway's "A Clean, Well-Lighted Place" (Chapter Five), in which the café is not merely a café, but an island of refuge from night, chaos, loneliness, old age, and impending death.

In some novels and stories, symbolic characters make brief cameo appearances. Such characters often are not well-rounded and fully known, but are seen fleetingly and remain slightly mysterious. In *Heart of Darkness,* a short novel by Joseph Conrad, a steamship company that hires men to work in the Congo maintains in its waiting room two women who knit black wool — like the classical Fates. Usually such a symbolic character is more a portrait than a person — or somewhat portraitlike, as Faulkner's Miss Emily, who twice appears at a window of her house "like the carven torso of an idol in a niche." Though Faulkner invests Miss Emily with life and vigor, he also clothes her in symbolic hints: she seems almost to personify the vanishing aristocracy of the antebellum south, still maintaining a black servant and being ruthlessly betrayed by a moneymaking Yankee. Sometimes a part of a character's body or an attribute may convey symbolic meaning: a baleful eye, as in Edgar Allan Poe's "The Tell-Tale Heart" (page 38).

Much as a symbolic whale holds more meaning than an ordinary whale, a **symbolic act** is a gesture with larger significance than usual. For the boy's father in Faulkner's "Barn Burning" (Chapter Five), the act of destroying a barn is no mere act of spite, but an expression of his profound hatred for anything not belonging to him. Faulkner adds that burning a barn reflects the father's memories of the "waste and extravagance of war"; and further adds that "the element of fire spoke to some deep mainspring" in his being. A symbolic act, however, doesn't have to be a gesture as large as starting a conflagration. Before setting out in pursuit of the great white whale, Melville's Captain Ahab in *Moby-Dick* deliberately snaps his tobacco pipe and throws it away, as if to suggest (among other things) that he will let no pleasure or pastime distract him from his vengeance.

Why do writers have to symbolize — why don't they tell us outright? One advantage of a symbol is that it is so compact, and yet so fully laden. Both starkly concrete and slightly mysterious, like Miss Emily's invisibly ticking watch, it may impress us with all the force of something beheld in a dream or in a nightmare. The watch suggests, among other things, the slow and invisible passage of time. What this symbol says, it says more fully and more memorably than could be said, perhaps, in a long essay on the subject.

To some extent (it may be claimed), all stories are symbolic. Merely by holding up for our inspection these characters and their actions, the writer lends them *some* special significance. But this is to think of *symbol* in an extremely broad and inclusive way. For the usual purposes of reading a story and understanding it, there is probably little point in looking for symbolism in every word, in every stick or stone, in every striking of a match, in every minor character. Still, to be on the alert for symbols when reading fiction is perhaps wiser than to ignore them. Not to admit that symbolic meanings may be present, or to refuse to think about them, would be another way to misread a story — or to read no further than its outer edges.

How, then, do you recognize a symbol in fiction when you meet it? Fortunately, the storyteller often gives the symbol particular emphasis. It may be mentioned repeatedly throughout the story; it may even supply the story with a title ("Araby," "Barn Burning," "A Clean, Well-Lighted Place"). At times, a crucial symbol will open a story or end it. Unless an object, act, or character is given some such special emphasis and importance, we may generally feel safe in taking it at face value. Probably it isn't a symbol if it points clearly and unmistakably toward some one meaning, like a whistle in a factory, whose blast at noon means lunch. But an object, an act, or a character is surely symbolic (and almost as surely displays high literary art) if, when we finish the story, we realize that it was that item — those gigantic eyes; that clean, well-lighted café; that burning of a barn — which led us to the author's theme, the essential meaning.

John Steinbeck
THE CHRYSANTHEMUMS   1938

John Steinbeck (1902 – 1968), was born in Salinas, California, in the fertile valley he remembers in "The Chrysanthemums." Off and on, he attended Stanford University, then sojourned in New York as a reporter and a bricklayer. After years of struggle to earn his bread from fiction, Steinbeck reached a large audience with Tortilla Flat *(1935), a loosely woven novel portraying Mexican-Americans in Monterey with fondness and sympathy. Great acclaim greeted* The Grapes of Wrath *(1939), the story of a family of Oklahoma farmers who, ruined by dust storms in the 1930s, join a mass migration to California. Like Ernest Hemingway and Stephen Crane, Steinbeck prided himself on his journalism: in World War II, he filed dispatches from battlefronts in Italy and Africa, and in 1966 he wrote a column from South Vietnam. Known widely behind the Iron Curtain, Steinbeck accepted an invitation to visit the Soviet Union, and reported his trip in* A Russian Journal *(1948). In 1962 he became the seventh American to win the Nobel prize for literature, but critics have never placed Steinbeck on the same high shelf with Faulkner and Hemingway. He wrote much, not all good, and yet his best work adds to an impressive total. Besides* The Grapes of Wrath, *it includes* In Dubious Battle *(1936) a novel of an apple-pickers' strike;* Of Mice and Men, *a powerful short novel (also a play) of comradeship between a hobo and a moron;* The Log from the Sea of Cortez, *a nonfiction account of a marine biological expedition; and the short stories in* The Long Valley *(1938). Through the fiction he wrote in his prime, Steinbeck maintains an appealing sympathy for the poor and downtrodden, the lonely and dispossessed.*

The high grey-flannel fog of winter closed off the Salinas Valley° from the sky and from all the rest of the world. On every side it sat like a lid on the mountains and made of the great valley a closed pot. On the broad, level land floor the gang plows bit deep and left the black earth shining like metal where the shares had cut. On the foothill ranches across the Salinas River, the yellow stubble fields seemed to be bathed in pale cold sunshine, but there was no sunshine in the valley now in December. The thick willow scrub along the river flamed with sharp and positive yellow leaves.

It was a time of quiet and of waiting. The air was cold and tender. A light wind blew up from the southwest so that the farmers were mildly hopeful of a good rain before long; but fog and rain do not go together.

Across the river, on Henry Allen's foothill ranch there was little work to be done, for the hay was cut and stored and the orchards were plowed up to receive the rain deeply when it should come. The cattle on the higher slopes were becoming shaggy and rough-coated.

Elisa Allen, working in her flower garden, looked down across the yard and saw Henry, her husband, talking to two men in business suits. The three of them stood by the tractor shed, each man with one foot on the side of the little Fordson. They smoked cigarettes and studied the machine as they talked.

Elisa watched them for a moment and then went back to her work. She 5
was thirty-five. Her face was lean and strong and her eyes were as clear as water. Her figure looked blocked and heavy in her gardening costume, a man's black hat pulled low down over her eyes, clod-hopper shoes, a figured print dress almost completely covered by a big corduroy apron with four big pockets

Salinas Valley: south of San Francisco in the Coast Ranges region of California.

to hold the snips, the trowel and scratcher, the seeds and the knife she worked with. She wore heavy leather gloves to protect her hands while she worked.

She was cutting down the old year's chrysanthemum stalks with a pair of short and powerful scissors. She looked down toward the men by the tractor shed now and then. Her face was eager and mature and handsome; even her work with the scissors was over-eager, over-powerful. The chrysanthemum stems seemed too small and easy for her energy.

She brushed a cloud of hair out of her eyes with the back of her glove, and left a smudge of earth on her cheek in doing it. Behind her stood the neat white farm house with red geraniums close-banked around it as high as the windows. It was a hard-swept looking little house with hard-polished windows, and a clean mud-mat on the front steps.

Elisa cast another glance toward the tractor shed. The strangers were getting into their Ford coupe. She took off a glove and put her strong fingers down into the forest of new green chrysanthemum sprouts that were growing around the old roots. She spread the leaves and looked down among the close-growing stems. No aphids were there, no sowbugs or snails or cutworms. Her terrier fingers destroyed such pests before they could get started.

Elisa started at the sound of her husband's voice. He had come near quietly, and he leaned over the wire fence that protected her flower garden from cattle and dogs and chickens.

"At it again," he said. "You've got a strong new crop coming."   10

Elisa straightened her back and pulled on the gardening glove again. "Yes. They'll be strong this coming year." In her tone and on her face there was a little smugness.

"You've got a gift with things," Henry observed. "Some of those yellow chrysanthemums you had this year were ten inches across. I wish you'd work out in the orchard and raise some apples that big."

Her eyes sharpened. "Maybe I could do it, too. I've a gift with things, all right. My mother had it. She could stick anything in the ground and make it grow. She said it was having planters' hands that knew how to do it."

"Well, it sure works with flowers," he said.

"Henry, who were those men you were talking to?"   15

"Why, sure, that's what I came to tell you. They were from the Western Meat Company. I sold those thirty head of three-year-old steers. Got nearly my own price, too."

"Good," she said. "Good for you."

"And I thought," he continued, "I thought how it's Saturday afternoon, and we might go into Salinas for dinner at a restaurant, and then to a picture show — to celebrate, you see."

"Good," she repeated. "Oh, yes. That will be good."

Henry put on his joking tone. "There's fights tonight. How'd you like   20 to go to the fights?"

"Oh, no," she said breathlessly. "No, I wouldn't like fights."

"Just fooling, Elisa. We'll go to a movie. Let's see. It's two now. I'm going to take Scotty and bring down those steers from the hill. It'll take us maybe two hours. We'll go in town about five and have dinner at the Cominos Hotel. Like that?"

"Of course I'll like it. It's good to eat away from home."

"All right, then. I'll go get up a couple of horses."

She said, "I'll have plenty of time to transplant some of these sets, I guess." 25

She heard her husband calling Scotty down by the barn. And a little later she saw the two men ride up the pale yellow hillside in search of the steers.

There was a little square sandy bed kept for rooting the chrysanthemums. With her trowel she turned the soil over and over, and smoothed it and patted it firm. Then she dug ten parallel trenches to receive the sets. Back at the chrysanthemum bed she pulled out the little crisp shoots, trimmed off the leaves of each one with her scissors and laid it on a small orderly pile.

A squeak of wheels and plod of hoofs came from the road. Elisa looked up. The country road ran along the dense bank of willows and cottonwoods that bordered the river, and up this road came a curious vehicle, curiously drawn. It was an old spring-wagon, with a round canvas top on it like the cover of a prairie schooner. It was drawn by an old bay horse and a little grey-and-white burro. A big stubble-bearded man sat between the cover flaps and drove the crawling team. Underneath the wagon, between the hind wheels, a lean and rangy mongrel dog walked sedately. Words were painted on the canvas, in clumsy, crooked letters. "Pots, pans, knives, sisors, lawn mores, Fixed." Two rows of articles, and the triumphantly definitive "Fixed" below. The black paint had run down in little sharp points beneath each letter.

Elisa, squatting on the ground, watched to see the crazy, loose-jointed wagon pass by. But it didn't pass. It turned into the farm road in front of her house, crooked old wheels skirling and squeaking. The rangy dog darted from between the wheels and ran ahead. Instantly the two ranch shepherds flew out at him. Then all three stopped, and with stiff and quivering tails, with taut straight legs, with ambassadorial dignity, they slowly circled, sniffing daintily. The caravan pulled up to Elisa's wire fence and stopped. Now the newcomer dog, feeling out-numbered, lowered his tail and retired under the wagon with raised hackles and bared teeth.

The man on the wagon seat called out, "That's a bad dog in a fight when he gets started." 30

Elisa laughed. "I see he is. How soon does he generally get started?"

The man caught up her laughter and echoed it heartily. "Sometimes not for weeks and weeks," he said. He climbed stiffly down, over the wheel. The horse and the donkey drooped like unwatered flowers.

Elisa saw that he was a very big man. Although his hair and beard were greying, he did not look old. His worn black suit was wrinkled and spotted with grease. The laughter had disappeared from his face and eyes the moment his laughing voice ceased. His eyes were dark, and they were full of the brooding that gets in the eyes of teamsters and of sailors. The calloused hands he rested on the wire fence were cracked, and every crack was a black line. He took off his battered hat.

"I'm off my general road, ma'am," he said. "Does this dirt road cut over across the river to the Los Angeles highway?"

Elisa stood up and shoved the thick scissors in her apron pocket. "Well, 35 yes, it does, but it winds around and then fords the river. I don't think your team could pull through the sand."

He replied with some asperity. "It might surprise you what them beasts can pull through."

"When they get started?" she asked.

He smiled for a second. "Yes. When they get started."

"Well," said Elisa, "I think you'll save time if you go back to the Salinas road and pick up the highway there."

He drew a big finger down the chicken wire and made it sing. "I ain't in any hurry, ma'am. I go from Seattle to San Diego and back every year. Takes all my time. About six months each way. I aim to follow nice weather." 40

Elisa took off her gloves and stuffed them in the apron pocket with the scissors. She touched the under edge of her man's hat, searching for fugitive hairs. "That sounds like a nice kind of a way to live," she said.

He leaned confidentially over the fence. "Maybe you noticed the writing on my wagon. I mend pots and sharpen knives and scissors. You got any of them things to do?"

"Oh, no," she said quickly. "Nothing like that." Her eyes hardened with resistance.

"Scissors is the worst thing," he explained. "Most people just ruin scissors trying to sharpen 'em, but I know how. I got a special tool. It's a little bobbit kind of thing, and patented. But it sure does the trick."

"No. My scissors are all sharp." 45

"All right, then. Take a pot," he continued earnestly, "a bent pot, or a pot with a hole. I can make it like new so you don't have to buy no new ones. That's a saving for you."

"No," she said shortly. "I tell you I have nothing like that for you to do."

His face fell to an exaggerated sadness. His voice took on a whining undertone. "I ain't had a thing to do today. Maybe I won't have no supper tonight. You see I'm off my regular road. I know folks on the highway clear from Seattle to San Diego. They save their things for me to sharpen up because they know I do it so good and save them money."

"I'm sorry," Elisa said irritably. "I haven't anything for you to do."

His eyes left her face and fell to searching the ground. They roamed about until they came to the chrysanthemum bed where she had been working. "What's them plants, ma'am?" 50

The irritation and resistance melted from Elisa's face. "Oh, those are chrysanthemums, giant whites and yellows. I raise them every year, bigger than anybody around here."

"Kind of a long-stemmed flower? Looks like a quick puff of colored smoke?" he asked.

"That's it. What a nice way to describe them."

"They smell kind of nasty till you get used to them," he said.

"It's a good bitter smell," she retorted, "not nasty at all." 55

He changed his tone quickly. "I like the smell myself." ·

"I had ten-inch blooms this year," she said.

The man leaned farther over the fence. "Look. I know a lady down the road a piece, has got the nicest garden you ever seen. Got nearly every kind of flower but no chrysanthemums. Last time I was mending a copper-bottom washtub for her (that's a hard job but I do it good), she said to me, 'If you ever run acrost some nice chrysanthemums I wish you'd try to get me a few seeds.' That's what she told me."

Elisa's eyes grew alert and eager. "She couldn't have known much about chrysanthemums. You *can* raise them from seed, but it's much easier to root the little sprouts you see there."

"Oh," he said. "I s'pose I can't take none to her, then." 60

"Why yes you can," Elisa cried. "I can put some in damp sand, and you can carry them right along with you. They'll take root in the pot if you keep them damp. And then she can transplant them."

"She'd sure like to have some, ma'am. You say they're nice ones?"

"Beautiful," she said. "Oh, beautiful." Her eyes shone. She tore off the battered hat and shook out her dark pretty hair. "I'll put them in a flower pot, and you can take them right with you. Come into the yard."

While the man came through the picket gate Elisa ran excitedly along the geranium-bordered path to the back of the house. And she returned carrying a big red flower pot. The gloves were forgotten now. She kneeled on the ground by the starting bed and dug up the sandy soil with her fingers and scooped it into the bright new flower pot. Then she picked up the little pile of shoots she had prepared. With her strong fingers she pressed them into the sand and tamped around them with her knuckles. The man stood over her. "I'll tell you what to do," she said. "You remember so you can tell the lady."

"Yes, I'll try to remember." 65

"Well, look. These will take root in about a month. Then she must set them out, about a foot apart in good rich earth like this, see?" She lifted a handful of dark soil for him to look at. "They'll grow fast and tall. Now remember this: In July tell her to cut them down, about eight inches from the ground."

"Before they bloom?" he asked.

"Yes, before they bloom." Her face was tight with eagerness. "They'll grow right up again. About the last of September the buds will start."

She stopped and seemed perplexed. "It's the budding that takes the most care," she said hesitantly. "I don't know how to tell you." She looked deep into his eyes, searchingly. Her mouth opened a little, and she seemed to be listening. "I'll try to tell you," she said. "Did you ever hear of planting hands?"

"Can't say I have, ma'am." 70

"Well, I can only tell you what it feels like. It's when you're picking off the buds you don't want. Everything goes right down into your fingertips. You watch your fingers work. They do it themselves. You can feel how it is. They pick and pick the buds. They never make a mistake. They're with the plant. Do you see? Your fingers and the plant. You can feel that, right up your arm. They know. They never make a mistake. You can feel it. When you're like that you can't do anything wrong. Do you see that? Can you understand that?"

She was kneeling on the ground looking up at him. Her breast swelled passionately.

The man's eyes narrowed. He looked away self-consciously. "Maybe I know," he said. "Sometimes in the night in the wagon there — "

Elisa's voice grew husky. She broke in on him, "I've never lived as you do, but I know what you mean. When the night is dark — why, the stars are sharp-pointed, and there's quiet. Why, you rise up and up! Every pointed star gets driven into your body. It's like that. Hot and sharp and — lovely."

Kneeling there, her hand went out toward his legs in the greasy black trousers. Her hesitant fingers almost touched the cloth. Then her hand dropped to the ground. She crouched low like a fawning dog.

He said, "It's nice, just like you say. Only when you don't have no dinner, it ain't."

She stood up then, very straight, and her face was ashamed. She held the flower pot out to him and placed it gently in his arms. "Here. Put it in your wagon, on the seat, where you can watch it. Maybe I can find something for you to do."

At the back of the house she dug in the can pile and found two old and battered aluminum saucepans. She carried them back and gave them to him. "Here, maybe you can fix these."

His manner changed. He became professional. "Good as new I can fix them." At the back of his wagon he set a little anvil, and out of an oily tool box dug a small machine hammer. Elisa came through the gate to watch him while he pounded out the dents in the kettles. His mouth grew sure and knowing. At a difficult part of the work he sucked his under-lip.

"You sleep right in the wagon?" Elisa asked.

"Right in the wagon, ma'am. Rain or shine I'm dry as a cow in there."

"It must be nice," she said. "It must be very nice. I wish women could do such things."

"It ain't the right kind of a life for a woman."

Her upper lip raised a little, showing her teeth. "How do you know? How can you tell?" she said.

"I don't know, ma'am," he protested. "Of course I don't know. Now here's your kettles, done. You don't have to buy no new ones."

"How much?"

"Oh, fifty cents'll do. I keep my prices down and my work good. That's why I have all them satisfied customers up and down the highway."

Elisa brought him a fifty-cent piece from the house and dropped it in his hand. "You might be surprised to have a rival some time. I can sharpen scissors, too. And I can beat the dents out of little pots. I could show you what a woman might do."

He put his hammer back in the oily box and shoved the little anvil out of sight. "It would be a lonely life for a woman, ma'am, and a scarey life, too, with animals creeping under the wagon all night." He climbed over the single-tree, steadying himself with a hand on the burro's white rump. He settled himself in the seat, picked up the lines. "Thank you kindly, ma'am," he said. "I'll do like you told me; I'll go back and catch the Salinas road."

"Mind," she called, "if you're long in getting there, keep the sand damp."

"Sand, ma'am? . . . Sand? Oh, sure. You mean around the chrysanthemums. Sure I will." He clucked his tongue. The beasts leaned luxuriously into their collars. The mongrel dog took his place between the back wheels. The wagon turned and crawled out the entrance road and back the way it had come, along the river.

Elisa stood in front of her wire fence watching the slow progress of the caravan. Her shoulders were straight, her head thrown back, her eyes half-closed, so that the scene came vaguely into them. Her lips moved silently, forming the words "Good-bye — good-bye." Then she whispered, "That's a bright direction. There's a glowing there." The sound of her whisper startled her. She shook herself free and looked about to see whether anyone had been listening. Only the dogs had heard. They lifted their heads toward her from their sleeping in the dust, and then stretched out their chins and settled asleep again. Elisa turned and ran hurriedly into the house.

In the kitchen she reached behind the stove and felt the water tank. It was full of hot water from the noonday cooking. In the bathroom she tore off her soiled clothes and flung them into the corner. And then she scrubbed herself with a little block of pumice, legs and thighs, loins and chest and arms, until her skin was scratched and red. When she had dried herself she stood in front of a mirror in her bedroom and looked at her body. She tightened her stomach and threw out her chest. She turned and looked over her shoulder at her back.

After a while she began to dress, slowly. She put on her newest under-clothing and her nicest stockings and the dress which was the symbol of her prettiness. She worked carefully on her hair, penciled her eyebrows and rouged her lips.

Before she was finished she heard the little thunder of hoofs and the 95 shouts of Henry and his helper as they drove the red steers into the corral. She heard the gate bang shut and set herself for Henry's arrival.

His step sounded on the porch. He entered the house calling, "Elisa, where are you?"

"In my room, dressing. I'm not ready. There's hot water for your bath. Hurry up. It's getting late."

When she heard him splashing in the tub, Elisa laid his dark suit on the bed, and shirt and socks and tie beside it. She stood his polished shoes on the floor beside the bed. Then she went to the porch and sat primly and stiffly down. She looked toward the river road where the willow-line was still yellow with frosted leaves so that under the high grey fog they seemed a thin band of sunshine. This was the only color in the grey afternoon. She sat unmoving for a long time. Her eyes blinked rarely.

Henry came banging out of the door, shoving his tie inside his vest as he came. Elisa stiffened and her face grew tight. Henry stopped short and looked at her. "Why — why, Elisa. You look so nice!"

"Nice? You think I look nice? What do you mean by 'nice'?" 100

Henry blundered on. "I don't know. I mean you look different, strong and happy."

"I am strong? Yes, strong. What do you mean 'strong'?"

He looked bewildered. "You're playing some kind of a game," he said helplessly. "It's a kind of a play. You look strong enough to break a calf over your knee, happy enough to eat it like a watermelon."

For a second she lost her rigidity. "Henry! Don't talk like that. You didn't know what you said." She grew complete again. "I'm strong," she boasted. "I never knew before how strong."

Henry looked down toward the tractor shed, and when he brought his 105 eyes back to her, they were his own again. "I'll get out the car. You can put on your coat while I'm starting."

Elisa went into the house. She heard him drive to the gate and idle down his motor, and then she took a long time to put on her hat. She pulled it here and pressed it there. When Henry turned the motor off she slipped into her coat and went out.

The little roadster bounced along on the dirt road by the river, raising the birds and driving the rabbits into the brush. Two cranes flapped heavily over the willow-line and dropped into the river-bed.

Far ahead on the road Elisa saw a dark speck. She knew.

She tried not to look as they passed it, but her eyes would not obey. She whispered to herself sadly, "He might have thrown them off the road. That wouldn't have been much trouble, not very much. But he kept the pot," she explained. "He had to keep the pot. That's why he couldn't get them off the road."

The roadster turned a bend and she saw the caravan ahead. She swung full around toward her husband so she could not see the little covered wagon and the mismatched team as the car passed them.

In a moment it was over. The thing was done. She did not look back.

She said loudly, to be heard above the motor, "It will be good, tonight, a good dinner."

"Now you're changed again," Henry complained. He took one hand from the wheel and patted her knee. "I ought to take you in to dinner oftener. It would be good for both of us. We get so heavy out on the ranch."

"Henry," she asked, "could we have wine at dinner?"

"Sure we could. Say! That will be fine."

She was silent for a while; then she said, "Henry, at those prize fights, do the men hurt each other very much?"

"Sometimes a little, not often. Why?"

"Well, I've read how they break noses, and blood runs down their chests. I've read how the fighting gloves get heavy and soggy with blood."

He looked around at her. "What's the matter, Elisa? I didn't know you read things like that." He brought the car to a stop, then turned to the right over the Salinas River bridge.

"Do any women ever go to the fights?" she asked.

"Oh, sure, some. What's the matter, Elisa? Do you want to go? I don't think you'd like it, but I'll take you if you really want to go."

She relaxed limply in the seat. "Oh, no. No. I don't want to go. I'm sure I don't." Her face was turned away from him. "It will be enough if we can have wine. It will be plenty." She turned up her coat collar so he could not see that she was crying weakly — like an old woman.

Questions

1. When we first meet Elisa in her garden, with what details does Steinbeck delineate her character for us?
2. Elisa works inside a "wire fence that protected her flower garden from cattle and dogs and chickens" (paragraph 9). What does this wire fence suggest?
3. How would you describe Henry and Elisa's marriage? Cite details from the story to support your description.
4. For what motive does the traveling salesman take an interest in Elisa's chrysanthemums? What immediate effect does his interest have on Elisa?

5. For what possible purpose does Steinbeck give us such a detailed account of Elisa's preparations for her evening out? Notice her tearing off her soiled clothes, her scrubbing her body with pumice (paragraphs 93 – 94).
6. Of what significance to Elisa is the sight of the contents of the flower pot discarded in the road? Notice that, as her husband's car overtakes the covered wagon, Elisa averts her eyes; and then Steinbeck adds, "In a moment it was over. The thing was done. She did not look back" (paragraph 111). Explain this passage.
7. How do you interpret Elisa's asking for wine with dinner? How do you account for her new interest in prize fights?
8. In a sentence, try to state this short story's theme.
9. Why are Elisa Allen's chrysanthemums so important to this story? Sum up what you understand them to mean.

Alice Munro

WILD SWANS   1978

Alice Munro, one of the bright new comets of Canadian fiction, was born of farm parents in 1931 in Wingham in southwestern Ontario, an area whose small-town characters figure in her stories. She attended the University of Western Ontario and now lives in Clinton, Ontario. She is the mother of three daughters. Her books, all fiction, include Dance of the Happy Shades *(1968);* Lives of Girls and Women *(1971);* Something I've Been Meaning to Tell You *(1974);* The Beggar Maid: Stories of Flo and Rose *(1982), first published in Canada as* Who Do You Think You Are? *(1978); and* The Moons of Jupiter *(1983). "The Wild Swans" comes from* The Beggar Maid, *a related collection of sensitive short stories about a stepmother and her daughter.*

Flo said to watch for White Slavers. She said this was how they operated: an old woman, a motherly or grandmotherly sort, made friends while riding beside you on a bus or train. She offered you candy, which was drugged. Pretty soon you began to droop and mumble, were in no condition to speak for yourself. Oh, help, the woman said, my daughter (granddaughter) is sick, please somebody help me get her off so that she can recover in the fresh air. Up stepped a polite gentleman, pretending to be a stranger, offering assistance. Together, at the next stop, they hustled you off the train or bus, and that was the last the ordinary world ever saw of you. They kept you a prisoner in the White Slave place (to which you had been transported drugged and bound so you wouldn't even know where you were), until such time as you were thoroughly degraded and in despair, your insides torn up by drunken men and invested with vile disease, your mind destroyed by drugs, your hair and teeth fallen out. It took about three years, for you to get to this state. You wouldn't want to go home, then, maybe couldn't remember home, or find your way if you did. So they let you out on the streets.

Flo took ten dollars and put it in a little cloth bag which she sewed to the strap of Rose's slip. Another thing likely to happen was that Rose would get her purse stolen.

Watch out, Flo said as well, for people dressed up as ministers. They were the worst. That disguise was commonly adopted by White Slavers, as well as those after your money.

Rose said she didn't see how she could tell which ones were disguised.

Flo had worked in Toronto once. She had worked as a waitress in a coffee shop in Union Station. That was how she knew all she knew. She never saw sunlight, in those days, except on her days off. But she saw plenty else. She saw a man cut another man's stomach with a knife, just pull out his shirt and do a tidy cut, as if it was a watermelon not a stomach. The stomach's owner just sat looking down surprised, with no time to protest. Flo implied that that was nothing, in Toronto. She saw two bad women (that was what Flo called whores, running the two words together, like badminton) get into a fight, and a man laughed at them, other men stopped and laughed and egged them on, and they had their fists full of each other's hair. At last the police came and took them away, still howling and yelping.

She saw a child die of a fit, too. Its face was black as ink.

"Well I'm not scared," said Rose provokingly. "There's the police, anyway."

"Oh, them! They'd be the first ones to diddle you!"

She did not believe anything Flo said on the subject of sex. Consider the undertaker.

A little bald man, very neatly dressed, would come into the store sometimes and speak to Flo with a placating expression.

"I only wanted a bag of candy. And maybe a few packages of gum. And one or two chocolate bars. Could you go to the trouble of wrapping them?"

Flo in her mock-deferential tone would assure him that she could. She wrapped them in heavy-duty white paper, so they were something like presents. He took his time with the selection, humming and chatting, then dawdled for a while. He might ask how Flo was feeling. And how Rose was, if she was there.

"You look pale. Young girls need fresh air." To Flo he would say, "You work too hard. You've worked hard all your life."

"No rest for the wicked," Flo would say agreeably.

When he went out she hurried to the window. There it was—the old black hearse with its purple curtains.

"He'll be after them today!" Flo would say as the hearse rolled away at a gentle pace, almost a funeral pace. The little man had been an undertaker, but he was retired now. The hearse was retired too. His sons had taken over the undertaking and bought a new one. He drove the old hearse all over the country, looking for women. So Flo said. Rose could not believe it. Flo said he gave them the gum and the candy. Rose said he probably ate them himself. Flo said he had been seen, he had been heard. In mild weather he drove with the windows down, singing, to himself or to somebody out of sight in the back.

Her brow is like the snowdrift
Her throat is like the swan

Flo imitated him singing. Gently overtaking some woman walking on a back road, or resting at a country crossroads. All compliments and courtesy and chocolate bars, offering a ride. Of course every woman who reported being asked said she had turned him down. He never pestered anybody, drove politely on. He called in at houses, and if the husband was home he seemed to like just as well as anything to sit and chat. Wives said that was all he ever did anyway but Flo did not believe it.

"Some women are taken in," she said. "A number." She liked to speculate on what the hearse was like inside. Plush. Plush on the walls and the roof and the floor. Soft purple, the color of the curtains, the color of dark lilacs.

All nonsense, Rose thought. Who could believe it, of a man that age?

Rose was going to Toronto on the train for the first time by herself. She had been once before, but that was with Flo, long before her father died. They took along their own sandwiches and bought milk from the vendor on the train. It was sour. Sour chocolate milk. Rose kept taking tiny sips, unwilling to admit that something so much desired could fail her. Flo sniffed it, then hunted up and down the train until she found the old man in his red jacket, with no teeth and the tray hanging around his neck. She invited him to sample the chocolate milk. She invited people nearby to smell it. He let her have some ginger ale for nothing. It was slightly warm.

"I let him know," Flo said looking around after he had left. "You have to let them know." ₂₀

A woman agreed with her but most people looked out the window. Rose drank the warm ginger ale. Either that, or the scene with the vendor, or the conversation Flo and the agreeing woman now got into about where they came from, why they were going to Toronto, and Rose's morning constipation which was why she was lacking color, or the small amount of chocolate milk she had got inside her, caused her to throw up in the train toilet. All day long she was afraid people in Toronto could smell vomit on her coat.

This time Flo started the trip off by saying, "Keep an eye on her, she's never been away from home before!" to the conductor, then looking around and laughing, to show that was jokingly meant. Then she had to get off. It seemed the conductor had no more need for jokes than Rose had, and no intention of keeping an eye on anybody. He never spoke to Rose except to ask for her ticket. She had a window seat, and was soon extraordinarily happy. She felt Flo receding, West Hanratty flying away from her, her own wearying self discarded as easily as everything else. She loved the towns less and less known. A woman was standing at her back door in her nightgown, not caring if everybody on the train saw her. They were traveling south, out of the snow belt, into an earlier spring, a tenderer sort of landscape. People could grow peach trees in their backyards.

Rose collected in her mind the things she had to look for in Toronto. First, things for Flo. Special stockings for her varicose veins. A special kind of cement for sticking handles on pots. And a full set of dominoes.

For herself Rose wanted to buy hair-remover to put on her arms and legs, and if possible an arrangement of inflatable cushions, supposed to reduce your hips and thighs. She thought they probably had hair-remover in the drugstore in Hanratty, but the woman in there was a friend of Flo's and told everything.

She told Flo who bought hair dye and slimming medicine and French safes. As for the cushion business, you could send away for it but there was sure to be a comment at the Post Office, and Flo knew people there as well. She also planned to buy some bangles, and an angora sweater. She had great hopes of silver bangles and powder-blue angora. She thought they could transform her, make her calm and slender and take the frizz out of her hair, dry her underarms and turn her complexion to pearl.

The money for these things, as well as the money for the trip, came from a prize Rose had won, for writing an essay called "Art and Science in the World of Tomorrow." To her surprise, Flo asked if she could read it, and while she was reading it, she remarked that they must have thought they had to give Rose the prize for swallowing the dictionary. Then she said shyly, "It's very interesting."

She would have to spend the night at Cela McKinney's. Cela McKinney was her father's cousin. She had married a hotel manager and thought she had gone up in the world. But the hotel manager came home one day and sat down on the dining room floor between two chairs and said, "I am never going to leave this house again." Nothing unusual had happened, he had just decided not to go out of the house again, and he didn't, until he died. That had made Cela McKinney odd and nervous. She locked her doors at eight o'clock. She was also very stingy. Supper was usually oatmeal porridge, with raisins. Her house was dark and narrow and smelled like a bank.

The train was filling up. At Brantford a man asked if she would mind if he sat down beside her.

"It's cooler out than you'd think," he said. He offered her part of his newspaper. She said no thanks.

Then lest he think her rude she said it really was cooler. She went on looking out the window at the spring morning. There was no snow left, down here. The trees and bushes seemed to have a paler bark than they did at home. Even the sunlight looked different. It was as different from home, here, as the coast of the Mediterranean would be, or the valleys of California.

"Filthy windows, you'd think they'd take more care," the man said. "Do you travel much by train?"

She said no.

Water was lying in the fields. He nodded at it and said there was a lot this year.

"Heavy snows."

She noticed his saying *snows,* a poetic-sounding word. Anyone at home would have said *snow.*

"I had an unusual experience the other day. I was driving out in the country. In fact I was on my way to see one of my parishioners, a lady with a heart condition — "

She looked quickly at his collar. He was wearing an ordinary shirt and tie and a dark blue suit.

"Oh, yes," he said. "I'm a United Church minister. But I don't always wear my uniform. I wear it for preaching in. I'm off duty today.

"Well as I said I was driving through the country and I saw some Canada geese down on a pond, and I took another look, and there were some swans down with them. A whole great flock of swans. What a lovely sight they were.

They would be on their spring migration, I expect, heading up north. What a spectacle. I never saw anything like it."

Rose was unable to think appreciatively of the wild swans because she was afraid he was going to lead the conversation from them to Nature in general and then to God, the way a minister would feel obliged to do. But he did not, he stopped with the swans.

"A very fine sight. You would have enjoyed them."   40

He was between fifty and sixty years old, Rose thought. He was short, and energetic-looking, with a square ruddy face and bright waves of gray hair combed straight up from his forehead. When she realized he was not going to mention God she felt she ought to show her gratitude.

She said they must have been lovely.

"It wasn't even a regular pond, it was only some water lying in a field. It was just luck the water was lying there and they came down and I came driving by at the right time. Just luck. They come in at the east end of Lake Erie, I think. But I never was lucky enough to see them before."

She turned by degrees to the window, and he returned to his paper. She remained slightly smiling, so as not to seem rude, not to seem to be rejecting conversation altogether. The morning really was cool, and she had taken down her coat off the hook where she put it when she first got on the train, she had spread it over herself, like a lap robe. She had set her purse on the floor when the minister sat down, to give him room. He took the sections of the paper apart, shaking and rustling them in a leisurely, rather showy, way. He seemed to her the sort of person who does everything in a showy way. A ministerial way. He brushed aside the sections he didn't want at the moment. A corner of newspaper touched her leg, just at the edge of her coat.

She thought for some time that it was the paper. Then she said to herself,   45
what if it is a hand? That was the kind of thing she could imagine. She would sometimes look at men's hands, at the fuzz on their forearms, their concentrating profiles. She would think about everything they could do. Even the stupid ones. For instance the driver-salesman who brought the bread to Flo's store. The ripeness and confidence of manner, the settled mixture of ease and alertness with which he handled the bread truck. A fold of mature belly over the belt did not displease her. Another time she had her eye on the French teacher at school. Not a Frenchman at all, really, his name was McLaren, but Rose thought teaching French had rubbed off on him, made him look like one. Quick and sallow; sharp shoulders; hooked nose and sad eyes. She saw him lapping and coiling his way through slow pleasures, a perfect autocrat of indulgences. She had a considerable longing to be somebody's object. Pounded, pleasured, reduced, exhausted.

But what if it was a hand? What if it really was a hand? She shifted slightly, moved as much as she could toward the window. Her imagination seemed to have created this reality, a reality she was not prepared for at all. She found it alarming. She was concentrating on that leg, that bit of skin with the stocking over it. She could not bring herself to look. Was there a pressure, or was there not? She shifted again. Her legs had been, and remained, tightly closed. It was. It was a hand. It was a hand's pressure.

Please don't. That was what she tried to say. She shaped the words in her mind, tried them out, then couldn't get them past her lips. Why was that? The embarrassment, was it, the fear that people might hear? People were all around them, the seats were full.

It was not only that.

She did manage to look at him, not raising her head but turning it cautiously. He had tilted his seat back and closed his eyes. There was his dark blue suit sleeve, disappearing under the newspaper. He had arranged the paper so that it overlapped Rose's coat. His hand was underneath, simply resting, as if flung out in sleep.

Now, Rose could have shifted the newspaper and removed her coat. If he was not asleep, he would have been obliged to draw back his hand. If he was asleep, if he did not draw it back, she could have whispered, *Excuse me,* and set his hand firmly on his own knee. This solution, so obvious and foolproof, did not occur to her. And she would have to wonder, why not? The minister's hand was not, or not yet, at all welcome to her. It made her feel uncomfortable, resentful, slightly disgusted, trapped and wary. But she could not take charge of it, to reject it. She could not insist that it was there, when he seemed to be insisting that it was not. How could she declare him responsible, when he lay there so harmless and trusting, resting himself before his busy day, with such a pleased and healthy face? A man older than her father would be, if he were living, a man used to deference, an appreciator of Nature, delighter in wild swans. If she did say *Please don't* she was sure he would ignore her, as if overlooking some silliness or impoliteness on her part. She knew that as soon as she said it she would hope he had not heard.

But there was more to it than that. Curiosity. More constant, more imperious, than any lust. A lust in itself, that will make you draw back and wait, wait too long, risk almost anything, just to see what will happen. *To see what will happen.*

The hand began, over the next several miles, the most delicate, the most timid, pressures and investigations. Not asleep. Or if he was, his hand wasn't. She did feel disgust. She felt a faint, wandering nausea. She thought of flesh: lumps of flesh, pink snouts, fat tongues, blunt fingers, all on their way trotting and creeping and lolling and rubbing, looking for their comfort. She thought of cats in heat rubbing themselves along the top of board fences, yowling with their miserable complaint. It was pitiful, infantile, this itching and shoving and squeezing. Spongy tissues, inflamed membranes, tormented nerve-ends, shameful smells; humiliation.

All that was starting. His hand, that she wouldn't ever have wanted to hold, that she wouldn't have squeezed back, his stubborn patient hand was able, after all, to get the ferns to rustle and the streams to flow, to waken a sly luxuriance.

Nevertheless, she would rather not. She would still rather not. Please remove this, she said out the window. Stop it, please, she said to the stumps and barns. The hand moved up her leg past the top of her stocking to her bare skin, had moved higher, under her suspender, reached her underpants and the lower part of her belly. Her legs were still crossed, pinched together. While her legs stayed crossed she could lay claim to innocence, she had not admitted anything. She could still believe that she would stop this in a minute. Nothing was going to happen, nothing more. Her legs were never going to open.

But they were. They were. As the train crossed the Niagara Escarpment above Dundas, as they looked down at the preglacial valley, the silver-wooded rubble of little hills, as they came sliding down to the shores of Lake Ontario, she would make this slow, and silent, and definite, declaration, perhaps disappointing as much as satisfying the hand's owner. He would not lift his eyelids, his face would not alter, his fingers would not hesitate, but would go powerfully and discreetly to work. Invasion, and welcome, and sunlight flashing far and wide on the lake water; miles of bare orchards stirring round Burlington.

This was disgrace, this was beggary. But what harm in that, we say to ourselves at such moments, what harm in anything, the worse the better, as we ride the cold wave of greed, of greedy assent. A stranger's hand, or root vegetables or humble kitchen tools that people tell jokes about; the world is tumbling with innocent-seeming objects ready to declare themselves, slippery and obliging. She was careful of her breathing. She could not believe this. Victim and accomplice she was borne past Glassco's Jams and Marmalades, past the big pulsating pipes of oil refineries. They glided into suburbs where bedsheets, and towels used to wipe up intimate stains, flapped leeringly on the clotheslines, where even the children seemed to be frolicking lewdly in the school-yards, and the very truckdrivers stopped at the railway crossings must be thrusting their thumbs gleefully into curled hands. Such cunning antics now, such popular visions. The gates and towers of the Exhibition Grounds came into view, the painted domes and pillars floated marvelously against her eyelids' rosy sky. Then flew apart in celebration. You could have had such a flock of birds, wild swans, even, wakened under one big dome together, exploding from it, taking to the sky.

She bit the edge of her tongue. Very soon the conductor passed through the train, to stir the travelers, warn them back to life.

In the darkness under the station the United Church minister, refreshed, opened his eyes and got his paper folded together, then asked if she would like some help with her coat. His gallantry was self-satisfied, dismissive. No, said Rose, with a sore tongue. He hurried out of the train ahead of her. She did not see him in the station. She never saw him again in her life. But he remained on call, so to speak, for years and years, ready to slip into place at a critical moment, without even any regard, later on, for husband or lovers. What recommended him? She could never understand it. His simplicity, his arrogance, his perversely appealing lack of handsomeness, even of ordinary grown-up masculinity? When he stood up she saw that he was shorter even than she had thought, that his face was pink and shiny, that there was something crude and pushy and childish about him.

Was he a minister, really, or was that only what he said? Flo had mentioned people who were not ministers, dressed up as if they were. Not real ministers dressed as if they were not. Or, stranger still, men who were not real ministers pretending to be real but dressed as if they were not. But that she had come as close as she had, to what could happen, was an unwelcome thing. Rose walked through Union Station feeling the little bag with the ten dollars rubbing at her, knew she would feel it all day long, rubbing its reminder against her skin.

She couldn't stop getting Flo's messages, even with that. She remembered, because she was in Union Station, that there was a girl named Mavis working here, in the Gift Shop, when Flo was working in the coffee shop.

Mavis had warts on her eyelids that looked like they were going to turn into sties but they didn't, they went away. Maybe she had them removed, Flo didn't ask. She was very good-looking, without them. There was a movie star in those days she looked a lot like. The movie star's name was Frances Farmer.

Frances Farmer. Rose had never heard of her.

That was the name. And Mavis went and bought herself a big hat that dipped over one eye and a dress entirely made of lace. She went off for the weekend to Georgian Bay, to a resort up there. She booked herself in under the name of Florence Farmer. To give everybody the idea she was really the other one, Frances Farmer, but calling herself Florence because she was on holiday and didn't want to be recognized. She had a little cigarette holder that was black and mother-of-pearl. She could have been arrested, Flo said. For the *nerve.*

Rose almost went over to the Gift Shop, to see if Mavis was still there and if she could recognize her. She thought it would be an especially fine thing, to manage a transformation like that. To dare it; to get away with it, to enter on preposterous adventures in your own, but newly named, skin.

QUESTIONS

1. By what hints does Munro indicate Rose's age and her level of sophistication?
2. What sort of person is Flo? Cite passages that reveal her attitude toward sex. What effect on Rose do her warnings seem to have?
3. Where in the early part of the story do you find *foreshadowing?* (The word is defined on page 9.)
4. What, if anything, does the minister's mention of the wild swans contribute to our understanding of his character? What part does his appreciation of the swans play in Rose's behavior toward him?
5. What forces conspire to prevent Rose from asking her seatmate to take his hand off her leg? How would you explain her apparent lack of resistance to his advances?
6. Where in "Wild Swans" does the point of view shift? What do these shifts contribute to the story's effect?
7. How are the references to the retired undertaker and his old hearse, Cela McKinney and her hotel manager husband, and the shopgirl named Mavis more than entertaining digressions?
8. What is the tone of Munro's story? What passages make it clear to you?
9. Reread the passages that refer to wild swans. What do the swans suggest?
10. What other details in the story are suggestive enough to be called symbolic?
11. What similarities do you find between this story and "Where Are You Going, Where Have You Been?" by Joyce Carol Oates (in Stories for Further Reading)? In what vital ways are the two stories *not* alike?

SUGGESTIONS FOR WRITING

1. Reexamine one of these stories you have already read: "A Rose for Emily," "The Tell-Tale Heart," "Araby," "Greasy Lake," "Barn Burning," "A Clean, Well-Lighted Place," "The Lottery," "Revelation," "The Open Boat." Reread carefully, looking for rich hints. In writing, indicate what actions and objects now seem to you symbolic in their suggestions. Do these actions or objects point toward any central theme in the story? (Note: Watch out for Poe. He eschews messages, and his stories keep away from central themes.)

2. For an alternate topic, look for symbols in a story you have not read before. In the Stories for Further Reading, you might take a look at "The Birthmark," "The Garden-Party," "A Hunger Artist," "The Portable Phonograph," "The Night of the Curlews," and "Where Are You Going, Where Have You Been?"
3. Write a short comment inspired by the title "Absolutely Nothing Is Symbolic" or "There Isn't a Thing You Can't Make a Symbol of." Draw upon your experiences in reading the stories in this chapter, or any other literature. Give concrete examples.
4. Pick a tangible *thing* that intrigues you — an animal, a plant, or another part of nature; a house or another man-made object. Recall it, observe it, meditate on it. Then write an opening paragraph for a story that will make a symbol of that object, doing your best to fill the passage with hints. For inspiration, look back over John Steinbeck's "The Chrysanthemums" and Alice Munro's "Wild Swans."

9 Evaluating a Story

When we **evaluate** a story, we consider it and place a value on it. Perhaps we decide that it is a masterpiece, or a bit of trash, or (like most fiction we read) a work of some value in between. No cut-and-dried method of judgment will work on every story, and so in this chapter I have none to propose. Still, there are things we can look for in a story — usually clear indications of its author's competence.

In judging the quality of a baseball glove, we first have to be aware that a catcher's mitt differs — for good reasons — from a first baseman's glove. It is no less true that, before evaluating a story, we need to recognize its nature. To see, for instance, that a story is a fable (or perhaps a tale) may save us from condemning it as a failed short story.

Good critics of literature have at least a working knowledge of some of its conventions. By **conventions** we mean usual devices and features of a literary work, by which we can recognize its kind. When in movies or on television we watch a yarn about a sinister old mansion full of horrors, we recognize the conventions of that long-lived species of fiction, the **Gothic story.** *The Castle of Otranto, A Gothic Story* (1764), by English author Horace Walpole, started the genre, supplied its name, and established its favorite trappings. In Walpole's short novel, Otranto is a cobwebbed ruin full of underground passages and massive doors that slam unexpectedly. There are awful objects: a statue that bleeds, a portrait that steps from its frame, a giant helmet that falls and leaves its victim "dashed to pieces." Atmosphere is essential to a Gothic story: dusty halls, shadowy landscapes, whispering servants "seen at a distance imperfectly through the dusk" (I quote from Anne Radcliffe's novel *The Mysteries of Udolpho,* 1794). In Charlotte Brontë's *Jane Eyre* (1847), we find the model for a legion of heroines in the Gothic fiction of our own day. In the best-selling Gothic romances of Victoria Holt, Phyllis A. Whitney, and others, young women similarly find love while working as governesses in ominous mansions. Lacking for English castles, American authors of Gothic fiction have had to make do with dark old houses — like those in Nathaniel Hawthorne's novel *The House of the Seven Gables* and in the short stories of Edgar Allan Poe, such as "The Tell-Tale Heart" (page 38). William Faulkner, who brought the tradition to Mississippi, gives "A Rose for Emily" some familiar conventions: a rundown mansion, a mysterious servant, a madwoman, a hideous secret. But Faulkner's story, in its portrait of an aristocrat who refuses to admit that her world has vanished, goes far beyond Gothic conventions. Evidently, when you set up court as a judge of stories, to recognize such conventions will be an advantage. Knowing a Gothic story for what it is, you won't condemn it for lacking "realism." And to be aware of the Gothic elements in "A Rose for Emily" may help you see how original Faulkner manages to be, though employing some handed-down conventions.

Is the story a piece of commercial fiction tailored to a formula, or is it unique in its design? You can't demand the subtlety of a Katherine Anne Porter of a writer of hard-boiled detective stories. Neither can you put down "The Jilting of Granny Weatherall" for lacking slam-bang action. Some stories are no more than light, entertaining bits of fluff — no point in damning them, unless you dislike fluff or find them written badly. Of course, you are within your rights to prefer solidity to fluff, or to prefer a Porter story to a typical paperback romance by a hack writer. James Thurber's "The Catbird Seat," though a simpler and briefer story than Leo Tolstoi's "The Death of Ivan Ilych," is no less finished, complete, and satisfactory a work of art. Yet, considered in another light, Tolstoi's short novel may well seem a greater work than Thurber's. It reveals greater meaning and enfolds more life.

Masterpieces often have flaws; and so, whenever we can, we need to consider a story in its entirety. Some novels by Thomas Hardy and by Theodore Dreiser impress (on the whole), despite passages of stilted dialogue and other clumsy writing. If a story totally fails to enlist our sympathies, probably it suffers from some basic ineptitude: choice of an inappropriate point of view, a style ill suited to its theme, or possibly insufficient knowledge of human beings. In some ineffectual stories, things important to the writer (and to the story) remain private and unmentioned. In other stories, the writer's interests may be perfectly clear but they may not interest the reader, for they are not presented with sufficient art.

Some stories fail from **sentimentality,** a defect in a work whose writer seems to feel tremendous emotion and implies that we too should feel it, but does not provide us enough reason to share such feelings. Sentimentality is rampant in televised weekday afternoon soap operas, whose characters usually palpitate with passion for reasons not quite known, and who speak in melodramatic tones as if heralding the end of the world. In some fiction, conventional objects (locks of baby hair, posthumously awarded medals, pressed roses) frequently signal, "Let's have a good cry!" Revisiting home after her marriage, the character Amelia in William Makepeace Thackeray's *Vanity Fair* effuses about the bed she slept in when a virgin: "Dear little bed! how many a long night had she wept on its pillow."[1] Teary sentimentality is more common in nineteenth-

---

[1]Sentimentality in fiction is older than the Victorians. Popular in eighteenth-century England, the **sentimental novel** (or **novel of sensibility**) specialized in characters whose ability to shed

century fiction than in ours. We have gone to the other extreme, some critics think, into a sentimentality of the violent and the hard-boiled. But in a grossly sentimental work of any kind, failure inheres in our refusal to go along with the author's implied attitudes. We laugh when we are expected to cry, feel delight when we are supposed to be horrified.

In evaluating a story, we may usefully ask a few questions:

1. What is the tone of the story? By what means and how effectively is it communicated?

2. What is the point of view? Does it seem appropriate and effective in this story? Imagine the story told from a different point of view; would such a change be for the worse or for the better?

3. Does the story show us unique and individual scenes, events, and characters — or weary stereotypes?

4. Are any symbols evident? If so, do they direct us to the story's central theme, or do they distract us from it?

5. How appropriate to the theme of the story, and to its subject matter, are its tone and style? Is it ever difficult or impossible to sympathize with the attitudes of the author (insofar as we can tell what they are)?

6. Does our interest in the story mainly depend on following its plot, on finding out what will happen next? Or does the author go beyond the events to show us what they mean? Are the events (however fantastic) credible, or are they incredibly melodramatic? Does the plot greatly depend upon farfetched coincidence?

7. Has the writer caused characters, events, and settings to come alive? Are they full of breath and motion, or simply told about in the abstract ("She was a lovable girl whose life had been highly exciting")? Unless the story is a fable or a tale, which need no detailed description or deep portrayal of character, then we may well expect the story to contain enough vividly imagined detail to make us believe in it.

Suggestions for Writing

1. In a short essay, take two stories that you find differing markedly in quality and evaluate them, giving evidence to support your judgments. Stories similar enough to compare might include two character studies of women, as in "Revelation" and "The Chrysanthemums."

2. Write a blast against a story in this book that you dislike intensely. Stick to the text of the story in making your criticisms and support your charges with plenty of evidence.

3. By comparing two stories that strike you as similar (" 'The Lottery' and 'The Hunger Artist': Two Stories of Human Sacrifice"), evaluate them.

---

quick and copious tears signified their virtuous hearts. Oliver Goldsmith's *The Vicar of Wakefield* (1766) and Henry Mackenzie's *The Man of Feeling* (1771) are classics of the genre. An abundance of tears does not prevent such novels from having merit.

10 Reading a Novel

Among the forms of imaginative literature in our language, the novel has been the favorite of both writers and readers for more than two hundred years. Broadly defined, a **novel** is a book-length story in prose, whose author tries to create the sense that while we read, we experience actual life.

This sense of actuality, also found in artful short stories, may be the quality that sets the novel apart from other long prose narratives. Why do we not apply the name *novel* to, for instance, *Gulliver's Travels*? In his marvel-filled account of Lemuel Gulliver's voyages among pygmies, giants, civilized horses, and noxious humanoid swine, Jonathan Swift does not seem primarily to care if we find his story credible. Though he arrays the adventures of Gulliver in painstaking detail (and, ironically, has Gulliver swear to the truth of them), Swift neither attempts nor achieves a convincing illusion of life. For his book is a fantastic satire that finds resemblances between noble horses and man's reasoning faculties, between debased apes and man's kinship with the beasts.

Unlike other major literary forms — drama, lyric, ballad, and epic — the novel is a relative newcomer. Originally, the drama in ancient Greece came alive only when actors performed it; the epic or heroic poem (from the classic *Iliad* through the Old English *Beowulf*), only when a bard sang or chanted it. But the English novel came to maturity in literate times, in the eighteenth century, and by its nature was something different: a story to be communicated silently, at whatever moment and at whatever pace (whether quickly or slowly and meditatively) the reader desired.

Some definitions of the novel would more strictly limit its province. "The Novel is a picture of real life and manners, and of the time in which it was written," declared Clara Reeve in 1785, thus distinguishing the novel from the romance, which "describes what never happened nor is likely to happen." By so specifying that the novel depicts life in the present day, the critic was probably observing the derivation of the word *novel*. Akin to the French word for "news" *(nouvelles)*, it comes from the Italian *novella* ("something new and small"), a term applied to a newly made story taking place in recent times, and not a traditional story taking place long ago.

Also drawing a line between novel and romance, Nathaniel Hawthorne, in his preface to *The House of the Seven Gables* (1851), restricted the novel "not merely to the possible, but to the probable and ordinary course of man's experience." A **romance** had no such limitations. Such a definition would deny the name of *novel* to any fantastic or speculative story — to, say, the gothic novel and the science fiction novel. Carefully bestowed, the labels *novel* and *romance* may be useful to distinguish between the true-to-life story of usual people in ordinary places (such as George Eliot's *Silas Marner* or John Updike's *Couples*) and the larger-than-life story of daring deeds and high adventure, set in the past or future or in some timeless land (such as Walter Scott's *Ivanhoe* or J. R. R. Tolkien's *Lord of the Rings*). But the labels are difficult to apply to much modern fiction, in which ordinary life is sometimes mingled with outlandishness. Who can say that James Joyce's *Ulysses* is not a novel, though it contains moments of dream and drunken hallucination? (At one moment, a cake of soap rises where the moon ought to be.) And yet the total effect, as in any successful novel, is a sense of the actual.

This sense of the actual is, perhaps, the hallmark of a novel, whether or not the events it relates are literally possible. To achieve this sense, novelists have employed many devices, and frequently have tried to pass off their storytelling as reporting. Nathaniel Hawthorne, in his introduction to *The Scarlet Letter,* gives a minute account of his finding documents on which he claims to base his novel, tied with a faded red ribbon and gathering dust in a customshouse. More recently, Vladimir Nabokov's *Pale Fire* (1962) tells its story in the form of a scholarly edition of a 999-line poem, complete with a biographical commentary by a friend of the late poet. Samuel Richardson's casting *Pamela* (1740) into the form of personal letters helped lend the story an appearance of being not invented, but discovered. Another method favored by early novelists was to write as though setting down a memoir or an autobiography. Daniel Defoe, whose skill in feigning such memoirs was phenomenal, even succeeded in writing the supposedly true confessions of a woman retired from a life of crime, *Moll Flanders* (1722), and in maintaining a vivid truthfulness:

> Going through Aldersgate Street, there was a pretty little child who had been at a dancing-school, and was going home all alone; and my prompter, like a true devil, set me upon this innocent creature. I talked to it, and it prattled to me again, and I took it by the hand and led it along till I came to a paved alley that goes into Bartholomew Close, and I led it in there. The child said that was not its way home. I said, "Yes, my dear, it is; I'll show you the way home." The child had a little necklace on of gold beads, and I had my eye upon that, and in the dark of the alley I stooped, pretending to mend the child's clog that was loose, and took off her necklace, and the child never felt it, and so led the child on again.

Here, I say, the devil put me upon killing the child in the dark alley, that it might not cry, but the very thought frighted me so that I was ready to drop down; but I turned the child about and bade it go back again. . . . The last affair left no great concern upon me, for as I did the poor child no harm, I only said to myself, I had given the parents a just reproof for their negligence in leaving the poor little lamb to come home by itself, and it would teach them to take more care of it another time.

What could sound more like the voice of an experienced child-robber than this manner of excusing her crime, and even justifying it?

Informed that a student had given up the study of mathematics to become a novelist, the logician David Hilbert drily remarked, "It was just as well: he did not have enough imagination to become a first-rate mathematician."[1] It is true that some novelists place great emphasis on research and notetaking. Arthur Halley, author of bestsellers such as *Wheels* (about the Detroit car industry) and *Airport,* reportedly starts work on a novel by interviewing people in whatever glamorous profession he plans to expose, gathering stacks of note cards to make sure that his slightest detail is accurate. Clearly, however, any novel can grow to completion only through a procedure of creation, selection, and arrangement. Raw facts cannot leap into a novel by themselves — whether the novel is a paperback shocker about a famous crime, or Theodore Dreiser's impressive study of a murder case, inspired by newspaper accounts, *An American Tragedy.*

In "The Open Boat," Stephen Crane brings high literary art to bear upon his own experience. The result is a short story based on fact. More recently, we have heard much about the **nonfiction novel,** in which the author presents actual people and events in story form. Norman Mailer, in *The Executioner's Song* (1979), chronicles the life and death of Gary Gilmore, the Utah murderer who demanded his own execution. Truman Capote's *In Cold Blood* (1966) sets forth an account of crime and punishment in Kansas, based on interviews with the accused and other principals. Perhaps the name "nonfiction novel" (Capote's name for it) or "true life novel" (as Mailer calls his Gilmore story) is newer than the form. In the past, writers of autobiography have cast their memoirs into what looks like novel form: Richard Wright in *Black Boy* (1945), William Burroughs in *Junkie* (1953). Derived not from the author's memory but from his reporting, John Hersey's *Hiroshima* (1946) reconstructs the lives of six survivors of the atom bomb as if they were fictional. In reading such works we may nearly forget we are reading literal truth, so well do the techniques of the novel lend remembered facts an air of immediacy.

A familiar kind of fiction that claims a basis in fact is the **historical novel,** a detailed reconstruction of life in another time, perhaps in another place. In some historical novels the author attempts a faithful picture of daily life in another era, as does Robert Graves in *I, Claudius* (1934), a novel

[1]Quoted by William H. Gass, *Fiction and the Figures of Life* (New York: Knopf, 1970).

of patrician Rome. More often, history is a backdrop for an exciting story of love and heroic adventure. Nathaniel Hawthorne's *The Scarlet Letter* (set in Puritan Boston), Herman Melville's *Moby-Dick* (set in the heyday of Yankee whalers), and Stephen Crane's *The Red Badge of Courage* (set in the battlefields of the Civil War) are historical novels in that their authors lived considerably later than the scenes and events that they depicted — and strove for truthfulness, by imaginative means.

Other varieties of novel will be familiar to anyone who scans the racks of paperback books in any drugstore: the mystery or detective novel, the Western novel, the science fiction novel, and other enduring types. Classified according to less well-known species, novels are sometimes said to belong to a category if they contain some recognizable kind of structure or theme. Such a category is the **bildungsroman** (German for a "novel of growth or development"), sometimes called the **apprenticeship novel** after its classic example, *Wilhelm Meister's Apprenticeship* (1796) by Johann Wolfgang von Goethe. This is the kind of novel in which a youth struggles toward maturity, seeking, perhaps, some consistent world view or philosophy of life. Sometimes the apprenticeship novel is evidently the author's recollection of his own early life: James Joyce's *Portrait of the Artist as a Young Man* and Mark Twain's *Tom Sawyer*.

In a **picaresque novel** (another famous category), a likable scoundrel wanders through adventures, living by his wits, duping the straight citizenry. The name comes from Spanish: *Pícaro*, "rascal" or "rogue." The classic picaresque novel is the anonymous Spanish *Life of Lazarillo de Tormes* (1554), imitated by many English writers, among them Henry Fielding in his story of a London thief and racketeer, *Jonathan Wild* (1743). Mark Twain's *Huckleberry Finn* owes something to the tradition; like early picaresque novels, it is told in episodes rather than in one all-unifying plot and is narrated in the first person by a hero at odds with respectable society ("dismal regular and decent," Huck Finn calls it). In Twain's novel, however, the traveling swindlers who claim to be a duke and a dauphin are much more typical rogues of picaresque fiction than Huck himself, an honest innocent. Modern novels worthy of the name include J. P. Donleavy's *The Ginger Man* (1965), Saul Bellow's *The Adventures of Augie March* (1953), and Erica Jong's *Fanny* (1981).

Mainly (but not merely) a description of size, the term **short novel** refers to a narrative midway in length between a short story and a novel (the latter, according to E. M. Forster, has to have at least 50,000 words). Generally a short novel, like a short story, is focused on just one or two characters but, unlike a short story, has room to reveal them in greater fullness and depth, sometimes taking in a longer span of time. A short novel is included in this book: Leo Tolstoi's *The Death of Ivan Ilych*. Sometimes a short novel is also called a **novelette** (a name formerly much used by magazines that featured long fiction), or a **nouvelle,** or a **novella;** but these names are out of fashion.

Trying to perceive a novel as a whole, we may find it helpful to look for the same elements that we have noticed in reading short stories. By asking ourselves leading questions, we may be drawn more deeply into the novel's world, and may come to recognize and appreciate the techniques of the novelist. Does the novel have themes, or an overall theme? Who is its main character? What is the author's kind of narrative voice? What do we know about the tone, style, and use of irony? Why is this novel written from one point of view rather than from another? If the novel in question is large and thickly populated, it may help to read it with a pencil, taking brief notes. Forced to put the novel aside and later return to it, the reader may find that the notes refresh the memory. Notetaking habits differ, but perhaps these might be no more than, say, "Theme introduced, p. 27," or, "Old clothes dealer, p. 109 — walking symbol?" Some readers find it useful to list briefly whatever each chapter accomplishes. Others make lists of a novel's characters, especially when reading classic Russian novels in which the reader has to recall that Alexey Karamazov is also identified by his pet name Aloysha, or that, in Leo Tolstoi's *Anna Karenina*, Princess Catherine Alexándrovna Shcherbátskaya and "Kitty" are one and the same.

Once our reading of a novel is finished and we prepare to discuss it or write about it, it may be a good idea to browse through it again, rereading brief portions. This method of overall browsing may also help when first approaching a bulky and difficult novel. Just as an explorer mapping unfamiliar territory may find it best to begin by taking an aerial view of it, so too the reader approaching an exceptionally thick and demanding novel may wish, at the start, to look for its general shape. This is the method of some professional book reviewers, who size up a novel (even an easy-to-read spy story, because they are not reading for pleasure) by skimming the first chapter, a middle chapter or two, and the last chapter; then going back and browsing at top speed through the rest. Reading a novel in this grim fashion, of course, the reviewer does not really know it thoroughly, any more than a tourist knows the mind and heart of a foreign people after just strolling in a capital city and riding a tour bus to a few monuments. The reviewer's method will, however, provide a general notion of what the author is doing, and at the very least will tell something of her tone, style, point of view, and competence. We suggest this method only as a way to *approach* a book that, otherwise, the reader might not want to approach at all. It may be a comfort in studying some obdurate-looking or highly experimental novel, such as James Joyce's *Ulysses* or Henry James's *The Sacred Fount*. But the reader will find it necessary to return to the book, in order to know it, and to read it honestly, in detail. There is, of course, no short cut to novel reading, and probably the best method is to settle in comfort and read the book through: with your own eyes, not with the borrowed glasses of literary criticism.

The death of the novel is continually being predicted. The competition of television drama is too much for it, some believe; indeed, some evidence says that such competition is taking hold. In Brittany, France, when antigovernment protesters blew up the only television transmitter in the province, booksellers the very next day reported their business increased by as much as twenty percent. But recently in England and North America, television dramas have been sending people in vast numbers back to the books dramatized: Tolstoi's *War and Peace*, Evelyn Waugh's *Brideshead Revisited*. Meanwhile, each year new novels by the hundreds continue to appear, their authors wistfully looking for a public. A chosen few reach tens of thousands of readers through book clubs, and, through paperback reprint editions, occasionally millions more. To forecast the end of the novel seems risky. For the novel exercises the imagination of the beholder. At any hour, at a touch of the hand, it opens and (with no warm-up) begins to speak. Once printed, it consumes no further energy. Often so small it may be carried in a pocket, it may yet survive by its ability to contain multitudes (a "capacious vessel," Henry James called it): a thing both a work of art and an amazingly compact system for the storage and retrieval of imagined life.

SUGGESTIONS FOR WRITING

1. In one carefully thought-out paragraph, try to sum up what you believe Tolstoi is saying in his short novel, *The Death of Ivan Ilych* (in Stories for Further Reading).
2. Compare Tolstoi's short novel with another story of spiritual awakening: Flannery O'Connor's "Revelation," or Isaac Bashevis Singer's "Gimpel the Fool." In each, what brings about the enlightenment of the central character?
3. Compare the last thoughts of Ivan Ilych with the last thoughts of Katherine Anne Porter's Granny Weatherall.
4. Topic for a long term paper: Read either *War and Peace* or *Anna Karenina* and show how some theme present in *Ivan Ilych* is essential to it as well.
5. Read a novel chosen from a list provided by your instructor, or chosen with your instructor's approval. Selecting some element in it that interests you, write an essay in which you demonstrate the importance to the book of that one element. You might write, for instance, on "The Character of the Monster in Mary Shelley's *Frankenstein*"; for an essay on theme, "A Plea for Paganism in D. H. Lawrence's *The Plumed Serpent*"; "Violence in John Irving's *The Hotel New Hampshire*"; or "Symbolism in *The Scarlet Letter*" (or in *The Great Gatsby*). (Suggestion: You might find it helpful to read the discussion of the method of analysis in "Writing about a Story," page 425.)

Stories for Further Reading

For human intercourse, as soon as we look at it for its own sake and not as a social adjunct, is seen to be haunted by a specter. We cannot understand each other, except in a rough-and-ready way; we cannot reveal ourselves, even when we want to; what we call intimacy is only a makeshift; perfect knowledge is an illusion. But in the novel we can know people perfectly, and, apart from the general pleasure of reading, we can find here a compensation for their dimness in life. In this direction fiction is truer than history, because it goes beyond the evidence, and each of us knows from his own experience that there is something beyond the evidence, and even if the novelist has not got it correctly, well — he has tried.

— E. M. Forster, *Aspects of the Novel*

Leo Tolstoi

THE DEATH OF IVAN ILYCH   1886

Translated by Louise and Aylmer Maude

Leo Tolstoi (1828 – 1910), who inherited the title of Count, was born into a family who owned vast lands in Tula province, Russia. As a young man disgruntled with self and schooling, he left Kazan University without taking a degree. After a period of fast living in Moscow and St. Petersburg, he became an army officer and took part in the siege of Sevastopol in the Crimean War. Returning to his estate, Tolstoi opened a school for the children of serfs, based on the ideas (then radical) that learning should be a joy and that individuals should be taught according to their needs. In 1862 he married young, well-educated Sophia Bers. Thirteen children followed, and Tolstoi's years of tremendous achievement as a novelist. About 1876, after a religious illumination, Tolstoi became convinced that one should do good, eschew alcohol, tobacco, meat, and violence, and stop owning things. These tenets brought him into conflict with his wife and family, the Russian Orthodox Church, and the Czarist government. Tolstoi renounced his lands and his book royalties. He dressed like a peasant, made his own boots, and dug potatoes. From his driven pen poured books, tracts, and articles expounding his radically Christian moral and social ideas. In What Is Art? *(1898) he held that artists have a God-given duty to produce only what most people can understand and appreciate. In his seventh decade Tolstoi returned to the novel, seeing in fiction a means to preach. Yet, impressive though they are,* The Kreutzer Sonata *(1891) and* Resurrection *(1899) have never won readers' love as have his earlier masterpieces* War and Peace *(1863 – 69), that immense saga of Russian society before, during, and after Napoleon's invasion, and* Anna Karenina *(1875 – 77), a compassionate history of the decline and fall of a woman who defies convention.*

I

During an interval in the Melvinski trial in the large building of the Law Courts, the members and public prosecutor met in Ivan Egorovich Shebek's private room, where the conversation turned on the celebrated Krasovski case. Fëdor Vasilievich warmly maintained that it was not subject to their jurisdiction, Ivan Egorovich maintained the contrary, while Peter Ivanovich, not having entered into the discussion at the start, took no part in it but looked through the *Gazette* which had just been handed in.

"Gentlemen," he said, "Ivan Ilych has died!"

"You don't say so!"

"Here, read it yourself," replied Peter Ivanovich, handing Fëdor Vasilievich the paper still damp from the press. Surrounded by a black border were the words: "Praskovya Fëdorovna Goloviná, with profound sorrow, informs relatives and friends of the demise of her beloved husband Ivan Ilych Golovin,

Member of the Court of Justice, which occurred on February the 4th of this year 1882. The funeral will take place on Friday at one o'clock in the afternoon."

Ivan Ilych had been a colleague of the gentlemen present and was liked by them all. He had been ill for some weeks with an illness said to be incurable. His post had been kept open for him, but there had been conjectures that in case of his death Alexeev might receive his appointment, and that either Vinnikov or Shtabel would succeed Alexeev. So on receiving the news of Ivan Ilych's death the first thought of each of the gentlemen in that private room was of the changes and promotions it might occasion among themselves or their acquaintances.

"I shall be sure to get Shtabel's place or Vinnikov's," thought Fëdor Vasilievich. "I was promised that long ago, and the promotion means an extra eight hundred rubles a year for me besides the allowance."

"Now I must apply for my brother-in-law's transfer from Kaluga," thought Peter Ivanovich. "My wife will be very glad, and then she won't be able to say that I never do anything for her relations."

"I thought he would never leave his bed again," said Peter Ivanovich aloud. "It's very sad."

"But what really was the matter with him?"

"The doctors couldn't say — at least they could, but each of them said something different. When last I saw him I thought he was getting better."

"And I haven't been to see him since the holidays. I always meant to go."

"Had he any property?"

"I think his wife had a little — but something quite trifling."

"We shall have to go to see her, but they live so terribly far away."

"Far away from you, you mean. Everything's far away from your place."

"You see, he never can forgive my living on the other side of the river," said Peter Ivanovich, smiling at Shebek. Then, still talking of the distances between different parts of the city, they returned to the Court.

Besides considerations as to the possible transfers and promotions likely to result from Ivan Ilych's death, the mere fact of the death of a near acquaintance aroused, as usual, in all who heard of it the complacent feeling that "it is he who is dead and not I."

Each one thought or felt, "Well, he's dead but I'm alive!" But the more intimate of Ivan Ilych's acquaintances, his so-called friends, could not help thinking also that they would now have to fulfil the very tiresome demands of propriety by attending the funeral service and paying a visit of condolence to the widow.

Fëdor Vasilievich and Peter Ivanovich had been his nearest acquaintances. Peter Ivanovich had studied law with Ivan Ilych and had considered himself to be under obligations to him.

Having told his wife at dinner-time of Ivan Ilych's death and of his conjecture that it might be possible to get her brother transferred to their circuit, Peter Ivanovich sacrificed his usual nap, put on his evening clothes, and drove to Ivan Ilych's house.

At the entrance stood a carriage and two cabs. Leaning against the wall in the hall downstairs near the cloak-stand was a coffin-lid covered with cloth of gold, ornamented with gold cord and tassels, that had been polished up with metal powder. Two ladies in black were taking off their fur cloaks. Peter Ivanovich recognized one of them as Ivan Ilych's sister, but the other was a stranger to him. His colleague Schwartz was just coming downstairs, but on seeing Peter Ivanovich enter he stopped and winked at him, as if to say: "Ivan Ilych has made a mess of things — not like you and me."

Schwartz's face with his Piccadilly whiskers and his slim figure in evening dress had as usual an air of elegant solemnity which contrasted with the playfulness of his character and had a special piquancy here, or so it seemed to Peter Ivanovich.

Peter Ivanovich allowed the ladies to precede him and slowly followed them upstairs. Schwartz did not come down but remained where he was, and Peter Ivanovich understood that he wanted to arrange where they should play bridge that evening. The ladies went upstairs to the widow's room, and Schwartz with seriously compressed lips but a playful look in his eyes, indicated by a twist of his eyebrows the room to the right where the body lay.

Peter Ivanovich, like everyone else on such occasions, entered feeling uncertain what he would have to do. All he knew was that at such times it is always safe to cross oneself. But he was not quite sure whether one should make obeisances while doing so. He therefore adopted a middle course. On entering the room he began crossing himself and made a slight movement resembling a bow. At the same time, as far as the motion of his head and arm allowed, he surveyed the room. Two young men — apparently nephews, one of whom was a high-school pupil — were leaving the room, crossing themselves as they did so. An old woman was standing motionless, and a lady with strangely arched eyebrows was saying something to her in a whisper. A vigorous, resolute Church Reader, in a frock-coat, was reading something in a loud voice with an expression that precluded any contradiction. The butler's assistant, Gerasim, stepping lightly in front of Peter Ivanovich, was strewing something on the floor. Noticing this, Peter Ivanovich was immediately aware of a faint odor of a decomposing body.

The last time he had called on Ivan Ilych, Peter Ivanovich had seen 25 Gerasim in the study. Ivan Ilych had been particularly fond of him and he was performing the duty of a sick nurse.

Peter Ivanovich continued to make the sign of the cross, slightly inclining his head in an intermediate direction between the coffin, the Reader, and the icons on the table in a corner of the room. Afterwards, when it seemed to him that this movement of his arm in crossing himself had gone on too long, he stopped and began to look at the corpse.

The dead man lay, as dead men always lie, in a specially heavy way, his rigid limbs sunk in the soft cushions of the coffin, with the head forever bowed on the pillow. His yellow waxen brow with bald patches over his sunken temples was thrust up in the way peculiar to the dead, the protruding nose seeming to press on the upper lip. He was much changed and had grown even thinner since Peter Ivanovich had last seen him, but, as is always the case with the dead, his face was handsomer and above all more dignified than when he was alive. The expression on the face said that what was necessary had been accomplished, and accomplished rightly. Besides this there was in that expression a reproach and a warning to the living. This warning seemed to Peter Ivanovich out of place, or at least not applicable to him. He felt a certain discomfort and so he hurriedly crossed himself once more and turned and went out of the door — too hurriedly and too regardless of propriety, as he himself was aware.

Schwartz was waiting for him in the adjoining room with legs spread wide apart and both hands toying with his top-hat behind his back. The mere sight of that playful, well-groomed, and elegant figure refreshed Peter Ivanovich. He felt that Schwartz was above all these happenings and would not surrender to any depressing influences. His very look said that this incident of a church service for Ivan Ilych could not be a sufficient reason for infringing the order of the session — in other words, that it would certainly not prevent his unwrapping a new pack of cards and shuffling them that evening while a footman placed four fresh candles on the table: in fact, that there was no reason for supposing that this incident would hinder their spending the evening agreeably. Indeed he said this in a whisper as Peter Ivanovich passed him, proposing that they should meet for a game at Fëdor Vasilievich's. But apparently Peter Ivanovich was not destined to play bridge that evening. Praskovya Fëdorovna (a short, fat woman who despite all efforts to the contrary had continued to broaden steadily from her shoulders downwards and who had the same extraordinarily arched eyebrows as the lady who had been standing by the coffin), dressed all in black, her head covered with lace, came out of her own room with some other ladies, conducted them to the room where the dead body lay, and said: "The service will begin immediately. Please go in."

Schwartz, making an indefinite bow, stood still, evidently neither accepting nor declining this invitation. Praskovya Fëdorovna, recognizing Peter Ivanovich, sighed, went close up to him, took his hand, and said: "I know you were a true friend of Ivan Ilych . . ." and looked at him awaiting some suitable response. And Peter Ivanovich knew that, just as it had been the right thing to cross himself in that room, so what he had to do here was to press her hand, sigh, and say, "Believe me. . . ." So he did all this and as he did it felt that the desired result had been achieved: that both he and she were touched.

"Come with me. I want to speak to you before it begins," said the widow. "Give me your arm." 30

Peter Ivanovich gave her his arm and they went to the inner rooms, passing Schwartz, who winked at Peter Ivanovich compassionately.

"That does for our bridge! Don't object if we find another player. Perhaps you can cut in when you do escape," said his playful look.

Peter Ivanovich sighed still more deeply and despondently, and Praskovya Fëdorovna pressed his arm gratefully. When they reached the drawing-room, upholstered in pink cretonne and lighted by a dim lamp, they sat down at the table — she on a sofa and Peter Ivanovich on a low pouffe, the springs of which yielded spasmodically under his weight. Praskovya Fëdorovna had been on the point of warning him to take another seat, but felt that such a warning was out of keeping with her present condition and so changed her mind. As he sat down on the pouffe Peter Ivanovich recalled how Ivan Ilych had arranged this room and had consulted him regarding this pink cretonne with green leaves. The whole room was full of furniture and knick-knacks, and on her way to the sofa the lace of the widow's black shawl caught on the carved edge of the table. Peter Ivanovich rose to detach it, and the springs of the pouffe, relieved of his weight, rose also and gave him a push. The widow began detaching her shawl herself, and Peter Ivanovich again sat down, suppressing the rebellious springs of the pouffe under him. But the widow had not quite freed herself and Peter Ivanovich got up again, and again the pouffe rebelled and even creaked. When this was all over she took out a clean cambric handkerchief and began to weep. The episode with the shawl and the struggle with the pouffe had cooled Peter Ivanovich's emotions and he sat there with a sullen look on his face. This awkward situation was interrupted by Sokolov, Ivan Ilych's butler, who came to report that the plot in the cemetery that Praskovya Fëdorovna had chosen would cost two hundred rubles. She stopped weeping and, looking at Peter Ivanovich with the air of a victim, remarked in French that it was very hard for her. Peter Ivanovich made a silent gesture signifying his full conviction that it must indeed be so.

"Please smoke," she said in a magnanimous yet crushed voice, and turned to discuss with Sokolov the price of the plot for the grave.

Peter Ivanovich while lighting his cigarette heard her inquiring very circumstantially into the prices of different plots in the cemetery and finally decide which she would take. When that was done she gave instructions about engaging the choir. Sokolov then left the room.

"I look after everything myself," she told Peter Ivanovich, shifting the albums that lay on the table; and noticing that the table was endangered by his cigarette-ash, she immediately passed him an ashtray, saying as she did so: "I consider it an affectation to say that my grief prevents my attending to practical affairs. On the contrary, if anything can — I won't say console me, but — distract me, it is seeing to everything concerning him." She again took out her handkerchief as if preparing to cry, but suddenly, as if mastering her feeling, she shook herself and began to speak calmly. "But there is something I want to talk to you about."

Peter Ivanovich bowed, keeping control of the springs of the pouffe, which immediately began quivering under him.

"He suffered terribly the last few days."

"Did he?" said Peter Ivanovich.

"Oh, terribly! He screamed unceasingly, not for minutes but for hours. For the last three days he screamed incessantly. It was unendurable. I cannot understand how I bore it; you could hear him three rooms off. Oh, what I have suffered!"

"Is it possible that he was conscious all that time?" asked Peter Ivanovich.

"Yes," she whispered. "To the last moment. He took leave of us a quarter of an hour before he died, and asked us to take Volodya away."

The thought of the sufferings of this man he had known so intimately, first as a merry little boy, then as a school-mate, and later as a grown-up colleague, suddenly struck Peter Ivanovich with horror, despite an unpleasant consciousness of his own and this woman's dissimulation. He again saw that brow, and that nose pressing down on the lip, and felt afraid for himself.

"Three days of frightful suffering and then death! Why, that might suddenly, at any time, happen to me," he thought, and for a moment felt terrified. But — he did not himself know how — the customary reflection at once occurred to him that this had happened to Ivan Ilych and not to him, and that it should not and could not happen to him, and that to think that it could would be yielding to depression which he ought not to do, as Schwartz's expression plainly showed. After which reflection Peter Ivanovich felt reassured, and began to ask with interest about the details of Ivan Ilych's death, as though death was an accident natural to Ivan Ilych but certainly not to himself.

After many details of the really dreadful physical sufferings Ivan Ilych 45 had endured (which details he learnt only from the effect those sufferings had produced on Praskovya Fëdorovna's nerves) the widow apparently found it necessary to get to business.

"Oh, Peter Ivanovich, how hard it is! How terribly, terribly hard!" and she again began to weep.

Peter Ivanovich sighed and waited for her to finish blowing her nose. When she had done so he said, "Believe me . . ." and she again began talking and brought out what was evidently her chief concern with him — namely, to question him as to how she could obtain a grant of money from the government on the occasion of her husband's death. She made it appear that she was asking Peter Ivanovich's advice about her pension, but he soon saw that she already knew about that to the minutest detail, more even than he did himself. She knew how much could be got out of the government in consequence of her husband's death, but wanted to find out whether she could not possibly extract something more. Peter Ivanovich tried to think of some means of doing so, but after reflecting for a while and, out of propriety, condemning the government for its niggardliness, he said he thought that nothing more could be got. Then she sighed and evidently began to devise means of getting rid of her visitor. Noticing this, he put out his cigarette, rose, pressed her hand, and went out into the anteroom.

In the dining-room where the clock stood that Ivan Ilych had liked so much and had bought at an antique shop, Peter Ivanovich met a priest and a few acquaintances who had come to attend the service, and he recognized Ivan Ilych's daughter, a handsome young woman. She was in black and her slim figure appeared slimmer than ever. She had a gloomy, determined, almost angry expression, and bowed to Peter Ivanovich as though he were in some way to blame. Behind her, with the same offended look, stood a wealthy young man, an examining magistrate, whom Peter Ivanovich also knew and who was her fiancé, as he had heard. He bowed mournfully to them and was about to pass into the death-chamber, when from under the stairs appeared the figure of Ivan Ilych's schoolboy son, who was extremely like his father. He seemed a little Ivan Ilych, such as Peter Ivanovich remembered when they studied law together. His tear-stained eyes had in them the look that is seen in the eyes of boys of thirteen or fourteen who are not pure-minded. When he saw Peter Ivanovich he scowled morosely and shamefacedly. Peter Ivanovich nodded to him and entered the death-chamber. The service began: candles, groans, incense, tears, and sobs. Peter Ivanovich stood looking gloomily down at his feet. He did not look once at the dead man, did not yield to any depressing influence, and was one of the first to leave the room. There was no one in the anteroom, but Gerasim darted out of the dead man's room, rummaged with his strong hands among the fur coats to find Peter Ivanovich's, and helped him on with it.

"Well, friend Gerasim," said Peter Ivanovich, so as to say something. "It's a sad affair, isn't it?"

"It's God's will. We shall all come to it some day," said Gerasim, display- 50
ing his teeth — the even, white teeth of a healthy peasant — and, like a man
in the thick of urgent work, he briskly opened the front door, called the
coachman, helped Peter Ivanovich into the sledge, and sprang back to the
porch as if in readiness for what he had to do next.

Peter Ivanovich found the fresh air particularly pleasant after the smell
of incense, the dead body, and carbolic acid.

"Where to, sir?" asked the coachman.

"It's not too late even now. . . . I'll call round on Fëdor Vasilievich."

He accordingly drove there and found them just finishing the first rubber, so that it was quite convenient for him to cut in.

II

Ivan Ilych's life had been most simple and most ordinary and therefore 55
most terrible.

He had been a member of the Court of Justice, and died at the age of
forty-five. His father had been an official who after serving in various minis-
tries and departments in Petersburg had made the sort of career which brings
men to positions from which by reason of their long service they cannot be
dismissed, though they are obviously unfit to hold any responsible position,
and for whom therefore posts are specially created, which though fictitious
carry salaries of from six to ten thousand rubles that are not fictitious, and in
receipt of which they live on to a great age.

Such was the Privy Councillor and superfluous member of various superfluous institutions, Ilya Epimovich Golovin.

He had three sons, of whom Ivan Ilych was the second. The eldest son
was following in his father's footsteps only in another department, and was
already approaching that stage in the service at which a similar sinecure would
be reached. The third son was a failure. He had ruined his prospects in a
number of positions and was now serving in the railway department. His
father and brothers, and still more their wives, not merely disliked meeting
him, but avoided remembering his existence unless compelled to do so. His
sister had married Baron Greff, a Petersburg official of her father's type. Ivan
Ilych was *le phénix de la famille*° as people said. He was neither as cold and formal
as his elder brother nor as wild as the younger, but was a happy mean between
them — an intelligent, polished, lively, and agreeable man. He had studied
with his younger brother at the School of Law, but the latter had failed to
complete the course and was expelled when he was in the fifth class. Ivan Ilych
finished the course well. Even when he was at the School of Law he was just
what he remained for the rest of his life: a capable, cheerful, good-natured, and
sociable man, though strict in the fulfillment of what he considered to be his
duty: and he considered his duty to be what was so considered by those in
authority. Neither as a boy nor as a man was he a toady, but from early youth
was by nature attracted to people of high station as a fly is drawn to the light,
assimilating their ways and views of life and establishing friendly relations
with them. All the enthusiasms of childhood and youth passed without leav-

le phénix de la famille: "the prize of the family."

ing much trace on him; he succumbed to sensuality, to vanity, and latterly among the highest classes to liberalism, but always within limits which his instinct unfailingly indicated to him as correct.

At school he had done things which had formerly seemed to him very horrid and made him feel disgusted with himself when he did them; but when later on he saw that such actions were done by people of good position and that they did not regard them as wrong, he was able not exactly to regard them as right, but to forget about them entirely or not be at all troubled at remembering them.

Having graduated from the School of Law and qualified for the tenth rank of the civil service, and having received money from his father for his equipment, Ivan Ilych ordered himself clothes at Scharmer's, the fashionable tailor, hung a medallion inscribed *respice finem*° on his watch-chain, took leave of his professor and the prince who was patron of the school, had a farewell dinner with his comrades at Donon's first-class restaurant, and with his new and fashionable portmanteau, linen, clothes, shaving and other toilet appliances, and a travelling rug all purchased at the best shops, he set off for one of the provinces where, through his father's influence, he had been attached to the Governor as an official for special service.

In the province Ivan Ilych soon arranged as easy and agreeable a position for himself as he had had at the School of Law. He performed his official tasks, made his career, and at the same time amused himself pleasantly and decorously. Occasionally he paid official visits to country districts, where he behaved with dignity both to his superiors and inferiors, and performed the duties entrusted to him, which related chiefly to the sectarians°, with an exactness and incorruptible honesty of which he could not but feel proud.

In official matters, despite his youth and taste for frivolous gaiety, he was exceedingly reserved, punctilious, and even severe; but in society he was often amusing and witty, and always good-natured, correct in his manner, and *bon enfant*°, as the Governor and his wife — with whom he was like one of the family — used to say of him.

In the province he had an affair with a lady who made advances to the elegant young lawyer, and there was also a milliner; and there were carousals with aides-de-camp who visited the district, and after-supper visits to a certain outlying street of doubtful reputation; and there was too some obsequiousness to his chief and even to his chief's wife, but all this was done with such a tone of good breeding that no hard names could be applied to it. It all came under the heading of the French saying: *"Il faut que jeunesse se passe."*° It was all done with clean hands, in clean linen, with French phrases, and above all among people of the best society and consequently with the approval of people of rank.

So Ivan Ilych served for five years and then came a change in his official life. The new and reformed judicial institutions were introduced, and new men were needed. Ivan Ilych became such a new man. He was offered the post of examining magistrate, and he accepted it though the post was in another province and obliged him to give up the connections he had formed and to

respice finem: "Think of the end (of your life)."
sectarians: dissenters from the Orthodox Church.
bon enfant: like a well-behaved child.
"Il faut que jeunesse se passe": "Youth doesn't last."

make new ones. His friends met to give him a send-off; they had a group-photograph taken and presented him with a silver cigarette-case, and he set off to his new post.

As examining magistrate Ivan Ilych was just as *comme il faut*° and decorous 65
a man, inspiring general respect and capable of separating his official duties from his private life, as he had been when acting as an official on special service. His duties now as examining magistrate were far more interesting and attractive than before. In his former position it had been pleasant to wear an undress uniform made by Scharmer, and to pass through the crowd of petitioners and officials who were timorously awaiting an audience with the Governor, and who envied him as with free and easy gait he went straight into his chief's private room to have a cup of tea and a cigarette with him. But not many people had been directly dependent on him — only police officials and the sectarians when he went on special missions — and he liked to treat them politely, almost as comrades, as if he were letting them feel that he who had the power to crush them was treating them in this simple, friendly way. There were then but few such people. But now, as an examining magistrate, Ivan Ilych felt that everyone without exception, even the most important and self-satisfied, was in his power, and that he need only write a few words on a sheet of paper with a certain heading, and this or that important, self-satisfied person would be brought before him in the role of an accused person or a witness, and if he did not choose to allow him to sit down, would have to stand before him and answer his questions. Ivan Ilych never abused his power; he tried on the contrary to soften its expression, but the consciousness of it and of the possibility of softening its effect, supplied the chief interest and attraction of his office. In his work itself, especially in his examinations, he very soon acquired a method of eliminating all considerations irrelevant to the legal aspect of the case, and reducing even the most complicated case to a form in which it would be presented on paper only in its externals, completely excluding his personal opinion of the matter, while above all observing every prescribed formality. The work was new and Ivan Ilych was one of the first men to apply the new Code of 1864°.

On taking up the post of examining magistrate in a new town, he made new acquaintances and connections, placed himself on a new footing, and assumed a somewhat different tone. He took up an attitude of rather dignified aloofness towards the provincial authorities, but picked out the best circle of legal gentlemen and wealthy gentry living in the town and assumed a tone of slight dissatisfaction with the government, of moderate liberalism, and of enlightened citizenship. At the same time, without at all altering the elegance of his toilet, he ceased shaving his chin and allowed his beard to grow as it pleased.

Ivan Ilych settled down very pleasantly in this new town. The society there, which inclined towards opposition to the Governor, was friendly, his salary was larger, and he began to play *vint*°, which he found added not a little to the pleasure of life, for he had a capacity for cards, played good-humoredly, and calculated rapidly and astutely, so that he usually won.

comme il faut: "as required," rule-abiding.
Code of 1864: The emancipation of the serfs in 1861 was followed by a thorough all-round reform of judicial proceedings. [Translators' note.]
vint: a form of bridge. [Translators' note.]

After living there for two years he met his future wife, Praskovya Fëdorovna Mikhel, who was the most attractive, clever, and brilliant girl of the set in which he moved, and among other amusements and relaxations from his labors as examining magistrate, Ivan Ilych established light and playful relations with her.

While he had been an official on special service he had been accustomed to dance, but now as an examining magistrate it was exceptional for him to do so. If he danced now, he did it as if to show that though he served under the reformed order of things, and had reached the fifth official rank, yet when it came to dancing he could do it better than most people. So at the end of an evening he sometimes danced with Praskovya Fëdorovna, and it was chiefly during these dances that he captivated her. She fell in love with him. Ivan Ilych had at first no definite intention of marrying, but when the girl fell in love with him he said to himself: "Really, why shouldn't I marry?"

Praskovya Fëdorovna came of a good family, was not bad-looking, and had some little property. Ivan Ilych might have aspired to a more brilliant match, but even this was good. He had his salary, and she, he hoped, would have an equal income. She was well connected, and was a sweet, pretty, and thoroughly correct young woman. To say that Ivan Ilych married because he fell in love with Praskovya Fëdorovna and found that she sympathized with his views of life would be as incorrect as to say that he married because his social circle approved of the match. He was swayed by both these considerations: the marriage gave him personal satisfaction, and at the same time it was considered the right thing by the most highly placed of his associates.

So Ivan Ilych got married.

The preparations for marriage and the beginning of married life, with its conjugal caresses, the new furniture, new crockery, and new linen, were very pleasant until his wife became pregnant — so that Ivan Ilych had begun to think that marriage would not impair the easy, agreeable, gay, and always decorous character of his life, approved of by society and regarded by himself as natural, but would even improve it. But from the first months of his wife's pregnancy, something new, unpleasant, depressing, and unseemly, and from which there was no way of escape, unexpectedly showed itself.

His wife, without any reason — *de gaieté de cœur*° as Ivan Ilych expressed it to himself — began to disturb the pleasure and propriety of their life. She began to be jealous without any cause, expected him to devote his whole attention to her, found fault with everything, and made coarse and ill-mannered scenes.

At first Ivan Ilych hoped to escape from the unpleasantness of this state of affairs by the same easy and decorous relation to life that had served him heretofore: he tried to ignore his wife's disagreeable moods, continued to live in his usual easy and pleasant way, invited friends to his house for a game of cards, and also tried going out to his club or spending his evenings with friends. But one day his wife began upbraiding him so vigorously, using such coarse words, and continued to abuse him every time he did not fulfil her demands, so resolutely and with such evident determination not to give way till he submitted — that is, till he stayed at home and was bored just as she was

de gaieté de cœur: "from pure whim."

— that he became alarmed. He now realized that matrimony — at any rate with Praskovya Fëdorovna — was not always conducive to the pleasures and amenities of life, but on the contrary often infringed both comfort and propriety, and that he must therefore entrench himself against such infringement. And Ivan Ilych began to seek for means of doing so. His official duties were the one thing that imposed upon Praskovya Fëdorovna, and by means of his official work and the duties attached to it he began struggling with his wife to secure his own independence.

With the birth of their child, the attempts to feed it and the various failures in doing so, and with the real and imaginary illnesses of mother and child, in which Ivan Ilych's sympathy was demanded but about which he understood nothing, the need of securing for himself an existence outside his family life became still more imperative. 75

As his wife grew more irritable and exacting and Ivan Ilych transferred the center of gravity of his life more and more to his official work, so did he grow to like his work better and become more ambitious than before.

Very soon, within a year of his wedding, Ivan Ilych had realized that marriage, though it may add some comforts to life, is in fact a very intricate and difficult affair towards which in order to perform one's duty, that is, to lead a decorous life approved of by society, one must adopt a definite attitude just as towards one's official duties.

And Ivan Ilych evolved such an attitude towards married life. He only required of it those conveniences — dinner at home, housewife, and bed — which it could give him, and above all that propriety of external forms required by public opinion. For the rest he looked for light-hearted pleasure and propriety, and was very thankful when he found them, but if he met with antagonism and querulousness he at once retired into his separate fenced-off world of official duties, where he found satisfaction.

Ivan Ilych was esteemed a good official, and after three years was made Assistant Public Prosecutor. His new duties, their importance, the possibility of indicting and imprisoning anyone he chose, the publicity his speeches received, and the success he had in all these things, made his work still more attractive.

More children came. His wife became more and more querulous and ill-tempered, but the attitude Ivan Ilych had adopted towards his home life rendered him almost impervious to her grumbling. 80

After seven years' service in that town he was transferred to another province as Public Prosecutor. They moved, but were short of money and his wife did not like the place they moved to. Though the salary was higher the cost of living was greater, besides which two of their children died and family life became still more unpleasant for him.

Praskovya Fëdorovna blamed her husband for every inconvenience they encountered in their new home. Most of the conversations between husband and wife, especially as to the children's education, led to topics which recalled former disputes, and those disputes were apt to flare up again at any moment. There remained only those rare periods of amorousness which still came to them at times but did not last long. These were islets at which they anchored for a while and then again set out upon that ocean of veiled hostility which showed itself in their aloofness from one another. This aloofness might have grieved Ivan Ilych had he considered that it ought not to exist, but he now regarded the position as normal, and even made it the goal at which he aimed in family life. His aim was to free himself more and more from those unpleasantnesses and to give them a semblance of harmlessness and propriety. He attained this by spending less and less time with his family, and when obliged to be at home he tried to safeguard his position by the presence of outsiders. The chief thing, however, was that he had his official duties. The whole interest of his life now centered in the official world and that interest absorbed him. The consciousness of his power, being able to ruin anybody he wished to ruin, the importance, even the external dignity of his entry into court, or meetings with his subordinates, his success with superiors and inferiors, and above all his masterly handling of cases, of which he was conscious — all this gave him pleasure and filled his life, together with chats with his colleagues, dinners, and bridge. So that on the whole Ivan Ilych's life continued to flow as he considered it should do — pleasantly and properly.

So things continued for another seven years. His eldest daughter was already sixteen, another child had died, and only one son was left, a schoolboy and a subject of dissension. Ivan Ilych wanted to put him in the School of Law, but to spite him Praskovya Fëdorovna entered him at the High School. The daughter had been educated at home and had turned out well: the boy did not learn badly either.

III

So Ivan Ilych lived for seventeen years after his marriage. He was already a Public Prosecutor of long standing, and had declined several proposed transfers while awaiting a more desirable post, when an unanticipated and unpleasant occurrence quite upset the peaceful course of his life. He was expecting to be offered the post of presiding judge in a University town, but Happe somehow came to the front and obtained the appointment instead. Ivan Ilych became irritable, reproached Happe, and quarrelled both with him and with his immediate superiors — who became colder to him and again passed him over when other appointments were made.

This was in 1880, the hardest year of Ivan Ilych's life. It was then that it became evident on the one hand that his salary was insufficient for them to live on, and on the other that he had been forgotten, and not only this, but that what was for him the greatest and most cruel injustice appeared to others a quite ordinary occurrence. Even his father did not consider it his duty to help him. Ivan Ilych felt himself abandoned by everyone, and that they regarded his position with a salary of 3,500 rubles as quite normal and even fortunate. He alone knew that with the consciousness of the injustices done him, with his wife's incessant nagging, and with the debts he had contracted by living beyond his means, his position was far from normal.

In order to save money that summer he obtained leave of absence and went with his wife to live in the country at her brother's place.

In the country, without his work, he experienced *ennui* for the first time in his life, and not only *ennui* but intolerable depression, and he decided that it was impossible to go on living like that, and that it was necessary to take energetic measures.

Having passed a sleepless night pacing up and down the veranda, he decided to go to Petersburg and bestir himself, in order to punish those who had failed to appreciate him and to get transferred to another ministry.

Next day, despite many protests from his wife and her brother, he started for Petersburg with the sole object of obtaining a post with a salary of five thousand rubles a year. He was no longer bent on any particular department, or tendency, or kind of activity. All he now wanted was an appointment to another post with a salary of five thousand rubles, either in the administration, in the banks, with the railways, in one of the Empress Marya's Institutions°, or even in the customs — but it had to carry with it a salary of five thousand rubles and be in a ministry other than that in which they had failed to appreciate him.

And this quest of Ivan Ilych's was crowned with remarkable and unexpected success. At Kursk an acquaintance of his, F. I. Ilyin, got into the first-class carriage, sat down beside Ivan Ilych, and told him of a telegram just received by the Governor of Kursk announcing that a change was about to take place in the ministry: Peter Ivanovich was to be superseded by Ivan Semënovich.

The proposed change, apart from its significance for Russia, had a special significance for Ivan Ilych, because by bringing forward a new man, Peter Petrovich, and consequently his friend Zachar Ivanovich, it was highly favorable for Ivan Ilych, since Zachar Ivanovich was a friend and colleague of his.

In Moscow this news was confirmed, and on reaching Petersburg Ivan Ilych found Zachar Ivanovich and received a definite promise of an appointment in his former department of Justice.

A week later he telegraphed to his wife: "Zachar in Miller's place. I shall receive appointment on presentation of report."

Thanks to this change of personnel, Ivan Ilych had unexpectedly obtained an appointment in his former ministry which placed him two stages above his former colleagues besides giving him five thousand rubles salary and three thousand five hundred rubles for expenses connected with his removal. All his ill humor towards his former enemies and the whole department vanished, and Ivan Ilych was completely happy.

He returned to the country more cheerful and contented than he had been for a long time. Praskovya Fëdorovna also cheered up and a truce was arranged between them. Ivan Ilych told of how he had been fêted by everybody in Petersburg, how all those who had been his enemies were put to shame and now fawned on him, how envious they were of his appointment, and how much everybody in Petersburg had liked him.

Praskovya Fëdorovna listened to all this and appeared to believe it. She did not contradict anything, but only made plans for their life in the town to which they were going. Ivan Ilych saw with delight that these plans were his plans, that he and his wife agreed, and that, after a stumble, his life was regaining its due and natural character of pleasant lightheartedness and decorum.

Ivan Ilych had come back for a short time only, for he had to take up his new duties on the 10th of September. Moreover, he needed time to settle

Empress Marya's Institutions: orphanages.

into the new place, to move all his belongings from the province, and to buy and order many additional things: in a word, to make such arrangements as he had resolved on, which were almost exactly what Praskovya Fëdorovna too had decided on.

Now that everything had happened so fortunately, and that he and his wife were at one in their aims and moreover saw so little of one another, they got on together better than they had done since the first years of marriage. Ivan Ilych had thought of taking his family away with him at once, but the insistence of his wife's brother and her sister-in-law, who had suddenly become particularly amiable and friendly to him and his family, induced him to depart alone.

So he departed, and the cheerful state of mind induced by his success and by the harmony between his wife and himself, the one intensifying the other, did not leave him. He found a delightful house, just the thing both he and his wife had dreamt of. Spacious, lofty reception rooms in the old style, a convenient and dignified study, rooms for his wife and daughter, a study for his son — it might have been specially built for them. Ivan Ilych himself superintended the arrangements, chose the wallpapers, supplemented the furniture (preferably with antiques which he considered particularly *comme il faut*), and supervised the upholstering. Everything progressed and progressed and approached the ideal he had set himself: even when things were only half completed they exceeded his expectations. He saw what a refined and elegant character, free from vulgarity, it would all have when it was ready. On falling asleep he pictured to himself how the reception-room would look. Looking at the yet unfinished drawing-room he could see the fireplace, the screen, the what-not, the little chairs dotted here and there, the dishes and plates on the walls, and the bronzes, as they would be when everything was in place. He was pleased by the thought of how his wife and daughter, who shared his taste in this matter, would be impressed by it. They were certainly not expecting as much. He had been particularly successful in finding, and buying cheaply, antiques which gave a particularly aristocratic character to the whole place. But in his letters he intentionally understated everything in order to be able to surprise them. All this so absorbed him that his new duties — though he liked his official work — interested him less than he had expected. Sometimes he even had moments of absentmindedness during the Court Sessions, and would consider whether he should have straight or curved cornices for his curtains. He was so interested in it all that he often did things himself, rearranging the furniture, or rehanging the curtains. Once when mounting a stepladder to show the upholsterer, who did not understand, how he wanted the hangings draped, he made a false step and slipped, but being a strong and agile man he clung on and only knocked his side against the knob of the window frame. The bruised place was painful but the pain soon passed, and he felt particularly bright and well just then. He wrote: "I feel fifteen years younger." He thought he would have everything ready by September, but it dragged on till mid-October. But the result was charming not only in his eyes but to everyone who saw it.

In reality it was just what is usually seen in the houses of people of moderate means who want to appear rich, and therefore succeed only in resembling others like themselves: there were damasks, dark wood, plants, 100 rugs, and dull and polished bronzes — all the things people of a certain class have in order to resemble other people of that class. His house was so like the others that it would never have been noticed, but to him it all seemed to be quite exceptional. He was very happy when he met his family at the station and brought them to the newly furnished house all lit up, where a footman in a white tie opened the door into the hall decorated with plants, and when they went on into the drawing-room and the study uttering exclamations of delight. He conducted them everywhere, drank in their praises eagerly, and beamed with pleasure. At tea that evening, when Praskovya Fëdorovna among other things asked him about his fall, he laughed and showed them how he had gone flying and had frightened the upholsterer.

"It's a good thing I'm a bit of an athlete. Another man might have been killed, but I merely knocked myself, just here; it hurts when it's touched, but it's passing off already — it's only a bruise."

So they began living in their new home — in which, as always happens, when they got thoroughly settled in they found they were just one room short — and with the increased income, which as always was just a little (some five hundred rubles) too little, but it was all very nice.

Things went particularly well at first, before everything was finally arranged and while something had still to be done: this thing bought, that thing ordered, another thing moved, and something else adjusted. Though there were some disputes between husband and wife, they were both so well satisfied and had so much to do that it all passed off without any serious quarrels. When nothing was left to arrange it became rather dull and something seemed to be lacking, but they were then making acquaintances, forming habits, and life was growing fuller.

Ivan Ilych spent his mornings at the law courts and came home to dinner, and at first he was generally in a good humor, though he occasionally became irritable just on account of his house. (Every spot on the tablecloth or the upholstery, and every broken window-blind string, irritated him. He had devoted so much trouble to arranging it all that every disturbance of it distressed him.) But on the whole his life ran its course as he believed life should do: easily, pleasantly, and decorously.

He got up at nine, drank his coffee, read the paper, and then put on his undress uniform and went to the law courts. There the harness in which he worked had already been stretched to fit him and he donned it without a hitch: petitioners, inquiries at the chancery, the chancery itself, and the sittings public and administrative. In all this the thing was to exclude everything fresh and vital, which always disturbs the regular course of official business, and to admit only official relations with people, and then only on official grounds. A man would come, for instance, wanting some information. Ivan Ilych, as one in whose sphere the matter did not lie, would have nothing to do with him: but if the man had some business with him in his official capacity, something that could be expressed on officially stamped paper, he would do everything, positively everything he could within the limits of such relations, and in doing so would maintain the semblance of friendly human relations, that is, would observe the courtesies of life. As soon as the official relations ended, so did everything else. Ivan Ilych possessed this capacity to separate his real life from the official side of affairs and not mix the two, in the highest degree, and by

105

long practice and natural aptitude had brought it to such a pitch that sometimes, in the manner of a virtuoso, he would even allow himself to let the human and official relations mingle. He let himself do this just because he felt that he could at any time he chose resume the strictly official attitude again and drop the human relation. And he did it all easily, pleasantly, correctly, and even artistically. In the intervals between the sessions he smoked, drank tea, chatted a little about politics, a little about general topics, a little about cards, but most of all about official appointments. Tired, but with the feelings of a virtuoso — one of the first violins who has played his part in an orchestra with precision — he would return home to find that his wife and daughter had been out paying calls, or had a visitor, and that his son had been to school, had done his homework with his tutor, and was duly learning what is taught at High Schools. Everything was as it should be. After dinner, if they had no visitors, Ivan Ilych sometimes read a book that was being much discussed at the time, and in the evening settled down to work, that is, read official papers, compared the depositions of witnesses, and noted paragraphs of the Code applying to them. This was neither dull nor amusing. It was dull when he might have been playing bridge, but if no bridge was available it was at any rate better than doing nothing or sitting with his wife. Ivan Ilych's chief pleasure was giving little dinners to which he invited men and women of good social position, and just as his drawing-room resembled all other drawing-rooms so did his enjoyable little parties resemble all other such parties.

Once they even gave a dance. Ivan Ilych enjoyed it and everything went off well, except that it led to a violent quarrel with his wife about the cakes and sweets. Praskovya Fëdorovna had made her own plans, but Ivan Ilych insisted on getting everything from an expensive confectioner and ordered too many cakes, and the quarrel occurred because some of those cakes were left over and the confectioner's bill came to forty-five rubles. It was a great and disagreeable quarrel. Praskovya Fëdorovna called him "a fool and an imbecile," and he clutched at his head and made angry allusions to divorce.

But the dance itself had been enjoyable. The best people were there, and Ivan Ilych had danced with Princess Trufonova, a sister of the distinguished founder of the Society "Bear my Burden."

The pleasures connected with his work were pleasures of ambition; his social pleasures were those of vanity; but Ivan Ilych's greatest pleasure was playing bridge. He acknowledged that whatever disagreeable incident happened in his life, the pleasure that beamed like a ray of light above everything else was to sit down to bridge with good players, not noisy partners, and of course to four-handed bridge (with five players it was annoying to have to stand out, though one pretended not to mind), to play a clever and serious game (when the cards allowed it), and then to have supper and drink a glass of wine. After a game of bridge, especially if he had won a little (to win a large sum was unpleasant), Ivan Ilych went to bed in specially good humor.

So they lived. They formed a circle of acquaintances among the best people and were visited by people of importance and by young folk. In their views as to their acquaintances, husband, wife, and daughter were entirely agreed, and tacitly and unanimously kept at arm's length and shook off the various shabby friends and relations who, with much show of affection, gushed into the drawing-room with its Japanese plates on the walls. Soon these shabby friends ceased to obtrude themselves and only the best people remained in the Golovins' set.

Young men made up to Lisa, and Petrishchev, an examining magistrate 110 and Dmitri Ivanovich Petrischev's son and sole heir, began to be so attentive to her that Ivan Ilych had already spoken to Praskovya Fëdorovna about it, and considered whether they should not arrange a party for them, or get up some private theatricals.

So they lived, and all went well, without change, and life followed pleasantly.

IV

They were all in good health. It could not be called ill health if Ivan Ilych sometimes said that he had a queer taste in his mouth and felt some discomfort in his left side.

But this discomfort increased and, though not exactly painful, grew into a sense of pressure in his side accompanied by ill humor. And his irritability became worse and worse and began to mar the agreeable, easy, and correct life that had established itself in the Golovin family. Quarrels between husband and wife became more and more frequent, and soon the ease and amenity disappeared and even the decorum was barely maintained. Scenes again became frequent, and very few of those islets remained on which husband and wife could meet without an explosion. Praskovya Fëdorovna now had good reason to say that her husband's temper was trying. With characteristic exaggeration she said he had always had a dreadful temper, and that it had needed all her good nature to put up with it for twenty years. It was true that now the quarrels were started by him. His bursts of temper always came just before dinner, often just as he began to eat his soup. Sometimes he noticed that a plate or dish was chipped, or the food was not right, or his son put his elbow on the table, or his daughter's hair was not done as he liked it, and for all this he blamed Praskovya Fëdorovna. At first she retorted and said disagreeable things to him, but once or twice he fell into such a rage at the beginning of dinner that she realized it was due to some physical derangement brought on by taking food, and so she restrained herself and did not answer, but only hurried to get the dinner over. She regarded this self-restraint as highly praiseworthy. Having come to the conclusion that her husband had a dreadful temper and made her life miserable, she began to feel sorry for herself, and the more she pitied herself the more she hated her husband. She began to wish he would die; yet she did not want him to die because then his salary would cease. And this irritated her against him still more. She considered herself dreadfully unhappy just because not even his death could save her, and though she concealed her exasperation, that hidden exasperation of hers increased his irritation also.

After one scene in which Ivan Ilych had been particularly unfair and after which he had said in explanation that he certainly was irritable but that it was due to his not being well, she said that if he was ill it should be attended to, and insisted on his going to see a celebrated doctor.

He went. Everything took place as he had expected and as it always does. 115 There was the usual waiting and the important air assumed by the doctor, with which he was so familiar (resembling that which he himself assumed in court), and the sounding and listening, and the questions which called for answers that were foregone conclusions and were evidently unnecessary, and the look of importance which implied that "if only you put yourself in our hands we will arrange everything — we know indubitably how it has to be done, always in the same way for everybody alike." It was all just as it was in the law courts. The doctor put on just the same air towards him as he himself put on towards an accused person.

The doctor said that so-and-so indicated that there was so-and-so inside the patient, but if the investigation of so-and-so did not confirm this, then he must assume that and that. If he assumed that and that, then . . . and so on. To Ivan Ilych only one question was important: was his case serious or not? But the doctor ignored that inappropriate question. From his point of view it was not the one under consideration, the real question was to decide between a floating kidney, chronic catarrh, or appendicitis. It was not a question of Ivan Ilych's life or death, but one between a floating kidney and appendicitis. And that question the doctor solved brilliantly, as it seemed to Ivan Ilych, in favor of the appendix, with the reservation that should an examination of the urine give fresh indications the matter would be reconsidered. All this was just what Ivan Ilych had himself brilliantly accomplished a thousand times in dealing with men on trial. The doctor summed up just as brilliantly, looking over his spectacles triumphantly and even gaily at the accused. From the doctor's summing up Ivan Ilych concluded that things were bad, but that for the doctor, and perhaps for everybody else, it was a matter of indifference, though for him it was bad. And this conclusion struck him painfully, arousing in him a great feeling of pity for himself and of bitterness towards the doctor's indifference to a matter of such importance.

He said nothing of this, but rose, placed the doctor's fee on the table, and remarked with a sigh: "We sick people probably often put inappropriate questions. But tell me, in general, is this complaint dangerous, or not? . . ."

The doctor looked at him sternly over his spectacles with one eye, as if to say: "Prisoner, if you will not keep to the questions put to you, I shall be obliged to have you removed from the court."

"I have already told you what I consider necessary and proper. The analysis may show something more." And the doctor bowed.

Ivan Ilych went out slowly, seated himself disconsolately in his sledge, and drove home. All the way home he was going over what the doctor had said, trying to translate those complicated, obscure, scientific phrases into plain language and find in them an answer to the question: "Is my condition bad? Is it very bad? Or is there as yet nothing much wrong?" And it seemed to him that the meaning of what the doctor had said was that it was very bad. Everything in the streets seemed depressing. The cabmen, the houses, the passers-by, and the shops, were dismal. His ache, this dull gnawing ache that never ceased for a moment, seemed to have acquired a new and more serious significance from the doctor's dubious remarks. Ivan Ilych now watched it with a new and oppressive feeling.

He reached home and began to tell his wife about it. She listened, but in the middle of his account his daughter came in with her hat on, ready to go out with her mother. She sat down reluctantly to listen to this tedious story,

120

but could not stand it long, and her mother too did not hear him to the end.

"Well, I am very glad," she said. "Mind now to take your medicine regularly. Give me the prescription and I'll send Gerasim to the chemist's." And she went to get ready to go out.

While she was in the room Ivan Ilych had hardly taken time to breathe, but he sighed deeply when she left it.

"Well," he thought, "perhaps it isn't so bad after all."

He began taking his medicine and following the doctor's directions, which had been altered after the examination of the urine. But then it happened that there was a contradiction between the indications drawn from the examination of the urine and the symptoms that showed themselves. It turned out that what was happening differed from what the doctor had told him, and that he had either forgotten, or blundered, or hidden something from him. He could not, however, be blamed for that, and Ivan Ilych still obeyed his orders implicitly and at first derived some comfort from doing so.

From the time of his visit to the doctor, Ivan Ilych's chief occupation was the exact fulfilment of the doctor's instructions regarding hygiene and the taking of medicine, and the observation of his pain and his excretions. His chief interests came to be people's ailments and people's health. When sickness, deaths, or recoveries were mentioned in his presence, especially when the illness resembled his own, he listened with agitation which he tried to hide, asked questions, and applied what he heard to his own case.

The pain did not grow less, but Ivan Ilych made efforts to force himself to think that he was better. And he could do this so long as nothing agitated him. But as soon as he had any unpleasantness with his wife, any lack of success in his official work, or held bad cards at bridge, he was at once acutely sensible of his disease. He had formerly borne such mischances, hoping soon to adjust what was wrong, to master it and attain success, or make a grand slam. But now every mischance upset him and plunged him into despair. He would say to himself: "There now, just as I was beginning to get better and the medicine had begun to take effect, comes this accursed misfortune, or unpleasantness. . . ." And he was furious with the mishap, or with the people who were causing the unpleasantness and killing him, for he felt that this fury was killing him but could not restrain it. One would have thought that it should have been clear to him that this exasperation with circumstances and people aggravated his illness, and that he ought therefore to ignore unpleasant occurrences. But he drew the very opposite conclusion: he said that he needed peace, and he watched for everything that might disturb it and became irritable at the slightest infringement of it. His condition was rendered worse by the fact that he read medical books and consulted doctors. The progress of his disease was so gradual that he could deceive himself when comparing one day with another — the difference was so slight. But when he consulted the doctors it seemed to him that he was getting worse, and even very rapidly. Yet despite this he was continually consulting them.

That month he went to see another celebrity, who told him almost the same as the first had done but put his questions rather differently, and the interview with this celebrity only increased Ivan Ilych's doubts and fears. A friend of a friend of his, a very good doctor, diagnosed his illness again quite differently from the others, and though he predicted recovery, his questions and suppositions bewildered Ivan Ilych still more and increased his doubts. A homoeopathist diagnosed the disease in yet another way, and prescribed medicine which Ivan Ilych took secretly for a week. But after a week, not feeling any improvement and having lost confidence both in the former doctor's treatment and in this one's, he became still more despondent. One day a lady acquaintance mentioned a cure effected by a wonder-working icon. Ivan Ilych caught himself listening attentively and beginning to believe that it had occurred. This incident alarmed him. "Has my mind really weakened to such an extent?" he asked himself. "Nonsense! It's all rubbish. I mustn't give way to nervous fears but having chosen a doctor must keep strictly to his treatment. That is what I will do. Now it's all settled. I won't think about it, but will follow the treatment seriously till summer, and then we shall see. From now there must be no more of this wavering!" This was easy to say but impossible to carry out. The pain in his side oppressed him and seemed to grow worse and more incessant, while the taste in his mouth grew stranger and stranger. It seemed to him that his breath had a disgusting smell, and he was conscious of a loss of appetite and strength. There was no deceiving himself: something terrible, new, and more important than anything before in his life, was taking place within him of which he alone was aware. Those about him did not understand or would not understand it, but thought everything in the world was going on as usual. That tormented Ivan Ilych more than anything. He saw that his household, especially his wife and daughter who were in a perfect whirl of visiting, did not understand anything of it and were annoyed that he was so depressed and so exacting, as if he were to blame for it. Though they tried to disguise it he saw that he was an obstacle in their path, and that his wife had adopted a definite line in regard to his illness and kept to it regardless of anything he said or did. Her attitude was this: "You know," she would say to her friends, "Ivan Ilych can't do as other people do, and keep to the treatment prescribed for him. One day he'll take his drops and keep strictly to his diet and go to bed in good time, but the next day unless I watch him he'll suddenly forget his medicine, eat sturgeon — which is forbidden — and sit up playing cards till one o'clock in the morning."

"Oh, come, when was that?" Ivan Ilych would ask in vexation. "Only once at Peter Ivanovich's."

"And yesterday with Shebek." 130

"Well, even if I hadn't stayed up, this pain would have kept me awake."

"Be that as it may you'll never get well like that, but will always make us wretched."

Praskovya Fëdorovna's attitude to Ivan Ilych's illness, as she expressed it both to others and to him, was that it was his own fault and was another of the annoyances he caused her. Ivan Ilych felt that this opinion escaped her involuntarily — but that did not make it easier for him.

At the law courts too, Ivan Ilych noticed, or thought he noticed, a strange attitude towards himself. It sometimes seemed to him that people were watching him inquisitively as a man whose place might soon be vacant. Then again, his friends would suddenly begin to chaff him in a friendly way about his low spirits, as if the awful, horrible, and unheard-of thing that was going on within him, incessantly gnawing at him and irresistibly drawing him away, was a very agreeable subject for jests. Schwartz in particular irritated him by his jocularity, vivacity, and *savoir-faire*, which reminded him of what he himself had been ten years ago.

Friends came to make up a set and they sat down to cards. They dealt, bending the new cards to soften them, and he sorted the diamonds in his hand and found he had seven. His partner said "No trumps" and supported him with two diamonds. What more could be wished for? It ought to be jolly and lively. They would make a grand slam. But suddenly Ivan Ilych was conscious of that gnawing pain, that taste in his mouth, and it seemed ridiculous that in such circumstances he should be pleased to make a grand slam.

He looked at his partner Mikhail Mikhaylovich, who rapped the table with his strong hand and instead of snatching up the tricks pushed the cards courteously and indulgently towards Ivan Ilych that he might have the pleasure of gathering them up without the trouble of stretching out his hand for them. "Does he think I am too weak to stretch out my arm?" thought Ivan Ilych, and forgetting what he was doing he over-trumped his partner, missing the grand slam by three tricks. And what was most awful of all was that he saw how upset Mikhail Mikhaylovich was about it but did not himself care. And it was dreadful to realize why he did not care.

They all saw that he was suffering, and said: "We can stop if you are tired. Take a rest." Lie down? No, he was not at all tired, and he finished the rubber. All were gloomy and silent. Ivan Ilych felt that he had diffused this gloom over them and could not dispel it. They had supper and went away, and Ivan Ilych was left alone with the consciousness that his life was poisoned and was poisoning the lives of others, and that this poison did not weaken but penetrated more and more deeply into his whole being.

With this consciousness, and with physical pain besides the terror, he must go to bed, often to lie awake the greater part of the night. Next morning he had to get up again, dress, go to the law courts, speak, and write; or if he did not go out, spend at home those twenty-four hours a day each of which was a torture. And he had to live thus all alone on the brink of an abyss, with no one who understood or pitied him.

V

So one month passed and then another. Just before the New Year his brother-in-law came to town and stayed at their house. Ivan Ilych was at the law courts and Praskovya Fëdorovna had gone shopping. When Ivan Ilych came home and entered his study he found his brother-in-law there — a healthy, florid man — unpacking his portmanteau himself. He raised his head on hearing Ivan Ilych's footsteps and looked up at him for a moment without a word. That stare told Ivan Ilych everything. His brother-in-law opened his mouth to utter an exclamation of surprise but checked himself, and that action confirmed it all.

"I have changed, eh?"

"Yes, there is a change."

And after that, try as he would to get his brother-in-law to return to the subject of his looks, the latter would say nothing about it. Praskovya Fëdorovna came home and her brother went out to her. Ivan Ilych locked the door and began to examine himself in the glass, first full face, then in profile. He took up a portrait of himself taken with his wife, and compared it with what he saw in the glass. The change in him was immense. Then he bared his arms to the elbow, looked at them, drew the sleeves down again, sat down on an ottoman, and grew blacker than night.

"No, no, this won't do!" he said to himself, and jumped up, went to the table, took up some law papers, and began to read them, but could not continue. He unlocked the door and went into the reception-room. The door leading to the drawing-room was shut. He approached it on tiptoe and listened.

"No, you are exaggerating!" Praskovya Fëdorovna was saying.

"Exaggerating! Don't you see it? Why, he's a dead man! Look at his eyes — there's no light in them. But what is it that is wrong with him?"

"No one knows. Nikolaevich said something, but I don't know what. And Leshchetitsky° said quite the contrary. . . ."

Ivan Ilych walked away, went to his own room, lay down, and began musing: "The kidney, a floating kidney." He recalled all the doctors had told him of how it detached itself and swayed about. And by an effort of imagination he tried to catch that kidney and arrest it and support it. So little was needed for this, it seemed to him. "No, I'll go to see Peter Ivanovich° again." He rang, ordered the carriage, and got ready to go.

"Where are you going, Jean?" asked his wife, with a specially sad and exceptionally kind look.

This exceptionally kind look irritated him. He looked morosely at her.

"I must go to see Peter Ivanovich."

He went to see Peter Ivanovich, and together they went to see his friend, the doctor. He was in, and Ivan Ilych had a long talk with him.

Reviewing the anatomical and physiological details of what in the doctor's opinion was going on inside him, he understood it all.

There was something, a small thing, in the vermiform appendix. It might all come right. Only stimulate the energy of one organ and check the activity of another, then absorption would take place and everything would come right. He got home rather late for dinner, ate his dinner, and conversed cheerfully, but could not for a long time bring himself to go back to work in his room. At last, however, he went to his study and did what was necessary, but the consciousness that he had put something aside — an important, intimate matter which he would revert to when his work was done — never left him. When he had finished his work he remembered that this intimate matter was the thought of his vermiform appendix. But he did not give himself up to it, and went to the drawing-room for tea. There were callers there, including the examining magistrate who was a desirable match for his daughter, and they were conversing, playing the piano, and singing. Ivan Ilych, as Praskovya Fëdorovna remarked, spent that evening more cheerfully than usual, but he never for a moment forgot that he had postponed the important matter of the appendix. At eleven o'clock he said good-night and went to his bedroom. Since his illness he had slept alone in a small room next to his study. He undressed and took up a novel by Zola, but instead of reading it he fell into thought, and

145

150

Nikolaevich, Leshchetitsky: two doctors, the latter a celebrated specialist. [Translators' note.]
Peter Ivanovich: That was the friend whose friend was a doctor. [Translators' note.]

in his imagination that desired improvement in the vermiform appendix occurred. There was the absorption and evacuation and the re-establishment of normal activity. "Yes, that's it!" he said to himself. "One need only assist nature, that's all." He remembered his medicine, rose, took it, and lay down on his back watching for the beneficent action of the medicine and for it to lessen the pain. "I need only take it regularly and avoid all injurious influences. I am already feeling better, much better." He began touching his side: it was not painful to the touch. "There, I really don't feel it. It's much better already." He put out the light and turned on his side. . . . "The appendix is getting better, absorption is occurring." Suddenly he felt the old, familiar, dull, gnawing pain, stubborn and serious. There was the same familiar loathsome taste in his mouth. His heart sank and he felt dazed. "My God! My God!" he muttered. "Again, again! and it will never cease." And suddenly the matter presented itself in a quite different aspect. "Vermiform appendix! Kidney!" he said to himself. "It's not a question of appendix or kidney, but of life and . . . death. Yes, life was there and now it is going, going and I cannot stop it. Yes. Why deceive myself? Isn't it obvious to everyone but me that I'm dying, and that it's only a question of weeks, days . . . it may happen this moment. There was light and now there is darkness. I was here and now I'm going there! Where?" A chill came over him, his breathing ceased, and he felt only the throbbing of his heart.

"When I am not, what will there be? There will be nothing. Then where shall I be when I am no more? Can this be dying? No, I don't want to!" He jumped up and tried to light the candle, felt for it with trembling hands, dropped candle and candlestick on the floor, and fell back on his pillow.

"What's the use? It makes no difference," he said to himself, staring with wide-open eyes into the darkness. "Death. Yes, death. And none of them know or wish to know it, and they have no pity for me. Now they are playing." (He heard through the door the distant sound of a song and its accompaniment.) "It's all the same to them, but they will die too! Fools! I first, and they later, but it will be the same for them. And now they are merry . . . the beasts!"

Anger choked him and he was agonizingly, unbearably miserable. "It is impossible that all men have been doomed to suffer this awful horror!" He raised himself.

"Something must be wrong. I must calm myself — must think it all over from the beginning." And he again began thinking. "Yes, the beginning of my illness: I knocked my side, but I was still quite well that day and the next. It hurt a little, then rather more. I saw the doctors, then followed despondency and anguish, more doctors, and I drew nearer to the abyss. My strength grew less and I kept coming nearer and nearer, and now I have wasted away and there is no light in my eyes. I think of the appendix — but this is death! I think of mending the appendix, and all the while here is death! Can it really be death?" Again terror seized him and he gasped for breath. He leant down and began feeling for the matches, pressing with his elbow on the stand beside the bed. It was in his way and hurt him, he grew furious with it, pressed on it still harder, and upset it. Breathless and in despair he fell on his back, expecting death to come immediately.

Meanwhile the visitors were leaving. Praskovya Fëdorovna was seeing them off. She heard something fall and came in.

"What has happened?"

"Nothing. I knocked it over accidentally."

She went out and returned with a candle. He lay there panting heavily, like a man who has run a thousand yards, and stared upwards at her with a fixed look.

"What is it, Jean?"

"No . . . o . . . thing. I upset it." ("Why speak of it? She won't understand," he thought.)

And in truth she did not understand. She picked up the stand, lit his candle, and hurried away to see another visitor off. When she came back he still lay on his back, looking upwards.

"What is it? Do you feel worse?"

"Yes."

She shook her head and sat down.

"Do you know, Jean, I think we must ask Leshchetitsky to come and see you here."

This meant calling in the famous specialist, regardless of expense. He smiled malignantly and said "No." She remained a little longer and then went up to him and kissed his forehead.

While she was kissing him he hated her from the bottom of his soul and with difficulty refrained from pushing her away.

"Good-night. Please God you'll sleep."

"Yes."

VI

Ivan Ilych saw that he was dying, and he was in continual despair.

In the depth of his heart he knew he was dying, but not only was he not accustomed to the thought, he simply did not and could not grasp it.

The syllogism he had learnt from Kiezewetter's Logic: "Caius is a man, men are mortal, therefore Caius is mortal," had always seemed to him correct as applied to Caius, but certainly not as applied to himself. That Caius — man in the abstract — was mortal, was perfectly correct, but he was not Caius, not an abstract man, but a creature quite, quite separate from all others. He had been little Vanya, with a mamma and a papa, with Mitya and Volodya, with the toys, a coachman and a nurse, afterwards with Katenka and with all the joys, griefs, and delights of childhood, boyhood, and youth. What did Caius know of the smell of that striped leather ball Vanya had been so fond of? Had Caius kissed his mother's hand like that, and did the silk of her dress rustle so for Caius? Had he rioted like that at school when the pastry was bad? Had Caius been in love like that? Could Caius preside at a session as he did? "Caius really was mortal, and it was right for him to die; but for me, little Vanya, Ivan Ilych, with all my thoughts and emotions, it's altogether a different matter. It cannot be that I ought to die. That would be too terrible."

Such was his feeling.

"If I had to die like Caius I should have known it was so. An inner voice would have told me so, but there was nothing of the sort in me and I and all my friends felt that our case was quite different from that of Caius. And now here it is!" he said to himself. "It can't be. It's impossible! But here it is. How is this? How is one to understand it?"

He could not understand it, and tried to drive this false, incorrect, morbid thought away and to replace it by other proper and healthy thoughts. But that thought, and not the thought only but the reality itself, seemed to come and confront him.

And to replace that thought he called up a succession of others, hoping to find in them some support. He tried to get back into the former current of thoughts that had once screened the thought of death from him. But strange to say, all that had formerly shut off, hidden, and destroyed his consciousness of death, no longer had that effect. Ivan Ilych now spent most of his time in attempting to re-establish that old current. He would say to himself: "I will take up my duties again — after all I used to live by them." And banishing all doubts he would go to the law courts, enter into conversation with his colleagues, and sit carelessly as was his wont, scanning the crowd with a thoughtful look and leaning both his emaciated arms on the arms of his oak chair; bending over as usual to a colleague and drawing his papers nearer he would interchange whispers with him, and then suddenly raising his eyes and sitting erect would pronounce certain words and open the proceedings. But suddenly in the midst of those proceedings the pain in his side, regardless of the stage the proceedings had reached, would begin its own gnawing work. Ivan Ilych would turn his attention to it and try to drive the thought of it away, but without success. *It* would come and stand before him and look at him, and he would be petrified and the light would die out of his eyes, and he would again begin asking himself whether *It* alone was true. And his colleagues and subordinates would see with surprise and distress that he, the brilliant and subtle judge, was becoming confused and making mistakes. He would shake himself, try to pull himself together, manage somehow to bring the sitting to a close, and return home with the sorrowful consciousness that his judicial labors could not as formerly hide from him what he wanted them to hide, and could not deliver him from *It*. And what was worst of all was that *It* drew his attention to itself not in order to make him take some action but only that he should look at *It*, look it straight in the face: look at it and, without doing anything, suffer inexpressibly.

And to save himself from this condition Ivan Ilych looked for consolations — new screens — and new screens were found and for a while seemed to save him, but then they immediately fell to pieces or rather became transparent, as if *It* penetrated them and nothing could veil *It*.

In these latter days he would go into the drawing-room he had arranged — that drawing-room where he had fallen and for the sake of which (how bitterly ridiculous it seemed) he had sacrificed his life — for he knew that his illness originated with that knock. He would enter and see that something had scratched the polished table. He would look for the cause of this and find that it was the bronze ornamentation of an album, that had got bent. He would take up the expensive album which he had lovingly arranged, and feel vexed with his daughter and her friends for their untidiness — for the album was torn here and there and some of the photographs turned upside down. He would put it carefully in order and bend the ornamentation back into position. Then it would occur to him to place all those things in another corner of the room, near

180

the plants. He could call the footman, but his daughter or wife would come to help him. They would not agree, and his wife would contradict him, and he would dispute and grow angry. But that was all right, for then he did not think about *It. It* was invisible.

But then, when he was moving something himself, his wife would say: "Let the servants do it. You will hurt yourself again." And suddenly *It* would flash through the screen and he would see it. It was just a flash, and he hoped it would disappear, but he would involuntarily pay attention to his side. "It sits there as before, gnawing just the same!" And he could no longer forget *It*, but could distinctly see it looking at him from behind the flowers. "What is it all for?"

"It really is so! I lost my life over that curtain as I might have done when storming a fort. Is that possible? How terrible and how stupid. It can't be true! It can't, but it is."

He would go to his study, lie down, and again be alone with *It*: face to face with *It*. And nothing could be done with *It* except to look at it and shudder.

VII

How it happened it is impossible to say because it came about step by step, unnoticed, but in the third month of Ivan Ilych's illness, his wife, his daughter, his son, his acquaintances, the doctors, the servants, and above all he himself, were aware that the whole interest he had for other people was whether he would soon vacate his place, and at last release the living from the discomfort caused by his presence and be himself released from his sufferings.

He slept less and less. He was given opium and hypodermic injections of morphine, but this did not relieve him. The dull depression he experienced in a somnolent condition at first gave him a little relief, but only as something new, afterwards it became as distressing as the pain itself or even more so.

Special foods were prepared for him by the doctors' orders, but all those foods became increasingly distasteful and disgusting to him.

For his excretions also special arrangements had to be made, and this was a torment to him every time — a torment from the uncleanliness, the unseemliness, and the smell, and from knowing that another person had to take part in it.

But just through this most unpleasant matter, Ivan Ilych obtained comfort. Gerasim, the butler's young assistant, always came in to carry the things out. Gerasim was a clean, fresh peasant lad, grown stout on town food and always cheerful and bright. At first the sight of him, in his clean Russian peasant costume, engaged on that disgusting task embarrassed Ivan Ilych.

Once when he got up from the commode too weak to draw up his trousers, he dropped into a soft armchair and looked with horror at his bare, enfeebled thighs with the muscles so sharply marked on them.

Gerasim with a firm light tread, his heavy boots emitting a pleasant smell of tar and fresh winter air, came in wearing a clean Hessian apron, the sleeves of his print shirt tucked up over his strong, bare young arms; and refraining from looking at his sick master out of consideration for his feelings, and restraining the joy of life that beamed from his face, he went up to the commode.

"Gerasim!" said Ivan Ilych in a weak voice.

Gerasim started, evidently afraid he might have committed some blunder, and with a rapid movement turned his fresh, kind, simple young face which just showed the first downy signs of a beard.

"Yes, sir?"

"That must be very unpleasant for you. You must forgive me. I am helpless."

"Oh, why, sir," and Gerasim's eyes beamed and he showed his glistening white teeth, "what's a little trouble? It's a case of illness with you, sir."

And his deft strong hands did their accustomed task, and he went out of the room stepping lightly. Five minutes later he as lightly returned.

Ivan Ilych was still sitting in the same position in the armchair.

"Gerasim," he said when the latter had replaced the freshly-washed utensil. "Please come here and help me." Gerasim went up to him. "Lift me up. It is hard for me to get up, and I have sent Dmitri away."

Gerasim went up to him, grasped his master with his strong arms deftly but gently, in the same way that he stepped — lifted him, supported him with one hand, and with the other drew up his trousers and would have set him down again, but Ivan Ilych asked to be led to the sofa. Gerasim, without an effort and without apparent pressure, led him, almost lifting him, to the sofa and placed him on it.

"Thank you. How easily and well you do it all!"

Gerasim smiled again and turned to leave the room. But Ivan Ilych felt his presence such a comfort that he did not want to let him go.

"One thing more, please move up that chair. No, the other one — under my feet. It is easier for me when my feet are raised."

Gerasim brought the chair, set it down gently in place, and raised Ivan Ilych's legs on to it. It seemed to Ivan Ilych that he felt better while Gerasim was holding up his legs.

"It's better when my legs are higher," he said. "Place that cushion under them."

Gerasim did so. He again lifted the legs and placed them, and again Ivan Ilych felt better while Gerasim held his legs. When he set them down Ivan Ilych fancied he felt worse.

"Gerasim," he said. "Are you busy now?"

"Not at all, sir," said Gerasim, who had learnt from the townsfolk how to speak to gentlefolk.

"What have you still to do?"

"What have I to do? I've done everything except chopping the logs for tomorrow."

"Then hold my legs up a bit higher, can you?"

"Of course I can. Why not?" And Gerasim raised his master's legs higher and Ivan Ilych thought that in that position he did not feel any pain at all.

"And how about the logs?"

"Don't trouble about that, sir. There's plenty of time."

Ivan Ilych told Gerasim to sit down and hold his legs, and began to talk to him. And strange to say it seemed to him that he felt better while Gerasim held his legs up.

After that Ivan Ilych would sometimes call Gerasim and get him to hold his legs on his shoulders, and he liked talking to him. Gerasim did it all easily, willingly, simply, and with a good nature that touched Ivan Ilych. Health, strength, and vitality in other people were offensive to him, but Gerasim's strength and vitality did not mortify but soothed him.

What tormented Ivan Ilych most was the deception, the lie, which for some reason they all accepted, that he was not dying but was simply ill, and that he only need keep quiet and undergo a treatment and then something very good would result. He, however, knew that do what they would nothing would come of it, only still more agonizing suffering and death. This deception tortured him — their not wishing to admit what they all knew and what he knew, but wanting to lie to him concerning his terrible condition, and wishing and forcing him to participate in that lie. Those lies — lies enacted over him on the eve of his death and destined to degrade this awful, solemn act to the level of their visitings, their curtains, their sturgeon for dinner — were a terrible agony for Ivan Ilych. And strangely enough, many times when they were going through their antics over him he had been within a hairbreadth of calling out to them: "Stop lying! You know and I know that I am dying. Then at least stop lying about it!" But he had never had the spirit to do it. The awful, terrible act of his dying was, he could see, reduced by those about him to the level of a casual, unpleasant, and almost indecorous incident (as if someone entered a drawing-room diffusing an unpleasant odor) and this was done by that very decorum which he had served all his life long. He saw that no one felt for him, because no one even wished to grasp his position. Only Gerasim recognized it and pitied him. And so Ivan Ilych felt at ease only with him. He felt comforted when Gerasim supported his legs (sometimes all night long) and refused to go to bed, saying: "Don't you worry, Ivan Ilych. I'll get sleep enough later on," or when he suddenly became familiar and exclaimed: "If you weren't sick it would be another matter, but as it is, why should I grudge a little trouble?" Gerasim alone did not lie; everything showed that he alone understood the facts of the case and did not consider it necessary to disguise them, but simply felt sorry for his emaciated and enfeebled master. Once when Ivan Ilych was sending him away he even said straight out: "We shall all of us die, so why should I grudge a little trouble?" — expressing the fact that he did not think his work burdensome, because he was doing it for a dying man and hoped someone would do the same for him when his time came.

Apart from this lying, or because of it, what most tormented Ivan Ilych was that no one pitied him as he wished to be pitied. At certain moments after prolonged suffering he wished most of all (though he would have been ashamed to confess it) for someone to pity him as a sick child is pitied. He longed to be petted and comforted. He knew he was an important functionary, that he had a beard turning grey, and that therefore what he longed for was impossible, but still he longed for it. And in Gerasim's attitude towards him there was something akin to what he wished for, and so that attitude comforted him. Ivan Ilych wanted to weep, wanted to be petted and cried over, and then his colleague Shebek would come, and instead of weeping and being petted, Ivan Ilych would assume a serious, severe, and profound air, and by force of habit would express his opinion on a decision of the Court of Cassation and would stubbornly insist on that view. This falsity around him and within him did more than anything else to poison his last days.

VIII

It was morning. He knew it was morning because Gerasim had gone, and Peter the footman had come and put out the candles, drawn back one of the curtains, and begun quietly to tidy up. Whether it was morning or evening, Friday or Sunday, made no difference, it was all just the same: the gnawing, unmitigated, agonizing pain, never ceasing for an instant, the consciousness of life inexorably waning but not yet extinguished, the approach of that ever dreaded and hateful Death which was the only reality, and always the same falsity. What were days, weeks, hours, in such a case?

"Will you have some tea, sir?"

"He wants things to be regular, and wishes the gentlefolk to drink tea in the morning," thought Ivan Ilych, and only said "No."

"Wouldn't you like to move onto the sofa, sir?"

"He wants to tidy up the room, and I'm in the way. I am uncleanliness and disorder," he thought, and said only:

"No, leave me alone."

The man went on bustling about. Ivan Ilych stretched out his hand. Peter came up, ready to help.

"What is it, sir?"

"My watch."

Peter took the watch which was close at hand and gave it to his master.

"Half-past eight. Are they up?"

"No, sir, except Vladimir Ivanovich" (the son) "who has gone to school. Praskovya Fëdorovna ordered me to wake her if you asked for her. Shall I do so?"

"No, there's no need to." "Perhaps I'd better have some tea," he thought, and added aloud: "Yes, bring me some tea."

Peter went to the door, but Ivan Ilych dreaded being left alone. "How can I keep him here? Oh yes, my medicine." "Peter, give me my medicine." "Why not? Perhaps it may still do some good." He took a spoonful and swallowed it. "No, it won't help. It's all tomfoolery, all deception," he decided as soon as he became aware of the familiar, sickly, hopeless taste. "No, I can't believe in it any longer. But the pain, why this pain? If it would only cease just for a moment!" And he moaned. Peter turned towards him. "It's all right. Go and fetch me some tea."

Peter went out. Left alone Ivan Ilych groaned not so much with pain, terrible though that was, as from mental anguish. Always and forever the same, always these endless days and nights. If only it would come quicker! If only *what* would come quicker? Death, darkness? . . . No, no! Anything rather than death!

When Peter returned with the tea on a tray, Ivan Ilych stared at him for a time in perplexity, not realizing who and what he was. Peter was disconcerted by that look and his embarrassment brought Ivan Ilych to himself.

"Oh, tea! All right, put it down. Only help me to wash and put on a clean shirt."

And Ivan Ilych began to wash. With pauses for rest, he washed his hands and then his face, cleaned his teeth, brushed his hair, and looked in the glass. He was terrified by what he saw, especially by the limp way in which his hair clung to his pallid forehead.

While his shirt was being changed he knew that he would be still more frightened at the sight of his body, so he avoided looking at it. Finally he was ready. He drew on a dressing-gown, wrapped himself in a plaid, and sat down in the armchair to take his tea. For a moment he felt refreshed, but soon as he began to drink the tea he was again aware of the same taste, and the pain also returned. He finished it with an effort, and then lay down stretching out his legs, and dismissed Peter.

Always the same. Now a spark of hope flashes up, then a sea of despair rages, and always pain; always pain, always despair, and always the same. When alone he had a dreadful and distressing desire to call someone, but he knew beforehand that with others present it would be still worse. "Another dose of morphine — to lose consciousness. I will tell him, the doctor, that he must think of something else. It's impossible, impossible, to go on like this."

An hour and another pass like that. But now there is a ring at the door bell. Perhaps it's the doctor? It is. He comes in fresh, hearty, plump, and cheerful, with that look on his face that seems to say: "There now, you're in a panic about something, but we'll arrange it all for you directly!" The doctor knows this expression is out of place here, but he has put it on once for all and can't take it off — like a man who has put on a frock-coat in the morning to pay a round of calls.

The doctor rubs his hands vigorously and reassuringly.   240

"Brr! How cold it is! There's such a sharp frost; just let me warm myself!" he says, as if it were only a matter of waiting till he was warm, and then he would put everything right.

"Well now, how are you?"

Ivan Ilych feels that the doctor would like to say: "Well, how are our affairs?" but that even he feels that this would not do, and says instead: "What sort of a night have you had?"

Ivan Ilych looks at him as much as to say: "Are you really never ashamed of lying?" But the doctor does not wish to understand this question, and Ivan Ilych says: "Just as terrible as ever. The pain never leaves me and never subsides. If only something . . ."

"Yes, you sick people are always like that. . . . There, now I think I am   245 warm enough. Even Praskovya Fëdorovna, who is so particular, could find no fault with my temperature. Well, now I can say good-morning," and the doctor presses his patient's hand.

Then, dropping his former playfulness, he begins with a most serious face to examine the patient, feeling his pulse and taking his temperature, and then begins the sounding and auscultation.

Ivan Ilych knows quite well and definitely that all this is nonsense and pure deception, but when the doctor, getting down on his knee, leans over him, putting his ear first higher then lower, and performs various gymnastic movements over him with a significant expression on his face, Ivan Ilych submits to it all as he used to submit to the speeches of the lawyers, though he knew very well that they were all lying and why they were lying.

The doctor, kneeling on the sofa, is still sounding him when Praskovya Fëdorovna's silk dress rustles at the door and she is heard scolding Peter for not having let her know of the doctor's arrival.

She comes in, kisses her husband, and at once proceeds to prove that she has been up a long time already, and only owing to a misunderstanding failed to be there when the doctor arrived.

Ivan Ilych looks at her, scans her all over, sets against her the whiteness and plumpness and cleanness of her hands and neck, the gloss of her hair, and the sparkle of her vivacious eyes. He hates her with his whole soul. And the thrill of hatred he feels for her makes him suffer from her touch.

Her attitude towards him and his disease is still the same. Just as the doctor had adopted a certain relation to his patient which he could not abandon, so had she formed one towards him — that he was not doing something he ought to do and was himself to blame, and that she reproached him lovingly for this — and she could not now change that attitude.

"You see he doesn't listen to me and doesn't take his medicine at the proper time. And above all he lies in a position that is no doubt bad for him — with his legs up."

She described how he made Gerasim hold his legs up.

The doctor smiled with a contemptuous affability that said: "What's to be done? These sick people do have foolish fancies of that kind, but we must forgive them."

When the examination was over the doctor looked at his watch, and then Praskovya Fëdorovna announced to Ivan Ilych that it was of course as he pleased, but she had sent today for a celebrated specialist who would examine him and have a consultation with Michael Danilovich (their regular doctor).

"Please don't raise any objections. I am doing this for my own sake," she said ironically, letting it be felt that she was doing it all for his sake and only said this to leave him no right to refuse. He remained silent, knitting his brows. He felt that he was so surrounded and involved in a mesh of falsity that it was hard to unravel anything.

Everything she did for him was entirely for her own sake, and she told him she was doing for herself what she actually was doing for herself, as if that was so incredible that he must understand the opposite.

At half-past eleven the celebrated specialist arrived. Again the sounding began and the significant conversations in his presence and in another room, about the kidneys and the appendix, and the questions and answers, with such an air of importance that again, instead of the real question of life and death which now alone confronted him, the question arose of the kidney and appendix which were not behaving as they ought to and would now be attacked by Michael Danilovich and the specialist and forced to amend their ways.

The celebrated specialist took leave of him with a serious though not hopeless look, and in reply to the timid question Ivan Ilych, with eyes glistening with fear and hope, put to him as to whether there was a chance of recovery, said that he could not vouch for it but there was a possibility. The look of hope with which Ivan Ilych watched the doctor out was so pathetic that Praskovya Fëdorovna, seeing it, even wept as she left the room to hand the doctor his fee.

The gleam of hope kindled by the doctor's encouragement did not last long. The same room, the same pictures, curtains, wallpaper, medicine bottles, were all there, and the same aching suffering body, and Ivan Ilych began to moan. They gave him a subcutaneous injection and he sank into oblivion.

It was twilight when he came to. They brought him his dinner and he swallowed some beef tea with difficulty, and then everything was the same again and night was coming on.

After dinner, at seven o'clock, Praskovya Fëdorovna came into the room in evening dress, her full bosom pushed up by her corset, and with traces of powder on her face. She had reminded him in the morning that they were going to the theatre. Sarah Bernhardt was visiting the town and they had a box, which he had insisted on their taking. Now he had forgotten about it and her toilet offended him, but he concealed his vexation when he remembered that he had himself insisted on their securing a box and going because it would be an instructive and aesthetic pleasure for the children.

Praskovya Fëdorovna came in, self-satisfied but yet with a rather guilty air. She sat down and asked how he was, but, as he saw, only for the sake of asking and not in order to learn about it, knowing that there was nothing to learn — and then went on to what she really wanted to say: that she would not on any account have gone but that the box had been taken and Helen and their daughter were going, as well as Petrishchev (the examining magistrate, their daughter's fiancé), and that it was out of the question to let them go alone; but that she would have much preferred to sit with him for a while; and he must be sure to follow the doctor's orders while she was away.

"Oh, and Fëdor Petrovich" (the fiancé) "would like to come in. May he? And Lisa?"

"All right." 265

Their daughter came in in full evening dress, her fresh young flesh exposed (making a show of that very flesh which in his own case caused so much suffering), strong, healthy, evidently in love, and impatient with illness, suffering, and death, because they interfered with her happiness.

Fëdor Petrovich came in too, in evening dress, his hair curled *à la Capoul°*, a tight stiff collar round his long sinewy neck, an enormous white shirt-front, and narrow black trousers tightly stretched over his strong thighs. He had one white glove tightly drawn on, and was holding his opera hat in his hand.

Following him the schoolboy crept in unnoticed, in a uniform, poor little fellow, and wearing gloves. Terribly dark shadows showed under his eyes, the meaning of which Ivan Ilych knew well.

His son had always seemed pathetic to him, and now it was dreadful to see the boy's frightened look of pity. It seemed to Ivan Ilych that Vasya was the only one besides Gerasim who understood and pitied him.

They all sat down and again asked how he was. A silence followed. Lisa 270 asked her mother about the opera-glasses, and there was an altercation between mother and daughter as to who had taken them and where they had been put. This occasioned some unpleasantness.

Fëdor Petrovich inquired of Ivan Ilych whether he had ever seen Sarah Bernhardt. Ivan Ilych did not at first catch the question, but then replied: "No, have you seen her before?"

"Yes, in *Adrienne Lecouvreur.*"

Praskovya Fëdorovna mentioned some rôles in which Sarah Bernhardt

à la Capoul: imitating the hair-do of Victor Capoul, a contemporary French singer.

was particularly good. Her daughter disagreed. Conversation sprang up as to the elegance and realism of her acting — the sort of conversation that is always repeated and is always the same.

In the midst of the conversation Fëdor Petrovich glanced at Ivan Ilych and became silent. The others also looked at him and grew silent. Ivan Ilych was staring with glittering eyes straight before him, evidently indignant with them. This had to be rectified, but it was impossible to do so. The silence had to be broken, but for a time no one dared to break it and they all became afraid that the conventional deception would suddenly become obvious and the truth become plain to all. Lisa was the first to pluck up courage and break that silence, but by trying to hide what everybody was feeling, she betrayed it.

"Well, if we are going it's time to start," she said, looking at her watch,   275 a present from her father, and with a faint and significant smile at Fëdor Petrovich relating to something known only to them. She got up with a rustle of her dress.

They all rose, said good-night, and went away.

When they had gone it seemed to Ivan Ilych that he felt better; the falsity had gone with them. But the pain remained — that same pain and that same fear that made everything monotonously alike, nothing harder and nothing easier. Everything was worse.

Again minute followed minute and hour followed hour. Everything remained the same and there was no cessation. And the inevitable end of it all became more and more terrible.

"Yes, send Gerasim here," he replied to a question Peter asked.

IX

His wife returned late at night. She came in on tiptoe, but he heard her,   280 opened his eyes, and made haste to close them again. She wished to send Gerasim away and to sit with him herself, but he opened his eyes and said: "No, go away."

"Are you in great pain?"

"Always the same."

"Take some opium."

He agreed and took some. She went away.

Till about three in the morning he was in a state of stupefied misery. It   285 seemed to him that he and his pain were being thrust into a narrow, deep black sack, but though they were pushed further and further in they could not be pushed to the bottom. And this, terrible enough in itself, was accompanied by suffering. He was frightened yet wanted to fall through the sack, he struggled but yet cooperated. And suddenly he broke through, fell, and regained consciousness. Gerasim was sitting at the foot of the bed dozing quietly and patiently, while he himself lay with his emaciated stockinged legs resting on Gerasim's shoulders; the same shaded candle was there and the same unceasing pain.

"Go away, Gerasim," he whispered.

"It's all right, sir. I'll stay a while."

"No. Go away."

He removed his legs from Gerasim's shoulders, turned sideways onto his arm, and felt sorry for himself. He only waited till Gerasim had gone into the next room and then restrained himself no longer but wept like a child. He wept on account of his helplessness, his terrible loneliness, the cruelty of man, the cruelty of God, and the absence of God.

"Why hast Thou done all this? Why hast Thou brought me here? Why, why dost Thou torment me so terribly?" 290

He did not expect an answer and yet wept because there was no answer and could be none. The pain again grew more acute, but he did not stir and did not call. He said to himself: "Go on! Strike me! But what is it for? What have I done to Thee? What is it for?"

Then he grew quiet and not only ceased weeping but even held his breath and became all attention. It was as though he were listening not to an audible voice but to the voice of his soul, to the current of thoughts arising within him.

"What is it you want?" was the first clear conception capable of expression in words, that he heard.

"What do you want? What do you want?" he repeated to himself.

"What do I want? To live and not to suffer," he answered. 295

And again he listened with such concentrated attention that even his pain did not distract him.

"To live? How?" asked his inner voice.

"Why, to live as I used to — well and pleasantly."

"As you lived before, well and pleasantly?" the voice repeated.

And in imagination he began to recall the best moments of his pleasant life. But strange to say none of those best moments of his pleasant life now seemed at all what they had then seemed — none of them except the first recollections of childhood. There, in childhood, there had been something really pleasant with which it would be possible to live if it could return. But the child who had experienced that happiness existed no longer, it was like a reminiscence of somebody else. 300

As soon as the period began which had produced the present Ivan Ilych, all that had then seemed joys now melted before his sight and turned into something trivial and often nasty.

And the further he departed from childhood and the nearer he came to the present the more worthless and doubtful were the joys. This began with the School of Law. A little that was really good was still found there — there was lightheartedness, friendship, and hope. But in the upper classes there had already been fewer of such good moments. Then during the first years of his official career, when he was in the service of the Governor, some pleasant moments again occurred; they were the memories of love for a woman. Then all became confused and there was still less of what was good; later on again there was still less that was good, and the further he went the less there was. His marriage, a mere accident, then the disenchantment that followed it, his wife's bad breath and the sensuality and hypocrisy: then that deadly official life and those preoccupations about money, a year of it, and two, and ten, and twenty, and always the same thing. And the longer it lasted the more deadly it became. "It is as if I had been going downhill while I imagined I was going up. And that is really what it was. I was going up in public opinion, but to the same extent life was ebbing away from me. And now it is all done and there is only death."

"Then what does it mean? Why? It can't be that life is so senseless and horrible. But if it really has been so horrible and senseless, why must I die and die in agony? There is something wrong!"

"Maybe I did not live as I ought to have done," it suddenly occurred to him. "But how could that be, when I did everything properly?" he replied, and immediately dismissed from his mind this, the sole solution of all the riddles of life and death, as something quite impossible.

"Then what do you want now? To live? Live how? Live as you lived in the law courts when the usher proclaimed 'The judge is coming!' The judge is coming, the judge!" he repeated to himself. "Here he is, the judge. But I am not guilty!" he exclaimed angrily. "What is it for?" And he ceased crying, but turning his face to the wall continued to ponder on the same question: Why, and for what purpose, is there all this horror? But however much he pondered he found no answer. And whenever the thought occurred to him, as it often did, that it all resulted from his not having lived as he ought to have done, he at once recalled the correctness of his whole life and dismissed so strange an idea.

X

Another fortnight passed. Ivan Ilych now no longer left his sofa. He would not lie in bed but lay on the sofa, facing the wall nearly all the time. He suffered ever the same unceasing agonies and in his loneliness pondered always on the same insoluble question: "What is this? Can it be that it is Death?" And the inner voice answered: "Yes, it is Death."

"Why these sufferings?" And the voice answered, "For no reason — they just are so." Beyond and besides this there was nothing.

From the very beginning of his illness, ever since he had first been to see the doctor, Ivan Ilych's life had been divided between two contrary and alternating moods: now it was despair and the expectation of this uncomprehended and terrible death, and now hope and an intently interested observation of the functioning of his organs. Now before his eyes there was only a kidney or an intestine that temporarily evaded its duty, and now only that incomprehensible and dreadful death from which it was impossible to escape.

These two states of mind had alternated from the very beginning of his illness, but the further it progressed the more doubtful and fantastic became the conception of the kidney, and the more real the sense of impending death.

He had but to call to mind what he had been three months before and what he was now, to call to mind with what regularity he had been going downhill, for every possibility of hope to be shattered.

Latterly during that loneliness in which he found himself as he lay facing the back of the sofa, a loneliness in the midst of a populous town and surrounded by numerous acquaintances and relations but that yet could not have been more complete anywhere — either at the bottom of the sea or under the earth — during that terrible loneliness Ivan Ilych had lived only in memories of the past. Pictures of his past rose before him one after another. They always began with what was nearest in time and then went back to what was most remote — to his childhood — and rested there. If he thought of the stewed prunes that had been offered him that day, his mind went back to the raw shrivelled French plums of his childhood, their peculiar flavor and the flow of saliva when he sucked their stones, and along with the memory of that taste came a whole series of memories of those days: his nurse, his brother, and their toys. "No, I mustn't think of that. . . . It is too painful," Ivan Ilych said to himself, and brought himself back to the present — to the button on the back of the sofa and the creases in its morocco. "Morocco is expensive, but it does not wear well: there had been a quarrel about it. It was a different kind of quarrel and a different kind of morocco that time when we tore father's portfolio and were punished, and mamma brought us some tarts. . . ." And again his thoughts dwelt on his childhood, and again it was painful and he tried to banish them and fix his mind on something else.

Then again together with that chain of memories another series passed through his mind — of how his illness had progressed and grown worse. There also the further back he looked the more life there had been. There had been more of what was good in life and more of life itself. The two merged together. "Just as the pain went on getting worse and worse, so my life grew worse and worse," he thought. "There is one bright spot there at the back, at the beginning of life, and afterwards all becomes blacker and blacker and proceeds more and more rapidly — in inverse ratio to the square of the distance from death," thought Ivan Ilych. And the example of a stone falling downwards with increasing velocity entered his mind. Life, a series of increasing sufferings, flies further and further towards its end — the most terrible suffering. "I am flying. . . ." He shuddered, shifted himself, and tried to resist, but was already aware that resistance was impossible, and again, with eyes weary of gazing but unable to cease seeing what was before them, he stared at the back of the sofa and waited — awaiting that dreadful fall and shock and destruction.

"Resistance is impossible!" he said to himself. "If I could only understand what it is all for! But that too is impossible. An explanation would be possible if it could be said that I have not lived as I ought to. But it is impossible to say that," and he remembered all the legality, correctitude, and propriety of his life. "That at any rate can certainly not be admitted," he thought, and his lips smiled ironically as if someone could see that smile and be taken in by it. "There is no explanation! Agony, death. . . . What for?"

XI

Another two weeks went by in this way and during that fortnight an event occurred that Ivan Ilych and his wife had desired. Petrishchev formally proposed. It happened in the evening. The next day Praskovya Fëdorovna came into her husband's room considering how best to inform him of it, but that very night there had been a fresh change for the worse in his condition. She found him still lying on the sofa but in a different position. He lay on his back, groaning and staring fixedly straight in front of him.

She began to remind him of his medicines, but he turned his eyes towards her with such a look that she did not finish what she was saying; so great an animosity, to her in particular, did that look express.

"For Christ's sake let me die in peace!" he said.

She would have gone away, but just then their daughter came in and went up to say good morning. He looked at her as he had done at his wife, and in reply to her inquiry about his health said dryly that he would soon free

315

them all of himself. They were both silent and after sitting with him for a while went away.

"Is it our fault?" Lisa said to her mother. "It's as if we were to blame! I am sorry for papa, but why should we be tortured?"

The doctor came at his usual time. Ivan Ilych answered "Yes" and "No," never taking his angry eyes from him, and at last said: "You know you can do nothing for me, so leave me alone."

"We can ease your sufferings."   320

"You can't even do that. Let me be."

The doctor went into the drawing-room and told Praskovya Fëdorovna that the case was very serious and that the only resource left was opium to allay her husband's sufferings, which must be terrible.

It was true, as the doctor said, that Ivan Ilych's physical sufferings were terrible, but worse than the physical sufferings were his mental sufferings, which were his chief torture.

His mental sufferings were due to the fact that one night, as he looked at Gerasim's sleepy, good-natured face with its prominent cheekbones, the question suddenly occurred to him: "What if my whole life has really been wrong?"

It occurred to him that what had appeared perfectly impossible before,   325
namely that he had not spent his life as he should have done, might after all be true. It occurred to him that his scarcely perceptible attempts to struggle against what was considered good by the most highly placed people, those scarcely noticeable impulses which he had immediately suppressed, might have been the real thing, and all the rest false. And his professional duties and the whole arrangement of his life and of his family, and all his social and official interests, might all have been false. He tried to defend all those things to himself and suddenly felt the weakness of what he was defending. There was nothing to defend.

"But if that is so," he said to himself, "and I am leaving this life with the consciousness that I have lost all that was given me and it is impossible to rectify it — what then?"

He lay on his back and began to pass his life in review in quite a new way. In the morning when he saw first his footman, then his wife, then his daughter, and then the doctor, their every word and movement confirmed to him the awful truth that had been revealed to him during the night. In them he saw himself — all that for which he had lived — and saw clearly that it was not real at all, but a terrible and huge deception which had hidden both life and death. This consciousness intensified his physical suffering tenfold. He groaned and tossed about, and pulled at his clothing which choked and stifled him. And he hated them on that account.

He was given a large dose of opium and became unconscious, but at noon his sufferings began again. He drove everybody away and tossed from side to side.

His wife came to him and said:

"Jean, my dear, do this for me. It can't do any harm and often helps.   330
Healthy people often do it."

He opened his eyes wide.

"What? Take communion? Why? It's unnecessary! However . . ."

She began to cry.

"Yes, do, my dear. I'll send for our priest. He is such a nice man."

"All right. Very well," he muttered.

When the priest came and heard his confession, Ivan Ilych was softened and seemed to feel a relief from his doubts and consequently from his sufferings, and for a moment there came a ray of hope. He again began to think of the vermiform appendix and the possibility of correcting it. He received the sacrament with tears in his eyes.

When they laid him down again afterwards he felt a moment's ease, and the hope that he might live awoke in him again. He began to think of the operation that had been suggested to him. "To live! I want to live!" he said to himself.

His wife came in to congratulate him after his communion, and when uttering the usual conventional words she added:

"You feel better, don't you?"

Without looking at her he said "Yes."

Her dress, her figure, the expression of her face, the tone of her voice, all revealed the same thing. "This is wrong, it is not as it should be. All you have lived for and still live for is falsehood and deception, hiding life and death from you." And as soon as he admitted that thought, his hatred and his agonizing physical suffering again sprang up, and with that suffering a consciousness of the unavoidable, approaching end. And to this was added a new sensation of grinding shooting pain and a feeling of suffocation.

The expression of his face when he uttered that "yes" was dreadful. Having uttered it, he looked her straight in the eyes, turned on his face with a rapidity extraordinary in his weak state and shouted:

"Go away! Go away and leave me alone!"

XII

From that moment the screaming began that continued for three days, and was so terrible that one could not hear it through two closed doors without horror. At the moment he answered his wife he realized that he was lost, that there was no return, that the end had come, the very end, and his doubts were still unsolved and remained doubts.

"Oh! Oh! Oh!" he cried in various intonations. He had begun by screaming "I won't!" and continued screaming on the letter O.

For three whole days, during which time did not exist for him, he struggled in that black sack into which he was being thrust by an invisible, resistless force. He struggled as a man condemned to death struggles in the hands of the executioner, knowing that he cannot save himself. And every moment he felt that despite all his efforts he was drawing nearer and nearer to what terrified him. He felt that his agony was due to his being thrust into that black hole and still more to his not being able to get right into it. He was hindered from getting into it by his conviction that his life had been a good one. That very justification of his life held him fast and prevented his moving forward, and it caused him most torment of all.

Suddenly some force struck him in the chest and side, making it still harder to breathe, and he fell through the hole and there at the bottom was a light. What had happened to him was like the sensation one sometimes experiences in a railway carriage when one thinks one is going backwards while one is really going forwards and suddenly becomes aware of the real direction.

"Yes, it was all not the right thing," he said to himself, "but that's no matter. It can be done. But what *is* the right thing?" he asked himself, and suddenly grew quiet.

This occurred at the end of the third day, two hours before his death. Just then his schoolboy son had crept softly in and gone up to the bedside. The dying man was still screaming desperately and waving his arms. His hand fell on the boy's head, and the boy caught it, pressed it to his lips, and began to cry.

At that very moment Ivan Ilych fell through and caught sight of the light, and it was revealed to him that though his life had not been what it should have been, this could still be rectified. He asked himself, "What *is* the right thing?" and grew still, listening. Then he felt that someone was kissing his hand. He opened his eyes, looked at his son, and felt sorry for him. His wife came up to him and he glanced at her. She was gazing at him open-mouthed, with undried tears on her nose and cheek and a despairing look on her face. He felt sorry for her too.

"Yes, I am making them wretched," he thought. "They are sorry, but it will be better for them when I die." He wished to say this but had not the strength to utter it. "Besides, why speak? I must act," he thought. With a look at his wife he indicated his son and said: "Take him away . . . sorry for him . . . sorry for you too. . . ." He tried to add, "Forgive me," but said "forgo" and waved his hand, knowing that He whose understanding mattered would understand.

And suddenly it grew clear to him that what had been oppressing him and would not leave him was all dropping away at once from two sides, from ten sides, and from all sides. He was sorry for them, he must act so as not to hurt them: release them and free himself from these sufferings. "How good and how simple!" he thought. "And the pain?" he asked himself. "What has become of it? Where are you, pain?"

He turned his attention to it.

"Yes, here it is. Well, what of it? Let the pain be."

"And death . . . where is it?"

He sought his former accustomed fear of death and did not find it. "Where is it? What death?" There was no fear because there was no death.

In place of death there was light.

"So that's what it is!" he suddenly exclaimed aloud. "What joy!"

To him all this happened in a single instant, and the meaning of that instant did not change. For those present his agony continued for another two hours. Something rattled in his throat, his emaciated body twitched, then the gasping and rattle became less and less frequent.

"It is finished!" said someone near him.

He heard these words and repeated them in his soul.

"Death is finished," he said to himself. "It is no more!"

He drew in a breath, stopped in the midst of a sigh, stretched out, and died.

Nathaniel Hawthorne

THE BIRTHMARK   1846

Nathaniel Hawthorne (1804 – 1864) was born in the clipper-ship seaport of Salem, Massachusetts, son of a merchant captain and grandson of a judge at the notorious Salem witchcraft trials. Hawthorne takes a keen interest in New England's sin-and-brimstone Puritan past in many of his stories and in The Scarlet Letter *(1848), that enduring novel of a woman taken in adultery. After college, Hawthorne lived at home and trained to be a writer. Only when his first collection,* Twice-Told Tales *(1837), made money did he feel secure enough to marry Sophia Peabody and settle in the Old Manse in Concord, Massachusetts. Three more novels followed* The Scarlet Letter: The House of the Seven Gables *(1851, a story tinged with nightmarish humor),* The Blithedale Romance *(1852, drawn from his short, disgruntled stay at a Utopian commune, Brook Farm), and* The Marble Faun *(1860, inspired by a stay in Italy). Hawthorne wrote for children, too, retelling classic legends in* The Wonder Book *(1852) and* Tanglewood Tales *(1853). At Bowdoin College, he had been a classmate of Franklin Pierce; later, when Pierce ran for President of the United States, Hawthorne wrote him a campaign biography. The victorious Pierce appointed his old friend American counsel at Liverpool, England. With his contemporary Edgar Allan Poe, Hawthorne sped the transformation of the American short story from popular magazine filler into a form of art.*

In the latter part of the last century there lived a man of science, an eminent proficient in every branch of natural philosophy, who not long before our story opens had made experience of a spiritual affinity more attractive than any chemical one. He had left his laboratory to the care of an assistant, cleared his fine countenance from the furnace smoke, washed the stain of acids from his fingers, and persuaded a beautiful woman to become his wife. In those days when the comparatively recent discovery of electricity and other kindred mysteries of Nature seemed to open paths into the region of miracle, it was not unusual for the love of science to rival the love of woman in its depth and absorbing energy. The higher intellect, the imagination, the spirit, and even the heart might all find their congenial aliment in pursuits which, as some of their ardent votaries believed, would ascend from one step of powerful intelligence to another, until the philosopher should lay his hand on the secret of creative force and perhaps make new worlds for himself. We know not whether Aylmer possessed this degree of faith in man's ultimate control over Nature. He had devoted himself, however, too unreservedly to scientific studies ever to be weaned from them by any second passion. His love for his young wife might prove the stronger of the two; but it could only be by intertwining itself with his love of science, and uniting the strength of the latter to his own.

Such a union accordingly took place, and was attended with truly remarkable consequences and a deeply impressive moral. One day, very soon after their marriage, Aylmer sat gazing at his wife with a trouble in his countenance that grew stronger until he spoke.

"Georgiana," said he, "has it never occurred to you that the mark upon your cheek might be removed?"

"No, indeed," said she, smiling; but perceiving the seriousness of his manner, she blushed deeply. "To tell you the truth it has been so often called a charm that I was simple enough to imagine it might be so."

"Ah, upon another face perhaps it might," replied her husband; "but never on yours. No, dearest Georgiana, you came so nearly perfect from the hand of Nature that this slightest possible defect, which we hesitate whether to term a defect or a beauty, shocks me, as being the visible mark of earthly imperfection." 5

"Shocks you, my husband!" cried Georgiana, deeply hurt; at first reddening with momentary anger, but then bursting into tears. "Then why did you take me from my mother's side? You cannot love what shocks you!"

To explain this conversation it must be mentioned that in the center of Georgiana's left cheek there was a singular mark, deeply interwoven, as it were, with the texture and substance of her face. In the usual state of her complexion — a healthy though delicate bloom — the mark wore a tint of deeper crimson, which imperfectly defined its shape amid the surrounding rosiness. When she blushed it gradually became more indistinct, and finally vanished amid the triumphant rush of blood that bathed the whole cheek with its brilliant glow. But if any shifting motion caused her to turn pale there was the mark again, a crimson stain upon the snow, in what Aylmer sometimes deemed an almost fearful distinctness. Its shape bore not a little similarity to the human hand, though of the smallest pygmy size. Georgiana's lovers were wont to say that some fairy at her birth hour had laid her tiny hand upon the infant's cheek, and left this impress there in token of the magic endowments that were to give her such sway over all hearts. Many a desperate swain would have risked life for the privilege of pressing his lips to the mysterious hand. It must not be concealed, however, that the impression wrought by this fairy sign manual varied exceedingly, according to the difference of temperament in the beholders. Some fastidious persons — but they were exclusively of her own sex — affirmed that the bloody hand, as they chose to call it, quite destroyed the effect of Georgiana's beauty, and rendered her countenance even hideous. But it would be as reasonable to say that one of those small blue stains which sometimes occur in the purest statuary marble would convert the Eve of Powers to a monster. Masculine observers, if the birthmark did not heighten their admiration, contented themselves with wishing it away, that the world might possess one living specimen of ideal loveliness without the semblance of a flaw. After his marriage — for he thought little or nothing of the matter before — Aylmer discovered that this was the case with himself.

Had she been less beautiful — if Envy's self could have found aught else to sneer at — he might have felt his affection heightened by the prettiness of this mimic hand, now vaguely portrayed, now lost, now stealing forth again and glimmering to and fro with every pulse of emotion that throbbed within her heart; but seeing her otherwise so perfect, he found this one defect grow more and more intolerable with every moment of their united lives. It was the fatal flaw of humanity which Nature, in one shape or another, stamps ineffaceably on all her productions, either to imply that they are temporary and finite, or that their perfection must be wrought by toil and pain. The crimson hand expressed the ineludible grip in which mortality clutches the highest and purest of earthly mould, degrading them into kindred with the lowest, and even with the very brutes, like whom their visible frames return to dust. In this manner, selecting it as the symbol of his wife's liability to sin, sorrow, decay, and death, Aylmer's somber imagination was not long in rendering the birthmark a frightful object, causing him more trouble and horror than ever Georgiana's beauty, whether of soul or sense, had given him delight.

At all the seasons which should have been their happiest, he invariably and without intending it, nay, in spite of a purpose to the contrary, reverted to this one disastrous topic. Trifling as it at first appeared, it so connected itself with innumerable trains of thought and modes of feeling that it became the central point of all. With the morning twilight Aylmer opened his eyes upon his wife's face and recognized the symbol of imperfection; and when they sat together at the evening hearth his eyes wandered stealthily to her cheek, and beheld, flickering with the blaze of the wood fire, the spectral hand that wrote mortality where he would fain have worshipped. Georgiana soon learned to shudder at his gaze. It needed but a glance with the peculiar expression that his face often wore to change the roses of her cheek into a deathlike paleness, amid which the crimson hand was brought strongly out, like a bas-relief of ruby on the whitest marble.

Late one night when the lights were growing dim, so as hardly to betray   10
the stain on the poor wife's cheek, she herself, for the first time, voluntarily took up the subject.

"Do you remember, my dear Aylmer," said she, with a feeble attempt at a smile, "have you any recollection of a dream last night about this odious hand?"

"None! none whatever!" replied Aylmer, starting; but then he added, in a dry, cold tone, affected for the sake of concealing the real depth of his emotion, "I might well dream of it; for before I fell asleep it had taken a pretty firm hold of my fancy."

"And you did dream of it?" continued Georgiana, hastily; for she dreaded lest a gush of tears should interrupt what she had to say. "A terrible dream! I wonder that you can forget it. Is it possible to forget this one expression? — 'It is in her heart now; we must have it out!' Reflect, my husband; for by all means I would have you recall that dream."

The mind is in a sad state when Sleep, the all-involving, cannot confine her specters within the dim region of her sway, but suffers them to break forth, affrighting this actual life with secrets that perchance belong to a deeper one. Aylmer now remembered his dream. He had fancied himself with his servant Aminadab° attempting an operation for the removal of the birthmark; but the deeper went the knife, the deeper sank the hand, until at length its tiny grasp appeared to have caught hold of Georgiana's heart; whence, however, her husband was inexorably resolved to cut or wrench it away.

When the dream had shaped itself perfectly in his memory, Aylmer sat   15

Aminadab: Spelled backward, the name becomes *bad anima* — "bad soul" or "evil spirit."

in his wife's presence with a guilty feeling. Truth often finds its way to the mind close muffled in robes of sleep, and then speaks with uncompromising directness of matters in regard to which we practice an unconscious self-deception during our waking moments. Until now he had not been aware of the tyrannizing influence acquired by one idea over his mind, and of the lengths which he might find in his heart to go for the sake of giving himself peace.

"Aylmer," resumed Georgiana, solemnly. "I know not what may be the cost to both of us to rid me of this fatal birthmark. Perhaps its removal may cause cureless deformity; or it may be the stain goes as deep as life itself. Again: do we know that there is a possibility, on any terms, of unclasping the firm grip of this little hand which was laid upon me before I came into the world?"

"Dearest Georgiana, I have spent much thought upon the subject," hastily interrupted Aylmer. "I am convinced of the perfect practicability of its removal."

"If there be the remotest possibility of it," continued Georgiana, "let the attempt be made at whatever risk. Danger is nothing to me; for life, while this hateful mark makes me the object of your horror and disgust — life is a burden which I would fling down with joy. Either remove this dreadful hand, or take my wretched life! You have deep science. All the world bears witness of it. You have achieved great wonders. Cannot you remove this little, little mark, which I cover with the tips of two small fingers? Is this beyond your power, for the sake of your own peace, and to save your poor wife from madness?"

"Noblest, dearest, tenderest wife," cried Aylmer, rapturously, "doubt not my power. I have already given this matter the deepest thought — thought which might almost have enlightened me to create a being less perfect than yourself. Georgiana, you have led me deeper than ever into the heart of science. I feel myself fully competent to render this dear cheek as faultless as its fellow; and then, most beloved, what will be my triumph when I shall have corrected what Nature left imperfect in her fairest work! Even Pygmalion, when his sculptured woman assumed life, felt not greater ecstasy than mine will be."

"It is resolved, then," said Georgiana, faintly smiling. "And, Aylmer, spare me not, though you should find the birthmark take refuge in my heart at last."

Her husband tenderly kissed her cheek — her right cheek — not that which bore the impress of the crimson hand.

The next day Aylmer apprised his wife of a plan that he had formed whereby he might have opportunity for the intense thought and constant watchfulness which the proposed operation would require; while Georgiana, likewise, would enjoy the perfect repose essential to its success. They were to seclude themselves in the extensive apartments occupied by Aylmer as a laboratory, and where, during his toilsome youth, he had made discoveries in the elemental powers of Nature that had roused the admiration of all the learned societies in Europe. Seated calmly in this laboratory, the pale philosopher had investigated the secrets of the highest cloud region and of the profoundest mines; he had satisfied himself of the causes that kindled and kept alive the fires of the volcano; and had explained the mystery of fountains, and how it is that they gush forth, some so bright and pure, and others with such rich medicinal virtues, from the dark bosom of the earth. Here, too, at an earlier period, he had studied the wonders of the human frame, and attempted to fathom the very process by which Nature assimilates all her precious influences from earth and air, and from the spiritual world, to create and foster man, her masterpiece. The latter pursuit, however, Aylmer had long laid aside in unwilling recognition of the truth — against which all seekers sooner or later stumble — that our great creative Mother, while she amuses us with apparently working in the broadest sunshine, is yet severely careful to keep her own secrets, and, in spite of her pretended openness, shows us nothing but results. She permits us, indeed, to mar, but seldom to mend, and, like a jealous patentee, on no account to make. Now, however, Aylmer resumed these half-forgotten investigations; not, of course, with such hopes or wishes as first suggested them; but because they involved much physiological truth and lay in the path of his proposed scheme for the treatment of Georgiana.

As he led her over the threshold of the laboratory, Georgiana was cold and tremulous. Aylmer looked cheerfully into her face, with intent to reassure her, but was so startled with the intense glow of the birthmark upon the whiteness of her cheek that he could not restrain a strong convulsive shudder. His wife fainted.

"Aminadab! Aminadab!" shouted Aylmer, stamping violently on the floor.

Forthwith there issued from an inner apartment a man of low stature, but 25 bulky frame, with shaggy hair hanging about his visage, which was grimed with the vapors of the furnace. This personage had been Aylmer's under-worker during his whole scientific career, and was admirably fitted for that office by his great mechanical readiness, and the skill with which, while incapable of comprehending a single principle, he executed all the details of his master's experiments. With his vast strength, his shaggy hair, his smoky aspect, and the indescribable earthiness that incrusted him, he seemed to represent man's physical nature; while Aylmer's slender figure, and pale, intellectual face, were no less apt a type of the spiritual element.

"Throw open the door of the boudoir, Aminadab," said Aylmer, "and burn a pastil°."

"Yes, master," answered Aminadab, looking intently at the lifeless form of Georgiana; and then he muttered to himself, "If she were my wife, I'd never part with that birthmark."

When Georgiana recovered consciousness she found herself breathing an atmosphere of penetrating fragrance, the gentle potency of which had recalled her from her deathlike faintness. The scene around her looked like enchantment. Aylmer had converted those smoky, dingy, somber rooms, where he had spent his brightest years in recondite pursuits, into a series of beautiful apartments not unfit to be the secluded abode of a lovely woman. The walls were hung with gorgeous curtains, which imparted the combination of grandeur and grace that no other species of adornment can achieve; and as they fell from the ceiling to the floor, their rich and ponderous folds, concealing all angles and straight lines, appeared to shut in the scene from infinite space. For aught

pastil: a pellet of aromatic paste, burned to deodorize the air.

Georgiana knew, it might be a pavilion among the clouds. And Aylmer, excluding the sunshine, which would have interfered with his chemical processes, had supplied its place with perfumed lamps, emitting flames of various hue, but all uniting in a soft, impurpled radiance. He now knelt by his wife's side, watching her earnestly, but without alarm; for he was confident in his science, and felt that he could draw a magic circle round her within which no evil might intrude.

"Where am I? Ah, I remember," said Georgiana, faintly; and she placed her hand over her cheek to hide the terrible mark from her husband's eyes.

"Fear not, dearest!" exclaimed he. "Do not shrink from me! Believe me, 30 Georgiana, I even rejoice in this single imperfection, since it will be such a rapture to remove it."

"Oh, spare me!" sadly replied his wife. "Pray do not look at it again. I never can forget that convulsive shudder."

In order to soothe Georgiana, and, as it were, to release her mind from the burden of actual things, Aylmer now put in practice some of the light and playful secrets which science had taught him among its profounder lore. Airy figures, absolutely bodiless ideas, and forms of unsubstantial beauty came and danced before her, imprinting their momentary footsteps on beams of light. Though she had some indistinct idea of the method of these optical phenomena, still the illusion was almost perfect enough to warrant the belief that her husband possessed sway over the spiritual world. Then again, when she felt a wish to look forth from her seclusion, immediately, as if her thoughts were answered, the procession of external existence flitted across a screen. The scenery and the figures of actual life were perfectly represented, but with that bewitching, yet indescribable difference which always makes a picture, an image, or a shadow so much more attractive than the original. When wearied of this, Aylmer bade her cast her eyes upon a vessel containing a quantity of earth. She did so, with little interest at first; but was soon startled to perceive the germ of a plant shooting upward from the soil. Then came the slender stalk; the leaves gradually unfolded themselves; and amid them was a perfect and lovely flower.

"It is magical!" cried Georgiana. "I dare not touch it."

"Nay, pluck it," answered Aylmer — "pluck it, and inhale its brief perfume while you may. The flower will wither in a few moments and leave nothing save its brown seed vessels; but thence may be perpetuated a race as ephemeral as itself."

But Georgiana had no sooner touched the flower than the whole plant 35 suffered a blight, its leaves turning coal-black as if by the agency of fire.

"There was too powerful a stimulus," said Aylmer, thoughtfully.

To make up for this abortive experiment, he proposed to take her portrait by a scientific process of his own invention. It was to be effected by rays of light striking upon a polished plate of metal. Georgiana assented; but, on looking at the result, was affrighted to find the features of the portrait blurred and indefinable; while the minute figure of a hand appeared where the cheek should have been. Aylmer snatched the metallic plate and threw it into a jar of corrosive acid.

Soon, however, he forgot these mortifying failures. In the intervals of study and chemical experiment he came to her flushed and exhausted, but seemed invigorated by her presence, and spoke in glowing language of the resources of his art. He gave a history of the long dynasty of the alchemists, who spent so many ages in quest of the universal solvent by which the golden principle might be elicited from all things vile and base. Aylmer appeared to believe that, by the plainest scientific logic, it was altogether within the limits of possibility to discover this long-sought medium; "but," he added, "a philosopher who should go deep enough to acquire the power would attain too lofty a wisdom to stoop to the exercise of it." Not less singular were his opinions in regard to the elixir vitæ. He more than intimated that it was at his option to concoct a liquid that should prolong life for years, perhaps interminably; but that it would produce a discord in Nature which all the world, and chiefly the quaffer of the immortal nostrum, would find cause to curse.

"Aylmer, are you in earnest?" asked Georgiana, looking at him with amazement and fear. "It is terrible to possess such power, or even to dream of possessing it."

"Oh, do not tremble, my love," said her husband. "I would not wrong 40 either you or myself by working such inharmonious effects upon our lives; but I would have you consider how trifling, in comparison, is the skill requisite to remove this little hand."

At the mention of the birthmark, Georgiana, as usual, shrank as if a redhot iron had touched her cheek.

Again Aylmer applied himself to his labors. She could hear his voice in the distant furnace room giving directions to Aminadab, whose harsh, uncouth, misshapen tones were audible in response, more like the grunt or growl of a brute than human speech. After hours of absence, Aylmer reappeared and proposed that she should now examine his cabinet of chemical products and natural treasures of the earth. Among the former he showed her a small vial, in which, he remarked, was contained a gentle yet most powerful fragrance, capable of impregnating all the breezes that blow across a kingdom. They were of inestimable value, the contents of that little vial; and, as he said so, he threw some of the perfume into the air and filled the room with piercing and invigorating delight.

"And what is this?" asked Georgiana, pointing to a small crystal globe containing a gold-colored liquid. "It is so beautiful to the eye that I could imagine it the elixir of life."

"In one sense it is," replied Aylmer; "or, rather, the elixir of immortality. It is the most precious poison that ever was concocted in this world. By its aid I could apportion the lifetime of any mortal at whom you might point your finger. The strength of the dose would determine whether he were to linger out years, or drop dead in the midst of a breath. No king on his guarded throne could keep his life if I, in my private station, should deem that the welfare of millions justified me in depriving him of it."

"Why do you keep such a terrific drug?" inquired Georgiana in horror. 45

"Do not mistrust me, dearest," said her husband, smiling; "its virtuous potency is yet greater than its harmful one. But see! here is a powerful cosmetic. With a few drops of this in a vase of water, freckles may be washed away as easily as the hands are cleansed. A stronger infusion would take the blood out of the cheek, and leave the rosiest beauty a pale ghost."

"Is it with this lotion that you intend to bathe my cheek?" asked Georgiana, anxiously.

"Oh, no," hastily replied her husband; "this is merely superficial. Your case demands a remedy that shall go deeper."

In his interviews with Georgiana, Aylmer generally made minute inquiries as to her sensations and whether the confinement of the rooms and the temperature of the atmosphere agreed with her. These questions had such a particular drift that Georgiana began to conjecture that she was already subjected to certain physical influences, either breathed in with the fragrant air or taken with her food. She fancied likewise, but it might be altogether fancy, that there was a stirring up of her system — a strange, indefinite sensation creeping through her veins, and tingling, half painfully, half pleasurably, at her heart. Still, whenever she dared to look into the mirror, there she beheld herself pale as a white rose and with the crimson birthmark stamped upon her cheek. Not even Aylmer now hated it so much as she.

To dispel the tedium of the hours which her husband found it necessary to devote to the processes of combination and analysis, Georgiana turned over the volumes of his scientific library. In many dark old tomes she met with chapters full of romance and poetry. They were the works of philosophers of the middle ages, such as Albertus Magnus, Cornelius Agrippa, Paracelsus, and the famous friar who created the prophetic Brazen Head°. All these antique naturalists stood in advance of their centuries, yet were imbued with some of their credulity, and therefore were believed, and perhaps imagined themselves to have acquired from the investigation of Nature a power above Nature, and from physics a sway over the spiritual world. Hardly less curious and imaginative were the early volumes of the Transactions of the Royal Society, in which the members, knowing little of the limits of natural possibility, were continually recording wonders or proposing methods whereby wonders might be wrought.

But to Georgiana the most engrossing volume was a large folio from her husband's own hand, in which he had recorded every experiment of his scientific career, its original aim, the methods adopted for its development, and its final success or failure, with the circumstances to which either event was attributable. The book, in truth, was both the history and emblem of his ardent, ambitious, imaginative, yet practical and laborious life. He handled physical details as if there were nothing beyond them; yet spiritualized them all, and redeemed himself from materialism by his strong and eager aspiration

50

Albertus Magnus . . . Brazen Head: medieval experimental scientists popularly supposed to be magicians. Albertus Magnus, or Saint Albert the Great (1206 – 1280), was a learned German scholar, teacher, and philosopher. He made contributions to botany, zoology, and astronomy, and succeeded in producing arsenic in his laboratory. Heinrich Cornelius Agrippa (1486 – 1535), German physician and theologian, wrote a treatise on the occult. He figures in early legends of Faust, who traded his soul in exchange for knowledge and power. Paracelsus (born Theophrastus Bombastus von Hohenheim, 1493? – 1541), Swiss physician and alchemist, introduced several drugs to medicine and proved that goiter in a parent can cause cretinism in a child. According to one story, he tried to grow babies in bottles. The "famous friar" was Roger Bacon, English Franciscan (c. 1220 – 1284?), author of an encyclopedia of scientific knowledge. In a popular story, the basis of Robert Greene's play *Friar Bacon and Friar Bungay* (1594), Bacon with the help of the Devil constructs a talking head of brass. It utters the words "Time is," "Time was," and "Time is past," then smashes to bits.

towards the infinite. In his grasp the veriest clod of earth assumed a soul. Georgiana, as she read, reverenced Aylmer and loved him more profoundly than ever, but with a less entire dependence on his judgment than heretofore. Much as he had accomplished, she could not but observe that his most splendid successes were almost invariably failures, if compared with the ideal at which he aimed. His brightest diamonds were the merest pebbles, and felt to be so by himself, in comparison with the inestimable gems which lay hidden beyond his reach. The volume, rich with achievements that had won renown for its author, was yet as melancholy a record as ever mortal hand had penned. It was the sad confession and continual exemplification of the shortcomings of the composite man, the spirit burdened with clay and working in matter, and of the despair that assails the higher nature at finding itself so miserably thwarted by the earthly part. Perhaps every man of genius in whatever sphere might recognize the image of his own experience in Aylmer's journal.

So deeply did these reflections affect Georgiana that she laid her face upon the open volume and burst into tears. In this situation she was found by her husband.

"It is dangerous to read in a sorcerer's books," said he with a smile, though his countenance was uneasy and displeased. "Georgiana, there are pages in that volume which I can scarcely glance over and keep my senses. Take heed lest it prove as detrimental to you."

"It has made me worship you more than ever," said she.

"Ah, wait for this one success," rejoined he, "then worship me if you will. I shall deem myself hardly unworthy of it. But come, I have sought you for the luxury of your voice. Sing to me, dearest."

So she poured out the liquid music of her voice to quench the thirst of his spirit. He then took his leave with a boyish exuberance of gayety, assuring her that her seclusion would endure but a little longer, and that the result was already certain. Scarcely had he departed when Georgiana felt irresistibly impelled to follow him. She had forgotten to inform Aylmer of a symptom which for two or three hours past had begun to excite her attention. It was a sensation in the fatal birthmark, not painful, but which induced a restlessness throughout her system. Hastening after her husband, she intruded for the first time into the laboratory.

The first thing that struck her eye was the furnace, that hot and feverish worker, with the intense glow of its fire, which by the quantities of soot clustered above it seemed to have been burning for ages. There was a distilling apparatus in full operation. Around the room were retorts, tubes, cylinders, crucibles, and other apparatus of chemical research. An electrical machine stood ready for immediate use. The atmosphere felt oppressively close, and was tainted with gaseous odors which had been tormented forth by the processes of science. The severe and homely simplicity of the apartment, with its naked walls and brick pavement, looked strange, accustomed as Georgiana had become to the fantastic elegance of her boudoir. But what chiefly, indeed almost solely, drew her attention, was the aspect of Aylmer himself.

He was pale as death, anxious and absorbed, and hung over the furnace as if it depended upon his utmost watchfulness whether the liquid which it was distilling should be the draught of immortal happiness or misery. How different from the sanguine and joyous mien that he had assumed for Georgiana's encouragement!

"Carefully now, Aminadab; carefully, thou human machine; carefully, thou man of clay!" muttered Aylmer, more to himself than his assistant. "Now, if there be a thought too much or too little, it is all over."

"Ho! ho!" mumbled Aminadab. "Look, master! Look!" 60

Aylmer raised his eyes hastily, and at first reddened, then grew paler than ever, on beholding Georgiana. He rushed towards her and seized her arm with a grip that left the print of his fingers upon it.

"Why do you come hither? Have you no trust in your husband?" cried he, impetuously. "Would you throw the blight of that fatal birthmark over my labors? It is not well done. Go, prying woman, go!"

"Nay, Aylmer," said Georgiana with the firmness of which she possessed no stinted endowment, "it is not you that have a right to complain. You mistrust your wife; you have concealed the anxiety with which you watch the development of this experiment. Think not so unworthily of me, my husband. Tell me all the risk we run, and fear not that I shall shrink; for my share in it is far less than your own."

"No, no, Georgiana!" said Aylmer, impatiently; "it must not be."

"I submit," replied she calmly. "And, Aylmer, I shall quaff whatever 65 draught you bring me; but it will be on the same principle that would induce me to take a dose of poison if offered by your hand."

"My noble wife," said Aylmer, deeply moved, "I knew not the height and depth of your nature until now. Nothing shall be concealed. Know, then, that this crimson hand, superficial as it seems, has clutched its grasp into your being with a strength of which I had no previous conception. I have already administered agents powerful enough to do aught except to change your entire physical system. Only one thing remains to be tried. If that fail us we are ruined."

"Why did you hesitate to tell me this?" asked she.

"Because, Georgiana," said Aylmer, in a low voice, "there is danger."

"Danger? There is but one danger — that this horrible stigma shall be left upon my cheek!" cried Georgiana. "Remove it, remove it, whatever be the cost, or we shall both go mad!"

"Heaven knows your words are too true," said Aylmer, sadly. "And 70 now, dearest, return to your boudoir. In a little while all will be tested."

He conducted her back and took leave of her with a solemn tenderness which spoke far more than his words how much was now at stake. After his departure Georgiana became rapt in musings. She considered the character of Aylmer, and did it completer justice than at any previous moment. Her heart exulted, while it trembled, at his honorable love — so pure and lofty that it would accept nothing less than perfection nor miserably make itself contented with an earthlier nature than he had dreamed of. She felt how much more precious was such a sentiment than that meaner kind which would have borne with the imperfection for her sake, and have been guilty of treason to holy love by degrading its perfect idea to the level of the actual; and with her whole spirit she prayed that, for a single moment, she might satisfy his highest and deepest conception. Longer than one moment she well knew it could not be; for his spirit was ever on the march, ever ascending, and each instant required something that was beyond the scope of the instant before.

The sound of her husband's footsteps aroused her. He bore a crystal goblet containing a liquor colorless as water, but bright enough to be the draught of immortality. Aylmer was pale; but it seemed rather the consequence of a highly-wrought state of mind and tension of spirit than of fear or doubt.

"The concoction of the draught has been perfect," said he, in answer to Georgiana's look. "Unless all my science have deceived me, it cannot fail."

"Save on your account, my dearest Aylmer," observed his wife, "I might wish to put off this birthmark of mortality by relinquishing mortality itself in preference to any other mode. Life is but a sad possession to those who have attained precisely the degree of moral advancement at which I stand. Were I weaker and blinder it might be happiness. Were I stronger, it might be endured hopefully. But, being what I find myself, methinks I am of all mortals the most fit to die."

"You are fit for heaven without tasting death!" replied her husband. "But 75 why do we speak of dying? The draught cannot fail. Behold its effect upon this plant."

On the window seat there stood a geranium diseased with yellow blotches, which had overspread all its leaves. Aylmer poured a small quantity of the liquid upon the soil in which it grew. In a little time, when the roots of the plant had taken up the moisture, the unsightly blotches began to be extinguished in a living verdure.

"There needed no proof," said Georgiana, quietly. "Give me the goblet, I joyfully stake all upon your word."

"Drink, then, thou lofty creature!" exclaimed Aylmer, with fervid admiration. "There is no taint of imperfection on thy spirit. Thy sensible frame, too, shall soon be all perfect."

She quaffed the liquid and returned the goblet to his hand.

"It is grateful," said she with a placid smile. "Methinks it is like water 80 from a heavenly fountain; for it contains I know not what of unobtrusive fragrance and deliciousness. It allays a feverish thirst that had parched me for many days. Now, dearest, let me sleep. My earthly senses are closing over my spirit like the leaves around the heart of a rose at sunset."

She spoke the last words with a gentle reluctance, as if it required almost more energy than she could command to pronounce the faint and lingering syllables. Scarcely had they loitered through her lips ere she was lost in slumber. Aylmer sat by her side, watching her aspect with the emotions proper to a man the whole value of whose existence was involved in the process now to be tested. Mingled with this mood, however, was the philosophic investigation characteristic of the man of science. Not the minutest symptom escaped him. A heightened flush of the cheek, a slight irregularity of breath, a quiver of the eyelid, a hardly perceptible tremor through the frame — such were the details which, as the moments passed, he wrote down in his folio volume. Intense thought had set its stamp upon every previous page of that volume, but the thoughts of years were all concentrated upon the last.

While thus employed, he failed not to gaze often at the fatal hand, and not without a shudder. Yet once, by a strange and unaccountable impulse, he pressed it with his lips. His spirit recoiled, however, in the very act; and

Georgiana, out of the midst of her deep sleep, moved uneasily and murmured as if in remonstrance. Again Aylmer resumed his watch. Nor was it without avail. The crimson hand, which at first had been strongly visible upon the marble paleness of Georgiana's cheek, now grew more faintly outlined. She remained not less pale than ever; but the birthmark, with every breath that came and went, lost somewhat of its former distinctness. Its presence had been awful; its departure was more awful still. Watch the stain of the rainbow fading out the sky, and you will know how that mysterious symbol passed away.

"By Heaven! it is well-nigh gone!" said Aylmer to himself, in almost irrepressible ecstasy. "I can scarcely trace it now. Success! success! And now it is like the faintest rose color. The lightest flush of blood across her cheek would overcome it. But she is so pale!"

He drew aside the window curtain and suffered the light of natural day to fall into the room and rest upon her cheek. At the same time he heard a gross, hoarse chuckle, which he had long known as his servant Aminadab's expression of delight.

"Ah, clod! ah, earthly mass!" cried Aylmer, laughing in a sort of frenzy, 85 "you have served me well! Matter and spirit — earth and heaven — have both done their part in this! Laugh, thing of the senses! You have earned the right to laugh."

These exclamations broke Georgiana's sleep. She slowly unclosed her eyes and gazed into the mirror which her husband had arranged for that purpose. A faint smile flitted over her lips when she recognized how barely perceptible was now that crimson hand which had once blazed forth with such disastrous brilliancy as to scare away all their happiness. But then her eyes sought Aylmer's face with a trouble and anxiety that he could by no means account for.

"My poor Aylmer!" murmured she.

"Poor? Nay, richest, happiest, most favored!" exclaimed he. "My peerless bride, it is successful! You are perfect!"

"My poor Aylmer," she repeated, with a more than human tenderness, "you have aimed loftily; you have done nobly. Do not repent that with so high and pure a feeling, you have rejected the best the earth could offer. Aylmer, dearest Aylmer, I am dying!"

Alas! it was too true! The fatal hand had grappled with the mystery of 90 life, and was the bond by which an angelic spirit kept itself in union with a mortal frame. As the last crimson tint of the birthmark — that sole token of human imperfection — faded from her cheek, the parting breath of the now perfect woman passed into the atmosphere, and her soul, lingering a moment near her husband, took its heavenward flight. Then a hoarse, chuckling laugh was heard again! Thus ever does the gross fatality of earth exult in its invariable triumph over the immortal essence which, in this dim sphere of half development, demands the completeness of a higher state. Yet, had Aylmer reached a profounder wisdom, he need not thus have flung away the happiness which would have woven his mortal life of the selfsame texture with the celestial. The momentary circumstance was too strong for him; he failed to look beyond the shadowy scope of time, and, living once for all in eternity, to find the perfect future in the present.

Virginia Woolf

A Haunted House   1921

Virginia Woolf (1882 – 1941), born in London, was educated mostly at home, where she read widely and deeply in the large personal library of her father, Sir Leslie Stephen, a prominent critic and editor. In 1904 she moved to London's Bloomsbury district, taking a dominant place in the Bloomsbury Group, a lively circle of young highbrows including biographer Lytton Strachey and economist John Maynard Keynes. With her husband Leonard Woolf, she established the influential Hogarth Press, publishing her own novels, the stories of her friend Katherine Mansfield, and the first English translations of Sigmund Freud's works. Woolf's fiction displays her keen interest in psychology. Mrs. Dalloway *(1920) reveals the minds of its characters as flowing streams of consciousness;* To the Lighthouse *(1927) abounds in dream symbols, sexual and otherwise. During World War II, saddened by bombing raids and by her long struggle with recurrent mental illness, Woolf took her life. A brilliant critic and essayist, she has seemed a writer of heightened importance to recent feminists, who especially admire* A Room of One's Own *(1929) and* Three Guineas *(1938).*

Whatever hour you woke there was a door shutting. From room to room they went, hand in hand, lifting here, opening there, making sure — a ghostly couple.

"Here we left it," she said. And he added, "Oh, but here too!" "It's upstairs," she murmured. "And in the garden," he whispered. "Quietly," they said, "or we shall wake them."

But it wasn't that you woke us. Oh, no. "They're looking for it; they're drawing the curtain," one might say, and so read on a page or two. "Now they've found it," one would be certain, stopping the pencil on the margin. And then, tired of reading, one might rise and see for oneself, the house all empty, the doors standing open, only the wood pigeons bubbling with content and the hum of the threshing machine sounding from the farm. "What did I come in here for? What did I want to find?" My hands were empty. "Perhaps it's upstairs then?" The apples were in the loft. And so down again, the garden still as ever, only the book had slipped into the grass.

But they had found it in the drawing-room. Not that one could ever see them. The window panes reflected apples, reflected roses; all the leaves were green in the glass. If they moved in the drawing-room, the apple only turned its yellow side. Yet, the moment after, if the door was opened, spread about the floor, hung upon the walls, pendant from the ceiling — what? My hands were empty. The shadow of a thrush crossed the carpet; from the deepest wells of silence the wood pigeon drew its bubble of sound. "Safe, safe, safe," the pulse of the house beat softly. "The treasure buried; the room . . ." the pulse stopped short. Oh, was that the buried treasure?

A moment later the light had faded. Out in the garden then? But the trees   5
spun darkness for a wandering beam of sun. So fine, so rare, coolly sunk

beneath the surface the beam I sought always burnt behind the glass. Death was the glass; death was between us; coming to the woman first, hundreds of years ago, leaving the house, sealing all the windows; the rooms were darkened. He left it, left her, went North, went East, saw the stars turned in the Southern sky; sought the house, found it dropped beneath the Downs. "Safe, safe, safe," the pulse of the house beat gladly. "The Treasure yours."

The wind roars up the avenue. Trees stoop and bend this way and that. Moonbeams splash and spill wildly in the rain. But the beam of the lamp falls straight from the window. The candle burns stiff and still. Wandering through the house, opening the windows, whispering not to wake us, the ghostly couple seek their joy.

"Here we slept," she says. And he adds, "Kisses without number." "Waking in the morning — " "Silver between the trees — " "Upstairs — " "In the garden — " "When summer came — " "In winter snowtime — " The doors go shutting far in the distance, gently knocking like the pulse of a heart.

Nearer they come; cease at the doorway. The wind falls, the rain slides silver down the glass. Our eyes darken; we hear no steps beside us; we see no lady spread her ghostly cloak. His hands shield the lantern. "Look," he breathes. "Sound asleep. Love upon their lips."

Stooping, holding their silver lamp above us, long they look and deeply. Long they pause. The wind drives straightly; the flame stoops slightly. Wild beams of moonlight cross both floor and wall, and, meeting, stain the faces bent; the faces pondering; the faces that search the sleepers and seek their hidden joy.

"Safe, safe, safe," the heart of the house beats proudly. "Long   10 years — " he sighs. "Again you found me." "Here," she murmurs, "sleeping; in the garden reading; laughing, rolling apples in the loft. Here we left our treasure — " Stooping, their light lifts the lids upon my eyes. "Safe! safe! safe!" the pulse of the house beats wildly. Waking, I cry "Oh, is this *your* buried treasure? The light in the heart."

Katherine Mansfield

THE GARDEN-PARTY   1922

Katherine Mansfield Beauchamp (1888 – 1923), who shortened her byline, was born into a sedate Victorian family in New Zealand, daughter of a successful businessman. At fifteen she emigrated to England to attend school and did not ever permanently return Down Under. In 1918, after a time of wild-oat sowing in bohemian London, she married the journalist and critic John Middleton Murray. All at once, Mansfield found herself struggling to define her sexual identity, to earn a living by her pen, to endure World War I (in which her brother was killed in action), and to survive the ravages of tuberculosis. She died at thirty-four, in France, at a spiritualist commune where she had sought to regain her health. Mansfield wrote no novels, but during her brief career concentrated on the short story, in which form of art she has few peers. Bliss *(1920) and* The Garden-Party and Other

Stories (1922) were greeted with an acclaim that has continued; her Short Stories were collected in 1937. Some celebrate life, others wryly poke fun at it. Many reveal, in ordinary lives, small incidents that open like doorways into significances.

And after all the weather was ideal. They could not have had a more perfect day for a garden-party if they had ordered it. Windless, warm, the sky without a cloud. Only the blue was veiled with a haze of light gold, as it is sometimes in early summer. The gardener had been up since dawn, mowing the lawns and sweeping them, until the grass and the dark flat rosettes where the daisy plants had been seemed to shine. As for the roses, you could not help feeling they understood that roses are the only flowers that impress people at garden-parties; the only flowers that everybody is certain of knowing. Hundreds, yes, literally hundreds, had come out in a single night; the green bushes bowed down as though they had been visited by archangels.

Breakfast was not yet over before the men came to put up the marquee°.

"Where do you want the marquee put, mother?"

"My dear child, it's no use asking me. I'm determined to leave everything to you children this year. Forget I am your mother. Treat me as an honored guest."

But Meg could not possibly go and supervise the men. She had washed her hair before breakfast, and she sat drinking her coffee in a green turban, with a dark wet curl stamped on each cheek. Jose, the butterfly, always came down in a silk petticoat and a kimono jacket.

"You'll have to go, Laura; you're the artistic one."

Away Laura flew, still holding her piece of bread-and-butter. It's so delicious to have an excuse for eating out of doors, and besides, she loved having to arrange things; she always felt she could do it so much better than anybody else.

Four men in their shirt-sleeves stood grouped together on the garden path. They carried staves covered with rolls of canvas, and they had big tool-bats slung on their backs. They looked impressive. Laura wished now that she had not got the bread-and-butter, but there was nowhere to put it, and she couldn't possibly throw it away. She blushed and tried to look severe and even a little bit short-sighted as she came up to them.

"Good morning," she said, copying her mother's voice. But that sounded so fearfully affected that she was ashamed, and stammered like a little girl, "Oh — er — have you come — is it about the marquee?"

"That's right, miss," said the tallest of the men, a lanky, freckled fellow, and he shifted his tool-bag, knocked back his straw hat and smiled down at her. "That's about it." 10

His smile was so easy, so friendly that Laura recovered. What nice eyes he had, small, but such a dark blue! And now she looked at the others, they were smiling too. "Cheer up, we won't bite," their smile seemed to say. How

marquee: a large, showy tent or canopy supported by poles, to be set up for the party.

very nice workmen were! And what a beautiful morning! She mustn't mention the morning; she must be businesslike. The marquee.

"Well, what about the lily-lawn? Would that do?"

And she pointed to the lily-lawn with the hand that didn't hold the bread-and-butter. They turned, they stared in the direction. A little fat chap thrust out his under-lip, and the tall fellow frowned.

"I don't fancy it," said he. "Not conspicuous enough. You see, with a thing like a marquee," and he turned to Laura in his easy way, "you want to put it somewhere where it'll give you a bang slap in the eye, if you follow me."

Laura's upbringing made her wonder for a moment whether it was quite respectful of a workman to talk to her of bangs slap in the eye. But she did quite follow him.

"A corner of the tennis-court," she suggested. "But the band's going to be in one corner."

"H'm, going to have a band, are you?" said another of the workmen. He was pale. He had a haggard look as his dark eyes scanned the tennis-court. What was he thinking?

"Only a very small band," said Laura gently. Perhaps he wouldn't mind so much if the band was quite small. But the tall fellow interrupted.

"Look here, miss, that's the place. Against those trees. Over there. That'll do fine."

Against the karakas. Then the karaka-trees would be hidden. And they were so lovely, with their broad, gleaming leaves, and their clusters of yellow fruit. They were like trees you imagined growing on a desert island, proud, solitary, lifting their leaves and fruits to the sun in a kind of silent splendor. Must they be hidden by a marquee?

They must. Already the men had shouldered their staves and were making for the place. Only the tall fellow was left. He bent down, pinched a sprig of lavender, put his thumb and forefinger to his nose and snuffed up the smell. When Laura saw that gesture she forgot all about the karakas in her wonder at him caring for things like that — caring for the smell of lavender. How many men that she knew would have done such a thing? Oh, how extraordinarily nice workmen were, she thought. Why couldn't she have workmen for friends rather than the silly boys she danced with and who came to Sunday night supper? She would get on much better with men like these.

It's all the fault, she decided, as the tall fellow drew something on the back of an envelope, something that was to be looped up or left to hang, of these absurd class distinctions. Well, for her part, she didn't feel them. Not a bit, not an atom. . . . And now there came the chock-chock of wooden hammers. Some one whistled, some one sang out, "Are you right there, matey?" "Matey!" The friendliness of it, the — the — Just to prove how happy she was, just to show the tall fellow how at home she felt, and how she despised stupid conventions, Laura took a big bite of her bread-and-butter as she stared at the little drawing. She felt just like a work-girl.

"Laura, Laura, where are you? Telephone, Laura!" a voice cried from the house.

"Coming!" Away she skimmed, over the lawn, up the path, up the steps, across the veranda, and into the porch. In the hall her father and Laurie were brushing their hats ready to go to the office.

"I say, Laura," said Laurie very fast, "you might just give a squiz at my coat before this afternoon. See if it wants pressing." 25

"I will," said she. Suddenly she couldn't stop herself. She ran at Laurie and gave him a small, quick squeeze. "Oh, I do love parties, don't you?" gasped Laura.

"Ra-ther," said Laurie's warm, boyish voice, and he squeezed his sister too, and gave her a gentle push. "Dash off to the telephone, old girl."

The telephone. "Yes, yes; oh yes. Kitty? Good morning, dear. Come to lunch? Do, dear. Delighted of course. It will only be a very scratch meal — just the sandwich crusts and broken meringue-shells and what's left over. Yes, isn't it a perfect morning? Your white? Oh, I certainly should. One moment — hold the line. Mother's calling." And Laura sat back. "What, mother? Can't hear."

Mrs. Sheridan's voice floated down the stairs. "Tell her to wear that sweet hat she had on last Sunday."

"Mother says you're to wear that *sweet* hat you had on last Sunday. Good. 30 One o'clock. Bye-bye."

Laura put back the receiver, flung her arms over her head, took a deep breath, stretched and let them fall. "Huh," she sighed, and the moment after the sigh she sat up quickly. She was still, listening. All the doors in the house seemed to be open. The house was alive with soft, quick steps and running voices. The green baize door that led to the kitchen regions swung open and shut with a muffled thud. And now there came a long, chuckling absurd sound. It was the heavy piano being moved on its stiff castors. But the air! If you stopped to notice, was the air always like this? Little faint winds were playing chase, in at the tops of the windows, out at the doors. And there were two tiny spots of sun, one on the inkpot, one on a silver photograph frame, playing too. Darling little spots. Especially the one on the inkpot lid. It was quite warm. A warm little silver star. She could have kissed it.

The front door bell pealed, and there sounded the rustle of Sadie's print skirt on the stairs. A man's voice murmured; Sadie answered, careless, "I'm sure I don't know. Wait. I'll ask Mrs. Sheridan."

"What is it, Sadie?" Laura came into the hall.

"It's the florist, Miss Laura."

It was, indeed. There, just inside the door, stood a wide, shallow tray full 35 of pots of pink lilies. No other kind. Nothing but lilies — canna lilies, big pink flowers, wide open, radiant, almost frighteningly alive on bright crimson stems.

"O-oh, Sadie!" said Laura, and the sound was like a little moan. She crouched down as if to warm herself at that blaze of lilies; she felt they were in her fingers, on her lips, growing in her breast.

"It's some mistake," she said faintly. "Nobody ever ordered so many. Sadie, go and find mother."

But at that moment Mrs. Sheridan joined them.

"It's quite right," she said calmly. "Yes, I ordered them. Aren't they lovely?" She pressed Laura's arm. "I was passing the shop yesterday, and I saw them in the window. And I suddenly thought for once in my life I shall have enough canna lilies. The garden-party will be a good excuse."

"But I thought you said you didn't mean to interfere," said Laura. Sadie had gone. The florist's man was still outside at his van. She put her arm round her mother's neck and gently, very gently, she bit her mother's ear.

"My darling child, you wouldn't like a logical mother, would you? Don't do that. Here's the man."

He carried more lilies still, another whole tray.

"Bank them up, just inside the door, on both sides of the porch, please," said Mrs. Sheridan. "Don't you agree, Laura?"

"Oh, I *do*, mother."

In the drawing-room Meg, Jose and good little Hans had at last succeeded in moving the piano.

"Now, if we put this chesterfield against the wall and move everything out of the room except the chairs, don't you think?"

"Quite."

"Hans, move these tables into the smoking-room, and bring a sweeper to take these marks off the carpet and — one moment, Hans — " Jose loved giving orders to the servants, and they loved obeying her. She always made them feel they were taking part in some drama. "Tell mother and Miss Laura to come here at once."

"Very good, Miss Jose."

She turned to Meg. "I want to hear what the piano sounds like, just in case I'm asked to sing this afternoon. Let's try over 'This Life is Weary.' "

Pom! Ta-ta-ta *Tee-*ta! The piano burst out so passionately that Jose's face changed. She clasped her hands. She looked mournfully and enigmatically at her mother and Laura as they came in.

This Life is *Wee-*ary,
A Tear — a Sigh.
A Love that *Chan-*ges,
   This Life is *Wee-*ary,
A Tear — a Sigh.
A Love that *Chan-*ges,
And then . . . Goodbye!

But at the word "Goodbye," and although the piano sounded more desperate than ever, her face broke into a brilliant, dreadfully unsympathetic smile.

"Aren't I in good voice, mummy?" she beamed.

This Life is *Wee-*ary,
Hope comes to Die.
A Dream — a *Wa-*kening.

But now Sadie interrupted them. "What is it, Sadie?"

"If you please, m'm, cook says have you got the flags for the sand-wiches?"

"The flags for the sandwiches, Sadie?" echoed Mrs. Sheridan dreamily. And the children knew by her face that she hadn't got them. "Let me see." And she said to Sadie firmly, "Tell cook I'll let her have them in ten minutes."

Sadie went.

"Now, Laura," said her mother quickly. "Come with me into the smoking-room. I've got the names somewhere on the back of an envelope. You'll have to write them out for me. Meg, go upstairs this minute and take that wet thing off your head. Jose, run and finish dressing this instant. Do you hear me, children, or shall I have to tell your father when he comes home to-night? And — and, Jose, pacify cook if you do go into the kitchen, will you? I'm terrified of her this morning."

The envelope was found at last behind the dining-room clock, though how it had got there Mrs. Sheridan could not imagine.

"One of you children must have stolen it out of my bag, because I remember vividly — cream cheese and lemon-curd. Have you done that?" 60

"Yes."

"Egg and —" Mrs. Sheridan held the envelope away from her. "It looks like mice. It can't be mice, can it?"

"Olive, pet," said Laura, looking over her shoulder.

"Yes, of course, olive. What a horrible combination it sounds. Egg and olive."

They were finished at last, and Laura took them off to the kitchen. She 65 found Jose there pacifying the cook, who did not look at all terrifying.

"I have never seen such exquisite sandwiches," said Jose's rapturous voice. "How many kinds did you say there were, cook? Fifteen?"

"Fifteen, Miss Jose."

"Well, cook, I congratulate you."

Cook swept up crusts with the long sandwich knife, and smiled broadly.

"Godber's has come," announced Sadie, issuing out of the pantry. She 70 had seen the man pass the window.

That meant the cream puffs had come. Godber's were famous for their cream puffs. Nobody ever thought of making them at home.

"Bring them in and put them on the table, my girl," ordered cook.

Sadie brought them in and went back to the door. Of course Laura and Jose were far too grown-up to really care about such things. All the same, they couldn't help agreeing that the puffs looked very attractive. Very. Cook began arranging them, shaking off the extra icing sugar.

"Don't they carry one back to all one's parties?" said Laura.

"I suppose they do," said practical Jose, who never liked to be carried 75 back. "They look beautifully light and feathery, I must say."

"Have one each, my dears," said cook in her comfortable voice. "Yer ma won't know."

Oh, impossible. Fancy cream puffs so soon after breakfast. The very idea made one shudder. All the same, two minutes later Jose and Laura were licking their fingers with that absorbed inward look that only comes from whipped cream.

"Let's go into the garden, out by the back way," suggested Laura. "I want to see how the men are getting on with the marquee. They're such awfully nice men."

But the back door was blocked by cook, Sadie, Godber's man and Hans. Something had happened. 80

"Tuk-tuk-tuk," clucked cook like an agitated hen. Sadie had her hand clapped to her cheek as though she had toothache. Hans's face was screwed up in the effort to understand. Only Godber's man seemed to be enjoying himself; it was his story.

"What's the matter? What's happened?"

"There's been a horrible accident," said Cook. "A man killed."

"A man killed! Where? How? When?"

But Godber's man wasn't going to have his story snatched from under his very nose.

"Know those little cottages just below here, miss?" Know them? Of course, she knew them. "Well, there's a young chap living there, name of Scott, a carter. His horse shied at a traction-engine, corner of Hawke Street this morning, and he was thrown out on the back of his head. Killed."

"Dead!" Laura stared at Godber's man.

"Dead when they picked him up," said Godber's man with relish. "They were taking the body home as I come up here." And he said to the cook, "He's left a wife and five little ones."

"Jose, come here." Laura caught hold of her sister's sleeve and dragged her through the kitchen to the other side of the green baize door. There she paused and leaned against it. "Jose!" she said, horrified, "however are we going to stop everything?"

"Stop everything, Laura!" cried Jose in astonishment. "What do you mean?"

"Stop the garden-party, of course." Why did Jose pretend?

But Jose was still more amazed. "Stop the garden-party? My dear Laura, don't be so absurd. Of course we can't do anything of the kind. Nobody expects us to. Don't be so extravagant."

"But we can't possibly have a garden-party with a man dead just outside the front gate."

That really was extravagant, for the little cottages were in a lane to themselves at the very bottom of a steep rise that led up to the house. A broad road ran between. True, they were far too near. They were the greatest possible eyesore, and they had no right to be in that neighborhood at all. They were little mean dwellings painted a chocolate brown. In the garden patches there was nothing but cabbage stalks, sick hens and tomato cans. The very smoke coming out of their chimneys was poverty-stricken. Little rags and shreds of smoke, so unlike the great silvery plumes that uncurled from the Sheridans' chimneys. Washerwomen lived in the lane and sweeps and a cobbler, and a man whose house-front was studded all over with minute bird-cages. Children swarmed. When the Sheridans were little they were forbidden to set foot there because of the revolting language and of what they might catch. But since they were grown up, Laura and Laurie on their prowls sometimes walked through. It was disgusting and sordid. They came out with a shudder. But still one must go everywhere; one must see everything. So through they went.

"And just think of what the band would sound like to that poor woman," said Laura.

"Oh, Laura!" Jose began to be seriously annoyed. "If you're going to stop a band playing every time some one has an accident, you'll lead a very strenuous life. I'm every bit as sorry about it as you. I feel just as sympathetic." Her eyes hardened. She looked at her sister just as she used to when they were little and fighting together. "You won't bring a drunken workman back to life by being sentimental," she said softly.

"Drunk! Who said he was drunk?" Laura turned furiously on Jose. She said, just as they had used to say on those occasions, "I'm going straight up to tell mother."

"Do, dear," cooed Jose.

"Mother, can I come into your room?" Laura turned the big glass door-knob.

"Of course, child. Why, what's the matter? What's given you such a color?" And Mrs. Sheridan turned round from her dressing-table. She was trying on a new hat. 100

"Mother, a man's been killed," began Laura.

"*Not* in the garden?" interrupted her mother.

"No, no!"

"Oh, what a fright you gave me!" Mrs. Sheridan sighed with relief, and took off the big hat and held it on her knees.

"But listen, mother," said Laura. Breathless, half-choking, she told the dreadful story. "Of course, we can't have our party, can we?" she pleaded. "The band and everybody arriving. They'd hear us, mother; they're nearly neighbors!" 105

To Laura's astonishment her mother behaved just like Jose; it was harder to bear because she seemed amused. She refused to take Laura seriously.

"But, my dear child, use your common sense. It's only by accident we've heard of it. If some one had died there normally — and I can't understand how they keep alive in those poky little holes — we should still be having our party, shouldn't we?"

Laura had to say "yes" to that, but she felt it was all wrong. She sat down on her mother's sofa and pinched the cushion frill.

"Mother, isn't it really terribly heartless of us?" she asked.

"Darling!" Mrs. Sheridan got up and came over to her, carrying the hat. Before Laura could stop her she had popped it on. "My child!" said her mother, "the hat is yours. It's made for you. It's much too young for me. I have never seen you look such a picture. Look at yourself!" And she held up her hand-mirror. 110

"But, mother," Laura began again. She couldn't look at herself; she turned aside.

This time Mrs. Sheridan lost patience just as Jose had done.

"You are being very absurd, Laura," she said coldly. "People like that don't expect sacrifices from us. And it's not very sympathetic to spoil every-body's enjoyment as you're doing now."

"I don't understand," said Laura, and she walked quickly out of the room into her own bedroom. There, quite by chance, the first thing she saw was this charming girl in the mirror, in her black hat trimmed with gold daisies, and a long black velvet ribbon. Never had she imagined she could look like that. Is mother right? she thought. And now she hoped her mother was right. Am I being extravagant? Perhaps it was extravagant. Just for a moment she had another glimpse of that poor woman and those little children, and the body being carried into the house. But it all seemed blurred, unreal, like a picture in the newspaper. I'll remember it again after the party's over, she decided. And somehow that seemed quite the best plan. . . .

Lunch was over by half-past one. By half-past two they were all ready for the fray. The green-coated band had arrived and was established in a corner of the tennis-court.

"My dear!" trilled Kitty Maitland, "aren't they too like frogs for words? You ought to have arranged them round the pond with the conductor in the middle on a leaf."

Laurie arrived and hailed them on his way to dress. At the sight of him Laura remembered the accident again. She wanted to tell him. If Laurie agreed with the others, then it was bound to be all right. And she followed him into the hall.

"Laurie!"

"Hallo!" He was half-way upstairs, but when he turned round and saw Laura he suddenly puffed out his cheeks and goggled his eyes at her. "My word, Laura! You do look stunning," said Laurie, "What an absolutely topping hat!"

Laura said faintly "Is it?" and smiled up at Laurie, and didn't tell him
after all.

Soon after that people began coming in streams. The band struck up; the hired waiters ran from the house to the marquee. Wherever you looked there were couples strolling, bending to the flowers, greeting, moving on over the lawn. They were like bright birds that had alighted in the Sheridans' garden for this one afternoon, on their way to — where? Ah, what happiness it is to be with people who all are happy, to press hands, press cheeks, smile into eyes.

"Darling Laura, how well you look!"

"What a becoming hat, child!"

"Laura, you look quite Spanish. I've never seen you look so striking."

And Laura, glowing, answered softly, "Have you had tea? Won't you
have an ice? The passion-fruit ices really are rather special." She ran to her father and begged him. "Daddy darling, can't the band have something to drink?"

And the perfect afternoon slowly ripened, slowly faded, slowly its petals closed.

"Never a more delightful garden-party . . ." "The greatest success . . ." "Quite the most . . ."

Laura helped her mother with the good-byes. They stood side by side in the porch till it was all over.

"All over, all over, thank heaven," said Mr. Sheridan. "Round up the others, Laura. Let's go and have some fresh coffee. I'm exhausted. Yes, it's been very successful. But oh, these parties, these parties! Why will you children insist on giving parties!" And they all of them sat down in the deserted marquee.

"Have a sandwich, daddy dear. I wrote the flag."

"Thanks." Mr. Sheridan took a bite and the sandwich was gone. He took another. "I suppose you didn't hear of a beastly accident that happened to-day?" he said.

"My dear," said Mrs. Sheridan, holding up her hand, "we did. It nearly ruined the party. Laura insisted we should put it off."

"Oh, mother!" Laura didn't want to be teased about it.

"It was a horrible affair all the same," said Mr. Sheridan. "The chap was married too. Lived just below in the lane, and leaves a wife and half a dozen kiddies, so they say."

An awkward little silence fell. Mrs. Sheridan fidgeted with her cup. 135 Really, it was very tactless of father . . .

Suddenly she looked up. There on the table were all those sandwiches, cakes, puffs, all uneaten, all going to be wasted. She had one of her brilliant ideas.

"I know," she said. "Let's make up a basket. Let's send that poor creature some of this perfectly good food. At any rate, it will be the greatest treat for the children. Don't you agree? And she's sure to have neighbors calling in and so on. What a point to have it all ready prepared. Laura!" She jumped up. "Get me the big basket out of the stairs cupboard."

"But, mother, do you really think it's a good idea?" said Laura.

Again, how curious, she seemed to be different from them all. To take scraps from their party. Would the poor woman really like that?

"Of course! What's the matter with you today? An hour or two ago you 140 were insisting on us being sympathetic, and now — "

Oh, well! Laura ran for the basket. It was filled, it was heaped by her mother.

"Take it yourself, darling," said she. "Run down just as you are. No, wait, take the arum lilies too. People of that class are so impressed by arum lilies."

"The stems will ruin her lace frock," said practical Jose.

So they would. Just in time. "Only the basket, then. And, Laura!" — her mother followed her out of the marquee — "don't on any account — "

"What, mother?" 145

No, better not put such ideas into the child's head! "Nothing! Run along."

It was just growing dusky as Laura shut their garden gates. A big dog ran by like a shadow. The road gleamed white, and down below in the hollow the little cottages were in deep shade. How quiet it seemed after the afternoon. Here she was going down the hill to somewhere where a man lay dead, and she couldn't realize it. Why couldn't she? She stopped a minute. And it seemed to her that kisses, voices, tinkling spoons, laughter, the smell of crushed grass were somehow inside her. She had no room for anything else. How strange! She looked up at the pale sky, and all she thought was, "Yes, it was the most successful party."

Now the broad road was crossed. The lane began, smoky and dark. Women in shawls and men's tweed caps hurried by. Men hung over the palings; the children played in the doorways. A low hum came from the mean little cottages. In some of them there was a flicker of light, and a shadow, crab-like, moved across the window. Laura bent her head and hurried on. She wished now she had put on a coat. How her frock shone! And the big hat with the velvet streamer — if only it was another hat! Were the people looking at her? They must be. It was a mistake to have come; she knew all along it was a mistake. Should she go back even now?

No, too late. This was the house. It must be. A dark knot of people stood outside. Beside the gate an old, old woman with a crutch sat in a chair, watching. She had her feet on a newspaper. The voices stopped as Laura drew near. The group parted. It was as though she was expected, as though they had known she was coming here.

Laura was terribly nervous. Tossing the velvet ribbon over her shoulder, 150 she said to a woman standing by, "Is this Mrs. Scott's house?" and the woman, smiling queerly, said, "It is, my lass."

Oh, to be away from this! She actually said, "Help me, God," as she walked up the tiny path and knocked. To be away from those staring eyes, or to be covered up in anything, one of those women's shawls even. I'll just leave the basket and go, she decided. I shan't even wait for it to be emptied.

Then the door opened. A little woman in black showed in the gloom.

Laura said, "Are you Mrs. Scott?" But to her horror the woman answered, "Walk in please, miss," and she was shut in the passage.

"No," said Laura, "I don't want to come in. I only want to leave this basket. Mother sent — "

The little woman in the gloomy passage seemed not to have heard her. 155 "Step this way, please, miss," she said in an oily voice, and Laura followed her.

She found herself in a wretched little low kitchen, lighted by a smoky lamp. There was a woman sitting before the fire.

"Em," said the little creature who had let her in. "Em! It's a young lady." She turned to Laura. She said meaningly, "I'm 'er sister, Miss. You'll excuse 'er, won't you?"

"Oh, but of course!" said Laura. "Please, please don't disturb her. I — I only want to leave — "

But at that moment the woman at the fire turned round. Her face, puffed up, red, with swollen eyes and swollen lips, looked terrible. She seemed as though she couldn't understand why Laura was there. What did it mean? Why was this stranger standing in the kitchen with a basket? What was it all about? And the poor face puckered up again.

"All right, my dear," said the other. "I'll thank the young lady." 160

And again she began, "You'll excuse her, miss, I'm sure," and her face, swollen too, tried an oily smile.

Laura only wanted to get out, to get away. She was back in the passage. The door opened. She walked straight through into the bedroom, where the dead man was lying.

"You'd like a look at 'im, wouldn't you?" said Em's sister, and she brushed past Laura over to the bed. "Don't be afraid, my lass — " and now her voice sounded fond and sly, and fondly she drew down the sheet — " 'e looks a picture. There's nothing to show. Come along, my dear."

Laura came.

There lay a young man, fast asleep — sleeping so soundly, so deeply, 165 that he was far, far away from them both. Oh, so remote, so peaceful. He was dreaming. Never wake him up again. His head was sunk in the pillow, his eyes were closed; they were blind under the closed eyelids. He was given up to his dream. What did garden-parties and baskets and lace frocks matter to him? He was far from all those things. He was wonderful, beautiful. While they were laughing and while the band was playing, this marvel had come to the lane. Happy . . . happy. . . . All is well, said that sleeping face. This is just as it should be. I am content.

But all the same you had to cry, and she couldn't go out of the room without saying something to him. Laura gave a loud childish sob.

"Forgive my hat," she said.

And this time she didn't wait for Em's sister. She found her way out of the door, down the path, past all those dark people. At the corner of the lane she met Laurie.

He stepped out of the shadow. "Is that you, Laura?"

"Yes."

"Mother was getting anxious. Was it all right?"

"Yes, quite. Oh, Laurie!" She took his arm, she pressed up against him.

"I say, you're not crying, are you?" asked her brother.

Laura shook her head. She was.

Laurie put his arm round her shoulder. "Don't cry," he said in his warm, loving voice. "Was it awful?"

"No," sobbed Laura. "It was simply marvelous. But, Laurie — " She stopped, she looked at her brother. "Isn't life," she stammered, "isn't life — " But what life was she couldn't explain. No matter. He quite understood.

"Isn't it, darling?" said Laurie.

Franz Kafka

A Hunger Artist   1924

Translated by Willa and Edwin Muir

Franz Kafka (1883 – 1924) was born into a German-speaking Jewish family in Prague, Czechoslovakia (then part of Austria). After taking a doctor's degree in law, he settled into the routine of a government claims investigator. By night when he couldn't sleep he toiled on stories. Kafka's work is rich in macabre humor and unforgettable nightmares: the long story The Metamorphosis *(1915), for instance, begins with the great line, "As Gregor Samsa awoke one morning from uneasy dreams he found himself transformed in his bed into a gigantic insect." Kafka was a writer of such impeccably high standards that he could bring himself to publish little in his lifetime; he never finished his major novels* The Trial *and* The Castle. *Both depict huge, remote, bumbling, irresponsible bureaucracies in whose power an individual feels helplessly isolated. Before he died, Kafka left his friend Max Brod orders to burn his incomplete manuscripts; Brod pondered, but didn't obey. Kafka, who succumbed to tuberculosis, did not live to see his stories appear startlingly prophetic to readers looking back on them by the later light of the Holocaust. Only after World War II did his work achieve international fame.*

During these last decades the interest in professional fasting has markedly diminished. It used to pay very well to stage such great performances under one's own management, but today that is quite impossible. We live in a different world now. At one time the whole town took a lively interest in the hunger artist; from day to day of his fast the excitement mounted; every-

298   Stories for Further Reading

body wanted to see him at least once a day; there were people who bought season tickets for the last few days and sat from morning till night in front of his small barred cage; even in the nighttime there were visiting hours, when the whole effect was heightened by torch flares; on fine days the cage was set out in the open air, and then it was the children's special treat to see the hunger artist; for their elders he was often just a joke that happened to be in fashion, but the children stood open-mouthed, holding each other's hands for greater security, marveling at him as he sat there pallid in black tights, with his ribs sticking out so prominently, not even on a seat but down among straw on the ground, sometimes giving a courteous nod, answering questions with a constrained smile, or perhaps stretching an arm through the bars so that one might feel how thin it was, and then again withdrawing deep into himself, paying no attention to anyone or anything, not even to the all-important striking of the clock that was the only piece of furniture in his cage, but merely staring into vacancy with half-shut eyes, now and then taking a sip from a tiny glass of water to moisten his lips.

Besides casual onlookers there were also relays of permanent watchers selected by the public, usually butchers, strangely enough, and it was their task to watch the hunger artist day and night, three of them at a time, in case he should have some secret recourse to nourishment. This was nothing but a formality, instituted to reassure the masses, for the initiates knew well enough that during his fast the artist would never in any circumstances, not even under forcible compulsion, swallow the smallest morsel of food; the honor of his profession forbade it. Not every watcher, of course, was capable of understanding this, there were often groups of night watchers who were very lax in carrying out their duties and deliberately huddled together in a retired corner to play cards with great absorption, obviously intending to give the hunger artist the chance of a little refreshment, which they supposed he could draw from some private hoard. Nothing annoyed the artist more than such watchers; they made him miserable; they made his fast seem unendurable; sometimes he mastered his feebleness sufficiently to sing during their watch for as long as he could keep going, to show them how unjust their suspicions were. But that was of little use; they only wondered at his cleverness in being able to fill his mouth even while singing. Much more to his taste were the watchers who sat close up to the bars, who were not content with the dim night lighting of the hall but focused him in the full glare of the electric pocket torch given them by the impresario. The harsh light did not trouble him at all. In any case he could never sleep properly, and he could always drowse a little, whatever the light, at any hour, even when the hall was thronged with noisy onlookers. He was quite happy at the prospect of spending a sleepless night with such watchers; he was ready to exchange jokes with them, to tell them stories out of his nomadic life, anything at all to keep them awake and demonstrate to them again that he had no eatables in his cage and that he was fasting as not one of them could fast. But his happiest moment was when the morning came and an enormous breakfast was brought them, at his expense, on which they flung themselves with the keen appetite of healthy men after a weary night of wakefulness. Of course there were people who argued that this breakfast was an unfair attempt to bribe the watchers, but that was going rather too far, and when they were invited to take on a night's vigil without a breakfast, merely for the sake of the cause, they made themselves scarce, although they stuck stubbornly to their suspicions.

Such suspicions, anyhow, were a necessary accompaniment to the profession of fasting. No one could possibly watch the hunger artist continuously, day and night, and so no one could produce first-hand evidence that the fast had really been rigorous and continuous; only the artist himself could know that; he was therefore bound to be the sole completely satisfied spectator of his own fast. Yet for other reasons he was never satisfied; it was not perhaps mere fasting that had brought him to such skeleton thinness that many people had regretfully to keep away from his exhibitions, because the sight of him was too much for them, perhaps it was dissatisfaction with himself that had worn him down. For he alone knew, what no other initiate knew, how easy it was to fast. It was the easiest thing in the world. He made no secret of this, yet people did not believe him; at the best they set him down as modest, most of them, however, thought he was out for publicity or else was some kind of cheat who found it easy to fast because he had discovered a way of making it easy, and then had the impudence to admit the fact, more or less. He had to put up with all that, and in the course of time had got used to it, but his inner dissatisfaction always rankled, and never yet, after any term of fasting — this must be granted to his credit — had he left the cage of his own free will. The longest period of fasting was fixed by his impresario at forty days, beyond that term he was not allowed to go, not even in great cities, and there was good reason for it, too. Experience had proved that for about forty days the interest of the public could be stimulated by a steadily increasing pressure of advertisement, but after that the town began to lose interest, sympathetic support began notably to fall off; there were of course local variations as between one town and another or one country and another, but as a general rule forty days marked the limit. So on the fortieth day the flower-bedecked cage was opened, enthusiastic spectators filled the hall, a military band played, two doctors entered the cage to measure the results of the fast, which were announced through a megaphone, and finally two young ladies appeared, blissful at having been selected for the honor, to help the hunger artist down the few steps leading to a small table on which was spread a carefully chosen invalid repast. And at this very moment the artist always turned stubborn. True, he would entrust his bony arms to the outstretched helping hands of the ladies bending over him, but stand up he would not. Why stop fasting at this particular moment, after forty days of it? He had held out for a long time, an illimitably long time; why stop now, when he was in his best fasting form, or rather, not yet quite in his best fasting form? Why should he be cheated of the fame he would get for fasting longer, for being not only the record hunger artist of all time, which presumably he was already, but for beating his own record by a performance beyond human imagination, since he felt that there were no limits to his capacity for fasting? His public pretended to admire him so much, why should it have so little patience with him; if he could endure fasting longer, why shouldn't the public endure it? Besides, he was tired, he was comfortable sitting in the straw, and now he was supposed to lift himself to his full height and go down to a meal the very thought of which gave him a nausea that only the presence of the ladies kept him from betraying, and even that with an effort. And he looked up into the eyes of the ladies who were apparently so friendly and in reality so cruel, and shook his head, which felt too heavy on its strengthless neck. But then there happened yet again what always happened. The impresario came forward, without a word — for the band made speech impossible — lifted his arms in the air above the artist, as if inviting Heaven to look down upon its creature here in the straw, this suffering martyr, which indeed he was, although in quite another sense; grasped him around the emaciated waist, with exaggerated caution, so that the frail condition he was in might be appreciated; and committed him to the care of the blenching ladies, not without secretly giving him a shaking so that his legs and body tottered and swayed. The artist now submitted completely; his head rolled on his breast as if it had landed there by chance; his body was hollowed out; his legs in a spasm of self-preservation clung close to each other at the knees, yet scraped on the ground as if it were not really solid ground, as if they were only trying to find solid ground; and the whole weight of his body, a featherweight after all, relapsed onto one of the ladies, who, looking round for help and panting a little — this post of honor was not at all what she had expected it to be — first stretched her neck as far as she could to keep her face at least free from contact with the artist, then finding this impossible, and her more fortunate companion not coming to her aid but merely holding extended on her own trembling hand the little bunch of knucklebones that was the artist's, to the great delight of the spectators burst into tears and had to be replaced by an attendant who had long been stationed in readiness. Then came the food, a little of which the impresario managed to get between the artist's lips, while he sat in a kind of half-fainting trance, to the accompaniment of cheerful patter designed to distract the public's attention from the artist's condition; after that, a toast was drunk to the public, supposedly prompted by a whisper from the artist in the impresario's ear; the band confirmed it with a mighty flourish, the spectators melted away, and no one had any cause to be dissatisfied with the proceedings, no one except the hunger artist himself, he only, as always.

So he lived for many years, with small regular intervals of recuperation, in visible glory, honored by the world, yet in spite of that troubled in spirit, and all the more troubled because no one would take his trouble seriously. What comfort could he possibly need? What more could he possibly wish for? And if some good-natured person, feeling sorry for him, tried to console him by pointing out that his melancholy was probably caused by fasting, it could happen, especially when he had been fasting for some time, that he reacted with an outburst of fury and to the general alarm began to shake the bars of his cage like a wild animal. Yet the impresario had a way of punishing these outbreaks which he rather enjoyed putting into operation. He would apologize publicly for the artist's behavior, which was only to be excused, he admitted, because of the irritability caused by fasting; a condition hardly to be understood by well-fed people; then by natural transition he went on to mention the artist's equally incomprehensible boast that he could fast for much longer than he was doing; he praised the high ambition, the good will, the great self-denial undoubtedly implicit in such a statement; and then quite simply countered it by bringing out photographs, which were also on sale to the public, showing the artist on the fortieth day of a fast lying in bed almost dead from exhaustion. This perversion of the truth, familiar to the artist though it was, always unnerved him afresh and proved too much for him. What was a consequence of the premature ending of his fast was here presented as the cause of it! To fight against this lack of understanding, against a whole world of non-understanding, was impossible. Time and again in good faith he stood by the bars listening to the impresario, but as soon as the photographs appeared he always let go and sank with a groan back on to his straw, and the reassured public could once more come close and gaze at him.

A few years later when the witnesses of such scenes called them to mind, ⁵ they often failed to understand themselves at all. For meanwhile the aforementioned change in public interest had set in; it seemed to happen almost overnight; there may have been profound causes for it, but who was going to bother about that; at any rate the pampered hunger artist suddenly found himself deserted one fine day by the amusement seekers, who went streaming past him to other more favored attractions. For the last time the impresario hurried him over half Europe to discover whether the old interest might still survive here and there; all in vain; everywhere, as if by secret agreement, a positive revulsion from professional fasting was in evidence. Of course it could not really have sprung up so suddenly as all that, and many premonitory symptoms which had not been sufficiently remarked or suppressed during the rush and glitter of success now came retrospectively to mind, but it was now too late to take any countermeasures. Fasting would surely come into fashion again at some future date, yet that was no comfort for those living in the present. What, then, was the hunger artist to do? He had been applauded by thousands in his time and could hardly come down to showing himself in a street booth at village fairs, and as for adopting another profession, he was not only too old for that but too fanatically devoted to fasting. So he took leave of the impresario, his partner in an unparalleled career, and hired himself to a large circus; in order to spare his own feelings he avoided reading the conditions of his contract.

A large circus with its enormous traffic in replacing and recruiting men, animals and apparatus can always find a use for people at any time, even for a hunger artist, provided of course that he does not ask too much, and in this particular case anyhow it was not only the artist who was taken on but his famous and long-known name as well; indeed considering the peculiar nature of his performance, which was not impaired by advancing age, it could not be objected that here was an artist past his prime, no longer at the height of his professional skill, seeking a refuge in some quiet corner of a circus; on the contrary, the hunger artist averred that he could fast as well as ever, which was entirely credible; he even alleged that if he were allowed to fast as he liked, and this was at once promised him without more ado, he could astound the world by establishing a record never yet achieved, a statement which certainly provoked a smile among the other professionals, since it left out of account the change in public opinion, which the hunger artist in his zeal conveniently forgot.

He had not, however, actually lost his sense of the real situation and took it as a matter of course that he and his cage should be stationed, not in the middle of the ring as a main attraction, but outside, near the animal cages, on a site that was after all easily accessible. Large and gaily painted placards made a frame for the cage and announced what was to be seen inside it. When the public came thronging out in the intervals to see the animals, they could hardly avoid passing the hunger artist's cage and stopping there for a moment; perhaps they might even have stayed longer had not those pressing behind them in the narrow gangway, who did not understand why they should be held up on their way towards the excitements of the menagerie, made it impossible for anyone to stand gazing quietly for any length of time. And that was the reason why the hunger artist, who had of course been looking forward to these visiting hours as the main achievement of his life, began instead to shrink from them. At first he could hardly wait for the intervals; it was exhilarating to watch the crowds come streaming his way, until only too soon — not even the most obstinate self-deception, clung to almost consciously, could hold out against the fact — the conviction was borne in upon him that these people, most of them, to judge from their actions, again and again, without exception, were all on their way to the menagerie. And the first sight of them from the distance remained the best. For when they reached his cage he was at once deafened by the storm of shouting and abuse that arose from the two contending factions, which renewed themselves continuously, of those who wanted to stop and stare at him — he soon began to dislike them more than the others — not out of real interest but only out of obstinate self-assertiveness, and those who wanted to go straight on to the animals. When the first great rush was past, the stragglers came along, and these, whom nothing could have prevented from stopping to look at him as long as they had breath, raced past with long strides, hardly even glancing at him, in their haste to get to the menagerie in time. And all too rarely did it happen that he had a stroke of luck, when some father of a family fetched up before him with his children, pointed a finger at the hunger artist and explained at length what the phenomenon meant, telling stories of earlier years when he himself had watched similar but much more thrilling performances, and the children, still rather uncomprehending, since neither inside nor outside school had they been sufficiently prepared for this lesson — what did they care about fasting? — yet showed by the brightness of their intent eyes that new and better times might be coming. Perhaps, said the hunger artist to himself many a time, things would be a little better if his cage were set not quite so near the menagerie. That made it too easy for people to make their choice, to say nothing of what he suffered from the stench of the menagerie, the animals' restlessness by night, the carrying past of raw lumps of flesh for the beasts of prey, the roaring at feeding times, which depressed him continually. But he did not dare to lodge a complaint with the management; after all, he had the animals to thank for the troops of people who passed his cage, among whom there might always be one here and there to take an interest in him, and who could tell where they might seclude him if he called attention to his existence and thereby to the fact that, strictly speaking, he was only an impediment on the way to the menagerie.

A small impediment, to be sure, one that grew steadily less. People grew familiar with the strange idea that they could be expected, in times like these, to take an interest in a hunger artist, and with this familiarity the verdict went out against him. He might fast as much as he could, and he did so; but nothing could save him now, people passed him by. Just try to explain to anyone the art of fasting! Anyone who has no feeling for it cannot be made to understand it. The fine placards grew dirty and illegible, they were torn down; the little notice board telling the number of fast days achieved, which at first was changed carefully every day, had long stayed at the same figure, for after the first few weeks even this small task seemed pointless to the staff; and so the artist simply fasted on and on, as he had once dreamed of doing, and it was no trouble to him, just as he had always foretold, but no one counted the days, no one, not even the artist himself, knew what records he was already breaking, and his heart grew heavy. And when once in a time some leisurely passer-by stopped, made merry over the old figure on the board and spoke of swindling, that was in its way the stupidest lie ever invented by indifference and inborn malice, since it was not the hunger artist who was cheating; he was working honestly, but the world was cheating him of his reward.

Many more days went by, however, and that too came to an end. An overseer's eye fell on the cage one day and he asked the attendants why this perfectly good cage should be left standing there unused with dirty straw inside it; nobody knew, until one man, helped out by the notice board, remembered about the hunger artist. They poked into the straw with sticks and found him in it. "Are you still fasting?" asked the overseer. "When on earth do you mean to stop?" "Forgive me, everybody," whispered the hunger artist; only the overseer, who had his ear to the bars, understood him. "Of course," said the overseer, and tapped his forehead with a finger to let the attendants know what state the man was in, "we forgive you." "I always wanted you to admire my fasting," said the hunger artist. "We do admire it," said the overseer, affably. "But you shouldn't admire it," said the hunger artist. "Well, then we don't admire it," said the overseer, "but why shouldn't we admire it?" "Because I have to fast, I can't help it," said the hunger artist. "What a fellow you are," said the overseer; "and why can't you help it?" "Because," said the hunger artist, lifting his head a little and speaking, with his lips pursed, as if for a kiss, right into the overseer's ear, so that no syllable might be lost, "because I couldn't find the food I liked. If I had found it, believe me, I should have made no fuss and stuffed myself like you or anyone else." These were his last words, but in his dimming eyes remained the firm though no longer proud persuasion that he was still continuing to fast.

"Well, clear this out now!" said the overseer, and they buried the hunger 10 artist, straw and all. Into the cage they put a young panther. Even the most insensitive felt it refreshing to see this wild creature leaping around the cage that had so long been dreary. The panther was all right. The food he liked was brought him without hesitation by the attendants; he seemed not even to miss his freedom; his noble body, furnished almost to the bursting point with all that it needed, seemed to carry freedom around with it too; somewhere in his jaws it seemed to lurk; and the joy of life streamed with such ardent passion from his throat that for the onlookers it was not easy to stand the shock of it. But they braced themselves, crowded round the cage, and did not want ever to move away.

D. H. Lawrence

THE ROCKING-HORSE WINNER 1933

David Herbert Lawrence (1885 – 1930) was born in Nottinghamshire, England, child of a coalminer and a schoolteacher who hated her husband's toil and vowed that her son should escape it. He took up fiction writing, attaining early success. During World War I, Lawrence and his wife were unjustly suspected of treason (he because of his pacifism, she because of her aristocratic German birth). After the armistice they left England and, seeking a climate healthier for Lawrence, who suffered from tuberculosis, wandered in Italy, France, Australia, Mexico, and the American Southwest. Lawrence is an impassioned spokesman for our unconscious, instinctive natures, which we moderns (he argues) have neglected in favor of our overweening intellects. In Lady Chatterley's Lover *(1928), he strove to restore explicit sexuality to English fiction. The book, which today seems tame and repetitious, was long banned in Britain and the United States. Deeper Lawrence novels include* Sons and Lovers *(1913), a veiled account of his breaking away from his fiercely possessive mother;* The Rainbow *(1915);* Women in Love *(1921); and* The Plumed Serpent *(1926), about a revival of pagan religion in Mexico. Besides fiction, Lawrence left a rich legacy of poetry, essays, criticism (*Studies in Classic American Literature, *1923, is espe-cially shrewd and funny), and travel writing. Lawrence exerted deep influence on others, both by the message in his work and by his personal magnetism.*

There was a woman who was beautiful, who started with all the advantages, yet she had no luck. She married for love, and the love turned to dust. She had bonny children, yet she felt they had been thrust upon her, and she could not love them. They looked at her coldly, as if they were finding fault with her. And hurriedly she felt she must cover up some fault in herself. Yet what it was that she must cover up she never knew. Nevertheless, when her children were present, she always felt the center of her heart go hard. This troubled her, and in her manner she was all the more gentle and anxious for her children, as if she loved them very much. Only she herself knew that at the center of her heart was a hard little place that could not feel love, no, not for anybody. Everybody else said of her: "She is such a good mother. She adores her children." Only she herself, and her children themselves, knew it was not so. They read it in each other's eyes.

There were a boy and two little girls. They lived in a pleasant house, with a garden, and they had discreet servants, and felt themselves superior to anyone in the neighborhood.

Although they lived in style, they felt always an anxiety in the house. There was never enough money. The mother had a small income, and the father had a small income, but not nearly enough for the social position which they had to keep up. The father went in to town to some office. But though he had good prospects, these prospects never materialized. There was always the grinding sense of the shortage of money, though the style was always kept up.

At last the mother said: "I will see if *I* can't make something." But she did not know where to begin. She racked her brains, and tried this thing and the other, but could not find anything successful. The failure made deep lines come into her face. Her children were growing up, they would have to go to school. There must be more money, there must be more money. The father, who was always very handsome and expensive in his tastes, seemed as if he never *would* be able to do anything worth doing. And the mother, who had a great belief in herself, did not succeed any better, and her tastes were just as expensive.

And so the house came to be haunted by the unspoken phrase: *There* 5 *must be more money! There must be more money!* The children could hear it all the time, though nobody said it aloud. They heard it at Christmas, when the expensive and splendid toys filled the nursery. Behind the shining modern rocking-horse, behind the smart doll's house, a voice would start whispering: "There *must* be more money! There *must* be more money!" And the children would stop playing, to listen for a moment. They would look into each other's eyes, to see if they had all heard. And each one saw in the eyes of the other two that they too had heard. "There *must* be more money! There *must* be more money!"

It came whispering from the springs of the still-swaying rocking-horse, and even the horse, bending his wooden, champing head, heard it. The big doll, sitting so pink and smirking in her new pram, could hear it quite plainly, and seemed to be smirking all the more self-consciously because of it. The foolish puppy, too, that took the place of the teddy-bear, he was looking so extraordinarily foolish for no other reason but that he heard the secret whisper all over the house: "There *must* be more money!"

Yet nobody ever said it aloud. The whisper was everywhere, and therefore no one spoke it. Just as no one ever says: "We are breathing!" in spite of the fact that breath is coming and going all the time.

"Mother," said the boy Paul one day, "why don't we keep a car of our own? Why do we always use uncle's, or else a taxi?"

"Because we're the poor members of the family," said the mother.

"But why *are* we, mother?" 10

"Well — I suppose," she said slowly and bitterly, "it's because your father has no luck."

The boy was silent for some time.

"Is luck money, mother?" he asked rather timidly.

"No, Paul. Not quite. It's what causes you to have money."

"Oh!" said Paul vaguely. "I thought when Uncle Oscar said *filthy lucker,* 15 it meant money."

"*Filthy lucre* does mean money," said the mother. "But it's lucre, not luck."

"Oh!" said the boy. "Then what *is* luck, mother?"

"It's what causes you to have money. If you're lucky you have money. That's why it's better to be born lucky than rich. If you're rich, you may lose your money. But if you're lucky, you will always get more money."

"Oh! Will you? And is father not lucky?"

"Very unlucky, I should say," she said bitterly. 20

The boy watched her with unsure eyes.

"Why?" he asked.

"I don't know. Nobody ever knows why one person is lucky and another unlucky."

"Don't they? Nobody at all? Does *nobody* know?"

"Perhaps God. But He never tells."

"He ought to, then. And aren't you lucky either, mother?"

"I can't be, if I married an unlucky husband."

"But by yourself, aren't you?"

"I used to think I was, before I married. Now I think I am very unlucky indeed."

"Why?"

"Well — never mind! Perhaps I'm not really," she said.

The child looked at her, to see if she meant it. But he saw, by the lines of her mouth, that she was only trying to hide something from him.

"Well, anyhow," he said stoutly, "I'm a lucky person."

"Why?" said his mother, with a sudden laugh.

He stared at her. He didn't even know why he had said it.

"God told me," he asserted, brazening it out.

"I hope He did, dear!" she said, again with a laugh, but rather bitter.

"He did, mother!"

"Excellent!" said the mother, using one of her husband's exclamations.

The boy saw she did not believe him; or, rather, that she paid no attention to his assertion. This angered him somewhat, and made him want to compel her attention.

He went off by himself, vaguely, in a childish way, seeking for the clue to "luck." Absorbed, taking no heed of other people, he went about with a sort of stealth, seeking inwardly for luck. He wanted luck, he wanted it, he wanted it. When the two girls were playing dolls in the nursery, he would sit on his big rocking-horse, charging madly into space, with a frenzy that made the little girls peer at him uneasily. Wildly the horse careered, the waving dark hair of the boy tossed, his eyes had a strange glare in them. The little girls dared not speak to him.

When he had ridden to the end of his mad little journey, he climbed down and stood in front of his rocking-horse, staring fixedly into its lowered face. Its red mouth was slightly open, its big eye was wide and glassy-bright.

"Now!" he would silently command the snorting steed. "Now, take me to where there is luck! Now take me!"

And he would slash the horse on the neck with the little whip he had asked Uncle Oscar for. He *knew* the horse could take him to where there was luck, if only he forced it. So he would mount again, and start on his furious ride, hoping at last to get there. He knew he could get there.

"You'll break your horse, Paul!" said the nurse.

"He's always riding like that! I wish he'd leave off!" said his elder sister Joan.

But he only glared down on them in silence. Nurse gave him up. She could make nothing of him. Anyhow he was growing beyond her.

One day his mother and his Uncle Oscar came in when he was on one of his furious rides. He did not speak to them.

"Hallo, you young jockey! Riding a winner?" said his uncle.

"Aren't you growing too big for a rocking-horse? You're not a very little 50
boy any longer, you know," said his mother.

But Paul only gave a blue glare from his big, rather close-set eyes. He
would speak to nobody when he was in full tilt. His mother watched him with
an anxious expression on her face.

At last he suddenly stopped forcing his horse into the mechanical gallop,
and slid down.

"Well, I got there!" he announced fiercely, his blue eyes still flaring, and
his sturdy long legs straddling apart.

"Where did you get to?" asked his mother.

"Where I wanted to go," he flared back at her. 55

"That's right, son!" said Uncle Oscar. "Don't you stop till you get there.
What's the horse's name?"

"He doesn't have a name," said the boy.

"Gets on without all right?" asked the uncle.

"Well, he has different names. He was called Sansovino last week."

"Sansovino, eh? Won the Ascot. How did you know his name?" 60

"He always talks about horse-races with Bassett," said Joan.

The uncle was delighted to find that his small nephew was posted with
all the racing news. Bassett, the young gardener, who had been wounded in
the left foot in the war and had got his present job through Oscar Cresswell,
whose batman he had been, was a perfect blade of the "turf." He lived in the
racing events, and the small boy lived with him.

Oscar Cresswell got it all from Bassett.

"Master Paul comes and asks me, so I can't do more than tell him, sir,"
said Bassett, his face terribly serious, as if he were speaking of religious matters.

"And does he ever put anything on a horse he fancies?" 65

"Well — I don't want to give him away — he's a young sport, a fine
sport, sir. Would you mind asking him himself? He sort of takes a pleasure in
it, and perhaps he'd feel I was giving him away, sir, if you don't mind."

Bassett was serious as a church.

The uncle went back to his nephew and took him off for a ride in the
car.

"Say, Paul, old man, do you ever put anything on a horse?" the uncle
asked.

The boy watched the handsome man closely. 70

"Why, do you think I oughtn't to?" he parried.

"Not a bit of it. I thought perhaps you might give me a tip for the
Lincoln."

The car sped on into the country, going down to Uncle Oscar's place in
Hampshire.

"Honor bright?" said the nephew.

"Honor bright, son!" said the uncle. 75

"Well, then, Daffodil."

"Daffodil! I doubt it, sonny. What about Mirza?"

"I only know the winner," said the boy. "That's Daffodil."

"Daffodil, eh?"

There was a pause. Daffodil was an obscure horse comparatively. 80

"Uncle!"

"Yes, son?"

"You won't let it go any further, will you? I promised Bassett."

"Bassett be damned, old man! What's he got to do with it?"

"We're partners. We've been partners from the first. Uncle, he lent me my first five shillings, which I lost. I promised him, honor bright, it was only between me and him; only you gave me that ten-shilling note I started winning with, so I thought you were lucky. You won't let it go any further, will you?"

The boy gazed at his uncle from those big, hot, blue eyes, set rather close together. The uncle stirred and laughed uneasily.

"Right you are, son! I'll keep your tip private. Daffodil, eh? How much are you putting on him?"

"All except twenty pounds," said the boy. "I keep that in reserve."

The uncle thought it a good joke.

"You keep twenty pounds in reserve, do you, you young romancer? What are you betting, then?"

"I'm betting three hundred," said the boy gravely. "But it's between you and me, Uncle Oscar! Honor bright?"

The uncle burst into a roar of laughter.

"It's between you and me all right, you young Nat Gould," he said, laughing. "But where's your three hundred?"

"Bassett keeps it for me. We're partners."

"You are, are you! And what is Bassett putting on Daffodil?"

"He won't go quite as high as I do, I expect. Perhaps he'll go a hundred and fifty."

"What, pennies?" laughed the uncle.

"Pounds," said the child, with a surprised look at his uncle. "Basset keeps a bigger reserve than I do."

Between wonder and amusement Uncle Oscar was silent. He pursued the matter no further, but he determined to take his nephew with him to the Lincoln races.

"Now, son," he said, "I'm putting twenty on Mirza, and I'll put five for you on any horse you fancy. What's your pick?"

"Daffodil, uncle."

"No, not the fiver on Daffodil!"

"I should if it was my own fiver," said the child.

"Good! Good! Right you are! A fiver for me and a fiver for you on Daffodil."

The child had never been to a race-meeting before, and his eyes were blue fire. He pursed his mouth tight, and watched. A Frenchman just in front had put his money on Lancelot. Wild with excitement, he flayed his arms up and down, yelling, *"Lancelot! Lancelot!"* in his French accent.

Daffodil came in first, Lancelot second, Mirza third. The child, flushed and with eyes blazing, was curiously serene. His uncle brought him four five-pound notes, four to one.

"What am I to do with these?" he cried, waving them before the boy's eyes.

"I suppose we'll talk to Bassett," said the boy. "I expect I have fifteen hundred now; and twenty in reserve; and this twenty."

His uncle studied him for some moments.

"Look here, son!" he said. "You're not serious about Bassett and that fifteen hundred, are you?" 110

"Yes, I am. But it's between you and me, uncle. Honor bright!"

"Honor bright all right, son! But I must talk to Bassett."

"If you'd like to be a partner, uncle, with Bassett and me, we could all be partners. Only, you'd have to promise, honor bright, uncle, not to let it go beyond us three. Bassett and I are lucky, and you must be lucky, because it was your ten shillings I started winning with. . . ."

Uncle Oscar took both Bassett and Paul into Richmond Park for an afternoon, and there they talked.

"It's like this, you see, sir," Bassett said. "Master Paul would get me 115 talking about racing events, spinning yarns, you know, sir. And he was always keen on knowing if I'd made or if I'd lost. It's about a year since, now, that I put five shillings on Blush of Dawn for him — and we lost. Then the luck turned, and with that ten shillings he had from you, that we put on Singhalese. And since that time, it's been pretty steady, all things considering. What do you say, Master Paul?"

"We're all right when we're sure," said Paul. "It's when we're not quite sure that we go down."

"Oh, but we're careful then," said Bassett.

"But when are you *sure?*" smiled Uncle Oscar.

"It's Master Paul, sir," said Bassett, in a secret, religious voice. "It's as if he had it from heaven. Like Daffodil, now, for the Lincoln. That was as sure as eggs."

"Did you put anything on Daffodil?" asked Oscar Cresswell. 120

"Yes, sir. I made my bit."

"And my nephew?"

Bassett was obstinately silent, looking at Paul.

"I made twelve hundred, didn't I, Bassett? I told uncle I was putting three hundred on Daffodil."

"That's right," said Bassett, nodding. 125

"But where's the money?" asked the uncle.

"I keep it safe locked up, sir. Master Paul he can have it any minute he likes to ask for it."

"What, fifteen hundred pounds?"

"And twenty! And *forty,* that is, with the twenty he made on the course."

"It's amazing!" said the uncle. 130

"If Master Paul offers you to be partners, sir, I would, if I were you; if you'll excuse me," said Bassett.

Oscar Cresswell thought about it.

"I'll see the money," he said.

They drove home again, and sure enough, Bassett came round to the garden-house with fifteen hundred pounds in notes. The twenty pounds reserve was left with Joe Glee, in the Turf Commission deposit.

"You see, it's all right, uncle, when I'm *sure!* Then we go strong, for all 135 we're worth. Don't we, Bassett?"

"We do that, Master Paul."

"And when are you sure?" said the uncle, laughing.

"Oh, well, sometimes I'm *absolutely* sure, like about Daffodil," said the boy; "and sometimes I have an idea; and sometimes I haven't even an idea, have I, Bassett? Then we're careful, because we mostly go down."

"You do, do you! And when you're sure, like about Daffodil, what makes you sure, sonny?"

"Oh, well, I don't know," said the boy uneasily. "I'm sure, you know, uncle; that's all." 140

"It's as if he had it from heaven, sir," Bassett reiterated.

"I should say so!" said the uncle.

But he became a partner. And when the Leger was coming on, Paul was "sure" about Lively Spark, which was a quite inconsiderable horse. The boy insisted on putting a thousand on the horse, Bassett went for five hundred, and Oscar Cresswell two hundred. Lively Spark came in first, and the betting had been ten to one against him. Paul had made ten thousand.

"You see," he said, "I was absolutely sure of him."

Even Oscar Cresswell had cleared two thousand. 145

"Look here, son," he said, "this sort of thing makes me nervous."

"It needn't, uncle! Perhaps I shan't be sure again for a long time."

"But what are you going to do with your money?" asked the uncle.

"Of course," said the boy, "I started it for mother. She said she had no luck, because father is unlucky, so I thought if *I* was lucky, it might stop whispering."

"What might stop whispering?" 150

"Our house. I *hate* our house for whispering."

"What does it whisper?"

"Why — why" — the boy fidgeted — "why, I don't know. But it's always short of money, you know, uncle."

"I know it, son, I know it."

"You know people send mother writs, don't you, uncle?" 155

"I'm afraid I do," said the uncle.

"And then the house whispers, like people laughing at you behind your back. It's awful, that is! I thought if I was lucky . . ."

"You might stop it," added the uncle.

The boy watched him with big blue eyes, that had an uncanny cold fire in them, and he said never a word.

"Well, then!" said the uncle. "What are we doing?" 160

"I shouldn't like mother to know I was lucky," said the boy.

"Why not, son?"

"She'd stop me."

"I don't think she would."

"Oh!" — and the boy writhed in an odd way — "I *don't* want her to know, uncle." 165

"All right, son! We'll manage it without her knowing."

They managed it very easily. Paul, at the other's suggestion, handed over five thousand pounds to his uncle, who deposited it with the family lawyer, who was then to inform Paul's mother that a relative had put five thousand pounds into his hands, which sum was to be paid out a thousand pounds at a time, on the mother's birthday, for the next five years.

"So she'll have a birthday present of a thousand pounds for five successive years," said Uncle Oscar. "I hope it won't make it all the harder for her later."

Paul's mother had her birthday in November. The house had been "whispering" worse than ever lately, and, even in spite of his luck, Paul could not bear up against it. He was very anxious to see the effect of the birthday letter, telling his mother about the thousand pounds.

When there were no visitors, Paul now took his meals with his parents,   170
as he was beyond the nursery control. His mother went into town nearly every day. She had discovered that she had an odd knack of sketching furs and dress materials, so she worked secretly in the studio of a friend who was the chief "artist" for the leading drapers. She drew the figures of ladies in furs and ladies in silk and sequins for the newspaper advertisements. This young woman artist earned several thousand pounds a year, but Paul's mother only made several hundreds, and she was again dissatisfied. She so wanted to be first in something, and she did not succeed, even in making sketches for drapery advertisements.

She was down to breakfast on the morning of her birthday. Paul watched her face as she read the letters. He knew the lawyer's letter. As his mother read it, her face hardened and became more expressionless. Then a cold, determined look came on her mouth. She hid the letter under the pile of others, and said not a word about it.

"Didn't you have anything nice in the post for your birthday, mother?" said Paul.

"Quite moderately nice," she said, her voice cold and absent.

She went away to town without saying more.

But in the afternoon Uncle Oscar appeared. He said Paul's mother had   175
had a long interview with the lawyer, asking if the whole five thousand could not be advanced at once, as she was in debt.

"What do you think, uncle?" said the boy.

"I leave it to you, son."

"Oh, let her have it, then! We can get some more with the other," said the boy.

"A bird in the hand is worth two in the bush, laddie!" said Uncle Oscar.

"But I'm sure to *know* for the Grand National; or the Lincolnshire; or else   180
the Derby. I'm sure to know for *one* of them," said Paul.

So Uncle Oscar signed the agreement, and Paul's mother touched the whole five thousand. Then something very curious happened. The voices in the house suddenly went mad, like a chorus of frogs on a spring evening. There were certain new furnishings, and Paul had a tutor. He was *really* going to Eton, his father's school, in the following autumn. There were flowers in the winter, and a blossoming of the luxury Paul's mother had been used to. And yet the voices in the house, behind the sprays of mimosa and almond blossom, and from under the piles of iridescent cushions, simply trilled and screamed in a sort of ecstasy: "There *must* be more money! Oh-h-h; there *must* be more money. Oh, now, now-w! Now-w-w — there *must* be more money! — more than ever! More than ever!"

It frightened Paul terribly. He studied away at his Latin and Greek with his tutors. But his intense hours were spent with Bassett. The Grand National had gone by: he had not "known," and had lost a hundred pounds. Summer was at hand. He was in agony for the Lincoln. But even for the Lincoln he didn't "know," and he lost fifty pounds. He became wild-eyed and strange, as if something were going to explode in him.

"Let it alone, son! Don't you bother about it!" urged Uncle Oscar. But it was as if the boy couldn't really hear what his uncle was saying.

"I've got to know for the Derby! I've got to know for the Derby!" the child reiterated, his big blue eyes blazing with a sort of madness.

His mother noticed how overwrought he was.   185

"You'd better go to the seaside. Wouldn't you like to go now to the seaside, instead of waiting? I think you'd better," she said, looking down at him anxiously, her heart curiously heavy because of him.

But the child lifted his uncanny blue eyes.

"I couldn't possibly go before the Derby, mother!" he said. "I couldn't possibly!"

"Why not?" she said, her voice becoming heavy when she was opposed. "Why not? You can still go from the seaside to see the Derby with your Uncle Oscar, if that's what you wish. No need for you to wait here. Besides, I think you care too much about these races. It's a bad sign. My family has been a gambling family, and you won't know till you grow up how much damage it has done. But it has done damage. I shall have to send Bassett away, and ask Uncle Oscar not to talk racing to you, unless you promise to be reasonable about it; go away to the seaside and forget it. You're all nerves!"

"I'll do what you like, mother, so long as you don't send me away till   190
after the Derby," the boy said.

"Send you away from where? Just from this house?"

"Yes," he said, gazing at her.

"Why, you curious child, what makes you care about this house so much, suddenly? I never knew you loved it."

He gazed at her without speaking. He had a secret within a secret, something he had not divulged, even to Bassett or to his Uncle Oscar.

But his mother, after standing undecided and a little bit sullen for some   195
moments, said:

"Very well, then! Don't go to the seaside till after the Derby, if you don't wish it. But promise me you won't let your nerves go to pieces. Promise you won't think so much about horse-racing and *events,* as you call them!"

"Oh, no," said the boy casually. "I won't think much about them, mother. You needn't worry. I wouldn't worry, mother, if I were you."

"If you were me and I were you," said his mother, "I wonder what we *should* do!"

"But you know you needn't worry, mother, don't you?" the boy repeated.

"I should be awfully glad to know it," she said wearily.   200

"Oh, well, you *can,* you know. I mean, you *ought* to know you needn't worry," he insisted.

"Ought I? Then I'll see about it," she said.

Paul's secret of secrets was his wooden horse, that which had no name. Since he was emancipated from a nurse and a nursery-governess, he had had his rocking-horse removed to his own bedroom at the top of the house.

"Surely, you're too big for a rocking-horse!" his mother had remonstrated.

"Well, you see, mother, till I can have a *real* horse, I like to have *some* sort of animal about," had been his quaint answer.

"Do you feel he keeps you company?" she laughed.

"Oh, yes! He's very good, he always keeps me company, when I'm there," said Paul.

So the horse, rather shabby, stood in an arrested prance in the boy's bedroom.

The Derby was drawing near, and the boy grew more and more tense. He hardly heard what was spoken to him, he was very frail, and his eyes were really uncanny. His mother had sudden strange seizures of uneasiness about him. Sometimes, for half-an-hour, she would feel a sudden anxiety about him that was almost anguish. She wanted to rush to him at once, and know he was safe.

Two nights before the Derby, she was at a big party in town, when one of her rushes of anxiety about her boy, her first-born, gripped her heart till she could hardly speak. She fought with the feeling, might and main, for she believed in common-sense. But it was too strong. She had to leave the dance and go downstairs to telephone to the country. The children's nursery-governess was terribly surprised and startled at being rung up in the night.

"Are the children all right, Miss Wilmot?"

"Oh, yes, they are quite all right."

"Master Paul? Is he all right?"

"He went to bed as right as a trivet. Shall I run up and look at him?"

"No," said Paul's mother reluctantly. "No! Don't trouble. It's all right. Don't sit up. We shall be home fairly soon." She did not want her son's privacy intruded upon.

"Very good," said the governess.

It was about one o'clock when Paul's mother and father drove up to their house. All was still. Paul's mother went to her room and slipped off her white fur cloak. She had told her maid not to wait up for her. She heard her husband downstairs, mixing a whisky-and-soda.

And then, because of the strange anxiety at her heart, she stole upstairs to her son's room. Noiselessly she went along the upper corridor. Was there a faint noise? What was it?

She stood, with arrested muscles, outside his door, listening. There was a strange, heavy, and yet not loud noise. Her heart stood still. It was a soundless noise, yet rushing and powerful. Something huge, in violent, hushed motion. What was it? What in God's name was it? She ought to know. She felt that she knew the noise. She knew what it was.

Yet she could not place it. She couldn't say what it was. And on and on it went, like a madness.

Softly, frozen with anxiety and fear, she turned the door-handle.

The room was dark. Yet in the space near the window, she heard and saw something plunging to and fro. She gazed in fear and amazement.

Then suddenly she switched on the light, and saw her son, in his green pajamas, madly surging on the rocking-horse. The blaze of light suddenly lit him up, as he urged the wooden horse, and lit her up, as she stood, blonde, in her dress of pale green and crystal, in the doorway.

"Paul!" she cried. "Whatever are you doing?"

"It's Malabar!" he screamed, in a powerful, strange voice. "It's Malabar!" ₂₂₅

His eyes blazed at her for one strange and senseless second, as he ceased urging his wooden horse. Then he fell with a crash to the ground, and she, all her tormented motherhood flooding upon her, rushed to gather him up.

But he was unconscious, and unconscious he remained, with some brainfever. He talked and tossed, and his mother sat stonily by his side.

"Malabar! It's Malabar! Bassett, Bassett, I *know!* It's Malabar!"

So the child cried, trying to get up and urge the rocking-horse that gave him his inspiration.

"What does he mean by Malabar?" asked the heart-frozen mother. ₂₃₀

"I don't know," said the father stonily.

"What does he mean by Malabar?" she asked her brother Oscar.

"It's one of the horses running for the Derby," was the answer.

And, in spite of himself, Oscar Cresswell spoke to Bassett, and himself put a thousand on Malabar: at fourteen to one.

The third day of the illness was critical: they were waiting for a ₂₃₅ change. The boy, with his rather long, curly hair, was tossing ceaselessly on the pillow. He neither slept nor regained consciousness, and his eyes were like blue stones. His mother sat, feeling her heart had gone, turned actually into a stone.

In the evening, Oscar Cresswell did not come, but Bassett sent a message, saying could he come up for one moment, just one moment? Paul's mother was very angry at the intrusion, but on second thought she agreed. The boy was the same. Perhaps Bassett might bring him to consciousness.

The gardener, a shortish fellow with a little brown moustache, and sharp little brown eyes, tiptoed into the room, touched his imaginary cap to Paul's mother, and stole to the bedside, staring with glittering, smallish eyes, at the tossing, dying child.

"Master Paul!" he whispered. "Master Paul! Malabar came in first all right, a clean win. I did as you told me. You've made over seventy thousand pounds, you have; you've got over eighty thousand. Malabar came in all right, Master Paul."

"Malabar! Malabar! Did I say Malabar, mother? Did I say Malabar? Do you think I'm lucky, mother? I knew Malabar, didn't I? Over eighty thousand pounds! I call that lucky, don't you, mother? Over eighty thousand pounds! I knew, didn't I know I knew? Malabar came in all right. If I ride my horse till I'm sure, then I tell you, Bassett, you can go as high as you like. Did you go for all you were worth, Bassett?"

"I went a thousand on it, Master Paul." ₂₄₀

"I never told you, mother, that if I can ride my horse, and *get there,* then I'm absolutely sure — oh, absolutely! Mother, did I ever tell you? I *am* lucky!"

"No, you never did," said the mother.

But the boy died in the night.

And even as he lay dead, his mother heard her brother's voice saying to her: "My God, Hester, you're eighty-odd thousand to the good, and a poor devil of a son to the bad. But, poor devil, poor devil, he's best gone out of a life where he rides his rocking-horse to find a winner."

Edith Wharton

ROMAN FEVER

Edith Wharton (1862 – 1937), born Edith Newbold Jones, grew up in a world she later dissected in her fiction: that of wealthy New York socialites. Although her parents frowned on her ambition to write — after all, why would she need money? — young Edith set out to perfect her own elegant, forceful prose style. In her early twenties she began placing stories in popular magazines, and kept on to become America's most celebrated woman author. A long, unhappy marriage to Edward Wharton, a rich nonreader thirteen years her senior, was cheered by the building of The Manse, a stately home in the Berkshires outside Lenox, Massachusetts. Divorced in 1913, she settled permanently in France. During World War I, she worked tirelessly to aid refugees. Friendship with American novelist Henry James inspired Wharton still more thoroughly to study her craft. Among her twenty-seven books of fiction are the novels The House of Mirth *(1905),* The Custom of the Country *(1913),* Summer *(1917), and* The Age of Innocence *(1920). Today her best-known novel may be that short, powerful tale of thwarted lovers in a New England village,* Ethan Frome *(1911). Besides, Wharton wrote fine ghost stories, memoirs, and a critical study,* The Writing of Fiction *(1925). As her biographer R. W. B. Lewis has shown in* Edith Wharton *(1975), she was a generous, wise, and impassioned woman whose best stories refuse to go away.*

I

From the table at which they had been lunching two American ladies of ripe but well-cared-for middle age moved across the lofty terrace of the Roman restaurant and, leaning on its parapet, looked first at each other, and then down on the outspread glories of the Palatine and the Forum, with the same expression of vague but benevolent approval.

As they leaned there a girlish voice echoed up gaily from the stairs leading to the court below. "Well, come along, then," it cried, not to them but to an invisible companion, "and let's leave the young things to their knitting"; and a voice as fresh laughed back: "Oh, look here, Babs, not actually *knitting* — " "Well, I mean figuratively," rejoined the first. "After all, we haven't left our poor parents much else to do. . . ." and at that point the turn of the stairs engulfed the dialogue.

The two ladies looked at each other again, this time with a tinge of smiling embarrassment, and the smaller and paler one shook her head and colored slightly.

"Barbara!" she murmured, sending an unheard rebuke after the mocking voice in the stairway.

The other lady, who was fuller, and higher in color, with a small deter- 5 mined nose supported by vigorous black eyebrows, gave a good-humored laugh. "That's what our daughters think of us!"

Her companion replied by a deprecating gesture. "Not of us individually. We must remember that. It's just the collective modern idea of Mothers. And you see — " Half-guiltily she drew from her handsomely mounted black handbag a twist of crimson silk run through by two fine knitting needles. "One never knows," she murmured. "The new system has certainly given us a good deal of time to kill; and sometimes I get tired just looking — even at this." Her gesture was now addressed to the stupendous scene at their feet.

The dark lady laughed again, and they both relapsed upon the view, contemplating it in silence, with a sort of diffused serenity which might have been borrowed from the spring effulgence of the Roman skies. The luncheon hour was long past, and the two had their end of the vast terrace to themselves. At its opposite extremity a few groups, detained by a lingering look at the outspread city, were gathering up guidebooks and fumbling for tips. The last of them scattered, and the two ladies were alone on the air-washed height.

"Well, I don't see why we shouldn't just stay here," said Mrs. Slade, the lady of the high color and energetic brows. Two derelict basket chairs stood near, and she pushed them into the angle of the parapet, and settled herself in one, her gaze upon the Palatine. "After all, it's still the most beautiful view in the world."

"It always will be, to me," assented her friend Mrs. Ansley, with so slight a stress on the "me" that Mrs. Slade, though she noticed it, wondered if it were not merely accidental, like the random underlinings of old-fashioned letter writers.

"Grace Ansley was always old-fashioned," she thought; and added 10 aloud, with a retrospective smile: "It's a view we've both been familiar with for a good many years. When we first met here we were younger than our girls are now. You remember?"

"Oh, yes, I remember," murmured Mrs. Ansley, with the same undefinable stress. "There's that headwaiter wondering," she interpolated. She was evidently far less sure than her companion of herself and of her rights in the world.

"I'll cure him of wondering," said Mrs. Slade, stretching her hand toward a bag as discreetly opulent-looking as Mrs. Ansley's. Signing to the headwaiter, she explained that she and her friend were old lovers of Rome, and would like to spend the end of the afternoon looking down on the view — that is, if it did not disturb the service? The headwaiter, bowing over her gratuity, assured her that the ladies were most welcome, and would be still more so if they would condescend to remain for dinner. A full-moon night, they would remember. . . .

Mrs. Slade's black brows drew together, as though references to the moon were out of place and even unwelcome. But she smiled away her frown as the headwaiter retreated. "Well, why not? We might do worse. There's no knowing, I suppose, when the girls will be back. Do you even know back from *where*? I don't!"

Mrs. Ansley again colored slightly. "I think those young Italian aviators we met at the Embassy invited them to fly to Tarquinia for tea. I suppose they'll want to wait and fly back by moonlight."

"Moonlight — moonlight! What a part it still plays. Do you suppose 15 they're as sentimental as we were?"

"I've come to the conclusion that I don't in the least know what they are," said Mrs. Ansley. "And perhaps we didn't know much more about each other."

"No; perhaps we didn't."

Her friend gave her a shy glance. "I never should have supposed you were sentimental, Alida."

"Well, perhaps I wasn't." Mrs. Slade drew her lids together in retrospect; and for a few moments the two ladies, who had been intimate since childhood, reflected how little they knew each other. Each one, of course, had a label ready to attach to the other's name; Mrs. Delphin Slade, for instance, would have told herself, or anyone who asked her, that Mrs. Horace Ansley, twenty-five years ago, had been exquisitely lovely — no, you wouldn't believe it, would you? . . . though, of course, still charming, distinguished. . . . Well, as a girl she had been exquisite; far more beautiful than her daughter Barbara, though certainly Babs, according to the new standards at any rate, was more effective — had more *edge,* as they say. Funny where she got it, with those two nullities as parents. Yes; Horace Ansley was — well, just the duplicate of his wife. Museum specimens of old New York. Good-looking, irreproachable, exemplary. Mrs. Slade and Mrs. Ansley had lived opposite each other — actually as well as figuratively — for years. When the drawing-room curtains in No. 20 East 73rd Street were renewed, No. 23, across the way, was always aware of it. And of all the movings, buyings, travels, anniversaries, illnesses — the tame chronicle of an estimable pair. Little of it escaped Mrs. Slade. But she had grown bored with it by the time her husband made his big *coup* in Wall Street, and when they bought in upper Park Avenue had already begun to think: "I'd rather live opposite a speakeasy for a change; at least one might see it raided." The idea of seeing Grace raided was so amusing that (before the move) she launched it at a woman's lunch. It made a hit, and went the rounds — she sometimes wondered if it had crossed the street, and reached Mrs. Ansley. She hoped not, but didn't much mind. Those were the days when respectability was at a discount, and it did the irreproachable no harm to laugh at them a little.

A few years later, and not many months apart, both ladies lost their husbands. There was an appropriate exchange of wreaths and condolences, and a brief renewal of intimacy in the half-shadow of their mourning; and now, after another interval, they had run across each other in Rome, at the same hotel, each of them the modest appendage of a salient daughter. The similarity of their lot had again drawn them together, lending itself to mild jokes, and the mutual confession that, if in old days it must have been tiring to "keep up" with daughters, it was now, at times, a little dull not to.

No doubt, Mrs. Slade reflected, she felt her unemployment more than poor Grace ever would. It was a big drop from being the wife of Delphin Slade to being his widow. She had always regarded herself (with a certain conjugal pride) as his equal in social gifts, as contributing her full share to the making of the exceptional couple they were: but the difference after his death was irremediable. As the wife of the famous corporation lawyer, always with an international case or two on hand, every day brought its exciting and unexpected obligation: the impromptu entertaining of eminent colleagues from abroad, the hurried dashes on legal business to London, Paris or Rome, where the entertaining was so handsomely reciprocated; the amusement of hearing in her wake: "What, that handsome woman with the good clothes and the eyes is Mrs. Slade — *the* Slade's wife? Really? Generally the wives of celebrities are such frumps."

Yes; being *the* Slade's widow was a dullish business after that. In living up to such a husband all her faculties had been engaged; now she had only her daughter to live up to, for the son who seemed to have inherited his father's gifts had died suddenly in boyhood. She had fought through that agony because her husband was there, to be helped and to help; now, after the father's death, the thought of the boy had become unbearable. There was nothing left but to mother her daughter; and dear Jenny was such a perfect daughter that she needed no excessive mothering. "Now with Babs Ansley I don't know that I *should* be so quiet," Mrs. Slade sometimes half-enviously reflected; but Jenny, who was younger than her brilliant friend, was that rare accident, an extremely pretty girl who somehow made youth and prettiness seem as safe as their absence. It was all perplexing — and to Mrs. Slade a little boring. She wished that Jenny would fall in love — with the wrong man, even; that she might have to be watched, out-maneuvered, rescued. And instead, it was Jenny who watched her mother, kept her out of drafts, made sure that she had taken her tonic. . . .

Mrs. Ansley was much less articulate than her friend, and her mental portrait of Mrs. Slade was slighter, and drawn with fainter touches. "Alida Slade's awfully brilliant; but not as brilliant as she thinks," would have summed it up; though she would have added, for the enlightenment of strangers, that Mrs. Slade had been an extremely dashing girl; much more so than her daughter, who was pretty, of course, and clever in a way, but had none of her mother's — well, "vividness," someone had once called it. Mrs. Ansley would take up current words like this, and cite them in quotation marks, as unheard-of audacities. No; Jenny was not like her mother. Sometimes Mrs. Ansley thought Alida Slade was disappointed; on the whole she had had a sad life. Full of failures and mistakes; Mrs. Ansley had always been rather sorry for her. . . .

So these two ladies visualized each other, each through the wrong end of her little telescope.

II

For a long time they continued to sit side by side without speaking. It seemed as though, to both, there was a relief in laying down their somewhat futile activities in the presence of the vast Memento Mori which faced them. Mrs. Slade sat quite still, her eyes fixed on the golden slope of the Palace of the Caesars, and after a while Mrs. Ansley ceased to fidget with her bag, and she too sank into meditation. Like many intimate friends, the two ladies had never before had occasion to be silent together, and Mrs. Ansley was slightly embarrassed by what seemed, after so many years, a new stage in their intimacy, and one with which she did not yet know how to deal.

Suddenly the air was full of that deep clangor of bells which periodically covers Rome with a roof of silver. Mrs. Slade glanced at her wristwatch. "Five o'clock already," she said, as though surprised.

Mrs. Ansley suggested interrogatively: "There's bridge at the Embassy at five." For a long time Mrs. Slade did not answer. She appeared to be lost in contemplation, and Mrs. Ansley thought the remark had escaped her. But after a while she said, as if speaking out of a dream: "Bridge, did you say? Not unless you want to. . . . But I don't think I will, you know."

"Oh, no," Mrs. Ansley hastened to assure her. "I don't care to at all. It's so lovely here; and so full of old memories, as you say." She settled herself in her chair, and almost furtively drew forth her knitting. Mrs. Slade took sideway note of this activity, but her own beautifully cared-for hands remained motionless on her knee.

"I was just thinking," she said slowly, "what different things Rome stands for to each generation of travelers. To our grandmothers, Roman fever; to our mothers, sentimental dangers — how we used to be guarded! — to our daughters, no more dangers than the middle of Main Street. They don't know it — but how much they're missing!"

The long golden light was beginning to pale, and Mrs. Ansley lifted her knitting a little closer to her eyes. "Yes; how we were guarded!" 30

"I always used to think," Mrs. Slade continued, "that our mothers had a much more difficult job than our grandmothers. When Roman fever stalked the streets it must have been comparatively easy to gather in the girls at the danger hour; but when you and I were young, with such beauty calling us, and the spice of disobedience thrown in, and no worse risk than catching cold during the cool hour after sunset, the mothers used to be put to it to keep us in — didn't they?"

She turned again toward Mrs. Ansley, but the latter had reached a delicate point in her knitting. "One, two, three — slip two; yes, they must have been," she assented, without looking up.

Mrs. Slade's eyes rested on her with a deepened attention. "She can knit — in the face of *this*! How like her. . . ."

Mrs. Slade leaned back, brooding, her eyes ranging from the ruins which faced her to the long green hollow of the Forum, the fading glow of the church fronts beyond it, and the outlying immensity of the Colosseum. Suddenly she thought: "It's all very well to say that our girls have done away with sentiment and moonlight. But if Babs Ansley isn't out to catch that young aviator — the one who's a Marchese — then I don't know anything. And Jenny has no chance beside her. I know that too. I wonder if that's why Grace Ansley likes the two girls to go everywhere together? My poor Jenny as a foil — !" Mrs. Slade gave a hardly audible laugh, and at the sound Mrs. Ansley dropped her knitting.

"Yes — ?" 35

"I — oh, nothing. I was only thinking how your Babs carries everything before her. That Campolieri boy is one of the best matches in Rome. Don't look so innocent, my dear — you know he is. And I was wondering, ever so respectfully, you understand . . . wondering how two such exemplary characters as you and Horace had managed to produce anything quite so dynamic." Mrs. Slade laughed again, with a touch of asperity.

Mrs. Ansley's hands lay inert across her needles. She looked straight out at the great accumulated wreckage of passion and splendor at her feet. But her small profile was almost expressionless. At length she said: "I think you overrate Babs, my dear."

Mrs. Slade's tone grew easier. "No; I don't. I appreciate her. And perhaps envy you. Oh, my girl's perfect; if I were a chronic invalid I'd — well, I think I'd rather be in Jenny's hands. There must be times . . . but there! I always wanted a brilliant daughter . . . and never quite understood why I got an angel instead."

Mrs. Ansley echoed her laugh in a faint murmur. "Babs is an angel too."

"Of course — of course! But she's got rainbow wings. Well, they're wandering by the sea with their young men; and here we sit . . . and it all brings back the past a little too acutely."

Mrs. Ansley had resumed her knitting. One might almost have imagined (if one had known her less well, Mrs. Slade reflected) that, for her also, too many memories rose from the lengthening shadows of those august ruins. But no; she was simply absorbed in her work. What was there for her to worry about? She knew that Babs would almost certainly come back engaged to the extremely eligible Campolieri. "And she'll sell the New York house, and settle down near them in Rome, and never be in their way . . . she's much too tactful. But she'll have an excellent cook, and just the right people in for bridge and cocktails . . . and a perfectly peaceful old age among her grandchildren."

Mrs. Slade broke off this prophetic flight with a recoil of self-disgust. There was no one of whom she had less right to think unkindly than of Grace Ansley. Would she never cure herself of envying her? Perhaps she had begun too long ago.

She stood up and leaned against the parapet, filling her troubled eyes with the tranquilizing magic of the hour. But instead of tranquilizing her the sight seemed to increase her exasperation. Her gaze turned toward the Colosseum. Already its golden flank was drowned in purple shadow, and above it the sky curved crystal clear, without light or color. It was the moment when afternoon and evening hang balanced in midheaven.

Mrs. Slade turned back and laid her hand on her friend's arm. The gesture was so abrupt that Mrs. Ansley looked up, startled.

"The sun's set. You're not afraid, my dear?"

"Afraid — ?"

"Of Roman fever or pneumonia? I remember how ill you were that winter. As a girl you had a very delicate throat, hadn't you?"

"Oh, we're all right up here. Down below, in the Forum, it does get deathly cold, all of a sudden . . . but not here."

"Ah, of course you know because you had to be so careful." Mrs. Slade turned back to the parapet. She thought: "I must make one more effort not to hate her." Aloud she said: "Whenever I look at the Forum from up here, I remember that story about a great-aunt of yours, wasn't she? A dreadfully wicked great-aunt?"

"Oh, yes; great-aunt Harriet. The one who was supposed to have sent her young sister out to the Forum after sunset to gather a night-blooming flower for her album. All our great-aunts and grandmothers used to have albums of dried flowers."

Mrs. Slade nodded. "But she really sent her because they were in love with the same man — "

"Well, that was the family tradition. They said Aunt Harriet confessed it years afterward. At any rate, the poor little sister caught the fever and died. Mother used to frighten us with the story when we were children."

"And you frightened *me* with it, that winter when you and I were here as girls. The winter I was engaged to Delphin."

Mrs. Ansley gave a faint laugh. "Oh, did I? Really frightened you? I don't believe you're easily frightened."

"Not often; but I was then. I was easily frightened because I was too happy. I wonder if you know what that means?"

"I — yes . . ." Mrs. Ansley faltered.

"Well, I suppose that was why the story of your wicked aunt made such an impression on me. And I thought: "There's no more Roman fever, but the Forum is deathly cold after sunset — especially after a hot day. And the Colosseum's even colder and damper.'"

"The Colosseum — ?"

"Yes. It wasn't easy to get in, after the gates were locked for the night. Far from easy. Still, in those days it could be managed; it *was* managed, often. Lovers met there who couldn't meet elsewhere. You knew that?"

"I — I dare say. I don't remember."

"You don't remember? You don't remember going to visit some ruins or other one evening, just after dark, and catching a bad chill? You were supposed to have gone to see the moon rise. People always said that expedition was what caused your illness."

There was a moment's silence; then Mrs. Ansley rejoined: "Did they? It was all so long ago."

"Yes. And you got well again — so it didn't matter. But I suppose it struck your friends — the reason given for your illness, I mean — because everybody knew you were so prudent on account of your throat, and your mother took such care of you. . . . You *had* been out late sight-seeing, hadn't you, that night?"

"Perhaps I had. The most prudent girls aren't always prudent. What made you think of it now?"

Mrs. Slade seemed to have no answer ready. But after a moment she broke out: "Because I simply can't bear it any longer — !"

Mrs. Ansley lifted her head quickly. Her eyes were wide and very pale. "Can't bear what?"

"Why — your not knowing that I've always known why you went."

"Why I went — ?"

"Yes. You think I'm bluffing, don't you? Well, you went to meet the man I was engaged to — and I can repeat every word of the letter that took you there."

While Mrs. Slade spoke Mrs. Ansley had risen unsteadily to her feet. Her bag, her knitting and gloves, slid in a panic-stricken heap to the ground. She looked at Mrs. Slade as though she were looking at a ghost.

"No, no — don't," she faltered out.

"Why not? Listen, if you don't believe me. 'My one darling, things can't go on like this. I must see you alone. Come to the Colosseum immediately after dark tomorrow. There will be somebody to let you in. No one whom you need fear will suspect' — but perhaps you've forgotten what the letter said?"

Mrs. Ansley met the challenge with an unexpected composure. Steadying herself against the chair she looked at her friend, and replied: "No; I know it by heart too."

"And the signature? 'Only *your* D.S.' Was that it? I'm right, am I? That was the letter that took you out that evening after dark?"

Mrs. Ansley was still looking at her. It seemed to Mrs. Slade that a slow struggle was going on behind the voluntarily controlled mask of her small quiet face. "I shouldn't have thought she had herself so well in hand," Mrs. Slade reflected, almost resentfully. But at this moment Mrs. Ansley spoke. "I don't know how you knew. I burnt that letter at once."

"Yes; you would, naturally — you're so prudent!" The sneer was open now. "And if you burnt the letter you're wondering how on earth I know what was in it. That's it, isn't it?"

Mrs. Slade waited, but Mrs. Ansley did not speak.

"Well, my dear, I know what was in the letter because I wrote it!"

"You wrote it?"

"Yes."

The two women stood for a minute staring at each other in the last golden light. Then Mrs. Ansley dropped back into her chair. "Oh," she murmured, and covered her face with her hands.

Mrs. Slade waited nervously for another word or movement. None came, and at length she broke out: "I horrify you."

Mrs. Ansley's hands dropped to her knee. The face they uncovered was streaked with tears. "I wasn't thinking of you. I was thinking — it was the only letter I ever had from him!"

"And I wrote it. Yes; I wrote it! But I was the girl he was engaged to. Did you happen to remember that?"

Mrs. Ansley's head drooped again. "I'm not trying to excuse myself . . . I remembered. . . ."

"And still you went?"

"Still I went."

Mrs. Slade stood looking down on the small bowed figure at her side. The flame of her wrath had already sunk, and she wondered why she had ever thought there would be any satisfaction in inflicting so purposeless a wound on her friend. But she had to justify herself.

"You do understand? I'd found out — and I hated you, hated you. I knew you were in love with Delphin — and I was afraid; afraid of you, of your quiet ways, your sweetness . . . your . . . well, I wanted you out of the way, that's all. Just for a few weeks; just till I was sure of him. So in a blind fury I wrote that letter. . . . I don't know why I'm telling you now."

"I suppose," said Mrs. Ansley slowly, "it's because you've always gone on hating me."

"Perhaps. Or because I wanted to get the whole thing off my mind." She paused. "I'm glad you destroyed the letter. Of course I never thought you'd die."

Mrs. Ansley relapsed into silence, and Mrs. Slade, leaning above her, was conscious of a strange sense of isolation, of being cut off from the warm current of human communion. "You think me a monster!"

"I don't know. . . . It was the only letter I had, and you say he didn't write it?"

"Ah, how you care for him still!"

"I cared for that memory," said Mrs. Ansley.

Mrs. Slade continued to look down on her. She seemed physically reduced by the blow — as if, when she got up, the wind might scatter her like a puff of dust. Mrs. Slade's jealousy suddenly leapt up again at the sight. All these years the woman had been living on that letter. How she must have loved him, to treasure the mere memory of its ashes! The letter of the man her friend was engaged to. Wasn't it she who was the monster?

"You tried your best to get him away from me, didn't you? But you failed; and I kept him. That's all."

"Yes. That's all."

"I wish now I hadn't told you. I'd no idea you'd feel about it as you do; I thought you'd be amused. It all happened so long ago, as you say; and you must do me the justice to remember that I had no reason to think you'd ever taken it seriously. How could I, when you were married to Horace Ansley two months afterward? As soon as you could get out of bed your mother rushed you off to Florence and married you. People were rather surprised — they wondered at its being done so quickly; but I thought I knew. I had an idea you did it out of *pique* — to be able to say you'd got ahead of Delphin and me. Girls have such silly reasons for doing the most serious things. And your marrying so soon convinced me that you'd never really cared."

"Yes. I suppose it would," Mrs. Ansley assented.   100

The clear heaven overhead was emptied of all its gold. Dusk spread over it, abruptly darkening the Seven Hills. Here and there lights began to twinkle through the foliage at their feet. Steps were coming and going on the deserted terrace — waiters looking out of the doorway at the head of the stairs, then reappearing with trays and napkins and flasks of wine. Tables were moved, chairs straightened. A feeble string of electric lights flickered out. Some vases of faded flowers were carried away, and brought back replenished. A stout lady in a dust coat suddenly appeared, asking in broken Italian if anyone had seen the elastic band which held together her tattered Baedeker. She poked with her stick under the table at which she had lunched, the waiters assisting.

The corner where Mrs. Slade and Mrs. Ansley sat was still shadowy and deserted. For a long time neither of them spoke. At length Mrs. Slade began again: "I suppose I did it as a sort of joke — "

"A joke?"

"Well, girls are ferocious sometimes, you know. Girls in love especially. And I remember laughing to myself all that evening at the idea that you were waiting around there in the dark, dodging out of sight, listening for every sound, trying to get in — Of course I was upset when I heard you were so ill afterward."

Mrs. Ansley had not moved for a long time. But now she turned slowly   105 toward her companion. "But I didn't wait. He'd arranged everything. He was there. We were let in at once," she said.

Mrs. Slade sprang up from her leaning position. "Delphin there? They let you in? — Ah, now you're lying!" she burst out with violence.

Mrs. Ansley's voice grew clearer, and full of surprise. "But of course he was there. Naturally he came — "

"Came? How did he know he'd find you there? You must be raving!"

Mrs. Ansley hesitated, as though reflecting. "But I answered the letter. I told him I'd be there. So he came."

Mrs. Slade flung her hands up to her face. "Oh, God — you answered! I never thought of your answering. . . ." 110

"It's odd you never thought of it, if you wrote the letter."

"Yes. I was blind with rage."

Mrs. Ansley rose, and drew her fur scarf about her. "It is cold here. We'd better go. . . . I'm sorry for you," she said, as she clasped the fur about her throat.

The unexpected words sent a pang through Mrs. Slade. "Yes; we'd better go." She gathered up her bag and cloak. "I don't know why you should be sorry for me," she muttered.

Mrs. Ansley stood looking away from her toward the dusky secret mass 115 of the Colosseum. "Well — because I didn't have to wait that night."

Mrs. Slade gave an unquiet laugh. "Yes; I was beaten there. But I oughtn't to begrudge it to you, I suppose. At the end of all these years. After all, I had everything; I had him for twenty-five years. And you had nothing but that one letter that he didn't write."

Mrs. Ansley was again silent. At length she turned toward the door of the terrace. She took a step, and turned back, facing her companion.

"I had Barbara," she said, and began to move ahead of Mrs. Slade toward the stairway.

Eudora Welty
A WORN PATH   1941

Eudora Welty was born in 1909 in Jackson, Mississippi, daughter of an insurance company president. She grew up within a stone's throw of the state capitol and still lives in her childhood home. Like William Faulkner, another Mississippi writer, she has stayed close to her roots for practically all her life, except for short sojourns at the University of Wisconsin, where she took her B.A., and in New York City, where she studied advertising. Although she is a novelist distinguished for The Robber Bridegroom *(1942),* Delta Wedding *(1946),* The Ponder Heart *(1954), and* Losing Battles *(1970), many critics think her finest work is in the short-story form.* The Collected Stories of Eudora Welty *(1980) gathers the work of more than forty years. Welty's other books include memoirs,* The Optimist's Daughter *(1972) and* One Writer's Beginnings *(1984), and* The Eye of the Story *(1977), a book of sympathetic criticism on the fiction of writers including Willa Cather, Virginia Woolf, Katherine Anne Porter, and Isak Dinesen.*

It was December — a bright frozen day in the early morning. Far out in the country there was an old Negro woman with her head tied in a red rag, coming along a path through the pinewoods. Her name was Phoenix Jackson. She was very old and small and she walked slowly in the dark pine shadows, moving a little from side to side in her steps, with the balanced heaviness and lightness of a pendulum in a grandfather clock. She carried a thin, small cane made from an umbrella, and with this she kept tapping the frozen earth in front of her. This made a grave and persistent noise in the still air, that seemed meditative like the chirping of a solitary little bird.

She wore a dark striped dress reaching down to her shoe tops, and an equally long apron of bleached sugar sacks, with a full pocket: all neat and tidy, but every time she took a step she might have fallen over her shoelaces, which dragged from her unlaced shoes. She looked straight ahead. Her eyes were blue with age. Her skin had a pattern all its own of numberless branching wrinkles and as though a whole little tree stood in the middle of her forehead, but a golden color ran underneath, and the two knobs of her cheeks were illumined by a yellow burning under the dark. Under the red rag her hair came down on her neck in the frailest of ringlets, still black, and with an odor like copper.

Now and then there was a quivering in the thicket. Old Phoenix said, "Out of my way, all you foxes, owls, beetles, jack rabbits, coons and wild animals! . . . Keep out from under these feet, little bobwhites. . . . Keep the big wild hogs out of my path. Don't let none of those come running my direction. I got a long way." Under her small black-freckled hand her cane, limber as a buggy whip, would switch at the brush as if to rouse up any hiding things.

On she went. The woods were deep and still. The sun made the pine needles almost too bright to look at, up where the wind rocked. The cones dropped as light as feathers. Down in the hollow was the mourning dove — it was not too late for him.

The path ran up a hill. "Seem like there is chains about my feet, time I ⁵ get this far," she said, in the voice of argument old people keep to use with themselves. "Something always take a hold of me on this hill — pleads I should stay."

After she got to the top she turned and gave a full, severe look behind her where she had come. "Up through pines," she said at length. "Now down through oaks."

Her eyes opened their widest, and she started down gently. But before she got to the bottom of the hill a bush caught her dress.

Her fingers were busy and intent, but her skirts were full and long, so that before she could pull them free in one place they were caught in another. It was not possible to allow the dress to tear. "I in the thorny bush," she said. "Thorns, you doing your appointed work. Never want to let folks pass, no sir. Old eyes thought you was a pretty little *green* bush."

Finally, trembling all over, she stood free, and after a moment dared to stoop for her cane.

"Sun so high!" she cried, leaning back and looking, while the thick tears ¹⁰ went over her eyes. "The time getting all gone here."

At the foot of this hill was a place where a log was laid across the creek. "Now comes the trial," said Phoenix.

Putting her right foot out, she mounted the log and shut her eyes. Lifting her skirt, leveling her cane fiercely before her, like a festival figure in some parade, she began to march across. Then she opened her eyes and she was safe on the other side.

"I wasn't as old as I thought," she said.

But she sat down to rest. She spread her skirts on the bank around her and folded her hands over her knees. Up above her was a tree in a pearly cloud of mistletoe. She did not dare to close her eyes, and when a little boy brought her a plate with a slice of marble-cake on it she spoke to him. "That would be acceptable," she said. But when she went to take it there was just her own hand in the air.

So she left that tree, and had to go through a barbed-wire fence. There she had to creep and crawl, spreading her knees and stretching her fingers like a baby trying to climb the steps. But she talked loudly to herself: she could not let her dress be torn now, so late in the day, and she could not pay for having her arm or her leg sawed off if she got caught fast where she was.

At last she was safe through the fence and risen up out in the clearing. Big dead trees, like black men with one arm, were standing in the purple stalks of the withered cotton field. There sat a buzzard.

"Who you watching?"

In the furrow she made her way along.

"Glad this not the season for bulls," she said, looking sideways, "and the good Lord made his snakes to curl up and sleep in the winter. A pleasure I don't see no two-headed snake coming around that tree, where it come once. It took a while to get by him, back in the summer."

She passed through the old cotton and went into a field of dead corn. It whispered and shook and was taller than her head. "Through the maze now," she said, for there was no path.

Then there was something tall, black, and skinny there, moving before her.

At first she took it for a man. It could have been a man dancing in the field. But she stood still and listened, and it did not make a sound. It was as silent as a ghost.

"Ghost," she said sharply, "who be you the ghost of? For I have heard of nary death close by."

But there was no answer — only the ragged dancing in the wind.

She shut her eyes, reached out her hand, and touched a sleeve. She found a coat and inside that an emptiness, cold as ice.

"You scarecrow," she said. Her face lighted. "I ought to be shut up for good," she said with laughter. "My senses is gone. I too old. I the oldest people I ever know. Dance, old scarecrow," she said, "while I dancing with you."

She kicked her foot over the furrow, and with mouth drawn down, shook her head once or twice in a little strutting way. Some husks blew down and whirled in streamers about her skirts.

Then she went on, parting her way from side to side with the cane, through the whispering field. At last she came to the end, to a wagon track where the silver grass blew between the red ruts. The quail were walking around like pullets, seeming all dainty and unseen.

"Walk pretty," she said. "This the easy place. This the easy going."

She followed the track, swaying through the quiet bare fields, through the little strings of trees silver in their dead leaves, past cabins silver from weather, with the doors and windows boarded shut, all like old women under a spell sitting there. "I walking in their sleep," she said, nodding her head vigorously.

In a ravine she went where a spring was silently flowing through a hollow log. Old Phoenix bent and drank. "Sweet-gum makes the water sweet," she said, and drank more. "Nobody know who made this well, for it was here when I was born."

The track crossed a swampy part where the moss hung as white as lace from every limb. "Sleep on, alligators, and blow your bubbles." Then the track went into the road.

Deep, deep the road went down between the high green-colored banks. Overhead the live-oaks met, and it was as dark as a cave.

A black dog with a lolling tongue came up out of the weeds by the ditch. 35 She was meditating, and not ready, and when he came at her she only hit him a little with her cane. Over she went in the ditch, like a little puff of milkweed.

Down there, her senses drifted away. A dream visited her, and she reached her hand up, but nothing reached down and gave her a pull. So she lay there and presently went to talking. "Old woman," she said to herself, "that black dog come up out of the weeds to stall you off, and now there he sitting on his fine tail, smiling at you."

A white man finally came along and found her — a hunter, a young man, with his dog on a chain.

"Well, Granny!" he laughed. "What are you doing there?"

"Lying on my back like a June-bug waiting to be turned over, mister," she said, reaching up her hand.

He lifted her up, gave her a swing in the air, and set her down. "Anything 40 broken, Granny?"

"No sir, them old dead weeds is springy enough," said Phoenix, when she had got her breath. "I thank you for your trouble."

"Where do you live, Granny?" he asked, while the two dogs were growling at each other.

"Away back yonder, sir, behind the ridge. You can't even see it from here."

"On your way home?"

"No sir, I going to town." 45

"Why, that's too far! That's as far as I walk when I come out myself, and I get something for my trouble." He patted the stuffed bag he carried, and there hung down a little closed claw. It was one of the bob-whites, with its beak hooked bitterly to show it was dead. "Now you go on home, Granny!"

"I bound to go to town, mister," said Phoenix. "The time come around."

He gave another laugh, filling the whole landscape. "I know you old colored people! Wouldn't miss going to town to see Santa Claus!"

But something held old Phoenix very still. The deep lines in her face went into a fierce and different radiation. Without warning, she had seen with her own eyes a flashing nickel fall out of the man's pocket onto the ground.

"How old are you, Granny?" he was saying. 50

"There is no telling, mister," she said, "no telling."

Then she gave a little cry and clapped her hands and said, "Git on away from here, dog! Look! Look at that dog!" She laughed as if in admiration. "He ain't scared of nobody. He a big black dog." She whispered, "Sic him!"

"Watch me get rid of that cur," said the man. "Sic him, Pete! Sic him!"

Phoenix heard the dogs fighting, and heard the man running and throwing sticks. She even heard a gunshot. But she was slowly bending forward by that time, further and further forward, the lids stretched down over her eyes, as if she were doing this in her sleep. Her chin was lowered almost to her knees. The yellow palm of her hand came out from the fold of her apron. Her fingers slid down and along the ground under the piece of money with the grace and care they would have in lifting an egg from under a setting hen. Then she slowly straightened up, she stood erect, and the nickel was in her apron pocket. A bird flew by. Her lips moved. "God watching me the whole time. I come to stealing."

The man came back, and his own dog panted about them. "Well, I scared him off that time," he said, and then he laughed and lifted his gun and pointed it at Phoenix.

She stood straight and faced him.

"Doesn't the gun scare you?" he said, still pointing it.

"No, sir, I seen plenty go off closer by, in my day, and for less than what I done," she said, holding utterly still.

He smiled, and shouldered the gun. "Well, Granny," he said, "you must be a hundred years old, and scared of nothing. I'd give you a dime if I had any money with me. But you take my advice and stay home, and nothing will happen to you."

"I bound to go on my way, mister," said Phoenix. She inclined her head in the red rag. Then they went in different directions, but she could hear the gun shooting again and again over the hill.

She walked on. The shadows hung from the oak trees to the road like curtains. Then she smelled wood-smoke, and smelled the river, and she saw a steeple and the cabins on their steep steps. Dozens of little black children whirled around her. There ahead was Natchez shining. Bells were ringing. She walked on.

In the paved city it was Christmas time. There were red and green electric lights strung and crisscrossed everywhere, and all turned on in the daytime. Old Phoenix would have been lost if she had not distrusted her eyesight and depended on her feet to know where to take her.

She paused quietly on the sidewalk where people were passing by. A lady came along in the crowd, carrying an armful of red-, green- and silver-wrapped presents; she gave off perfume like the red roses in hot summer, and Phoenix stopped her.

"Please, missy, will you lace up my shoe?" She held up her foot.

"What do you want, Grandma?"

"See my shoe," said Phoenix. "Do all right for out in the country, but wouldn't look right to go in a big building."

"Stand still then, Grandma," said the lady. She put her packages down on the sidewalk beside her and laced and tied both shoes tightly.

"Can't lace 'em with a cane," said Phoenix. "Thank you, missy. I doesn't mind asking a nice lady to tie up my shoe, when I gets out on the street."

Moving slowly and from side to side, she went into the big building, and into a tower of steps, where she walked up and around and around until her feet knew to stop.

She entered a door, and there she saw nailed up on the wall the document 70
that had been stamped with the gold seal and framed in the gold frame, which
matched the dream that was hung up in her head.

"Here I be," she said. There was a fixed and ceremonial stiffness over her
body.

"A charity case, I suppose," said an attendant who sat at the desk before
her.

But Phoenix only looked above her head. There was sweat on her face,
the wrinkles in her skin shone like a bright net.

"Speak up, Grandma," the woman said. "What's your name? We must
have your history, you know. Have you been here before? What seems to be
the trouble with you?"

Old Phoenix only gave a twitch to her face as if a fly were bothering her. 75

"Are you deaf?" cried the attendant.

But then the nurse came in.

"Oh, that's just old Aunt Phoenix," she said. "She doesn't come for
herself — she has a little grandson. She makes these trips just as regular as
clockwork. She lives away back off the Old Natchez Trace." She bent down.
"Well, Aunt Phoenix, why don't you just take a seat? We won't keep you
standing after your long trip." She pointed.

The old woman sat down, bolt upright in the chair.

"Now, how is the boy?" asked the nurse. 80

Old Phoenix did not speak.

"I said, how is the boy?"

But Phoenix only waited and stared straight ahead, her face very solemn
and withdrawn into rigidity.

"Is his throat any better?" asked the nurse. "Aunt Phoenix, don't you
hear me? Is your grandson's throat any better since the last time you came for
the medicine?"

With her hands on her knees, the old woman waited, silent, erect and 85
motionless, just as if she were in armor.

"You mustn't take up our time this way, Aunt Phoenix," the nurse said.
"Tell us quickly about your grandson, and get it over. He isn't dead, is he?"

At last there came a flicker and then a flame of comprehension across her
face, and she spoke.

"My grandson. It was my memory had left me. There I sat and forgot
why I made my long trip."

"Forgot?" The nurse frowned. "After you came so far?"

Then Phoenix was like an old woman begging a dignified forgiveness for 90
waking up frightened in the night. "I never did go to school, I was too old at
the Surrender," she said in a soft voice. "I'm an old woman without an education. It was my memory fail me. My little grandson, he is just the same, and
I forgot it in the coming."

"Throat never heals, does it?" said the nurse, speaking in a loud, sure
voice to old Phoenix. By now she had a card with something written on it, a
little list. "Yes. Swallowed lye. When was it? — January — two, three years
ago —"

Phoenix spoke unasked now. "No, missy, he not dead, he just the same.
Every little while his throat begin to close up again, and he not able to swallow.

He not get his breath. He not able to help himself. So the time come around, and I go on another trip for the soothing medicine."

"All right. The doctor said as long as you came to get it, you could have it," said the nurse. "But it's an obstinate case."

"My little grandson, he sit up there in the house all wrapped up, waiting by himself," Phoenix went on. "We is the only two left in the world. He suffer and it don't seem to put him back at all. He got a sweet look. He going to last. He wear a little patch quilt and peep out holding his mouth open like a little bird. I remembers so plain now. I not going to forget him again, no, the whole enduring time. I could tell him from all the others in creation."

"All right." The nurse was trying to hush her now. She brought her a $_{95}$ bottle of medicine. "Charity," she said, making a check mark in a book.

Old Phoenix held the bottle close to her eyes, and then carefully put it into her pocket.

"I thank you," she said.

"It's Christmas time, Grandma," said the attendant. "Could I give you a few pennies out of my purse?"

"Five pennies is a nickel," said Phoenix stiffly.

"Here's a nickel," said the attendant. $_{100}$

Phoenix rose carefully and held out her hand. She received the nickel and then fished the other nickel out of her pocket and laid it beside the new one. She stared at her palm closely, with her head on one side.

Then she gave a tap with her cane on the floor.

"This is what come to me to do," she said. "I going to the store and buy my child a little windmill they sells, made out of paper. He going to find it hard to believe there such a thing in the world. I'll march myself back where he waiting, holding it straight up in this hand."

She lifted her free hand, gave a little nod, turned around, and walked out of the doctor's office. Then her slow step began on the stairs, going down.

Walter Van Tilburg Clark
THE PORTABLE PHONOGRAPH   1942

Walter Van Tilburg Clark (1909 – 1971), born in Maine, moved at age eight to Reno, where his father, Walter Ernest Clark, was president of the state university. As a young man he taught English and coached sports for ten years in the public schools of Cazenovia, New York, while taking his Ph.D. at Colgate University. In 1945 he went back West, living in Taos, New Mexico; Virginia City, Nevada; and Reno, where he ended his days as writer-in-residence back at the University of Nevada, his alma mater. Though Clark's writing career began with poetry, he is best remembered for his fiction, all published in one decade. The first of three novels, The Ox-Bow Incident *(1940), was declared a minor classic as soon as it appeared. Clark sets it in Nevada cattle country, and explores events that follow the lynching of three men wrongly accused of murder. Hollywood turned it into a notable movie.* The City of Trembling Leaves *(1945), evidently autobi-*

ographical, traces the boyhood of an aspiring composer. The Track of the Cat *(1949), a novel about the hunt for a marauding panther, and a volume of short stories,* The Watchful Gods *(1950), closed his major work. Clark's fiction wholly identifies with the American West, and its themes are those of the frontier: survival in the face of hostile nature, imposition of law upon anarchy.*

The red sunset, with narrow, black cloud strips like threats across it, lay on the curved horizon of the prairie. The air was still and cold, and in it settled the mute darkness and greater cold of night. High in the air there was wind, for through the veil of the dusk the clouds could be seen gliding rapidly south and changing shapes. A sensation of torment, of two-sided, unpredictable nature, arose from the stillness of the earth air beneath the violence of the upper air. Out of the sunset, through the dead, matted grass and isolated weed stalks of the prairie, crept the narrow and deeply rutted remains of a road. In the road, in places, there were crusts of shallow, brittle ice. There were little islands of an old oiled pavement in the road too, but most of it was mud, now frozen rigid. The frozen mud still bore the toothed impress of great tanks, and a wanderer on the neighboring undulations might have stumbled, in this light, into large, partially filled-in and weed-grown cavities, their banks channeled and beginning to spread into badlands. These pits were such as might have been made by falling meteors, but they were not. They were the scars of gigantic bombs, their rawness already made a little natural by rain, seed and time. Along the road there were rakish remnants of fence. There was also, just visible, one portion of tangled and multiple barbed wire still erect, behind which was a shelving ditch with small caves, now very quiet and empty, at intervals in its back wall. Otherwise there was no structure or remnant of a structure visible over the dome of the darkling earth, but only, in sheltered hollows, the darker shadows of young trees trying again.

Under the wuthering arch of the high wind a V of wild geese fled south. The rush of their pinions sounded briefly, and the faint, plaintive notes of their expeditionary talk. Then they left a still greater vacancy. There was the smell and expectation of snow, as there is likely to be when the wild geese fly south. From the remote distance, toward the red sky, came faintly the protracted howl and quick yap-yap of a prairie wolf.

North of the road, perhaps a hundred yards, lay the parallel and deeply intrenched course of a small creek, lined with leafless alders and willows. The creek was already silent under ice. Into the bank above it was dug a sort of cell, with a single opening, like the mouth of a mine tunnel. Within the cell there was a little red of fire, which showed dully through the opening, like a reflection or a deception of the imagination. The light came from the chary burning of four blocks of poorly aged peat, which gave off a petty warmth and much acrid smoke. But the precious remnants of wood, old fence posts and timbers from the long-deserted dugouts, had to be saved for the real cold, for the time when a man's breath blew white, the moisture in his nostrils stiffened at once when he stepped out, and the expansive blizzards paraded for days over the vast open, swirling and settling and thickening, till the dawn of the cleared day when the sky was a thin blue-green and the terrible cold, in which a man could not live for three hours unwarmed, lay over the uniformly drifted swell of the plain.

Around the smoldering peat four men were seated cross-legged. Behind them, traversed by their shadows, was the earth bench, with two old and dirty army blankets, where the owner of the cell slept. In a niche in the opposite wall were a few tin utensils which caught the glint of the coals. The host was rewrapping in a piece of daubed burlap, four fine, leather-bound books. He worked slowly and very carefully, and at last tied the bundle securely with a piece of grass-woven cord. The other three looked intently upon the process, as if a great significance lay in it. As the host tied the cord, he spoke. He was an old man, his long, matted beard and hair gray to nearly white. The shadows made his brows and cheekbones appear gnarled, his eyes and cheeks deeply sunken. His big hands, rough with frost and swollen by rheumatism, were awkward but gentle at their task. He was like a prehistoric priest performing a fateful ceremonial rite. Also his voice had in it a suitable quality of deep, reverent despair, yet perhaps, at the moment, a sharpness of selfish satisfaction.

"When I perceived what was happening," he said, "I told myself, 'It is   5
the end. I cannot take much; I will take these.'

"Perhaps I was impractical," he continued. "But for myself, I do not regret, and what do we know of those who will come after us? We are the doddering remnant of a race of mechanical fools. I have saved what I love; the soul of what was good in us here; perhaps the new ones will make a strong enough beginning not to fall behind when they become clever."

He rose with slow pain and placed the wrapped volumes in the niche with his utensils. The others watched him with the same ritualistic gaze.

"Shakespeare, the Bible, *Moby-Dick, The Divine Comedy,*" one of them said softly. "You might have done worse; much worse."

"You will have a little soul left until you die," said another harshly. "That is more than is true of us. My brain becomes thick, like my hands." He held the big, battered hands, with their black nails, in the glow to be seen.

"I want paper to write on," he said. "And there is none."   10

The fourth man said nothing. He sat in the shadow farthest from the fire, and sometimes his body jerked in its rags from the cold. Although he was still young, he was sick, and coughed often. Writing implied a greater future than he now felt able to consider.

The old man seated himself laboriously, and reached out, groaning at the movement, to put another block of peat on the fire. With bowed heads and averted eyes, his three quests acknowledged his magnanimity.

"We thank you, Doctor Jenkins, for the reading," said the man who had named the books.

They seemed then to be waiting for something. Doctor Jenkins understood, but was loath to comply. In an ordinary moment he would have said nothing. But the words of *The Tempest,* which he had been reading, and the religious attention of the three, made this an unusual occasion.

"You wish to hear the phonograph," he said grudgingly.   15

The two middle-aged men stared into the fire, unable to formulate and expose the enormity of their desire.

Walter Van Tilburg Clark   333

The young man, however, said anxiously, between suppressed coughs, "Oh, please," like an excited child.

The old man rose again in his difficult way, and went to the back of the cell. He returned and placed tenderly upon the packed floor, where the firelight might fall upon it, an old, portable phonograph in a black case. He smoothed the top with his hand, then opened it. The lovely green-felt-covered disk became visible.

"I have been using thorns as needles," he said. "But tonight, because we have a musician among us" — he bent his head to the young man, almost invisible in the shadow — "I will use a steel needle. There are only three left."

The two middle-aged men stared at him in speechless adoration. The one with the big hands, who wanted to write, moved his lips, but the whisper was not audible.

"Oh, don't," cried the young man, as if he were hurt. "The thorns will do beautifully."

"No," the old man said. "I have become accustomed to the thorns — but they are not really good. For you, my young friend, we will have good music tonight.

"After all," he added generously, and beginning to wind the phonograph, which creaked, "they can't last forever."

"No, nor we," the man who needed to write said harshly. "The needle, by all means."

"Oh, thanks," said the young man. "Thanks," he said again, in a low, excited voice, and then stifled his coughing with a bowed head.

"The records, though," said the old man when he had finished winding, "are a different matter. Already they are very worn. I do not play them more than once a week. One, once a week, that is what I allow myself.

"More than a week I cannot stand it; not to hear them," he apologized.

"No, how could you?" cried the young man. "And with them here like this."

"A man can stand anything," said the man who wanted to write, in his harsh, antagonistic voice.

"Please, the music," said the young man.

"Only the one," said the old man. "In the long run we will remember more that way."

He had a dozen records with luxuriant gold and red seals. Even in that light the others could see that the threads of the records were becoming worn. Slowly he read out the titles, and the tremendous, dead names of the composers and the artists and the orchestras. The three worked upon the names in their minds, carefully. It was difficult to select from such a wealth what they would at once most like to remember. Finally the man who wanted to write named Gershwin's "New York."

"Oh, no," cried the sick young man, and then could say nothing more because he had to cough. The others understood him, and the harsh man withdrew his selection and waited for the musician to choose.

The musician begged Doctor Jenkins to read the titles again, very slowly, so that he could remember the sounds. While they were read, he lay back against the wall, his eyes closed, his thin, horny hand pulling at his light beard, and listened to the voices and the orchestras and the single instruments in his mind.

When the reading was done he spoke despairingly. "I have forgotten," he complained. "I cannot hear them clearly." 35

"There are things missing," he explained.

"I know," said Doctor Jenkins. "I thought that I knew all of Shelley by heart. I should have brought Shelley."

"That's more soul than we can use," said the harsh man. *"Moby-Dick* is better.

"By God, we can understand that," he emphasized.

The doctor nodded. 40

"Still," said the man who had admired the books, "we need the absolute if we are to keep a grasp on anything.

"Anything but these sticks and peat clods and rabbit snares," he said bitterly.

"Shelley desired an ultimate absolute," said the harsh man. "It's too much," he said. "It's no good; no earthly good."

The musician selected a Debussy nocturne. The others considered and approved. They rose to their knees to watch the doctor prepare for the playing, so that they appeared to be actually in an attitude of worship. The peat glow showed the thinness of their bearded faces, and the deep lines in them, and revealed the condition of their garments. The other two continued to kneel as the old man carefully lowered the needle onto the spinning disk, but the musician suddenly drew back against the wall again, with his knees up, and buried his face in his hands.

At the first notes of the piano the listeners were startled. They stared at each other. Even the musician lifted his head in amazement, but then quickly bowed it again, strainingly, as if he were suffering from a pain he might not be able to endure. They were all listening deeply, without movement. The wet, blue-green notes tinkled forth from the old machine, and were individual, delectable presences in the cell. The individual, delectable presences swept into a sudden tide of unbearably beautiful dissonance, and then continued fully the swelling and ebbing of that tide, the dissonant inpourings, and the resolutions, and the diminishments, and the little, quiet wavelets of interlude lapping between. Every sound was piercing and singularly sweet. In all the men except the musician, there occurred rapid sequences of tragically heightened recollection. He heard nothing but what was there. At the final, whispering disappearance, but moving quietly, so that the others would not hear him and look at him, he let his head fall back in agony, as if it were drawn there by the hair, and clenched the fingers of one hand over his teeth. He sat that way while the others were silent, and until they began to breathe again normally. His drawn-up legs were trembling violently. 45

Quickly Doctor Jenkins lifted the needle off, to save it, and not to spoil the recollection with scraping. When he had stopped the whirling of the sacred disk, he courteously left the phonograph open and by the fire, in sight.

The others, however, understood. The musician rose last, but then abruptly, and went quickly out at the door without saying anything. The others stopped at the door and gave their thanks in low voices. The doctor nodded magnificently.

"Come again," he invited, "in a week. We will have the 'New York.'"

When the two had gone together, out toward the rimmed road, he stood in the entrance, peering and listening. At first there was only the resonant boom of the wind overhead, and then, far over the dome of the dead, dark plain, the wolf cry lamenting. In the rifts of clouds the doctor saw four stars flying. It impressed the doctor that one of them had just been obscured by the beginning of a flying cloud at the very moment he heard what he had been listening for, a sound of suppressed coughing. It was not near by, however. He believed that down against the pale alders he could see the moving shadow.

With nervous hands he lowered the piece of canvas which served as his 50 door, and pegged it at the bottom. Then quickly and quietly, looking at the piece of canvas frequently, he slipped the records into the case, snapped the lid shut, and carried the phonograph to his couch. There, pausing often to stare at the canvas and listen, he dug earth from the wall and disclosed a piece of board. Behind this there was a deep hole in the wall, into which he put the phonograph. After a moment's consideration, he went over and reached down his bundle of books and inserted it also. Then, guardedly, he once more sealed up the hole with the board and the earth. He also changed his blankets, and the grass-stuffed sack which served as a pillow, so that he could lie facing the entrance. After carefully placing two more blocks of peat on the fire, he stood for a long time watching the stretched canvas, but it seemed to billow naturally with the first gusts of a lowering wind. At last he prayed, and got in under his blankets, and closed his smoke-smarting eyes. On the inside of the bed, next the wall, he could feel with his hand, the comfortable piece of lead pipe.

Isak Dinesen

A Sailor Boy's Tale   1942

Isak Dinesen was the pen name of Karen Dinesen von Blixen (1885 – 1962), Danish author who wrote in English. In 1913 she married her distant cousin, Baron Bror Blixen, and began a seventeen-year-long attempt to grow coffee in Kenya — a world she recalls beautifully in Out of Africa *(1937). (This memoir omits the love life made graphic in the 1985 film version with Meryl Streep.) Syphilis contracted from her husband, though temporarily arrested, later recurred; it was gradually to waste her to death. In 1931, divorced, shattered in health, her English lover killed in an air crash, her coffee plantation lost on the auction block, Dinesen returned to Denmark. There at age forty-six she turned to writing to pay her debts, determinedly signing her stories* Isak *("he who laughs"). Elegant in style, rich in surprise, shining with arch wit and a disturbing sense of the macabre, Dinesen's work quickly attained a large American audience. She wrote* Seven Gothic Tales *(1934);* Winter's Tales *(1942);* The Angelic Avengers *(1944), a novel subtly protesting against the Nazi occupation, published in wartime under the pen name Pierre Andrezel;* Last Tales *(1957); and* Shadows on the Grass *(1961), a later view of Africa. Her mission as a storyteller, she wrote, was "to make others confound fiction and reality in order to render them, for an hour, mysteriously happy."*

The barque *Charlotte* was on her way from Marseille to Athens, in grey weather, on a high sea, after three days' heavy gale. A small sailor-boy, named Simon, stood on the wet, swinging deck, held on to a shroud, and looked up towards the drifting clouds, and to the upper top-gallant yard of the main-mast.

A bird, that had sought refuge upon the mast, had got her feet entangled in some loose tackle-yarn of the halliard, and, high up there, struggled to get free. The boy on the deck could see her wings flapping and her head turning from side to side.

Through his own experience of life he had come to the conviction that in this world everyone must look after himself, and expect no help from others. But the mute, deadly fight kept him fascinated for more than an hour. He wondered what kind of bird it would be. These last days a number of birds had come to settle in the barque's rigging: swallows, quails, and a pair of peregrine falcons; he believed that this bird was a peregrine falcon. He remembered how, many years ago, in his own country and near his home, he had once seen a peregrine falcon quite close, sitting on a stone and flying straight up from it. Perhaps this was the same bird. He thought: "That bird is like me. Then she was there, and now she is here."

At that a fellow-feeling rose in him, a sense of common tragedy; he stood looking at the bird with his heart in his mouth. There were none of the sailors about to make fun of him; he began to think out how he might go up by the shrouds to help the falcon out. He brushed his hair back and pulled up his sleeves, gave the deck round him a great glance, and climbed up. He had to stop a couple of times in the swaying rigging.

It was indeed, he found when he got to the top of the mast, a peregrine   5 falcon. As his head was on a level with hers, she gave up her struggle, and looked at him with a pair of angry, desperate yellow eyes. He had to take hold of her with one hand while he got his knife out, and cut off the tackle-yarn. He was scared as he looked down, but at the same time he felt that he had been ordered up by nobody, but that this was his own venture, and this gave him a proud, steadying sensation, as if the sea and the sky, the ship, the bird and himself were all one. Just as he had freed the falcon, she hacked him in the thumb, so that the blood ran, and he nearly let her go. He grew angry with her, and gave her a clout on the head, then he put her inside his jacket, and climbed down again.

When he reached the deck the mate and the cook were standing there, looking up; they roared to him to ask what he had had to do in the mast. He was so tired that the tears were in his eyes. He took the falcon out and showed her to them, and she kept still within his hands. They laughed and walked off. Simon set the falcon down, stood back and watched her. After a while he reflected that she might not be able to get up from the slippery deck, so he caught her once more, walked away with her and placed her upon a bolt of canvas. A little after she began to trim her feathers, made two or three sharp jerks forward, and then suddenly flew off. The boy could follow her flight above the troughs of the grey sea. He thought: "There flies my falcon."

When the *Charlotte* came home, Simon signed aboard another ship, and two years later he was a light hand on the schooner *Hebe* lying at Bodø, high up on the coast of Norway, to buy herrings.

To the great herring-markets of Bodø ships came together from all corners of the world; here were Swedish, Finnish and Russian boats, a forest of masts, and on shore a turbulent, irregular display of life, with many languages spoken, and mighty fights. On the shore booths had been set up, and the Lapps, small yellow people, noiseless in their movements, with watchful eyes, whom Simon had never seen before, came down to sell bead-embroidered leather-goods. It was April, the sky and the sea were so clear that it was difficult to hold one's eyes up against them — salt, infinitely wide, and filled with bird-shrieks — as if someone were incessantly whetting invisible knives, on all sides, high up in Heaven.

Simon was amazed at the lightness of these April evenings. He knew no geography, and did not assign it to the latitude, but he took it as a sign of an unwonted good-will in the Universe, a favor. Simon had been small for his age all his life, but this last winter he had grown, and had become strong of limb. That good luck, he felt, must spring from the very same source as the sweetness of the weather, from a new benevolence in the world. He had been in need of such encouragement, for he was timid by nature; now he asked for no more. The rest he felt to be his own affair. He went about slowly, and proudly.

One evening he was ashore with land-leave, and walked up to the booth of a small Russian trader, a Jew who sold gold watches. All the sailors knew that his watches were made from bad metal, and would not go, still they bought them, and paraded them about. Simon looked at these watches for a long time, but did not buy. The old Jew had divers goods in his shop, and amongst others a case of oranges. Simon had tasted oranges on his journeys; he bought one and took it with him. He meant to go up on a hill, from where he could see the sea, and suck it there.

As he walked on, and had got to the outskirts of the place, he saw a little girl in a blue frock, standing at the other side of a fence and looking at him. She was thirteen or fourteen years old, as slim as an eel, but with a round, clear, freckled face, and a pair of long plaits. The two looked at one another.

"Who are you looking out for?" Simon asked, to say something. The girl's face broke into an ecstatic, presumptuous smile. "For the man I am going to marry, of course," she said. Something in her countenance made the boy confident and happy; he grinned a little at her. "That will perhaps be me," he said. "Ha, ha," said the girl, "he is a few years older than you, I can tell you." "Why," said Simon, "you are not grown up yourself." The little girl shook her head solemnly. "Nay," she said, "but when I grow up I will be exceedingly beautiful, and wear brown shoes with heels, and a hat." "Will you have an orange?" asked Simon, who could give her none of the things she had named. She looked at the orange and at him. "They are very good to eat," said he. "Why do you not eat it yourself then?" she asked. "I have eaten so many already," said he, "when I was in Athens. Here I had to pay a mark for it." "What is your name?" asked she. "My name is Simon," said he. "What is yours?" "Nora," said the girl. "What do you want for your orange now, Simon?"

When he heard his name in her mouth Simon grew bold. "Will you give

10

me a kiss for the orange?" he asked. Nora looked at him gravely for a moment. "Yes," she said, "I should not mind giving you a kiss." He grew as warm as if he had been running quickly. When she stretched out her hand for the orange he took hold of it. At that moment somebody in the house called out for her. "That is my father," said she, and tried to give him back the orange, but he would not take it. "Then come again tomorrow," she said quickly, "then I will give you a kiss." At that she slipped off. He stood and looked after her, and a little later went back to his ship.

Simon was not in the habit of making plans for the future, and now he did not know whether he would be going back to her or not.

The following evening he had to stay aboard, as the other sailors were going ashore, and he did not mind that either. He meant to sit on the deck with the ship's dog, Balthasar, and to practise upon a concertina that he had purchased some time ago. The pale evening was all around him, the sky was faintly roseate, the sea was quite calm, like milk-and-water, only in the wake of the boats going inshore it broke into streaks of vivid indigo. Simon sat and played; after a while his own music began to speak to him so strongly that he stopped, got up and looked upwards. Then he saw that the full moon was sitting high on the sky.

The sky was so light that she hardly seemed needed there; it was as if she had turned up by a caprice of her own. She was round, demure and presumptuous. At that he knew that he must go ashore, whatever it was to cost him. But he did not know how to get away, since the others had taken the yawl with them. He stood on the deck for a long time, a small lonely figure of a sailor-boy on a boat, when he caught sight of a yawl coming in from a ship farther out, and hailed her. He found that it was the Russian crew from a boat named *Anna,* going ashore. When he could make himself understood to them, they took him with them; they first asked him for money for his fare, then, laughing, gave it back to him. He thought: "These people will be believing that I am going in to town, wenching." And then he felt, with some pride, that they were right, although at the same time they were infinitely wrong, and knew nothing about anything.

When they came ashore they invited him to come in and drink in their company, and he would not refuse, because they had helped him. One of the Russians was a giant, as big as a bear; he told Simon that his name was Ivan. He got drunk at once, and then fell upon the boy with a bear-like affection, pawed him, smiled and laughed into his face, made him a present of a gold watch-chain, and kissed him on both cheeks. At that Simon reflected that he also ought to give Nora a present when they met again, and as soon as he could get away from the Russians he walked up to a booth that he knew of, and bought a small blue silk handkerchief, the same color as her eyes.

It was Saturday evening, and there were many people amongst the houses; they came in long rows, some of them singing, all keen to have some fun that night. Simon, in the midst of this rich, bawling life under the clear moon, felt his head light with the flight from the ship and the strong drinks. He crammed the handkerchief in his pocket; it was silk, which he had never touched before, a present for his girl.

He could not remember the path up to Nora's house, lost his way, and came back to where he had started. Then he grew deadly afraid that he should be too late, and began to run. In a small passage between two wooden huts he ran straight into a big man, and found that it was Ivan once more. The Russian folded his arms round him and held him. "Good! Good!" he cried in high glee, "I have found you, my little chicken. I have looked for you everywhere, and poor Ivan has wept because he lost his friend." "Let me go, Ivan," cried Simon. "Oho," said Ivan, "I shall go with you and get you what you want. My heart and my money are all yours, all yours; I have been seventeen years old myself, a little lamb of God, and I want to be so again tonight." "Let me go," cried Simon, "I am in a hurry." Ivan held him so that it hurt, and patted him with his other hand. "I feel it, I feel it," he said. "Now trust to me, my little friend. Nothing shall part you and me. I hear the others coming; we will have such a night together as you will remember when you are an old grand-papa."

Suddenly he crushed the boy to him, like a bear that carries off a sheep. The odious sensation of male bodily warmth and the bulk of a man close to him made the lean boy mad. He thought of Nora waiting, like a slender ship in the dim air, and of himself, here, in the hot embrace of a hairy animal. He struck Ivan with all his might. "I shall kill you, Ivan," he cried out, "if you do not let me go." "Oh, you will be thankful to me later on," said Ivan, and began to sing. Simon fumbled in his pocket for his knife, and got it opened. He could not lift his hand, but he drove the knife, furiously, in under the big man's arm. Almost immediately he felt the blood spouting out, and running down in his sleeve. Ivan stopped short in the song, let go his hold of the boy and gave two long deep grunts. The next second he tumbled down on his knees. "Poor Ivan, poor Ivan," he groaned. He fell straight on his face. At that moment Simon heard the other sailors coming along, singing, in the by-street.

He stood still for a minute, wiped his knife, and watched the blood spread into a dark pool underneath the big body. Then he ran. As he stopped for a second to choose his way, he heard the sailors behind him scream out over their dead comrade. He thought: "I must get down to the sea, where I can wash my hand." But at the same time he ran the other way. After a little while he found himself on the path that he had walked on the day before, and it seemed as familiar to him as if he had walked it many hundred times in his life.

He slackened his pace to look around, and suddenly saw Nora standing on the other side of the fence; she was quite close to him when he caught sight of her in the moonlight. Wavering and out of breath he sank down on his knees. For a moment he could not speak. The little girl looked down at him. "Good evening, Simon," she said in her small coy voice. "I have waited for you a long time," and after a moment she added: "I have eaten your orange."

"Oh, Nora," cried the boy. "I have killed a man." She stared at him, but did not move. "Why did you kill a man?" she asked after a moment. "To get here," said Simon. "Because he tried to stop me. But he was my friend." Slowly he got on to his feet. "He loved me!" the boy cried out, and at that burst into tears. "Yes," said she slowly and thoughtfully. "Yes, because you must be here in time." "Can you hide me?" he asked. "For they are after me." "Nay," said Nora, "I cannot hide you. For my father is the parson here at Bodø, and he would be sure to hand you over to them, if he knew that you had killed a man." "Then," said Simon, "give me something to wipe my hands on." "What is the matter with your hands?" she asked, and took a little step forward. He stretched out his hands to her. "Is that your own blood?" she asked. "No," said he, "it is his." She took the step back again. "Do you hate me now?" he asked. "No, I do not hate you," said she. "But do put your hands at your back."

As he did so she came up close to him, at the other side of the fence, and clasped her arms round his neck. She pressed her young body to his, and kissed him tenderly. He felt her face, cool as the moonlight, upon his own, and when she released him, his head swam, and he did not know if the kiss had lasted a second or an hour. Nora stood up straight, her eyes wide open. "Now," she said slowly and proudly, "I promise you that I will never marry anybody, as long as I live." The boy kept standing with his hands on his back, as if she had tied them there. "And now," she said, "you must run, for they are coming." They looked at one another. "Do not forget Nora," said she. He turned and ran.

He leapt over a fence, and when he was down amongst the houses he walked. He did not know at all where to go. As he came to a house, from where music and noise streamed out, he slowly went through the door. The room was full of people; they were dancing in here. A lamp hung from the ceiling, and shone down on them; the air was thick and brown with the dust rising from the floor. There were some women in the room, but many of the men danced with each other, and gravely or laughingly stamped the floor. A moment after Simon had come in the crowd withdrew to the walls to clear the floor for two sailors, who were showing a dance from their own country.

Simon thought: "Now, very soon, the men from the boat will come round to look for their comrade's murderer, and from my hands they will know that I have done it." These five minutes during which he stood by the wall of the dancing-room, in the midst of the gay, sweating dancers, were of great significance to the boy. He himself felt it, as if during this time he grew up, and became like other people. He did not entreat his destiny, nor complain. Here he was, he had killed a man, and had kissed a girl. He did not demand any more from life, nor did life now demand more from him. He was Simon, a man like the men round him, and going to die, as all men are going to die.

He only became aware of what was going on outside him, when he saw that a woman had come in, and was standing in the midst of the cleared floor, looking round her. She was a short, broad old woman, in the clothes of the Lapps, and she took her stand with such majesty and fierceness as if she owned the whole place. It was obvious that most of the people knew her, and were a little afraid of her, although a few laughed; the din of the dancing-room stopped when she spoke.

"Where is my son?" she asked in a high shrill voice, like a bird's. The next moment her eyes fell on Simon himself, and she steered through the crowd, which opened up before her, stretched out her old skinny, dark hand, and took him by the elbow. "Come home with me now," she said. "You need not dance here tonight. You may be dancing a high enough dance soon."

Simon drew back, for he thought that she was drunk. But as she looked him straight in the face with her yellow eyes, it seemed to him that he had met her before, and that he might do well in listening to her. The old woman pulled him with her across the floor, and he followed her without a word. "Do not birch your boy too badly, Sunniva," one of the men in the room cried to her. "He has done no harm, he only wanted to look at the dance."

At the same moment as they came out through the door, there was an alarm in the street, a flock of people came running down it, and one of them, as he turned into the house, knocked against Simon, looked at him and the old woman, and ran on.

While the two walked along the street, the old woman lifted up her skirt, and put the hem of it into the boy's hand. "Wipe your hand on my skirt," she said. They had not gone far before they came to a small wooden house, and stopped; the door to it was so low that they must bend to get through it. As the Lapp-woman went in before Simon, still holding on to his arm, the boy looked up for a moment. The night had grown misty; there was a wide ring round the moon.

The old woman's room was narrow and dark, with but one small window to it; a lantern stood on the floor and lighted it up dimly. It was all filled with reindeer skins and wolf skins, and with reindeer horn, such as the Lapps use to make their carved buttons and knife-handles, and the air in here was rank and stifling. As soon as they were in, the woman turned to Simon, took hold of his head, and with her crooked fingers parted his hair and combed it down in Lapp fashion. She clapped a Lapp cap on him and stood back to glance at him. "Sit down on my stool, now," she said. "But first take out your knife." She was so commanding in voice and manner that the boy could not but choose to do as she told him; he sat down on the stool, and he could not take his eyes off her face, which was flat and brown, and as if smeared with dirt in its net of fine wrinkles. As he sat there he heard many people come along outside, and stop by the house; then someone knocked at the door, waited a moment and knocked again. The old woman stood and listened, as still as a mouse.

"Nay," said the boy and got up. "This is no good, for it is me that they are after. It will be better for you to let me go out to them." "Give me your knife," said she. When he handed it to her, she stuck it straight into her thumb, so that the blood spouted out, and she let it drip all over her skirt. "Come in, then," she cried.

The door opened, and two of the Russian sailors came and stood in the opening; there were more people outside. "Has anybody come in here?" they asked. "We are after a man who has killed our mate, but he has run away from us. Have you seen or heard anybody this way?" The old Lapp-woman turned upon them, and her eyes shone like gold in the lamplight. "Have I seen or heard anyone?" she cried. "I have heard you shriek murder all over the town. You frightened me, and my poor silly boy there, so that I cut my thumb as I was ripping the skin-rug that I sew. The boy is too scared to help me, and the rug is all ruined. I shall make you pay me for that. If you are looking for a murderer, come in and search my house for me, and I shall know you when we meet again." She was so furious that she danced where she stood, and jerked her head like an angry bird of prey.

The Russian came in, looked round the room, and at her and her blood-stained hand and skirt. "Do not put a curse on us now, Sunniva," he said timidly. "We know that you can do many things when you like. Here is a mark to pay you for the blood you have spilled." She stretched out her hand, and he placed a piece of money in it. She spat on it. "Then go, and there shall be no bad blood between us," said Sunniva, and shut the door after them. She stuck her thumb in her mouth, and chuckled a little.

The boy got up from his stool, stood straight up before her and stared into her face. He felt as if he were swaying high up in the air, with but a small hold. "Why have you helped me?" he asked her. "Do you not know?" she answered. "Have you not recognized me yet? But you will remember the peregrine falcon which was caught in the tackle-yarn of your boat, the *Charlotte,* as she sailed in the Mediterranean. That day you climbed up by the shrouds of the top-gallantmast to help her out, in a stiff wind, and with a high sea. That falcon was me. We Lapps often fly in such a manner, to see the world. When I first met you I was on my way to Africa, to see my younger sister and her children. She is a falcon too, when she chooses. By that time she was living at Takaunga, within an old ruined tower, which down there they call a minaret." She swathed a corner of her skirt round her thumb, and bit at it. "We do not forget," she said. "I hacked your thumb, when you took hold of me; it is only fair that I should cut my thumb for you tonight."

She came close to him, and gently rubbed her two brown, claw-like fingers against his forehead. "So you are a boy," she said, "who will kill a man rather than be late to meet your sweetheart? We hold together, the females of this earth. I shall mark your forehead now, so that the girls will know of that, when they look at you, and they will like you for it." She played with the boy's hair, and twisted it round her finger.

"Listen now, my little bird," said she. "My great grandson's brother-in-law is lying with his boat by the landing-place at this moment; he is to take a consignment of skins out to a Danish boat. He will bring you back to your boat, in time, before your mate comes. The *Hebe* is sailing tomorrow morning, is it not so? But when you are aboard, give him back my cap for me." She took up his knife, wiped it in her skirt and handed it to him. "Here is your knife," she said. "You will stick it into no more men; you will not need to, for from now you will sail the seas like a faithful seaman. We have enough trouble with our sons as it is."

The bewildered boy began to stammer his thanks to her. "Wait," said she, "I shall make you a cup of coffee, to bring back your wits, while I wash your jacket." She went and rattled an old copper kettle upon the fireplace. After a while she handed him a hot, strong, black drink in a cup without a handle to it. "You have drunk with Sunniva now," she said; "you have drunk down a little wisdom, so that in the future all your thoughts shall not fall like raindrops into the salt sea."

When he had finished and set down the cup, she led him to the door and opened it for him. He was surprised to see that it was almost clear morning. The house was so high up that the boy could see the sea from it, and a milky mist about it. He gave her his hand to say good-bye.

She stared into his face. "We do not forget," she said. "And you, you knocked me on the head there, high up in the mast. I shall give you that blow back." With that she smacked him on the ear as hard as she could, so that his head swam. "Now we are quits," she said, gave him a great, mischievous, shining glance, and a little push down the doorstep, and nodded to him.

In this way the sailor-boy got back to his ship, which was to sail the next morning, and lived to tell the story.

Isak Dinesen 343

Nagai Tatsuo

BRIEF ENCOUNTER 1948

Translated by Edward Seidensticker

Nagai Tatsuo (born in 1904) has written novels and essays over his long literary career, but is most highly esteemed in Japan as a writer of the short story. When poor health obliged him to drop out of school in his early teens, he set to work perfecting his craft as a writer. For decades he worked as an editor for Bungei Shunju, a major publishing firm, eventually becoming a director of the company and founding its branch in Manchuria. Expelled by the Red Chinese occupation in 1947, he returned to his native Tokyo. Nagai's stories portray, with gentle humor, touching moments in the lives of ordinary citizens in swiftly changing, Westernized, postwar Japan.

I must ask you to read a part of my letter before you begin the story proper:

> I received your letter and the enclosed money order. Thank you very much.
>
> Thank you for the remarkable news that the ring I left with you has joined your engagement ring and been reborn as a tooth. I find myself less surprised and sorry than wanting to tell how much it helped with the fresh, new view of life I mentioned to you.
>
> As you have shown in your own person, the gold tooth artlessly in place somewhere behind an eyetooth is especially pleasing when glimpsed in the smile of a woman in her middle twenties. (Was yours perhaps one into which your husband himself put all his affection and skill? Forgive me. I will say no more about your false tooth. Even by way of sympathy.) I only hope this: that the two rings, the symbol of your gloom and the symbol of my new, fresh mood, will become admirable new teeth for the good of the people of Tokyo.
>
> It occurs to me, as I stop writing for a minute to light a cigarette, that letter-writing scenes are disappearing from the movies. To be sure, telephones and telegraphs are relieving the race of the troublesome chore; but I feel a certain nostalgia for the expression on her face for those few seconds when, having laid down the pen, she raises the envelope to her lips. 5
>
> What was I going to say? At first, not used to the work, I was exhausted; but now a month has gone by, and, sound and healthy again, I am in with the youngsters, having the experience of life in the mines . . .

I had quite cleaned out the room.

The medium-sized Boston bag that held my belongings lay in the middle of the alcove, and twenty or thirty books were stacked against the wall. There was a newspaper on the desk by the window. The bedding was folded neatly in front of the cupboard, with the pillow on top, as if to weigh it down.

I said good-by at the main house, and when I came back to my six-mat room, somehow cut off, amputated from the human world, the red kitten was curled by the pillow.

I felt myself smiling. "And what do you think *you're* doing here?" In my hat and coat, I knelt by the bedding and stroked the animal softly. Its eyes still closed, it rolled over on its back, and, in a most excellent mood, purred for me.

It had been in the main house for three months or so, and it would come to see me several times every day. Although nearly forty, I had never kept a cat or a dog. This was the first time I had ever lived near a cat.

I put my ear to its stomach and listened for a moment to the purring. Then, going out to the corridor that faced the garden and led to the main house, I put on my shoes. I had a raincoat over my arm. They had told me in the main house that the forecast was for rain.

Since they had agreed to store everything I did not immediately need, the disposition of my assets could not have been simpler.

I left the door open a little, for the kitten.

Several days earlier I had told my brother that I thought I might go to see a foreign movie — I would be off in the mines for a while, and would not have another chance. This morning a note had come by messenger.

"I was not able to get tickets for *The Best Years of Our Lives*°. I enclose instead tickets for an English movie that is said to be very good, and with them an express ticket. The latter is for tomorrow. I will see you at the station."

The note was in my pocket when I got off at Shimbashi. I had come in from Hodogaya on the electric line, and I had been wondering all the way what to do. There were two tickets to *Brief Encounter*°, with the Japanese title *Aibiki*, "Assignation." I had no idea what sort of movie it was, but that was the title. It seemed to tease me, to jeer at me, to prod me.

My brother was too serious a sort to be teasing me with the two tickets, that much was sure; but it was ironical all the same, sending two tickets to a bachelor in his late thirties. What was I to do with the other?

As I walked down the stairs at Shimbashi I decided to invite A, who worked in an office behind the Ginza°.

I thought I would make a joke of it: "Someone gave me tickets to a movie called *Aibiki*, and I have them to get rid of. I know it's a little behind the times for two grown men to go to that sort of movie together, but I won't be seeing you again for a while. Come on along."

Unfortunately, A was out. Very well; I would give the ticket to someone in front of the theater. I crossed the bridge in the direction of the H Theater.

There were three or four people at the ticket window. I walked briskly up — and then changed my mind. There was a couple, and there were young

The Best Years of Our Lives: 1946 Samuel Goldwyn movie about American service people returning home from World War II.

Brief Encounter: This classic postwar English film (1945) portrays the fleeting, poignant, but unconsummated love between two middle-aged people already married. Rather than betray their mates, the two finally part, keeping stiff upper lips. Directed by David Lean with screenplay by Noel Coward, the film has touching performances by Celia Johnson and Trevor Howard as the almost-lovers.

the Ginza: busy shopping and entertainment area in Tokyo, concentrated on mile-long Ginza Street.

girls. The expression "a man in his forties" had come into my mind, and the image of middle-age accosting youth. After it, derisively, came those other terms that seemed applicable: "ex-soldier," "broken-down soldier," and the rest.

I went into the theater. The girl showed me to my seat. The next seat of course was vacant. As if asking them to sit down, I gave it to my hat and raincoat.

There was no reason at all to invite someone else just because I had two tickets. This was much better — I could spread out. The trouble with me was that I was still a prisoner of inflexible concepts.

People came in, the theater filled. The bell rang. The news went dizzy- 25
ingly in review.

Why was it, my brother had remarked the other day, that there was always something stale and musty about newsreels even when they had the latest scoops? The destruction after the storm was the same, whether the scene was Japan or America. The American woman, blown down the street, clung precariously to a telephone pole, and, frowning into the storm, she turned to the camera and smiled a childlike smile, as if to say that people *did* have interesting experiences.

The lights went on again when the newsreel was over. I felt somehow isolated from the crowd, but then the lights dimmed and the words "Brief Encounter" flashed against the rising curtain. I planted my elbow firmly on the arm of the vacant seat.

I had the aisle seat, and I felt a sort of pressure on my right. Someone, bent slightly forward, was standing there in the dark, waiting to be allowed past.

Automatically I looked back, but the only vacant seat was the one beside me. The ticket for it was in my pocket. I picked up my coat and hat nonetheless and put them on my knee.

The person bowed and slipped adroitly past. It was a woman in foreign 30
dress, leaving a faint perfume behind her. I heard her open her handbag. She seemed to be taking out her glasses. I felt even after she had sat down that she was fairly tall for a woman.

Life was new and fresh, clearly it was — I reaffirmed the philosophy I had acquired during the preceding half year. But how to explain the mystery of the seat beside me?

The dull confession of a plain, tired wife, in an atmosphere of indescriba- ble gloom. It began to pull at me. At first I resisted, but presently I was caught up in it.

There is no need here to recount the plot or to give my reactions, and indeed I am not qualified to. When I thought of it again some days later on the train, I suddenly thought too of *Earth,* that somber Japanese novel of peasant life, a cheap edition of which I had borrowed from a young comrade when I was stationed on the southern front. The movie was about a secret affair of a nameless woman in a small town, and the views of an ex-soldier are of no importance.

Yet I must mention something I would rather not: I thought again, for the first time in a great while, of my ex-wife, whom, a year before, I had let go without a shade of regret. Although no one could know that I had thought of her, I felt most ashamed of myself afterwards.

I was slightly dissatisfied with the last scene, in which the amiable   35
husband forgave the wife. She had not committed the final error, it is true, but
the affair had left her an empty shell. Perhaps that was what made me remember
my wife. On that point, at least, I was superior to the husband of the
movie.

Brief Encounter was over. I seem to have lost myself in thought, for the
woman was asking to be let by. I stood up. I followed her, and we were the
last to leave the theater.

The weather forecast had been accurate. The exit was screened by a
white curtain, a May rain. There were some ten young people caught without
umbrellas.

I stepped beyond them and lighted a cigarette. I was ready for the rain,
but felt no need to hurry. The woman too took a cigarette from a silver case.
There was a subtle quickness in her gestures, the movement from gesture to
gesture. She had on a dark green suit, and she was indeed tall for a woman.
I had glanced at her as she looked up into the sky, and been struck by the lashes
of the slightly narrowed eyes. A woman's age is among the things I am
incapable of judging, but she was not yet thirty, of that I was sure. Perhaps
twenty-four or twenty-five, perhaps twenty-seven.

"It's not going to stop, either," she said suddenly. The black eyes moved
toward me as she spoke.

"I'm afraid not." I looked at the rain hitting the pavement. Now and then   40
a couple under a single umbrella stumbled through the spray.

"I thought it was so near, and I wouldn't need an umbrella. Stupid of
me." A mischievous laugh came into the eyes. There was a trace of lipstick on
her cigarette. I had not realized that it was possible to color the lips such a calm,
tranquil color.

"It's near, is it?"

"Just over there." The eyes, still smiling, and a finger pointed to the left.
"Next door to the curio shop."

I spread open my raincoat. "I have this. I'm going in that direction
anyway — suppose I stop by and have someone come with an umbrella."

"Please don't bother. It's so near. I'll run on when I've made up my mind   45
to get wet. Really." She spoke briskly, but with no suggestion of wanting to
brush me aside.

"Suppose I do it this way." I pulled the coat over my head like a photographer,
and smiled at her. The people who were waiting for a lull in the rain
looked at us curiously.

Cocking her head a little to one side, she smiled back. I seemed to have
put her at ease.

"Really? I shouldn't ask you to — but may I?" She came a step or two
nearer. "The building next to the curio shop. A dentist named Suematsu. If you
could ask the girl at the reception desk to come with a coat and an umbrella,
I'd really be most grateful."

It pleased me to think that I was helping someone I would never see
again. I ran through the rain. But I still did not understand about that seat.

There was a compact little building some two hundred yards away,   50
around the corner from the curio shop. I had no trouble finding the dentist's
office on the second floor. "Suematsu Shingo, Doctor of Dental Surgery; Suematsu
Akira, Dentist," the sign said in horizontal characters. It also said that

Sunday was a holiday, and that the office was open only until two on Saturdays. Today was a Saturday.

Just inside the door there was a little window over the reception desk, where a girl of eighteen or nineteen was sitting. I told her my business, and she answered quietly.

Feeling somewhat nostalgic at the antiseptic smell of the office, I closed the door behind me. As I started down I could hear the rain below.

"Excuse me." Someone was calling from the head of the stairs.

It was the reception girl. Two umbrellas and an oil-cloth coat in hand, she stood by the wall, waiting for me to come up again.

"If I leave there will be no one here. Would you mind waiting till I get back?"   55

"Not at all, not at all."

She seemed to think that I was a friend of the woman's. Such a simple girl — should she be so trusting? There was something heart-warming about her. I walked slowly up and down before the Suematsu door.

"What a rain, and no sign of letting up. When did it begin?" The bright voice of the woman came from the stairs. Then she saw me, and once more I looked closely into her eyes. "Well! What a bother for you! That's our Miss Tateno, as easygoing as ever. She had you watch the place, did she? Come on in, now that you've gone to so much trouble. For just a minute. It would be strange to let him go like this, wouldn't it, Miss Tateno?"

Turning from me to the receptionist, she pushed open the door without letting me answer.

"It's strange to think it would be strange."   60

She laughed, and opened another door, to a clean little waiting room that could accommodate perhaps three or four people.

"Have a seat. I'll be back in a minute." I took off my wet coat and sat on the sofa.

In the quiet I could hear water, and, faintly, the sound of a comb running through someone's hair.

"What about the coffee in the thermos bottle? Yes, let's have that. You have some too." She spoke to the girl in a voice so quiet that I wondered how it could come from the same person. "It was a gloomy, gloomy movie. I'm exhausted." I next heard someone opening a can. "I don't say it wasn't interesting, but I wonder how it would be for a young person."

Miss Tateno looked much brighter when she came in with coffee. She   65
had changed from her office uniform. The place seemed more like a parlor.

"I shouldn't have asked you to wait. You must forgive me." She had on a blouse, I suppose you would call it — a clear, pale cerulean blue. (I know, having investigated these colors.) The sleeves were short, and the brooch was an ivory flower set in gold. I stood up.

"There was a terrible rainstorm in *Brief Encounter* too."

"Yes. I must look a little like the doctor."

"Maybe it feels good when you get as wet as that." The woman sat down lightly in the chair opposite me.

If one had praised the fairness of her complexion, she would probably   70
have answered: "Oh? And I've never done a thing for it. You should praise my father and mother."

But since in her hair, for all the careful attention that had gone into dressing it, there was a faint touch of calculated disarray, as of a keystone pulled slightly loose, so that the hair set off the beauty of the throat — since there was this air about her whole person, one could not doubt that a considerable sum had been invested in the almost unpowdered whiteness of the skin.

"You're going shopping in the rain?" She cast a quiet glance over my shoulder. "You are? Well, don't worry about me. I'll sit here with this gentleman a little longer, and then close the office."

Miss Tateno said nothing, but I gathered that she was leaving. The woman got up and went toward her.

"I'm sorry I had to say such unpleasant things. You must forgive me."

"Please don't apologize." 75

"You're not to worry. Understand? I'm completely over it now. I'll be in early Monday morning, looking very cheerful." She laughed softly. "Bye-bye."

I sensed that she had taken the girl's hand by way of apology. The "Bye-bye" had a high, clear ring to it.

"Something unpleasant happened, and I ran out to the movie. I felt dreadful, it was such a dismal movie." She had sat down again, and her eyes were still on the silver case after she had offered me a cigarette and taken one herself.

I wondered what the unpleasantness might have been, but did not feel that I could ask. Instead I turned the conversation to the matter that puzzled me. "I had two tickets to the movie, and the second one was a problem. It made me feel very useless."

"You should have taken your wife." 80

"Well, you see, as a matter of fact — " It was not a subject I found easy to talk about.

"May I ask if you were in the service? In the Navy, perhaps?"

"Precisely."

"I had two cousins in the Navy. Up until a few years ago I was rather popular with the young officers." But I did not want to talk about the past.

"And what did you do with the other ticket?" she asked. 85

"I wanted to invite a friend — a man, of course — but he was out. I went by myself."

"What a pity. And for a *Brief Encounter,* too."

"But here I am drinking coffee with you. Why did you take that seat?"

"That seat?" Her eyes narrowed questioningly, and there was a pause. "Oh! I took the wrong seat. How stupid of me!" For the first time I felt a touch of coquetry.

"I thought it a great privilege." 90

"I was upset and a little excited, and there was no usher. I go there often, it's so close, and I thought my seat ought to be about there. And I'm a little nearsighted."

"I see." I saw everything. I saw too that a slight case of myopia could make a woman's eyes rather seductive.

"I think it's letting up. You said you had business on the Ginza?"

"Nothing of any importance." I too looked out the window.

"If you're in no hurry, stay as long as you like. I have nothing to do myself." 95

"I go away tomorrow."

"How I envy you. Where are you going?"

"I'll be in Kyushu for a while."

"Men have all the advantages. On business."

"No money in it, as they say. I'm going to work. In a coal mine." 100

"Oh?"

"I've done all sorts of things to keep myself alive since I came back. I've come to the conclusion that it's not too difficult if keeping yourself alive is all you want. But everything seems so strange, now that the military blinkers are off. Everything seems so fresh and new, so alive, from the time I get up in the morning till I go to bed at night."

"You were a commander?"

"A lieutenant-commander at the end of the war. I didn't do so well when it came to promotions." I spoke rapidly. I did not want to talk about the past. "There was a kitten that used to come and see me all the time. It was very interesting. I had never liked cats — so cold and willful. But then I would watch that kitten, and it seemed strange that such an animal could have been born. Everything was interesting to it, even its own tail. It was never bored. If that liveliness to new impressions could go on say four or five years, a cat would be a remarkable beast."

"Isn't it the truth. They get so fat and sluggish when they are older. I 105 kept three cats once, but then it came to me that it was not very good form for a childless woman to be fond of cats, and I gave them away."

"I want to have all the experiences I can before I get fat and sluggish myself. I'm in a great hurry."

"And that's why you're going into a coal mine?"

"I want to do away with the ex-soldier."

"You'll join the Communist Party, then, and the labor movement?"

"Possibly. But the Party is too much like the service. It has no respect 110 for you as an individual." I sensed that I was being asked leading questions. And so I made a leading remark: "To someone like me it's a fairy story, a well-matched husband and wife running a clean little office together."

"A fairy story — it was at first." She looked at me again with that slightly quizzical expression, and immediately lowered her eyes. Her manner changed abruptly. She evidently did not mean to be taken by my lead. "You're kept busy, that's all, repairing bad teeth day after day. Unless someone has to have a difficult bridge made, you can hardly breathe for the boredom. I'd like to use heaps of gold and platinum on something really good."

With that, I remembered my business on the Ginza. I hesitated a second, then took a little wad of paper from my pocket. I had found it in the desk drawer when I cleaned the room that morning. "It's a little sudden, but could you use this?"

The delicately manicured hand took up the paper, and from it came an engagement ring.

I explained in some confusion: "I found it this morning when I was cleaning up. I wondered if I might be able to sell it on the Ginza. I know it would be more dashing if I were to drop it into the river from Kachidoki Bridge or somewhere, but I've never been much for romantic things, and I thought I'd put it up for sale instead."

"I could take it for you. Shall I?" 115

"It's been no use for a year — no, for much longer than that. It's not a question of the money," I added, when I saw a cloud come over her face.

The curve of her neck, slightly arched against the back of the chair, turned toward the window. She fingered the ring languidly. "Three grams, maybe four? Well, let me take it for you. I think the rain has stopped."

I too had been looking uncomfortably at the faint yellowish sunlight coming through the window. It was time to leave.

As the hand with the ring dropped to her lap, she took a deep breath, and two points came to life on her blouse. Then her face, propped on her other hand, turned to me with a delicate quickness, as if to dismiss something. "Excuse me. Here I am brooding when I have company." She hunched over, and the smiling face came nearer. "When I'm busy I usually have lunch just up the street. I've left a supply of rice there. I thought of having something today before I go home, and if you have nothing else to do, suppose you come along." Without waiting for my answer, she took her handbag from the little table. "The price of gold changes every day, but let me give you a thousand yen anyway. Business is business. I'll send the rest to your mine when I know exactly how much it comes to."

The frankness of the smooth-flowing words helped a little. 120

I waited in the hall.

She came out, her lips alive, and the office door closed sharply.

In the evening sunlight after the May rain, we crossed the bridge toward the Ginza. It is pointless, at such times, to describe life as "new and fresh."

She exchanged quiet greetings with the waiters and sat down opposite me.

"They say beer doesn't go well with it, but — " We emptied our glasses. 125

"Your husband?" The talk of drink gave me courage to mention something that had puzzled me.

"Oh, don't worry about 'your husband.' " As she poured more beer for me — indeed, by pouring more beer — she fended off my question. "Were you on the southern front for a long time?"

"Here and there for two years."

"And you were separated from your wife a year after you came back?"

"I guessed everything immediately. It wasn't fun, but I wanted to be rid 130 of the past, and I made a clean break with her. But that isn't a very pleasant subject."

"I'm sorry. That last scene of *Brief Encounter* — remember? Where the husband forgives the wife? It bothered me. It made me very sad to think how they would pass the years afterward. And so I brought it up. But no more."

True, that ending was no ending. Might we not better have left the matter to the critics, however?

"We got nothing at all from military life. Or one thing only. We islanders with our island minds can still remember Java or Luzon° when we see a sunset

Java or Luzon: islands in Indonesia and in the Philippines, both of which the Japanese army occupied in World War II.

like this. The sunrise some morning makes us all think of sunrises on the continent, while we plow our fields and row our boats. That is the one thing it gave us."

"Men have all the advantages." Her long eyelashes lowered, she watched the shining beads that rose from the bottom of the glass. It is dangerous to be too impressed by feminine poses at certain times. "Oh, yes. You mustn't forget to give me your Kyushu address."

I took out my card case. A long, narrow piece of paper came out with it.

She opened her handbag.

"I have a pen."

"Thank you." Idly, I turned over the piece of paper. It was the second theater ticket.

"Oh, good! Write on the back of that."

I looked at her and we laughed.

With a delicate fountain pen I wrote down the name of the mine and the dormitory.

"When I was in the south, the boys under me all had pictures of their girlfriends and their fiancées and their brides, and whenever they had a spare minute they would take out their pictures and look at them and show them off to the others. It was very strange, though — the habit would make them forget the real women."

She did not answer.

" 'Hey! What was my old woman's face like?' someone would say, and someone else would say, 'Now that you mention it, I can't remember my girl's face either. Be quiet a minute while I close my eyes and think.' It happened all the time."

"Interesting."

"How shall I describe it? The impulse to beautify women is always at work, and it builds up an image that moves away from the actual person. Even at my age."

"May I ask you to do the same with your image of me?" She tilted her head slightly and smiled.

"It may well happen."

Amused, I had my longest look into her eyes.

We parted at Tokyo Station, she to take the Central Line, I the Yokosuka Line. The next day I left for this mine.

A month later I had a registered letter from her:

First, our business.

The enclosed money order covers what I owe you for the item you left with me. I talked with a man we do business with, and bought it at the price he quoted.

It is becoming the cap for a young lady's second molar. She is a very pretty young lady and she is soon to be married. The lower bicuspid next to it will be capped with platinum, and for that I mean to use my own engagement ring.

The day I met you in that strange way was the day I decided on a divorce, after a great deal of unpleasantness. The reason is a most ordinary one, which I shall leave to your imagination.

I hesitated for a time about capping the teeth of a young girl soon to be married with two unlucky engagement rings, but then I came to think that they might be a sort of mascot for her in her new life.

I work hard, all day long. It is new and fresh, this not being anyone's wife.

I trust that you are taking care of yourself.

Have you noted any tendency to beautify my image?

The letter with which I began was my answer.

That is all there is to the story.

It would please me beyond measure if, among my readers, there should be some who felt like going back to reread the beginning.

160

Gabriel García Márquez
THE NIGHT OF THE CURLEWS   1953

Translated by Gregory Rabassa

Gabriel García Márquez, among the most eminent of living Latin American writers, was born in 1929 in Aracataca, a Caribbean port in Colombia, one of sixteen children of an impoverished telegraph operator. For a time he studied law in Bogotá, then became a reporter for a newspaper. Although he never joined the Communist party, García Márquez outspokenly advocated many left-wing proposals for reform. In 1954, despairing of any prospect for political change, he left Colombia to live in Mexico City. Though at nineteen he had completed a book of short stories, La hojorasca (Leafstorm), *he waited until 1955 to publish it. Soon he began to build a towering reputation among readers of Spanish. His celebrated novel,* Cien años de soledad (1967), *published in English as* One Hundred Years of Solitude (1969), *traces the history of a Colombian family through six generations. Called by Chilean poet Pablo Neruda "the greatest revelation in the Spanish language since* Don Quixote," *it has sold more than twelve million copies in thirty languages. In 1982 García Márquez was awarded the Nobel prize for literature. His fiction, rich in myth and invention, has reminded American readers of that of William Faulkner, another explorer of his native turf; indeed, García Márquez has called Faulkner "my master." Recently, he wrote the screenplay for* Eréndira (1984), *a film based on the title story from* Innocent Eréndira (1978). *"The Night of the Curlews" comes from the same collection.*

We were sitting, the three of us, around the table, when someone put a coin in the slot and the Wurlitzer played once more the record that had been going all night. The rest happened so fast that we didn't have time to think. It happened before we could remember where we were, before we could get back our sense of location. One of us reached his hand out over the counter, groping (we couldn't see the hand, we heard it), bumped into a glass, and then was still, with both hands resting on the hard surface. Then the three of us looked for ourselves in the darkness and found ourselves there, in the joints of the thirty fingers piled up on the counter. One of us said:

"Let's go."

And we stood up as if nothing had happened. We still hadn't had time to get upset.

In the hallway, as we passed, we heard the nearby music spinning out at us. We caught the smell of sad women sitting and waiting. We felt the prolonged emptiness of the hall before us while we walked toward the door, before the other smell came out to greet us, the sour smell of the woman sitting by the door. We said:

"We're leaving."   5

The woman didn't answer anything. We heard the creak of a rocking chair, rising up as she stood. We heard the footsteps on the loose board and the return of the woman again, when the hinges creaked once more and the door closed behind us.

We turned around. Right there, behind us, there was a harsh, cutting breeze of an invisible dawn, and a voice that said:

"Get out of the way, I'm coming through with this."

We moved back. And the voice spoke again:

"You're still against the door."   10

And only then, when we'd moved to all sides and had found the voice everywhere, did we say:

"We can't get out of here. The curlews have pecked out our eyes."

Then we heard several doors open. One of us let go of the other hands and we heard him dragging along in the darkness, weaving, bumping into the things that surrounded us. He spoke from somewhere in the darkness.

"We must be close," he said. "There's a smell of piled-up trunks around here."

We felt the contact of his hands again. We leaned against the wall and   15
another voice passed by then, but in the opposite direction.

"They might be coffins," one of us said.

The one who had dragged himself into the corner and was breathing beside us now said:

"They're trunks. Ever since I was little I've been able to tell the smell of stored clothing."

Then we moved in that direction. The ground was soft and smooth, fine earth that had been walked on. Someone held out a hand. We felt the contact with long, live skin, but we no longer felt the wall opposite.

"This is a woman," we said.   20

The other one, the one who had spoken of trunks, said:

"I think she's asleep."

The body shook under our hands, trembled, we felt it slip away, not as if it had got out of our reach, but as if it had ceased to exist. Still, after an instant in which we remained motionless, stiffened, leaning against each other's shoulders, we heard her voice.

"Who's there?" it said.

"It's us," we replied without moving.

The movement of the bed could be heard, the creaking and the shuffling of feet looking for slippers in the darkness. Then we pictured the seated woman, looking at us as when she still hadn't awakened completely.

"What are you doing here?" she asked.

And we answered.

"We don't know. The curlews pecked out our eyes."

The voice said that she'd heard something about that. That the newspapers had said that three men had been drinking in a courtyard where there were five or six curlews. Seven curlews. One of the men began singing like a curlew, imitating them.

"The worst was that he was an hour behind," she said. "That was when the birds jumped on the table and pecked out their eyes."

She said that's what the newspapers had said, but nobody had believed them. We said:

"If people had gone there, they'd have seen the curlews."

And the woman said:

"They did. The courtyard was full of people the next day, but the woman had already taken the curlews somewhere else."

When he turned around, the woman stopped speaking. There was the wall again. By just turning around we would find the wall. Around us, surrounding us, there was always a wall. One let go of our hands again. We heard him crawling again, smelling the ground, saying:

"Now I don't know where the trunks are. I think we're somewhere else now."

And we said:

"Come here. Somebody's here next to us."

We heard him come close. We felt him stand up beside us and again his warm breath hit us in the face.

"Reach out that way," we told him. "There's someone we know there."

He must have reached out, he must have moved toward the place we indicated, because an instant later he came back to tell us:

"I think it's a boy."

And we told him:

"Fine. Ask him if he knows us."

He asked the question. We heard the apathetic and simple voice of the boy, who said:

"Yes, I know you. You're the three men whose eyes were pecked out by the curlews."

Then an adult voice spoke. The voice of a woman who seemed to be behind a closed door, saying:

"You're talking to yourself again."

And the child's voice, unconcerned, said:

"No. The men who had their eyes pecked out by the curlews are here again."

There was a sound of hinges and then the adult voice, closer than the first time.

"Take them home," she said.

And the boy said:

"I don't know where they live." 55

And the adult voice said:

"Don't be mean. Everybody knows where they live ever since the night the curlews pecked their eyes out."

Then she went on in a different tone, as if she were speaking to us:

"What happened is that nobody wanted to believe it and they say it was a fake item made up by the papers to boost their circulation. No one has seen the curlews."

And he said: 60

"But nobody would believe me if I led them along the street."

We didn't move. We were still, leaning against the wall, listening to her. And the woman said:

"If this one wants to take you it's different. After all, nobody would pay much attention to what a boy says."

The child's voice cut in:

"If I go out onto the street with them and say that they're the men who 65 had their eyes pecked out by the curlews, the boys will throw stones at me. Everybody on the street says it couldn't have happened."

There was a moment of silence. Then the door closed again and the boy spoke:

"Besides, I'm reading *Terry and the Pirates*° right now."

Someone said in our ear:

"I'll convince him."

He crawled over to where the voice was. 70

"I like it," he said. "At least tell us what happened to Terry this week."

He's trying to gain his confidence, we thought. But the boy said:

"That doesn't interest me. The only thing I like are the colors."

"Terry's in a maze," we said.

And the boy said: 75

"That was Friday. Today's Sunday and what I like are the colors," and he said it with a cold, dispassionate, indifferent voice.

When the other one came back, we said:

"We've been lost for almost three days and we haven't had a moment's rest."

And one said:

"All right. Let's rest awhile, but without letting go of each other's 80 hands."

We sat down. An invisible sun began to warm us on the shoulders. But not even the presence of the sun interested us. We felt it there, everywhere, having already lost the notion of distance, time, direction. Several voices passed.

"The curlews pecked out our eyes," we said.

And one of the voices said:

Terry and the Pirates: newspaper comic strip of swashbuckling adventures in China.

"These here took the newspapers seriously."

The voices disappeared. And we kept on sitting, like that, shoulder to [85] shoulder, waiting, in that passing of voices, in that passing of images, for a smell or a voice that was known to us to pass. The sun was above our heads, still warming us. Then someone said:

"Let's go toward the wall again."

And the others, motionless, their heads lifted toward the invisible light:

"Not yet. Let's just wait till the sun begins to burn us on the face."

Tillie Olsen

I STAND HERE IRONING   1961

Tillie Olsen was born in Omaha in 1912, into a family of blue-collar workers who had fled Czarist Russia to escape persecution. Olsen grew up in poverty and quit school in eleventh grade to work. She later declared, "Public libraries were my college." As a member of the Young Communist League, she strove to organize Kansas City meat-packers, and was once thrown into jail. After her first husband deserted her, leaving her with one child, she married a printer and labor activist, Jack Olsen, by whom she had three more children. Although in the 1930s she published fiction in a distinguished little magazine, Partisan Review, *the demands of mother-hood, political activity, and factory and office jobs left her scant time to write until 1955. Then her youngest daughter began school and Olsen was awarded a creative-writing fellowship at Stanford University. Long a cru-sader for causes, she has been active in the recent feminist movement. "I Stand Here Ironing," from her first book,* Tell Me a Riddle *(1961), reads like autobiography. Olsen has since published* Yonnondio *(1974) an unfinished novel begun at age nineteen, and* Silences *(1978), a study of why writers — especially women writers — dry up. She holds several honorary degrees. In 1981 the city of San Francisco, where she has long resided, designated a Tillie Olsen day.*

I stand here ironing, and what you asked me moves tormented back and forth with the iron.

"I wish you would manage the time to come in and talk with me about your daughter. I'm sure you can help me understand her. She's a youngster who needs help and whom I'm deeply interested in helping."

"Who needs help." . . . Even if I came, what good would it do? You think because I am her mother I have a key, or that in some way you could use me as a key? She has lived for nineteen years. There is all that life that has happened outside of me, beyond me.

And when is there time to remember, to sift, to weigh, to estimate, to total? I will start and there will be an interruption and I will have to gather it all together again. Or I will become engulfed with all I did or did not do, with what should have been and what cannot be helped.

She was a beautiful baby. The first and only one of our five that was   5
beautiful at birth. You do not guess how new and uneasy her tenancy in her
now-loveliness. You did not know her all those years she was thought homely,
or see her poring over her baby pictures, making me tell her over and over how
beautiful she had been — and would be, I would tell her — and was now, to
the seeing eye. But the seeing eyes were few or nonexistent. Including mine.

I nursed her. They feel that's important nowadays. I nursed all the
children, but with her, with all the fierce rigidity of first motherhood, I did like
the books then said. Though her cries battered me to trembling and my breasts
ached with swollenness, I waited till the clock decreed.

Why do I put that first? I do not even know if it matters, or if it explains
anything.

She was a beautiful baby. She blew shining bubbles of sound. She loved
motion, loved light, loved color and music and textures. She would lie on the
floor in her blue overalls patting the surface so hard in ecstasy her hands and
feet would blur. She was a miracle to me, but when she was eight months old
I had to leave her daytimes with the woman downstairs to whom she was no
miracle at all, for I worked or looked for work and for Emily's father, who
"could no longer endure" (he wrote in his good-bye note) "sharing want with
us."

I was nineteen. It was the pre-relief, pre-WPA world of the depression.
I would start running as soon as I got off the streetcar, running up the stairs,
the place smelling sour, and awake or asleep to startle awake, when she saw
me she would break into a clogged weeping that could not be comforted, a
weeping I can hear yet.

After a while I found a job hashing at night so I could be with her days,   10
and it was better. But it came to where I had to bring her to his family and
leave her.

It took a long time to raise the money for her fare back. Then she got
chicken pox and I had to wait longer. When she finally came, I hardly knew
her, walking quick and nervous like her father, looking like her father, thin,
and dressed in a shoddy red that yellowed her skin and glared at the pock-
marks. All the baby loveliness gone.

She was two. Old enough for nursery school they said, and I did not
know then what I know now — the fatigue of the long day, and the lacerations
of group life in the kinds of nurseries that are only parking places for children.

Except that it would have made no difference if I had known. It was the
only place there was. It was the only way we could be together, the only way
I could hold a job.

And even without knowing, I knew. I knew the teacher that was evil
because all these years it has curdled into my memory, the little boy hunched
in the corner, her rasp, "why aren't you outside, because Alvin hits you? that's
no reason, go out, scaredy." I knew Emily hated it even if she did not clutch
and implore "don't go Mommy" like the other children, mornings.

She always had a reason why we should stay home. Momma, you look   15
sick. Momma, I feel sick. Momma, the teachers aren't there today, they're sick.
Momma, we can't go, there was a fire there last night. Momma, it's a holiday
today, no school, they told me.

But never a direct protest, never rebellion. I think of our others in their three-, four-year-oldness — the explosions, the tempers, the denunciations, the demands — and I feel suddenly ill. I put the iron down. What in me demanded that goodness in her? And what was the cost, the cost to her of such goodness?

The old man living in the back once said in his gentle way: "You should smile at Emily more when you look at her." What *was* in my face when I looked at her? I loved her. There were all the acts of love.

It was only with the others I remembered what he said, and it was the face of joy, and not of care or tightness or worry I turned to them — too late for Emily. She does not smile easily, let alone almost always as her brothers and sisters do. Her face is closed and sombre, but when she wants, how fluid. You must have seen it in her pantomimes, you spoke of her rare gift for comedy on the stage that rouses laughter out of the audience so dear they applaud and applaud and do not want to let her go.

Where does it come from, that comedy? There was none of it in her when she came back to me that second time, after I had had to send her away again. She had a new daddy now to learn to love, and I think perhaps it was a better time.

Except when we left her alone nights, telling ourselves she was old 20 enough.

"Can't you go some other time, Mommy, like tomorrow?" she would ask. "Will it be just a little while you'll be gone? Do you promise?"

The time we came back, the front door open, the clock on the floor in the hall. She rigid awake. "It wasn't just a little while. I didn't cry. Three times I called you, just three times, and then I ran downstairs to open the door so you could come faster. The clock talked loud. I threw it away, it scared me what it talked."

She said the clock talked loud again that night I went to the hospital to have Susan. She was delirious with the fever that comes before red measles, but she was fully conscious all the week I was gone and the week after we were home when she could not come near the new baby or me.

She did not get well. She stayed skeleton thin, not wanting to eat, and night after night she had nightmares. She would call for me, and I would rouse from exhaustion to sleepily call back: "You're all right, darling, go to sleep, it's just a dream," and if she still called, in a sterner voice, "now go to sleep, Emily, there's nothing to hurt you." Twice, only twice, when I had to get up for Susan anyhow, I went in to sit with her.

Now when it is too late (as if she would let me hold and comfort her like 25 I do the others) I get up and go to her at once at her moan or restless stirring. "Are you awake, Emily? Can I get you something?" And the answer is always the same: "No, I'm all right, go back to sleep, Mother."

They persuaded me at the clinic to send her away to a convalescent home in the country where "she can have the kind of food and care you can't manage for her, and you'll be free to concentrate on the new baby." They still send children to that place. I see pictures on the society page of sleek young women planning affairs to raise money for it, or dancing at the affairs, or decorating Easter eggs or filling Christmas stockings for the children.

They never have a picture of the children so I do not know if the girls still wear those gigantic red bows and the ravaged looks on the every other

Sunday when parents can come to visit "unless otherwise notified" — as we were notified the first six weeks.

Oh it is a handsome place, green lawns and tall trees and fluted flower beds. High up on the balconies of each cottage the children stand, the girls in their red bows and white dresses, the boys in white suits and giant red ties. The parents stand below shrieking up to be heard and the children shriek down to be heard, and between them the invisible wall: "Not to Be Contaminated by Parental Germs or Physical Affection."

There was a tiny girl who always stood hand in hand with Emily. Her parents never came. One visit she was gone. "They moved her to Rose Cottage," Emily shouted in explanation. "They don't like you to love anybody here."

She wrote once a week, the labored writing of a seven-year-old. "I am fine. How is the baby. If I write my leter nicly I will have a star. Love." There never was a star. We wrote every other day, letters she could never hold or keep but only hear read — once. "We simply do not have room for children to keep any personal possessions," they patiently explained when we pieced one Sunday's shrieking together to plead how much it would mean to Emily, who loved so to keep things, to be allowed to keep her letters and cards.

Each visit she looked frailer. "She isn't eating," they told us.

(They had runny eggs for breakfast or mush with lumps, Emily said later, I'd hold it in my mouth and not swallow. Nothing ever tasted good, just when they had chicken.)

It took us eight months to get her released home, and only the fact that she gained back so little of her seven lost pounds convinced the social worker.

I used to try to hold and love her after she came back, but her body would stay stiff, and after a while she'd push away. She ate little. Food sickened her, and I think much of life too. Oh she had physical lightness and brightness, twinkling by on skates, bouncing like a ball up and down up and down over the jump rope, skimming over the hill; but these were momentary.

She fretted about her appearance, thin and dark and foreign-looking at a time when every little girl was supposed to look or thought she should look a chubby blonde replica of Shirley Temple. The doorbell sometimes rang for her, but no one seemed to come and play in the house or be a best friend. Maybe because we moved so much.

There was a boy she loved painfully through two school semesters. Months later she told me how she had taken pennies from my purse to buy him candy. "Licorice was his favorite and I brought him some every day, but he still liked Jennifer better'n me. Why, Mommy?" The kind of question for which there is no answer.

School was a worry to her. She was not glib or quick in a world where glibness and quickness were easily confused with ability to learn. To her overworked and exasperated teachers she was an overconscientious "slow learner" who kept trying to catch up and was absent entirely too often.

I let her be absent, though sometimes the illness was imaginary. How different from my now-strictness about attendance with the others. I wasn't working. We had a new baby, I was home anyhow. Sometimes, after Susan grew old enough, I would keep her home from school, too, to have them all together.

Mostly Emily had asthma, and her breathing, harsh and labored, would fill the house with a curiously tranquil sound. I would bring the two old dresser mirrors and her boxes of collections to her bed. She would select beads and single earrings, bottle tops and shells, dried flowers and pebbles, old postcards and scraps, all sorts of oddments; then she and Susan would play Kingdom, setting up landscapes and furniture, peopling them with action.

Those were the only times of peaceful companionship between her and Susan. I have edged away from it, that poisonous feeling between them, that terrible balancing of hurts and needs I had to do between the two, and did so badly, those earlier years.

Oh there are conflicts between the others too, each one human, needing, demanding, hurting, taking — but only between Emily and Susan, no, Emily toward Susan that corroding resentment. It seems so obvious on the surface, yet it is not obvious. Susan, the second child, Susan, golden- and curly-haired and chubby, quick and articulate and assured, everything in appearance and manner Emily was not; Susan, not able to resist Emily's precious things, losing or sometimes clumsily breaking them; Susan telling jokes and riddles to company for applause while Emily sat silent (to say to me later: that was *my* riddle, Mother, I told it to Susan); Susan, who for all the five years' difference in age was just a year behind Emily in developing physically.

I am glad for that slow physical development that widened the difference between her and her contemporaries, though she suffered over it. She was too vulnerable for that terrible world of youthful competition, of preening and parading, of constant measuring of yourself against every other, of envy, "If I had that copper hair," "If I had that skin. . . ." She tormented herself enough about not looking like the others, there was enough of the unsureness, the having to be conscious of words before you speak, the constant caring — what are they thinking of me? without having it all magnified by the merciless physical drives.

Ronnie is calling. He is wet and I change him. It is rare there is such a cry now. That time of motherhood is almost behind me when the ear is not one's own but must always be racked and listening for the child cry, the child call. We sit for a while and I hold him, looking out over the city spread in charcoal with its soft aisles of light. *"Shoogily,"* he breathes and curls closer. I carry him back to bed, asleep. *Shoogily*. A funny word, a family word, inherited from Emily, invented by her to say: *comfort*.

In this and other ways she leaves her seal, I say aloud. And startle at my saying it. What do I mean? What did I start to gather together, to try and make coherent? I was at the terrible, growing years. War years. I do not remember them well. I was working, there were four smaller ones now, there was not time for her. She had to help be a mother, and housekeeper, and shopper. She had to set her seal. Mornings of crisis and near hysteria trying to get lunches packed, hair combed, coats and shoes found, everyone to school or Child Care on time, the baby ready for transportation. And always the paper scribbled on by a smaller one, the book looked at by Susan then mislaid, the homework not done. Running out to that huge school where she was one, she was lost, she was a drop; suffering over the unpreparedness, stammering and unsure in her classes.

There was so little time left at night after the kids were bedded down.

She would struggle over books, always eating (it was in those years she developed her enormous appetite that is legendary in our family) and I would be ironing, or preparing food for the next day, or writing V-mail to Bill, or tending the baby. Sometimes, to make me laugh, or out of her despair, she would imitate happenings or types at school.

I think I said once: "Why don't you do something like this in the school amateur show?" One morning she phoned me at work, hardly understandable through the weeping: "Mother, I did it. I won, I won; they gave me first prize; they clapped and clapped and wouldn't let me go."

Now suddenly she was Somebody, and as imprisoned in her difference as she had been in anonymity.

She began to be asked to perform at other high schools, even in colleges, then at city and statewide affairs. The first one we went to, I only recognized her that first moment when thin, shy, she almost drowned herself into the curtains. Then: Was this Emily? The control, the command, the convulsing and deadly clowning, the spell, then the roaring, stamping audience, unwilling to let this rare and precious laughter out of their lives.

Afterwards: You ought to do something about her with a gift like that — but without money or knowing how, what does one do? We have left it all to her, and the gift has as often eddied inside, clogged and clotted, as been used and growing.

She is coming. She runs up the stairs two at a time with her light graceful   50
step, and I know she is happy tonight. Whatever it was that occasioned your call did not happen today.

"Aren't you ever going to finish the ironing, Mother? Whistler painted his mother in a rocker. I'd have to paint mine standing over an ironing board." This is one of her communicative nights and she tells me everything and nothing as she fixes herself a plate of food out of the icebox.

She is so lovely. Why did you want me to come in at all? Why were you concerned? She will find her way.

She starts up the stairs to bed. "Don't get me up with the rest in the morning." "But I thought you were having midterms." "Oh, those," she comes back in, kisses me, and says quite lightly, "in a couple of years when we'll all be atom-dead they won't matter a bit."

She has said it before. She *believes* it. But because I have been dredging the past, and all that compounds a human being is so heavy and meaningful in me, I cannot endure it tonight.

I will never total it all. I will never come in to say: She was a child seldom   55
smiled at. Her father left me before she was a year old. I had to work her first six years when there was work, or I sent her home and to his relatives. There were years she had care she hated. She was dark and thin and foreign-looking in a world where the prestige went to blondeness and curly hair and dimples, she was slow where glibness was prized. She was a child of anxious, not proud, love. We were poor and could not afford for her the soil of easy growth. I was a young mother, I was a distracted mother. There were other children pushing up, demanding. Her younger sister seemed all that she was not. There were years she did not want me to touch her. She kept too much in herself, her life was such she had to keep too much in herself. My wisdom came too late. She has much to her and probably little will come of it. She is a child of her age, of depression, of war, of fear.

Let her be. So all that is in her will not bloom — but in how many does it? There is still enough left to live by. Only help her to know — help make it so there is cause for her to know — that she is more than this dress on the ironing board, helpless before the iron.

Philip Roth
THE CONVERSION OF THE JEWS   1959

Philip Roth, called "the inventor of the Jewish novel of manners," was born in 1933 in Newark, New Jersey. He first attended college on the local campus of Rutgers University, later transferred to Bucknell, completed his M.A. degree at the University of Chicago, and served a year in the Army. Although now a writer full time, he has taught fiction writing at three universities: Iowa, Pennsylvania, and Princeton. Roth's first book, the collection of stories Goodbye, Columbus *(1955), from which we take "The Conversion of the Jews," won him immediate fame.* Portnoy's Complaint, *a sardonically comic novel of a man's sexual obsession, topped the bestseller list in 1969. Three novels about a writer named Zuckerman have been collected as* Zuckerman Bound *(1985). Roth has also written plays and literary criticism, notably* Reading Myself and Others *(1975).*

"You're a real one for opening your mouth in the first place," Itzie said. "What do you open your mouth all the time for?"

"I didn't bring it up, Itz, I didn't," Ozzie said.

"What do you care about Jesus Christ for anyway?"

"I didn't bring up Jesus Christ. He did. I didn't even know what he was talking about. Jesus is historical, he kept saying. Jesus is historical." Ozzie mimicked the monumental voice of Rabbi Binder.

"Jesus was a person that lived like you and me," Ozzie continued.   5 "That's what Binder said — "

"Yeah? . . . So what! What do I give two cents whether he lived or not. And what do you gotta open your mouth!" Itzie Lieberman favored closed-mouthedness, especially when it came to Ozzie Freedman's questions. Mrs. Freedman had to see Rabbi Binder twice before about Ozzie's questions and this Wednesday at four-thirty would be the third time. Itzie preferred to keep *his* mother in the kitchen; he settled for behind-the-back subtleties such as gestures, faces, snarls and other less delicate barnyard noises.

"He was a real person, Jesus, but he wasn't like God, and we don't believe he is God." Slowly, Ozzie was explaining Rabbi Binder's position to Itzie, who had been absent from Hebrew School the previous afternoon.

"The Catholics," Itzie said helpfully, "they believe in Jesus Christ, that he's God." Itzie Lieberman used "the Catholics" in its broadest sense — to include the Protestants.

Ozzie received Itzie's remark with a tiny head bob, as though it were a footnote, and went on. "His mother was Mary, and his father probably was Joseph," Ozzie said. "But the New Testament says his real father was God."

"His *real* father?"

"Yeah," Ozzie said, "that's the big thing, his father's supposed to be God."

"Bull."

"That's what Rabbi Binder says, that it's impossible — "

"Sure it's impossible. That stuff's all bull. To have a baby you gotta get laid," Itzie theologized. "Mary hadda get laid."

"That's what Binder says: 'The only way a woman can have a baby is to have intercourse with a man.'"

"He said *that*, Ozz?" For a moment it appeared that Itzie had put the theological question aside. "He said that, intercourse?" A little curled smile shaped itself in the lower half of Itzie's face like a pink mustache. "What you guys do, Ozz, you laugh or something?"

"I raised my hand."

"Yeah? Whatja say?"

"That's when I asked the question."

Itzie's face lit up. "Whatja ask about — intercourse?"

"No, I asked the question about God, how if He could create the heaven and earth in six days, and make all the animals and the fish and the light in six days — the light especially, that's what always gets me, that He could make the light. Making fish and animals, that's pretty good — "

"That's damn good." Itzie's appreciation was honest but unimaginative: it was as though God had just pitched a one-hitter.

"But making light . . . I mean when you think about it, it's really something," Ozzie said. "Anyway, I asked Binder if He could make all that in six days, and He could *pick* the six days He wanted right out of nowhere, why couldn't He let a woman have a baby without having intercourse."

"You said intercourse, Ozz, to Binder?"

"Yeah."

"Right in class?"

"Yeah."

Itzie smacked the side of his head.

"I mean, no kidding around," Ozzie said, "that'd really be nothing. After all that other stuff, that'd practically be nothing."

Itzie considered a moment. "What'd Binder say?"

"He started all over again explaining how Jesus was historical and how he lived like you and me but he wasn't God. So I said I understood that. What I wanted to know was different."

What Ozzie wanted to know was always different. The first time he had wanted to know how Rabbi Binder could call the Jews "The Chosen People" if the Declaration of Independence claimed all men to be created equal. Rabbi Binder tried to distinguish for him between political equality and spiritual legitimacy, but what Ozzie wanted to know, he insisted vehemently, was different. That was the first time his mother had to come.

Then there was the plane crash. Fifty-eight people had been killed in a plane crash at La Guardia°. In studying a casualty list in the newspaper his mother had discovered among the list of those dead eight Jewish names (his

La Guardia: a New York City airport.

grandmother had nine but she counted Miller as a Jewish name); because of the eight she said the plane crash was "a tragedy." During free-discussion time on Wednesday Ozzie had brought to Rabbi Binder's attention this matter of "some of his relations" always picking out the Jewish names. Rabbi Binder had begun to explain cultural unity and some other things when Ozzie stood up at his seat and said that what he wanted to know was different. Rabbi Binder insisted that he sit down and it was then that Ozzie shouted that he wished all fifty-eight were Jews. That was the second time his mother came.

"And he kept explaining about Jesus being historical, and so I kept asking him. No kidding, Itz, he was trying to make me look stupid."

"So what he finally do?"   35

"Finally he starts screaming that I was deliberately simple-minded and a wise guy, and that my mother had to come, and this was the last time. And that I'd never get bar-mitzvahed if he could help it. Then, Itz, then he starts talking in that voice like a statue, real slow and deep, and he says that I better think over what I said about the Lord. He told me to go to his office and think it over." Ozzie leaned his body towards Itzie. "Itz, I thought it over for a solid hour, and now I'm convinced God could do it."

Ozzie had planned to confess his latest transgression to his mother as soon as she came home from work. But it was a Friday night in November and already dark, and when Mrs. Freedman came through the door she tossed off her coat, kissed Ozzie quickly on the face, and went to the kitchen table to light the three yellow candles, two for the Sabbath and one for Ozzie's father.

When his mother lit the candles she would move her two arms slowly towards her, dragging them through the air, as though persuading people whose minds were half made up. And her eyes would get glassy with tears. Even when his father was alive Ozzie remembered that her eyes had gotten glassy, so it didn't have anything to do with his dying. It had something to do with lighting the candles.

As she touched the flaming match to the unlit wick of a Sabbath candle, the phone rang, and Ozzie, standing only a foot from it, plucked it off the receiver and held it muffled to his chest. When his mother lit candles Ozzie felt there should be no noise; even breathing, if you could manage it, should be softened. Ozzie pressed the phone to his breast and watched his mother dragging whatever she was dragging, and he felt his own eyes get glassy. His mother was a round, tired, gray-haired penguin of a woman whose gray skin had begun to feel the tug of gravity and the weight of her own history. Even when she was dressed up she didn't look like a chosen person. But when she lit candles she looked like something better; like a woman who knew momentarily that God could do anything.

After a few mysterious minutes she was finished. Ozzie hung up the   40
phone and walked to the kitchen table where she was beginning to lay the two places for the four-course Sabbath meal. He told her that she would have to see Rabbi Binder next Wednesday at four-thirty, and then he told her why. For the first time in their life together she hit Ozzie across the face with her hand.

All through the chopped liver and chicken soup part of the dinner Ozzie cried; he didn't have any appetite for the rest.

On Wednesday, in the largest of the three basement classrooms of the synagogue, Rabbi Marvin Binder, a tall, handsome, broad-shouldered man of thirty with thick strong-fibered black hair, removed his watch from his pocket and saw that it was four o'clock. At the rear of the room Yakov Blotnik, the seventy-one-year-old custodian, slowly polished the large window, mumbling to himself, unaware that it was four o'clock or six o'clock, Monday or Wednesday. To most of the students Yakov Blotnik's mumbling, along with his brown curly beard, scythe nose, and two heel-trailing black cats, made of him an object of wonder, a foreigner, a relic, towards whom they were alternately fearful and disrespectful. To Ozzie the mumbling had always seemed a monotonous, curious prayer; what made it curious was that old Blotnik had been mumbling so steadily for so many years, Ozzie suspected he had memorized the prayers and forgotten all about God.

"It is now free-discussion time," Rabbi Binder said. "Feel free to talk about any Jewish matter at all — religion, family, politics, sports — "

There was silence. It was a gusty, clouded November afternoon and it did not seem as though there ever was or could be a thing called baseball. So nobody this week said a word about that hero from the past, Hank Greenberg — which limited free discussion considerably.

And the soul-battering Ozzie Freedman had just received from Rabbi Binder had imposed its limitation. When it was Ozzie's turn to read aloud from the Hebrew book the rabbi had asked him petulantly why he didn't read more rapidly. He was showing no progress. Ozzie said he could read faster but that if he did he was sure not to understand what he was reading. Nevertheless, at the rabbi's repeated suggestion Ozzie tried, and showed a great talent, but in the midst of a long passage he stopped short and said he didn't understand a word he was reading, and started in again at a drag-footed pace. Then came the soul-battering.

Consequently when free-discussion time rolled around none of the students felt too free. The rabbi's invitation was answered only by the mumbling of feeble old Blotnik.

"Isn't there anything at all you would like to discuss?" Rabbi Binder asked again, looking at his watch. "No questions or comments?"

There was a small grumble from the third row. The rabbi requested that Ozzie rise and give the rest of the class the advantage of his thought.

Ozzie rose. "I forget it now," he said, and sat down in his place.

Rabbi Binder advanced a seat towards Ozzie and poised himself on the edge of the desk. It was Itzie's desk and the rabbi's frame only a dagger's-length away from his face snapped him to sitting attention.

"Stand up again, Oscar," Rabbi Binder said calmly, "and try to assemble your thoughts."

Ozzie stood up. All his classmates turned in their seats and watched as he gave an unconvincing scratch to his forehead.

"I can't assemble any," he announced, and plunked himself down.

"Stand up!" Rabbi Binder advanced from Itzie's desk to the one directly in front of Ozzie; when the rabbinical back was turned Ozzie gave it five-fingers off the tip of his nose, causing a small titter in the room. Rabbi Binder was too absorbed in squelching Ozzie's nonsense once and for all to bother with titters. "Stand up, Oscar. What's your question about?"

Ozzie pulled a word out of the air. It was the handiest word. "Religion." 55
"Oh, now you remember?"
"Yes."
"What is it?"
Trapped, Ozzie blurted the first thing that came to him. "Why can't He make anything He wants to make!"
As Rabbi Binder prepared an answer, a final answer, Itzie, ten feet behind 60 him, raised one finger on his left hand, gestured it meaningfully towards the rabbi's back, and brought the house down.

Binder twisted quickly to see what had happened and in the midst of the commotion Ozzie shouted into the rabbi's back what he couldn't have shouted to his face. It was a loud, toneless sound that had the timbre of something stored inside for about six days.

"You don't know! You don't know anything about God!"
The rabbi spun back towards Ozzie. "What?"
"You don't know — you don't — "
"Apologize, Oscar, apologize!" It was a threat. 65
"You don't — "
Rabbi Binder's hand flicked out at Ozzie's cheek. Perhaps it had only been meant to clamp the boy's mouth shut, but Ozzie ducked and the palm caught him squarely on the nose.

The blood came in a short, red spurt on to Ozzie's shirt front.

The next moment was all confusion. Ozzie screamed, "You bastard, you bastard!" and broke for the classroom door. Rabbi Binder lurched a step backwards, as though his own blood had started flowing violently in the opposite direction, then gave a clumsy lurch forward and bolted out the door after Ozzie. The class followed after the rabbi's huge blue-suited back, and before old Blotnik could turn from his window, the room was empty and everyone was headed full speed up the three flights leading to the roof.

If one should compare the light of the day to the life of man: sunrise to 70 birth; sunset — the dropping down over the edge — to death; then as Ozzie Freedman wiggled through the trapdoor of the synagogue roof, his feet kicking backwards bronco-style at Rabbi Binder's outstretched arms — at that moment the day was fifty years old. As a rule, fifty or fifty-five reflects accurately the age of late afternoons in November, for it is in that month, during those hours, that one's awareness of light seems no longer a matter of seeing, but of hearing: light begins clicking away. In fact, as Ozzie locked shut the trapdoor in the rabbi's face, the sharp click of the bolt into the lock might momentarily have been mistaken for the sound of the heavier gray that had just throbbed through the sky.

With all his weight Ozzie kneeled on the locked door; any instant he was certain that Rabbi Binder's shoulder would fling it open, splintering the wood into shrapnel and catapulting his body into the sky. But the door did not move and below him he heard only the rumble of feet, first loud then dim, like thunder rolling away.

A question shot through his brain. "Can this be *me?*" For a thirteen-year-old who had just labeled his religious leader a bastard, twice, it was not an improper question. Louder and louder the question came to him — "Is it me?

Is it me?" — until he discovered himself no longer kneeling, but racing crazily towards the edge of the roof, his eyes crying, his throat screaming, and his arms flying everywhichway as though not his own.

"Is it me? Is it me Me Me Me Me! It has to be me — but is it!"

It is the question a thief must ask himself the night he jimmies open his first window, and it is said to be the question with which bridegrooms quiz themselves before the altar.

In the few wild seconds it took Ozzie's body to propel him to the edge 75 of the roof, his self-examination began to grow fuzzy. Gazing down at the street, he became confused as to the problem beneath the question: was it, is-it-me-who-called-Binder-a-bastard? or, is-it-me-prancing-around-on-the-roof? However, the scene below settled all, for there is an instant in any action when whether it is you or somebody else is academic. The thief crams the money in his pockets and scoots out the window. The bridegroom signs the hotel register for two. And the boy on the roof finds a streetful of people gaping at him, necks stretched backwards, faces up, as though he were the ceiling of the Hayde Planetarium. Suddenly you know it's you.

"Oscar! Oscar Freedman!" A voice rose from the center of the crowd, a voice that, could it have been seen, would have looked like the writing on scroll. "Oscar Freedman, get down from there. Immediately!" Rabbi Binder was pointing one arm stiffly up at him; and at the end of that arm, one finger aimed menacingly. It was the attitude of a dictator, but one — the eyes confessed all — whose personal valet had spit neatly in his face.

Ozzie didn't answer. Only for a blink's length did he look towards Rabbi Binder. Instead his eyes began to fit together the world beneath him, to sort out people from places, friends from enemies, participants from spectators. In little jagged starlike clusters his friends stood around Rabbi Binder, who was still pointing. The topmost point on a star compounded not of angels but of five adolescent boys was Itzie. What a world it was, with those stars below, Rabbi Binder below . . . Ozzie, who a moment earlier hadn't been able to control his own body, started to feel the meaning of the word control: he felt Peace and he felt Power.

"Oscar Freedman, I'll give you three to come down."

Few dictators give their subjects three to do anything; but, as always, Rabbi Binder only looked dictatorial.

"Are you ready, Oscar?" 80

Ozzie nodded his head yes, although he had no intention in the world — the lower one or the celestial one he'd just entered — of coming down even if Rabbi Binder should give him a million.

"All right then," said Rabbi Binder. He ran a hand through his black Samson hair as though it were the gesture prescribed for uttering the first digit. Then, with his other hand cutting a circle out of the small piece of sky around him, he spoke. "One!"

There was no thunder. On the contrary, at that moment, as though "one" was the cue for which he had been waiting, the world's least thunderous person appeared on the synagogue steps. He did not so much come out the synagogue door as lean out, onto the darkening air. He clutched at the doorknob with one hand and looked up at the roof.

"Oy!"

Yakov Blotnik's old mind hobbled slowly, as if on crutches, and though 85 he couldn't decide precisely what the boy was doing on the roof, he knew it wasn't good — that is, it wasn't-good-for-the-Jews. For Yakov Blotnik life had fractionated itself simply: things were either good-for-the-Jews or no-good-for-the-Jews.

He smacked his free hand to his in-sucked cheek, gently. "Oy, Gut!" And then quickly as he was able, he jacked down his head and surveyed the street. There was Rabbi Binder (like a man at an auction with only three dollars in his pocket, he had just delivered a shaky "Two!"); there were the students, and that was all. So far it-wasn't-so-bad-for-the-Jews. But the boy had to come down immediately, before anybody saw. The problem: how to get the boy off the roof?

Anybody who has ever had a cat on the roof knows how to get him down. You call the fire department. Or first you call the operator and you ask her for the fire department. And the next thing there is great jamming of brakes and clanging of bells and shouting of instructions. And then the cat is off the roof. You do the same thing to get a boy off the roof.

That is, you do the same thing if you are Yakov Blotnik and you once had a cat on the roof.

When the engines, all four of them, arrived, Rabbi Binder had four times given Ozzie the count of three. The big hook-and-ladder swung around the corner and one of the firemen leaped from it, plunging headlong towards the yellow fire hydrant in front of the synagogue. With a huge wrench he began to unscrew the top nozzle. Rabbi Binder raced over to him and pulled at his shoulder.

"There's no fire . . ."   90

The fireman mumbled back over his shoulder and, heatedly, continued working at the nozzle.

"But there's no fire, there's no fire . . ." Binder shouted. When the fireman mumbled again, the rabbi grasped his face with both his hands and pointed it up at the roof.

To Ozzie it looked as though Rabbi Binder was trying to tug the fire-man's head out of his body, like a cork from a bottle. He had to giggle at the picture they made: it was a family portrait — rabbi in black skullcap, fireman in red fire hat, and the little yellow hydrant squatting beside like a kid brother, bareheaded. From the edge of the roof Ozzie waved at the portrait, a one-handed, flapping, mocking wave; in doing it his right foot slipped from under him. Rabbi Binder covered his eyes with his hands.

Firemen work fast. Before Ozzie had even regained his balance, a big, round, yellowed net was being held on the synagogue lawn. The firemen who held it looked up at Ozzie with stern, feelingless faces.

One of the firemen turned his head towards Rabbi Binder. "What, is the   95
kid nuts or something?"

Rabbi Binder unpeeled his hands from his eyes, slowly, painfully, as if they were tape. Then he checked: nothing on the sidewalk, no dents in the net.

"Is he gonna jump, or what?" the fireman shouted.

In a voice not at all like a statue, Rabbi Binder finally answered. "Yes, yes, I think so . . . He's been threatening to . . ."

Threatening to? Why, the reason he was on the roof, Ozzie remembered, was to get away; he hadn't even thought about jumping. He had just run to get away, and the truth was that he hadn't really headed for the roof as much as he'd been chased there.

"What's his name, the kid?"

"Freedman," Rabbi Binder answered. "Oscar Freedman."

The fireman looked up at Ozzie. "What is it with you, Oscar? You gonna jump, or what?"

Ozzie did not answer. Frankly, the question had just arisen.

"Look, Oscar, if you're gonna jump, jump — and if you're not gonna jump, don't jump. But don't waste our time, willya?"

Ozzie looked at the fireman and then at Rabbi Binder. He wanted to see Rabbi Binder cover his eyes one more time.

"I'm going to jump."

And then he scampered around the edge of the roof to the corner, where there was no net below, and he flapped his arms at his sides, swishing the air and smacking his palms to his trousers on the downbeat. He began screaming like some kind of engine, "Wheeeee . . . wheeeeee," and leaning way out over the edge with the upper half of his body. The firemen whipped around to cover the ground with the net. Rabbi Binder mumbled a few words to Somebody and covered his eyes. Everything happened quickly, jerkily, as in a silent movie. The crowd, which had arrived with the fire engines, gave out a long, Fourth-of-July fireworks oooh-aahhh. In the excitement no one had paid the crowd much heed, except, of course, Yakov Blotnik, who swung from the doorknob counting heads. "Fier und tsvansik . . . finf und tsvantsik . . . Oy, Gut!°" It wasn't like this with the cat.

Rabbi Binder peeked through his fingers, checked the sidewalk and net. Empty. But there was Ozzie racing to the other corner. The firemen raced with him but were unable to keep up. Whenever Ozzie wanted to he might jump and splatter himself upon the sidewalk, and by the time the firemen scooted to the spot all they could do with their net would be to cover the mess.

"Wheeeee . . . wheeeee . . ."

"Hey, Oscar," the winded fireman yelled, "What the hell is this, a game or something?"

"Wheeeee . . . wheeeee . . ."

"Hey, Oscar — "

But he was off now to the other corner, flapping his wings fiercely. Rabbi Binder couldn't take it any longer — the fire engines from nowhere, the scream-ing suicidal boy, the net. He fell to his knees, exhausted, and with his hands curled together in front of his chest like a little dome, he pleaded, "Oscar, stop it, Oscar. Don't jump, Oscar. Please come down . . . Please don't jump."

And further back in the crowd a single voice, a single young voice, shouted a lone word to the boy on the roof.

"Jump!"

It was Itzie. Ozzie momentarily stopped flapping.

"Go ahead, Ozz — jump!" Itzie broke off his point of the star and coura-geously, with the inspiration not of a wise-guy but of a disciple, stood alone. "Jump, Ozz, jump!"

Still on his knees, his hands still curled, Rabbi Binder twisted his body back. He looked at Itzie, then, agonizingly, back to Ozzie.

Fier . . . Gut! Yiddish: "Twenty-four . . . twenty-five . . . Oh, God!"

"OSCAR, DON'T JUMP! PLEASE, DON'T JUMP . . . please please . . ."

"Jump!" This time it wasn't Itzie but another point of the star. By the time Mrs. Freedman arrived to keep her four-thirty appointment with Rabbi Binder, the whole little upside down heaven was shouting and pleading for Ozzie to jump, and Rabbi Binder no longer was pleading with him not to jump, but was crying into the dome of his hands.

Understandably Mrs. Freedman couldn't figure out what her son was doing on the roof. So she asked.

"Ozzie, my Ozzie, what are you doing? My Ozzie, what is it?"

Ozzie stopped wheeeeeing and slowed his arms down to a cruising flap, the kind birds use in soft winds, but he did not answer. He stood against the low, clouded, darkening sky — light clicked down swiftly now, as on a small gear — flapping softly and gazing down at the small bundle of a woman who was his mother.

"What are you doing, Ozzie?" She turned towards the kneeling Rabbi Binder and rushed so close that only a paper-thickness of dusk lay between her stomach and his shoulders.

"What is my baby doing?"

Rabbi Binder gaped up at her but he too was mute. All that moved was the dome of his hands; it shook back and forth like a weak pulse.

"Rabbi, get him down! He'll kill himself. Get him down, my only baby . . ."

"I can't," Rabbi Binder said, "I can't . . ." and he turned his handsome head towards the crowd of boys behind him. "It's them. Listen to them."

And for the first time Mrs. Freedman saw the crowd of boys, and she heard what they were yelling.

"He's doing it for them. He won't listen to me. It's them." Rabbi Binder spoke like one in a trance.

"For them?"

"Yes."

"Why for them?"

"They want him to . . ."

Mrs. Freedman raised her two arms upward as though she were conducting the sky. "For them he's doing it!" And then in a gesture older than pyramids, older than prophets and floods, her arms came slapping down to her sides. "A martyr I have. Look!" She tilted her head to the roof. Ozzie was still flapping softly. "My martyr."

"Oscar, come down, *please,*" Rabbi Binder groaned.

In a startlingly even voice Mrs. Freedman called to the boy on the roof. "Ozzie, come down, Ozzie. Don't be a martyr, my baby."

As though it were a litany, Rabbi Binder repeated her words. "Don't be a martyr, my baby. Don't be a martyr."

"Gawhead, Ozz — *be* a Martin!" It was Itzie. "Be a Martin, be a Martin," and all the voices joined in singing for Martindom, whatever *it* was. "Be a Martin, be a Martin . . ."

Somehow when you're on a roof the darker it gets the less you can hear. All Ozzie knew was that two groups wanted two new things; his friends were spirited and musical about what they wanted; his mother and the rabbi were even-toned, chanting, about what they didn't want. The rabbi's voice was without tears now and so was his mother's.

The big net stared up at Ozzie like a sightless eye. The big, clouded sky pushed down. From beneath it looked like a gray corrugated board. Suddenly, looking up into that unsympathetic sky, Ozzie realized all the strangeness of what these people, his friends, were asking: they wanted him to jump, to kill himself; they were singing about it now — it made them that happy. And there was an even greater strangeness: Rabbi Binder was on his knees, trembling. If there was a question to be asked now it was not "Is it me?" but rather "Is it us? . . . Is it us?"

Being on the roof, it turned out, was a serious thing. If he jumped would the singing become dancing? Would it? What would jumping stop? Yearningly, Ozzie wished he could rip open the sky, plunge his hands through, and pull out the sun; and on the sun, like a coin, would be stamped JUMP or DON'T JUMP.

Ozzie's knees rocked and sagged a little under him as though they were setting him for a dive. His arms tightened, stiffened, froze, from shoulders to fingernails. He felt as if each part of his body were going to vote as to whether he should kill himself or not — and each part as though it were independent of *him.*

The light took an unexpected click down and the new darkness, like a gag, hushed the friends singing for this and the mother and rabbi chanting for that.

Ozzie stopped counting votes, and in a curiously high voice, like one who 145 wasn't prepared for speech, he spoke.

"Mamma?"

"Yes, Oscar."

"Mamma, get down on your knees, like Rabbi Binder."

"Oscar — "

"Get down on your knees," he said, "or I'll jump." 150

Ozzie heard a whimper, then a quick rustling, and when he looked down where his mother had stood he saw the top of a head and beneath that a circle of dress. She was kneeling beside Rabbi Binder.

He spoke again. "Everybody kneel." There was the sound of everybody kneeling.

Ozzie looked around. With one hand he pointed towards the synagogue entrance. "Make *him* kneel."

There was a noise, not of kneeling, but of body-and-cloth stretching. Ozzie could hear Rabbi Binder saying in a gruff whisper, ". . . or he'll *kill* himself," and when next he looked there was Yakov Blotnik off the doorknob and for the first time in his life upon his knees in the Gentile posture of prayer.

As for the firemen — it is not as difficult as one might imagine to hold 155 a net taut while you are kneeling.

Ozzie looked around again; and then he called to Rabbi Binder.

"Rabbi?"

"Yes, Oscar."

"Rabbi Binder, do you believe in God?"

"Yes." 160

"Do you believe God can do Anything?" Ozzie leaned his head out into the darkness. "Anything?"

"Oscar, I think — "

"Tell me you believe God can do Anything."

There was a second's hesitation. Then: "God can do Anything."

"Tell me you believe God can make a child without intercourse." 165

"He can."

"Tell me!"

"God," Rabbi Binder admitted, "can make a child without intercourse."

"Mamma, you tell me."

"God can make a child without intercourse," his mother said. 170

"Make *him* tell me." There was no doubt who *him* was.

In a few moments Ozzie heard an old comical voice say something to the increasing darkness about God.

Next, Ozzie made everybody say it. And then he made them all say they believed in Jesus Christ — first one at a time, then all together.

When the catechizing was through it was the beginning of evening. From the street it sounded as if the boy on the roof might have sighed.

"Ozzie?" A woman's voice dared to speak. "You'll come down now?" 175

There was no answer, but the woman waited, and when a voice finally did speak it was thin and crying, and exhausted as that of an old man who has just finished pulling the bells.

"Mamma, don't you see — you shouldn't hit me. He shouldn't hit me. You shouldn't hit me about God, Mamma. You should never hit anybody about God — "

"Ozzie, please come down now."

"Promise me, promise me you'll never hit anybody about God."

He had asked only his mother, but for some reason everyone kneeling 180 in the street promised he would never hit anybody about God.

Once again there was silence.

"I can come down now, Mamma," the boy on the roof finally said. He turned his head both ways as though checking the traffic lights. "Now I can come down . . ."

And he did, right into the center of the yellow net that glowed in the evening's edge like an overgrown halo.

Joyce Carol Oates

WHERE ARE YOU GOING, WHERE HAVE YOU BEEN? 1970

Joyce Carol Oates was born in 1938 into a blue-collar family in Lockport, New York. As a college student she won a Mademoiselle *magazine award for fiction. After graduation from Syracuse with top honors, she took a master's degree in English at the University of Wisconsin and went on to teach at universities: Detroit, Windsor (Ontario), and Princeton. She now lives in New Jersey, where together with her husband, Raymond Smith, she directs the Ontario Review Press, literary publishers. An amazingly prolific writer, Oates so far has produced forty-four books of stories; novels including* Them, *winner of a National Book Award in 1970,* Solstice *(1985), and* Marya *(1986); poetry, plays, and literary criticism. Violence and the macabre inhabit the world of her best stories, but Oates has insisted that these elements in her work are never gratuitous.*

For Bob Dylan

Her name was Connie. She was fifteen and she had a quick nervous giggling habit of craning her neck to glance into mirrors, or checking other people's faces to make sure her own was all right. Her mother, who noticed everything and knew everything and who hadn't much reason any longer to look at her own face, always scolded Connie about it. "Stop gawking at yourself, who are you? You think you're so pretty?" she would say. Connie would raise her eyebrows at these familiar complaints and look right through her mother, into a shadowy vision of herself as she was right at that moment: she knew she was pretty and that was everything. Her mother had been pretty once too, if you could believe those old snapshots in the album, but now her looks were gone and that was why she was always after Connie.

"Why don't you keep your room clean like your sister? How've you got your hair fixed — what the hell stinks? Hair spray? You don't see your sister using that junk."

Her sister June was twenty-four and still lived at home. She was a secretary in the high school Connie attended, and if that wasn't bad enough — with her in the same building — she was so plain and chunky and steady that Connie had to hear her praised all the time by her mother and her mother's sisters. June did this, June did that, she saved money and helped clean the house and cooked and Connie couldn't do a thing, her mind was all filled with trashy daydreams. Their father was away at work most of the time and when he came home he wanted supper and he read the newspaper at supper and after supper he went to bed. He didn't bother talking much to them, but around his bent head Connie's mother kept picking at her until Connie wished her mother was dead and she herself was dead and it was all over. "She makes me want to throw up sometimes," she complained to her friends. She had a high, breathless, amused voice which made everything she said sound a little forced, whether it was sincere or not.

There was one good thing: June went places with girl friends of hers, girls who were just as plain and steady as she, and so when Connie wanted to do that her mother had no objections. The father of Connie's best girl friend drove the girls the three miles to town and left them off at a shopping plaza, so that they could walk through the stores or go to a movie, and when he came to pick them up again at eleven he never bothered to ask what they had done.

They must have been familiar sights, walking around that shopping plaza in their shorts and flat ballerina slippers that always scuffed the sidewalk, with charm bracelets jingling on their thin wrists; they would lean together to whisper and laugh secretly if someone passed by who amused or interested them. Connie had long dark blond hair that drew anyone's eye to it, and she wore part of it pulled up on her head and puffed out and the rest of it she let

5

fall down her back. She wore a pull-over jersey blouse that looked one way when she was at home and another way when she was away from home. Everything about her had two sides to it, one for home and one for anywhere that was not home: her walk that could be childlike and bobbing, or languid enough to make anyone think she was hearing music in her head, her mouth which was pale and smirking most of the time, but bright and pink on these evenings out, her laugh which was cynical and drawling at home — "Ha, ha, very funny" — but high-pitched and nervous anywhere else, like the jingling of the charms on her bracelet.

Sometimes they did go shopping or to a movie, but sometimes they went across the highway, ducking fast across the busy road, to a drive-in restaurant where older kids hung out. The restaurant was shaped like a big bottle, though squatter than a real bottle, and on its cap was a revolving figure of a grinning boy who held a hamburger aloft. One night in mid-summer they ran across, breathless with daring, and right away someone leaned out a car window and invited them over, but it was just a boy from high school they didn't like. It made them feel good to be able to ignore him. They went up through the maze of parked and cruising cars to the bright-lit, fly-infested restaurant, their faces pleased and expectant as if they were entering a sacred building that loomed out of the night to give them what haven and what blessing they yearned for. They sat at the counter and crossed their legs at the ankles, their thin shoulders rigid with excitement, and listened to the music that made everything so good: the music was always in the background like music at a church service, it was something to depend upon.

A boy named Eddie came in to talk with them. He sat backwards on his stool, turning himself jerkily around in semi-circles and then stopping and turning again, and after a while he asked Connie if she would like something to eat. She said she did and so she tapped her friend's arm on her way out — her friend pulled her face up into a brave droll look — and Connie said she would meet her at eleven, across the way. "I just hate to leave her like that," Connie said earnestly, but the boy said that she wouldn't be alone for long. So they went out to his car and on the way Connie couldn't help but let her eyes wander over the windshields and faces all around her, her face gleaming with a joy that had nothing to do with Eddie or even this place; it might have been the music. She drew her shoulders up and sucked in her breath with the pure pleasure of being alive, and just at that moment she happened to glance at a face just a few feet from hers. It was a boy with shaggy black hair, in a convertible jalopy painted gold. He stared at her and then his lips widened into a grin. Connie slit her eyes at him and turned away, but she couldn't help glancing back and there he was still watching her. He wagged a finger and laughed and said, "Gonna get you, baby," and Connie turned away again without Eddie noticing anything.

She spent three hours with him, at the restaurant where they ate hamburgers and drank Cokes in wax cups that were always sweating, and then down an alley a mile or so away, and when he left her off at five to eleven only the movie house was still open at the plaza. Her girl friend was there, talking with a boy. When Connie came up the two girls smiled at each other and Connie said, "How was the movie?" and the girl said, "*You* should know." They rode off with the girl's father, sleepy and pleased, and Connie couldn't help but look at the darkened shopping plaza with its big empty parking lot and its signs that were faded and ghostly now, and over at the drive-in restaurant where cars were still circling tirelessly. She couldn't hear the music at this distance.

Next morning June asked her how the movie was and Connie said, "So-so."

She and that girl and occasionally another girl went out several times a week that way, and the rest of the time Connie spent around the house — it was summer vacation — getting in her mother's way and thinking, dreaming, about the boys she met. But all the boys fell back and dissolved into a single face that was not even a face, but an idea, a feeling, mixed up with the urgent insistent pounding of the music and the humid night air of July. Connie's mother kept dragging her back to the daylight by finding things for her to do or saying, suddenly, "What's this about the Pettinger girl?" 10

And Connie would say nervously, "Oh, her. That dope." She always drew thick clear lines between herself and such girls, and her mother was simple and kindly enough to believe her. Her mother was so simple, Connie thought, that it was maybe cruel to fool her so much. Her mother went scuffling around the house in old bedroom slippers and complained over the telephone to one sister about the other, then the other called up and the two of them complained about the third one. If June's name was mentioned her mother's tone was approving, and if Connie's name was mentioned it was disapproving. This did not really mean she disliked Connie and actually Connie thought that her mother preferred her to June because she was prettier, but the two of them kept up a pretense of exasperation, a sense that they were tugging and struggling over something of little value to either of them. Sometimes, over coffee, they were almost friends, but something would come up — some vexation that was like a fly buzzing suddenly around their heads — and their faces went hard with contempt.

One Sunday Connie got up at eleven — none of them bothered with church — and washed her hair so that it could dry all day long, in the sun. Her parents and sister were going to a barbecue at an aunt's house and Connie said no, she wasn't interested, rolling her eyes to let her mother know just what she thought of it. "Stay home alone then," her mother said sharply. Connie sat out back in a lawn chair and watched them drive away, her father quiet and bald, hunched around so that he could back the car out, her mother with a look that was still angry and not at all softened through the windshield, and in the back seat poor old June all dressed up as if she didn't know what a barbecue was, with all the running yelling kids and the flies. Connie sat with her eyes closed in the sun, dreaming and dazed with the warmth about her as if this were a kind of love, the caresses of love, and her mind slipped over onto thoughts of the boy she had been with the night before and how nice he had been, how sweet it always was, not the way someone like June would suppose but sweet, gentle, the way it was in movies and promised in songs; and when she opened her eyes she hardly knew where she was, the back yard ran off into weeds and a fence-line of trees and behind it the sky was perfectly blue and still. The asbestos "ranch house" that was now three years old startled her — it looked small. She shook her head as if to get awake.

It was too hot. She went inside the house and turned on the radio to drown out the quiet. She sat on the edge of her bed, barefoot, and listened for an hour and a half to a program called XYZ Sunday Jamboree, record after record of hard, fast, shrieking songs she sang along with, interspersed by exclamations from "Bobby King": "An' look here you girls at Napoleon's — Son and Charley want you to pay real close attention to this song coming up!"

And Connie paid close attention herself, bathed in a glow of slow-pulsed joy that seemed to rise mysteriously out of the music itself and lay languidly about the airless little room, breathed in and breathed out with each gentle rise and fall of her chest.

After a while she heard a car coming up the drive. She sat up at once, 15 startled, because it couldn't be her father so soon. The gravel kept crunching all the way in from the road — the driveway was long — and Connie ran to the window. It was a car she didn't know. It was an open jalopy, painted a bright gold that caught the sunlight opaquely. Her heart began to pound and her fingers snatched at her hair, checking it, and she whispered "Christ. Christ," wondering how bad she looked. The car came to a stop at the side door and the horn sounded four short taps as if this were a signal Connie knew.

She went into the kitchen and approached the door slowly, then hung out the screen door, her bare toes curling down off the step. There were two boys in the car and now she recognized the driver: he had shaggy, shabby black hair that looked crazy as a wig and he was grinning at her.

"I ain't late, am I?" he said.

"Who the hell do you think you are?" Connie said.

"Toldja I'd be out, didn't I?"

"I don't even know who you are." 20

She spoke sullenly, careful to show no interest or pleasure, and he spoke in a fast bright monotone. Connie looked past him to the other boy, taking her time. He had fair brown hair, with a lock that fell onto his forehead. His sideburns gave him a fierce, embarrassed look, but so far he hadn't even bothered to glance at her. Both boys wore sunglasses. The driver's glasses were metallic and mirrored everything in miniature.

"You wanta come for a ride?" he said.

Connie smirked and let her hair fall loose over one shoulder.

"Don'tcha like my car? New paint job," he said. "Hey."

"What?" 25

"You're cute."

She pretended to fidget, chasing flies away from the door.

"Don'tcha believe me, or what?" he said.

"Look, I don't even know who you are," Connie said in disgust.

"Hey, Ellie's got a radio, see. Mine's broke down." He lifted his friend's 30 arm and showed her the little transistor the boy was holding, and now Connie began to hear the music. It was the same program that was playing inside the house.

"Bobby King?" she said.

"I listen to him all the time. I think he's great."

"He's kind of great," Connie said reluctantly.

"Listen, that guy's *great*. He knows where the action is."

Connie blushed a little, because the glasses made it impossible for her 35 to see just what this boy was looking at. She couldn't decide if she liked him or if he was just a jerk, and so she dawdled in the doorway and wouldn't come down or go back inside. She said, "What's all that stuff painted on your car?"

"Can'tcha read it?" He opened the door very carefully, as if he was afraid it might fall off. He slid out just as carefully, planting his feet firmly on the ground, the tiny metallic world in his glasses slowing down like gelatine hardening and in the midst of it Connie's bright green blouse. "This here is my name, to begin with," he said. ARNOLD FRIEND was written in tarlike black letters on the side, with a drawing of a round grinning face that reminded Connie of a pumpkin, except it wore sunglasses. "I wanta introduce myself, I'm Arnold Friend and that's my real name and I'm gonna be your friend, honey, and inside the car's Ellie Oscar, he's kinda shy." Ellie brought his transistor radio up to his shoulder and balanced it there. "Now these numbers are a secret code, honey," Arnold Friend explained. He read off the numbers 33, 19, 17 and raised his eyebrows at her to see what she thought of that, but she didn't think much of it. The left rear fender had been smashed and around it was written, on the gleaming gold background: DONE BY CRAZY WOMAN DRIVER. Connie had to laugh at that. Arnold Friend was pleased at her laughter and looked up at her. "Around the other side's a lot more — you wanta come and see them?"

"No."

"Why not?"

"Why should I?"

"Don'tcha wanta see what's on the car? Don'tcha wanta go for a ride?"   40

"I don't know."

"Why not?"

"I got things to do."

"Like what?"

"Things."   45

He laughed as if she had said something funny. He slapped his thighs. He was standing in a strange way, leaning back against the car as if he were balancing himself. He wasn't tall, only an inch or so taller than she would be if she came down to him. Connie liked the way he was dressed, which was the way all of them dressed: tight faded jeans stuffed into black, scuffed boots, a belt that pulled his waist in and showed how lean he was, and a white pull-over shirt that was a little soiled and showed the hard small muscles of his arms and shoulders. He looked as if he probably did hard work, lifting and carrying things. Even his neck looked muscular. And his face was a familiar face, somehow: the jaw and chin and cheeks slightly darkened, because he hadn't shaved for a day or two, and the nose long and hawk-like, sniffing as if she were a treat he was going to gobble up and it was all a joke.

"Connie, you ain't telling the truth. This is your day set aside for a ride with me and you know it," he said, still laughing. The way he straightened and recovered from his fit of laughing showed that it had been all fake.

"How do you know what my name is?" she said suspiciously.

"It's Connie."

"Maybe and maybe not."   50

"I know my Connie," he said, wagging his finger. Now she remembered him even better, back at the restaurant, and her cheeks warmed at the thought of how she sucked in her breath just at the moment she passed him — how she must have looked to him. And he had remembered her. "Ellie and I come out here especially for you," he said. "Ellie can sit in back. How about it?"

"Where?"

"Where what?"

"Where're we going?"

He looked at her. He took off the sunglasses and she saw how pale the skin around his eyes was, like holes that were not in shadow but instead in light. His eyes were chips of broken glass that catch the light in an amiable way. He smiled. It was as if the idea of going for a ride somewhere, to some place, was a new idea to him.

"Just for a ride, Connie sweetheart."

"I never said my name was Connie," she said.

"But I know what it is. I know your name and all about you, lots of things," Arnold Friend said. He had not moved yet but stood still leaning back against the side of his jalopy. "I took a special interest in you, such a pretty girl, and found out all about you like I know your parents and sister are gone somewheres and I know where and how long they're going to be gone, and I know who you were with last night, and your best girl friend's name is Betty. Right?"

He spoke in a simple lilting voice, exactly as if he were reciting the words to a song. His smile assured her that everything was fine. In the car Ellie turned up the volume on his radio and did not bother to look around at them.

"Ellie can sit in the back seat," Arnold Friend said. He indicated his friend with a casual jerk of his chin, as if Ellie did not count and she should not bother with him.

"How'd you find out all that stuff?" Connie said.

"Listen: Betty Schultz and Tony Fitch and Jimmy Pettinger and Nancy Pettinger," he said, in a chant. "Raymond Stanley and Bob Hutter — "

"Do you know all those kids?"

"I know everybody."

"Look, you're kidding. You're not from around here."

"Sure."

"But — how come we never saw you before?"

"Sure you saw me before," he said. He looked down at his boots, as if he were a little offended. "You just don't remember."

"I guess I'd remember you," Connie said.

"Yeah?" He looked up at this, beaming. He was pleased. He began to mark time with the music from Ellie's radio, tapping his fists lightly together. Connie looked away from his smile to the car, which was painted so bright it almost hurt her eyes to look at it. She looked at that name, ARNOLD FRIEND. And up at the front fender was an expression that was familiar — MAN THE FLYING SAUCERS. It was an expression kids had used the year before, but didn't use this year. She looked at it for a while as if the words meant something to her that she did not yet know.

"What're you thinking about? Huh?" Arnold Friend demanded. "Not worried about your hair blowing around in the car, are you?"

"No."

"Think I maybe can't drive good?"

"How do I know?"

"You're a hard girl to handle. How come?" he said. "Don't you know I'm your friend? Didn't you see me put my sign in the air when you walked by?"

"What sign?"

"My sign." And he drew an X in the air, leaning out toward her. They were maybe ten feet apart. After his hand fell back to his side the X was still in the air, almost visible. Connie let the screen door close and stood perfectly still inside it, listening to the music from her radio and the boy's blend together. She stared at Arnold Friend. He stood there so stiffly relaxed, pretending to be relaxed, with one hand idly on the door handle as if he were keeping himself up that way and had no intention of ever moving again. She recognized most things about him, the tight jeans that showed his thighs and buttocks and the greasy leather boots and the tight shirt, and even that slippery friendly smile of his, that sleepy dreamy smile that all the boys used to get across ideas they didn't want to put into words. She recognized all this and also the singsong way he talked, slightly mocking, kidding, but serious and a little melancholy, and she recognized the way he tapped one fist against the other in homage to the perpetual music behind him. But all these things did not come together.

She said suddenly, "Hey, how old are you?"

His smile faded. She could see then that he wasn't a kid, he was much older — thirty, maybe more. At this knowledge her heart began to pound faster.

"That's a crazy thing to ask. Can'tcha see I'm your own age?"

"Like hell you are."

"Or maybe a coupla years older, I'm eighteen."

"Eighteen?" she said doubtfully.

He grinned to reassure her and lines appeared at the corners of his mouth. His teeth were big and white. He grinned so broadly his eyes became slits and she saw how thick the lashes were, thick and black as if painted with a black tarlike material. Then he seemed to become embarrassed, abruptly, and looked over his shoulder at Ellie. "*Him,* he's crazy," he said. "Ain't he a riot, he's a nut, a real character." Ellie was still listening to the music. His sunglasses told nothing about what he was thinking. He wore a bright orange shirt unbuttoned halfway to show his chest, which was a pale, bluish chest and not muscular like Arnold Friend's. His shirt collar was turned up all around and the very tips of the collar pointed out past his chin as if they were protecting him. He was pressing the transistor radio up against his ear and sat there in a kind of daze, right in the sun.

"He's kinda strange," Connie said.

"Hey, she says you're kinda strange! Kinda strange!" Arnold Friend cried. He pounded on the car to get Ellie's attention. Ellie turned for the first time and Connie saw with shock that he wasn't a kid either — he had a fair, hairless face, cheeks reddened slightly as if the veins grew too close to the surface of his skin, the face of a forty-year-old baby. Connie felt a wave of dizziness rise in her at this sight and she stared at him as if waiting for something to change the shock of the moment, make it all right again. Ellie's lips kept shaping words, mumbling along with the words blasting in his ear.

"Maybe you two better go away," Connie said faintly.

"What? How come?" Arnold Friend cried. "We come out here to take you for a ride. It's Sunday." He had the voice of the man on the radio now. It was the same voice, Connie thought. "Don'tcha know it's Sunday all day and honey, no matter who you were with last night today you're with Arnold Friend and don't you forget it! — Maybe you better step out here," he said, and this last was in a different voice. It was a little flatter, as if the heat was finally getting to him.

"No. I got things to do."

"Hey." 90

"You two better leave."

"We ain't leaving until you come with us."

"Like hell I am — "

"Connie, don't fool around with me. I mean, I mean, don't fool *around*," he said, shaking his head. He laughed incredulously. He placed his sunglasses on top of his head, carefully, as if he were indeed wearing a wig, and brought the stems down behind his ears. Connie stared at him, another wave of dizziness and fear rising in her so that for a moment he wasn't even in focus but was just a blur, standing there against his gold car, and she had the idea that he had driven up the driveway all right but had come from nowhere before that and belonged nowhere and that everything about him and even about the music that was so familiar to her was only half real.

"If my father comes and sees you — " 95

"He ain't coming. He's at a barbecue."

"How do you know that?"

"Aunt Tillie's. Right now they're — uh — they're drinking. Sitting around," he said vaguely, squinting as if he were staring all the way to town and over to Aunt Tillie's backyard. Then the vision seemed to get clear and he nodded energetically. "Yeah. Sitting around. There's your sister in a blue dress, huh? And high heels, the poor sad bitch — nothing like you, sweetheart! And your mother's helping some fat woman with the corn, they're cleaning the corn — husking the corn — "

"What fat woman?" Connie cried.

"How do I know what fat woman. I don't know every goddam fat 100 woman in the world!" Arnold Friend laughed.

"Oh, that's Mrs. Hornby. . . . Who invited her?" Connie said. She felt a little light-headed. Her breath was coming quickly.

"She's too fat. I don't like them fat. I like them the way you are, honey," he said, smiling sleepily at her. They stared at each other for a while, through the screen door. He said softly, "Now what you're going to do is this: you're going to come out that door. You're going to sit up front with me and Ellie's going to sit in the back, the hell with Ellie, right? This isn't Ellie's date. You're my date. I'm your lover, honey."

"What? You're crazy — "

"Yes, I'm your lover. You don't know what that is but you will," he said. "I know that too. I know all about you. But look: it's real nice and you couldn't ask for nobody better than me, or more polite. I always keep my word. I'll tell you how it is, I'm always nice at first, the first time. I'll hold you so tight you won't think you have to try to get away or pretend anything because you'll know you can't. And I'll come inside you where it's all secret and you'll give in to me and you'll love me — "

"Shut up! You're crazy!" Connie said. She backed away from the door. 105
She put her hands against her ears as if she'd heard something terrible, something not meant for her. "People don't talk like that, you're crazy," she muttered. Her heart was almost too big now for her chest and its pumping made sweat break out all over her. She looked out to see Arnold Friend pause and then take a step toward the porch lurching. He almost fell. But, like a clever drunken man, he managed to catch his balance. He wobbled in his high boots and grabbed hold of one of the porch posts.

"Honey?" he said. "You still listening?"

"Get the hell out of here!"

"Be nice, honey. Listen."

"I'm going to call the police — "

He wobbled again and out of the side of his mouth came a fast spat curse, 110
an aside not meant for her to hear. But even this "Christ!" sounded forced. Then he began to smile again. She watched this smile come, awkward as if he were smiling from inside a mask. His whole face was a mask, she thought wildly, tanned down onto his throat but then running out as if he had plastered make-up on his face but had forgotten about his throat.

"Honey — ? Listen, here's how it is. I always tell the truth and I promise you this: I ain't coming in that house after you."

"You better not! I'm going to call the police if you — if you don't — "

"Honey," he said, talking right through her voice, "honey, I'm not coming in there but you are coming out here. You know why?"

She was panting. The kitchen looked like a place she had never seen before, some room she had run inside but which wasn't good enough, wasn't going to help her. The kitchen window had never had a curtain, after three years, and there were dishes in the sink for her to do — probably — and if you ran your hand across the table you'd probably feel something sticky there.

"You listening, honey? Hey?" 115

" — going to call the police — "

"Soon as you touch the phone I don't need to keep my promise and can come inside. You won't want that."

She rushed forward and tried to lock the door. Her fingers were shaking. "But why lock it," Arnold Friend said gently, talking right into her face. "It's just a screen door. It's just nothing." One of his boots was at a strange angle, as if his foot wasn't in it. It pointed out to the left, bent at the ankle. "I mean, anybody can break through a screen door and glass and wood and iron or anything else if he needs to, anybody at all and specially Arnold Friend. If the place got lit up with a fire honey you'd come running out into my arms, right into my arms and safe at home — like you knew I was your lover and'd stopped fooling around. I don't mind a nice shy girl but I don't like no fooling around." Part of those words were spoken with a slight rhythmic lilt, and Connie somehow recognized them — the echo of a song from last year, about a girl rushing into her boy friend's arms and coming home again —

Connie stood barefoot on the linoleum floor, staring at him. "What do you want?" she whispered.

"I want you," he said. 120

"What?"

"Seen you that night and thought, that's the one, yes sir. I never needed to look any more."

"But my father's coming back. He's coming to get me. I had to wash my hair first — " She spoke in a dry, rapid voice, hardly raising it for him to hear.

"No, your daddy is not coming and yes, you had to wash your hair and you washed it for me. It's nice and shining and all for me, I thank you, sweetheart," he said, with a mock bow, but again he almost lost his balance. He had to bend and adjust his boots. Evidently his feet did not go all the way down; the boots must have been stuffed with something so that he would seem taller. Connie stared out at him and behind him Ellie in the car, who seemed to be looking off toward Connie's right, into nothing. This Ellie said, pulling the words out of the air one after another as if he were just discovering them, "You want me to pull out the phone?"

"Shut your mouth and keep it shut," Arnold Friend said, his face red   125
from bending over or maybe from embarrassment because Connie had seen his boots. "This ain't none of your business."

"What — what are you doing? What do you want?" Connie said. "If I call the police they'll get you, they'll arrest you — "

"Promise was not to come in unless you touch that phone, and I'll keep that promise," he said. He resumed his erect position and tried to force his shoulders back. He sounded like a hero in a movie, declaring something important. He spoke too loudly and it was as if he were speaking to someone behind Connie. "I ain't made plans for coming in that house where I don't belong but just for you to come out to me, the way you should. Don't you know who I am?"

"You're crazy," she whispered. She backed away from the door but did not want to go into another part of the house, as if this would give him permission to come through the door. "What do you. . . . You're crazy, you . . ."

"Huh? What're you saying, honey?"

Her eyes darted everywhere in the kitchen. She could not remember   130
what it was, this room.

"This is how it is, honey: you come out and we'll drive away, have a nice ride. But if you don't come out we're gonna wait till your people come home and then they're all going to get it."

"You want that telephone pulled out?" Ellie said. He held the radio away from his ear and grimaced, as if without the radio the air was too much for him.

"I toldja shut up, Ellie," Arnold Friend said, "you're deaf, get a hearing aid, right? Fix yourself up. This little girl's no trouble and's gonna be nice to me, so Ellie keep to yourself, this ain't your date — right? Don't hem in on me. Don't hog. Don't crush. Don't bird dog. Don't trail me," he said in a rapid meaningless voice, as if he were running through all the expressions he'd learned but was no longer sure which one of them was in style, then rushing on to new ones, making them up with his eyes closed, "Don't crawl under my fence, don't squeeze in my chipmunk hole, don't sniff my glue, suck my popsicle, keep your own greasy fingers on yourself!" He shaded his eyes and peered in at Connie, who was backed against the kitchen table. "Don't mind him honey he's just a creep. He's a dope. Right? I'm the boy for you and like I said you come out here nice like a lady and give me your hand, and nobody else gets hurt, I mean, your nice old bald-headed daddy and your mummy and your sister in her high heels. Because listen: why bring them in this?"

"Leave me alone," Connie whispered.

"Hey, you know that old woman down the road, the one with the chickens and stuff — you know her?" 135

"She's dead!"

"Dead? What? You know her?" Arnold Friend said.

"She's dead — "

"Don't you like her?"

"She's dead — she's — she isn't here any more — " 140

"But don't you like her, I mean, you got something against her? Some grudge or something?" Then his voice dipped as if he were conscious of a rudeness. He touched the sunglasses perched on top of his head as if to make sure they were still there. "Now you be a good girl."

"What are you going to do?"

"Just two things, or maybe three," Arnold Friend said. "But I promise it won't last long and you'll like me that way you get to like people you're close to. You will. It's all over for you here, so come on out. You don't want your people in any trouble, do you?"

She turned and bumped against a chair or something, hurting her leg, but she ran into the back room and picked up the telephone. Something roared in her ear, a tiny roaring, and she was so sick with fear that she could do nothing but listen to it — the telephone was clammy and very heavy and her fingers groped down to the dial but were too weak to touch it. She began to scream into the phone, into the roaring. She cried out, she cried for her mother, she felt her breath start jerking back and forth in her lungs as if it were something Arnold Friend were stabbing her with again and again with no tenderness. A noisy sorrowful wailing rose all about her and she was locked inside it the way she was locked inside the house.

After a while she could hear again. She was sitting on the floor with her 145 wet back against the wall.

Arnold Friend was saying from the door, "That's a good girl. Put the phone back."

She kicked the phone away from her.

"No, honey. Pick it up. Put it back right."

She picked it up and put it back. The dial tone stopped.

"That's a good girl. Now you come outside." 150

She was hollow with what had been fear, but what was now just an emptiness. All that screaming had blasted it out of her. She sat, one leg cramped under her, and deep inside her brain was something like a pinpoint of light that kept going and would not let her relax. She thought, I'm not going to see my mother again. She thought, I'm not going to sleep in my bed again. Her bright green blouse was all wet.

Arnold Friend said, in a gentle-loud voice that was like a stage voice, "The place where you came from ain't there any more, and where you had in mind to go is cancelled out. This place you are now — inside your daddy's house — is nothing but a cardboard box I can knock down any time. You know that and always did know it. You hear me?"

She thought, I have got to think. I have to know what to do.

"We'll go out to a nice field, out in the country here where it smells so nice and it's sunny," Arnold Friend said. "I'll have my arms around you so you won't need to try to get away and I'll show you what love is like, what it does. The hell with this house! It looks solid all right," he said. He ran a fingernail down the screen and the noise did not make Connie shiver, as it would have the day before. "Now put your hand on your heart, honey. Feel that? That feels solid too but we know better, be nice to me, be sweet like you can because what else is there for a girl like you but to be sweet and pretty and give in? — and get away before her people come back?"

She felt her pounding heart. Her hand seemed to enclose it. She thought for the first time in her life that it was nothing that was hers, that belonged to her, but just a pounding, living thing inside this body that wasn't really hers either. 155

"You don't want them to get hurt," Arnold Friend went on. "Now get up, honey. Get up all by yourself."

She stood.

"Now turn this way. That's right. Come over here to me — Ellie, put that away, didn't I tell you? You dope. You miserable creepy dope," Arnold Friend said. His words were not angry but only part of an incantation. The incantation was kindly. "Now come out through the kitchen to me honey and let's see a smile, try it, you're a brave sweet little girl and now they're eating corn and hotdogs cooked to bursting over an outdoor fire, and they don't know one thing about you and never did and honey you're better than them because not a one of them would have done this for you."

Connie felt the linoleum under her feet; it was cool. She brushed her hair back out of her eyes. Arnold Friend let go of the post tentatively and opened his arms for her, his elbows pointing in toward each other and his wrists limp, to show that this was an embarrassed embrace and a little mocking, he didn't want to make her self-conscious.

She put out her hand against the screen. She watched herself push the door slowly open as if she were safe back somewhere in the other doorway, watching this body and this head of long hair moving out into the sunlight where Arnold Friend waited. 160

"My sweet little blue-eyed girl," he said, in a half-sung sigh that had nothing to do with her brown eyes but was taken up just the same by the vast sunlit reaches of the land behind him and on all sides of him, so much land that Connie had never seen before and did not recognize except to know that she was going to it.

Toni Cade Bambara

MY MAN BOVANNE   1972

Toni Cade Bambara, born in New York in 1939, grew up on low-rent streets in Harlem and the city's Bedford-Stuyvesant district. After taking her master's degree at City College, she worked for the New York State Welfare Department as a case investigator. Later, she studied dance and film-making, and directed a recreation program for psychiatric patients at New York City's Metropolitan Hospital. When her fiction began to spread her fame, she received (and accepted) invitations to teach at Duke, Stephens, and Emory. In recent years she has served Spelman College in Atlanta as writer-in-residence. Bambara's fiction books include Gorilla, My Love *(1972),* The Sea Birds Are Still Alive: Collected Stories *(1977), and* The Salt Eaters *(1980). As a storyteller, Bambara has been especially devoted to correcting stereotyped images of black women.*

Blind people got a hummin jones° if you notice. Which is understandable completely once you been around one and notice what no eyes will force you into to see people, and you get past the first time, which seems to come out of nowhere, and it's like you in church again with fat-chest ladies and old gents gruntin a hum low in the throat to whatever the preacher be saying. Shakey Bee bottom lip all swole up with Sweet Peach° and me explainin how come the sweet-potato bread was a dollar-quarter this time stead of dollar regular and he say uh hunh he understand, then he break into this *thizzin* kind of hum which is quiet, but fiercesome just the same, if you ain't ready for it. Which I wasn't. But I got used to it and the onliest time I had to say somethin bout it was when he was playin checkers on the stoop one time and he commenst to hummin quite churchy seem to me. So I says, "Look here Shakey Bee, I can't beat you and Jesus too." He stop.

So that's how come I asked My Man Bovanne to dance. He ain't my man mind you, just a nice ole gent from the block that we all know cause he fixes things and the kids like him. Or used to fore Black Power° got hold their minds and mess em around till they can't be civil to ole folks. So we at this benefit for my niece's cousin who's runnin for somethin with this Black party somethin or other behind her. And I press up close to dance with Bovanne who blind and I'm hummin and he hummin, chest to chest like talkin. Not jammin my breasts into the man. Wasn't bout tits. Was bout vibrations. And he dug it and asked me what color dress I had on and how my hair was fixed and how I was doin without a man, not nosy but nice-like, and who was at this affair and was the canapés dainty-stingy or healthy enough to get hold of proper. Comfy and cheery is what I'm tryin to get across. Touch talkin like the heel of the hand on the tambourine or on a drum.

But right away Joe Lee come up on us and frown for dancin so close to the man. My own son who knows what kind of warm I am about; and don't grown men all call me long distance and in the middle of the night for a little Mama comfort? But he frown. Which ain't right since Bovanne can't see and defend himself. Just a nice old man who fixes toasters and busted irons and bicycles and things and changes the lock on my door when my men friends get messy. Nice man. Which is not why they invited him. Grass roots you see. Me and Sister

a hummin jones: the habit of humming to express a craving for satisfaction.
Sweet Peach: snuff.
Black Power: militant civil rights movement that in the 1960s began gaining influence, especially among the young.

Taylor and the woman who does heads° at Mamies and the man from the barber shop, we all there on account of we grass roots. And I ain't never been souther than Brooklyn Battery and no more country than the window box on my fire escape. And just yesterday my kids tellin me to take them countrified rags off my head and be cool. And now can't get Black enough to suit 'em. So everybody passin sayin My Man Bovanne. Big deal, keep steppin and don't even stop a minute to get the man a drink or one of them cute sandwiches or tell him what's goin on. And him standin there with a smile ready case someone do speak he want to be ready. So that's how come I pull him on the dance floor and we dance squeezin past the tables and chairs and all them coats and people standin round up in each other face talkin bout this and that but got no use for this blind man who mostly fixed skates and skooters for all these folks when they were just kids. So I'm pressed up close and we touch talkin with the hum. And here come my daughter cuttin her eye at me° like she do when she tell me about my "apolitical" self like I got hoof and mouf disease and there ain't no hope at all. And I don't pay her no mind and just look up in Bovanne shadow face and tell him his stomach like a drum and he laugh. Laugh real loud. And here come my youngest, Task, with a tap on my elbow like he the third grade monitor and I'm cuttin up on the line to assembly.

"I was just talkin on the drums," I explained when they hauled me into the kitchen. I figured drums was my best defense. They can get ready for drums what with all this heritage business. And Bovanne stomach just like that drum Task give me when he come back from Africa. You just touch it and it hum thizzm, thizzm. So I stuck to the drum story. "Just drummin that's all."

"Mama, what are you talkin about?"   5

"She had too much to drink," say Elo to Task cause she don't hardly say nuthin to me direct no more since that ugly argument about my wigs.

"Look here Mama," say Task, the gentle one. "We just trying to pull your coat. You were makin a spectacle of yourself out there dancing like that."

"Dancin like what?"

Task run a hand over his left ear like his father for the world and his father before that.

"Like a bitch in heat," say Elo.   10

"Well uhh, I was goin to say like one of them sex-starved ladies gettin on in years and not too discriminating. Know what I mean?"

I don't answer cause I'll cry. Terrible thing when your own children talk to you like that. Pullin me out the party and hustlin me into some stranger's kitchen in the back of a bar just like the damn police. And ain't like I'm old old. I can still wear me some sleeveless dresses without the meat hangin off my arm. And I keep up with some thangs through my kids. Who ain't kids no more. To hear them tell it. So I don't say nuthin.

"Dancin with that tom°," say Elo to Joe Lee, who leanin on the folks'

does heads: fixes hair in a beauty shop.

cuttin her eye at me: throwing me a look that could kill.

tom: an Uncle Tom, slang for a black who, like the stereotyped good old loyal slave in Harriet Beecher Stowe's pre-Civil War novel of plantation life, *Uncle Tom's Cabin,* obligingly submits to mistreatment and white rule.

freezer. "His feet can smell a cracker° a mile away and go into their shuffle number post haste. And them eyes. He could be a little considerate and put on some shades. Who wants to look into them blown-out fuses that — "

"Is this what they call the generation gap?" I say.

"Generation gap," spits Elo, like I suggested castor oil and fricassee 15 possum in the milk-shakes or somethin. "That's a white concept for a white phenomenon. There's no generation gap among Black people. We are a col — "

"Yeh, well never mind," says Joe Lee. "The point is Mama . . . well, it's pride. You embarrass yourself and us too dancin like that."

"I wasn't shame." Then nobody say nuthin. Them standin there in they pretty clothes with drinks in they hands and gangin up on me, and me in the third-degree chair and nary a olive to my name. Felt just like the police got hold to me.

"First of all," Task say, holdin up his hand and tickin off the offenses, "the dress. Now that dress is too short, Mama, and too low-cut for a woman your age. And Tamu's going to make a speech tonight to kick off the campaign and will be introducin you and expecting you to organize the council of elders — "

"Me? Didn nobody ask me nuthin. You mean Nisi? She change her name?"

"Well, Norton was supposed to tell you about it. Nisi wants to introduce 20 you and then encourage the older folks to form a Council of the Elders to act as an advisory — "

"And you going to be standing there with your boobs out and that wig on your head and that hem up to your ass. And people'll say, 'Ain't that the horny bitch that was grindin with the blind dude?' "

"Elo, be cool a minute," say Task, gettin to the next finger. "And then there's the drinkin. Mama, you know you can't drink cause next thing you know you be laughin loud and carryin on," and he grab another finger for the loudness. "And then there's the dancin. You been tattooed on the man for four records straight and slow draggin even on the fast numbers. How you think that look for a woman your age?"

"What's my age?"

"What?"

"I'm axin you all a simple question. You keep talkin bout what's proper 25 for a woman my age. How old am I anyhow?" And Joe Lee slams his eyes shut and squinches up his face to figure. And Task run a hand over his ear and stare into his glass like the ice cubes goin calculate for him. And Elo just starin at the top of my head like she goin rip the wig off any minute now.

"Is your hair braided up under that thing? If so, why don't you take it off? You always did do a neat cornroll°."

"Uh huh," cause I'm thinkin how she couldn't undo her hair fast enough talking bout cornroll so countrified. None of which was the subject. "How old, I say?"

"Sixtee-one or — "

---

cracker: a rural white supremacist.
cornroll: a style of braided hair.

"You a damn lie Joe Lee Peoples."

"And that's another thing," say Task on the fingers.   30

"You know what you all can kiss," I say, gettin up and brushin the wrinkles out my lap.

"Oh, Mama," Elo say, puttin a hand on my shoulder like she hasn't done since she left home and the hand landin light and not sure it supposed to be there. Which hurt me to my heart. Cause this was the child in our happiness fore Mr. Peoples die. And I carried that child strapped to my chest till she was nearly two. We was close is what I'm tryin to tell you. Cause it was more me in the child than the others. And even after Task it was the girlchild I covered in the night and wept over for no reason at all less it was she was a chub-chub like me and not very pretty, but a warm child. And how did things get to this, that she can't put a sure hand on me and say Mama we love you and care about you and you entitled to enjoy yourself cause you a good woman?

"And then there's Reverend Trent," say Task, glancin from left to right like they hatchin a plot and just now lettin me in on it. "You were suppose to be talking with him tonight, Mama, about giving us his basement for campaign headquarters and — "

"Didn nobody tell me nuthin. If grass roots mean you kept in the dark I can't use it. I really can't. And Reven Trent a fool anyway the way he tore into the widow man up there on Edgecomb cause he wouldn't take in three of them foster children and the woman not even comfy in the ground yet and the man's mind messed up and — "

"Look here," say Task. "What we need is a family conference so we can   35 get all this stuff cleared up and laid out on the table. In the meantime I think we better get back into the other room and tend to business. And in the meantime, Mama, see if you can't get to Reverend Trent and — "

"You want me to belly rub with the Reven, that it?"

"Oh damn," Elo say and go through the swingin door.

"We'll talk about all this at dinner. How's tomorrow night, Joe Lee?" While Joe Lee being self-important I'm wonderin who's doin the cookin and how come no body ax me if I'm free and do I get a corsage and things like that. Then Joe nod that it's O.K. and he go through the swingin door and just a little hubbub come through from the other room. Then Task smile his smile, lookin just like his daddy, and he leave. And it just me and this stranger's kitchen, which was a mess I wouldn't never let my kitchen look like. Poison you just to look at the pots. Then the door swing the other way and it's My Man Bovanne standin there sayin Miss Hazel but lookin at the deep fry and then at the steam table, and most surprised when I come up on him from the other direction and take him on out of there. Pass the folks pushin up towards the stage where Nisi and some other people settin and ready to talk, and folks gettin to the last of the sandwiches and the booze fore they settle down in one spot and listen serious. And I'm thinkin bout tellin Bovanne what a lovely long dress Nisi got on and the earrings and her hair piled up in a cone and the people bout to hear how we all gettin screwed and gotta form our own party and everybody there listenin and lookin. But instead I just haul the man on out of there, and Joe Lee and his wife look at me like I'm terrible, but they ain't said boo to the man yet. Cause he blind and old and don't nobody there need him since they grown up and don't need they skates fixed no more.

"Where we goin, Miss Hazel?" Him knowin all the time.

"First we gonna buy you some dark sunglasses. Then you comin with   40
me to the supermarket so I can pick up tomorrow's dinner, which is going to
be a grand thing proper and you invited. Then we going to my house."

"That be fine. I surely would like to rest my feet." Bein cute, but you
got to let men play out they little show, blind or not. So he chat on bout how
tired he is and how he appreciate me takin him in hand this way. And I'm
thinkin I'll have him change the lock on my door first thing. Then I'll give the
man a nice warm bath with jasmine leaves in the water and a little Epsom salt
on the sponge to do his back. And then a good rubdown with rose water and
olive oil. Then a cup of lemon tea with a taste in it. And a little talcum, some
of that fancy stuff Nisi mother sent over last Christmas. And then a massage,
a good face massage round the forehead which is the worrying part. Cause you
gots to take care of the older folks. And let them know they still needed to
run the mimeo machine° and keep the spark plugs clean and fix the mailboxes
for folks who might help us get the breakfast program goin, and the school
for the little kids and the campaign and all. Cause old folks in the nation. That
what Nisi was sayin and I mean to do my part.

"I imagine you are a very pretty woman, Miss Hazel."

"I surely am," I say just like the hussy my daughter always say I was.

Ursula K. LeGuin

THE WIFE'S STORY   1982

*Ursula K. LeGuin was born in 1929 in Berkeley, California, the daughter
of Theodora Kroeber, a folklorist, and Alfred L. Kroeber, an anthropologist.
After graduation from Radcliffe, she took an M.A. degree at Columbia.
LeGuin, who launched her successful career as a writer while rearing three
children and holding a job, first won a devoted following for her stories in
science fiction magazines.* Roncannon's World *(1966) was her first book;
another early novel,* The Left Hand of Darkness *(1969), has been called
a classic in its field. Like the novels of Kurt Vonnegut, Jr., LeGuin's work
has appealed beyond science fiction fandom to a wider audience. (LeGuin
remarks that she did not at first regard herself as a science fiction writer; it
was only when she began reading that genre herself that she realized the label
would apply.) Bringing a feminine sensibility to science fiction, she has
employed science fiction to criticize her own civilization. Many of her stories
create whole new cultures and civilizations, with some anthropological authority. Besides, she has written poetry and juvenile fiction, including the
trilogy of Earthsea novels beginning with* Wizard of Earthsea *(1968),
given a Globe-Hornbook children's book award. She lives in Portland,
Oregon. "The Wife's Tale" was originally written for an anthology entitled*
Changes.

---

mimeo machine: Mimeograph stencil duplicator, an inexpensive means to turn out propaganda.

He was a good husband, a good father. I don't understand it. I don't believe in it. I don't believe that it happened. I saw it happen but it isn't true. It can't be. He was always gentle. If you'd have seen him playing with the children, anybody who saw him with the children would have known that there wasn't any bad in him, not one mean bone. When I first met him he was still living with his mother, over near Spring Lake, and I used to see them together, the mother and the sons, and think that any young fellow that was that nice with his family must be one worth knowing. Then one time when I was walking in the woods I met him by himself coming back from a hunting trip. He hadn't got any game at all, not so much as a field mouse, but he wasn't cast down about it. He was just larking along enjoying the morning air. That's one of the things I first loved about him. He didn't take things hard, he didn't grouch and whine when things didn't go his way. So we got to talking that day. And I guess things moved right along after that, because pretty soon he was over here pretty near all the time. And my sister said — see, my parents had moved out the year before and gone south, leaving us the place — my sister said, kind of teasing but serious, "Well! If he's going to be here every day and half the night, I guess there isn't room for me!" And she moved out — just down the way. We've always been real close, her and me. That's the sort of thing doesn't ever change. I couldn't ever have got through this bad time without my sis.

Well, so he come to live here. And all I can say is, it was the happy year of my life. He was just purely good to me. A hard worker and never lazy, and so big and fine-looking. Everybody looked up to him, you know, young as he was. Lodge Meeting nights, more and more often they had him to lead the singing. He had such a beautiful voice, and he'd lead off strong, and the others following and joining in, high voices and low. It brings the shivers on me now to think of it, hearing it, nights when I'd stayed home from meeting when the children was babies — the singing coming up through the trees there, and the moonlight, summer nights, the full moon shining. I'll never hear anything so beautiful. I'll never know a joy like that again.

It was the moon, that's what they say. It's the moon's fault, and the blood. It was in his father's blood. I never knew his father, and now I wonder what become of him. He was from up Whitewater way, and had no kin around here. I always thought he went back there, but now I don't know. There was some talk about him, tales, that come out after what happened to my husband. It's something runs in the blood, they say, and it may never come out, but if it does, it's the change of the moon that does it. Always it happens in the dark of the moon. When everybody's home and asleep. Something comes over the one that's got the curse in his blood, they say, and he gets up because he can't sleep, and goes out into the glaring sun, and goes off all alone — drawn to find those like him.

And it may be so, because my husband would do that. I'd half rouse and say, "Where you going to?" and he'd say, "Oh, hunting, be back this evening," and it wasn't like him, even his voice was different. But I'd be so sleepy, and not wanting to wake the kids, and he was so good and responsible, it was no call of mine to go asking "Why?" and "Where?" and all like that.

So it happened that way maybe three times or four. He'd come back late, and worn out, and pretty near cross for one so sweet-tempered — not wanting to talk about it. I figured everybody got to bust out now and then, and nagging never helped anything. But it did begin to worry me. Not so much that he went, but that he come back so tired and strange. Even, he smelled strange. It made my hair stand up on end. I could not endure it and I said, "What is that — those smells on you? All over you!" And he said, "I don't know," real short, and made like he was sleeping. But he went down when he thought I wasn't noticing, and washed and washed himself. But those smells stayed in his hair, and in our bed, for days.

And then the awful thing. I don't find it easy to tell about this. I want to cry when I have to bring it to my mind. Our youngest, the little one, my baby, she turned from her father. Just overnight. He come in and she got scared-looking, stiff, with her eyes wide, and then she begun to cry and try to hide behind me. She didn't yet talk plain but she was saying over and over, "Make it go away! Make it go away!"

The look in his eyes, just for one moment, when he heard that. That's what I don't want ever to remember. That's what I can't forget. The look in his eyes looking at his own child.

I said to the child, "Shame on you, what's got into you!" — scolding, but keeping her right up close to me at the same time, because I was frightened too. Frightened to shaking.

He looked away then and said something like, "Guess she just waked up dreaming," and passed it off that way. Or tried to. And so did I. And I got real mad with my baby when she kept on acting crazy scared of her own dad. But she couldn't help it and I couldn't change it.

He kept away that whole day. Because he knew, I guess. It was just beginning dark of the moon.

It was hot and close inside, and dark, and we'd all been asleep some while, when something woke me up. He wasn't there beside me. I heard a little stir in the passage, when I listened. So I got up, because I could bear it no longer. I went out into the passage, and it was light there, hard sunlight coming in from the door. And I saw him standing just outside, in the tall grass by the entrance. His head was hanging. Presently he sat down, like he felt weary, and looked down at his feet. I held still, inside, and watched — I didn't know what for.

And I saw what he saw. I saw the changing. In his feet, it was, first. They got long, each foot got longer, stretching out, the toes stretching out and the foot getting long, and fleshy, and white. And no hair on them.

The hair begun to come away all over his body. It was like his hair fried away in the sunlight and was gone. He was white all over then, like a worm's skin. And he turned his face. It was changing while I looked. It got flatter and flatter, the mouth flat and wide, and the teeth grinning flat and dull, and the nose just a knob of flesh with nostril holes, and the ears gone, and the eyes gone blue — blue, with white rims around the blue — staring at me out of that flat, soft, white face.

He stood up then on two legs.

I saw him, I had to see him, my own dear love, turned into the hateful one.

I couldn't move, but as I crouched there in the passage staring out into the day I was trembling and shaking with a growl that burst out into a crazy,

10

15

awful howling. A grief howl and a terror howl and a calling howl. And the others heard it, even sleeping, and woke up.

It stared and peered, that thing my husband had turned into, and shoved its face up to the entrance of our house. I was still bound by mortal fear, but behind me the children had waked up, and the baby was whimpering. The mother anger come into me then, and I snarled and crept forward.

The man thing looked around. It had no gun, like the ones from the man places do. But it picked up a heavy fallen tree branch in its long white foot, and shoved the end of that down into our house, at me. I snapped the end of it in my teeth and started to force my way out, because I knew the man would kill our children if it could. But my sister was already coming. I saw her running at the man with her head low and her mane high and her eyes yellow as the winter sun. It turned on her and raised up that branch to hit her. But I come out of the doorway, mad with the mother anger, and the others all were coming answering my call, the whole pack gathering, there in that blind glare and heat of the sun at noon.

The man looked round at us and yelled out loud, and brandished the branch it held. Then it broke and ran, heading for the cleared fields and plowlands, down the mountainside. It ran, on two legs, leaping and weaving, and we followed it.

I was last, because love still bound the anger and the fear in me. I was running when I saw them pull it down. My sister's teeth were in its throat. I got there and it was dead. The others were drawing back from the kill, because of the taste of the blood, and the smell. The younger ones were cowering and some crying, and my sister rubbed her mouth against her forelegs over and over to get rid of the taste. I went up close because I thought if the thing was dead the spell, the curse must be done, and my husband could come back — alive, or even dead, if I could only see him, my true love, in his true form, beautiful. But only the dead man lay there white and bloody. We drew back and back from it, and turned and ran, back up into the hills, back to the woods of the shadows and the twilight and the blessed dark.

Criticism: On Fiction

The critical power is of lower rank than the creative. True, but in assenting to this proposition, one or two things are to be kept in mind. It is undeniable that the exercise of a creative power, that of a free creative activity, is the true function of man; it is proved to be so by man's finding in it his true happiness. But it is undeniable, also, that men may have the sense of exercising this free creative activity in other ways than in producing great works of literature or art; if it were not so, all but a very few men would be shut out from the true happiness of all men; they may have it in well-doing, they may have it in learning, they may have it even in criticizing.

— Matthew Arnold, "The Function of Criticism"

Edgar Allan Poe (1809 – 1849)
THE TALE AND ITS EFFECT

1842

Were we called upon, however, to designate that class of composition which, next to [a short lyric poem], should best fulfill the demands of high genius — should offer it the most advantageous field of exertion — we should unhesitatingly speak of the prose tale, as Mr. Hawthorne has here exemplified it. We allude to the short prose narrative, requiring from a half-hour to one or two hours in its perusal. The ordinary novel is objectionable, from its length, for reasons already stated in substance. As it cannot be read at one sitting, it deprives itself, of course, of the immense force derivable from *totality.* Worldly interests intervening during the pauses of perusal, modify, annul, or counteract; in a greater or less degree, the impressions of the book. But simple cessation in reading would, of itself, be sufficient to destroy the true unity. In the brief tale, however, the author is enabled to carry out the fullness of his intention, be it what it may. During the hour of perusal the soul of the reader is at the writer's control. There are no external or extrinsic influences — resulting from weariness or interruption.

A skillful literary artist has constructed a tale. If wise, he has not fashioned his thoughts to accommodate his incidents; but having conceived, with deliberate care, a certain unique or single *effect* to be wrought out, he then invents such incidents — he then combines such events as may best aid him in establishing this preconceived effect. If his very initial sentence tend not to the outbringing of this effect, then he has failed in his first step. In the whole composition there should be no word written, of which the tendency, direct or indirect, is not to the one pre-established design. And by such means, with such care and skill, a picture is at length painted which leaves in the mind of him who contemplates it with a kindred art, a sense of the fullest satisfaction. The idea of the tale has been presented unblemished, because undisturbed; and this is an end unattainable by the novel. Undue brevity is just as exceptionable here as in the poem; but undue length is yet more to be avoided.

— Twice-Told Tales, by Nathaniel Hawthorne: A Review

Charlotte Brontë (1816 – 1855)
THE WRITER'S PASSIVE WORK

1850

Whether it is right or advisable to create beings like Heathcliff°, I do not know: I scarcely think it is. But this I know: the writer who possesses the creative gift owns something of which he is not always master — something that, at times, strangely wills and works for itself. He may lay down rules and devise principles, and to rules and principles it will perhaps for years lie in subjection; and then, haply without any warning of revolt, there comes a time when it will no longer consent to "harrow the valleys, or be bound with a band

---

THE WRITER'S PASSIVE WORK. *Heathcliff:* Central character of the novel *Wuthering Heights:* "a man's shape animated by demon life" (in Charlotte Brontë's view).

in the furrow" — when it "laughs at the multitude of the city, and regards not the crying of the driver" — when, refusing absolutely to make ropes out of sea-sand any longer, it sets to work on statue-hewing, and you have a Pluto or Jove, a Tisiphone or a Psyche, a Mermaid or a Madonna, as Fate or Inspiration direct. Be the work grim or glorious, dread or divine, you have little choice left but quiescent adoption. As for you — the nominal artist — your share in it has been to work passively under dictates you neither delivered nor could question — that would not be uttered at your prayer, nor suppressed nor changed at your caprice. If the result be attractive, the World will praise you, who little deserve praise; if it be repulsive, the same World will blame you, who almost as little deserve blame.

— Preface to the Second Edition of *Wuthering Heights* (by Emily Brontë)

Gustave Flaubert (1821 – 1880)

THE LABOR OF STYLE   1854

Translated by Francis Steegmuller

I have just made a fresh copy of what I have written since New Year, or rather since the middle of February, for on my return from Paris I burned all my January work. It amounts to thirteen pages, no more, no less, thirteen pages in seven weeks. However, they are in shape, I think, and as perfect as I can make them. There are only two or three repetitions of the same word which must be removed, and two turns of phrase that are still too much alike. At last something is completed. It was a difficult transition: the reader had to be led gradually and imperceptibly from psychology to action. Now I am about to begin the dramatic, eventful part. Two or three more big pushes and the end will be in sight. By July or August I hope to tackle the denouement. What a struggle it has been! My God, what a struggle! Such drudgery! Such discouragement! I spent all last evening frantically poring over surgical texts. I am studying the theory of clubfeet. In three hours I devoured an entire volume on this interesting subject and took notes. I came upon some really fine sentences. "The maternal breast is an impenetrable and mysterious sanctuary, where . . . etc." An excellent treatise, incidentally. Why am I not young? How I should work! One ought to know everything, to write. All of us scribblers are monstrously ignorant. If only we weren't so lacking in stamina, what a rich field of ideas and similes we could tap! Books that have been the source of entire literatures, like Homer and Rabelais, contain the sum of all the knowledge of their times. They knew everything, those fellows, and we know nothing. Ronsard's poetics contain a curious precept: he advises the poet to become well versed in the arts and crafts — to frequent blacksmiths, goldsmiths, locksmiths, etc. — in order to enrich his stock of metaphors. And indeed that is the sort of thing that makes for rich and varied language. The sentences in a book must quiver like the leaves in a forest, all dissimilar in their similarity.

— Letter to Louise Colet, April 7, 1854,
during the writing of *Madame Bovary*

Nathaniel Hawthorne (1804 – 1864)

AMERICA AND THE LANDSCAPE OF ROMANCE 1860

The author proposes to himself merely to write a fanciful story, evolving a thoughtful moral, and did not purpose attempting a portraiture of Italian manners and character. . . . Italy, as the site of his Romance, was chiefly valuable to him as affording a sort of poetic or fairy precinct, where actualities would not be so terribly insisted upon as they are, and must needs be, in America. No author, without a trial, can conceive of the difficulty of writing a romance about a country where there is no shadow, no antiquity, no mystery, no picturesque and gloomy wrong, nor anything but a commonplace prosperity, in broad and simple daylight, as is happily the case with my dear native land. It will be very long, I trust, before romance-writers may find congenial and easily handled themes, either in the annals of our stalwart republic, or in any characteristic and probable events of our individual lives. Romance and poetry, like ivy, lichens, and wall-flowers, need ruin to make them grow.

— Preface to *The Marble Faun*

Thomas Hardy (1840 – 1928)

"THE WHOLE SECRET OF A LIVING STYLE" 1874

The whole secret of a living style and the difference between it and a dead style, lies in not having too much style — being, in fact, a little careless, or rather seeming to be, here and there. It brings wonderful life into the writing. . . .

Otherwise your style is like worn half-pence — all the fresh images rounded off by rubbing, and no crispness or movement at all.

It is, of course, simply a carrying into prose the knowledge I have acquired in poetry — that inexact rhymes and rhythms now and then are far more pleasing than correct ones.

— Note to himself, quoted by Florence Emily Hardy,
The Early Life of Thomas Hardy (London: Macmillan, 1928)

Henry James (1843 – 1916)

THE MIRROR OF A CONSCIOUSNESS 1908

This in fact I have ever found rather terribly the point — that the figures in any picture, the agents in any drama, are interesting only in proportion as they feel their respective situations; since the consciousness, on their part, of the complication exhibited forms for us their link of connection with it. But there are degrees of feeling — the muffled, the faint, the just sufficient, the barely intelligent, as we may say; and the acute, the intense, the complete, in a word — the power to be finely aware and richly responsible. It is those moved in this latter fashion who "get most" out of all that happens to them and who in so doing enable us, as readers of their record, as participators by a fond attention, also to get most. Their being finely aware — as Hamlet and Lear, say, are finely aware — *makes* absolutely the intensity of their adventure, gives the maximum of sense to what befalls them. We care, our curiosity and our sympathy care, comparatively little for what happens to the stupid, the coarse and the blind; care for it, and for the effects of it, at the most as helping to precipitate what happens to the more deeply wondering, to the really sentient. Hamlet and Lear are surrounded, amid their complications, by the stupid and the blind, who minister in all sorts of ways to their recorded fate. . . .

Verily even, I think, no "story" is possible without its fools — as most of the fine painters of life, Shakespeare, Cervantes and Balzac, Fielding, Scott, Thackeray, Dickens, George Meredith, George Eliot, Jane Austen, have abundantly felt. At the same time I confess I never see the *leading* interest of any human hazard but in a consciousness (on the part of the moved and moving creature) subject to fine intensification and wide enlargement. It is as mirrored in that consciousness that the gross fools, the headlong fools, the fatal fools play their part for us — they have much less to show us in themselves. The troubled life mostly at the center of our subject — whatever our subject, for the artistic hour, happens to be — embraces them and deals with them for its amusement and its anguish: they are apt largely indeed, on a near view, to be all the cause of its trouble. This means, exactly, that the person capable of feeling in the given case more than another of what is to be felt for it, and so serving in the highest degree to *record* it dramatically and objectively, is the only sort of person on whom we can count not to betray, to cheapen or, as we say, give away, the value and beauty of the thing. By so much as the affair matters *for* some such individual, by so much do we get the best there is of it, and by so much as it falls within the scope of a denser and duller, a more vulgar and more shallow capacity, do we get a picture dim and meager.

The great chroniclers have clearly always been aware of this; they have at least always either placed a mind of some sort — in the sense of a reflecting and coloring medium — in possession of the general adventure . . . or else paid signally, as to the interest created for their failure to do so.

— Preface to *The Princess Casamassima*

James Joyce (1882 – 1941)

EPIPHANIES   1904 – 1906

He° was passing through Eccles Street one evening, one misty evening, with all these thoughts dancing the dance of unrest in his brain when a trivial incident set him composing some ardent verses which he entitled a 'Villanelle of the Temptress.' A young lady was standing on the steps of one of those brown brick houses which seem the very incarnation of Irish paralysis. A young gentleman was leaning on the rusty railings of the area. Stephen as he

EPIPHANIES. *He:* Stephen Dedalus, protagonist of Joyce's novel (an early version of *Portrait of the Artist as a Young Man*), a young Dublin intellectual resembling Joyce himself.

passed on his quest heard the following fragment of colloquy out of which he received an impression keen enough to afflict his sensitiveness very severely.

THE YOUNG LADY — (drawling discreetly) . . . O, yes . . . I was . . . at the . . . cha . . . pel. . . .

THE YOUNG GENTLEMAN — (inaudibly) . . . I . . . (again inaudibly) . . . I . . .

THE YOUNG LADY — (softly) . . . O . . . but you're . . . ve . . . ry . . . wick . . . ed. . . .

This triviality made him think of collecting many such moments together in a book of epiphanies. By an epiphany he meant a sudden spiritual manifestation, whether in the vulgarity of speech or of gesture or in a memorable phase of the mind itself. He believed that it was for the man of letters to record these epiphanies with extreme care, seeing that they themselves are the most delicate and evanescent of moments. He told Cranly° that the clock of the Ballast Office was capable of an epiphany. Cranly questioned the inscrutable dial of the Ballast Office with his no less inscrutable countenance.

— Yes, said Stephen. I will pass it time after time, allude to it, refer to it, catch a glimpse of it. It is only an item in the catalogue of Dublin's street furniture. Then all at once I see it and I know at once what it is: epiphany . . .

— *Stephen Hero*

Virginia Woolf (1882 – 1941)
"A LUMINOUS HALO"   1919

Examine for a moment an ordinary mind on an ordinary day. The mind receives a myriad impressions — trivial, fantastic, evanescent, or engraved with the sharpness of steel. From all sides they come, an incessant shower of innumerable atoms; and as they fall, as they shape themselves into the life of Monday or Tuesday, the accent falls differently from of old; the moment of importance came not here but there; so that if a writer were a free man and not a slave, if he could write what he chose, not what he must, if he could base his work upon his own feeling and not upon convention, there would be no plot, no comedy, no tragedy, no love interest or catastrophe in the accepted style, and perhaps not a single button sewn on as the Bond Street tailors would have it. Life is not a series of gig lamps symmetrically arranged; but a luminous halo, a semi-transparent envelope surrounding us from the beginning of consciousness to the end. Is it not the task of the novelist to convey this varying, this unknown and uncircumscribed spirit, whatever aberration or complexity it may display, with as little mixture of the alien and external as possible? We are not pleading merely for courage and sincerity; we are suggesting that the proper stuff of fiction is a little other than custom would have us believe it.

It is, at any rate, in some such fashion as this that we seek to define the quality which distinguishes the work of several young writers, among whom Mr. James Joyce is the most notable, from that of their predecessors. They

Cranly: a fellow student.

attempt to come closer to life, and to preserve more sincerely and exactly what interests and moves them, even if to do so they must discard most of the conventions which are commonly observed by the novelist. Let us record the atoms as they fall upon the mind in the order in which they fall, let us trace the pattern, however disconnected and incoherent in appearance, which each sight or incident scores upon the consciousness. Let us not take it for granted that life exists more fully in what is commonly thought big than in what is commonly thought small.

— Modern Fiction, The Common Reader

Edith Wharton (1862 – 1937)

THE SHORT STORY AND THE NOVEL

1925

A curious distinction between the successful tale and the successful novel at once presents itself. It is safe to say (since the surest way of measuring achievement in art is by survival) that the test of the novel is that its people should be *alive*. No subject in itself, however fruitful, appears to be able to keep a novel alive; only the characters in it can. Of the short story the same cannot be said. Some of the greatest short stories owe their vitality entirely to the dramatic rendering of a situation. Undoubtedly the characters engaged must be a little more than puppets; but apparently, also, they may be a little less than individual human beings. In this respect the short story, rather than the novel, might be called the direct descendant of the old epic or ballad — of those earlier forms of fiction in all of which action was the chief affair, and the characters, if they did not remain mere puppets, seldom or never became more than types — such as the people, for instance, in Molière. The reason for the difference is obvious. Type, general character, may be set forth in a few strokes, but the progression, the unfolding of personality, of which the reader instinctively feels the need if the actors in the tale are to retain their individuality for him through a succession of changing circumstances — this slow but continuous growth requires space, and therefore belongs by definition to a larger, a symphonic plan.

The chief technical difference between the short story and the novel may therefore be summed up by saying that situation is the main concern of the short story, character of the novel; and it follows that the effect produced by the short story depends almost entirely on its form, or presentation. Even more — yes, and much more — than in the construction of the novel, the impression of vividness, of *presentness,* in the affair narrated, has to be sought, and made sure of beforehand, by that careful artifice which is the real carelessness of art. The short-story writer must not only know from what angle to present his anecdote if it is to give out all its fires, but must understand just *why* that particular angle and no other is the right one. He must therefore have turned his subject over and over, walked around it, so to speak, and applied to it those laws of perspective which Paolo Uccello called "so beautiful," before it can be offered to the reader as a natural unembellished fragment of experience, detached like a ripe fruit from the tree.

— The Writing of Fiction

William Faulkner (1897 – 1962)

"THE HUMAN HEART IN CONFLICT WITH ITSELF" 1950

Our tragedy today is a general and universal physical fear so long sustained by now that we can even bear it. There are no longer problems of the spirit. There is only the question: When will I be blown up? Because of this, the young man or woman writing today has forgotten the problems of the human heart in conflict with itself which alone can make good writing because only that is worth writing about, worth the agony and the sweat.

He must learn them again. He must teach himself that the basest of all things is to be afraid; and, teaching himself that, forget it forever, leaving no room in his workshop for anything but the old verities and truths of the heart, the old universal truths lacking which any story is ephemeral and doomed — love and honor and pity and pride and compassion and sacrifice. Until he does so, he labors under a curse. He writes not of love but of lust, of defeats in which nobody loses anything of value, of victories without hope and, worst of all, without pity or compassion. His griefs grieve on no universal bones, leaving no scars. He writes not of the heart but of the glands.

Until he relearns these things, he will write as though he stood among and watched the end of man. I decline to accept the end of man. It is easy enough to say that man is immortal simply because he will endure; that when the last ding-dong of doom has clanged and faded from the last worthless rock hanging tideless in the last red and dying evening, that even then there will still be one more sound: that of his puny inexhaustible voice, still talking. I refuse to accept this. I believe that man will not merely endure: he will prevail. He is immortal, not because he alone among creatures has an inexhaustible voice, but because he has a soul, a spirit capable of compassion and sacrifice and endurance. The poet's, the writer's, duty is to write about these things. It is his privilege to help man endure by lifting his heart, by reminding him of the courage and honor and hope and pride and compassion and pity and sacrifice which have been the glory of his past. The poet's voice need not merely be the record of man, it can be one of the props, the pillars to help him endure and prevail.

> — Speech of Acceptance for the award
> of the Nobel Prize for Literature

Frank O'Connor (1903 – 1966)

THE GREATEST ESSENTIAL OF A STORY 1957

INTERVIEWER: What is the greatest essential of a story?

O'CONNOR: You have to have a theme, a story to tell. Here's a man at the other side of the table and I'm talking to him; I'm going to tell him something that will interest him. As you know perfectly well, our principal difficulty at Harvard was a number of people who'd had affairs with girls or had had another interesting experience, and wanted to come in and tell about it, straight away. That is not a theme. A theme is something that is worth something to everybody. In fact, you wouldn't, if you'd ever been involved in a thing like this, grab a man in a pub and say, "Look, I had a girl out last night, under the Charles Bridge." That's the last thing you'd do. You grab somebody and say, "Look, an extraordinary thing happened to me yesterday — I met a man — he said this to me — " and that, to me, is a theme. The moment you grab somebody by the lapels and you've got something to tell, that's a real story. It means you want to tell him and think the story is interesting in itself. If you start describing your own personal experiences, something that's only of interest to yourself, then you can't express yourself, you cannot say, ultimately, what you think about human beings. The moment you say this, you're committed.

I'll tell you what I mean. We were down on the south coast of Ireland for a holiday and we got talkin' to this old farmer and he said his son, who was dead now, had gone to America. He'd married an American girl and she had come over for a visit, alone. Apparently her doctor had told her a trip to Ireland would do her good. And she stayed with the parents, had gone around to see his friends and other relations, and it wasn't till after she'd gone that they learned that the boy had died. Why didn't she tell them? There's your story. Dragging the reader in, making the reader a part of the story . . .

— Writers at Work: The Paris Review Interviews

Stanley Fish (b. 1938)

An eskimo "a rose for emily"   1980

The fact that it remains easy to think of a reading that most of us would dismiss out of hand does not mean that the text excludes it but that there is as yet no elaborated interpretive procedure for producing that text. . . . Norman Holland's analysis of Faulkner's "A Rose for Emily" is a case in point. Holland is arguing for a kind of psychoanalytic pluralism. The text, he declares, is "at most a matrix of psychological possibilities for its readers," but, he insists, "only some possibilities . . . truly fit the matrix": "One would not say, for example, that a reader of . . . 'A Rose for Emily' who thought the 'tableau' [of Emily and her father in the doorway] described an Eskimo was really responding to the story at all — only pursuing some mysterious inner exploration."

Holland is making two arguments: first, that anyone who proposes an Eskimo reading of "A Rose for Emily" will not find a hearing in the literary community. And that, I think, is right. ("We are right to rule out at least some readings.") His second argument is that the unacceptability of the Eskimo reading is a function of the text, of what he calls its "sharable promptuary" (p. 287), the public "store of structured language" (p. 287) that sets limits to the interpretations the words can accommodate. And that, I think, is wrong. The Eskimo reading is unacceptable because there is at present no interpretive strategy for producing it, no way of "looking" or reading (and remember, all acts of looking or reading are "ways") that would result in the emergence of obviously Eskimo meanings. This does not mean, however, that no such strategy could ever come into play, and it is not difficult to imagine the circumstances under which it would establish itself. One such circumstance would be the discovery of a letter in which Faulkner confides that he has always believed himself to be an Eskimo changeling. (The example is absurd only if one forgets Yeats's *Vision* or Blake's Swedenborgianism or James Miller's recent elaboration of a homosexual reading of *The Waste Land*). Immediately the workers in the Faulkner industry would begin to reinterpret the canon in the light of this newly revealed "belief" and the work of reinterpretation would involve the elaboration of a symbolic or allusive system (not unlike mythological or typological criticism) whose application would immediately transform the text into one informed everywhere by Eskimo meanings. It might seem that I am admitting that there is a text to be transformed, but the object of transformation would be the text (or texts) given by whatever interpretive strategies the Eskimo strategy was in the process of dislodging or expanding. The result would be that whereas we now have a Freudian "A Rose for Emily," a mythological "A Rose for Emily," a Christological "A Rose for Emily," a regional "A Rose for Emily," a sociological "A Rose for Emily," a linguistic "A Rose for Emily," we would in addition have an Eskimo "A Rose for Emily," existing in some relation of compatibility or incompatibility with the others.

Again the point is that while there are always mechanisms for ruling out readings, their source is not the text but the presently recognized interpretive strategies for producing the text. It follows, then, that no reading, however outlandish it might appear, is inherently an impossible one.

— *Is There a Text in This Class?*

Supplement: Writing

Writing about Literature

All of us have some powers of reasoning and perception. And when we come to a story, a poem, or a play, we can do little other than to trust whatever powers we have, like one who enters a shadowy room, clutching a decent candle.

After all, in the study of literature, common sense (poet Gerard Manley Hopkins said) is never out of place. For most of a class hour, a renowned English professor rhapsodized about the arrangement of the contents of W. H. Auden's *Collected Poems.* Auden, he claimed, was a master of thematic continuity, who had brilliantly placed the poems in the best possible order, in which (to the ingenious mind) they complemented each other. Near the end of the hour, his theories were punctured — with a great inaudible pop — when a student, timidly raising a hand, pointed out that Auden had arranged the poems in the book not according to theme but in alphabetical order according to the first word of each poem. The professor's jaw dropped: "Why didn't you say that sooner?" The student was apologetic: "I — I was afraid I'd sound too *ordinary.*"

Emerson makes a similar point in his essay, "The American Scholar": "Meek young men grow up in libraries, believing it their duty to accept the views which Cicero, which Locke, which Bacon have given; forgetful that Cicero, Locke, and Bacon were only young men in libraries when they wrote these books." Don't be afraid to state a conviction, though it seems obvious. Does it matter that you may be repeating something that, once upon a time or even just the other day, has been said before? There are excellent old ideas as well as new.

SOME APPROACHES TO LITERATURE

Most writers of critical essays follow a few familiar approaches to stories, poems, and plays. Underlying each of these four approaches is a specific way of regarding the nature of a work of literature.

1. *The Work by Itself.* This view assumes a story, poem, or play to be an individual entity, existing on its page, which we can read and understand in its own right, without necessarily studying the life of its author,

or the age in which it was written, or its possible effect on its readers. This is the approach in most papers written in response to college assignments; to study just the work (and not its backgrounds or its influence) does not require the student to spend prolonged time doing research in a library. The three common ways of writing a paper discussed in this book — explication, analysis, and comparison and contrast — deal mainly with the work of literature in itself.

2. *The Work as Imitation of Life.* Aristotle called the art of writing a tragedy *mimesis:* the imitation or re-creation of an action that is serious and complete in itself. From this classic theory in the *Poetics* comes the view that a work of literature in some ways imitates the world or the civilization in which it was produced. We can say that Ibsen's play *A Doll House* places before our eyes actors whose lifelike speeches and movements represent members of an upper-middle-class society in provincial Norway in the late nineteenth century and that the play reflects their beliefs and attitudes. Not only the subject and theme of a work imitate life in this view: John Ciardi remarked that the heroic couplet, dominant stanza form in poetry read by educated people in eighteenth-century England, reflects, in its exact form and its use of antitheses, the rhythms of the minuet — another contemporary form, fashionable also among the well-to-do: "now on this hand, now on that." The writer considering literature as imitation usually studies the world that the literary work imitates. He or she goes into the ideas underlying the writer's society, showing how the themes, assumptions, and conventions of the writer's work arose out of that time and that place. Obviously, this analysis takes more research than one can do for a weekly paper; it is usually the approach taken for a book or a dissertation, or perhaps an honors thesis or a term paper. (The other two approaches we will mention also take research.) Reasonably short studies of the relation between the work and its world are, however, sometimes possible: "World War II as Seen in Henry Reed's 'Naming of Parts' "; "Faulkner's 'Barn Burning': A Mirror of Mississippi?"

3. *The Work as Expression.* In this view, a work of literature expresses the feelings of the person who wrote it; therefore, to study it, one studies the author's life. Typical paper topics: *"A Glass Menagerie* and the Early Life of Tennessee Williams"; "Sylvia Plath's Lost Father and Her View of Him in 'Daddy.' " To write any truly deep-reaching biographical criticism takes research, clearly, but one could write a term paper on topics such as these by reading a biography.

Biographical criticism fell into temporary disrepute around 1920, when T. S. Eliot questioned the assumption that a poem has to be a personal statement of the poet's thoughts and emotions.[1] Eliot and other critics did much to clear the air of speculation that the "Ode on a Grecian Urn" may

---

[1] See Eliot's essay "Tradition and the Individual Talent," in *Selected Essays* (New York: Harcourt, 1932).

have been shaped by what Keats had had for breakfast. Evidently, in any search for what went on in an author's mind, and for the influence of life upon work, absolute certainty is unattainable. Besides, such an approach can be grossly reductive — holding, for example, that Shakespeare was sad when he wrote his tragedies and especially happy when he wrote *A Midsummer Night's Dream*. Still, some works do gain in meaning from even a slight knowledge of the author's biography. In reading *Moby-Dick*, it helps to know that Herman Melville served aboard a whaling vessel.

4. *The Work as Influence.* From this perspective, a literary work is a force that affects people. It stirs responses in them, rouses their emotions, perhaps argues for ideas that change their minds. The artist, said Tolstoi in a famous pronouncement *(What Is Art?)*, "hands on to others those feelings he himself has felt, that they too may be moved, and experience them." Part of the function of art, Tolstoi continued, is to enlighten and to lead its audience into an acceptance of better moral attitudes (religious faith, or a sense of social justice). The critic who takes this approach generally deals with the ideas that a literary work imparts and the reception of those ideas by a particular audience: "Did *Uncle Tom's Cabin* Cause the Civil War?"; "The Early Reception of Allen Ginsberg's *Howl*"; "Ed Bullins's Plays and Their Newly Proud Black Audience." As you can see, this whole approach is closely related to viewing a literary work as an imitation of life. Still another way of discussing a work's influence is to trace its effect upon other writers: "Robert Frost's Debt to Emily Dickinson"; "*Moby-Dick* and William Faulkner's *The Bear:* Two Threatened Wildernesses."

BEGINNING

Offered a choice of literary works to write about, you probably will do best if, instead of choosing what you think will impress your instructor, you choose what appeals to you. And how to find out what appeals? Whether you plan to write a short paper that requires no research beyond the story or poem or play itself, or a long term paper that will take you to the library, the first stage of your project is reading — and note taking. To concentrate your attention, one time-honored method is to read with a pencil, marking (if the book is yours) passages that stand out in importance, jotting brief notes in a margin (*"Key symbol — this foreshadows the ending"; "Dramatic irony"; "IDIOT!!!"*; or other possibly useful remarks). In a long story or poem or play, some students asterisk passages that cry for comparison; for instance, all the places in which they find the same theme or symbol. Later, at a glance, they can review the highlights of a work and, when writing a paper about it, quickly refer to evidence. This method shoots holes in a book's resale value, but many find the sacrifice worthwhile. Patient souls who dislike butchering a book prefer to take notes on looseleaf notebook paper, holding one sheet beside a page in the book and giving it the book's page number. Later, in writing a paper, they can place book page and companion note page together again. This method has the advantage of affording a lot of room for note taking; it is a good one for short poems closely packed with complexities.

But by far the most popular method of taking notes (besides writing on the pages of books) is to write on index cards — the 3 × 5 kind, for brief notes and titles; 5 × 8 cards for longer notes. Write on one side only; notes on the back of the card usually get overlooked later. Cards are easy to shuffle and, in organizing your material, to deal. To save work, instead of copying out on a card the title and author of a book you're taking a note from, just keep a numbered list of the books you're using. Then, when making a note, you need write only the book's identifying number on the card in order to identify your source. (Later, when writing footnotes, you can translate the number into title, author, and other information.)

Now that coin-operated photocopy machines are to be found in many libraries, you no longer need to spend hours copying by hand whole poems and longer passages. If accuracy is essential (surely it is) and if a poem or passage is long enough to be worth the investment of a few cents, you can lay photocopied material into place in your paper with transparent tape or rubber cement. The latest copyright law permits students and scholars to reproduce books and periodicals in this fashion; it does not, however, permit making a dozen or more copies for public sale.

Certain literary works, because they offer intriguing difficulties, have attracted professional critics by the score. On library shelves, great pha-lanxes of critical books now stand at the side of James Joyce's complex novels *Ulysses* and *Finnegans Wake,* and T. S. Eliot's allusive poem *The Waste Land.* The student who undertakes to study such works seriously is well advised to profit from the critics' labors. Chances are, too, that even in discussing a relatively uncomplicated work you will want to seek the aid of the finest critics. If you quote them, quote them exactly, in quotation marks, and give them credit. When employed in any but the most superlative student paper, a brilliant phrase (or even a not-so-brilliant sentence) from a renowned critic is likely to stand out like a golf ball in a garter snake's midriff, and most English instructors are likely to recognize it. If you rip off the critic's words, then go ahead and steal the whole essay, for good critics write in seamless unities. Then, when apprehended, you can exclaim — like the student whose term paper was found to be the work of a well-known scholar — "I've been robbed! That paper cost me twenty dollars!" But of course the worst rip-off is the one the student inflicted on himself, having got nothing for his money out of a college course but a little practice in touch typing.

Taking notes on your readings, you will want to jot down the title of every book you might refer to in your paper, and the page number of any passage you might wish to quote. Even if you summarize a critic's idea in your own words, rather than quote, you have to give credit to your source. Nothing is cheaper to give than proper credit. Certainly it's easier to take notes while you read than to have to run back to the library during the final typing.

Choose a topic appropriate to the assigned length of your paper. How do you know the probable length of your discussion until you write it? When in doubt, you are better off to define your topic narrowly. Your paper will be stronger if you go deeper into your subject than if you choose some gigantic subject and then find yourself able to touch on it only superficially. A thorough explication of a short story is hardly possible in a paper of 250 words. There are, in truth, four-line poems whose surface 250 words might only begin to scratch. A profound topic ("The Character of Shakespeare's Hamlet") might overflow a book; but a topic more narrowly defined ("Hamlet's Views of Acting"; "Hamlet's Puns") might result in a more nearly manageable term paper. You can narrow and focus a large topic while you work your way into it. A general interest in "Hemingway's Heroes" might lead you, in reading, taking notes, and thinking further, to the narrower topic, "Jake Barnes: Spokesman for Hemingway's Views of War."

Many student writers find it helpful, in defining a topic, to state an emerging idea for a paper in a provisional **thesis sentence:** a summing-up of the one main idea or argument that the paper will embody. (A thesis sentence is for your own use; you don't have to implant it in your paper unless your instructor asks for it.) A good statement of a thesis is not just a disembodied subject; it comes with both subject and verb. ("The Downfall of Oedipus Rex" is not yet a complete idea for a paper; "What Caused the Downfall of Oedipus Rex?" is.) A thesis sentence may help you see for yourself what the author is *saying about* a subject. Not a full thesis, and not a sentence, "The Isolation of City-dwellers in Edward Albee's *A Zoo Story*" might be a decent title for a paper. But it isn't a useful thesis because it doesn't indicate what one might say about that isolation (nor what Albee is saying about it). It may be obvious that isolation isn't desirable, but a clearer and more workable thesis sentence might be, "In *A Zoo Story* Albee shows how city-dwellers' isolation from one another prompts one city dweller to action"; the writer might well go on to demonstrate just what that action is.

DISCOVERING AND PLANNING

Writing is not likely to proceed in a straight line. Like thought, it often goes by fits and starts, by charges and retreats and mopping-up operations. All the while you take notes, you discover material to write about; all the while you tool over your topic in your mind, you plan. It is the nature of ideas, those headstrong things, to happen in any order they desire. While you continue to plan, while you write a draft, and while you revise, expect to keep discovering new thoughts — perhaps the best thoughts of all. If you do, be sure to let them in.

Topic in hand (which may get drastically changed as you continue), you begin to sort out your miscellaneous notes, thoughts, and impressions. If you can see that you haven't had enough ideas, you may wish to

brainstorm — to set yourself, say, fifteen minutes in which to write down as fast as you can all the ideas on your topic that come into your head, without worrying whether they are going to be useful. (You can look over the results and decide that later.) Another method of discovery is to **freewrite:** to write rapidly and uncritically, letting your thoughts tumble onto paper as fast as your pen, typewriter, or word processor can capture them. Sometimes these methods will goad the unconscious into coming up with unexpectedly good ideas; at least, you will generate more potentially useful raw material.

To outline or not to outline? Unless your topic, by its nature, suggests some obvious way to organize your paper ("An Explication of a Wordsworth Sonnet" might mean simply working through the poem line by line), then some kind of outline will probably help. In high school or other prehistoric times, you perhaps learned how to construct a beautiful outline, laid out with Roman numerals, capital letters, Arabic numerals, and lower-case letters. It was a thing of beauty and symmetry, and possibly even had something to do with paper writing. But if now you are skeptical of the value of outlining, reflect: not every outline needs to be detailed and elaborate. Some students, of course, find it helpful to outline in detail — particularly if they are planning a long term paper involving several literary works, comparing and contrasting several aspects of them. For a 500-word analysis of a short story's figures of speech, though, all you might need is a simple list of points to make, scribbled down in the order in which you will make them. This order is probably not, of course, the order in which the points first occurred to you. Thoughts, when they first come to mind, can be a confused rabble.

While granting the need for order in a piece of writing, the present writer confesses that he is a reluctant outliner. His tendency (or curse) is to want to keep whatever random thoughts occur to him; to polish his prose right then and there; and finally to try to juggle his disconnected paragraphs into something like logical order. The usual result is that he has large blocks of illogical thought left over. This process is wasteful, and if you can learn to live with an outline, then you belong to the legion of the blessed, and will never know the pain of scrapping pages that cost you hours. On the other hand, you will never know the joy of meandering — of bursting into words and surprising yourself. As novelist E. M. Forster remarked, "How do I know what I think until I see what I say?"

An outline, if you use one, is not meant to stand as an achievement in itself. It should — as Ezra Pound said literary criticism ought to do — consume itself and disappear. Here is a once-valuable outline not worth keeping — a very informal one that enabled a student to organize the paper that appears on page 430, "The Hearer of 'The Tell-Tale Heart.'" Before he wrote, the student jotted down the ideas that had occurred to him. Looking them over, he could see that certain ones predominated. Since the aim of his paper was to analyze Poe's story for its point of view, he began with some notes about the narrator of the story. His other leading ideas had emerged as questions: is the story supposed to be a ghost story or an account of a delusion? Can we read the whole thing as a nightmare, having no reality outside the narrator's mind? Having seen that his thoughts weren't a totally disconnected jumble, he drew connections. Going down his list, he numbered with the same numbers those ideas that belonged together.

> (Point of view) → 1 Killer is mad -- can listen in on Hell.
>
> 2 He is obsessed with the Evil Eye.
>
> 1 He thinks he is sane, we know he's mad.
>
> Old man rich -- a miser?
>
> 4 { Is this a ghost story? NO! Natural explanations for the heartbeat:
>
> His mind is playing tricks.
>
> Hears his own heart (Hoffman's idea).
>
> 3 Maybe the whole story is only his dream?
>
> Poe must have been crazy too.

The numbers now showed him the order in which he planned to take up each of his four chief ideas. Labeling with the number "1" his remarks about the narrator, he decided to open his paper with them, and to declare at once that they indicated the story's point of view. As you can tell from his finished paper, he discarded two notions that didn't seem to relate to his purpose: the point about the old man's wealth, and the speculation (which he realized he couldn't prove) that Poe himself was probably mad. Having completed this rough outline, he felt encouraged to return to Poe's story, and on rereading it, noticed a few additional points, which you will find in his paper. His outline didn't tell him exactly what to say at every moment, but it was clear and easy to follow.

DRAFTING AND REVISING

Seated at last, or striking some other businesslike stance,[2] you prepare to write, only to find yourself besieged with petty distractions. All of a sudden you remember a friend you had promised to call, some dry cleaning you were supposed to pick up, a neglected Coke (in another room)

---

[2]R. H. Super of the University of Michigan wrote a definitive biography of Walter Savage Landor while standing up, typing on a machine atop a filing cabinet.

growing warmer and flatter by the minute. If your paper is to be written, you have one course of action: to collar these thoughts and for the moment banish them.

When first you draft your paper — that is, when you write it out in the rough — you will probably do best to write rapidly. At this early stage, you don't need to be fussy about spelling, grammar, and punctuation. To be sure, those picayune details matter, but you can worry about them later on, when you are **editing** (combing through your draft repairing grammar, cutting excess words, making small verbal improvements) and **proofreading** (going over your finished paper line by line, checking it for typographical or other mistakes). Right now, it is more important to get your thoughts down on paper in a steady flow than to keep taking time out to check spellings in the dictionary. Forge ahead, and don't be too nastily self-critical. Perhaps when you write your draft you won't even want to look at all those notes on your reading that you collected so industriously. When you come to a place where a note will fit, you might just insert a reminder to yourself, such as SEE CARD 19, or SEE ARISTOTLE ON COMEDY.

Let us admit that writing about literature is a fussier kind of writing than turning out a narrative essay called, "My Most Exciting Experience." You may need to draft some of your paper slowly and painstakingly. You'll find yourself coping with all sorts of small problems, many of them simple and mechanical. What, for instance, will you call the author whose work you are dealing with? Decide at the outset. Most critics favor the author's last name alone: "Dickinson implies . . ." ("Miss Dickinson" or "Ms. Dickinson" may sound fussily polite; "Emily," too chummy.) Will you include footnotes in your paper and, if so, do you know how they work? (Some pointers on handling the pesky things will come in a few pages.)

You will want to give credit to any critics who helped you out, and properly to do so is to be painstaking. To paraphrase a critic, you do more than just rearrange the critic's words and phrases; you translate them into language of your own. Say you wish to refer to an insight of Randall Jarrell, who comments on the images of spider, flower, and moth in Robert Frost's poem "Design":

> Notice how the *heal-all,* because of its name, is the one flower in all the world picked to be the altar for this Devil's Mass; notice how holding up the moth brings something ritual and hieratic, a ghostly, ghastly formality to this priest and its sacrificial victim. . . .

It would be incorrect to say, without quotation marks:

```
Frost picks the heal-all as the one flower in all the world to be

the altar for this Devil's Mass.  There is a ghostly, ghastly
```

```
formality to the spider holding up the moth, like a priest holding

a sacrificial victim.
```

That rewording, although not exactly in Jarrell's language, manages to steal his memorable phrases without giving him credit. Nor is it sufficient just to list Jarrell's essay in a bibliography at the end of your paper. If you do, you are still a crook; you merely point to the scene of your crime. What is needed, clearly, is to think through Jarrell's words to the point he is making; and if you want to keep any of his striking phrases (and why not?), put them in quotation marks:

```
As Randall Jarrell points out, Frost portrays the spider as a kind

of priest in a Mass, or Black Mass, elevating the moth like an

object for sacrifice, with "a ghostly, ghastly formality."
```

To be scrupulous in your acknowledgment, tell where you found your quotation from Jarrell, citing the book and the page. (See "Documenting Your Sources," page 419.) But unless your instructor expects you to write such a formal, documented paper, the passage as it now stands would make sufficiently clear your source, and your obligation.

One more word of Dutch-uncle warning. In this book you are offered a vocabulary with which to discuss literature: a flurry of terms such as *irony, symbol,* and *image,* printed in **boldface** when first introduced. In your writing you may decide to enlist a few of them. And yet, critical terminology — especially if unfamiliar — can tempt a beginning critic to sling it about. Nothing can be less sophisticated, or more misleading, than a technical term grandly misapplied: "The *myth-symbolism* of this *rime scheme* leaves one aghast." Far better to choose plain words you're already at ease with. Your instructor, no doubt, has met many a critical term and is not likely to be impressed by the mere sight of another one. Knowingly selected and placed, a critical term can help sharpen a thought and make it easier to handle. Clearly it is less cumbersome to refer to the *tone* of a story than to have to say, "the way the author makes you feel that she feels about what she is talking about." But the paper-writer who declares, "The tone of this poem is full of ironic imagery," fries words to a hash — mixed up and indigestible.

When you write your first draft, by the way, leave plenty of space between lines and enormous margins. Then, when later thoughts come to you, you can easily squeeze them in.

Does any writer write with perfection on first try, and drop ideas with a single shot? Some writers have claimed to do so — among them the English novelist Anthony Trollope, who thought it "unmanly" not to write a thought right the first time. Jack Kerouac, leading novelist of the beat generation of the 1950s, believed in spontaneous prose. He used to write entire novels on uncut ribbons of teletype paper, thus saving himself the interruption of stopping at the bottom of each page. His specialty, though, was fiction of ecstasy and hallucination, not essays in explication, or comparison and contrast. For most of us, however, good writing is largely a matter of revising — of going back over our first thoughts word by word. Painstaking revision is more than a matter of tidying grammar and spelling: in the process of reconsidering our words, we sometimes discover fresher and sharper ideas. "Writing and rewriting," says John Updike, "are a constant search for what one is saying."

To achieve effective writing, you have to have the courage to be wild. Aware that no reader need see your rough drafts, you can treat them mercilessly — scissor them apart, rearrange their pieces, reassemble them into a stronger order, using staples or tape or glue. The art of revising calls for a textbook in itself, but here are a few simple suggestions:

1. Insofar as your deadline allows, be willing to revise as many times as need be.

2. Don't think of revision as the simple chore of fixing up spelling mistakes. That's proofreading, and it comes last. When you revise, be willing to cut and slash, to discover new insights, to move blocks of words around so that they follow in a stronger order. Stand ready to question your whole approach to a work of literature, to entertain the notion of throwing everything you have written into the wastebasket and starting over again.

3. At this stage, you may find it helpful to enlist outside advice — from your instructor, from your roommate or your mate, from any friend who will read your rough draft and give you a reaction. If you can enlist such a willing reader, ask: What isn't clear to you?

4. If you (or your willing reader) should find any places that aren't readily understandable, single them out for rewriting. After all, you don't need to revise a whole draft if only parts of it need work. Try rewriting any especially troublesome passage or paragraph.

5. Short, skimpy paragraphs of one or two sentences may indicate places that call for more thought, or more material. Can you supply them with more evidence, more explanation, more example and illustration?

6. A time-tested method of revising is to lay aside your manuscript for a while, forget about it, and then after a long interval (the Roman poet Horace recommended nine years, but obviously that won't do), go back to it for a fresh look. If you have time, take a nap or a walk, or at least a yawn and a stretch before you take yet another look.

7. When your paper is in a *last* draft — that's the time to edit it. Once you have your ideas in firm shape, you can check those uncertain spellings, look up the agreement of verbs in a grammar book or handbook, make your pronouns and numbers agree, cut needless words, pull out a weak

word and send in a stronger one. Back when you were drafting, to get prematurely fussy about such small things might have frozen you up. But once you feel satisfied that you have made yourself clear, you can be as fussy as you like.

If you type your papers, it is a great help to become a reasonably expert typist — one whose method is other than the Christopher Columbus method (to discover a key and land on it). Then you can revise while you retype. All to what end? "Each clear sentence," according to Robert Russell, "is that much ground stripped clean of the undergrowth of one's own confusion. Sometimes it's thrilling to feel you have written even a single paragraph that makes sense."[3]

THE FORM OF YOUR FINISHED PAPER

Now that you have smoothed your final draft as fleck-free as you can, your instructor may have specific advice for the form of your finished paper. If none is forthcoming, it is only reasonable

1. to choose standard letter-size (8½ × 11) paper;
2. to give your name at the top of your title page;
3. to leave an inch or more of margin on all four sides of each page, and a few inches of blank paper or an additional sheet after your conclusion, so that your instructor can offer comment;
4. to doublespace, or (if you handwrite) to use paper with widely spaced lines.

And what of titles of works discussed: when to put them in quotation marks, when to underline them? One rule of thumb is that titles of works shorter than book length rate quotation marks (poems, short stories, articles); but titles of books (including book-length poems: *The Odyssey*), plays, and periodicals take underlining. (In a manuscript to be set in type, an underline is a signal to the compositor to use *italics.*)

DOCUMENTING YOUR SOURCES

When you quote from other writers, when you lift their information, when you summarize or paraphrase their ideas, make sure you give them their due. Document everything you take. Identify the writer by name; cite the very book, magazine, newspaper, pamphlet, letter, or other source you are using, and the page or pages you are indebted to.

By so doing, you invite your readers to go to your original source and check up on you. Most readers won't bother, of course, but at least your

[3] *To Catch an Angel* (New York: Vanguard, 1962) 301.

invitation enlists their confidence. Besides, the duty to document keeps you carefully looking at your sources — and so helps keep your writing accurate and responsible.

The latest and most efficient way for writers to document their sources is that recommended in the *MLA Handbook for Writers of Research Papers,* 2nd ed. (New York: Modern Language Association of America, 1984). In the long run, whether you write an immense term paper citing a hundred sources or a short paper citing only three or four, the MLA's advice will save you and your reader time and trouble.

These pointers cannot take the place of the *MLA Handbook* itself; but the gist of the method is this. Begin by listing your sources: all the works from which you're going to quote, summarize, paraphrase, or take information. Later on, when you type up your paper in finished form, you're going to *end* it with a neat copy of this list (once called a *bibliography,* now entitled *Works Cited*). But right now, in writing your paper, every time you refer to one of these works, you need give only enough information to help a reader locate it in your Works Cited. Usually, you can just give (in parentheses) an author's last name and a page citation. You incorporate this information right in the text of your paper, most often at the end of a sentence:

```
One recent investigation has suggested that few people who

submit poems to small literary magazines bother to read

those magazines; or indeed, bother to read poems by any-

body else (Horton 108-09).
```

Say you will want to cite *two* books or magazine articles by Horton — how to tell them apart? In your text, condense the title of each article into a word or two.

```
One recent investigation has shown that few people who sub-

mit poems to small literary magazines bother to read those

magazines (Horton, "Magazines" 108-09).
```

If you have mentioned the name of the author in the body of your paper, you need give only the page number:

```
As a recent investigator, Louise Horton, has suggested, few

people who submit poems to small literary magazines bother

to read those magazines (108-09).
```

The beauty of this method is that you don't have to stop every two minutes to write a footnote identifying your source in full detail. At the end of your paper, in your list of works cited, your reader can find a fuller description of your source — in this case, a magazine article:

> Horton, Louise. "Who Reads Small Literary Magazines and What Good Do They Do?" Texas Review Spring/Summer 1984: 108-13.

It's imperative to keep citations in your text brief and snappy, lest they hinder the flow of your prose. You may wish to append a note supplying a passage of less important (yet possibly valuable) information or making careful qualifying statements ("On the other hand, not every expert agrees. John Binks finds that poets are often a little magazine's only cash customers; while Molly MacGuire maintains that . . ."). If you want to put in some such aside, and suspect that you couldn't give it in your text without interrupting your paper awkwardly, then cast it into a **footnote** (a note placed at the bottom of a page) or an **endnote** (a note placed at the end of a paper). Given a choice, most writers prefer endnotes. Far easier to collect all the notes at the end of a paper than to use footnotes — as any writer knows who has had to retype pages and pages again and again, to make the footnotes fit.[4]

How do you drop in such notes? The number of each consecutive note comes (following any punctuation) after the last word of a sentence. So that the number will stand out, you roll your typewriter carriage up a click (or order your word-processor to do a superscript), thus lifting the number slightly above the usual level of your prose.

> as other observers have claimed.[1]

When you come to type the footnote or endnote itself, skip five spaces, elevate the number again, skip a space, and proceed.

> [1] John Binks, to name only one such observer, finds . . .

Although now useful mainly for such slightly longwinded asides, footnotes and endnotes are time-honored ways to document *all* sources in a research paper. Indeed, some instructors still prefer them to the new MLA guidelines, and urge students to use such notes to indicate every writer cited. Though such notes take more work, they have the advantage

---

[4]Nowadays, some word-processing programs make life easier for footnoters by helping to format each footnote and by automatically dropping it in at the bottom of its page.

of hiding dull data away from your reader's eyes, enabling you to end sentences with powerful bangs and inconspicuous note numbers instead of whimpering parentheses (Glutz-Finnegan, *Lesser Corollary* 1029 – 30). Besides, in a brief paper containing only one citation or two, to use footnotes or endnotes may be simpler and less showy than to compile a Works Cited list that has only two entries. (For an example of a student paper with a single footnote, see page 430.)

Large-mindedly, the *MLA Handbook* tolerates the continued use of footnotes and endnotes for documentation — indeed, offers advice for their preparation, which we will follow here. If you do use footnotes or endnotes to document all your sources, here is how to format them. A note identifying a magazine article looks like this:

> [16] Louise Horton, "Who Reads Small Literary Magazines and What Good Do They Do?" Texas Review Spring/Summer 1984: 108-09.

Notice that, in notes, the author's first name comes first. (In a list of Works Cited, you work differently: you put last name first, so that you can readily arrange your list of authors in easy-to-consult alphabetical order.) A footnote or endnote for a reference to a book (and not a magazine article) looks like this:

> [17] Elizabeth Frank, Louise Bogan: A Portrait (New York: Knopf, 1985) 59-60.

Should you return later to cite another place in Frank's book, you need not repeat all its information. Just write:

> [18] Frank 192.

If in your paper you refer to *two* books by Elizabeth Frank, give the full title of each in the first note citing it. Then, if you cite it again, use a shortened form of its title:

> [19] Frank, Bogan 192.

Your readers should not have to interrupt their reading of your essay to glance down at a note simply to find out whom you are quoting. It is poor form to write:

> Dylan Thomas's poem "Fern Hill" is a memory of the poet's
>
> childhood: of his Aunt Ann Jones's farm, where he spent his
>
> holidays. "Time, which has an art to throw dust on all things,

broods over the poem."[1]   The farm, indeed, is a lost paradise -- a personal garden of Eden.

---

[1] William York Tindall, A Reader's Guide to Dylan Thomas (New York: Noonday, 1962) 268.

That is annoying, because the reader has to stop reading and look at the footnote to find out who made that resonant statement about Time brooding over the poem. A better way:

> "Time," as William York Tindall has observed, "which has an art
> to throw dust on all things, broods over the poem."[1]

---

[1] A Reader's Guide to Dylan Thomas (New York: Noonday, 1962) 268.

What to do now but hand in your paper? "And good riddance," you may feel, after such an expenditure of thinking, time, and energy. But a good paper is not only worth submitting, it is worth keeping. If you return to it, after a while, you may find to your surprise that it will preserve and even renew what you have learned.

KEEPING A JOURNAL

The essay is not, of course, the only medium in which you can write your responses to literature. Many instructors ask students to keep a **journal:** a day-to-day account of what they read and how they react to it. A great advantage in keeping a journal is that you can express your thoughts and feelings immediately, before they grow cold. You can set down all your miscellaneous reactions to what you read, whether or not they fit into a paper topic. (If you have to write a paper later on, your journal just might suggest topics galore.) Depending on what your instructor thinks essential, your journal may take in all your reading for the course; or you may concentrate on the work of some writer or writers, or on one kind of story. As you read (or afterward), you can jot down anything you notice that you wish to remember. Does a theme in a story, or a line of dialogue, strike you forcefully? Make a note of it. Does something in the story not make sense? Record your bewilderment. Your journal is personal: a place for you to sound off, to express your feelings. Don't just copy your class notes into it; don't simply quote the stories. Mere length of your entries will not impress your instructor, either: try for insights. A paragraph or two will probably suffice to set down your main reactions to most stories. In keeping a journal (a kind of writing primarily for yourself), you don't rewrite; and so you need not feel obliged to polish your prose. Your aim is to store information without delay: to wrap words around your reactions and observations.

Keeping a journal will be satisfying only if you keep it up to date. Record your feelings and insights while you still have a story freshly in mind. Get weeks behind and have to grind out a journal from scratch, the night before it is due, and the whole project will decay into meaningless drudgery. But faithfully do a little reading and a little writing every day or so, and you will find yourself keeping track of the life of your mind. When your journal is closed, you will have a lively record not only of the literature you have read, but also of your involvement with it.

Robert Wallace (b. 1932)
THE GIRL WRITING HER ENGLISH PAPER   1979

lies on one hip by the fire,
blond, in jeans.

The wreckage of her labor, elegant as Eden
or petals from a tree,
surrounds her —   5

a little farm, smoke rising from the ashtray,
book, notebooks, papers, fields;
a poem's furrows.

If the lights were to go out suddenly,
stars would be overhead,   10
their light come in.

Writing about a Story

Like any coherent, forceful essay, a good discussion of fiction doesn't just toss forth a random lot of impressions. It makes some point about which the writer feels strongly. In order to write a meaningful paper, then, you need something you *want* to say — a meaningful topic. For suggestions on finding such a topic (also some pointers on organizing, writing, revising, and finishing your paper), please see "Writing about Literature," which begins on page 409. The advice there may be applied to papers on fiction, poetry, and drama. Some methods especially useful for writing about stories are gathered in the present chapter.

Unlike a brief poem, or a painting you can take in with one long glance, a work of fiction — even a short story — may be too complicated to hold all at once in the mind's eye. Before you can write about it, you may need to give it two or more careful readings, and even then, as you begin to think further about it, you will probably have to thumb through it to reread passages. The first time through, perhaps it is best just to read attentively, open to whatever pleasure and wisdom the story may afford. On second look, you may find it useful to read with pencil in hand, either to mark your personal copy or to take notes to jog your memory. To see the design and meaning of a story need not be a boring chore — any more than it is to land a fighting fish and to study it with admiration.

In this chapter, all the discussions and examples refer to Edgar Allan Poe's short story "The Tell-Tale Heart" (page 38). If you haven't already read it, you can do so in only a few minutes, so that the rest of the chapter will make more sense to you.

EXPLICATING

Explication is the patient unfolding of meanings in a work of literature. An explication — that is, an essay that follows this method — proceeds carefully through a story, poem, or play, usually interpreting it line by line — perhaps even word by word. A good explication dwells on details, as well as on larger things. It brings them to the attention of a reader who might have missed them (the reader probably hasn't read so closely as the writer of the explication). Alert and willing to take pains, the writer of such an essay notices anything meaningful that isn't obvious, whether it is a colossal theme suggested by a symbol, or a little hint contained in a single word.

To write an honest explication of a story takes time and space, probably too much time and space to devote to a long and complex story unless you are writing a huge term paper, an honors thesis, or a dissertation. A thorough explication of Nathaniel Hawthorne's "The Birthmark" would be likely to run much longer than the rich and intriguing short story itself. Ordinarily, the method of explication is best suited to a paper that deals only with a short passage or section of a story: a key scene, a crucial conversation, a statement of theme, an opening or closing paragraph. Storytellers who are especially fond of language invite closer attention to their words than others do. Edgar Allan Poe, for one, is a poet sensitive to the rhythms of his sentences, and a symbolist whose stories abound in suggestions. Here is an explication, by a student, of a short but essential passage in "The Tell-Tale Heart." The passage occurs in the third paragraph of the story, and (to help us follow the explication) the student quotes it in full at the beginning of her paper.

By Lantern Light: An Explication of a Passage
in "The Tell-Tale Heart"

And every night, about midnight, I turned the latch of his door and opened it -- oh, so gently! And then, when I had made an opening sufficient for my head, I put in a dark lantern, all closed, closed, so that no light shone out, and then I thrust in my head. Oh, you would have laughed to see how cunningly I thrust it in! I moved it slowly -- very, very slowly, so that I might not disturb the old man's sleep. It took me an hour to place my whole head within the opening so far that I could see him as he lay upon his bed. Ha! -- would a madman have been so wise as this? And then, when my head was well in the room, I undid the lantern cautiously -- oh, so cautiously -- cautiously (for the hinges creaked) -- I undid it just so much that a single thin ray fell upon the vulture eye. And this I did for seven long nights -- every night just at midnight -- but I found the eye always closed; and so it was impossible to do the work; for it was not the old man who vexed me, but his Evil Eye.

Although Poe has indicated in the first lines of his story that the

person who addresses us is insane, it is only when we come to the

speaker's account of his preparations for murdering the old man that we

imagine him in action, and so find his madness fully revealed. Even more convincingly than his earlier words (for we might *possibly* think that someone who claims to hear things in heaven and hell is a religious mystic), these preparations reveal him to be mad. What strikes us is that they are so elaborate and meticulous. A significant detail is the exactness of his schedule for spying: "every night just at midnight." The words with which he describes his motions also convey the most extreme care (and I will indicate them with italics): "how *wisely* I proceeded -- with *what caution*," "I turned the latch of his door and opened it -- oh, *so gently*!" "how *cunningly* I thrust [my head] in! I moved it *slowly*, *very slowly*," "I undid the lantern *cautiously* -- oh, *so cautiously* -- *cautiously*." Taking a whole hour to intrude his head into the room, he asks, "Ha! would a madman be as wise as this?" But of course the word *wise* is unconsciously ironic, for clearly it is not wisdom the speaker displays, but an absurd degree of care, an almost fiendish ingenuity. Such behavior, I understand, is typical of certain mental illnesses. All his careful preparations that he thinks prove him sane only convince us instead that he is mad.

Obviously his behavior is self-defeating. He wants to catch the "vulture eye" open, and yet he takes all these pains not to disturb the old man's sleep. If he behaved logically, he might go barging into the bedroom with his lantern ablaze, shouting at the top of his voice. And yet, if we can see things his way, there *is* a strange logic to his reasoning. He regards the eye as a creature in itself, quite apart from its possessor. "It was not," he says, "the old man who vexed me, but his Evil Eye." Apparently, to be inspired to do his deed, the madman needs to behold the eye -- at least, this is my understanding of his remark, "I found the eye always closed; and so it was impossible to do the work." Poe's choice of the word *work*, by the way, is also revealing. Murder is made to seem a duty or a job; and anyone who so regards murder is either extremely cold-blooded, like a hired killer for a gangland assassination, or else deranged. Besides, the word suggests again the curious sense of detachment that the speaker feels toward the owner of the eye.

In still another of his assumptions, the speaker shows that he is madly logical, or operating on the logic of a dream. There seems a dreamlike relationship between his dark lantern "all closed, closed, so that no light shone out," and the sleeping victim. When the madman opens his lantern so that it emits a single ray, he is hoping that the eye in the old man's head will be open too, letting out its corresponding gleam. The latch that he turns so gently, too, seems like the eye, whose lid needs to be opened in order for the murderer to go ahead. It is as though the speaker is <u>trying</u> to get the eyelid to lift. By taking such great pains and by going through all this nightly ritual, he is practicing some kind of magic, whose rules are laid down not by our logic, but by the logic of dreams.

An unusually well-written paper, "By Lantern Light" cost the student two or three careful revisions. Rather than attempting to say something about *everything* in the passage from Poe, she selects only the details that strike her as most meaningful. In her very first sentence, she briefly shows us how the passage functions in the context of Poe's story: how it clinches our suspicions that the narrator is mad. In writing her paper, the student went by the following rough, simple outline — nothing more than a list of the points she wanted to express:

1. Speaker's extreme care and exactness -- typical of some mental illnesses.

2. Speaker doesn't act by usual logic but by a crazy logic.

3. Dreamlike connection between latch & lantern and old man's eye.

As she wrote, she followed her brief list, setting forth her ideas one at a time, one idea to a paragraph. There is a different (and still easier) way to organize an explication: just work through the original passage line by line or sentence by sentence. The danger of this procedure is that you may find yourself falling into a boring singsong: "In the first sentence I noticed . . . ," "In the next sentence . . . ," "Now in the third sentence . . . ," "Finally, in the last paragraph. . . ." (If you choose to organize an explication in such a way, then boldly vary your transitions.) Notice that the student who wrote "By Lantern Light" doesn't inch through the passage sentence by sentence, but freely takes up its details in whatever order she likes. Less fussy than Poe's madman, she neatly writes in three corrections, saving herself retyping. And why, in her first paragraph, does she change Poe's word *it* to *my head?* Coming upon a piece of a sentence quoted out of context, the reader might forget what *it* refers to — and so the writer places the alteration in brackets, to indicate that the changed words are her own.

In a long critical essay in which we don't adhere to one method all the way through, the method of explication may appear from time to time — as when the critic, in discussing a story, stops to unravel a particularly knotty passage. But useful as it may be to know how to write an explication of fiction, it is probably still more useful (in most literature courses) to know how to write an analysis.

ANALYZING

Assignment: "Write an **analysis** of a story or novel." What do you do? Following the method of analysis (from the Greek: "breaking up"), you separate a story or novel into its components, then (usually) select one part for close study. One likely topic for an analysis might be "The Character of James Thurber's Mr. Martin" (referring to "The Catbird Seat"), in which the writer would concentrate on showing us Martin's highly individual features and traits of personality. Other typical analyses might be written about, say, "Folk Humor in Mark Twain's *Huckleberry Finn,*" or "Gothic Elements in a Story by Joyce Carol Oates" (referring to "Where Are You Going, Where Have You Been?"), or "The Unidentified Narrator in 'A Rose for Emily.' " To be sure, no element of a story dwells in isolation from the story's other elements. In "The Tell-Tale Heart," the madness of the leading character apparently makes it necessary to tell the story from a special point of view and probably helps determine the author's choice of theme, setting, symbolism, tone, style, and ironies. But it would be mind-boggling to try to study all those elements simultaneously. For this reason, when we write an analysis we generally study just one element, though we may suggest — probably at the start of the essay — its relation to the whole story. Indeed, analysis is the method used in this book, in which, chapter by chapter, we have separated fiction into its components of plot, point of view, character, tone and style, and so on. If you have read the discussion on the plot of "Godfather Death" (page 6), or, the attempt to state the theme of Hemingway's "A Clean, Well-Lighted Place" (page 122), then you have already read some brief essays in analysis. Here is a student-written analysis of "The Tell-Tale Heart," dealing with just one element — the story's point of view.

The Hearer of the Tell-Tale Heart

Although there are many things we do not know about the narrator of
Edgar Allan Poe's story "The Tell-Tale Heart" -- is he a son? a servant?
a companion? -- there is one thing we are sure of from the start. He is
mad. In the opening paragraph, Poe makes the narrator's condition un-
mistakeable, not only from his excited and worked-up speech (full of
dashes and exclamation points), but also from his wild claims. He says
it is merely some disease which has sharpened his senses that has made
people call him crazy. Who but a madman, however, would say, "I heard
all things in the heaven and in the earth," and brag how his ear is a
kind of CB radio, listening in on Hell? Such a statement leaves no
doubt that the point of view in the story is an ironic one.

Because the participating narrator is telling his story in the
first person, some details in the story stand out more than others.
When the narrator goes on to tell how he watches the old man sleeping,
he rivets his attention on the old man's "vulture eye." When a ray from
his lantern finds the Evil Eye open, he says, "I could see nothing else
of the old man's face or person." Actually, the reader can see almost
nothing else about the old man anywhere in the rest of the story. All
we are told is that the old man treated the younger man well, and we
gather that the old man was rich, because his house is full of treasures.
We do not have a clear idea of what the old man looks like, though, nor
do we know how he talks, for we are not given any of his words. Our
knowledge of him is mainly confined to his eye and its effect on the
narrator. This confinement gives that symbolic eye a lot of importance
in the story. The narrator tells us all we know and directs our attention to parts of it.

This point of view raises an interesting question. Since we are
on the narrator
dependent/for all our information, how do we know the whole story
isn't just a nightmare in his demented mind? We have really no way to

be sure it isn't, as far as I can see. I assume, however, that there

really is a dark shuttered house and an old man and real policemen who

start snooping around when screams are heard in the neighborhood,

because it is a more memorable story if it is a crazy man's view of

reality than if it is all just a terrible dream. But we can't take

stock in the madman's interpretation of what happens. Poe keeps

putting distances between what the narrator says and what we are supposed

to think, apparently. For instance: the narrator has boasted that he

is calm and clear in the head, but as soon as he starts (in the second

paragraph) trying to explain why he killed the old man, we gather that

he is confused, to say the least. "I think it was his eye!" the narrator

exclaims, as if not quite sure. As he goes on to explain how he con-

ducted the murder, we realize that he is a man with a fixed idea working

with a patience that is certainly mad, almost diabolical.

Some readers might wonder if "The Tell-Tale Heart" is a story of the

supernatural. Is the heartbeat that the narrator hears a ghost come back

to haunt him? Here, I think, the point of view is our best guide to what

to believe. The simple explanation for the heartbeat is this: it is all

in the madman's mind. Perhaps he feels such guilt that he starts hearing

things. Another explanation is possible, one suggested by Daniel

Hoffman, a critic who has discussed the story: the killer hears the

sound of his own heart.[1] Hoffman's explanation (which I don't like as

well as mine) also is a natural one, and it fits the story as a whole.

Back when the narrator first entered the old man's bedroom to kill

him, the heartbeat sounded so loud to him that he was afraid the

neighbors would hear it too. Evidently they didn't, and so Hoffman may

be right in thinking that the sound was only that of his own heart

pounding in his ears. Whichever explanation you take, it is a more

down-to-earth and reasonable explanation than that (as the narrator

believes) the heart is still alive, even though its owner has been cut

to pieces. Then, too, the police keep chatting. If they heard the heartbeat too, wouldn't they leap to their feet, draw their guns, and look all around the room? As the author has kept showing us in the rest of the story, the narrator's view of things is ~~always~~ untrustworthy. You don't kill someone just because you dislike the look in his eye. You don't think that such a murder is funny. For all its Gothic atmosphere of the old dark house with a secret hidden inside, "The Tell-Tale Heart" is not a ghost story. We have only to see its point of view to know that it is a study in abnormal psychology.

---

[1] *Poe Poe Poe Poe Poe Poe Poe* (New York: Anchor, 1973), 227.

A temptation in writing an analysis is to want to include all sorts of insights that the writer proudly wishes to display, even though they aren't related to the main idea. In the preceding essay, the student resists this temptation admirably. In fairly plump and ample paragraphs, he works out his ideas, and he supports his contentions with specific references to Poe's story. Although his paper is not brilliantly written and contains no insight so fresh as the suggestion (by the writer of the first paper) that the madman's lantern is like the old man's head, still, it is a good brief analysis. By sticking faithfully to his purpose and by confronting the problems he raises ("how do we know the whole story isn't just a nightmare?"), the writer persuades us that he understands not only the story's point of view, but the story in its entirety.

Our analysis so far deals with one element in Poe's story: point of view. In another familiar writing assignment, the **card report,** one is asked to analyze a story into its *several* elements. Usually confined to the front and back of one 5 × 8-inch index card, such a report is just as challenging to write as an essay, if not more so. To do the job well, you have to see the story in its elements, then specify them succinctly and accurately. Here (on the following pages) is a typical card report listing and detailing the essentials of "The Tell-Tale Heart." In this assignment, the student was asked to include:

1. The title of the story and the date of its original publication.
2. The author's name and dates.
3. The name (if any) of the main character, together with a description of that character's dominant traits or features.
4. Other characters in the story, dealt with in the same fashion.
5. A short description of the setting.
6. The narrator of the story. (To identify him or her is, of course, to define the point of view from which the story is told.)

Story: "The Tell-Tale Heart," 1850
Author: Edgar Allan Poe (1809–1849)

    Central character: An unnamed younger man whom people call mad,
who claims that a nervous disease has greatly sharpened his sense
perceptions. He is proud of his own cleverness. Other characters:
The old man, whose leading feature is one pale blue, filmed eye; said
to be rich, kind, and lovable. Also three policemen, not individually
described.
    Setting: A shuttered house full of wind, mice, and treasures;
pitch dark even in the afternoon.
    Narrator: The madman himself.
    Events in summary: (1) Dreading one vulturelike eye of the old
man he shares a house with, a madman determines to kill its owner.
(2) Each night he spies on the sleeping old man, but finding the eye
shut, he stays his hand. (3) On the eighth night, finding the eye open,
he suffocates its owner beneath the mattress and conceals the dismembered body under the floor of the bedchamber. (4) Entertaining some
inquiring police officers in the very room where the body lies hidden,
the killer again hears (or thinks he hears) the beat of his victim's
heart. (5) Terrified, convinced that the police also hear the heartbeat growing louder, the killer confesses his crime.
    Tone: Horror at the events described, skepticism toward the
narrator's claims to be sane, revulsion (or at least detachment) from
his gaiety and laughter.

Front of Card

    7. A terse summary of the main events of the story, given in chronological order.

    8. A description of the general tone of the story, as well as it can be sensed: the author's apparent feelings toward the central character or the main events.

    9. Some comments on the style in which the story is written. (Brief illustrative quotations are helpful, insofar as space permits.)

    10. Whatever kinds of irony the story contains, and what they contribute to the story.

    11. In a sentence, the story's main theme.

    12. Leading symbols (if the story has any), with an educated guess at whatever each symbol suggests.

    13. Finally, an evaluation of the story as a whole, concisely setting forth the student's opinion of it. (Some instructors regard this as the most important part of the report, and most students find that, by the time they have so painstakingly separated the ingredients of the story, they have arrived at a definite opinion of it.)

    To fit so much on one card is, admittedly, somewhat like trying to engrave the Declaration of Independence on the head of a pin. The student who wrote this succinct report had to spoil a few trial cards before he was able to do it. Every word has to count, and making them count is a

Back of Card

discipline worthwhile in almost any sort of expository writing. Some students enjoy the challenge. In doing such a report, though you may feel
severely limited, you'll probably be surprised at how thoroughly you come
to understand a story. Besides, if you care to keep the card for future
reference, it won't take much storage room. A longer story, even a novel,
may be analyzed in the same way; but insist on taking a second card if you
are asked to analyze some especially hefty and complicated novel — say,
Leo Tolstoi's panoramic, thousand-page *War and Peace.*

COMPARING AND CONTRASTING

If you were to write on "The Humor of Frank O'Connor's 'First
Confession' and Alice Walker's 'Everyday Use,'" you would probably
employ one or two other methods. You might use **comparison,** placing the
two stories side by side and pointing out their similarities; or you might
use **contrast,** pointing out their differences. Most of the time, in dealing
with a pair of stories, you will find them similar in some ways and different
in others; and so you will be using both methods in writing your paper.
No law requires you to devote equal space to each method. You might have
to do more contrasting than comparing, or the other way around. If the

stories are obviously similar but subtly different, you will probably compare them briefly, listing the similarities, and then, at greater length, contrast them by calling attention to their important differences. If, however, the stories at first glance seem as different as peas from polecats, and yet they are in fact closely related, you'll probably spend most of your time comparing them rather than contrasting them. (You might not just compare and contrast, but also analyze, in that you might select one element of the stories for your investigation.) Other topics for papers involving two stories might be "The Experience of Coming of Age in James Joyce's 'Araby' and William Faulkner's 'Barn Burning'"; and "The Fascinated Prey: A Comparison of the Situations of Connie in Joyce Carol Oates's 'Where Are You Going, Where Have You Been?' and Rose in Alice Munro's 'Wild Swans.'"

Your paper, of course, will hang together better if you choose a pair of stories that apparently have much in common than if you choose two as unlike as cow and canteloupe. Before you start writing, think: Do the two stories you've selected throw some light on each other? An essay that likened W. Somerset Maugham's terse, ironic fable "The Appointment in Samarra" with William Faulkner's rich, complex "Barn Burning" just might reveal unexpected similarities. More likely, it would seem strained and pointless.

You can also write an essay in comparison and contrast that deals with just one story. You might consider, say, the attitudes of the younger waiter and the older waiter in Hemingway's "A Clean, Well-Lighted Place." In Flannery O'Connor's "Revelation," you might contrast Mrs. Turpin's smug view of herself with young Mary Grace's merciless view of her.

If your topic calls for both comparison and contrast, and you are dealing with two stories, don't write the first half of your paper all about one story, then pivot and write the second half about the other, never permitting the two to mingle. The result probably would not be a unified essay in contrast and comparison, but two separate commentaries yoked together. One workable way to organize such a paper is to make (before you begin) a brief list of points to look for in each story, then, as you write, to consider each point — first in one story and then in the other. Here is a simple outline for an essay bringing together William Faulkner's "A Rose for Emily" and Flannery O'Connor's "Revelation." The topic is "Two Would-be Aristocrats: The Characters of Emily Grierson and Mrs. Turpin."

1. Character's view of her own innate superiority

    a. Emily

    b. Mrs. Turpin

2. Author's evaluation of character's moral worth

    a. Emily

    b. Mrs. Turpin

3. Character's ability to change

    a. Emily

    b. Mrs. Turpin

It is best, however, not to follow such an outline in plodding, mechanical fashion ("Well, now it's time to whip over to Mrs. Turpin again"), lest your readers feel they are watching a back-and-forth tennis match. Some points are bound to interest you more than others, and, when they do, you will want to give them greater emphasis.

SUGGESTIONS FOR WRITING

What kinds of topics are likely to result in papers that will reveal something about works of fiction? Here is a list of typical topics, suitable to papers of various lengths, offered in the hope of stimulating your own ideas. For other topics, see Suggestions for Writing at the end of every chapter. For specific advice on finding a topic of your own, see Writing about Literature, page 413.

TOPICS FOR BRIEF PAPERS (250 – 500 words)

1. Consider a short story in which the central character has to make a decision or must take some decisive step that will alter the rest of his or her life. Faulkner's "Barn Burning" is one such story; another is Updike's "A & P." As concisely and as thoroughly as you can, explain the nature of the character's decision, the reasons for it, and its probable consequences (as suggested by what the author tells us).
2. Write an informal (rather than a complete) explication of the opening paragraph or first few lines of a story. Show us how it prepares us for what will happen. (An alternate topic: take instead a *closing* paragraph and sum up whatever insight it leaves us with.) Don't feel obliged to deal with everything in the passage, as you would do in writing a more nearly complete explication. Within this suggested word length, limit your discussion to whatever strikes you as most essential.
3. Make a card report (see page 432) on a short story in the Stories for Further Reading or one suggested by your instructor. Include all the elements in the report illustrated in this chapter (unless your instructor wishes you to emphasize some element or offers other advice).
4. Show how reading a specific short story caused you to change or modify an attitude or opinion you once had.
5. Just for fun, try writing a different ending to one of the short stories in this anthology. What does this exercise suggest about the wisdom of the author in ending things as done in the original? (Try to keep a sense of the author's style.)
6. Another wild idea: Write a *sequel* to one of your favorite short stories — or at least the beginning of a sequel, enough to give your reader a sense of it.
7. Argue from your own experience that a character in any story behaves (or doesn't behave) as people behave in life.

Topics for More Extended Papers (600 – 1,000 words)

1. Choose a short passage (one of, say, three or four sentences) in a story, a passage that interests you. Perhaps it will contain a decisive moment in a plot, a revealing comment on a character, or a statement of the story's major theme. Then write a reasonably thorough explication. Like the writer of the paper "By Lantern Light" (page 426), go through the passage in some detail, noticing words that especially convey the author's meanings.

2. Write an analysis of a short story, singling out an element such as the author's voice (tone, style, irony), point of view, character, theme, symbolism, or Gothic elements (if the story has any). Try to show how this element functions in the story as a whole. For a typical paper in response to this assignment, see "The Hearer of 'The Tell-Tale Heart' " (page 430).

3. Analyze a story in which a character experiences some realization or revelation. How does the writer prepare us for the moment of enlightenment? What is the nature of each realization or revelation? How does it affect the character? Stories to consider might include "Araby," "Greasy Lake," "Gimpel the Fool," "Revelation," "The Chrysanthemums," "The Death of Ivan Ilych," "The Garden-Party," and "Roman Fever."

4. Explore how humor functions in a story. What is funny? How is humor implied by the story's tone or style? Does humor help set forth a theme, or reveal character? Any of the following stories deserves exploration: "A & P," "First Confession," "Greasy Lake," "The Catbird Seat," "Gimpel the Fool," "Everyday Use," "Revelation," "A Hunger Artist," "Brief Encounter," "The Conversion of the Jews," and "My Man Bovanne."

5. For anyone interested in a career in teaching: Explain how you would teach a story, either to an imaginary class or to the class you belong to now. Perhaps you might arrange with your instructor to write about a story your class hasn't read yet; and then, after writing your paper, actually to teach the story in class.

6. See if you can discover a new Stephen Crane — another journalist who brings literary skill to reporting (as Crane does in "The Open Boat"). In an essay, examine some news story, interview, or feature that you think reads like excellent fiction. Point out whatever elements of good storytelling you find in it. (Is there a plot? Lively dialogue? Suspense? Vivid style? Thought-provoking theme? Rounded characters, or at least memorable ones? Shrewd choice of a point of view?) For such a story, consult your daily newspaper or a weekly news magazine. Supply a clipping or copy of your discovery along with your finished paper.

7. If your daily newspaper lacks literary quality but you'd like to try that last topic, see any of the following books. Each contains some reporting that will show you storytelling art:

> Nora Ephron, *Crazy Salad: Some Things About Women* (New York: Knopf, 1975). Includes a portrait of the first woman umpire and a cutthroat national baking competition.

> John Hersey, *Hiroshima* (New York: Knopf, 1946). The first atomic holocaust as seen by six survivors.

> Garrison Keillor, *Lake Wobegon Days* (New York: Viking, 1985). Gentle comic reports of a practically vanished small-town way of life.

> Larry L. King, *Of Outlaws, Con-men, Whores, Politicians, and Other Artists* (New York: Viking, 1978). Includes a memoir of a gambling contest, "Shoot-out with Amarillo Slim."

> Lillian Ross, *Reporting* (New York: Dodd, 1981). Seven classic essays in journalism, among them a profile of Ernest Hemingway.

Hunter S. Thompson, *The Great Shark Hunt* (New York: Summit Books, 1979). Reports of politics, sports, and pleasure-seeking in the 1960s and 1970s.

Tom Wolfe, *The Right Stuff* (New York: Farrar, 1979). The story of America's first astronauts.

TOPICS FOR LONG PAPERS (1,500 WORDS OR MORE)

1. Selecting a short story from the anthology in this book, or taking one suggested by your instructor, write an informal essay setting forth (as thoroughly as you can) your understanding of it. Point out any difficulties you encountered in first reading the story, for the benefit of other students who might meet the same difficulties. If you find particularly complicated passages, briefly explicate them. An ample statement of the meaning of the story probably will not deal only with plot or only with theme, but will also consider how the story is written and structured.

2. Dealing with a single element of fiction, write an analysis of Tolstoi's *The Death of Ivan Ilych,* or of some other long story that your instructor suggests.

3. Take a short story in which most of the events take place in the physical world (rather than inside some character's mind), and translate it into a one-act play, complete with stage directions. After you have done so, you might present a reading of it with the aid of other members of the class and then perhaps discuss what you had to do to the story to make a play of it.

4. Taking an author in this book whose work appeals to you, read at least three or four of his or her other stories. Then write an analysis of them, concentrating on an element of fiction that you find present in all.

5. Again going beyond this book to read other stories, compare and contrast two writers' handling of a similar theme. Let your essay build to a conclusion in which you state your opinion: which author's expression of theme is deeper, or more memorable?

Writing a Story

FINDING A STORY

Whether or not you aspire to be a new Doris Lessing or D. H. Lawrence, writing a story may reveal to you much firsthand knowledge. At the very least, you may learn some of the ways in which a good story is crafted, and you may acquire a keener sense of the art it requires. Then, when you read stories in the future, you will enjoy them as an insider does.

Not everyone, of course, is a born storyteller. If someone tells you of something that happened the other day and practically puts you to sleep, you realize that it takes both talent and skill to recognize a story worth telling and to narrate it effectively. Yet most people who can write expository prose clearly and vigorously can, with enough effort, write at least a brief story that will satisfy themselves, and perhaps others. Generally, the skilled writer of fiction is a skilled reader of fiction, too. Among famed storytellers, Erskine Caldwell, author of *Tobacco Road,* may be the only one to claim that reading never did him any good. Before you attempt a story of your own, you would do well to read the works of master storytellers — as many as possible. In this book, you'll find a fair sampling; but if you are serious about wanting to write stories, you will want to read whole collections by authors you admire. Read not only for entertainment, read critically. Notice how a story is woven together. For what possible purpose does the writer tell it from one point of view, instead of from another? What do the actions of the characters show us about the kinds of people they are? Are events given in chronological order? If not, what does the writer achieve by so departing from chronology? Such questions may seem dry, but if you apply them to living stories, they may help give you a few insights into the storyteller's art.

Some beginning writers, remarked Flannery O'Connor, think they know what a short story is until they try to write one — "Then they find themselves writing a sketch with an essay woven through it, or an editorial with a character in it, or a case history with a moral, or some other mongrel thing."[1] But what, exactly, is a story? According to O'Connor, it is a form of writing in which characters and events influence each other. "If you start with a real personality, a real character," she explained to an audience of aspiring writers, "then something is bound to happen."[2] This would seem another way of saying, "Character is action" — the words of a master storyteller, Henry James.[3]

For an event to be charged with meaning in fiction, it has to produce an effect on someone. E. M. Forster has explained, "Consider the death of a queen. If it is in a story we say, 'and then?' "[4] In such a story a writer might tell how the queen's death in some way altered the life of an obscure commoner. Read outstanding short stories of the past century and, in most, you will find a character led to act — or left, as a result of some dramatic event, deeply illumined and fundamentally changed. Most stories in this book exhibit the tradition that James defined: stories in which characters think, feel, and react, causing things to happen. Recently, however, many fiction writers have experimented with radically different concepts of character (discussed briefly in Chapter Four). As a result, in many contemporary stories, character seems hardly to matter and events sometimes occur without apparent human control. If recent fiction intrigues you, then closely read the stories of Franz Kafka, Gabriel García Márquez, T. Coraghessan Boyle, Joyce Carol Oates, and Alice Walker (all represented in this book), as well as those of John Barth, Donald Barthelme, Russell Edson, Samuel Beckett, and others. You will meet a few stories in which writers appear to devise new rules for storytelling. If you are a novice at writing fiction, however, you might do well, before trying to change the rules, first to watch a fair number of games.

Let us assume that you have a working sense of the nature of a short story. Where do you find a story to tell? Evidently, if you take Flannery O'Connor's advice and start with a "real character," then to unfold a story you have only to imagine that character in some dramatic situation or confrontation. Then you imagine how he or she will respond to it. In O'Connor's own story "Revelation," we see her procedure. First she establishes the nature of Mrs. Turpin, a racist prig full of smug self-congratulation. Then, after a flung textbook strikes Mrs. Turpin in the brow, O'Connor shows us her main character going through anguished change. Of course, there is no one approved and infallible method of story-finding. Writers begin with anything that sparks them into motion. Henry James could find the germ for a story — even for a whole novel — in an anecdote

---

[1]"The Nature and Aim of Fiction" in *Mystery and Manners,* ed. Sally and Robert Fitzgerald (New York: Farrar, 1961), 66.
[2]"Writing Short Stories," *Mystery* 106
[3]"Anthony Trollope" (1883), reprinted in part in *Theory of Fiction: Henry James,* ed. James E. Miller, Jr. (Lincoln: U of Nebraska P, 1972), 200.
[4]*Aspects of the Novel,* quoted by Eric S. Rabkin in the epigraph for his study *Narrative Suspense* (Ann Arbor: U of Michigan P, 1973).

told him at a dinner party. Another source of seedling stories, for novelist and short story writer J. F. Powers, is small human-interest items in a daily newspaper. Robert Ludlum, author of popular spy novels, says, "I start with an idea, with something that outrages, amuses, or interests me. Then I try to find the story line that will support the basic idea."[5] (Ludlum, no Flannery O'Connor-like prober of souls, writes a kind of fiction in which ingenious plot, not character, counts most.)

Endless stories surround you, if only you can recognize them. Your daily life may prove your most fruitful source. You need not live a story in order to write it, though: you can overhear it, or observe it in the lives of others. As an aid to memory, many distinguished fiction writers have kept notebooks. There, in rough form, they record whatever sticks in their minds as grist for stories. F. Scott Fitzgerald filled his notebook with "Things Overheard," "Nonsense and Stray Phrases," "Scenes," "Situations," and "Descriptions of Girls." Nathaniel Hawthorne jotted down hundreds of ideas for stories he meant to write. (One that didn't materialize: "A stove possessed by a Devil.") In his own profound notebooks, Henry James not only saved bits and scraps (such as names he thought up for possible characters), he analyzed his stories as he worked on them, listing problems and solutions. Some writers, whether or not they ever turn their notebooks into finished stories, find that notebook-keeping sharpens their powers of observation. Keep such a notebook, after your own fashion, and you may well find yourself opening your eyes wide to the stories that surround you, and also fine-tuning your ears.

THE PROCESS OF STORYTELLING

In the heyday of pulp magazines (so called for their cheap paper) many professional writers of fiction relied on a mechanical gadget called Plotto — a sort of writer's Ouija board. Constructing a story for *Dime Western* or *Spicy Detective,* a writer would spin a little tin arrow to a number, then look up the number in an accompanying book. A few spins would indicate all the necessary ingredients: type of hero, type of villain, setting, kind of conflict, complication ("an earthquake"), crisis, climax, and conclusion. When the writer cooked the ingredients into a story, the result brought a penny a word.

Some more highly literate storytellers, though they don't own a Plotto board, lay out the elements of a story before they write. One believer in thorough planning was P. G. Wodehouse, author of ingeniously plotted novels of screwball dwellers in posh mansions in rural England. Everything in a story, declared Wodehouse, should be carefully figured out

[5]Reply to a questioner, quoted by Robert Charm, "From Pen to Podium," Boston *Globe,* 11 May 1982: 15.

ahead of time: "Once you go saying to yourself, 'This is a pretty weak plot as it stands, but I'm such a hell of a writer that my magic touch will make it OK,' you're sunk."[6] Other writers, less insistent on firm scaffolding, begin writing with only a character or a situation in mind, letting themselves be surprised (along with the reader) as the story unfolds. Flannery O'Connor, it would seem, was such a writer. In her short story "Good Country People," a Bible salesman steals a woman's artificial leg. O'Connor has recalled that she didn't know he was going to do so until ten or twelve lines before she came to describe the theft. Yet, she later realized, the salesman's astonishing act followed from the kind of man he was and from the nature of his victim.[7]

Whether they lay plans carefully or casually, writers often will meet a surprise in the act of telling a story. At times a character will behave unpredictably, especially a lifelike character who grows larger under the pen. Tolstoi, who began writing *Anna Karenina* determined to condemn an unfaithful woman, found himself, as he wrote his immense novel, coming to view his adulterous main character with greater compassion. He had imagined Anna as physically unattractive and boorish in her manners, but his descriptions of her became kinder and more sympathetic as he wrote on.

Like runners who first limber up their muscles before hitting the track, some writers warm up before they write. George Fox, author of popular novels (*Amok, Without Music*) and filmscripts, starts out by writing "a lot of drivel about the hero's childhood, about the setting, about a certain car." Perhaps none of this "drivel" will appear in his finished story. As he writes a description of a character, perhaps things start to happen, and the story begins to move. Then Fox drops ten or twenty pages of warm-up exercise into his trashbasket. Hero and setting, he finds, have become vivid in his imagination.

Early in writing a story, you have to make crucial decisions. One is your choice of the person to narrate the story — the point of view. Tolstoi, in writing *The Death of Ivan Ilych*, at first cast his story into the form of a diary kept by Ivan during his last days. Later, as Tolstoi reviewed what he had written, he decided against this device. He then completely rewrote the story in the third person. No doubt he had realized that the story required a narrator able to see Ivan both from without and from within. Such a narrator, besides, could survive Ivan's death and portray his mourners. In effective storytelling, perhaps a writer's most important decision is to select the most appropriate point of view. How to decide which point of view is best? Try telling the story to yourself in different ways, as if through the eyes of different narrators.

[6]Interview with Gerald Clarke, *Paris Review* 64 (1975): 155.
[7]"Writing Short Stories," *Mystery and Manners* 100.

Still another decision that greatly matters is how thoroughly each part of your story needs to be told. Which events will you set forth in brief summaries, which in full scenes? Drawing a scene, you visualize it in detail. You thus enable your readers to see it in their minds' eye as if they beheld it on a stage or a screen. In John Updike's "A & P," most of the story takes place in one extended scene in a supermarket, including a few interior thoughts of Sammy, the narrator. That we may visualize the action, Updike includes plenty of physical details: the story takes place "under the fluorescent lights, against all those stacked packages," and the girls who trigger Sammy's big decision are described with loving care. For another vivid scene, see Faulkner's "Barn Burning," in which the boy's father marches into Major de Spain's mansion, streaking the rug with filth. In a well-told story, we usually find the most highly dramatic moments set forth in scenes. For as long as a scene transpires, the reader lives it.

In employing the method of **summary,** you tell what happens in fewer words. You boil down events to their essentials and set them forth in a more general way. In the Grimm brothers' "Godfather Death," we find summary in the statement, "It wasn't long before the young man had become the most famous doctor in the world." In this one sentence, the taleteller covers events that, if told in scenes, might have required many chapters. Summary is the method of narration most of us employ in conversation: "I was in a little car crash last night. A truck slammed me in the tailgate and stove in my rear end." In fiction, a story containing scenes may also employ summary — for the less dramatic events, perhaps, or for getting over a long expanse of time that doesn't need to be chronicled in detail. In Singer's "Gimpel the Fool" the narrator summarizes: "I wandered over the land and good people did not neglect me. After many years I became old and white. . . ." Here, Singer's apparent purpose isn't to give us a complete history of Gimpel's later life. Instead, it is to show that, during his years of wandering, the supposed fool becomes a wiser man. Summary may also be valuable to supply background information that the reader needs. With wonderful economy, D. H. Lawrence begins "The Rocking-Horse Winner" with a summary: "There was a woman who was beautiful, who started with all the advantages, yet she had no luck. She married for love, and the love turned to dust." In a few words, summary can convey all the information we need more effectively than many scenes.

To decide which events to summarize and which to depict in scenes is a challenge to many storytellers. Beginning writers sometimes tell too large a part of their story in sketchy summary form, neglecting to set forth the dramatic moments in detailed scenes — and therefore, failing to milk these moments for all they are worth. Still, good storytellers know that, although vivid scenes are what readers best remember, summary at times is indispensable. With a short passage of summary, the writer can move along quickly to a scene. Divide your story into scenes, P. G. Wodehouse advised, "and have as little stuff in between as possible."[8]

Some writers, when shifting scenes, don't even use summary. To waft a character from one place to another, they will end a scene, leave some white space, and open the next scene with the character already arrived at a destination. Perhaps they will use a **time-marker,** or a brief phrase of transition, to indicate that some while has gone by: *"An hour later"* — that's the time-marker — "Cassidy was shoving open the bleary glass door of the Tenth Precinct Station."

A word of warning: Don't pretend to feelings you don't feel, or attitudes you can't call your own. In later life, Eudora Welty recalled with amusement the opening line of a story she had written as a girl trying to maintain a sophistication she hadn't really had: "Monsieur Boule inserted a delicate dagger into Mademoiselle's left side and departed with a poised immediacy."[9]

Some storytellers work slowly, taking pains to find the right words on their first try. Others, like Frank O'Connor, dash off a rough draft of a story, saving the pains for later. O'Connor would start writing "any sort of rubbish which will cover the main outlines of the story," just to get it down in writing and be able to look at it. "When I draft a story I never think of writing nice sentences," he explained. "It's the design of the story which to me is most important, the thing that tells you there's a bad gap in the narrative here and you really ought to fill that up in some way or another."[10] Satisfied with his design, O'Connor would then work on the story's texture, rewriting a story as many as fifty times. " 'First Confession,' " he said, "has appeared in three quite different forms from the first day when *Lovat Dickson's Magazine* printed it, so I may now hope its ghost has ceased to haunt me."[11]

Not every writer of fiction believes in profound revision. "You know," Ann Beattie told a writers' conference, "I'm not capable of major revision at all. That's why I throw things out a lot."[12] D. H. Lawrence was another believer in letting first thoughts stand. If dissatisfied with a story, he would write the whole thing over from scratch. This strenuous custom accounts for there being at least three complete and separate versions of his novel *Lady Chatterley's Lover.*

At the opposite extreme is the "bleeder," the writer who lets go of each word as reluctantly as though it were a drop of blood. Perhaps the

---

[8]Interview with Clarke, 152.

[9]*One Writer's Beginnings* (Cambridge: Harvard UP, 1984), 85 – 6.

[10]Interview with Anthony Whittier, *Writers at Work: The Paris Review Interviews* (New York: Viking, 1959) 167 – 8.

[11]Foreword to the *Stories of Frank O'Connor* (New York: Knopf, 1952).

[12]Quoted by Gelarch Asayesh, news story on the New England Writers' Conference, Boston *Globe,* 8 July 1982.

most celebrated bleeder in literary history was Gustave Flaubert, who rewrote his work with masochistic devotion, seeking to reflect in his style the clarity and precision of classical music. "May I die like a dog," he wrote to a friend, "rather than hasten the ripening of a sentence by a single second!"[13] (See other remarks by Flaubert upon his labors, page 398; and for a conflicting view of style, the comment by Thomas Hardy, page 399.)

Most professional writers of fiction probably reside somewhere between perfectionism and "Oh, let it all hang out." If, in looking over what they have written they spy a passage they can improve, they improve it. Because it is usually easier to delete than to amplify, some write at great length, putting in everything they can think of, and then, in revising the story, shorten it. Georges Simenon, French writer of mystery novels, sometimes reduced his first versions by as much as half. Simenon declared that he hated "show-off writing," and so would strike out any word or sentence that called attention to its own cleverness. So stern was Simenon in his deletions that he rendered his prose almost totally colorless. In his way, James Thurber also distrusted too-obvious delight in one's own words. In writing a humorous story, he observed, "you're likely to be very gleeful with what you've first put down." But careful rewriting can transfer the glee from writer to reader. "You go over and over it . . . to make the piece sound less as if you were having a lot of fun with it yourself."[14]

If we can generalize at all, it may be safe to say that most professional writers first write a much rougher version of a story than they finish with. Although in some of his working habits Truman Capote may have been unique (he wrote *second* drafts on a peculiar kind of yellow paper), he was like most writers in bringing a story to completion stage by stage. After writing a first draft in longhand, Capote would type another draft, which he then retired for a week or a month. "When I take it out again," he said, "I read it as coldly as possible, then read it aloud to a friend or two, and decide what changes I want to make and whether or not I want to publish it." (Capote threw away hundreds of thousands of words that didn't seem publishable.) "But if all goes well, I type the final version on white paper."[15]

As you can see, professional writers of fiction tend to be patient and demanding self-critics. They cultivate an ability to step out of themselves and to inspect a story as though with a reader's eyes. To be sure, problems will appear, problems deeper than whether to delete an adjective. A major character may prove useless and a minor character may assume swaggering proportions. A plot that had rolled along smoothly may run into a pothole and fall apart. Mark Twain, in writing *Huckleberry Finn,* called his masterpiece "that damned book" as he struggled with it. For seven years he kept

[13]Letter to Maxim du Camp, June 19, 1852, *Selected Letters,* tr. Francis Steegmuller (New York: Vintage, 1957) 132.
[14]Interview with George Plimpton and Max Steele, *Writers* 88.
[15]Interview with Pati Hill, *Writers* 296 – 7.

casting aside his manuscript and returning to it. Something in him seemed unwilling to finish the book, and in the midst of his labors on it he took time out to produce his autobiographical *Life on the Mississippi* and an inferior but more tractable novel, *The Prince and the Pauper.* In spinning forth a story, every veteran writer of fiction perhaps has encountered knots. Fortunately, in trying to undo them, the writer has a powerful ally: the unconscious. Joyce Carol Oates has suggested a remedy for writer's block caused by running into deep problems. When the mind halts before a problem it can't solve, the writer had best put aside the story for a while, and sleep on it, until the trustworthy unconscious comes up with a solution.[16]

To write a novel that will soar to the top of bestseller lists and set every reviewer to babbling praise — this is a cherished American dream. In actuality, your chances of achieving great rewards from fiction are somewhat like your chances of winning a million dollars by playing black-jack at Las Vegas. Although a few professional writers make a living by regularly churning out paperback novels in some popular genre such as romance, Gothic, or science fiction, few serious first novelists meet much favor these days with readers or publishers. If you write short stories, you will find it even harder to reach a wide audience. Little magazines, with circulations of a few hundred dedicated readers, are today the principal medium for short fiction. Lately, however, hope for the short story has blossomed. Collections of stories by distinguished old hands (Eudora Welty, John Cheever) have proved bestsellers; and more and more publishers, including some university presses, have been welcoming volumes of stories.

Like poets, most short-story writers nowadays practice their demanding art for reasons other than the prospects of money and renown. What satisfactions reside in writing short stories? May you discover them, by writing a story that pleases you, your instructor, and your friends.

SUGGESTIONS FOR WRITING

1. Reviewing the illustrations of fable and tale in Chapter One (those by W. Somerset Maugham and the brothers Grimm), write a brief supernatural or fantastic tale, or a fable with a point to it.
2. In three separate paragraphs, try beginning a story in three distinctly different ways. You might try, for instance, relating an incident from three points of view; or try beginning a story with a summary, the opening of a scene, and a descriptive passage introducing a person or a setting.
3. Recount a dream you vividly remember, in which something exciting or astonishing occurred. (This is an exercise; the result does not have to be a complete story. You may find, though, that a longer story will suggest itself.)
4. Here is a writing exercise suggested by novelist R. V. Cassill. Take the first three paragraphs of a story you admire, and with the text open beside you, write three parallel paragraphs of careful imitation. Keep the same number of

[16]Cited by Rust Hills, *Writing in General and the Short Story in Particular* (Boston: Houghton, 1977) 191.

sentences, of the same general length and complexity. Imitate any proper names, characteristic detail, "emotional state of the characters." Reproduce the point of view. "In a word," says Cassill, "you cannot do this sort of imitation without thinking pretty nimbly about what you are doing. You are performing one of the kinds of thought that is part of original composition." (From *Writing Fiction,* New York: Pocket Books, 1962.)

5. Following George Fox's method of warming up, write ten or more pages of carefree exercise material, portraying in detail some strong and colorful character, or a weak and appealing one. If the character you envision interests you, try to imagine such a person confronted with some challenge. Then go on to write the story that ensues.

6. Recall some dramatic event in your life, or some event that you know from vivid secondhand reports. Bring it alive in the form of a scene, including dialogue and description if they seem necessary.

7. Write a skeletal novel in summary form, taking three or four pages to encompass all the main events in it. Then select one dramatic moment from your summary and present it in the form of a scene of about 1,000 to 2,000 words.

8. Invent names for ten or twelve imaginary characters, wildly assorted in age, walk of life, and personality. Then describe in two or three sentences the person each name suggests to you. (Here are three memorable fictional names from the novels of Henry James, for instance: Lambert Strether, Fleda Vetch, and Mrs. Bread.)

9. Following the procedure of J. F. Powers, scan a newspaper for some two-inch-long comic or touching story of relatively small news value but of much human interest. Write the tale or short story it suggests to you.

10. Choose a place you know well and write a story that might have happened there twenty-five, fifty, or a hundred years ago. An alternative idea might be to set your story in the future. (For inspiration, see "The Portable Phonograph" or a current science-fiction magazine.)

11. In a short story, show how a brief moment alters the course of a character's life. For illustrations of such stories, see "A & P," "Greasy Lake," "Revelation," and "The Jilting of Granny Weatherall."

Acknowledgments *(continued)*

Ursula K. LeGuin. "The Wife's Story" from *The Compass Rose: Short Stories by Ursula K. LeGuin.* Copyright © 1982 by Ursula LeGuin. Reprinted by permission of Harper & Row, Publishers, Inc.

Doris Lessing. "A Woman on a Roof" from *A Man and Two Women* by Doris Lessing. Copyright © 1958, 1962, 1963 by Doris Lessing. Reprinted by permission of Simon & Schuster, Inc., and Jonathan Clowes, Ltd., London, on behalf of Doris Lessing.

Katherine Mansfield. "The Garden-Party." Copyright 1922 by Alfred A. Knopf, Inc. and renewed 1950 by John Middleton Murry. Reprinted from *The Short Stories of Katherine Mansfield,* by permission of the publisher.

Gabriel García Márquez. "The Night of the Curlews" from *Innocent Erendira and Other Stories by Gabriel García Márquez,* translated by Gregory Rabassa. English translation copyright © 1978 by Harper and Row, Publishers, Inc. Reprinted by permission of Harper & Row, Publishers, Inc.

W. Somerset Maugham. "Appointment in Samarra" from *Sheppey* by W. Somerset Maugham. Copyright 1933 by W. Somerset Maugham. Reprinted by permission of Doubleday Company and A. P. Watt on behalf of The Executors of the Estate of Somerset Maugham.

Alice Munro. "Wild Swans" from *The Beggar Maid* and *Who Do You Think You Are?* Copyright © 1977, 1978 by Alice Munro. Reprinted by permission of Alfred A. Knopf, Inc. and Macmillan of Canada, a division of Canada Publishing Corporation.

Joyce Carol Oates. "Where Are You Going? Where Have You Been?" Reprinted from *The Wheel of Love* by Joyce Carol Oates by permission of the publisher, The Vanguard Press, Inc. Copyright © 1970, 1969, 1968, 1967, 1965 by The Vanguard Press Inc.

Flann O'Brien (pseud., Brian O'Nolan). "Two in One" from *A Flann O'Brien Reader,* edited by Stephen Jones (New York: The Viking Press, 1978, pp. 321–326). First printed in the *Journal of Irish Literature.* Copyright 1978 by the Estate of Flann O'Brien and copyright 1978 by Viking Penguin, Inc. Reprinted by permission of Brandt & Brandt Literary Agency.

Flannery O'Connor. "Revelation" from *Everything That Rises Must Converge* by Flannery O'Connor. Copyright © 1964, 1965 by the Estate of Mary Flannery O'Connor. Reprinted with the permission of Farrar, Straus & Giroux, Inc.

Frank O'Connor. "First Confession." Copyright 1951 by Frank O'Connor. Reprinted from *Collected Stories,* by Frank O'Connor, by permission of Alfred A. Knopf, Inc. and Joan Daves. Excerpt from interview with Frank O'Connor from *Writers at Work: The Paris Review Interviews,* First Series. Edited by Malcolm Cowley. Copyright © 1957, 1958 by The Paris Review, Inc. Reprinted by permission of Viking Penguin, Inc.

Tillie Olsen. "I Stand Here Ironing" excerpted from the book *Tell Me a Riddle* by Tillie Olsen. Copyright © 1956 by Tillie Olsen. Reprinted by permission of Delacorte Press/Seymour Lawrence.

Katharine Anne Porter. "The Jilting of Granny Weatherall." Copyright 1930, 1958 by Katharine Anne Porter. Reprinted from her volume *Flowering Judas and Other Stories* by permission of Harcourt Brace Jovanovich, Inc.

Philip Roth. "Conversion of the Jews" from *Goodbye, Columbus* by Philip Roth. Copyright © 1959 by Philip Roth. Reprinted by permission of Houghton Mifflin Company.

Isaac Bashevis Singer. "Gimpel the Fool" by Isaac Bashevis Singer, translated by Saul Bellow from *A Treasury of Yiddish Stories,* edited by Irving Howe and Eliezer Greenberg. Copyright 1953, renewed © 1981 by Isaac Bashevis Singer. Reprinted by permission of Viking Penguin Inc.

John Steinbeck. "The Chrysanthemums" from *The Long Valley* by John Steinbeck. Copyright 1937, © 1965 by John Steinbeck. Reprinted by permission of Viking Penguin Inc.

Nagai Tatsuo. "Brief Encounter," translated by Edward Seidensticker. From *Japan Quarterly* VII, 2 (1960). Copyright © 1960 by Nagai Tatsuo. Reprinted by permission of Nagai Tatsuo, Edward Seidensticker and *Japan Quarterly.*

James Thurber. "The Catbird Seat." Copyright © 1945 James Thurber. Copyright © 1973 Helen W. Thurber and Rosemary T. Sauers. From *The Thurber Carnival,* published by Harper & Row. Reprinted by permission.

Leo Tolstoy. "The Death of Ivan Ilych" from *The Death of Ivan Ilych and Other Stories* by Leo Tolstoy translated by Louise and Aylmer Maude. Reprinted by permission of Oxford University Press.

John Updike. "A & P." Copyright © 1962 by John Updike. Reprinted from *Pigeon Feathers and Other Stories,* by John Updike, by permission of Alfred A. Knopf, Inc. Originally appeared in *The New Yorker.*

Alice Walker. "Everyday Use" from *In Love & Trouble,* copyright © 1973 by Alice Walker. Reprinted by permission of Harcourt Brace Jovanovich, Inc.

Eudora Welty. "A Worn Path" from *A Curtain of Green and Other Stories,* copyright © 1941, 1969 by Eudora Welty. Reprinted by permission of Harcourt Brace Jovanovich, Inc.

Edith Wharton. "Roman Fever," (Copyright 1934 Liberty Magazine; copyright renewed 1962 William R. Tyler) in *Roman Fever and Other Stories.* Copyright © 1964 Charles Scribner's Sons. Reprinted with the permission of Charles Scribner's Sons. Excerpt from "Telling a Short Story," in *The Writing of Fiction.* Copyright 1925 by Charles Scribner's Sons, copyright renewed 1953 Frederick R. King. Reprinted with the permission of Charles Scribner's Sons.

E. B. White. "The Door" from *Poems and Sketches of E. B. White.* Copyright 1939, 1967 by E. B. White. Reprinted by permission of Harper and Row, Publishers, Inc.

Virginia Woolf. Excerpt from "Modern Fiction" from *The Common Reader,* First Series by Virginia Woolf. Copyright 1925 by Harcourt Brace Jovanovich, Inc., renewed 1953 by Leonard Woolf. Reprinted by permission of Harcourt Brace Jovanovich, Inc., the Author's Estate and The Hogarth Press. Virginia Woolf, "A Haunted House" from *A Haunted House and Other Stories* by Virginia Woolf. Copyright 1944, 1972 by Harcourt Brace Jovanovich, Inc. Reprinted by permission of Harcourt Brace Jovanovich, Inc., the Author's Estate and The Hogarth Press.

To the Student

As publishers, we realize that one way to improve education is to improve textbooks. We also realize that you, the student, very much determine the success or failure of textbooks. Although the instructor assigns them, the student buys and uses them. If enough of you don't like a book and do make your feelings known, the chances are your instructor will not assign it again.

Usually instructors but not students are asked about the quality of a textbook; their opinion alone is considered as revisions are planned or as new books are developed. Now, we would like to ask you about X. J. Kennedy's *An Introduction to Fiction, 4th Edition:* how you liked or disliked it; why it was interesting or dull; if it taught you anything. Please fill in this form and return it to us at: Little, Brown and Company, College English, 34 Beacon Street, Boston, MA 02108.

School:_____

Instructor's name:_____

Title of course:_____

1. Do you find this book too easy?_____too difficult?_____

   about right?_____

2. Which chapters do you find most interesting?_____

   _____

3. Which chapters do you find least interesting?_____

   _____

4. Which stories do you like most?_____

   _____

5. Do you particularly dislike any of the stories?_____

   _____

6. Which statement comes closest to expressing your feelings about reading and studying literature? (Please check one, or supply your own statement.)

   _____Love to read literature. It's my favorite subject.

   _____Usually enjoy reading most literature.

   _____Can take it or leave it.

_____ Usually find little of interest in most literature.

_____ Literature just is not for me.

Other: _____

7. Do you find this book helps you to enjoy fiction more than you did? _____

_____

8. Are the supplements "Writing about Literature," "Writing about a Story,"

and "Writing a Story" very useful? _____ somewhat useful? _____ of

no help? _____

9. In the sections about writing papers, do you prefer to see examples of

writing by students? _____ or by professional critics? _____

10. Do you intend to keep this book for your personal library? Yes _____

No _____

11. Any other comments or suggestions: _____

_____

_____

_____

12. May we quote you in our efforts to promote this book? Yes _____

No _____

Date: _____

Signature (optional): _____

Address (optional): _____